The Extraordinary Adventures
of a Russian Scientist
(Volume 1)

The Extraordinary Adventures of a Russian Scientist (Volume 1)

by
Georges Le Faure & Henri de Graffigny

translated, annotated and introduced by
Brian Stableford

A Black Coat Press Book

ISBN 978-1-934543-81-8. First Printing September 2009. Published by Black Coat Press, an imprint of Hollywood Comics.com, LLC, P.O. Box 17270, Encino, CA 91416.

Introduction

The first of four volumes of *Aventures extraordinaires d'un savant russe*, signed "G. Le Faure and H. de Graffigny" was published by Guillaume Edinger in 1888.[1] That first volume was an unusually lavish book illustrated with astronomical photographs, maps and drawings by various hands, and a preface by France's best-known popularizer of science, Camille Flammarion, who is also the novel's dedicatee. The second and third volumes of the original version appeared in a slightly less lavish format in 1889 and 1890, but Edinger appears to have ceased trading as a publisher thereafter, either because his enthusiastic political activities proved too much of a distraction, or because his recently-established and highly ambitious publishing program had stretched his finances to breaking point; at any rate, the assets of his firm were acquired by Arthème Fayard. After a long delay, Fayard issued the fourth and concluding volume of the *Aventures extraordinaires* in 1896, with illustrations distinctly inferior to those in the earlier volumes. The story told in the four volumes is a single continuous narrative whose subdivision was entirely arbitrary; it is here translated in two volumes as *The Extraordinary Adventures of a Russian Scientist*.

All four volumes of the original edition are now rare; the third and fourth are exceedingly difficult to find, thus making it very difficult for any modern reader to peruse the work in its entirety—even contemporary readers must have had difficulty, given the interruption of its publication. The historical importance of the work as an unprecedentedly ambitious scientific romance and a significant precursor of modern science fiction has, however, long been recognized, and a considerable effort has recently been made to make the whole text available in electronic form.

The version I have translated was obtained from ebooksgratuits.com, although the first two volumes are also available from other suppliers.

The two authors of *Aventures extraordinaires d'un savant russe* were both at the beginning of their careers in 1888, having published relatively little before

---

[1] Many bibliographical sources give 1889, that being the date on the copy currently available in electronic form, but several copies offered for sale on the internet at the time of writing are dated 1888, and one is described as being dated 1889 but actually published in October 1888 (it was not uncommon for volumes published late in a calendar year to be dated for the following year). Flammarion's preface is, however, dated November 1888, so it is unlikely that the book was published before then. The first volume was certainly reissued when the second volume was published, and the copies dated 1889 might be a second edition. Sources also differ as to the date of the third volume, some giving it as 1891.

that year, at least in book form. Whether they formed their partnership spontaneously or were brought together by Edinger to execute a plan formed by the publisher, it appears that theirs was a literary marriage of convenience; the evidence of their separate careers strongly suggests that Le Faure was appointed to be the provider of the action/adventure component of the work, while de Graffigny was to supply the science content. There is no way to be certain, but de Graffigny might well have provided a rough draft that was then given to Le Faure for expansion and melodramatic enhancement—a pattern of production employed in other notable partnerships in French scientific romance, including three collaborative works by between Paschal Grousset (*alias* André Laurie) and Jules Verne and the two-volume "Martian Epic" credited to Octave Joncquel and Théo Varlet.[2]

The senior writer of the present partnership, Georges Le Faure (1858-1953), went on to become a prolific writer of popular fiction, especially for younger readers. Much of his work was in a vaguely Vernian vein, although he never did anything else as ambitious as the *Aventures extraordinaires*, and he became conspicuously more modest in his imaginative reach once the four-volume novel was complete. While the early volumes of the *Aventures extraordinaires* were in progress, however, he was extremely enthusiastic in his production of scientific romances—so much so that when Fayard took over Edinger's assets, he was able to reissue a three-volume omnibus of Le Faure's other *Voyages scientifiques extraordinaires* in 1892-94, containing nine novels originally issued in 14 volumes. Le Faure became a regular contributor to the Vernian *Journal des Voyages* thereafter, sometimes using the pseudonym Georges Faber, but most of his contributions were non-speculative adventure stories. He wrote a good deal of popular fiction in that vein, his most successful single work being *Les Aventures de Sidi-Froussard* (1891), a comic "patriotic novel" about French colonial adventures in the Middle East. He also wrote *feuilleton* fiction in the "cape et épée" swashbuckling vein pioneered by Paul Féval, including a gargantuan 225-episode serial featuring one of the stock characters of French picaresque fiction, *Robert Macaire* (1896-98).

The most successful of Le Faure's scientific romances was probably *La Guerre sous l'eau* (1890; tr. as *War Under Water*), an English translation of which was issued in the USA by Cassell in 1892. It features the construction of a submarine powered by electricity and armed with powerful torpedoes by an international secret society dedicated to the destruction of the German Empire. *Les Robinsons lunaires* [The Lunar Castaways] (1892) was more ambitious, and more handsomely-illustrated, but once he had completed the nine novels reprinted in the Fayard omnibus, and had belatedly put an end to *Aventures extraordinaires d'un savant russe*, Le Faure seems to have decided that speculative work was not worth the necessary imaginative effort and abandoned it, although

---

[2] Available in a Black Coat Press edition, ISBN 978-1-934543-41-2.

modest speculative technologies are featured in peripheral roles in some of the adventure stories he produced in the 1920s. Very little is known about his life, the only biographical details on record being the dates of his birth and death.

"Henry de Graffigny" was the pseudonym of Raoul Marquis (1863-1942), an engineer by training and a popularizer of science by vocation. The idea of writing the *Aventures extraordinaires* is likely to have been his, if it was not Edinger's. De Graffigny had made his first tentative foray into the subgenre of Vernian romance in 1887, with *Voyages fantastiques* [Fantastic Voyages], which he followed up with *De la Terre aux étoiles* [From the Earth to the Stars] (1888)—a work that is not as extravagant as its title promises, only taking in the Moon, Venus and a ride on a comet, although it might be regarded as a preliminary prospectus for *Aventures extraordinaires d'un savant russe*, whose early phases follow the same route.

Both these works, aimed at a juvenile audience, were awkwardly didactic, and a third, *Contes d'un vieux savant* [An Old Scientist's Tales] (1888), used a fictional frame simply to dress up a series of scientific lectures; it is unsurprising that Edinger thought that de Graffigny was in urgent need of a collaborator skilled in melodrama if he were ever to produce something that aficionados of Vernian fiction might actually enjoy. More typical of de Graffigny's contemporary endeavors were *Le jeune electrician amateur* (1888) and a multivolume *Petite Encyclopédie Electro-Mécanique* (1889), both of which were reprinted several times.

Although he worked for much of his life as a scientific journalist before "retiring" in 1920, ostensibly to dedicate his life to "electroculture"—the application of electricity to agricultural endeavor—de Graffigny did make further excursions into Vernian romance following the conclusion of the *Aventures extraordinaires*. Like Le Faure, however, he stuck to inventions that were, by comparison, conspicuous by their modesty. In *A travers l'espace—aventures d'un aéronaute* [Across the Sky—Adventures of an Aeronaut] (1908), the North Pole is reached by balloon; *La ville aérienne* [The Aerial City] (1910) is another account of an advanced aerostat. Considering that de Graffigny knew by the time he wrote these two novels that his advocacy of heavier-than-air craft in the *Aventures extraordinaires* had been justified, their production may seem deliberately retrograde—and, indeed, probably was. He seems to have become an enthusiastic balloonist himself by the time he wrote them, and his journalistic endeavors championed lighter-than-air craft against their upstart kin.

The most imaginative work of the latter part of de Graffigny's career, *Voyage de cinq Américains dans les planets* [A Voyage to the Planets by Five Americans] (1925), appears to have been directly inspired by André Mas' *Les Allemands sur Venus* (1913)[3] and he maintained a steady flow of non-fictional

---

[3] Included in *The Germans on Venus*, a Black Coat Press anthology of French scientific romances, ISBN 978-1-934543-56-6.

7

publications on the possibility of interplanetary travel, culminating in the speculative enquiry *Irons-nous dans la lune?* [Shall we go to the Moon?] (1932).
This was one of the first full-length works advertising the possibility of building
a rocket capable of flying to the Moon, and it includes a bibliography of relevant
imaginary voyages, although it had been long anticipated in France by Mas' po-
pularizing efforts—Mas had also included such a bibliography in *Les Allemands
sur Venus*.

De Graffigny's last scientific romances in book form were *Electropolis,
roman scientifique* [Electropolis, a Scientific Romance] (1933), *Les Martyres du
Pôle* [The Polar Martyrs] (1934) and *Au fond des Abîmes* [The Abyssal Depths]
(1934). The plot of the first-named, in which a rich Englishman, intent on rege-
nerating the Mesopotamian desert, recruits a French engineer who has invented
a technology for producing electricity directly from solar energy, seems to have
been a fairly slavish copy of Otfrid von Hanstein's *Elektropolis, Die Stadt der
technisen Wunder* [Electropolis, the Technological Wonder State] (1928; tr. as
"Electropolis" in *Science Wonder Stories*, 1930), while the others are themati-
cally similar to Le Faure's *Un drame sous le banquise* [Drama Under the Ice-
Cap] (1926), so it seems that de Graffigny was still having difficulty designing
appropriate fictional vehicles for his technological speculations. Unsurprisingly,
Pierre Versins' *Encyclopédie de l'utopie et de la science-fiction* is dismissive of
de Graffigny's talents as a fiction writer, considering him distinctly inferior to
the admittedly-slapdash Le Faure, but Versins readily admits his significance as
a popularizer of science.

Although Le Faure and de Graffigny are both almost entirely forgotten today, Raoul Marquis left one curious literary legacy. His work as a scientific
journalist included editing the periodical *Euréka*, for which Louis-Ferdinand
Destouches, alias Céline, worked in 1916-19. Céline produced an unusually detailed and affectionate depiction of his employer in the flamboyant character of
"Courtial Roger-Marin des Pereires," editor of "the favorite periodical of the
petty artisan inventors of Paris," *Génie* [Genius], in Chapters 109-119 of his au-
tobiographical novel *Mort à crédit* (1936; tr. as *Death on the Instalment Plan*).
This pen-portrait of "Courtial" is now Marquis' main claim to modern fame.

"Courtial des Pereires, it must be stated," Céline wrote, "was absolutely
distinct from the general run of petty inventors; he dominated the entire crawling
swarm of subscribers to the magazine from a great height… His self-possession,
his absolute competence and his irresistible optimism rendered him invulnerable
to the direst assaults of the most extreme stupidity… He never stopped producing, planning, devising, asserting… He had to shield himself against an on-
slaught of ideas and tread warily… He was pursued by wild notions, went ca-
reering off on the track of some fascinating whimsy… Holding his brilliance in
check had put him to greater trouble and required more superhuman effort than
all the rest of his work. He told me so."

8

There is undoubtedly an element of parody in this description, and its flattery is undoubtedly exaggerated. "He had an X-ray mind," Céline alleges. "He needed only an hour's concentrated effort and furious application to knock the weightiest idiocies into shape for good and all, to reduce the most pretentious claptrap to the level of the *Génie* in terms comprehensible to the most recalcitrant blockheads among its slowest-witted readers... To Courtial, nothing was obscure."

This is not, alas, the man we meet in reading between the lines of the *Aventures extraordinaires*—but that was, we must recall, a much younger man, whose enthusiasm still far outweighed his achievements. In one respect, however, the editor described by Céline is still very definitely, and quintessentially, the co-author of the *Aventures extraordinaires*: "At Courtial's, we worked under the aegis of the great Flammarion; his signed portrait occupied the center of the window; his name was invoked as that of the Almighty Himself whenever there was the slightest argument, for a mere trifle. He was the touchstone, Providence, the real McCoy; we swore by him and him alone..."

The historical importance of the *Aventures extraordinaires d'un savant russe* is primarily derived from the fact that it was a determined and highly ambitious attempt to hybridize action-adventure fiction and the popularization of science to produce a new kind of fiction: one that had much in common with the "hard science fiction" that aficionados of the American-born science fiction genre distinguished when they thought it politic to discriminate between stories that were fundamentally faithful to known science and those which merely used a lexicon of imaginary entities—spaceships, aliens, robots and so on—as standard props of futuristic costume drama or as metaphorical and symbolic devices.

Authentic hard science fiction is very difficult to write, for a variety of reasons, and de Graffigny and Le Faure encountered all those reasons. They failed to solve any of the resultant problems, but that is not surprising; it is, in fact, arguable, that all the writers who have addressed them since have also failed, albeit less conspicuously, but in a remarkably similar fashion. This first attempt, like all pioneering exercises, seems ham-fisted in retrospect, but the *Aventures extraordinaires* certainly cannot be faulted for its boldness, and even if the difficulties its authors experienced in writing it proved so taxing that neither of them ever attempted anything remotely similar again, the novel remains a monument of sorts. It is the longest scientific romance ever written, and it was not until the final years of the 20th century that the science fiction genre produced a handful of longer works. It was the first scientific romance to attempt a tour of the entire Solar System, and the first to venture outside by means of faster-than-light travel. Only a handful of subsequent scientific romances made similar attempts, and the fact that writers active in the American science fiction genre eventually grasped the nettle of interstellar navigation more firmly and more securely is largely responsible for the eventual triumph of that genre over its European rivals—which entitles *Aventures extraordinaires d'un savant russe* to be one of the most important proto-science fiction novels produced by the earlier genre.

In setting out to write a pioneering analogue of a hard science fiction story, de Graffigny and Le Faure were not entirely lacking in earlier models. The most important of these were a handful of works by Jules Verne, who had written several moderately daring but ostensibly "hard" scientific romances before being reined in by his publisher, P.-J. Hetzel and constrained to exercise greater modesty in his inventions. One of them in particular, *Autour de la Lune* (1870; tr. as *Around the Moon*), provided a cardinal example which de Graffigny and Le Faure plundered in a wholesale fashion, and they also borrowed extravagantly from a more problematic model in *Hector Servadac* (1877), in which Verne had attempted to dabble in interplanetary tourism, but had eventually been let down by his own lack of conviction.

Despite the carefully-researched technical detail that he put into his novels, in order to follow Hetzel's explicitly didactic agenda, Verne was not particularly knowledgeable about science, nor even particularly sympathetic to technological progress. The one futuristic novel he wrote, which Hetzel advised him never to publish lest it ruin his reputation—*Paris au XXe siècle* (tr. as *Paris in the Twentieth Century*), which was eventually rediscovered and published in 1994—was markedly hostile to the prospects of a society that has wholeheartedly embraced the rewards of technological sophistication. Although he was always under pressure to maintain the rational plausibility of his work, Verne was not above the use of casual imaginative flourishes with no logical basis, nor was he unwilling simply to throw up his hands and decline to rationalize inventions for which there could be no logical basis, as he did at the end of *Hector Servadac*. He was, in consequence, not an ideal model for late 19th century would-be writers of hard science fiction—but he was, nevertheless, the only one who possessed the least vestige of credibility, and the only one who has set any kind of standard for reference.

The other models of scientifically-sophisticated speculative fiction that immediately recommended itself to the attention of de Graffigny and Le Faure were a handful of experimental works by their own novel's dedicatee and Raoul Marquis' ultimate hero, Camille Flammarion—the leading popularizer of science in France, at least in terms of his literary fecundity and his popularity. Like de Graffigny, Flammarion was infinitely more comfortable writing non-fiction than fiction, and had no obvious talent for the narrative techniques that were becoming standardized as the method and apparatus of the novel, but he was well aware that speculative non-fiction, playing with the imaginative possibilities opened up by scientific discovery, was itself a kind of fantasizing, which might potentially benefit from the adoption of various kinds of narrative devices.

Early in his career, Flammarion had experimented with several such devices, especially the items collected in *Récits de l'infini* (1872; tr. as *Stories of Infinity*), and most spectacularly of all in the longest of those items, *Lumen* (1866-

69; expanded for separate publication 1887). *Lumen* is cast as a series of philosophical dialogues, but the latter ones—taking some inspiration from Sir
Humphry Davy's *Consolations in Travel* (1830), which Flammarion translated
into French while his own work was in progress—describe a cosmic tour in
which the eponymous post-human spirit, who is able to travel faster than light
and also to seek reincarnation on other worlds, offers an account of the universe
embodying contemporary discoveries in astronomy and contemporary theories
of biological evolution.

There was already a long literary tradition of such visionary cosmic tours,
initially inspired by the theological debate regarding the plurality of worlds, and
the key works in the tradition had often tried to take advantage of advances in
astronomical science. Bernard de Fontenelle's clever, witty and enormously
popular *Entretiens sur la pluralité des mondes* (1696; tr. as *Conversations on the
Plurality of Worlds*) had established a particularly significant landmark in
France. Christian Huygens' *Kosmotheoros* (1698), by one of the most important
early pioneers of astronomy, was rapidly translated into French, as was Emanuel
Swedenborg's monumental *Arcana coelestia* (1749-1756), which represented
itself as an authentic divinely-inspired revelation of the cosmic schema but drew
heavily on the legacy of the mystic's former career as a scientist.

Although the most popular such work produced in France in the Age of
Enlightenment, Marie-Anne Roumier's *Voyages de Milord Céton dans les sept
planètes* [Lord Seaton's Journeys to the Seven Planets] (1765), concentrated
heavily on the moral aspects of its cosmic scheme, the cosmic voyage included
in Nicolas Restif de la Bretonne's *Les posthumes* [Posthumous Correspondence]
(written 1787-88; published 1802)[4] was much more preoccupied with the potential biological exoticism of other worlds. Had the latter work been more widely
read, it might have provided a more significant example, but it was regarded as
an essentially scandalous work and had vanished from sight by the time Flammarion became active; although Flammarion cites it in his exhaustive survey of
Les mondes imaginaires et les mondes réels (1864; expanded 1892)—which
compared astronomical and literary images of the worlds of the Solar System—
he does not appear actually to have read it, and seems to be relying on a rather
dismissive second-hand account.

At any rate, what all these previous works had in common, no matter how
much or how little influence they took from scientific sources, was that they all
were couched as visionary revelations, and were thus devoid of the narrative
substantiality—or "hardness"—that had developed as the central characteristic
of the novel. That had never seemed to be a significant limitation before the
middle of the 19th century, when all books had perforce to be addressed to an
intellectual elite, but with the advent of popular fiction—especially popular fiction aimed at younger readers—the packaging of didactic narratives as tales of

---

[4] Also included in *The Germans on Venus*, q.v.

adventure, in which imaginary journeys were disguised as actual experiences, came to be seen as necessary if readers were to be intimately engaged.

Flammarion and Verne were both admirers of Edgar Allan Poe, and they both took seriously the preface that Edgar Allan Poe had added to the 1840 version of "The Unparalleled Adventure of Hans Pfaall"—the version that Charles Baudelaire translated into French—in which Poe had appealed for greater "verisimilitude" in accounts of lunar voyages, in order to fit them to the expectations of modern wisdom and modern literature. Flammarion and Verne were both well aware, however, that Poe's own account of the cosmic schema, contained in *Eureka: An Essay on the Material and Spiritual Universe* (1848), had been cast, of necessity, as a visionary fantasy, and neither of them could see any way to combine the demand for verisimilitude with the adventurous reach required by cosmic tourism. Flammarion's only novel, *Stella* (1877), was a straightforward *bildungsroman* with only a hint of frankly-supernatural speculation, while Verne's initial attempt to put Poe's proposal into practice, *De la Terre à la Lune* (1865; tr. as *From the Earth to the Moon*) had focused on the building of a gun to fire a projectile at the Moon and had concluded modestly, with its firing.

Although he wrote *Autour de la Lune* as a sequel to *De la Terre à la Lune*, Verne's space-travelers are hamstrung by the author's inability or conscientious unwillingness to envisage any means of getting them off the Moon again were they to land on it, and are thus restricted to making a looping voyage around it, confining their observation of the alien world to staring through portholes and discussing their observations with the aid of a lunar map. Nor did Flammarion's fellow popularizers of science make any significant headway with this sort of problem; P.-J. Hetzel published Henri de Parville's *Un habitant de la planète Mars* (1865; tr. as *An Inhabitant of the Planet Mars*)[5] alongside Verne's early works, but Parville—a more prestigious, if less popular, popularizer than Flammarion—could find no more convenient narrative medium for his own cosmic vision than to represent it as a series of discussions conducted at a scientific conference. Although Flammarion borrowed that device in the first part of *La Fin du monde* (1894; tr. as *Omega: The End of the World*), it was by no means a satisfactory solution to the problem of transposing scientific speculation into a reader-friendly narrative form.

In setting out their initial prospectus for *Aventures extraordinaires d'un savant russe*, de Graffigny, Le Faure and Edinger were explicitly setting themselves the task of attempting to fill in the "verisimilitude gap" that Poe, Verne, Flammarion and Parville had all been unable to bridge. They knew, in making such plans, that they would have to improvise the narrative means that Verne had scrupulously declined to construct, in order to allow them to make ports of call within the Solar System and range much further afield than Verne's charac-

---

[5] Available in a Black Coat Press edition, ISBN 978-1-934543-45-0.

ters had been able to do. They were willing not only to copy and elaborate Verne's space gun, but also to appropriate the highly dubious means of interplanetary travel that he had used in *Hector Servadac*, even though they knew that they would have to face up to problems of rationalization that Verne had been unable to solve—and they knew, too, that they would need further improvisations of which no one had yet thought.

In retrospect, the attempts that de Graffigny and Le Faure made to design a sequence of space vehicles—each more powerful than the last, so as to be capable of taking their characters to the outer limits of the Solar System and beyond—inevitably seem woefully primitive, and are now very obviously lacking in the verisimilitude that the authors were trying to cultivate, but they did do their best, and it was probably the best that anyone could have been expected to do at the time. It is also very obvious, in retrospect, that they suffered an eventual failure of imagination and nerve similar to the one experienced by Verne in *Hector Servadac*, but much more exaggerated in consequence of their bolder ambitions—but that too is forgivable, given that they were attempting the unprecedented, and we now know that no one would do any better for at least 40 years.

It would be inappropriate to continue the discussion of the particular narrative moves employed by de Graffigny and Le Faure in advance of the reader's experience of the text, so I shall postpone my further remarks on those matters to footnotes and an afterword, but I do need to make some further observations here on the particular difficulties that arose in the translation of this exceedingly awkward text.

However the text was composed, the fact that it appears to have gone through more than one draft did not result in any manifest tidying, and if the proofs were read at all, they were not read very scrupulously. The published text is abundantly littered with errors of every possible sort, some of which are presumably typesetting errors, but many of which must have been incorporated into the manuscript. Many of the proper nouns cited in the text are misrendered, probably because the manuscript used for typesetting was dictated to an amanuensis who did not know how to spell them by an author whose memory sometimes let him down. The narrative is also liberally strewn with continuity errors, seemingly resulting from memory lapses on the part of the dictator. Given its extreme length, it is not surprising that the story is rambling, and that its later phases do not have much in common with its earlier ones, but it is not uncommon for relatively short stretches of the text to include numerous inconsistencies and blatant contradictions. More worryingly, given the text's loudly-proclaimed didactic aspirations, many of the mathematical calculations carried out by the characters are mistaken; although some of these miscalculations are due to careless rounding of the cited figures and others are undoubtedly transcription errors introduced by the amanuensis or the typesetter, some can only have arisen from the arithmetical carelessness of the originator of the calculations.

All of these errors caused problems in translation, because I had to decide in each case—or, at least, each case that I detected, given that a significant proportion will surely have escaped my attention—whether to correct the error without comment, leave it in place without comment, or call attention to its existence. With grosser errors, which arise from understandable mistakes made by 19th century astronomers or the fact that the authors' understanding of certain basic scientific principles is a trifle confused, I felt compelled to leave the text as it is and to attempt explanation of some of its more intriguing shortcomings as best I could in commentary footnotes. To do that for more trivial errors would, however, have been inappropriate and could easily have resulted in such an enormous proliferation of notes that the text would have become ridiculously cluttered. I therefore decided simply to make small corrections wherever I could, and to leave some uncorrectable continuity errors in place without comment, thus confining my explanatory remarks to more serious matters, in which the reader might obtain some benefit from my supplementary observations. I can only apologize for perpetuating any errors that I did not notice, or could not resolve. I have also made some minor alterations to the content and arrangement of the text in order to make it read more smoothly in English and adapt it to its new format; the most significant of these adaptations is the continuous numbering of the chapters (which, in the original, started anew in each subsequent volume).

Having said all that, it is worth emphasizing that many of the more glaring faults in the original text arose, not from the carelessness of its authors, but from the sheer impossibility of their task. Much of what they were attempting to do in combining and fusing the legacy of astronomical discovery with the norms and expectations of novelistic narrative is akin to mixing oil and water, and would surely have defeated the ingenuity any contemporary individual or group of collaborators. The internal evidence of the text suggests that the two authors were as temperamentally incompatible as the materials they provided, but a certain emergent frustration was probably inevitable—and there is a sense in which the evident tension between their contributions, and the gradual development of that tension into a more-or-less open enmity, merely adds a further dimension to the fascination of a unique text.

Brian Stableford

THE EXTRAORDINARY ADVENTURES
OF A RUSSIAN SCIENTIST

"Our minds feel an intense communication with these inaccessible worlds."
Camille Flammarion, *Les Terres du ciel*

PREFACE

To Messrs. G. Le Faure and H. de Graffigny

You ask me if I approve of the thinking that has presided over the elaboration of *The Extraordinary Adventures of a Russian Scientist*—which is to say, the publication of a scientific romance entirely based on Astronomy.

Not only do I approve, but I also congratulate you on the path that you have taken. Nowadays, in fact, Astronomy is more than a science that remains inaccessible or indifferent; it emerges from the realm of data as a living thing. It is what touches us most intimately; without it, we would be living blindly in the midst of an unknown universe. No intelligent being, no cultivated mind is nowadays a stranger to the splendid discoveries of Astronomy: discoveries that allow us to live in the bosom of grandiose visions of nature and put us in direct communication with the sublime realities of Creation.

This is not the first time that anyone has tried to describe a voyage through space. Lucian of Samosata opened the way to us nearly 2000 years ago, and Cyrano de Bergerac transported us in his ingenious celestial voyages, written 200 years ago, to the bosom of *The States and Empires of the Moon and Sun*. More recently still, Edgar Poe has recounted the adventures of a burger of Rotterdam,[6] rising in a balloon as far as our satellite and sending back news to the town of his birth by courtesy of an obliging Selenite. Other writers, too numerous to name, have followed the same path—but it was the imagination that played the greatest—almost the only—role in these imaginary excursions. Henceforth,

---

[6] Lucian's "True History" is a satire on travelers' tales in which a ship is carried to the Moon by a whirlwind. Cyrano's Swiftian trilogy, of which only the voyage to the Moon and part of the subsequent tour of the Solar System survive, was by far the boldest, broadest and most imaginative satire of its era, which is why it was only published in a partial and bowdlerized form. The Poe story to which Flammarion refers is, of course, "The Unparalleled Adventure of One Hans Pfaall."

science, being more advanced, can serve as a solid based for such compositions and use ingenious fabulation to frame the facts revealed by the marvelous telescopic discoveries of our times, offering intelligent minds of all ages reading-matter incomparably more enthralling, more instructive, and even more seductive than the over-refined novels of an empty and unhealthy literature that are thrown out daily as fodder for misguided minds and which leave in their wake neither truth, nor enlightenment, nor satisfaction.

The fact is that the study of the universe, in itself, exercises a profound and captivating charm upon all those who embark upon it. The fact is that one experiences intense joy in launching oneself, on the wings of the imagination, towards the worlds that gravitate, in concert with ours, in the immensity of the skies, towards the comets, mysterious messengers of infinity, and towards the stars, sparkling radiances at our zenith.

How many questions there are to resolve in this journey through the wide-open immensities of space! What are the causes of the changes produced on the surface of the Moon? What is the red spot, larger than the Earth, apparent on Jupiter? And who hollowed out those channels linking up all the seas of Mars? What is the physical constitution of those pale nebulas lost in the depths of the Heavens, and the transparent tails of comets? What worlds and what human-kinds are illuminated by the ruby, emerald and sapphire suns that constitute the systems of double stars?

How many more points there are to elucidate!

People who want to take account, therefore, without undue fatigue, of the general constitution of the Universe, understanding that our Earth and its inhabitants are moving in space, will follow you in your audacious fecund attempt, you who have undertaken the mission of transporting them through the magnificent panoramas of the Heavens. It is good to live in the contemplation of the beauties of nature; it is pleasant to fly through the etheric heights, in the realm of the imagination, sometimes to forget the vulgar things of life to travel for a little while among the indescribable marvels of that Infinity whose center is everywhere and circumference nowhere.

CAMILLE FLAMMARION
Juvisy Observatory,
November 1888

PUBLISHER'S ADVERTISEMENT

Far be it from us to presume to add to the lines that the reader has just read and interrupt him on the threshold of this work, now that the celebrated astronomer and writer, signatory of the preface, has opened the door with his high competence and incontestable authority. He has brought to light, better than we could, the points in which the present work differs from previous attempts; he has said, better than we could—and his affirmation is a guarantee—that in *The Extraordinary Adventures of a Russian Scientist* the reader who cares about scientific truths will be able, while perusing pages that are sometimes dramatic, often witty and always interesting, to bring himself up to date with astronomical discoveries, the most recent of which have amazed the scientific world in this very year.[7]

The point on which we wish to insist, however, is this:

Until today, the *more or less* scientific romances that have dealt with astronomy have scarcely spoken of anything but the Moon; none of them has taken its hero through the whole series of celestial worlds, without omitting any, from our humble satellite, the first stop on the voyage to the resplendent stars and further beyond, by way of the Sun and the telescopic planets, small or giant, of our Solar System. Messieurs Le Faure and de Graffigny have undertaken this difficult task and we are entitled to affirm, in accordance with Monsieur Camille Flammarion, that they have done well, for they have succeeded in framing within their story, in a most original form, all the scientific data that it are nowadays indispensable to Astronomical knowledge.

Two artists well-known to and admired by the public, L. Vallet and Henriot, with all the intelligence and talent of their pencils, have collaborated in making this book a marvel, which leaves the publications of the same sort that have so far appeared—we mean those intended for people of taste—far behind.

---

[7] There are, in fact, no references in the text to discoveries made in 1888, and the reader will eventually discover that the authors, mindful of the fact that the adventures they are relating were bound to take several years, took care to set the beginning of their narrative in the relatively distant past. The now-established convention that allows a writer to establish a narrative viewpoint in the future was quite unknown in the 19th century, when all narrative viewpoints were tacitly assumed to be speaking in the present unless the author took care to place them in a manuscript relic of the past.

Is there any need to add that in form and content, this work is addressed to everyone, to young lovers of exciting and instructive adventure stories as well as grown-ups entranced by a love of science.

Our last word must be to thank publicly the highly-esteemed scientific individual who has accepted the dedication of *The Extraordinary Adventures of a Russian Scientist*.

G. EDINGER

Chapter I
In which there is some mention of marriage and much talk of the Moon

It was snowing outside. The white flakes were falling softly and soundlessly, powdering the trees and the roofs of houses and covering the roadway with a thick carpet, on which the sleighs slid silently along.

Only the bells of the rare carriages passing through this remote quarter of St. Petersburg imparted a joyful tinkling to the heavy atmosphere, sometimes punctuated by the dry crack of a whip. Inside, a profound silence reigned, troubled only by the rumbling of an enormous enameled stove occupying the very center of the room and the monotonous tick-tock of a clock enclosed in a carved wooden frame and hung on the wall facing the door. In the embrasure of the window, slumped in a vast armchair, a young woman was lost in a reverie, her relaxed hands resting on a piece of embroidery that she had allowed to fall on her knees.

With her pale and symmetrically oval face, lit up by her large and prominent blue eyes, her straight and slender nose with pink and palpitating nostrils, her small mouth, hemmed by lips that were perhaps a little emphatic but adorably ruby-tinted, her well-shaped chin, hollowed by a little dimple, her flaxen-blonde hair curling naturally over her forehead and falling to her shoulders in two long, thick plaits, each tied at its extremity by a blue silk ribbon, the young woman represented the Russian feminine type in all its purity. Her slim shoulders, her scarcely-accentuated bosom, her slender and lissom figure, and her slightly thin arms indicated that she was 16 or 17 years old—but on seeing the gravity of her forehead and the grooves that were hollowed out at the corners of her lips, one might have thought her 20.

Suddenly, the clock chimed five. The young woman shivered, passed her hand over her eyes—the gesture of a sleeper waking up—and murmured:

"5 p.m... He won't come now. Madame Bakunin promised me, though..."

Her gaze fixed itself momentarily upon the snow, whose flakes were swirling in the air and softly flattening themselves upon the windows. "Perhaps it's the weather that's delayed him," she added, seeking to give herself the excuses that the latecomer might well offer. Her lips formed a charming moue. "If he loves me, though, as he told Madame Bakunin," she muttered, "the snow wouldn't stop him..."

As she finished this speech, a violent explosion resounded, shaking the house to its deepest foundations, giving the impression that it was about to be torn out of the ground. At the same time, the window-panes shattered. A side-table set against the wall and loaded with instruments of every sort collapsed with a frightful racket, spraying the floor with debris, and the tall bookcases arranged along the walls released mountains of volumes through their broken glass fronts.

A profound silence followed, untroubled even by the ticking of the clock, which had been stopped by the shock.

The young woman had stood up with a single motion, as if activated by a spring, but once standing she remained motionless, both hands leaning on the back of the armchair, more astonished than truly afraid, with her eyebrows frowning slightly and her eyelids half-closed, in the attitude of a person trying to take stock of a situation.

"Poor father," she eventually murmured, with a smile. "He'll end up blowing us up once and for all."

Suddenly, shaking her shoulders, which had caught an icy blast coming through the broken window-panes, she took a few steps toward a table and rang a bell.

A domestic came in immediately, dressed in a muzjik's long red blouse and cotton trousers sunk into calf-length boots.

"That will need repairing, Vassily," the young girl instructed, pointing to the window.

"Your old father's done it again," the servant muttered, between his teeth. Then, noticing the debris strewn on the floor, he lifted his arms to heaven in a fearful gesture. "Ah, Holy Virgin!" he exclaimed, in a voice choked with emotion. "What will your old father say? His beautiful telescope...his photographs...his lenses...his spectacles...his books...!" Vassily had dropped to his knees and was crawling across the carpet on all fours, pausing at each disaster he encountered to deliver further lamentations.

"Vassily!" said the young woman, impatiently. "The window, quickly. It's freezing cold in here...."

The domestic got up and ran out.

As soon as he had disappeared, a door opened and someone else burst into the room like a bomb. It was an old man of short stature, apparently some 60 years old, lively and alert, with a pink and white face like a doll's, haloed by wispy grey hair that left the top of his head exposed, as shiny as polished ivory. Little could be seen of his clothing but an immense leather apron that covered him almost entirely, which was stained, frayed and corroded by acids and other chemical products. His hands and arms, which were bare to the elbows, bore the scars of numerous burns. In one hand he was holding a thick glass mask covered with tightly-knit steel mesh; in the other he was brandishing a metal tube blackened by the effects of a powerful explosion.

"Ah, Selena, Selena!" he cried, running toward his daughter. "I've found it!" And the old man kissed the forehead that the young woman extended to him several times over. Showing her the tube that he was holding and putting his finger on a narrow fissure, whose length he traced, he went on in a vibrant tone: "See—the formula is found...and no one in the world will dispute it. One gram—you heard right—just one gram of this explosive material, ignited by a spark and expanded by a temperature of 450 degrees, produces 10 cubic meters of gas. Do you understand, Selena? 10 cubic meters of gas! In an ordinary rifle, I dispense with the cartridge and leave nothing but a disk as large, at the most, as a silver coin...and do you know what the explosion of that simple disk produces? No? Well, it produces a platinum bullet weighing 100 grams, with an initial velocity of 2000 meters per second, and projects it 16 kilometers..."

The young woman put her hands together and opened her mouth to reply, but the old man did not give her the time. "Do you understand what a revolution this is in ballistics? All known explosives, from gunpowder to dynamite, roburite, and even melinite, are sunk..."

He shook his tube with a terrible expression.

"With a kilogram of this, you see, Selena, I could send the city of St. Petersburg into the clouds, and with a few tons one could blast the Earth that carries us into little pieces." His face radiant and his eyes sparkling, he started striding back and forth along the length of the small room, taking steps as large as his small legs could contrive. Then, all of a sudden, he stopped short in front of his daughter. "And do you know," he exclaimed, "what I'm going to call my powder? I want you to be its godmother, and I baptize it *Selenite!*"

The young woman made a gesture of horror. "Give my name to such a frightful thing!" she cried. "Never, never..." And she added in a reproachful tone: "Well, father? Is it really the art of destroying your peers to which you've devoted so much time and effort?"

The old man started, as if offended by his daughter's words. "Is that really you talking, Selena?" he asked. How can you suppose me capable...? Don't worry; if I want to give you name to a substance as terrible as the one I've just succeeded in formulating, it's not to procure me the pleasure of destroying anything at all. The goal that I'm pursuing is more noble, more grandiose and more worthy of Mikhail Ossipoff, member of the Scientific Institute of St. Petersburg and Vozduhoplavatel."

In saying this he had raised himself up to the full height of his short stature, and it seemed that his attitude was ennobled. Then, suddenly softening, he moved closer to Selena, took her hands in his, drew her to his breast and held her there for a little while. "Dear child," he said, eventually, "*She* and you are my entire life, as you know very well. *She* occupies all my thoughts and you fill my entire heart. Often, at night, in my dreams, I see you, as beautiful and chaste as the Virgin, your gracious face aureoled in gold, like that of a saint, by her luminous disk."

"Father..." murmured the young woman, emotionally.

"Oh, I'm so happy today," he added. "So very happy—and I want you to share in my happiness." He undid his belt and, suddenly pensive, went to sit in a leather-clad armchair near the stove, where he remained, head bowed, letting a vague gaze filter through his half-lowered eyelids, while his lips muttered silent words. "Selena," he said, suddenly, looking at his daughter, who was standing before him, motionless and surprised, "I have something to confess to you."

"To me, father?" the young woman murmured, immediately becoming anxious.

"Yes, my girl; you're grown up now and I want to tell you about a project that I've been nursing for a long time."

Selena's anxiety increased. Her cheeks were colored by a sudden pinkness and her long silky eyelashes, suddenly lowered, mirrored a shadow on her pale complexion. Then, as her father opened his mouth to continue, the young woman put her finger over the old man's lips, with a gracefully coaxing gesture. "Me too, father," she stammered. "I have something to tell you."

He looked at her in surprise. "A secret! You too?" he said.

She nodded her head affirmatively.

"Bah! What can it be?"

By way of reply, the young woman sat down on Mikhail Ossipoff's knees, put her arms around his neck, leaned her head on the old man's shoulder, and said—in a low voice as if she were ashamed—"I'm in love."

"You're in love!" he groaned. "You're in love? What does that mean?"

Then, very rapidly with her eyes fixed on the floor, the young woman replied: "You know, grandfather, that I go every Thursday and Sunday to hear mass at Our Lady of Kazan…now, about two months ago, as I got up again after kneeling down for the elevation, my foot caught in my dress—and I would certainly have fallen if, by the greatest of luck, a young man had not been there and caught me by the arm…"

She stopped for a moment to get her breath back and waited for a word of encouragement—but her father remained silent. "Since that day," she went on, "I've seen that young man every Thursday and every Sunday, leaning on the same pillar, never taking his eyes off me as long as the mass lasts, looking at me with a great deal of respect, and also with…how shall I put it?…all in all, in a manner that troubles me and gives me pleasure at the same time. Then, one day, on the floor of the church, I found him near the font, offering me holy water…my fingers brushed his and—I don't know why—I suddenly started to tremble…so much that I had to take the arm of Maria Petrovna to come back to the house."

She fell silent again and darted a sideways glance at her father, who continued to listen in silence, without the slightest sign of approval or disapproval appearing on his motionless face. Emboldened by the old man's attitude, Selena went on: "A few days later, Maria Petrovna mentioned to me, as we were approaching the house, that a man had been following us since we came out of Our Lady of Kazan. Without seeing him, I guessed that it was him; I didn't turn round, so afraid was I of showing him how troubled I was. However, as Vassily came to open the door, I couldn't resist. I turned my head ever so slightly, and I saw him 15 paces behind, stopped at the corner of the street, his eyes fixed on me...

"That was a Thursday, I think, and on the following Sunday there was a dance at Madame Bakunin's house—only you weren't able to go with me because there was a big meeting of scientists that evening at the Observatory, to discuss an eclipse of...I don't remember...and when I went into Madame Bakunin's drawing room, the first person I saw was him, leaning on a window-sill, looking at me, smiling..."

Selena stopped, all a-tremble, expecting to see her father leap to his feet. He did not do anything. He did not even flinch. The she added: "A few minutes later, Madame Bakunin introduced me to him as an excellent waltzer, and I danced with him. Since then, I've gone back to Madame Bakunin's every Sunday evening, and I've always found him...increasingly friendly...increasingly gallant...to such a extent that I wasn't surprised when, a week ago, Madame Bakunin told me that he's in love with me, that he had asked to tell me so and to find out whether he might hope...then I hugged that good Madame Bakunin. She understood, and it was agreed that she would bring him here today to make his formal request...." After a short pause, she added: "He has a little money...he's a diplomat, and his name is Gontran de Flammermont."

The old man started at the name and, seizing his daughter's hands, he cried: "Did you say *Flammermont*? Did you just pronounce the name of Flammermont?"

"Yes, father," the young woman replied, startled. "His name is Flammermont, he loves me, and he was supposed to come today to ask you for my hand."

The old man stood up abruptly and began striding back and forth feverishly. "Flammermont here!" he murmured, raising his arms in the air. "Flammermont, who loves you and wants to become my son-in-law. Ah, I never hoped for a happiness so great..."

Selena opened her eyes wide. "Do you know him, then, father?" she stammered, astonished.

"Do I know him!" exclaimed the old man. "Who in the world of science does not know Flammermont, the French scientist whose discoveries have constituted such astonishing progress in the study of astronomy? There, in my library, I have all his works; I've read them and re-read them...I know them by heart. Oh, he's an astonishing man—truly astonishing!"

The young woman looked at her father with a fearful expression. "But it's a mix-up," she murmured. "Doubtless there is a French scientist who has that name, but Gontran is only a diplomat...he doesn't know anything about science, and even less about astronomy." The truth suddenly became obvious to her. The old man had not heard a single word of the explanations she had given him; his mind had obviously been absorbed by some astronomical problem and only the name of Flammermont—the last word Selena had pronounced—had attracted his attention.

As the young woman opened her mouth to correct the error into which her father had been caused to fall by his customary distraction, however, the electric doorbell rang, announcing a visitor.

"It's him," Selena murmured, flushed with emotion.

"It's him," Mikhail Ossipoff repeated, radiantly. Then, immediately looking down at his stained, frayed and burned clothing, he added: "I can't receive him decently like this. Keep him company, my dear child, while I change my clothes." Without waiting for a reply, he lifted up a curtain and disappeared.

At the same moment, Vassily opened the door and announced: "Monsieur le Comte Gontran de Flammermont." Standing aside, he ceded passage to a young man of about 25 or 26, with an elegant figure, well wrapped-up in an ir-reproachably-tailored frock-coat, holding his head high. His face was divided horizontally by a broad russet moustache with a military trim, set over a mouth suggestive of ironic wit. His rather small brown eyes shone with a bright gleam, opening beneath bushy eyebrows that met at the top of his nose like two curved sabers. His broad and clear forehead was framed by a forest of carefully-trimmed and combed hair the same color as his moustache.

"Mademoiselle," he said, bowing deeply and enveloping the young woman with a loving gaze. "Madame Bakunin, having been suddenly taken ill, was unable to accompany me; nevertheless, seeing how very impatient I was to know my fate, she asked me to come anyway, assuring me that you would be good enough to introduce me to your father...so, in spite of the slightly irregular nature of this step..."

Selena smiled delicately, and replied, blushing slightly: "Indeed, it's perhaps not very...diplomatic...but, at the end of the day, it's a case of *force majeure*...." She offered the young man a seat, very graciously, and said: "Excuse my father, Monsieur; he left me just a moment ago to exchange his laboratory clothes for a more suitable costume." Then, drawing nearer to the Comte de Flammermont, she added: "Oh, Monsieur, if you knew..."

He became instantly anxious and asked: "What's happened?"

As she was about to reply, Monsieur Ossipoff appeared, grotesquely clad in an outmoded frock-coat covering a crumpled shirt soiled by laboratory work, around the neck of which a creased white tie was knotted like a piece of string. Arms extended, he advanced toward the young man, who went to meet him.

"Excuse me, Monsieur," said Flammermont, "for coming in this fashion to disturb the work and study of the man of genius to whom Russia and the entire world owe so many fine and great discoveries."

"You're entirely excused, Monsieur," Ossipoff replied, "for it's a great pleasure for me to shake the hand of the author of *Les Continents du ciel* and *Astronomie du peuple...*"[8]

---

[8] The Flammermont to whom Ossipoff is referring is, of course, a fictional equivalent of Camille Flammarion (although Flammarion will subsequently be

Gontran looked at the old man, quite nonplussed, opening his eyes wide—then his gaze strayed to Selena, and his surprise increased further as he saw the young woman put a finger to her lips.

Monsieur Ossipoff noticed the young man's expression and said: "You seem surprised—but my dear Monsieur, Russia is not a land of savages. We are familiar with the scientific progress of other nations, and, with particular respect to you..." He took him by the hand in a familiar manner, drew him to one of the immense glass-fronted bookcases that were arranged along the wall, and showed him the shelves crammed with books. "There," he said, pointing to enormous folio volumes bound in morocco leather, on the spines of which shone inscriptions in gold leaf. "You have the place of honor, you see."

Gontran was stunned, for a glance darted at those volumes had just made him understand the confusion to which the old man was victim. They were all works from the pen of the celebrated French astronomer Flammermont: *Les Continents du ciel, L'Astronomie du peuple, Les Mondes planétaires, L'Atmosphère terrestre...*[9] Mikhail Ossipoff thought he was dealing with the author of those remarkable works, whereas he, Gontran de Flammermont, a Comte by birth and a diplomat by profession, was completely at a loss with regard to anything resembling science. The mere words "equation," "polynomial" and "bisection" gave him a migraine, and here he was, being confused with one of the scientists who were the glory of his country.

In truth, chance plays some strange tricks. Straight away, Gontran saw how close his matrimonial projects were to running aground, now that the old man believed that the man aspiring to the hand of his daughter was a scientist like himself, a man navigating the infinity of space, more familiar with the stars than the Earth, more interested in lunar volcanoes and sunspots than the high tides and volcanic eruptions of our own poor planet. Honest and frank by nature, however, he could not bring himself to entertain the scientist's error, and he said: "I don't know how your error arose, Monsieur Ossipoff, but I must humbly confess that I am not the man you believe me to be."

As if by magic, the old man's attitude changed. "What did you say, then?" he asked, addressing Selena, in an offended tone. "Didn't you tell me that this gentleman was named Flammermont?"

"Certainly, Father dear," the young woman replied, "but I didn't tell you that he was the scientist you assumed him to be."

---

cited under his own name too), and these titles are thinly-disguised equivalents of *Les Terres du ciel* (1877) and the frequently-updated *Astronomie populaire* (first published 1880). The former substitute text will play a considerable role in the plot, under the revised title *Les Continents célestes*.

[9] The additional titles cited here are equivalents of Flammarion's *La Pluralité des mondes habités* (1864) and *L'Atmosphère* (1873).

The old man immediately pulled away and stood up straight, with a suspicious expression. "What is Monsieur doing here, then?" he asked.

The Comte turned to Selena. "I thought," he murmured, "that your daughter had explained...."

Selena interrupted him. "I told you, Father, that Monsieur de Flammermont loves me, and that he was coming today to ask for my hand." Seeing the old man's contracted eyebrows and hostile attitude, she added, by way of mollification: "Moreover, Madame Bakunin and I only encouraged the gentleman to take such a step once we were sure that you and he had ideas in common."

Ossipoff's expression cheered up slightly. Gontran's reflected the most profound astonishment.

"Yes," Selena continued, addressing the young man with a knowing look, "Monsieur le Comte is more than a friend of the sciences; he is a fervent adept, who is by no means indifferent to the great progress that out epoch has seen. In addition to the diplomatic career that he is obliged to follow, he has continued to occupy himself with astronomy, chemistry, physics and many other things..."

Flammermont looked at the young woman in dismay.

The old scientist fixed the young man with an abruptly softened gaze. "You're welcome in my home, Monsieur," he said. "Please be seated." Indicating a chair to his visitor, he sank into his armchair.

Meanwhile, with a skilled maneuver, Selena placed herself on a tapestry pouf directly behind Gontran's chair. Once installed, half-concealed by the semi-darkness that reigned within the room, she leaned forward slightly and murmured: "Don't be afraid—let my father speak and rely on me."

Somewhat reassured by these words, the young man put on a brave face and set himself to face the anticipated assault as best he could.

"You're presumably related to the author of *Les Continents célestes*?" asked Ossipoff, after a moment's pause.

Gontran, who had been expecting the conversation to deal with his marriage request, took the chance of replying: "Indeed."

Immediately, as if he were extremely pleased with that reply, the old man rolled his armchair closer to the young man's chair.

"And you doubtless see a great deal of him?"

"As much as I can," Gontran replied, deciding to give the answers that the questions seemed to invite.

Ossipoff's face lit up. "In that case," he said, "you must be very familiar with his theories. I mean his real theories—those that he expresses in private."

"*Very familiar* might perhaps be putting it a bit strongly," Gontran said, afraid of saying too much, "but I dare say that I'm sufficiently up to date with the illustrious scientist's thinking." And he added, privately: *May the Devil roast me alive if I know a single thing about what my worthy namesake thinks.*

As for Ossipoff, he rubbed his hands together with an expression of perfect contentment. "Let's see, Monsieur le Comte," he said, point-blank. "What do you think, personally, about the Moon?"

The young man remained quite dazed for a few seconds, and was racking his brains in search of a reply that might satisfy the old scientist when the latter added: "I'll explain what I mean. Do you—like the majority of astronomers, who start from the position that that Moon has no atmosphere and that nothing is ever seen to move there—believe that our satellite is a dead world, deprived of any species of life, animal or vegetable?"

"Well, I certainly don't claim to be able to affirm anything," said Gontran, who did not want to compromise himself, "However, the most elementary reasoning and the simplest common sense lead us to think..."

"That the Moon is the dwelling of inhabitants of some sort," Ossipoff finished for him, utterly convinced that he had divined the meaning of the young man's ambiguous words, "and you're right." And he added, mentally, considering these words as a reflection of the theories of the celebrated Flammermont: *I always suspected that Flammermont thought so. One can read it between the lines of his books*. Then he continued, aloud: "So you're a partisan of the doctrine of the plurality of worlds?"

"It's the only one that responds to my intimate sentiments," the young man replied, decisively, not knowing the first thing about the doctrine to which the old man was referring, but having heard Selena whisper an affirmative response.

Ossipoff got up and started pacing around his study, with his forehead furrowed, absorbed in his thoughts. Them stopping in front of the young Frenchman, he said: "My daughter is right, my friend, to say that we have ideas in common. Yes, I can see that you're a lover of the great things that distinguish human beings from the brute whose regrettable instincts they so unfortunately retain. I'm glad to find that you consider the Moon to be a province annexed to this Earth on which we are condemned to crawl. For myself, I proclaim loudly that the Moon will sooner or later be one of our celestial colonies."

"But..." Gontran put in, with a negative gesture.

"You're doubtless saying to yourself that the colony in question might be very difficult to found," Ossipoff went on, "since science has not as yet imagined any means of locomotion by means of which to quit our terraqueous globe and travel 100,000 leagues through the void!"[10]

"That's true," said the young man, having all the trouble in the world keeping a straight face.

---

[10] The French *lieue* [league] is equivalent to four kilometers; the text continual use of the term is inconvenient, but simply to translate all the references into kilometers would falsify the original, so I have retained it despite the inevitable confusion with the English league, which is equivalent to three miles.

"Then again, you also think that the country to be colonized is frightful, and would make the most wretched habitation—because the telescope shows us nothing there but rocks languishing in an eternal silence and lit for 354 hours at a stretch by an implacable Sun, whose intensity is never assuaged by any cloud."[11]

Flammermont listened, making no movement, for fear that the slightest gesture might be interpreted by his interlocutor as a contradiction of theories dear to him.

Ossipoff went on. "As to that, I reply to you that, like Airy[12] and many other astronomers and cosmographers, I think that we should not be too hasty to draw conclusions on the basis of what our imperfect telescopes permit us to distinguish. The most powerful telescope, in fact, only allows us to see as much of the lunar surface as we could see if we were floating over it in a balloon at a height of 100 leagues..." The old man shrugged his shoulders—a gesture replete with commiseration. "Now, I ask you," he went on, "what can one see at a distanced of 100 leagues? Objects several 100 meters in height or width. Thus, the pyramids of Egypt, transported to the Moon, would remain invisible to our most powerful optical instruments! We are told that the Moon is a dead world, uninhabited and uninhabitable because we see it from too far away to distinguish its cities, its inhabitants, its plants and animals—but that's absurd!"

"It's true, though..." the diplomat began.

Ossipoff cut him off. "Oh, I see where you're going," he replied, wagging his index finger at him. "You're going to tell me that, although the Moon might be inhabited by creatures created expressly to live in a world that has neither clouds nor water, it doesn't follow that the Moon might be habitable by beings like us—in a word, that there's no proof that you could survive there if you were transported there, because that would require your conformation, in harmony with the forces active upon the Earth, to still—by some freak of chance—be in harmony with the conditions existing on our satellite."

Gontran was about to reply when, feeling himself pulled backwards by the tail of his coat, he understood that Selena was instructing him to be silent, and he shut up.

"To that," continued the scientist, "I shall reply with Hansen[13] that the Moon is shaped like an egg, whose smaller end faces the Earth and whose center

---

[11] The actual length of the Moon's axial rotation is about 656 hours, which implies a duration of daylight of 328 hours.

[12] George Airy (1801-1892) was the British Astronomer Royal from 1835-81. He published a significant volume of lunar observations in 1886, following 14 years of careful measurement.

[13] The Danish astronomer Peter Andreas Hansen (1795-1874) published a landmark work on the moon in 1838, although his name was more familiar in connection with "Hansen's Lunar Tables," issued in 1857, based on his observa-

of gravity is set 60 kilometers from the interior central point of the hemisphere that is unknown to us. Now, if an atmosphere and liquids exist on our satellite, of which I am convinced, they must in consequence be drawn into that hemisphere, being unable to remain for a long time in the one we see in consequence of the attraction of the Earth and the existence of that center of gravity." Here Ossipoff paused, looking victoriously at the young man, doubtless expecting some sign of approval that had not been expectable previously.

"You said it!" cried Flammermont, warmly. "Your deductions are correct, illustrious master, and for myself, I've always thought, contrary to popular opinion, that there must be inhabitants in the Moon and that terrestrial humankind might very well be able to adaptable to it." And he added, smiling: "As no one will ever be able to go and try it, though…"

"How do you know?" exclaimed Ossipoff, folding his arms and looking at the Comte in a challenging manner. "Is it the distance that scares you? Why make a fuss about the 96,000 leagues that separate us from the Moon? They're trivial by comparison with the millions and millions of leagues that constitute the radius of the Solar System. Is it, on the other hand, the means of crossing those 96,000 leagues that gives you pause? Remember, though, that terrestrial humanity is young in its own world, and if you take account of the continual march of progress, you'll surely admit that science and industry will one day furnish our descendants with a viable means of abandoning our worldlet in order to visit, not only the Moon—which will be invaded by legions of emigrants— but the entire Solar System." The old man had rise to his full height. Standing directly in front of the dazed Gontran, he was talking in a vibrant voice, as if inspired. "And that day," he added, in a mysterious voice, "might arrive sooner than you think."

Ossipoff went swiftly to his bookcase, opened it, and reached out towards the volumes piles on its shelves. "I possess all the imaginary voyages written since antiquity, of which other worlds are the object," he said. "It seems to me that the Moon has been the rendezvous of all the storytellers and pseudo-voyagers. Here, for example, is the *True History* written by Lucian of Samosata, 500 years before our era,[14] Plutarch's *The Face of the Man in the Moon*, Godwin's *Man in the Moone*, by an Englishman who imagined having himself drawn to our planet by a team of swans.[15] As we arrive at what I shall call the modern period, I can cite, among other works, *The States and Empires of the*

---

tions. He received the Royal Astronomical Society's Gold Medal in 1854 for the theory of lunar deformation that Ossipoff cites here, but it was subsequently discredited.

[14] This is presumably intended to imply that Lucian was active in the sixth century B.C.; in fact, he was active in the second century A.D.

[15] Actually, they were geese, and it was Godwin's Spanish protagonist, Domingo Gonsales, who claimed to have been transported by this means.

Sun and Moon by one of your compatriots, Cyrano de Bergerac, *Discoveries in the Moon* by the American Locke and voyages to the Moon by Edgar Poe, Dr. Cathelineau[16] and many others that there is no need to list, but which are there, side by side, resting from the numerous fatigues to which I have submitted them. Each voyager, impelled by his imagination, has adopted a particular means of locomotion...but it is necessary to admit that they are all scientifically implausible."

Flammermont, who had listened to this long tirade religiously, got to his feet, seeing that it was over. "Monsieur Ossipoff," he said, in a serious tone. "I should like to ask you a question."

"Go on."

"The charm of your conversation is so great, Monsieur," the young man said, "and I experienced such contentment in hearing the subjects that you have touched upon discussed in my presence, that I had totally forgotten the reason for my visit. That is a crime of treason against gallantry for which I beg Mademoiselle Selena's pardon." Then, bowing formally to the old man, he said in a grave voice: "Monsieur Ossipoff, I have the honor..."

The scientist put out his hand. "I know, I know," he said. "But we'll make that, if you wish, the object of a particular conversation...after tea. You're staying for tea aren't you?" Without waiting for the young man's response, Ossipoff made a sign to Selena.

Selena got up, took the samovar that was fuming and bubbling on the stove and poured the odorous amber liquid into three fine Japanese porcelain cups. Then, going cup in hand to Gontran—who was following her with his eyes, mute and almost ecstatic—she murmured: "Don't stand there without saying anything. Don't wait for my father to ask you another embarrassing question—take the initiative."

Very embarrassed, Gontran reflected momentarily, then, finally, having gravely absorbed a sip of tea, he said, not without a certain familiarity: "My God! Given that some people consider the Moon habitable by men of our species, it's entirely natural that it has always been the object of dreams and aspirations of celestial voyagers. What astonishes me is that they have not thought more often of visiting the mysterious stars, which sparkle so poetically in the transparent night."

Ossipoff leapt out of his chair and Selena bit her lip.

Gontran, not knowing what he had said, alternated his gaze between them, trying to divine the enormity of his words from their faces.

---

[16] The very obscure *Voyage à la lune* published in Paris in 1865 by someone named Fauré (who might or might not have been related to the co-author of the present text) and credited to "A. Cathelineau" is probably a translation of *A Voyage to the Moon* (1864) by the pseudonymous "Chrysostom Trueman", one of the more imaginatively-adventurous lunar voyages of the 19th century.

"If you think about it," said the old man, in a slightly disdainful tone, "and if you calculate, imaginatively, the colossal distances at which—and I'm not talking about the stars—the planets of the Solar System orbit the Sun, you'll understand the difficulty of traveling to such distant worlds. The Moon, which rotates around us every 27 and a half days, is the first stop, the first station, of any celestial voyage.

The crestfallen Flammermont bowed his head, obstinately fixing his eyes the bearskin run that covered the floorboards, as if he hoped to find an idea of genius there. "Of course, Monsieur Ossipoff," he said. "I'm not unaware of the immense distances that separate the stars in the sky, and the disposition of the universe, as you can well imagine, is in no way unfamiliar to me." And he added, in an emphatic tone, while leaning backwards in order to hear what Selena was whispering in his ear more clearly: "Who does not know that the Sun is immobile at the center of our Solar System, and that it sustains the planets in the powerful meshes of its gravitational attraction?" Carried away by the approving nods of Ossipoff's head, and feeling the necessity of completely dispelling the bad impression that his recent ill-chosen words has created, he went on: "Those planets...those planets...are, first of all..."

"First of all what?" asked the old man.

"Those planets, "Gontain repeated, leaning back far enough to lose his balance "are, first of all..." But Selena remained mute—for what reason, he did not know—and he could not do anything else but imitate her.

Surprised by this silence, Ossipoff looked at the young man, suddenly assailed by doubts regarding the cosmological knowledge of the man who aspired to be his son-in-law. "Well?" he said, with a sort of impatient astonishment. "Those planets...?"

Flammermont shook himself, as if emerging from a dream, and replied by pointing to Selena, who went to her father, a cup of tea in her hand, "Excuse me, Monsieur Ossipoff, if I have descended from the immensity to which I had risen up with you, but have I not before my very eyes, in your home, an image of celestial phenomena: this star gravitating around the Sun of science!"

The young woman blushed with contentment. As for Ossipoff, his forehead cleared and, flattered in his paternal affection and in his scientific pride, he looked at Gontran gratefully.

By a skillful maneuver the young woman had slipped behind her father's armchair, over which she leaned for a few seconds.

"But to get back to our conversation," the old man continued. "You were saying?" His body bent forward, with his elbows on his knees and his eyes closed, he was concentrating all his attention on Gontran's reply.

The latter shrugged his shoulders desperately, looking at Selena. Suddenly, she smiled radiantly, as if a stroke of genius had suddenly come to mind. Silently, she stepped away from the armchair, turned to the wall—which was covered by an immense blackboard designed for the scientist's algebraic calculations—

31

and seized a piece of chalk. In the middle of the board she drew a circle, which she labeled in distinct letters: *Sun*. Beside it, a slightly larger circle appeared, along with the word *Mercury*.

Immediately, following Selena's explanatory mime from the corner of his eye, the young man said, confidently: "The first of the planets we encounter as we move away from the Sun is Mercury..."

"Which rotates around the sun in 88 days," added Ossipoff. "That's right."

Selena continued to write and Gontran, his eyes fixed on the savior blackboard, continued emphatically: "After Mercury, there's Venus, the Earth's younger sister."

"Whose year is 280 days, indeed, and whose distance from the Sun is 26,000,000 leagues, as you so rightly say.[17] Next is our Earth, isn't it?"

"At 148,000,000 kilometers," added Gontran, reading the figure that appeared in enormous characters in the corner of the blackboard.

"Then we find...?"

"Mars," the young Comte hastened to say. "Mars, 52,000,000 leagues distant,[18] and finally...Jupiter...the colossal, monstrous Jupiter..." He had not hesitated to attribute these epithets to the planet he had just named because of the large circle by which Selena represented it on the blackboard.

The old scientist had raised his head abruptly, and the young woman briskly resumed her place, leaning on the back of the armchair.

"Yes," said Ossipoff, in a vibrant voice, "you're right to qualify as monstrous a world equivalent 1300 Earths like ours, and whose diameter is no less than 35,000 leagues. Jupiter! That gigantic world, which turns on its vertical axis in only 10 hours! Jupiter, which is escorted in its course by four satellites, two of which are as large as the planet Mercury!"

Impressed in spite of himself by the old man's enthusiasm, Gontran remained motionless, interested, submissive to these astonishing revelations about a world of which he was hearing mention for the first time.

"And after Jupiter," Ossipoff continued in the same tone, "we find Saturn, the gigantic Saturn, 355,000,000 leagues away from the central star, which rotates on its axis, in the midst of its seven rings, almost as rapidly as Jupiter."

The scientist stopped, fixing Flammermont with a gaze that altered Selena to the fact that the young man was about to be asked another embarrassing question—so she said: "Isn't it that planet of whose calendar has—didn't you tell me, father?—10,000 of our days, which is 27 years and 3 months?"

"Indeed, but..."

---

[17] Venus' "year" is approximately 225 days and its mean distance from the Sun is approximately 108 kilometers, or 27 million leagues.

[18] Mars' mean distance from the Sun is actually 228 million kilometers, or 57 million leagues.

"Saturn covers more than 100,000 leagues in its orbit,"[19] the young woman continued, "and drags with it, in its movement around the Sun, its cosmic rings and eight satellites..." She stopped. Seizing the old scientist's head in both hands, she tipped it back and kissed it. "Well, Father?" she said. "Am I an exceptional student, and am I a credit to my professor?"

Mikhail Ossipoff was radiant; he enveloped his daughter with a tender regard and exclaimed to Gontran: "And you thought I might give this child to the first comer—one of those down-to-earth idlers indifferent to the celestial marvels that surround us! But that would be a crime, my dear sir, and I would 100 times rather see Selena remain a daughter than have a son-in-law of whose education I could not first be convinced."

Flammermont was chilled to the marrow on hearing these words, whose forcefulness proved their sincerity.

"Then again," added the old man, in a mysterious tone, "I've had a great project in mind for many years, for the execution of which I'm counting count on the collaboration of a son-in-law—for a son-in-law is almost a son—in whom I can have complete confidence...while a stranger might deceive and steal from me...and I'd run the risk of having spent my life in sleepless nights and studies only for some wretch to deprive me, perhaps not of the honor of success, but at least of the honor of having made the attempt."

There was so much bitterness in these last words that Gontran, involuntarily moved, got up and went to squeeze the old scientist's hand. "Monsieur Ossipoff," he said, "be assured that you would have in me, if not a useful collaborator, at least a son filled with respect and devotion."

"Thank you, my friend—my son," stammered the old man, making an effort to hold back a tear that was balanced on the edge of his eyelid. I've taken aboard your proposal, your request...but as I said to you just now, I'll discuss that with you later. For the moment..."

Selena, for her part, had continued writing on the blackboard. Rapidly, with a few strokes of the chalk, she had completed the sidereal diagram.

Gontran, desirous of displaying the instant erudition that he had acquired by means of the young woman's subterfuge to his future father-in-law, exclaimed: "And when one thinks that beyond those giant worlds, whose relative proximity permits us to appreciate their dimensions, there are others, and yet others, and others still..." He darted a rapid glance at the blackboard and added: "Thus, we shall never know whether Uranus and Neptune, which is more than a billion leagues distant from the Sun, really are the outermost planets of the Solar System. At such a distance from the cosmic torch, those worlds must be inert and icy..."

---

[19] Actually it covers more than twice that—Graffigny appears to have multiplied the radius rather than the diameter by *pi* to obtain the circumference of the orbit.

"Wait, wait!" cried Mikhail Ossipoff. "What is the billion leagues at which one encounters the planet Neptune, in comparison to the sidereal desert in which the Solar System moves as a unit, borne by the central star!"

"The sidereal desert," the Comte de Flammermont repeated, mechanically.

Thinking that he detected a question in the tone in which these three words had been produced, the old scientist continued: "Represent by a meter the 37,000,000 leagues that separate our Earth from the Sun and the outermost planet—Neptune, about which we were speaking, which travels at million leagues from Apollo—would be 30 meters away. Now, to arrive at the zone of another sun, the nearest star to us, would require that step to be repeated 7,400 times—which represents 222 kilometers, on a scale of one meter per 37,000,000 leagues. 222 kilometers is the distance between St. Petersburg and Moscow. Such is the sidereal desert—and note that those 222 kilometers form, in reality, several trillion leagues, a figure so large as to be unimaginable."

Gontran, immobilized by the amazement into which these figures had thrown him, fixed the old man with a wide-eyed stare.

Ossipoff went on: "You know that light travels 77,000 leagues, or 304,000 kilometers, in a second; well, it takes three and a half years to reach the nearest star to ours.[20] As for sound, it only travels at 330 meters per second—so that, if that star exploded, the noise of the explosion would only reach us after 3,000,000 years."

"But then," said the Comte, quite bewildered, "given that a train only travels at 60 kilometers an hour, it would need...."

"To travel without interruption for 60,000,000 years before arriving at its journey's end—which is to say, at the star."

"In that case," Gontran said, ingenuously, "the stars that we see sparkling in the immensity of the Heavens might be long extinct, and yet continue to illuminate us, since their light takes centuries to reach us."

"Certainly." As he pronounced this word, Mikhail Ossipoff's eyes moved mechanically in the direction of the clock and he got up, murmuring: "9 p.m. already! It's time to go." Then, turning to Gontran, he said: "My friend, present your respects to my daughter, who will retire to her own room."

"Oh, Father!" murmured the young woman, in a pleading tone. "Don't go out tonight."

"Duty calls, my child," the old man replied.

"Just for this evening, for Monsieur's sake, make an exception and stay here..."

---

[20] The nearest star, Alpha Centauri, is actually 4.2 light years (approximately 9.4 trillion leagues) away, but measurements of stellar parallax—and hence of stellar distances—were still rather approximate in the 1880s.

"Monsieur is going with me," Ossipoff replied. "In any case, I don't want to delay the conversation that we must have with one another—and where I'm going, we'll have plenty of opportunity to chat."

Selena looked at her father with a curious expression, which surprised Flammermont. "May I, without indiscretion, know where you're taking me, Monsieur Ossipoff?" he asked.

"I'll tell you that in a little while, when we're alone."

"Oh, Father!" exclaimed Selena, reproachfully. "Don't you trust me?"

"It's not that, my child—but at the point I've reached, the utmost prudence is required." Addressing Gontran, he added, with a deep sigh: "Astronomy elevates minds, but—alas!—does not prevent certain hearts from crawling in the mud. Also…but I'll explain that later…come on!"

The diplomat was increasingly troubled by the old man's reticence, not to mention the fact that he dreaded having a scientific conversation with him in private—which would not take long to enlighten Ossipoff as to future son-in-law's complete ignorance of astronomical matters. He could not retreat, though. Already, the old scientist was waiting for him on the threshold, enveloped in a thick cloak, with his head covered by a fur cap with ear-flaps, clicking his tongue impatiently to tell him that he had to hasten his farewells.

Gontran took the delicate hand that Selena extended to him in his own, bowed like the gentlemen of the 18th century, and deposited a kiss thereupon that illuminated the young woman's cheek with a sudden blush, by courtesy of the emotion the caress invoked in her heart. She made no attempt to withdraw her hand and, with a slight smile, murmured in a low voice: "Be careful, Monsieur de Flammermont; remember that your happiness depends on the satisfactory replies that you make to my father."

Just like the baccalaureat, thought Gontran, and replied: "Alas, I'm direly afraid of making a false step, now that I no longer have my star to guide me."

Chapter II
In which Gontran conceives serious doubts about the cerebral stability of his future father-in-law.

The door in the vestibule was wide open, and Vassily was standing on the threshold in a threatening attitude, shaking his fist at several individuals assembled in the street, whom he was cursing in a most vehement fashion. The domestic's colorful language resonated continually with the words "dog," "thief' and "bandit"—to which the crowd responded with savage howls accompanied by powerfully compacted snowballs, one of which had already injured the unfortunate Vassily's nose.

At the sight of Mikhail Ossipoff the insults doubled in vigor and intensity; at the same time, a general discharge peppered the old scientist and his companion. Ossipoff went back into the house precipitately, but Gontran, whose patience was not the finest of his qualities, ran to his *droshky*, which was stationed in front of the door, seized the coachman's whip and made its long lash whistle as it fell upon the crowd several times over, stinging calves, shoulders and faces at random.

Within two minutes, the street was deserted.

"What's up with those brutes?" the Comte asked Vassily—who, forgetting the pain of his crushed nose, was writhing with laughter as he heard the howls of those attained by the vengeful lash.

"Those brutes accuse the old man of being a forger or a thief! There's even one who claims he's a nihilist!" Lifting his arms to the heavens in a gesture full of indignation, Vassily added: "The old man a nihilist! So, you understand, not wanting to hear that, I treated them as they deserved…and there you are!"

"But why do these people claim such things?" asked the young man.

"The domestic looked around to make sure that Ossipoff was not listening, and replied in a low voice: "It must be admitted that the old man isn't a good neighbor. I don't know what he does down there"—Vassily struck the floor-tiles in the vestibule with his boot-heel—"but there are explosions all the time, loud enough to make one think that the entire quarter is about to be blown up."

Gontran opened his eyes wide. "The thing is," Vassily went on, "that this evening, some time before you arrived, the entire house trembled. The windows broke, and all the old man's beautiful instruments rolled on the floor, along with a lot of his big books." Then, drawing the young man to edge of the roadway and leaning over to look more closely at the ground, the domestic pointed to a long hairline crack, which extended all the way across the street, and added: "That's more of the old man's work—that was also made just now, and it's what put the neighbors into the fury you just saw."

36

Gontran shook his head and murmured: "He's a peculiar old chap." And he added, with a little mocking laugh: "I hope he isn't taking me out by night to subject me to his experiments in ballistics...he's quite capable of sending me to the Moon, to see with my own eyes whether his theories are correct."

As he finished this private reflection, the old scientist arrived at a run. "Excuse me for having kept you waiting," he said, "but I'd forgotten some papers. We can go now." As he said this he climbed into the carriage.

Flammermont installed himself by his side and asked, not without a certain curiosity: "Where are we going?"

"Please would you tell your coachman to go to the Pulkova neighbnorhood. Once we get there, I'll tell him when to stop."

What a mystery! thought Gontran. *Those clowns might have been right after all...who knows whether the old lunatic might be taking me to a secret meeting of nihilists?* Nevertheless, he transmitted the old man's instructions to the coachman—who, shaking up his horses, touched them with the long and flexible lash of his whip, adding a particular clicking of the tongue to this stimulant. The animals departed at a fast trot and the droshky, sliding noiselessly over the snow, headed for the wealthier quarters of St. Petersburg.

The snow had stopped falling and the sky, very clear and cloudless, extended its dark blue cupola, studded with stars like golden nails, over the silent city. The two men, wrapped up in their furs to protect them from the cold—which was much more intense than it had been earlier in the evening—maintained silence, each absorbed in his own thoughts of very different sorts.

Gontran, his eyes vague, was thinking about Selena, whose grace and beauty had entirely seduced him. The vision of the young woman caused a little smile to form on the Comte's lips: a reflection of the great happiness with which his soul was filled. Sometimes, though, that smile disappeared, giving place of an anxious moue whenever Flammermont's gaze happened to fall upon his companion and he thought about the tête-à-tête that might cast a shadow over his love. Mentally, the young man went over in his memory all the names and figures with which the tea gracefully served by Selena had been seasoned, promising himself to utilize those astronomical notions and to get as much out of them as possible. *After all*, he thought, *I'm no more stupid than the next man, and this Monsieur Ossipoff is so distracted....* Then, after a moment, still privately, he added: *All the same, I'd rather go to a congress of nihilists...it would probably be more dangerous, but at least my love wouldn't be running any risk.*

For his part, Ossipoff was deep in thought—and, contrary to what Gontran supposed, the old scientist had not "set off for the Moon." He was entirely preoccupied with the situation—as the young man might have guessed had he noticed the many rapid glances that the old man darted at him on the sly. Moreover, it seemed that, in the course of their long familiarity with spectacles and telescopes, Ossipoff's eyes had acquired something of the property of magnifying lenses, and that they possessed a particular acuity, thanks to which he could sound the depths of the human soul as he sounded the immensity of the Heavens. With his brows slightly furrowed, his eyelids half-closed and his lips a trifle pinched, analyzing in his brain as if in an alembic, he concentrated inwardly all the particulars that his gaze had seized from the physiognomy and attitude of the young man, trying to divine the personality in the presence of which he found himself. Was this a father who wanted to determine the measure of happiness that the man who wanted to become his son-in-law might give to his daughter? Was it not rather a scientist desirous of knowing the extent to which he might confide in the natural collaborator that love had procured from him?

Meanwhile, the *droshky*, having gone along the right bank of the Neva, had crossed the river opposite the headquarters of the Admiralty and, leaving Garskovaya and the Nevsky Prospect on its left, had gone into the Voznesenskaya, which it followed for its entire length, drawn at a rapid trot by its horses, whose hooves kicked up clouds of powdery snow, bloodied by the red glare of its lanterns. Turning right, the carriage suddenly found itself in the suburbs of St. Petersburg and glided soundlessly for a quarter of an hour through the silent and sleepy streets of the Pulkova district.

Suddenly, the coachman pulled on his reins; the horses stopped and he leaned down from his seat to ask: "Where shall I go now, Monsieur le Comte?"

Gontran touched Mikhail Ossipoff's right arm. "The coachman wants to know which road he should take."

As if awakening with a start, the scientist sat up in the midst of his furs, darted a rapid glance outside, saw where they were and replied: "We get out here!" And, before Flammermont could raise any objection, Ossipoff jumped down on to the compacted snow and gestured an invitation to his companion to follow him. Then, addressing the coachman, he commanded: "Stay here and wait until we come back."

That said, he took Gontran's arm and, with more agility than one might have expected in a man of his age, drew him into a dark and narrow side-street, solely illuminated by the whiteness of the carpet of snow extended underfoot.

"For sure," the young man murmured, inaudibly, "we're going to attend some secret meeting at which various means of putting the Emperor of all the Russias to death will be discussed. In truth, here I am! This is a fine occupation for an attaché of the embassy of the French Republic!" And yet, the sweet image of Selena drew him onwards in spite of the reasoning that told him to stop. Not for an instant did he think of turning back, or even asking his guide a question. Love rendered him fatalistic and he thought, as the Orientals do: *what is written is written.*

Suddenly, the buildings bordering the right-hand side of the street vanished, giving place to a high wall, alongside which Mikhail Ossipoff and Gontran de Flammermont went on for some 50 meters. Then the old scientist suddenly stopped, rummaged in his thick furs, and brought a key out of his pocket.

He introduced it into the lock of a little door in the wall, which Gontran had not noticed.

"Have we arrived?" murmured the young man.

"Almost," Ossipoff replied, standing aside to let him go through the doorway, the door having turned silently on its hinges.

To his great surprise, the young Comte found himself in a vast courtyard, surrounded on three sides by a high wall similar to the one he had just passed along, thus forming a parallelogram whose fourth side was occupied by an imposing monument surmounted by a cupola rounded like the dome of a church.

What can that be? Gontran asked himself, darting curious glances around him while Ossipoff carefully closed the door again.

"If you'd care to follow me," said the old scientist, crossing the courtyard in the direction of the black and silent buildings that loomed up in front of them.

With the aid of another key Ossipoff opened a second door and pushed Gontran in front of him. The latter was slightly choked with emotion. The two men were now in pitch darkness.

"Give me your hand," whispered the old man in Gontran's ear, "and let yourself be led without fear...above all, be careful to make as little noise as possible."

An imposing silence reigned in this place, which Flammermont judged very high-ceilinged, on the basis of the sonority of the dull echoes that his steps, and those of his companion, awakened. A considerable coldness seemed to be descending upon his shoulders, and he thought that they must be moving beneath stone vaults. That was, however, all he could deduce regarding the mysterious dwelling—through which Mikhail Ossipoff was guiding him without any hesitation, in spite of the thick shadow that enveloped them, thus proving that it was all entirely familiar to him.

After successively climbing up and going down several flights of steps, opening and closing several doors, the scientist eventually pushed one last hinged door and said, in a low voice: "Here were are...stay here quietly, without moving, while I go put the light on." With these words he let go of Gontran's hand, headed confidently for the wall—avoiding objects whose mass could be vaguely divined in the darkness—and pushed a button. Immediately, a bright light sprang from an electric lamp, inundating the place where Ossipoff and his companion were with its radiance.

It was a vast circular room topped by a semicircular dome—the same one that Gontran had seen from outside—quite similar to the one surmounting the old Cornmarket in Paris, but not as large. In the middle of this cupola—to employ the technical term—on a carriage of cast iron and steel, stood a monstrous tube measuring 50 or 60 meters in length, with a diameter of about two meters.

The sight of this gigantic machine made Gontran open his eyes very wide, immediately reminding him of the mysterious occupations to which, according to popular rumor and the honest Vassily himself, Ossipoff devoted himself in the basement of his house. A connection was made in his mind between the terrible explosives that the scientist must be researching and this instrument. "A cannon!" he murmured, loud enough to be heard.

The old man started. "A telescope!" he replied.

Gontran bit his lip, furious with himself for the enormous stupidity of which he had just been guilty—but the thought of Selena immediately caused him to pull himself together, and he calmly replied: "That's what I meant."

"Of course," said Ossipoff, shaking his head with an ironic smile.

"Take note," the young man added, gravely, "that in making use of that expression, which seemed to surprise you, I was only repeating one that had been used in my presence one evening by my illustrious relative, Monsieur Flammermont."

Ossipoff's eyes widenened. "Yes," Gontran continued, imperturbably, "one evening when the celebrated Flammermont was with me and some other people at the Paris Observatory and he was explaining the mechanism of the large telescope that he generally uses for his observations, he compared the telescope to a cannon that sends the observer's soul to the stars."

The old scientist nodded his head approvingly. "Quite so," he murmured. "Quite so." If Gontran's ears had been keen enough to hear what the old man was saying to himself, however, he would have heard the private addition: *Flammermont only sends souls there, whereas I...* Then, turning to Gontran, he said: "I see by your words that you've guessed where we are."

"Of course," sad the young man, in a breezy tone. "We're in an observatory..."

"Yes, my friend, we're in the Pulkova Observatory,[21] and this instrument, which my illustrious master so rightly likens to a cannon, is our new telescope, one of the largest, best and most powerful in the entire world."

Gontran circled the instrument, making admiring gestures.

"Yes," Ossipoff went on, "its construction required nearly ten years of uninterrupted work, and its installation is a marvel of precision. I make no mention of the many thousands of roubles that its construction cost—that's a mere detail..."

While speaking, the old man had moved to a lectern on which an enormous volume stood open; it was the *Connaissance des temps* published by the Bureau of Longitudes in Paris.[22] He turned the pages with a rapid finger, and Gontran

---

[21] The Pulkova (or Pulkovo) Observatory had been active since 1839, and was the most important in Russia. Pulkova is actually 19 kilometers south of St. Petersburg rather than being a suburb of the city.

[22] Jean Picard's *La Connaissance du temps ou des mouvements célestes*, first issued in 1679, was the pioneering astronomical ephemeris, recording all the phenomena whose observation was anticipatable in a particular place; updated versions are still issued annually in many nations. It is unclear why this edition re-

saw him finally fix his eyes on one and murmur, while tracing lines with his index finger: "Passage of Biela's comet... eclipses of Saturn's satellites... occultation of Mars..." Ossipoff released a little exclamation: "Here's what I need!"

He quit the lectern, came back to the huge telescope, switched on a little lamp that illuminated the meridian circle and, thanks to a powerful clockwork mechanism that could be activated by the simple pressure of a finger, the enormous tube rose up vertically as easily as if it had weighed no more than a few 100 grams. When it was in the desired position in that dimension, Ossipoff pressed another button, and the telescope rotated horizontally, like a marine gun pivoting on its carriage. The scientist lifted his finger, and the gigantic tube became motionless.

Having done that, Ossipoff ran to the cupola and set the entire metallic dome in motion, rolling on its bronze castors, until it was in the desired position. Then, pulling on cords attached to the wall, he opened a trapdoor in the cupola immediately in front of the mouth of the telescopic canon, through which a segment of sky appeared.

Gontran had not missed a single one of the scientist's movements, but had been sufficiently clever not to manifest any astonishment, as if these various operations were quite familiar to him.

Ossipoff, pointing to the telescope, said: "Look!"

The young man put his eye to the ocular lens. He had to grab hold of the telescope in order to remain motionless and not step back, so great was his surprise and admiration.

"You recognize the Triesnecker Crater and its surroundings, in the equatorial region of the Moon, don't you?" said the old man.

"Of course," Gontran replied, briefly, entranced by the spectacle before his eyes. He seemed to be floating a few kilometers above an unknown world; high mountains projected their sharp and shiny peaks into space, betraying their prodigious elevation by the immense extent of the shadows that they extended over the plain. There was an inextricable confusion of pits, crevasses and gaping craters, and the young man felt his throat constrict with an indefinable emotion at the chaotic appearance of that grandiose landscape, seemingly fixed in eternal immobility.

Ossipoff had stopped the movement of the telescopic tube, though, and the Moon—then in its first quarter—successively presented its entire territory to Gontran's marveling eyes. The eastern region filed slowly past, with its crater-pimpled ground, its mysterious grooves, its abysms and dry seas. Eventually, the edge of the disk also appeared, and the Comte uttered an exclamation of surprise.

"What is it?" asked the old man.

---

fers to Biela's comet, which was observed to have split into two in 1846 and was not seen again after 1852.

"A star!" the young man exclaimed. "A star, about to pass behind the Moon."

"It's not a star," the scientist replied. "It's the planet Mars." Then, gripping Gontran's arm, he said, with suppressed emotion: "Look hard, and tell me exactly what you see."

"Certainly!" said the young man, naively. "I see a little reddish ball moving slowly forward, which is about to disappear...ah! Here's something strange...it's become slightly fainter...but I can still see it."

Ossipoff, whose eyes were fixed on the sidereal clock and who was counting the seconds in a whisper, replied, excitedly: "It's not the planet that you're seeing, for that disappeared behind the Moon 15 seconds ago, but simply its reflection."

"Ah!" said Gontran. "I can no longer see anything now."

He was about to quit the ocular lens, but Ossipoff held him in place, with unexpected force. "Stay there!" he commanded, giving the ocular lens a slight push. "And keep on looking."

Meekly, Flammermont remained still, widening his eyes. He was becoming impatient with standing still and seeing nothing when he exclaimed: "Ah! Now that's very strange... I can see the planet again, but it's on the other side of the Moon now."

"And yet it has not reappeared at the horizon," Ossipoff retorted, his eyes still fixed on the clock.

A few minutes ran by.

"There it is...there it is," the young man repeated. "It's two thirds visible. My word, the edge of the Moon is very dark at the place where the planet has emerged..."

These were undoubtedly the words that the old man was waiting for, for he uttered a cry—a cry of joy and of triumph—and, grabbing Gontran, he almost dragged him away from the telescope. Drawing him closer, he said: "You saw it, didn't you? You really saw it...I knew that you'd be convinced by your own eyes."

Breathlessly, he fixed the young man with staring eyes in which there was a strange gleam. Then, sitting down and indicating that his companion should do likewise, he murmured: "Bless the good fortune that permitted me to show you that this very day."

Gontran looked at him, quite astonished.

"You have just had, before your very eyes, material and palpable proof that all those who consider the Moon to be a dead star, uninhabited and uninhabitable, are grossly mistaken."

The young man contented himself with an approving nod of the head, afraid of compromising himself again by some imprudent remark.

"They say that the Moon has no atmosphere! And what do they base that on, I ask you? On the fact that the disk's surface is never veiled by any cloud and that the disk always presents the same appearance to us...on the fact that any atmosphere produces twilight, and that the bright and dark parts of the Moon are separated from one another by a clear-cut line presenting no gradation of light! Others have examined the spectrum of a star at the moment of its occultation and, not having remarked any change in the color of the spectrum, conclude that the atmosphere, which should have caused such a variation, is absent. Yet others, departing from the principle that lunar radiance is only the reflection of solar radiation, declare that the spectrum formed by the Moon's light ought to present absorption lines added to the solar spectrum by the lunar atmosphere! Now, all these observations prove, they say, that the Moon simply reflects solar light like a mirror, without the slightest atmosphere modifying it in any way whatsoever."

Ossipoff shrugged his shoulders, and added: "All that's plausible...but it's not true! You've just seen the proof of it yourself. Do you think that you would be able to perceive the planet Mars, even after its disappearance, if its rays had not been reflected—and what could have produced that reflection, I ask you, if not the lunar atmosphere? It's for the same reason that it was possible for you to perceive it at the other side of the disk before the conclusion of the occultation. Come on, frankly—does what I'm saying to you seem absurd?"

Gontran made a movement suggestive of indignation. "Which is to say," he replied, vibrantly, "that all of that is as clear and limpid as a rock pool."

"As for the twilight," Ossipoff went on, becoming progressively more animated, Schröter[23]—who was certainly not a donkey—has not only demonstrated the existence of lunar twilight, but has even found that its arc, measured in the direction of the tangential solar radiation, is two degrees 34 minutes, and that the atmospheric layers that illuminate the extremity of that arc must be 352 meters high. Is that conclusive?"

"Marvelously conclusive," retorted Gontran with magnificent self-composure.

The young man had rested his elbow on his knee and his chin in the palm of his hand; his expression was grave and his eyes were fixed on the scientist. He seemed to be following the other's explanations with perfect comprehension.

---

[23] Johann Hieronymus Schröter (1745-1816) had a private observatory at Lilienthal, near Bremen, from 1772 onwards; he published his landmark work on the Moon in 1791. He was an enthusiastic advocate of the plurality of worlds and of the principle of plenitude: the notion that God would not have created all those worlds without equipping every single one with inhabitants. He was, as Ossipoff observes, no donkey, but he made all his observations with this item of faith in mind, and found nothing to disprove his conviction that the Moon must be home to intelligent beings; in addition to the hopeful calculation of the depth of the lunar atmosphere cited here, he also thought he had seen evidence of cultivation on the lunar surface.

Ossipoff continued: "The astronomer Airy, referring to 295 occultations—that's not trivial, 295 occultations—concluded therefrom that the lunar radius is diminished by two degrees, in respect of the disappearance of stars behind the dark side of the Moon, and two degrees four in respect of their reappearance, similarly at the dark side. It therefore follows that the radius measured at occultations is inferior to the telescopic radius. To what, I ask you, can that diminution be attributed, if not the horizontal refraction of a lunar atmosphere?"

"As you say," the young man replied, seriously.

"Furthermore," Ossipoff continued, "if I were to enumerate all the various proofs gathered in different eras and by scientists who were not just anyone, in favor of the existence of a lunar atmosphere, it would take me several hours, at least. For myself, I can't explain the phenomenon to which the occultation of certain stars gives rise other than by an atmosphere that exists primarily on the hemisphere that we cannot see, but which is gradually brought toward the edge of the Moon by libration."

He looked at Gontran, seemingly waiting for his approval, which immediately translated itself into firmly pronounced words: "That's also my opinion." Then, resuming immediately: "Or rather that of my illustrious namesake."

Ossipoff sat up straight, and everything about his attitude testified to a great internal satisfaction.

"Now," added the young Comte, "it might perfectly well be that the Moon possesses an atmosphere different from ours."

The scientist seized his hand. "Ah!" he said, enthusiastically. "I see that you've read the *Astronomie de peuple*, for what you've just said is one of the suppositions made by Flammermont in favor of the lunar atmosphere. He admits not only that the proportions of oxygen and nitrogen in a celestial atmosphere might not be the same as in ours, but also that the atmosphere might be composed of other gases."

"After all," exclaimed Gontran, "what does it matter of what the atmosphere is composed, so long as it exists?" Then, suddenly becoming calmer, he said: "Monsieur Gontran, did you bring me to this Observatory in such great secrecy to talk about the Moon, and that alone?"

The scientist shivered, mistaking the meaning of the young man's words, and replied excitedly: "No, not at all—for, as I've told you, the Moon is, for me, only the first station of a celestial voyage, and I have every intention of taking you through the whole planetary and stellar immensity today."

Gontran smiled softly. "You haven't understood me, my dear Monsieur. I was trying to ask you whether we might touch on another question, just as interesting...from another point of view, perhaps, but..."

The old savant's eyes grew round. "Another question, as interesting as the Moon..." he murmured, doubtfully.

"To be sure, Monsieur Ossipoff," Gontran replied. "Astronomy is very fine...but love is no less pleasant...and you know that I love Mademoiselle Selena and that I came this evening to ask you for her hand..."

Ossipoff squinted, and fixed the young man with a penetrative stare. "Between the Moon and my daughter," he said, "there might not be as much distance as you suppose."

"About 96,000 leagues," replied Gontran, whose memory had chanced to retain that number—and he added, jokingly: "In astronomy, that distance is trivial, but in love..." A deep sigh completed the sentence.

The scientist remained silent for a moment, enveloping the young man with a piercing and studious gaze, as he had in the carriage. Eventually, he said: "I'll prove to you that in love, there are circumstances in which distance is trivial." He paused again, staring fixedly at Gontran, who pricked up his ears. "Monsieur le Comte de Flammermont," the old man said, eventually, is a serious voice, "do you love my daughter?"

"Profoundly, Monsieur Ossipoff."

"But have you considered that I am old, and that, once my daughter is married, I shall be alone in this world?"

"You're so rarely here," objected Gontran, who wished by this anodyne joke to offer a diversion to the self-pity that had taken possession of his companion.

The latter did, indeed, smile. "You're right," he replied, "but scientists have hearts like other men, and mine is filled solely by affection for my daughter..."

The young Comte seized his hands. "If I understand you correctly," he said, "you dread the solitude in which Mademoiselle Selena's marriage would leave you."

"Precisely—and that dread is so great in me that I have decided only to give my daughter to a man who will swear never to take her away from me."

"You have my oath, Monsieur Ossipoff," said the young man, with abundant frankness in his voice.

The old man shook his head.

"Do you not dread engaging yourself very lightly, Monsieur le Comte?" he asked, in a slightly ironic tone. "I love traveling, and the whim might take me..."

Gontran interrupted him, exclaiming: "Ah, Monsieur Ossipoff, you insult my love if you suppose it capable of balking at distances, however large they might be."

"There now!" observed the old scientist, with a little smile. "So you're of the same opinion as me, that distances are trivial, whether it's a matter of astronomy or love."

"Monsieur Ossipoff," exclaimed the young man, ardently, "I love Mademoiselle Selena with all my heart, and, if necessary, I would follow her to the ends of the Earth."

"And as far as the Moon?" added the old man, fixing him with a strange stare.

If Gontran had been able to observe the sudden transfiguration that had just overtaken the old man's physiognomy, he would doubtless have paid more attention to his words, but the thought of Selena filled him entirely, and he lifted his arms to the heavens, exclaiming: "Ah, if only there existed a single audacious soul sufficiently well-equipped to launch into space on the conquest of all those unknown worlds...if Selena's hand were the price, I would beg him to take me with him, to prove to you that millions, billions and trillions of leagues could not intimidate a love such as mine!"

He was a superb sight, standing up, his face raised towards the cupola of the observatory, through which a bright ray of moonlight then fell directly, his eyes shining, his lips half-open, his nostrils flared.

"Ah, my boy! Ah, my son!" And, uttering these two appellations in an affectionate tone, Monsieur Ossipoff threw his arms around the young man's neck and kissed him on both cheeks several times.

Surprised by this expansiveness, in which he only understood one thing—that it was an indication of the good progress of his matrimonial project—Flammermont looked at the old man, who abandoned the embrace and looked at him warmly. Then the scientist seized his hands, shook them, and shook them again, stammering: "Oh, my boy! My boy!"

"Monsieur Ossipoff," said the young man, "may I know...?"

"Eh? What?" cried the old man. "Didn't you just say that, to have Selena's hand, you'd go to the Moon in search of it...?"

"That's true...but for that, it would be necessary for your daughter to be on the Moon..."

Then, posing in front of Flammermont with a fiery gaze and his arms folded in a challenging manner, the little old man cried: "And what if this man, audacious enough to have dreamed of the conquest of the unknown worlds that scintillate above our heads, existed...if, not content with having dreamed, this man had resolved to put his dream into execution?"

Gontran looked at Ossipoff in bewilderment. He was beginning to think that his passion for astronomy had unbalanced the poor scientist's mind.

"Yes," the latter continued, "if, after 20 years of incessant work, uninterrupted studies and laborious vigils, I had contrived to render practicable that marvelous voyage that so many philosophers, thinkers and poets had made in imagination...if I were to say to you: 'I'm leaving for the Moon and the celestial immensity; if you love my daughter, come with me!'—what would you reply?"

Gontran examined him attentively—and even, it must be said, with a certain suspicion. This was the first time he had met the old man, and that acquaintance, hardly amounting to a few hours, did not permit him to estimate the exact extent of what he supposed to be Monsieur Ossipoff's madness. He knew, from having heard it said, that many madmen cannot tolerate contradiction, and that maniacs—even the gentlest and most inoffensive—are to be feared when anyone contradicts them. So, to the question that the scientist had just put to him, he replied without hesitation: "You ask that of me, Monsieur Ossipoff—of me, after what I said to you a little while ago! You ask me if I would follow Mademoiselle Selena to the Moon...but the Moon is too near...I'd rather that she went to the Sun!"

"The Sun will come later," the old man replied, gravely. Then, as he detected a certain pity in the young man's eyes, his eyebrows immediately contracted, and he said: "You think I'm mad, don't you? You're saying to yourself: 'The old man's lost his mind...but in addition to his mania he has a charming daughter...humor the mania to get the girl...' "

Gontran tried to protest.

"Well, my dear Comte, I'm not mad. What I've told you is perfectly serious and I haven't brought you here this evening merely to convince you that the impossibility, proposed by many scientists, of the habitability of the Moon—by virtue of the non-existence of a lunar atmosphere—is not an impossibility at all. That first point having been established by 20 years of study and observation, what then remains for the final settlement of the problem to which I've devoted my life? To find a means of traveling to our satellite! For several years, I've had the plans for a gigantic cannon in my notebook and a little while ago, before your visit, I carried out my last experiment with a special powder, whose effects are sufficient to send to the Moon...everything that I might wish to send there. So, the Moon is habitable and I have found a means of getting there. What have you to say to that?"

Ossipoff had been speaking softly, calmly, and without seeming to be prey to any cerebral overexcitement. That made Gontran all the more suspicious. This tranquility seemed to him to presage an imminent storm, and he decided to try to prevent that storm from bursting. To deceive the old man, therefore, and make him believe that he was taking him seriously, he said: "In your situation, Monsieur Ossipoff, I would have disdained to bother with the Moon, an overly familiar world deprived of freshness by all the studies of which it has been the object, and I would have turned my attention to another world, of a conformity more similar to that of our own planet and also less frequented by imaginary voyagers. Why not go to Mars, for instance?"

The old scientist's face lit up. "Ah, my young friend!" he said, cheerfully, "You're getting a taste for it, from what I can see, and your mind seeks adventures...a little while ago, you offered to go seek Selena on the Moon; now you're talking about Mars. I'm delighted to see your ideas taking such a direction so easily. But everything in its time...for the moment, it's a matter of going to the Moon—firstly, I repeat, because the celestial highway has its stations, just like a railway, at which it's necessary to stop, and then, I must admit, because my powder would be insufficient to permit us to travel millions of leagues...." He said this in the most natural tone in the world, although there was something akin to shame in his intonation at having to admit the imperfect nature of his explosive.

"But how can we continue our voyage, then?" asked Flammermont, earnestly. "Must we remain broken down on the Moon?"

"Why would we do that?"

"Well, if your powder is incapable of carrying us for long distances...."

"We'll find the means of continuing our voyage there," relied the old scientist, with a mysterious smile.

"That's a relief," said the young man, adding, privately: *It's odd; he seems to have full control of his reasoning...his ideas are connected with a precision and logic that would make one doubt the imbalance of his mind, if he were talking about any other subject...poor man. Humor his mania, then, until things get out of hand....* Then, in order to discover the full extent of the old man's thinking, he said aloud: "Without being indiscreet, might I know why you've brought me here in such great secrecy? For yours seems to me to be a very praiseworthy occupation, and there's no need for you not to dedicate yourself to it in broad daylight."

This observation, seemingly so simple, brought about an abrupt change in Monsieur Ossipoff's physiognomy. His expression suddenly darkened, his brows furrowed violently, his mouth turned down profoundly at each corner and he replied, in a low and chagrined tone: "The world is full of jealousy, my dear boy. Without being certain of it, I feel that I'm being watched, spied upon. Among scientists, one easily divines when a colleague has some project in mind that..."

"What!" exclaimed Gontran, earnestly. "Do you suppose that one of your colleagues wants to steal the fruit of so much work and effort from you?"

"God forbid," cried the old man, "that I should direct that insult against eminent men, my colleagues...but at the end of the day, I don't want my projects to be overtaken before I've even begun to put them into execution. That's why I've been coming here, for many years, every evening when I was certain that I wouldn't run into anyone—so that I'd be able to deliver myself, in complete solitude, to my studies and my research. I want the news of my departure to burst upon the scientific world like a bomb-blast...and as for you, as I told you at the house, your very pronounced taste for the sciences and your knowledge of astronomical matters leads me to consider you as the son-in-law I need. I want to associate you with my work; at the same time, your love for my daughter is a guarantee of your zeal and discretion."

With an energetic squeeze of the hand Gontran assured the scientist that he could count on his total devotion.

"That said," the old man continued, "we can go back to the house if you wish, where I'll make haste to explain the mechanism of the cannon I've invented, and carry out a further experiment with selenite—that's what I've baptized my powder—for your benefit." While speaking, Ossipoff was busy putting everything back in its place, so that no one would suspect the following day that the observatory had received a nocturnal visit.

When the light was out, the scientist took his companion by the hand and led him by the hand, as he had when they arrived, to the exit door.

Their footsteps left no tracks in the compacted snow, and when Ossipoff had locked the door to the street, the white carpet extended in the interior courtyard was as immaculate as if no one had entered it.

They found the coachman where they had left him, stamping his feet beside his motionless horses, warmly wrapped up in furs taken from the *droshky*.

As soon as Ossipoff and his companion were muffled in their warm cloaks and seated on the cushions, the coachman shook the reins and the horses, spurred on by the cold, set off like swallows, moving soundlessly through the deserted streets.

As they turned into the street in which Mikhail Ossipoff's small house was situated, two forms suddenly surged out of the shadow of the houses, and the coachman stopped his horses in response to an imperious gesture accompanied by a sonorously-pronounced instruction: "Halt!"

"What is it?" Ossipoff asked, leaning out—but he uttered an exclamation of surprise when he realized that the men who has stopped the *droshky* were two mounted policemen. The naked blades of their sabers gleamed in the moonlight.

One of the soldiers approached. "Where are you going, grandfather?" he asked, politely.

"Ah!" said the other policeman, excitedly, approaching in his turn. "Do you live near here, then?"

"My name is Mikhail Ossipoff, member of the Academy of Sciences," the scientist replied, "and I live in the small house you see over there."

It seemed that the policemen trembled on hearing the old man announce his name and quality; they contented themselves, however, with drawing aside slightly and saying: "That's all right. You may pass, grandfather."

The *droshky* resumed its course and Mikhail Ossipoff said to his astonished companion: "That often happens. The police have probably discovered some nihilist plot."

At these words, Gontran felt a small shiver run along his spine. Why? He would certainly have been unable to say. Then he turned round, his ears having caught a sound they had not heard before. The two policemen were galloping 20 paces behind the carriage. The young man frowned momentarily; then he shrugged his shoulders and resumed thinking about Selena.

The *droshky* finally stopped; they had arrived. As he got down, following his companion, Flammermont could not help looking around suspiciously. The street was deserted; the façade of the house was silent; everyone seemed to be asleep.

Ossipoff lifted up the copper knocker and brought it down several times, but the door remained closed. "That animal Vassily must be asleep," he grumbled. Taking a key from his pocket, he introduced it into the lock; the door opened and the scientist went into the dark vestibule, followed by Gontran. They had not taken three steps, though, when they were seized and immobilized by arms emerging from the darkness. At the same time, amid the clinking of sabers and spurs on the floor-tiles, a curt voice ordered: "Tie them up securely."

A suddenly-lit lantern showed the old man and his companion that the hallway was full of policemen and guardsmen. Vassily lay on the ground in a corner, bound and gagged, absolutely incapable of movement or speech.

"But there's been some error!" exclaimed the old man. "My name is Mikhail Ossipoff."

"That's exactly who we're looking for," replied a colonel of the guard, haughtily.

"But I protest!" howled he scientist. "I protest…I'll complain to the Tsar…I'll…"

He was unable to say any more; in response to a gesture from the colonel, two guardsmen had put a gag over his mouth, which they tied securely behind his head.

At first, Gontran made as if to resist; he even reached into his pocket in search of his revolver—but he was thrown brutally to the ground, then disarmed, tied up and gagged. He was already in his droshky, lying on his back and rolling his eyes furiously but powerless, when Mikhail Ossipoff was thrown in beside him, as carelessly as a bag of old clothes. Then two guardsmen sat down in the front of the carriage, while a dozen mounted policemen surrounded the *droshky*, with their fingers on the triggers of their revolvers.

"Where are we going, Colonel?" asked the coachman, in a tremulous voice.

"To the central prison," replied the officer, urging his horse to a trot—and the little troop son disappeared around the street corner, leaving Vassily, whom they had forgotten to set free, behind in the little house, along with Selena, who was sleeping peacefully in her bedroom, dreaming of the Moon and Gontran.

At the door of the house, two mounted policemen remained on watch, immobile in the whiteness of the snow.

Chapter III

How Fedor Sharp, the permanent secretary of the Academy of Sciences, turned out to be a blackguard.

"Well then, most honorable Monsieur Sharp?"

"Well then, most esteemed Monsieur Mileradovich!"

That said, the two men maintained silence, examining one another covertly with straight faces, as befitted persons conscious of the importance of their mission, but with a hint of mockery in their expressions that would certainly have given an attentive observer something to think about.

One of them, tall, thin and bony, seemed to be suspended limply within an ample black frock-coat tightly fitted about the breast, whose unusually long tails were draped over similarly black trousers, twisted around the ankles. On his feet he wore coarse leather shoes with thick laces, whose enormous hobnails clicked noisily on the tiles flooring the room with every step he took. Long, straight hair, vainly softened with abundant supplies of perfumed oil, fell over the collar of his frock-coat, which was shiny with grease; it framed a sharp-featured visage whose prominent cheekbones jutted out from a wrinkled and sickly hide. The face, lit by two little eyes profoundly sunk in their orbits but as bright as polished jet, was clean-shaven, with the exception of a prominent tuft of grey hair mounted beneath the chin, which descended to a considerable length over the breast, reminiscent of a billy-goat's beard.

The other was similar to all those men whose sedentary work and immoderate love of the dining-table have rounded their waists and rendered their complexion apoplectic.

The former was none other than Fedor Sharp, the permanent secretary of the Academy of Sciences. The other was named Mileradovich, and served the important function in St. Petersburg of a criminal magistrate. Both of them, at the moment we make their acquaintance—which is to say, the day after the one in which we witnessed the surprising arrest of Mikhail Ossipoff and Gontran de Flammermont—were in the scientist's laboratory, which they had been searching thoroughly for nearly three hours.

Mileradovich, sitting at a large table in front of a blank piece of paper, was taking notes from the dictation of Sharp, who was pacing back and forth across the room, nosing around, examining everything with extreme care, shaking flasks, lifting the lids of crucibles, looking at test-tubes, aided in his research by a large ledger that he held in his hands, at which he glanced frequently. Suddenly, while the examining magistrate was bent over his piece of paper, writing, Sharp had stopped in front of a rather large flask placed on a furnace that had gone cold, beside which was the blackened metal tube that Osssipoff, at the beginning of this story, had shown his daughter so triumphantly.

This discovery undoubtedly had a particular significance for the secretary of the St. Petersburg Academy of Sciences, for he could not suppress an exclamation of joyful surprise—and it was this exclamation that had prompted the examining magistrate to make the interrogative remark with which this chapter began. We have seen what response Monsieur Sharp had thought himself obliged to make to that inquiry. Then both of them shut up, the judge half-turning around in his seat in order to see his companion more clearly, the other standing with his back to the furnace, his hands holding the flask on which his ardent eyes were fixed.

"Well then," repeated Mileradovich, "what have you found, Monsieur Sharp?"

The latter pointed a thin and bony finger at the flask. "Here it is," he said.

A gleam of joy appeared in the judge's eyes. "Are you sure?" he asked.

"I won't be absolutely sure until I've carried out a careful analysis, and—more importantly—an experiment that will permit me to base my opinion on undeniable results...but something tells me, my most esteemed Monsieur Mileradovich, that this is definitely what we're looking for." And he put his hand on his heart.

The examining magistrate put down his pen and rubbed his hands together, manifesting a contentment that swelled his torso. Then, suddenly, he became motionless, his eyes fixed on his companion. "You know," he said, "this is a business from which we might obtain numerous advantages."

"What do you mean by that?" asked Sharp, in a singular tone.

"Why, if the Tsar is just, he'll give me a promotion and you the Order of Merit—at least."

"I'm not asking for anything," Sharp replied, promptly.

"Without asking, one may still accept."

The permanent secretary of the Academy of Sciences made an energetic gesture of protest. "I've only done my duty," he retorted, "and I don't hold that to be sufficient cause for the Tsar's gratitude. I was given a mission; I've carried it out, with no more thought of recompense than of denying myself...a few regrets that I've experienced in acting against my excellent colleague Monsieur Ossipoff." He pronounced these words with emphasis, raising his shining eyes, in which a tear seemed to be trembling, toward Heaven.

Mileradovich uttered a little mocking laugh. "That disinterest is very edifying, my most esteemed Monsieur Sharp," he said, "but you'll permit me, given that I don't have the same reasons as you"—he stressed the final phrase—"for not aspiring to the generosity of the Tsar, to rely on your support in extracting a few benefits from this affair, won't you?"

Monsieur Sharp undoubtedly thought that he could detect a threat in the rather strange tone in which these words had been pronounced, for, hurriedly setting the flask and the tube down on the furnace, he went precipitately to the judge and shook his hands with a strong grip. "Rely on me," he aid. "Rely on me..."

"It must be admitted," Mileradovich continued, after a short pause "that without this denunciation, the police would never have suspected that the St. Petersburg Institute was concealing such a dangerous conspirator in its bosom."

A slight redness tinted Monsieur Sharp's sallow complexion for a few seconds. "It's sometimes the most improbable things that are the truest," he replied, sententiously.

At that moment, there was a sound of sleigh-bells in the street, accompanied by the tramping feet of horses and a dull murmur of voices; then the bells and the hoofbeats suddenly stopped; only the murmur, transformed into shouts and vociferations, continued to rise in a crescendo.

"There they are," said the judge, with an expression of keen satisfaction.

"There they are," repeated Sharp, whose eyebrows immediately furrowed, in response to an intense annoyance.

Mileradovich invited his companion to sit down beside him; then he rang a bell, and a small, shifty and shabby individual, who had presumably been waiting in the next room, came in. He was the magistrate's clerk. In response to a sign from his superior, he sat down on a stool at the same table.

Scarcely were these preparations terminated when the door opened and a policeman appeared, stopping respectfully on the threshold. "The prisoners are here," he said.

"Bring in Mikhail Ossipoff," ordered Mileradovich, leaning back self-importantly in his chair.

Sharp, by contrast, who was sitting with his elbows on the table and his face hidden by his hands, appeared to be deep in thought. One might have thought that a violent battle had been joined within the man's soul; beneath his deeply-furrowed eyebrows, his little eyes were burning with dark fire; a profound wrinkle split his forehead vertically in two, and his sharp teeth bit his thin, pale lip until it bled. Finally, he recovered his composure, raised his head, folded his arms over his chest, fixed his eyes on the doorway through which the prisoner would enter, and waited impassively.

Mikhail Ossipoff appeared, his hands secured behind his back by a cord, each extremity of which was held by a guardsman with a revolver in his other hand.

At the sight of Sharp, the old scientist released a cry of joy. "You here, my dear friend!" he said, taking several steps forward in spite of the guards' efforts to hold him back.

"Me, Monsieur Ossipoff," the permanent secretary of the Academy of Science replied, coldly.

Had a bucket of cold water been poured over his head, Ossipoff could not have been more amazed than he was by the attitude and tone of his colleague and friend. He fixed Sharp with a stare full of astonishment and reproach, and said, not without bitterness: "I scarcely expected to see you here, Monsieur."

"Believe, Monsieur Ossipoff," the other relied, "that it was only with the greatest reluctance that I accepted the painful mission with which I am charged…but I am, before anything else, a faithful servant of the Tsar, and I could not do otherwise than obey him."

A mocking smile played upon Mileradovich's lips. "Have the accused sit down," ordered the magistrate.

At these words however, instead of sitting down on the stool that his guards indicated to him, Ossipoff leapt forward, red with anger. "Accused!" he cried. "Oh, so I'm accused—of what, pray?"

Mileradovich made a sign. The guards grabbed hold of Ossipoff and pushed down on his shoulders with all their strength, obliging him to sit down.

"Your name?" asked the magistrate.

"Mikhail Ossipoff."

"Your age?"

"59."

"Your profession?"

"Member of the St. Petersburg Academy of Sciences, correspondent of all the scientific societies of the world." And he added, raising his head proudly: "One of the glories of Russia, as the Tsar recently took the trouble to inform me."

A flood of bile rose to Monsieur Sharp's face; beneath his lowered eyelids, he directed a furious gaze at his colleague.

The magistrate continued: "Is the house in which we are located yours?"

"It's mine."

"This room is your laboratory, isn't it?"

"Of course."

"You recognize all the objects that are in it as yours?"

Ossipoff nodded his head affirmatively.

"As you also declare that you have fabricated all the substances to be found in your laboratory with your own hands?"

"Certainly." The scientist pronounced this word with an assurance punctuated with pride. Sharp felt it, and lowered his eyes.

The magistrate fell silent and perused the transcriptions that the clerk had made of Ossipoff's replies.

"Now that I've answered all your questions meekly," said the scientist, with exaggerated courtesy, "may I be permitted to ask you one?"

"Speak," Mileradovich replied.

"Why am I here, in my own house, with my hands bound and hidden from sight like a criminal, while strangers sit before me like judges, having turned my entire house upside-down?"

The rotund Mileradovich turned his round face, brightened by a sly smile, toward Sharp, shrugging his shoulder slightly in a gesture of commiseration. Then, addressing the old scientist, he said: "Although you have no right to ask that question, what we can tell you, knowing perfectly well what your case involves, and as it is customary—for form's sake—to inform an accused person of the accusation laid against him, is that you, Mikhail Ossipoff, have been accused of the crime of high treason."

The old man's amazement was so great that he kept silent, his tongue stuck to his palate, his eyes wide, his lips partly opened by an exclamation caught in his throat.

Mileradovich misinterpreted this expression and continued, emphasizing every syllable that fell upon the prisoner's skull like a blow from a sledgehammer: "You have conspired against the security of the State and the life of the Tsar."

Ossipoff felt as if his limbs had been broken by these words. Him, accused of wanting to overthrow the State! Him, accused of wanting to put Tsar Alexander to death![24] Him, in a word, a nihilist! Either the people who had accused him must be mad, or he was a victim of the grossest of misunderstandings. It was upon this latter supposition that his mind, momentarily deranged by this frightful accusation, eventually settled after a few seconds of reflection. He recovered the use of his limbs; his tongue loosened, and he burst into hearty laughter, extending his hand to Sharp—who looked at him through his spectacles, as stiff and stern in his chair as if he were carved in wood.

"Magistrate," said Ossipoff, when his hilarity had calmed down, "to your accusation I can only ay one thing: there has been an error. I only require, as a witness to that, Monsieur Sharp, here present, my excellent colleague in the Academy of Sciences, who will tell you whether Mikhail Ossipoff could ever be plausibly accused of nihilism."

In the face of the poor scientist's expectation, however, the permanent secretary of the St. Petersburg Academy of Sciences remained immobile and mute.

Mileradovich resumed speaking. "The very honorable Monsieur Sharp," he said, dryly, "has no say in this; the accusation that weighs upon you is no concern of his."

"If Monsieur Sharp has no say in this," retorted Ossipoff, becoming impatient, "what is he doing here?"

---

[24] The chronology of the novel has not yet been clarified within the text, so a contemporary reader would probably have assumed that this reference is to Alexander III, who had succeeded to the imperial throne in March 1881, after his father, Alexander II, was assassinated by nihilists. Dates subsequently included in the text, however, suggest that it actually refers to Alexander II, who was subject to a series of plots and assassination attempts in 1879 and 1880.

"He was appointed by the chief of police to assist me in the investigation that I had to carry out here—an investigation which, I must admit, clearly establishes your guilt and the truth of the accusation."

Ossipoff bowed his head, his ears buzzing with the two relevant words: "Guilt...accusation...guilt...accusation."

"For several months," Mileradovich went on, "your neighbors have been alarmed by your mysterious comings and goings, and your strange ways. You spend almost all your time here in your laboratory, rarely going out except at night, to undertake journeys through St. Petersburg whose objective no one knows."

The scientist raised his hand again and opened his mouth to reply, but the magistrate continued: "Loud explosions have been heard on several occasions emanating from your house. The neighboring dwellings have been shaken many times by powerful shocks that have even made deep cracks in the ground; flames have been seen through the ventilation shafts of this cellar. All of this is strange and incomprehensible..."

"Is that sufficient reason to treat me as a thief or an assassin?" demanded the indignant Ossipoff.

Without answering him, Mileradovich said, brutally: "Mikhail Ossipoff, in your own interests, I advice you to change your defensive strategy. A full confession might save your head from the severity of the Tsar."

"I have no fear of the severity of the Tsar," said the scientist. "I only ask for his justice."

Mileradovich shrugged his shoulders and glanced sideways at Monsieur Sharp, then continued: "What is it that you do?"

At these words, Sharp raised his had and stared at the accused.

"I carry out chemical experiments," Ossipoff replied.

"On explosives, isn't that so?" asked the magistrate.

"The principal object of my studies is, indeed, explosive compounds."

Miladerovitch rubbed his hands and leaned over his clerk to make sure that he as transcribing the accused responses accurately. "And for what purpose," he asked, in an insinuating tone, "are you seeking an explosive so ardently?"

"For a scientific purpose, you may be sure. What other purpose could I have?"

The magistrate laughed, and shook his head. "You're forgetting that the manufacture of explosives is the monopoly of the State—and, in consequence, strictly forbidden to individuals."

"But it's not a matter of manufacture—purely of research."

Miladerovich thumped the table forcefully with his fist. "If you continue to lie in this fashion," he growled, "I'll have you gagged. To devote yourself as secretly as you have to the manufacture of a powerful engine of destruction—selenite, as you call it..."

Ossipoff started.

"…You must, therefore, have a terrible goal—and you cannot be far from attaining that goal, for in consulting your records, Monsieur Sharp has discovered under yesterday's date the formula for a powder indispensable to the projects of the association of which you are a member."

The permanent secretary of the Academy of Sciences moved his thin and bony finger over the page of the enormous volume open in front of him, murmuring: "$KO_2AZO_5 + BaO + C_2O_4$"[25]

Mikhail Ossipoff raised his head and fixed his colleague with a profound stare.

"Fortunately," Mileradovich continued, "the attention of your neighbors had been attracted by your mysterious behavior and your dangerous exploits. The police, who were already watching, had been alerted by a friend of public security." Abruptly, he added: "Where were you coming from yesterday evening, when you were arrested with one of your accomplices?"

Ossipoff could not prevent himself from shrugging his shoulders. "Your error," he said, a trifle sarcastically, "is manifestly too gross for my replies to assist you to recognize it." And he fell silent, attentively examining Monsieur Sharp, who was still riffling through papers, making notes in a notebook open beside him.

"Clerk," said the irritated magistrate, "write that the accused refused to admit that he went to a nihilist meeting yesterday evening."

Ossipoff burst out laughing.

"And this," Mileradovich continued furiously, putting a piece of paper covered with names and numbers under the old scientist's nose. "What's this?"

"As to that," replied the accused, quite self-composed, "you can read as well as me."

"Jupiter…Mars…Saturn…Sirius, and a lot of other bizarre names," proclaimed the magistrate. "Do you deny that these are the pseudonyms that conceal the most dangerous of conspirators?"

The bewildered Ossipoff remained silent momentarily, then pointed at Sharp: "Have you asked Monsieur Sharp what he thinks of the theory you've just put forward?" he asked, sarcastically.

"Monsieur Sharp shares my feelings on the subject," Mileradovich replied, hotly.

---

[25] I have refrained from substituting N (nitrogen) for AZ (azote) in order to modernize this formula, which remains very odd, paying little heed to the principle of valency. At a later stage in the narrative, selenite is said to contain saltpeter—potassium nitrate, KNO_3—which is the key component of gunpowder, but that seems inherently unlikely, given that selenite is said to be more powerful than such high explosives as dynamite and roburite.

The permanent secretary of the Academy of Sciences started so violently that the enormous steel-rimmed spectacles sitting astride his nose leapt on to the table. "Pardon me," he said, "but I never told you that."

Mileradovich's apoplectic face turned a deeper shade of purple. "What!" he cried, folding his arms across his breast. "What did you say, then, when I showed you this list?"

"That they were the names of stars and planets."

"That's true—and what did I say to you?"

"As far as I can recall, you told me that the names of stars must serve to designate Monsieur Ossipoff's accomplices."

The magistrate's face lit up triumphantly. "And to that, what did you add?"

"Nothing," Sharp replied, hiding a sly smile.

"Therefore, you shared my opinion."

"Ah!" exclaimed he permanent secretary. "Pardon me, but I'm here to give you my opinion when you ask for it, not to give you a course in astronomy. You don't know what Mars, Saturn and so on are—that's your right—but don't make me out to be an imbecile." Having said that, he took a huge handkerchief from the pocket of his frock-coat and set about cleaning the lenses of his spectacles carefully.

Mileradovich, slightly vexed, shrugged his shoulders. "I may not know anything about astronomy," he said, "but, with all due respect, most honored Monsieur Sharp, you don't know all the tricks employed by rogues to escape the police." Addressing himself to Ossipoff, he went on: "Your precautions were clever, but you've been caught, and, in your own interests, I strongly advise you to make a full confession."

He leaned against the table, advancing is luminous face towards the scientist, and lowered his voice confidentially, saying: "Come on, the fate that awaits you is as certain as it is that Monsieur Sharp and I are honest men, while you're nothing but a scoundrel. If you persist in denial, you'll be hanged. Right! With regard to each of these names of stars, give me the name of your accomplice, and I promise to commute your sentence to banishment."

"Truly, Magistrate," Ossipoff retorted, "You speak marvelously, and it's obvious that treason doesn't cause you any difficulty."

Monsieur Sharp's spectacles glinted vividly, and the furious Mileradovich cried: "Clerk, write that the accused has accomplices, but that he refuses to name them."

"Eh? For the excellent reason that I don't have any. Now, if it will give you pleasure, write: Uranus, Neptune, Betelgeuse, Capella…but I warn you that they're stars."

Behind his spectacles, Monsieur Sharp narrowed his eyes, allowing a sharp glance to filter through his lashes. "So why have you occupied yourself with so many stars?" he asked. "What can astronomy and ballistics possible have in common?"

Ossipoff turned to his colleague and, in spite of the feeling of foreboding that Sharp's attitude and language inspired in him, he might well have been about to release some confidence regarding the gigantic project that he had mentioned to Gontran de Flammermont, when a frightful racket broke out in the next room. It was like the noise of a fight, mingled with exclamations in the Russian language and heavily emphasized French curses.

Monsieur Sharp looked at the examining magistrate, who leaned toward the clerk to instruct him to go and see what was happening. The shifty and shabby little man put down his penholder, pushed back his stool, and headed for the door at a slow pace. Scarcely had he opened it, however, when a tumultuous group was precipitated into the room, to Monsieur Sharp's great amazement and the considerable alarm of the portly Mileradovich, who stood up hurriedly in order to put the entire breadth of the table between him and the newcomers.

As for Mikhail Ossipoff, maintained immobile in his seat by the guardsmen in charge of him, he recognized among those who had just invaded the laboratory Gontran de Flammermont—who, although his hands were tied behind his back, was energetically shaking four policeman hanging on to his clothing, as a wild boar does to dogs that have collared it.

"Where's this magistrate?" cried the young Frenchman, in a thunderous voice. "Where is he? Show him to me, if he exists!"

Seeing the prisoner solidly contained by his guards, Mileradovich recovered his assurance somewhat, and responded in a less-than-firm voice: "You're asking for a magistrate, Monsieur? Here I am."

The Comte de Flammermont, dragging his guardsmen, launched himself to the table behind which Mileradovich was entrenched.

"Ah! So you're the magistrate!" he exclaimed, his lips tremulous with anger and his eyes aflame. "It's on your orders that I've been treated as a criminal and am still, at the present moment, bound like gallows-prey. Well, since you're the magistrate, I demand that you set me free forthwith. I warn you that every minute that goes by aggravates your offence, as I also warn you that when I leave here I shall address, through the medium of my ambassador, observations to your government..."

Stunned by this torrent of words, and disturbed by the young man's self-confidence, Mileradovic kept silent.

The Comte went on, in a calmer tone: "I am outraged, Monsieur, by the manner in which Russians treat the representatives of a friendly nation. No one behaves in such a manner. It's necessary to come to your nation of Russia to be treated as brutally." Then, wrath taking possession of him more fully, he cried: "Well, what are you waiting for?"

The investigating magistrate had recovered his self-possession. "Just one thing, Monsieur," he replied, with obsequious politeness. "For you to tell me who you are and on what your claim is based."

Gontran started violently. "Who I am?" he shouted. "You ask me who I am! Didn't you know that when you had me arrested?"

"The orders concerned Mikhail Ossipoff alone," Mileradovich replied. "Seeing that he was accompanied, the guardsmen took the person accompanying him for an accomplice and thought they ought to arrest him too—for which I cannot blame them until you have proved to me..."

"That my name is Comte Gontran de Flammermont and that I belong to the diplomatic service!" the young man continued. "Send one of your men to the French embassy and it will not be long before you have proof of the gross error that you have committed."

"Not me, but the guardsmen," the investigating magistrate protested, swiftly, beginning to dread, on account of Gontran's tone and attitude, that he had taken a wrong turn. So saying, he scribbled a few lines hastily on a piece of paper, which he gave to one of the police agents saying; "Hurry up!"

The man went out at a run.

Then, in order to conciliate the prisoner, in case he really had made the gross error of arresting a member of the French embassy, the magistrate gave orders that his hands should be untied and that a chair should be brought for him.

Instead of sitting down, though, Gontran ran to Ossipoff.

"And you!" he cried. "My dear, venerable Monsieur Ossipoff, can they not recognize, equally, that they are mistaken in subjecting you to such shameful treatment?"

The old scientist smiled sadly. "Alas," he said, "personally, I do not have the honor, as you do, of belonging to the diplomatic service."

"But all the scientists of the world will protest!" Gontran retorted, vehemently.

Ossipoff nodded his head in the direction of Sharp, who was watching the scene mutely and motionlessly, and said: "This gentleman is the permanent secretary of the St. Petersburg Academy of Sciences, and his mission is to prove to the judge the crime of which I am accused."

The young man's eyes widened and he exclaimed: "The crime of which you're accused! You're accused of a crime! Good God, what is it?"

"I belong to the terrible association of nihilists," the old man replied, ironically. "Yesterday, when we were arrested, we were coming back from a secret conference of the conspirators, which probably had the objective of organizing a new attempt on the Tsar's life."

Gontran burst out laughing. "What kind of fairy tale is that?" he cried.

"It's not a fairy tale, it's the truth; at least, the investigating magistrate, enlightened by Monsieur Sharp's advice, says so."

"What! But yesterday evening we were at Pulkova Observatory—didn't you tell these gentlemen that?"

A rapid gleam flashed in the year of the permanent secretary of the Academy of Sciences, and Mileradovich cried: "You spent the evening at the Observatory? Do you swear that's true?"

"We swear it," replied the two men, in unison—and the Comte de Flammermont added: "It's my own *droshky* that took us there."

The investigating magistrate sniggered. "Your coachman, under interrogation, stated that he stopped the carriage in a deserted street where he waited for you for nearly two hours—which led me to suppose that you had taken precautions to ensure that no one knew where you were going." He paused briefly, then went on: "You'll agree with me that going to the Observatory to study the stars is not an occupation that needs to be surrounded by such mystery."

Gontran bit his lip, remembering that the old scientist had indeed arranged things in such a manner as not to leave any trace of his visit in the observatory. Despairing of that alibi, which escaped him as well as Ossipoff, he looked at the latter with eyes that seemed to say: "Why, then, did you keep silent, instead of proving your innocence…which would have been very easy."

To this mute interrogation, Mikhail Ossipoff as about to make a mute response, when the policeman that the examining magistrate had dispatched to the French embassy came back, out of breath. Without saying a word, he handed Mileradovich a large envelope, whose red wax seals the fat man broke with feverish fingers.

As the magistrate progressed in reading the hastily-written lines, the set of his features visibly altered. Finally, he straightened up, bowed to Gontran, and said: "You're free to go, Monsieur le Comte. Be assured that I regret what has happened most sincerely. The police sometimes have a heavy hand, which weighs blindly upon the innocent as well as the guilty, but they frankly admit their error when it is demonstrated to them, and try to make reparation."

"That's good, Monsieur," Flammermont replied, dryly. "As far as I'm concerned, I know what I have to do. However, from what you have just said, I retain one thing: the police make reparation for their error when it is demonstrated to them. Why, then, are you not giving the order for Monsieur Ossipoff, who is as innocent as I am, to be set free?"

Mileradovich shook his head. "As for Ossipoff," he said, "his case is as clear as his crime is conclusive…the gallows awaits him."

"But that's an infamy!" cried Gontron.

"Monsieur de Flammermont," Sharp retorted, in a menacing tone, "permit me to tell you that here, as in France, there are laws designed to obtain respect for justice and its representatives. Don't oblige us to apply them."

"Defend yourself!" the young man cried, turning to Ossipoff. "Prove that they've taken a false path—that, far from thinking of killing the Tsar, you think only of giving one more glory to your fatherland, that the purpose of this powder that accuses you is not to destroy anything whatsoever, but quite the contrary…"

The old man put out his hands excitedly to implore Gontran to be silent. "Say no more, Monsieur le Comte," he said, in a firm voice. "All that you might say, and all that I might say, would be futile. I sense that I have been caught in the meshes of a terrible plot, whose apparent objective I can deduce. If I'm not mistaken, I'm doomed…"

"But I shall save you!" exclaimed Gontran, with superb alacrity.

Ossipoff shook his head. "Alas, I know my country. I know that it's impossible to prove one's innocence of a crime such as the one of which I'm accused."

"But the Tsar is just!"

"Yes, but they'll blind him, if it's in their interests…"

"But you have proofs of your innocence. Produce them, and this terrible but absurd accusation will fall apart."

The old man stood up straight, and replied hoarsely: "Remember what I told you yesterday evening—and see how accurate my presentiments were. I have been suspected, spied upon, and now…" He fell silent, sensing Sharp's eyes fixed upon him. Then he continued, firmly: "It's hardly probable that I'll see you again. Farewell, then—and be assured that, whatever fate awaits me, I shall submit to it with resignation if you will swear to protect my Selena, my poor daughter, whom my disappearance will leave without protection…without support." Moved by the thought of his child, the old man stopped, strangling a sob in his throat, and a tear rolled along the edge of his eyelid. "Swear, Gontran!" he went on. "Swear!"

"On all that I hold most sacred in the world," Gontran relied, "I swear to love Selena, to respect her, to defend her and to do everything possible with her to save you." He leaned toward the old man, kissed him on the forehead and went out of the laboratory without even deigning to look at the magistrate and his companion.

In the vestibule, he bumped into Vassily.

"Oh, Monsieur le Comte!" the domestic exclaimed. "You're free! And my master…?"

Gontran made a despairing gesture.

Vassily immediately launched into lamentations, which the young man immediately cut short. "Save your wailing for later," he said, "and take me to Mademoiselle Selena."

"Mademoiselle Selena?" Vassily repeated. "What do you want with her?"

"I need to talk to her. Take me to her room—or, rather, ask her in my name to come down."

"Neither of those things is possible," retorted the domestic, shaking his head.

"Why not?"

"Because Mademoiselle's room is locked, and the key is in the hands of a guardsman who is standing guard at the door."

Gontran reflected momentarily, and said: "Take me all the same; I'll figure something out."

After going up 20 stairs behind Vassily, the Comte found himself on a landing in which a patrolling policeman was marching back and forth, looking profoundly bored. At the sight of the newcomers, he came forward and demanded rudely: "What are you doing here?"

"Tell him," Gontran said to Vassily, "that I want to talk to Mademoiselle Ossipoff.

The domestic translated the reply into Russian. The guardsman burst into brutal laughter. "It's not possible to speak to the young lady," he replied.

"Why?" asked Vassily, on the Comte's instruction.

"Because that's the orders."

The Comte took a gold coin from his pocket, which ignited a covetous gleam in the policeman's eye.

"Offer him this," said Flammermont, "if he'll let me talk to Mademoiselle Ossipoff for five minutes."

The guardsman undoubtedly guessed the meaning of these words, for he took the key out of his pocket, introduced it into the lock, activated the bolt and stuck out his hand, into which Vassily dropped the gold coin. Then the man opened the door, and Gontran went into the room.

Selena was sitting in an armchair, her face buried in her hands, sobbing. At the sound of the door opening she raised her head and, seeing Flammermont, ran towards him with her arms extended. "My father!" she cried.

"Alas, Mademoiselle, Monsieur Ossipoff, your father, is a prisoner—the victim of a police error or an odious plot."

"A prisoner? But that's infamous! It's horrible! I want to see him." So saying, she went to the door.

"That's not possible," said Gontran. "There's a guard there, who won't let you pass. I had to bribe him in order to get in."

The young woman wrung her hands desperately. "But they can't take my father away without me seeing him, without me embracing him."

Gontran shook his head. "Alas," he murmured, "it's more than probable that the magistrate will refuse you that concession...but I've come to find you in order to assure you of my entire devotion and to tell you that you can count on me no matter what, for anything."

"You must save my father, Monsieur. You must save him...."

"I'll run to the embassy, and through the intermediary of my ambassador, I'll ask for an audience with the Tsar. If I don't succeed in that first interview, I'll try to obtain a second, and take you with me...your tears and prayers might perhaps obtain justice..."

"But of what is my poor father accused?" she asked.

"They claim that he's a member of an association of nihilists."

One might have thought that this reply had fallen on the young woman's head like the blow of a sledgehammer; she shut her eyes and would have fallen on the floor if Gontran had not caught her in his arms.

"Here, Vassily, to me!" he shouted.

The domestic came in, followed by the guardsman, who made a sign to Flammermont to leave the room—and when the Comte turned a deaf ear, declaring that he would not abandon Selena in her present state, the domestic said; "Go, Monsieur le Comte…this man is capable of locking all three of us in…and who would busy himself trying to free my poor master then?"

Gontran, in distress, lifted the young woman's inert hand to his lips, and then went out precipitately, went down the stairs four at a time and launched himself into the street like a madman, elbowing his way pitilessly through the curiosity-seekers massed in front of the little house.

In the laboratory, the interrogation was drawing to a conclusion. The magistrate Mileradovich had conducted it as spitefully as possible, tightening a net of insidious and ambiguous questions around the accused. He was already furious at having seen the Comte de Flammermont escape, and dreaded that the superb affair which might bring him so many benefits—as we saw at the beginning of the chapter—might be aborted.

The old scientist only made brief and perfunctory replies, and only when the demands became more incisive and venomous. Finally, Ossipoff lost patience, and cried: "My colleague, Monsieur Sharp, permanent secretary of the Institute of Sciences, knows perfectly well that your accusation is ridiculous, and that I am neither an assassin nor an agent hired by any secret society."

Sharp stood up and put his hand on his heart. "God is my witness," he said, in a tearful voice, "that I have only fulfilled a painful duty here, which hurts me…it hurts me to have to analyze the work of a former colleague. But having been drafted and designated as an expert witness by the chief of police, I have been obliged, whether I liked it or not, to study your notebooks and render an account by an examination of your laboratory of the kind of work in which you have involved yourself."

Ossipoff shivered and asked: "And your investigations…?"

"…Have discovered certain indications that I could not do otherwise than communicate to the magistrate. For me, as for any scientist who might examine your laboratory and your books, it is indisputable—and you have admitted it yourself—that you have fabricated a terrible explosive. With what purpose? I don't know, and I leave it to the law to construct hypotheses, whose value I shall not attempt to estimate, desirous of confining myself strictly to my expert role."

Ossipoff allowed himself to be convinced by the utterly sincere tone in which these words were pronounced, and unreservedly took back the dire thoughts concerning Monsieur Sharp that had crossed his mind a little while before. Then again, what would happen to him if he could not prove his innocence of the crimes of which he was accused? Must he renounce forever the project of celestial exploration that he had cherished for so long, and to which he had dedicated a substantial part of his life? And must he abandon all hope of ever holding his daughter, his dear Selena, in his arms again? He resolved to confide partially in his colleague, in order at least to have one advocate convinced of the reality of his assertions involved in the legal proceedings.

"Magistrate," he said, in a slightly tremulous voice, "I ask your permission to converse with Monsieur Sharp privately for a few moments."

Mileradovich turned to the expert, whose mask had become impassive in response to these words. "Did you hear the prisoner?" he said.

"Yes."

"Do you consent?"

Sharp nodded his head.

The magistrate made a sign to the policemen, instructing them to go away, and got up from his own chair. Followed by his clerk, he headed for the door. "I'll give you ten minutes," he said to Ossipoff, in a gruff tone. Then, turning to the expert, he added: "As for you, my dear sir, I recommend the greatest prudence. These people are extremely dangerous."

The permanent secretary smiled in a strange fashion and the magistrate went out. Left alone, the two scientists looked at one another silently, each attempting to deduce what the other was thinking.

It was Mikhail who spoke first. "In truth, my dear Sharp," he exclaimed, with a forcefulness he could not restrain, "how could you consider me guilty, having known me for so many years?"

"What?" retorted the permanent secretary. "My dear Ossipoff, it's not for me to make any judgment whatsoever…in doing that, I would be surpassing the duty that has been entrusted to me."

"But it's not prohibited for you to interpret the results of your investigation in a manner favorable to me."

Sharp drew nearer to the accused. "I'd like nothing better," he said, "but you'll have to help me."

"What do you mean?" asked Ossipoff, surprised.

"This powder that forms the basis of the most terrible accusation that can be held over the head of a Russian—what is its exact formula?" He had pronounced these words in a breathless voice, the words whistling through clenched teeth, and he had put his hands on Ossipoff's shoulders, looking at him in anxious anticipation of the reply that might be given to him.

Seized by a presentiment, the prisoner stepped back and replied: "But you found the formula in my records."

"No—it's incomplete. I know enough chemistry to understand that one of the constituent elements of this *selenite* is missing."

"What does it matter?"

"It matters to me," Sharp growled. "If you want to save your head, you must give me the entire formula."

"And if I refuse…?"

"You'll go to the gallows within a month, if I say so," Sharp sniggered.

"Wretch!" cried Ossipoff. "Tell me frankly that everything that has befallen me is your work and that you want to steal the fruit of my labor."

"The formula?" the permanent secretary repeated, coldly. "I need that formula."

Impelled by anger and indignation, Mikhail Ossipoff made a movement so abrupt that the cords tying his hands broke. Heedless of anything but fury, the little old man rushed at Monsieur Sharp and grabbed him by the throat.

The permanent secretary, surprised by this unexpected attack, moved back precipitately, but his legs encountered the chair left vacant by Mileradovich and he fell backwards, dragging Ossipoff—who did not let go—down with him.

Hearing the noise of the struggle, the magistrate raced into the laboratory, followed by the guardsmen, who tore Ossipoff away from the unfortunate Sharp within the blink of an eye. They gagged him, tied him up, and transported him, in response to Mileradovich's orders, to a secure carriage—which, to the cheers of the crowd, set off on the road to Roggatznaya Prison.

Half an hour later, Mikhail Ossipoff was thrown into a cell, whose threshold he would only cross again to go to the scaffold, unless the Tsar's clemency sent him to Siberia.

Chapter IV
In which Providence presents itself to Selena
in the form of Alcide Fricoulet

A month went by, during which Selena passed between the extreme alternatives of wild optimism and profound despair. Had it not been for Gontran de Flammermont, who visited her every day and found means of renewing her courage, the poor young woman would undoubtedly have died; but the embassy attaché was so very skillful in persuading Mademoiselle Ossipoff—although he did not believe a word of it—that the judges could not be so blind as not to recognize the error made by the police, that Selena's tears eventually dried up. Whenever Gontran took her back to the threshold of the little house her expression was more serene and her heart less inflamed.

One evening—which was, we repeat, a month after the old scientist's arrest—Flammermont was preparing to leave the lodgings in the Avenue Voinnensky that he occupied, not far from the embassy, when a loud altercation became audible in the antechamber. He opened his door and said: "What is it, Jean?" Jean was the manservant he had brought from Paris.

"It's some kind of Cossack, Monsieur le Comte, who wants to force his way in and talk to Monsieur."

Gontran immediately recognized Mademoiselle Ossipoff's *muzjik*, and ran to him. "Selena?" he asked, his throat anxiously constricted.

"Mademoiselle is well," Vassily replied, "but my poor master..." And the servant dissolved in tears.

Seized by a presentiment, Gontran said: "Have you had news?"

"Condemned, Monsieur le Comte!" stammered Vassily, amid his sobs. "They've passed sentence on him!"

The young man shuddered. Although he had expected the outcome, the news struck him hard. A question was burning his lips, but he remained silent, fearful of the response. To what had Ossipoff been sentenced—death or deportation? Considering things coldly, the former was certainly preferable to the latter; what is death, as a torture, compared with life without liberty? But what about Selena? What a terrible blow it would be for the young woman if it were necessary for her to renounce all hope—however far-fetched it might be—of ever holding her adored father in her arms again. The blow might kill her.

At that thought, poor Gontran felt his heartbeat slow down, as if life were about to abandon him.

"The swine!" moaned Vassily, still weeping. "The poor old fellow! It'll kill him for sure."

These few words brought the Comte some relief. The fate that had befallen Ossipoff and inspired such mortal apprehension in Vassily was not the gallows. He breathed deeply and said: "Where are they sending him?"

The *muzjik* raised his arms to Heaven. "That I don't know," he said. "The police are keeping it secret."

Gontran picked up his hat and put on his cloak. "Does Mademoiselle Ossipoff know about her father's condemnation?" he asked, as they went downstairs.

"I don't think so," Vassily replied. "I was hanging around the court and learned it from a guardsman—then I ran to warn you straight away, in order that you could tell poor Mademoiselle yourself."

"You did well, Vassily," the young man said. "Go back to the house, and don't say anything to your mistress. I'll get more information." Climbing into his droshky, he instructed the coachman to take him to the chief of police.

As he got down again, an individual hurrying down the steps bumped into him in such a rude fashion that the young Comte cried, in a furious voice: "What the Devil's the matter with that stupid fool!"

The other stopped short, politely raised the traveling cap he was wearing, and said: "A thousand apologies, Monsieur, I'm merely clumsy!" And he added, cheerfully: "You'll permit me, however, to bless my stupidity—for, in consequence of it, I've been able to hear the melodious tones of my native language again." Bowing again, he was about to leave when Gontran put a hand on his arm and drew him towards the carriage in such a manner that the light of the lantern fell full on his face.

The young Comte saw a rounded face, in which two very bright black eyes shone, as piercing as a drill. Beneath a snub nose was a mouth like the gash of a saber, edged with highly-colored lips. Here and there, irregularly-planted tufts of black hair formed what is known in vulgar terms as a "gardener's beard." The man was certainly not handsome; in fact, he was ugly, but in a rather appealing way. Furthermore, a rare intelligence was visible in the broad and high forehead, topped by a shock of thick curly hair. As for the rest of the body, although it was wrapped up in a thick fur cloak, it was evident nevertheless that it was thin and lanky. The length of the arms allowed the length of the legs to be presumed. The hands were beefy and the feet could easily stand comparison with miniature boats.

"My God, Monsieur!" said Gontran, hesitantly. "Aren't you Alcide Fricoulet?"

The other uttered an exclamation of surprise. "How do you know my name?" he stammered.

Without answering, the Comte de Flammermont threw his arms around the other's neck, crying: "Alcide! Alcide! Don't you recognize me?"

Somewhat troubled by this sudden manifestation of amity, the stranger detached himself from the Comte's grip, murmuring: "There must be some mistake, Monsieur, for I confess…"

"Don't you remember Gontran...Gontran de Flammermont?"

With a joyful gesture, the other threw his hat into the air—it fell into the snow—and simultaneously precipitated himself upon the young Comte, squeezing his arms and crying: "Gontran! Gontran! Fancy seeing you here!" Then, after a momentary pause: "But what are you doing in St. Petersburg?"

The young Comte started. "Didn't I write to you several times? Didn't you get my letters? Don't you know that I'm at the French embassy?"

Alcide Fricoulet slapped his forehead. "Of course! That's right...but I've been so busy, I completely forgot."

"And you," said Monsieur de Flammermont, "how does it come about that I meet you on the bank of the Neva, 500 leagues from the Boulevard Montparnasse?"

"I'm only passing through...I'm leaving tomorrow for the Nertchinsk district, where I'm to survey a mine in the capacity of an engineer. If you've nothing better to do, let's spend the evening together."

The young Comte did not reply immediately. He lowered his head, thoughtfully. Then he said: "Come on—climb into my droshky and wait for me, without getting impatient. It's absolutely necessary for me to talk to the chief of police with regard to a matter about which I'll talk you later."

While Alcide Fricoulet installed himself under the warm fur covers, Gontran slowly climbed the steps and disappeared into the interior of the somber building. When he took his seat in the *droshky* again after a quarter of an hour, beside his friend, the latter was struck by the change in his expression.

"What's up?" Fricoulet asked, solicitously.

"I've...something very unpleasant to do."

"Something very unpleasant?" the other repeated, in an interrogative tone.

Then, impelled by the urgent need a man has to share his troubles with his friend, as he shares his joys, Flammermont briefly told his friend about the affair in which he was mixed up.

At the first words that were said to him, Fricoulet cried: "But I know this story...it's made a great deal of noise in Paris. You must know that Ossipoff is held in high esteem there in the scientific world, which is very upset by his arrest."

Gontran explained how, softly and without him quite being aware of it, the seed of love had germinated in his heart, and how he had perceived one day that the love in question had put down such solid roots that he could not imagine dislodging it.

While the young Comte was speaking, Fricoulet fidgeted on the cushions of the carriage, frowning, clicking is tongue, and eventually giving signs of the most profound discontentment. "Well, of course," he finally cried, no longer able to contain himself, "if you let a woman into your life...it doesn't surprise me that all these misfortunes have descended upon you."

Without paying any heed to this sally, Gontran concluded by saying: "In brief, I decided to ask for Selena's hand."

The strangeness of the name made Fricoulet forget his ill-humor. "Selena!" he exclaimed. "The girl you're in love with is called Selena? Only a scientist—and a Russian scientist, at that—could name his daughter after the Moon."

"After the Moon?" repeated the Comte. "Why after the Moon?"

Fricoulet was astounded. "What!" he exclaimed. "You're in love...your beloved has a bizarre name that isn't to be found in any calendar,[26] and you don't bother to investigate the etymology of the name?" Folding his arms in a gesture of comic indignation, he went on: "The roots of your love, Monsieur le Comte, do not appear to have extended to the determination of Greek roots. What do you do in the diplomatic service, to neglect the mother tongue in this fashion? If you had Burnouf[27] a little more present in your memory, you'd know that Selena comes from Selene, which means the Moon." Then, with a slightly ironic smile, he added: "I'll wager that your fiancée is blonde—blonde and pale, like Phoebe on a beautiful spring night..." He paused momentarily and resumed, with a mocking laugh: "Anyway, what does her coloring matter? A woman, blonde, brunette or redhead, is still a man's evil genius."

The Comte shrugged his shoulders, and murmured: "You haven't changed. I remember you had that same horror of women..."

"A horror that I count on preserving until death!" exclaimed Fricoulet.

"At least until you, too, encounter..."

Fricoulet grabbed his friend by the arm. "Shut up!" he said. "Shut up! The merest suggestion of that sort upsets me...for two pins I'd jump out of the carriage." Then, calming down, he added: "And the end of your story?"

"Oh, there's not much more to tell," Gontran continued. "The unfortunate Ossipoff, victim of an odious plot, was arrested, accused of nihilism and plotting against the Tsar's life—and, in spite of all my efforts and those of my friends, he's been condemned to deportation this very day."

"Damnation!" murmured Fricoulet. "Deportation to Siberia is a death-sentence." Privately, he added: *One father-in-law less—that's one fewer black cloud on the conjugal horizon.* As Flammermont shook his head, he said aloud: "The chance that brought you so unexpectedly into contact with me might send Ossipoff to the mines for which I'm bound."

"I've just been told that Ossipoff will be leaving St. Petersburg for Moscow tomorrow, to join a convoy of deportees bound for Ekaterinburg."

---

[26] Which is to say that it is not the name of a saint, as all names in a Catholic country like France are supposed to be.

[27] Jean-Louis Burnouf (1775-1844) was the Professor of Latin Eloquence at the Collège de France and produced many of the Latin translations used in the French educational system during the 19th century.

"Ah, yes!" murmured the engineer. "I know there are important platinum mines there."

The *droshky* had stopped outside Ossipoff's house. Vassily, who was doubtless on the lookout for the young Comte, opened the door and came out to meet him. At the sight of Fricoulet, the *muzjik* raised his lambskin cap and stood aside.

"Do you live here?" asked the engineer.

"No, it's Mademoiselle Ossipoff's house."

Fricoulet moved as if to throw off the furs that were covering him, but Flammermont murmured to him in a pleading tone: "Please wait for me here. I might need your advice...in any case, we can't part so abruptly." Without waiting for his friend's reply, he followed Vassily.

At the sound of the door opening, Selena swiftly got to her feet and came towards Gontran, her arms outstretched. Her face was pale and her eyes were still red with the tears she had shed during the day. Since misfortune had befallen her, the young woman had worn mourning-dress, and the black that enveloped her from head to foot made her unpolished ivory skin seem more translucent and diaphanous than ever, while her long gilded plaits hung down more heavily.

As on every other day, her first words posed the question that invariably began their conversation: "Is there any news?" And her gaze plunged into that of the young Comte in order to divine the truth, afraid that, for love of her, he might seek to hide it from her.

Contrary to his habit, Gontran did not reply. Without letting go of the young woman's hands, he led her to a sofa on which he made her sit down, applying gentle pressure. He sat down beside her.

Troubled by his silence, Selena cried; "There is something!"

Mutely, not having the courage to break her heart by announcing the fatal news, Gontran nodded his head.

"Oh, my God!" she moaned. Dolorously, she bowed her head, with her eyelids closed and her lips convulsively taut, like a mortally-wounded bird falling lifeless on to the ground.

"Selena," murmured the young man, fearfully.

But Mademoiselle Ossipoff had a valiant nature, which pitiless fate could bend but not break. She raised her head again, looked Gontran in the face, and stammered: "They've condemned him, haven't they?"

"Yes," said Gontran, in a low voice.

"The wretches!" she cried. Then she went on: "But the Tsar is just...he's merciful...he'll have mercy...you'll go with me, won't you, Gontran? You promised me. I'll throw myself at the Tsar's feet and beg him to let my father go..." When the Comte remained silent, she realized that she was deluding herself, and that it was necessary to abandon all hope. Then terror seized her; the sinister vision of the scaffold loomed up before her. She uttered a cry of horror, shielded her face with her hands, and murmured: "Death! My God, death!"

"No!" Gontran made haste to reply. "Deportation."

She shuddered, seizing is hand, and said in a strangled voiced: "Then why give up attempting further measures?"

He hesitated momentarily; then, having nothing else to say now that he had been cornered by the truth, he said: "Because, at dawn tomorrow, Monsieur Ossipoff will already be on his way to Moscow."

Selena cried out, sat up very straight and repeated: "To Moscow!"

"Yes, on his way to Ekaterinburg."

The young woman made a despairing gesture. "Him! Him, condemned to the mines, like a thief, like a murderer! Oh, the wretches! The villains!" She fell silent, her features contorted by pain, her eyes shining indignantly. Then, suddenly raising her head again, and shaking her closed fist, she said: "But we'll save him, Monsieur de Flammermont. We'll take that man innocent away from them."

"What can we do?" the young man murmured, pensively. "What imaginable means…? What subterfuge could we employ?

Selena stamped her foot and cried, with a certain bitterness in her voice: "I thought that a great man from your country had declared that the word *impossible* was not French! Are you backing out?"

"No—but I'm intimidated by the innumerable difficulties that now stand between us and our goal. There's no question of saving your father on Russian territory, before he's taken into the Siberian desert…measures are taken to prevent any escape attempt, and anything we did would only make the situation worse."

Selena bowed her lead, thus admitting the wisdom of what Flammermont had just said.

Suddenly, the latter got up and went to the door of the room. "I had a chance encounter today with one of my good childhood friends—a young French scientist who knows Monsieur Ossipoff by reputation and is keenly interested in his unfortunate fate. Would you allow me to introduce him to you?" As Selena remained silent, he went on: "He's a worthy fellow, very ingenious and knowledgeable. I brought him here because I thought he might be useful to us."

"Have him come in," Mademoiselle Ossipoff replied. "He's welcome in advance; he already has all my gratitude."

A few moments later, Gontran came back into the room, followed by the young engineer. "Dear Mademoiselle," he said, addressing Selena, "permit me to introduce one of my good friends, a French scientist, Monsieur Alcide Fricoulet, an engineer by profession and a prolific inventor."

Selena offered the newcomer a chair, then sat down. Smiling sadly, she said, graciously: "You're doubly welcome, Monsieur. As a friend of Monsieur de Flammermont, the doors of this house are open to you no less widely than they are to you in your capacity as a scientist."

Alcide Fricoulet bowed in recognition of this amicable speech. "Mademoiselle," he replied, "my friend Gontran, who told me a little while ago about the great misfortune that has overtaken you, came to find me to ask my advice. Alas, I have no pretension to bring you any great wisdom...but feeble as my resources are, they are entirely at your disposal." He turned to the young Comte and said: "Let's deliberate, then." Addressing himself to Selena, he added: "Do you have any maps of Russia?"

The young woman rang a bell. Vassily came back with a gigantic map, which was opened up on Ossipoff's work-table.

For a few minutes, Fricolet remained hunched over the canvas, attentively examining the map of Siberia, carefully measuring the distance that separated the mines of Ekaterinburg from St. Petersburg and verifying the height of the Ural Mountains. As his study progressed and he took account of the difficulties to be overcome, his brows furrowed and his lips elongated into a significant moue.

"Diabolical country!" he grumbled. Then, lifting his head: "Unless the circumstances are exceptional," he said, "I believe that it's impossible to escape from Siberia."

"You also despair, Monsieur!" cried Selena.

The engineer put out his hand sand said: "I said 'unless the circumstances are exceptional,' Mademoiselle. So, I continue: the passes are guarded, it's said, by observation-posts. It would be necessary to follow the mountains as far as Urenburg, cross plains devoid of vegetation, continually pursued by the Kirghiz tribesmen who hunt for escaped prisoners." Shaking his head energetically, he declared: "A man on his own, with no one to rely on but himself, cannot flee the mines; he would inevitably be recaptured, whether he were on foot or mounted on a sturdy horse, or even if he followed the rivers of the region by boat."

"But then," said Gontran, whose face had grown longer as his friend spoke, "if you declare all mans of escape impracticable...if one cannot save oneself by land or by water, nothing else remains..."

"What about air!" exclaimed Fricoulet. "Do you, by chance, consider the aerial route inferior to the others?"

"A balloon!" exclaimed the young Comte, in a tone that was half-incredulous and half-enthusiastic.

The engineer shrugged his shoulders. "A balloon!" he repeated, rather disdainfully. "Good God—what could you do with one of those? When you want to go to Siberia, it will take you to Norway...you know full well that such machines are not dirigible."

Gontran lowered his head. "What, then?" he murmured.

Alcide Fricoulet remained motionless, his brow furrowed as if contracted by a violent mental effort, with a vague and indecisive gaze filtering through his lowered eyelids. Suddenly, he straightened up and addressed Flammermont: "I repeat," he said, vibrantly, "that the air is the only way by which it will be possible for us to make an attempt to save Monsieur Ossipoff."

"The air...the air!" Gontrant objected. "That's all very well...but we need a means of making use of it."

"I think I've found that means."

Selena leapt out of her chair and seized the young scientist's hands. "Oh, Monsieur, don't lead us on! Don't give me vain hope! If you undertake to save my father, he must be saved!"

"Mademoiselle," Fricoulet replied, gravely, "I will undertake to attempt the impossible—that's all an honest man can do." He turned to the young Comte. "Are you ready for any sacrifice?" he asked.

"Even that of my life," replied Gontran, vibrantly.

In spite of the gravity of the situation, an imperceptible smile creased Fricoulet's lips. "I'm not asking as much as that," he said.

"What do you need, then?"

"First of all, that you can act freely—and for that, you must hand in your resignation."

"I'll see the ambassador this evening," the young diplomat replied, unhesitatingly, "and while waiting for my resignation to be accepted by the Ministry of Foreign Affairs, I'll obtain an immediate leave of absence."

Selena looked at Gontran, her eyes moist with tears. "Oh, Gontran," she murmured, her voice full of gratitude.

He took her hands, squeezed them gently, and replied: "What's that little sacrifice, if, by that means, I can dry up your tears and bring a smile back to your lips?"

Fricoulet shrugged his shoulders slightly. *All the same*, he thought, *not one of these people in love can find other things to say than the phrases repeated endlessly since the creation of Adam and Eve.*

"What are you muttering between your teeth?" asked the Comte, turning round.

"I'm saying that your resignation isn't the only thing I need. I'll also need 50,000 francs."

"This evening, again, I'll write to my lawyer to tell him to send me the money." Then he whispered in his friend's ear: "You do well not to be too demanding, for that's almost all that remains of my fortune."

"Gontran," said Selena, "I don't want...."

"It's for your father's sake, Mademoiselle Ossipoff," Fricoulet replied.

The young woman blushed, and murmured: "I don't want Monsieur de Flammermont to ruin himself, though."

"Ah!" cried the young man, hotly. "Have I not millions to sacrifice for you?"

"In that case," said Fricoulet, coolly. "Mikhail Ossipoff shall be saved. Tomorrow, we'll take the train to Paris, and there we'll make all our preparations for the prisoner's escape."

Gontran nodded towards Selena. "I can't leave her alone here," he said.

Fricoulet frowned. "Oh, women!" he groaned. Then, after a momentary pause: "Well then, stay in St. Petersburg until everything's ready, when I'll summon you to join me."

"But explain—what do you intend to do? Tell us what your plan is."

"My plan is quite simple. I said just now that the only practicable way to free Mikhail Ossipoff is by air, and that's the truth…but as balloons aren't dirigible, it's a matter of constructing a high-speed apparatus capable of flying through the air at will."

"But you mocked me just now when I pronounced the word *balloon*."

"Indeed…in order for me to be master of my means of locomotion, it will have to be heavier than air."

Gontran opened his astonished eyes wide; his more-than-insufficient scientific knowledge overwhelmed by this declaration.

"You don't seem very convinced," observed Fricoulet, sarcastically.

The young Comte smiled, for Selena's benefit, and replied: "In the absence of the worthy Monsieur Ossipoff, I can admit to you that I'm a mere savage in matters of science, and that I don't understand…"

"Bah! You don't need to understand…do you trust me?"

"Blindly."

"Well then, don't ask me for explanations that, apart from possibly bringing a little enlightenment to your mind, will only delay us…" He looked at the clock and got up abruptly. "Don't forget that I arrived here yesterday evening after 35 hours of traveling, and that I must catch the earliest possible train tomorrow morning." He suddenly slapped his forehead and looked at Gontran and Selena alternately, with a startled expression.

"What is it?" they asked, simultaneously, gripped by the same presentiment that some impossibility had just sprung to the young engineer's mind.

"It's…it's…that everything we've just said is all very well, but…"

"But?" repeated the others, anxiously.

Alcide Fricoulet burst out laughing, folded his arms, and said "What about my mine at Nertchinsk?"

Gontran looked at Selena, pale with desolation. "That's true," he murmured. "I'd forgotten that you were merely passing through St. Petersburg and that a brilliant position was waiting for you there."

Mademoiselle Ossipoff covered her face with her hands to hide the tears running down her cheeks. In spite of the scant sympathy that the weaker sex inspired in him, the young engineer was moved by the sight of that poignant distress. He looked at Mademoiselle Ossipoff gravely and it was evident from his

75

profound gaze and his anxiously-pursed lips that a fierce combat was raging within him.

"To the Devil with them!" he said, suddenly. "Let me mines at Nerchinsk be exploited by whomsoever might wish. Things will remain as we just left them. I leave for Paris tomorrow."

Selena raised her head again and a radiant smile lit up her pale and tearful face.

Gontran threw himself on his friend's hands and shook them repeatedly. "Alcide, Alcide! How shall we ever be able to thank you?"

The engineer shrugged his shoulders. "Quite simply," he said. "Promise me that if, as I firmly hope, I succeed in contriving Monsieur Ossipoff's escape…promise me in his name to make me part of the great celestial excursion he has in mind."

Selena clapped her hands and cried: "Oh, I'll gladly do that."

"In that case," Fricoulet relied, "far from owing me anything, Mademoiselle, it's me who'll be in your debt…for pleasure trips to the Moon aren't organized every day, and I shan't be displeased to go and see with my own eyes the extent to which the Selenites have made progress in technology."

Two months after this conversation, Serena said to Monsieur de Flammermont; "What do you think has become of Monsieur Fricoulet, my dear friend?"

"Well," said the young Comte, rather embarrassed by the question, "I really don't know what to think, I confess…my letters go unanswered, and the telegram I sent him a week ago has met the same fate as my letters."

"Well, do you want to know what I think?" the young woman continued, in a strange tone. "Your friend Fricoulet, who, in the grip of I don't know what sentiment, made us so many fine promises here, has simply had second thoughts and has gone to Nerchinsk."

Monsieur de Flammermont started. "What are you saying, Mademoiselle?" he exclaimed.

"What must be the truth," she said, bitterly. "Monsieur Fricoulet has probably realized that it was stupid to sacrifice his interests for an old man he does not even know…and that's all there is to it!"

"But that's impossible! A fortnight after Alcide's departure, I received word from my lawyer that he had given him the 50,000 francs in person."

Selena shook her head. "Perhaps," she said, pensively, "he employed that money in unsuccessful attempts and, not daring to tell you, for the sake of self-respect or some other reason…he's playing dead."

"I know Fricoulet," cried the young Comte. "He's a stout fellow, and honest…I'd swear to that…let's wait a little longer."

Mademoiselle Ossipoff remained silent for a moment, then, in a slightly bitter voice, said: "Wait…always wait…and in the meantime, out there in those hellish mines, in company with bandits, my poor father is eking out his miserable life, accusing me—his daughter—of doing nothing to save him."

"But what could you do?" asked Gontran.

"Attempt to join him—and, if I can't help him to escape, at least share his fate."

"But you're not thinking of doing that!"

"I'm thinking of it so seriously, Monsieur de Flammermont, that everything is ready for my departure."

The young man could not believe his ears.

"You're going!" he said. "You're leaving! But you know perfectly well that it's forbidden for the families of deportees to go to Siberia."

"I know that—but I've taken my precautions to deflect suspicion and avoid police surveillance."

As he looked at her in astonishment, she went to a cupboard, opened it, and took out the complete costume of a Lithuanian peasant, which she laid out on a chair.

"You see," she said. "With these clothes, I'll be able to travel, and no one will know that it's Mademoiselle Ossipoff, that daughter of one of the members of the St. Petersburg Institute, thus clad, going to join her father in Siberia."

"But you won't be able to get across the frontier."

She picked up a map, which she opened. "Look," she said. "See how exact my plan is. From here, I take the railway as far as Urenburg. There I abandon my Russian peasant's costume and buy gypsy clothing in a bazaar, by courtesy of which I slip through with one of the nomadic bands who go into Siberia every spring in order to earn a living there by going to village to village giving theatrical performances."

"But that's crazy!" cried Gontran. "You can't do that!"

"Crazy or not, Monsieur de Flammermont," the young woman said, in a firm voice, "I've decided to put the plan I've just briefly described to you into action, point by point."

The young Comte was speechless. He sensed, given Mademoiselle Ossipoff's resolute tone, than any contradiction would be futile. "And when are you leaving?" he asked, in a tremulous voice.

"Tomorrow."

"So soon!" he cried, taking her by the hands.

"I've already delayed too long. Think about the man who's suffering all alone…out there."

"Permit me to accompany you as far as Urenburg," he begged.

"I don't even want you to come to St. Petersburg Station; the least imprudence might attract the attention of the police."

Gontran made a despairing gesture. "So my dream is ended!" he stammered.

"No," she said, forcefully. "Don't despair, any more than I despair. We shall see one another again, I swear…there is something that tells me so."

She had pronounced these words with such a profound conviction that Gontran felt a flicker of hope reignite in his heart—and when he took his leave of Mademoiselle Ossipoff he too was persuaded that the old man might escape his guards.

The next day, however, despite Selena's prohibition, he could not resist the desire to see her one last time; he borrowed Vassily's clothes and went to the railway station some time before the departure of the train. Hidden in a corner, concealed behind a pillar, he saw Mademoiselle Ossipoff arrive, more charming than ever in her peasant's costume. As if her heart had warned her that he was there, the young woman paraded an indifferent gaze all around her, and finally perceived the man who was devouring her with his eyes. She signaled to him that she had seen him, and then, presenting her ticket, mingled with the other travelers who were crowding the platform.

He followed her, saw her climb into a third class carriage, at the door of which she stayed, leaning out in order that he could see her until the last moment. Finally, the engine released a strident whistle-blast, and the train moved off. Selena put her fingers to her lips then, and blew a kiss in the direction in which de Flammermont was standing, motionless. Then, moved by the desolation in which she had left him, she took her seat and wept silently.

Nothing any longer retained Gontran in St. Petersburg, his resignation having been accepted. Scarcely eight hours after Selena had left the city, he had buckled up his suitcase and was about to set off for Paris, when, on the very even of his departure, he received a telegram which read: *Everything ready. Come. Fricoulet.*

Flammermont uttered a cry of surprise. "Good lad!" he said. "I knew as soon as he promised that he would do the impossible to keep his word." But his radiant face suddenly darkened and his joy turned to depression as he thought of Selena, who had not had the patience to wait and would now leave Urenburg to launch herself into the Siberian wilderness, exposed to 1000 dangers. "Provided that she gets as far as Ekaterinburg," he murmured, "Fricoulet will be able to rescue two instead of one."

Two and a half day later, he disembarked in Paris and had himself taken to the Boulevard Montparnasse, where Alcide had lodgings beneath the very roof of a tall house.

The young scientist's apartments were nothing less than sumptuous. They consisted, in total, of two vast mansard rooms, from the windows of which one could see the whole of north Paris extended in a vast panorama.

One of the two rooms was a library that also served as a study, an observatory, a smoking-room and, if necessary, a drawing-room. The other served as a laboratory and bedroom, as was indicated by a little iron cot with a mattress as thin as a pancake and a blanket as thin as an onion-skin, extending from a recess in the wall. On a tiled hearth with a movable glass chimney-hood stood earthenware stoves, vessels in sandstone and glass, and a huge alembic with a cooling coil. Sets of shelves garnishing the wall were overloaded with bottles of chemical compounds, test tubes, flat-bottomed flasks and long-necked flasks. The large table in front of the window supported a chemical balance, an assay-balance in a glass case, a powerful microscope with freshly-made slides and test-tubes for the study of the "infinitely small."

In the other room—the library—there were immense glass-fronted cases instead of stoves; some contained numerous dissimilar volumes whose worn spines testified to continual use, others enclosed physics apparatus: electric machines of every sort, pneumatic pumps, voltaic batteries, photographic apparatus, lenses, telescopes, etc. The only furniture in this room was a threadbare settee, a few chairs and a side-table—no mirrors, let alone paintings, and no curtains on the windows. Master Fricoulet, without being a cenobite, was absolutely disdainful of all these useless objects; his books and apparatus were sufficient to all his needs, along with a collection of pipes, more-or-less cleaned out, suspended from the wall.

"You!" he cried, leaping toward his friend.

"Aren't you expecting me?" asked Gontran, a trifle astonished.

"Certainly, but...not for a few days." And he added, with an ironic smile: "I didn't suppose you'd be able to tear yourself away so quickly."

The young Comte's face suddenly changed expression. "Alas," he said, "Selena left last week." In a few heart-rending sentences, he brought Fricoulet up to date.

"Oh, women!" cried the young engineer. "They're all the same! The best of them, you know, isn't worth *that*." And he clicked his thumbnail disdainfully against his teeth. Then, abruptly he added: "You're not too tired to come with me?"

"Where to?"

"A place near Nogent-sur-Marne."

"To do what?"

"To see the body of my apparatus."

"Let's go."

An hour later, the two friends got down from a tram in front of the Fort de Vincennes and set off into the shady by-ways of the woods. Having gone through Fontenay, Fricoulet took a little-used side-street and stopped in front of a door furnished with a sturdy lock, into which he introduced a key he had taken from his pocket. The door opened and the two men went into in a vast uncultivated field nearly 800 square meters, at the back of which was a hangar.

"I don't see your famous apparatus!" said Gontran. "Where is it?"

"In that hangar over there. It's not assembled, because the engine isn't finished, and besides, there's not enough room...to carry four people, I needed to make my bird quite large."

"Your bird!" exclaimed the young Comte.

Fricoulet smiled. "When you've seen it, you'll understand why I call it that." So saying, he opened the hangar door, and Gontran then saw a dozen bizarrely-constructed and carefully-polished metallic sections laid out on the ground. There were also rolled-up pieces of silk and fabrics of every sort. Along the walls, on special mountings, were all kinds of tools and equipment used by carpenters and mechanics.

Gontran seemed disappointed. "That's all that there is to your...bird?" he murmured.

"What! All that there is! Do you think I've been wasting my time?"

Gontran pointed to the pieces of silk. "Are you making a balloon?"

"Not at all...it's an *aeroplane*." Reading an entirely natural question in his friend's eyes, he added: "You know what a kite is, and you understand why it rises into the air: because it's held against the wind by means of a string attached to the ground; the stability of the apparatus comes from that traction and wind-resistance. Well, suppose one thing: I get rid of the string and replace it by a *propeller* that draws the apparatus forward, with exactly the same speed as the person who holds the end of the string contrives. Doesn't it seem to you that the result will be the same?"[28]

"Which is to say that the kite will remain immobile if the resistance doesn't change...but if it varies, it will fall or move forward...."

Fricoulet nodded approvingly.

"Oh, if only Monsieur Ossipoff, who believes that he will only have an astronomer for a son-in-law, were here to hear me talking like this!" cried Gontran, comically. "What joy he would experience in observing that my knowledge also extends to mechanics!" The, in a more serious tone, he immediately added: "But you don't intend to carry me in a kite?"

"Why not?" countered the engineer, with the utmost calm.

Flammermont looked at his friend; then, placing his forefinger on his forehead and shaking his head, he said: "Are you...?"

"You think I'm mad!" cried Fricoulet. "Well, look, listen and try to understand."

He picked up a piece of charcoal that was lying on the ground and set about sketching a machine on the white wall of the hangar, in broad strokes, which made Gontran open his eyes wide.

"What's that?" the latter asked.

---

[28] I have transcribed Graffigny and Le Faure's "*aéroplane*" and "*propulseur*" directly into English, just as the eventual inventors of actual aircraft did, although the authors—in common with their contemporaries—have not understood the actual principle that was eventually to facilitate heavier-than-air flight (which is to do with pressure differences above and below a fast-moving wing).

"This," the young engineer exclaimed, "is my kite! Here, first of all, is a large surface of glossy silk—you can see the rolls of silk to your right—which will be about 400 square meters, in order to constitute, in case of damage to the machine, an immense and effective parachute. You understand the design, don't you?"

"Thus far, it's as clear as a rock-pool. But what I understand better is what a parachute is for...brrr...you're sending shivers down my spine..."

"Here—at what I call the head, the front of the kite—I install two helices made of silk bordered by steel wire, three meters in diameter..."

"Which are probably these machines here," Gontran put in, pointing with the end of his walking-stick at the bizarre twisted plates that had immediately attracted his attention.

"Yes," replied the engineer, smiling at the expression, "they're those machines there. Now, these machines—as you call them—are moved at 300 cycles per minute by a steam-engine of my own design...would you like me to explain my design?"

"No, no!" cried the Comte, with veritable alarm. "My head's already reeling somewhat with what you've told me—not to mention that you'd be wasting your time. Where do you put this motor, though? Not on the silk, surely?"

"Why not?" Making a cross in the very center of the kite, Fricolet said: "Here's my motor."

"But what about its weight? And that of the fire, and the water...?"

"Patience...we'll get to that shortly. For the moment, here's my kite drawn forwards, thanks to the helices, with a speed that can be as much as 50 meters a second. At any rate, that speed is sufficient for the air to present sufficient resistance to sustain the entire apparatus.

"But once launched," said Gontran, banteringly, "your kite will go straight ahead, without being able to deviate from a straight line—and, as you said to me in St. Petersburg, speaking of balloons, you'll head for Norway went you want to land in Siberia."

Fricoulet shrugged his shoulders. "Smart thinking!" he said. "Doesn't the rudder count for anything?" As he spoke, three strokes of the charcoal added a triangular surface, like a fish's tail, to the rear of the apparatus. "Here," he said, is what will steer our aerial boat."

"That's very good!" retorted Flammermont. "But tell me about the motor."

"I'd like to—but that won't be as obvious to you. Anyway, my motor is composed of a high-pressure boiler in a serpentine form, so as to be incapable of exploding, and containing only 500 grams of water. By virtue of the great heat generated by the combustion of the liquid hydrocarbons burned in a lamp, the 500 grams of water are transformed into vapor at a pressure of 500 atmospheres and work upon both faces of an exceedingly light piston, whose shaft is directly articulated to the crank-shafts of the spindles of the propulsive helices."

"Oof!" said Gontran. "What a sentence!"

"My dear chap, scientific explanations scarcely lend themselves to oratorical flourishes. I continue: after relaxation by working in a second cylinder, the vapor is brought back to a condenser in which it is liquefied, and from which a pump extracts it to return it to the boiler—in that manner, virtually all the dead weight of water and the fuel brought with it is dispensed with. Do you understand?"

"Hardly any of it…but one thing I do understand is that the motor, with all its accessories, still weighs something."

"My kite can support a load of 700 kilos!" the young inventor cried, triumphantly. "It can travel 1000 kilometers in a single flight."

Gontran was dumbfounded.

"What do you have to say to that?"

"Nothing—absolutely nothing," retorted the Comte. Then, suddenly throwing his arms around the young engineer's neck, he exclaimed: "You're a genius, Fricoulet!"

"Pooh!" said the other. "You'd never have dreamed of saying that to me, you mocker, if my kite weren't going to bring a smile to Mademoiselle Selena's lips."

"Ah, my friend," Gontran riposted, "I shall owe my happiness to you!"

"What a madman!" growled Fricoulet. "Has any free creature ever been seen so desirous of being in chains?" Then, meeting Gontran's eyes, he said, curtly: "Don't ever blame me if the honeymoon you're anticipating changes color and goes red…for I tell you straight out, in spite of our friendship—or, rather, because of it, that I wouldn't be doing what I'm doing if it weren't a matter of rendering to science a man as eminent as Monsieur Ossipoff." And having delivered this speech in a single breath, the young engineer fell silent.

Gontran, who was long familiar with his friend's antipathy toward marriage, shrugged his shoulders gently. "As regards Ossipoff," was all he said, "how will we let him know we're coming?"

"He already knows," Fricoulet replied, sullenly.

The Comte's mouth fell open. "Ossipoff already knows!" he said. "But who's told him?"

"I have," said the other, laconically. Taking out his watch, he murmured: "In two hours, I have to be at the Cail factory to inspect my motor. Have you anything else to ask me?"

"I'd like to ask one question."

"Go on."

"When will your bird be able to take to the air?"

Without hesitation, Fricoulet replied: "My aeroplane will be ready on July 20… I'll be carrying out trials until the end of the month. I've allowed three days for fitting it out completely and furnishing the stocks of food and provisions of every sort. That will take us to August 3. We'll leave on the evening of August 4."

"In six weeks!" Gontran exclaimed.

"Yes, in six weeks—and on the morning of August 8, we'll be flying over Ekaterinburg."

"As long as we don't break our heads on the way," observed Flammermont.

"Very true," Fricoulet replied. And he added, shrugging his shoulders: "Well, it'll end that way or by marriage!"

Alcide Fricoulet definitely did not like women.

Chapter V
Ossipoff's Removal

About 500 *versts* from the Kammenoy Poyas—the "stone belt"—as the Russians call the chain of the Ural Mountains, at 56 degrees 51 minutes north latitude and 38 degrees 18 minutes east longitude, stands the town of Ekaterinburg, the center of a crowd of mines and forges. It was there, after a frightful two month journey, his body broken by fatigue and suffering but his morale still resistant, that Mikhail Ossipoff arrived with an entire column of convicts, composed for the most part of condemned criminals.

The day after his arrival, separated from his companions and escorted by two policemen in blue tunics and copper helmets, the old man was taken to the police station. There, in the presence of the *smotritel*—the inspector—he was stripped to the waist in order to establish his identity with reference to a description. Then he was given the number 7327 which would henceforth replace any other status in his regard.

When these various formalities were complete, the inspector said to his secretary: "Go and see if Ismail Krekov is here."

The other came back a few minutes later with a huge devil of a man clad entirely in furs, with a bearskin cap pulled down to his eyes. His face was almost completely hidden by a thick black beard, into which the emphatically curved lips imported a scarlet stain.

"Ismail Krekov," said the inspector, "this is the man you're waiting for."

The newcomer approached the old scientist. "Your name is Mikhail Ossipoff?" he asked.

"That's me," replied the scientist, in some surprise.

"Ah!" said the other, moving around the prisoner, examining him from top to toe.

The inspector stamped his foot impatiently. "Get on with it!" he said. "What are you waiting for, Ismail Krekov?"

"I want to verify that it's really the man I've been told about," the other replied, gravely.

"Imbecile," murmured the inspector. "Since you've never seen him before, how can you possibly know whether it's him? Go on—take delivery of your man and get out."

Meekly, Ismail Krekov bent over a large ledger that was opened for him, put his signature in the place that was indicated to him, and went out, giving Mikhail Ossipoff a signal to follow him."

Outside the door of the police station, a telega hitched to two horses was waiting. Ismail Krekov climbed into it. The old man took his place beside him and the two horses, spurred on by a vigorous crack of the whip, carried the light vehicle through the suburbs of the town.

The last houses soon disappeared; then, turning abruptly off the highway, the telega went into a narrow road that climbed rather steeply along the side of a mountain. The driver let his horses slow down, and turned to his companion. "Well," he said, "you can count yourself very lucky."

"Yes?" said Mikhail Ossipoff, evasively.

"Just imagine that three days ago, when I received the letter recommending you to me, my book-keeper—a convict like you—had just died. Then, as they told me that you were a man sufficiently educated to keep books, I asked the smotritel to let me have you."

"Ah!" said Ossipoff, making every effort to hide his astonishment. "You received a letter mentioning me?"

"Yes, three days ago. A French engineer that I had with me for some years to supervise the mine of which I have the commission wrote to me warmly recommending you. So, as he'd rendered me such good service and I retained fond memories of him, and as I also had need of another book-keeper to replace the one who died...I'm taking you on. Are you content?"

"Thank you," said Ossipoff, simply. His amazement was so great that he did not think of offering further thanks to the man for the great service he was doing him in taking him out of the hellish mine-work. He wondered what friend could have written from Paris to recommend him, given that he had never left St. Petersburg and had no connection with the French capital. Unable to answer that question, he accepted the matter philosophically, silently blessing that person to whom he owed the amelioration of his fate without knowing who it was.

These things happened at about the same time that Selena and Gontran de Flammermont were leaving St. Petersburg, a week apart, the former to travel through the many dangers of the Siberian steppes to join her father, the latter in response to the appeal of his friend Fricoulet, whose telegram summoned him to Paris.

During the early days of his sojourn, Ossipoff found a diversion from his chagrin in the exploitation of the mine and the chemical operations necessary to the treatment of the platinum extracted from the serpentine rocks of the mountain.

Separated by repeated washing from the earth and sand that contained it, the platinum is then plunged into a bath of *aqua regia*,[29] in which the gold and iron mixed in with it are dissolved. The *aqua regia* is then concentrated further and the metal dissolves with the other substances still attached to it: rhodium, palladium and iridium. The decanted solution is evaporated almost to dryness to remove the excess *aqua regia* and decompose these metallic substances more

---

[29] *Aqua regia* (*eau royale* in French) is a mixture of sulphuric and nitric acid, which serves as an exceedingly powerful inorganic solvent.

fully. Then the liquor is treated with ammonium chlorhydrate, which yields a precipitate of platinum ammonium chloride. This precipitate, washed, dried and heated to red heat, then constitutes the gray "platinum sponge" from which metallic platinum is recoverable. This powder was the end-product of the mine and factory that Ismail Krekov directed; it was then sent to Moscow, where it was founded in a special process to manufacture actual ingots.

Almost all the convicts employed by Ismail Krekov, with sallow complexions, untidy beards and haggard eyes, bore on their foreheads and cheeks, branded by hot irons, the three letters of the infamous stigmatum *vor*, meaning "thief." They were also recognizable by squares of black cloth sewn on the backs of their greatcoats. Murderers wore red squares and arsonists yellow ones.

Although Mikhail Ossipoff, employed in the administration offices, had no communication with his companions in captivity by day, when evening came he had to return to the *isba*—a kind of small hut built of mud—that he shared with another convict, on whose back was a red square. He was a murderer, and on the first evening they spent together, Yegor—that was the man's name—told Ossipoff his story in such cynical detail that the old man could not help shivering.

"What about you?" asked the bandit, when he had finished. "Why are you here?"

In order not to irritate his companion, the scientist acquainted him briefly with the odious plot that had led to his condemnation. The other remained pensive. The following evening, as Ossipoff was about to go to bed, Yegor drew him to the window of the *isba* and, showing him the star-strewn sky, said to him: "Tell me a little about all that."

Initially surprised, the scientist looked at his companion, doubting that he was serious—but, seeing the bandit's grave expression and curious gaze, he began to explain to him in simple terms, understandable to a naïve intelligence, the principles of the universal mechanism. Then he passed on to the organization of the celestial system, and spoke for two hours—forgetting, by involving himself thus is a subject so dear to him, the horrible situation in which he found himself.

Every evening, it was the same. The bandit was increasingly captivated by he scientist's explanations. Gradually, the scientist felt his initial reserve melt away and a certain sympathy for the unfortunate penetrated his heart.

"Ah!" said Yegor, one day, with a deep sigh, extending his hand toward the silvery disk of the Moon. "I wish I could see it at closer range."

"We'd need a telescope for that," Ossipoff replied.

The following morning, as the old man went into the little room that served as his office, he was told that Krekov wanted to see him in his study.

The concessionaire had a letter in his hand. "Your friend in Paris," he said to Ossipoff, "has written asking me to give you this—which, he assures me, will give you great pleasure. As I'm pleased with you, I don't see any objection to doing as he asks." So saying, he pointed to a long, narrow object set on the table, carefully packaged in cloth and straw.

The old man opened the package excitedly, and his eyes were delighted by the appearance of a magnificent telescope. He uttered a cry of joy and his tremulous hands almost dropped the precious object.

"Take it away," said Ismail Krekov. "This evening, when your day's work is done, you can amuse yourself at your leisure."

One can imagine how slowly the hours passed for the old scientist. A telescope! That object alone brought him back to life. Thanks to that, he could continue his studies and seek to forget his misery in the stars.

When he arrived at his *isba*, Yegor had not yet come back from the mine. Without losing a minute, Ossipoff, having focused his telescope, aimed it at the vault where a myriad of stars were scintillating. To his surprise, though, the instrument's field remained dark; not a single star was visible. It was as if a thick veil were extended between the scientist's eye and the objective lens.

Thinking that a foreign body had slipped into the interior of the instrument, Ossipoff dismantled it completely, then examined the various parts one by one with extreme care. Suddenly, he released a muffled exclamation. A small piece of collodion was stuck to one of the lenses, about the size of a thumbnail.

His throat constricted by emotion and his heart beating with unimaginable violence, the old scientist realized that the collodion seemed to be dotted with imperceptible black spots. Immediately, he suspected that he was dealing with a photographic reduction; placing one of the magnifying lenses of the telescope over the reduction, he was able to read these words:

We are watching over you and working to save you. We shall be in Ekaterinburg between August 7 and 8, arriving by air.

It was signed *Gontran de Flammermont.*

Ossipoff required all his will-power not to scream with joy. He had not been abandoned! People were working on his behalf! They were going to save him! Was that really possible, in truth? He re-read the blessed note several times. Yes, it had been written, definitely written, and the day of his deliverance was fixed for August 8, and it was signed Flammermont. So the mysterious friend who had written to Ismail Krekov must be the young Comte. Ah, the brave lad! How happy he was that Selena loved a man like that!

Gradually recovering his composure, though, the scientist hastened to scrape away the collodion. Then he reassembled the telescope and, incapable of surrendering himself to his favorite study that evening, was about to got to bed when there was a sound of footsteps outside. The door was violently shoved open and two men—two convicts—came into the *isba* carrying an unfortunate covered in blood by the feet and head. By the light of the lantern, Ossipoff recognized his nightly companion.

Without saying a word, the prisoners deposited their comrade on his bed and left.

"Yegor!" cried the old man.

The injured man opened his eyes with difficulty, gazed silently at Ossipoff for a moment, then beckoned to him to come closer. "I'm dead," he murmured, in a feeble voice. "A section of rock collapsed on me. I only have a few hours to live, but I want to tell you something before I die."

"Speak," said the old man, putting his ear close t the dying man's mouth.

The latter made a violent effort, sat up in his bed and pointed to the hearth. "There," he said, in a voice punctuated by gurgling. "There, under the stones…a fortune…found in the mine…ten years ago…for you…for you…under the stones…" He slumped backwards; his limbs twisted, then became motionless. He was dead!

Ossipoff, deeply moved, spent the entire night sitting up with the cadaver, then returned to his duties the following day without even trying to establish the veracity of Yegor's last words.

It was not until several days afterwards that, alone in his *isba* one evening, the cloudy weather rendering any astronomical study impossible, the old man suddenly shivered as his eyes fixed themselves mechanically on the hearth, remembering the dead man's revelation. Having carefully locked the door and extended his only blanket over the window, he went to the hearth, knelt down and, with the aid of an iron pick, lifted up the stones of the fireplace. A hole then appeared, into which he shone the light of his lantern. He recoiled, his eyes dazzled by the many glints thrown off by the heap of rubies, emeralds and tourmalines—the smallest of which was as broad as a thumb—that filled the hole he had uncovered.

"A fortune!" he exclaimed. "Yes, the man was telling the truth. There's a fortune here!"

He remained pensive for a moment, kneeling on the compacted earth that served as the *isba*'s floor; his honest man's soul rebelled at the thought of taking possession of these precious stones, and his initial impulse was to take them to Ismail Krekov—but he reflected that the man was merely a concessionaire and that, by virtue of the laws of the empire, precious stones found on Russian territory belonged to the Tsar. It was not, therefore, Ismail Krekov who would get the benefit of the treasure accumulated by the bandit Yegor, but the Emperor.

Now, the Emperor….

Mikhail Ossipoff remained hesitant for part of the night, but by morning his decision was made. He had resolved to use the fortune that had fallen so unexpectedly into his hands for the realization of his famous project. *The Emperor will be frustrated*, he thought, *but Russia will gain thereby*. He replaced the stones in the fireplace and kept Yegor's secret to himself.

Meanwhile, a singular animation had reigned in the streets of Ekaterinburg for a week, occasioned by the annual fair held in the town—an event of great importance—between mid-July and the end of August.

The closer the time fixed by Gontran de Flamermont approached, the more Ossipoff trembled lest the slightest incident might upset his savior's plans. Finally, one Sunday morning—August 8 [30]—having hidden the precious stones left to him by Yegor in his telescope, and having suspended the aforesaid telescope around his neck beneath his goatskin cloak, the old man asked Ismail Krekov for permission to go into the town to make a tour of the fête. It was not a favor that he was asking; the penitentiary administration deemed it a good idea to keep up the convicts' spirits by means of a few treats, to the extent that the convicts had permission to mingle with the crowds, provided that they wore the coats identifying them as "state workers."

Having arrived in Ekaterinburg, Ossipoff, drawn along by the irresistible tide of curiosity-seekers soon found himself in the large town square—where, it seemed, all the attractions of the fair were gathered. These attractions mostly consisted of bands of bohemians who devoted themselves to strange exercises in the open air: singing, dancing, and performing feats of strength and skill, to the great amazement of onlookers.

As one might imagine, these distractions were of no interest to Ossipoff; once in the square he had but one end: to get through the crowd that pressed around him to an isolated isba where he might rest and await developments in peace.

Suddenly, a voice rose up from a circle of curiosity-seekers that made the old man shudder. Instinctively, with a force of which he had not thought himself capable, he cut through the human tide to arrive in the front rank of a circle, in the middle of which a young woman with a swarthy face, clad in a gaudy Bohemian costume, was making a little white kid dance to the accompaniment of her voice.

"Selena!" cried the old man.

"Father! My dear Father!" exclaimed the young gypsy girl in her turn, fainting into Ossipoff's arms.

Then, without paying any heed to the murmurs of the crowd, which did not like its entertainments to be so abruptly interrupted, he took the young woman to one of the isbas bordering the square.

"You, here!" he said. "My poor child! But how?"

Briefly, the young woman told the old man what had happened. She told him about Fricoulet's visit, the confidence that she had in him, her subsequent impatience, and the decision she had made to come and find her father, if not to save him, at least to ameliorate the rigors of his captivity.

---

[30] The assertion that the crucial date of August 8 falls on a Sunday might have been made at hazard, without reference to a calendar, but it may be worth noting that August 8 fell on a Sunday in 1880. This is inconsistent with information provided subsequently in the text, but I shall make some attempt to clarify the inconsistencies in an afterword.

"But I've had news from Monsieur de Flammermont!" Ossipoff exclaimed. He told Selena what he had found in the telescope sent to him from Paris, and then added: "Do you know what their plan is?"

"I have absolutely no idea," the young woman replied. "I only know one thing: Monsieur Fricoulet intended to construct an apparatus specifically designed for aerial navigation. That's all."

"Do you know that it's today that they're supposed to arrive in Ekaterinburg?"

Selena uttered a cry of joy. "Today! Oh, my dear Father!" Putting her arms around the old man's neck, she kissed him tenderly on both cheeks.

Suddenly, a policeman appeared at the door of the isba. He paused momentarily on the threshold, putting his hand over his eye like an eye-shade, scanning the interior of the *isba*, then advanced towards Ossipoff.

"Number 7357?" he said, roughly.

"That's me," the old scientist replied.

"Is this your daughter?" the representative of the authorities asked, turning to Selena. The old man nodded his head affirmatively. "I'm placing you both under arrest," he declared. Turning to the door, he made a gesture. Ten policemen came into the isba then, threw themselves on the old man and his daughter, and put heavy chains on their hands and feet.

"What crime have we committed?" asked Ossipoff.

"You're planning to escape."

"What proof do you have?" retorted the scientist.

"The *Korosse* will explain that." The *Korosse* was the equivalent of a commissaire.

Shoving the prisoner outside, the policemen set off for the police station. Crossing the marketplace was not accomplished without difficulty; in spite of the brutality with which the policemen pushed the crowds back, the latter were enthusiastic to see the prisoners—whose wretched appearance moved them to pity—at closer range. Muffled rumors even began to circulate in the crowd, and the policemen, sensing a sentiment on the part of the peasants favorable to their captives, were looking at one another anxiously, when one of them suddenly shouted: "Don't you love the Tsar any longer, that you complain on behalf of those who have tried to put him to death?"

The first ranks of the curiosity-seekers moved backwards, several voices repeating: "They've tried to kill the Tsar!"

"They're witches," the policeman added.

At this word, a frightful cry of rage emerged from multitudinous throats. "Witches! Witches!" they repeated.

"They'll curse the crops!"

"They'll make the livestock die!"

"Death to the witches!" cried one voice.

Immediately, the entire audience howled: "Hang them! Hang them!"

Faced with the hostile inclinations of the crowd, the anxiety of the policemen increased—for it was as much their duty to prevent the prisoners being lynched as to prevent them from escaping, and it was certainly the former fate that was in store for the unfortunate Ossipoff and his daughter.

In vain, the policemen struck out pitilessly to the right and the left with their cudgels, belaboring the peasants; the latter, rendered furious, fought fiercely to take possession of the quarry they coveted.

Suddenly, a policeman treacherously grabbed by the legs fell backwards, and was disarmed and tied up before he had time to get up. This capture increased the assailants' courage. Uttering a loud cry, they surged forward unanimously, throwing themselves on the procession and breaking it up in spite of the determination with which the guards defended their prisoners.

Within a few minutes, they were put out of action. Ossipoff and Selena passed into the hands of the convicts, who dragged them to the middle of the fairground, where there was a gigantic fir-tree, whose enormous branches extended horizontally a few meters from the ground.

"My child! My beloved Selena!" murmured the old man, divining the barbarians' intention.

The young woman looked at her father boldly. "Don't worry about me, Father," she said, in a firm voice. "I'll show these wretches what courage innocence can give a girl like me."

Tugged and jostled by the men, pinched and insulted by the women, the two prisoners were no more than ten meters from the fatal tree when a sharp whistling sound suddenly disturbed the air so terribly that the entire crowd looked up.

In the blue sky, directly above Ekaterinburg, a black dot was floating, visibly increasing in size, seemingly descending vertically upon the town—and the same whistling sound continued to make itself heard.

"A hailstorm! A hailstorm!" cried a voice. "The witches are drawing it down upon us! Put them to death!"

But the dot was still growing, and something like a plume of smoke could now be seen emerging from it. Amazement was then transformed into fear, and the same cry emerged simultaneously from hundreds of throats: "A dragon! A dragon!"

Ossipoff stared like everyone else, in spite of the imminent death that awaited him, impassively seeking an explanation for this surprising phenomenon.

Suddenly, Selena uttered a cry of joy. Leaning toward her father's ear, she murmured: "It's them! It's Monsieur de Flammermont and his friend."

Meanwhile, the bravest of the peasants were dragging the prisoners into the middle of the square when the ground began to shake in the distance and several voices shouted: "The Cossacks! The Cossacks!"

It was, indeed, a platoon of cavalry, which was galloping forward under orders to recover the prisoners from the crowd. There was a frightful tumult, in which the voices of women and children trampled by the horses mingled with howls of anguish from the men pricked by the Cossacks' lances.

Suddenly, the astonishing smoke-belching apparatus descended like a thunderbolt from the upper atmosphere and stopped dead 20 meters above the ground, reminiscent of a gigantic bird hovering with its wings extended. Then two gunshots rang out and two peasants, one of whom had been clinging to Ossipoff and the other to his daughter, rolled on the ground, screaming hideously—and a formidable voice that seemed to come from the sky rose above the hubbub, shouting: "Ossipoff! Look out! Hold on!"

At the same time, a cable unwound, bearing a strange apparatus at its extremity, like two spools connected to a horseshoe. The branches of the horseshoe collided with the chains shackling the scientist's hands and feet, and, so to speak, gathered them together so that they now seemed to form a single mass of iron. Instinctively, Selena threw herself into her father's arms; he clasped her desperately to his breast, and both of them, lifted up by an unknown force, lost their footing.

"Well done!" cried a voice that Ossipoff recognized as Flammermont's. "Well done! Hang on! You're saved!"

The old man and the young woman were already 15 meters above the ground, suspended in mid-air by the cable that supplied the electric current to the electromagnet, while the Cossacks, recovering from their surprise and furious at seeing the prisoners escape them so miraculously, took aim at the fugitives and opened fire.

Ossipoff released a cry of pain; a bullet had just struck him in the shoulder, and it required an uncommon strength of will for him to hold on to Selena, clasped in his arms. Gontran, however, galvanized by the danger to the woman he loved, redoubled his efforts and imparted a vertiginous rapidity to the winch that was reeling in the cable.

In a few seconds, the electromagnet had rejoined the aeroplane, and the Comte de Flammermont, aided by Fricoulet, pulled Ossipoff and his daughter on to the deck. Then, leaving his friend to take care of the two fugitives, the engineer leaned over the guard-rail and looked down at the crowd swarming beneath them, shouting threats at the aeroplane, while the Cossacks reloaded their weapons in response to orders given to them by their commanding officer, who was pointing at the apparatus.

Fricoulet knew that a general discharge might tear the fabric of the aircraft apart. "So much the worse for them," he growled. Bending down, he took several shiny metal spheres from a box that was open at his feet, and dropped them on the enemy.

The soldiers were already taking aim when frightful screams burst forth; as they hit the ground the spheres had exploded, producing a black cloud—through which the engineer saw several dismounted cossacks writhing in horrible convulsions, while their maddened horses bucked and pranced in the midst of the fearful crowd.

"Let's go!" he cried.

Gontran, who had hurried to the side of the unconscious Selena, abandoned the young woman, ran to a tap and turned it. Instantly, the aeroplane rose upwards, splitting the air with its deep and continuous sound. It was soon at such a height that Ekaterinburg appeared as no more than a cluster of little black dots lost in the immensity the Siberian waste. Then it stopped.

Fricoulet turned round then, and saw Ossipoff, who was staring at him in astonishment. "My dear Gontran," he said, "would you do me the honor of introducing me to Monsieur Ossipoff?" He drew nearer and, with his hat raised and his body inclined, as casually as if he had been standing in his laboratory, he waited.

The young Comte approached in his turn and pointed to his friend. "Monsieur Ossipoff," he said, "will you permit me to introduce to you Monsieur Alcide Fricoulet, my best friend?"

"And a passionate admirer of your work," the engineer added, cordially shaking the hand that the old man held out to him. Then, immediately, he said: "Let me look at your wound."

"Are you a physician, then, Monsieur Fricoulet?" Ossipoff asked, taking off his fur cloak.

"Is he a physician?" cried the Comte de Flammermont, laughing. "Ah, Monsieur Ossipoff, when you know my friend Alcide better, you won't ask him whether he's this or that. He's everything: physicist, chemist, mathematician, botanist, electrician, mechanic, astronomer…and I don't know what else."

"You're an astronomer?" asked the old scientist, excitedly.

"Gontran exaggerates," Fricoulet replied, smiling. "I'm little more of an astronomer than he is, which is to say…" He bit his lip, understanding from his friend's furious expression that he was about to commit a gaffe. He leaned over the wound to conceal his confusion, which prevented him from seeing the singular expression with which the old man had greeted his last words. "It's nothing," he said, eventually, having made a careful examination of Ossipoff's shoulder. "A mere scratch. The angle of the shot was acute; the bullet only grazed the clavicle and rebounded, according to the angle of reflection." He turned away to fetch the bandages that a careful man always carries with him from a box.

Ossipoff took advantage of the pause to murmur in Gontran's ear: "I'm afraid that your friend's science has more breadth than depth."

"Bah! Why's that?"

"He knows too many things. Then there's what he said about you—a true scientist isn't jealous of other people's knowledge."

Gontran had enormous difficulty keeping his face straight.

At that moment, Fricoulet returned; he dressed the bloody bullet-wound with the skill of a consummate surgeon, then put a simple spica bandage around the shoulder and helped the scientist put his coat on again.

As Flammermont, returning to Selena, took the young woman's hands in his own and looked at her anxiously she opened her eyes. "Saved!" she stammered, in a weak voice.

"Yes, my dear Selena, saved—and reunited forever, for nothing shall separate us now."

"I will ask you, nevertheless to let Mademoiselle alone for a few moments," said Fricoulet, cheerfully, coming forward, "for if we don't intend to stay here, it's time to thin about the destination of our journey."

"Where are we going?" asked Selena.

"To Paris, Mademoiselle."

"To Paris?" repeated Ossipoff, surprised. "What are we going to do in Paris?"

"Isn't it our only refuge?" Gontran replied. "Don't you know that you no longer own anything, that your fortune has been confiscated; even your little house has been sold. Henceforth, Russian territory is forbidden to you."

Mikhail Ossipoff lowered his head, suddenly plunged into painful reflection. He saw himself banished from society, hunted everywhere as a criminal, even though he was innocent of the crime of which he had been accused. The sly and sinister face of his former colleague in the Institute of Sciences appeared before his eyes: Sharp, into whose possession all his papers had fallen, and who might, at this very moment, be putting into operation his scientific ideas, the results of an entire life dedicated to research.

Meanwhile, Fricoulet was preparing to leave; having darted a rapid glance around him, to make sure that everything was ready, he was consulting the compass, with one hand on the tap controlling the steam and the other on the wheel operating the rudder, when a voice whispered in his ear: "Monsieur Fricoulet, I have a favor to ask you."

He turned round. Selena was standing beside him.

"A favor? Of me, Mademoiselle? What is it?" he asked, suppressing a gesture of impatience.

"Quietly," she said, darting a sideways glance at her father, who was still absorbed in his dark thoughts. Blushing slightly, she added: "I want to talk to you about Gontran."

"Very well, then," muttered Fricoulet. "Here I am, reduced to the state of a confidante on tragedy."

"I don't know," she continued, "whether Gontran has told you...."

"That he loves you! Yes, Mademoiselle, Gontran has told me that..."

She shook her head. "It's not that. Has he told you that, in order to get into my father's good graces, he was obliged to feign scientific knowledge of which he does not know the first thing!"

"Oh, yes!" said the engineer, laughing. "He mentioned that to me, vaguely. Well, what has it got to do with me?"

She remained silent for a moment, as if embarrassed, then went on: "This: I want to ask you—you, who are a true scientist—to help him out a little, when my father asks him embarrassing questions…for you understand quite well that I know very little myself, and that my stock will be quickly exhausted."

"Ah!" said Fricoulet, smiling. "I understand. I remember when I used to whisper his lessons to him in college. Very well! It's understood, Mademoiselle, that you can count on me."

She thanked him with a smile and went to sit down beside her father.

Fricoulet, annoyed by the promise he had just made—for he now found himself, a hardened bachelor, constrained to assist his friend's marriage—privately called himself a coward for lending a hand to such a comedy. Selena was so polite and gracious, though, and she has asked him in such a charming fashion! He turned the tap. The vapor acted more powerfully on the spindle of the helices, and they began to turn with vertiginous speed, drawing the aeroplane, which had been motionless, through the air.

Ossipoff had raised his head. "With a favorable wind," he said to Gontran, "how long do you think it will take us to reach Paris?"

It was Fricoulet who replied. "30 or 40 hours. The aeroplane can easily make the journey at 100 or 150 kilometers an hour."

"A nice speed," murmured the scientist, marveling, while alternating his gaze between the motor, the propellers and the rudder. He added: "Is it you, Monsieur Fricoulet, who imagined and built this apparatus?"

"Built, yes, Monsieur, but imagined, no—all the honor of its invention belongs to my friend Gontran." Obviously, the young engineer was in a hurry to prove to Selena that he was a man of his word; at the same time, he was by no means reluctant to increase Gontran's matrimonial anxieties by putting the wind up him.

Flammermont looked at his friend in frank alarm. Him, the inventor of the aeroplane! What was that about? He understood immediately, though, from the tender and affectionate gaze that Ossipoff directed at him, that Fricoulet simply wanted to raise him up a peg or two in his future father-in-law's estimation.

"Ah, my dear Gontran," the old man said, eventually, "I can't congratulate you enough on having succeeded in bringing this construction to fruition. For many years, without being able to succeed, inventors have been desperately trying to develop devices totally different in kind from those unstable floating vessels called aerostatic balloons, capable of flying by mechanical means."

"It's in France that the matter has been examined most exhaustively," Gontran declared, with an assurance that made Fricoulet smile. "Going back as far as

1863, a whole host of projects has been mounted by Nadar, La Landelle, Ponton d'Amécourt, Bright, Pénaud, and so on."[31]

Selena heard to the young man speak, amazed by all this science of which the Comte de Flammermont, as a clever fellow, had made provision. He had foreseen that the aeroplane would become an object of discussion, and had wanted to be able to play his part.

"The list of those who've made efforts in this direction is certainly long," said Fricoulet, "but who among them has succeeded in proving anything? Who among them has ever shown a heavier-than-air apparatus"—he emphasized these words—"taking off and steering through the air."

Ossipoff looked the young man up and down. "If you will permit," he said, "one of my compatriots, named Philips,[32] imagined a helical propeller with four horizontal branches fixed to a spherical hub, which was nothing more than a little aeolipile filled with water. When the shell was put on the fire, the water that it contained heated up and was transformed into vapor, which escaped through

---

[31] The significance of 1863 is that a *Societé d'encouragement pour la locomotion aérienne au moyen d'appareils plus lourds que l'air* [Society for the Encouragement of Aerial Locomotion by means of Heavier-than-Air Machines] was founded in that year in Paris, under the presidency of "Nadar" (Gaspard-Félix Tournachon, 1820-1910). Gabriel de La Landelle (1812-1886) and Gustave Ponton d'Amécourt (1825-1888) were also founder members, as was Jules Verne, who was the organization's secretary. After building *Le Géant* [The Giant]—the balloon that inspired Verne to write *Cinq semaines en ballon* (1863; tr. as *Five Weeks in a Balloon*) and launch his career as a popular writer—Nadar became convinced that the future of aeronautics belonged to heavier-than-air craft. La Landelle, who had long been a prolific writer of popular maritime romances, coined a new term for the speculative technology in *Aviation, ou Navigation aérienne sans ballon* (1863), shortly after his experimental collaborator Ponton had coined the term "hélicoptère" in an 1861 patent application for a steam-powered helicopter. Alphonse Pénaud (1850-1880) made numerous model aircraft powered by rubber bands in the 1870s, including some whose airscrews spun vertically (as in Graffigny's model and actual heavier-than-air craft) rather than horizontally—it was a copy of one of these that allegedly inspired the Wright brothers. Crucially, however, none of these experimenters realized, any more than Graffigny did, how a fixed wing was able to obtain lift, so the society members and their successors were unable to make any significant progress in developing the technology in the 19th century. Henry Bright had taken out an even earlier patent for a helicopter in 1859, but remains historically obscure; Graffigny almost certainly found his name in a brief citation in Verne's *Robur le conquérant* (1886; tr. as *The Clipper of the Clouds*).

[32] I can find no other reference to this strangely-named Russian pioneer, who conducted his alleged experiments in what is now Warsaw.

little holes bored at a convenient place in the branches of the propeller. By means of the reaction the escaping vapor produced, the hub and its wings turned, much as a hydraulic turnpike does; the propeller lifted itself up into the air by means of a screw effect, and climbed rapidly. I saw a trial in Varsovia in 1845."

Gontran chuckled disdainfully. "But could that apparatus work on a large scale?" he asked. "I recall seeing Ponton d'Amécourt's aluminum steam-helicopter in a museum. I've also read a description of a very similar mechanism designed by the Italian Forlanini[33]—but that sort of thing hasn't made much headway."

In the face of Gontran's aplomb, Fricoulet had difficulty maintaining a serious expression; he knew what his friend's scientific knowledge amounted to better than anyone.

"That's precisely why, my dear son," the old scientist retorted, "I find the result you've obtained marvelous…if you had only had to copy it, that would have been quite simple."

"Gontran invented—which was easier," said Fricoulet.

"The most difficult thing," Osipoff continued, "was to obtain a mechanism of surprising lightness…"

"Why is that?" asked Fricoulet, impassively.

Osipoff did not reply at first, but leaned toward his daughter's ear. "This little gentleman," he said, "is beginning to annoy me with his mania for speaking when no one is speaking to him…just to show off the fact that he knows something." The old man clicked his tongue and frowned; with his mouth curled sarcastically, he said in a curt tone: "You know, I suppose that the intensity of gravity at the surface of our world causes bodies to fall at a velocity of 4.9 meters in the first second;[34] thus, it is necessary to counter that force. Now, it has been established that a one horsepower steam engine, which can lift a weight of 75 kilograms to a height of one meter, applied to an ascensional helix, only renders it capable of lifting a weight of 15 kilograms."

"Why tell me that?"

---

[33] Enrico Forlanini (1848-1930) designed a steam-powered helicopter in 1877, which rose to a height of 13 meters and remained airborne for 20 seconds—a significant achievement at the time.

[34] The actual acceleration due to gravity at the Earth's surface is 9.8 meters per second per second; it is the accelerative force that is the key figure, in accordance with Newton's second law, not the velocity at any particular moment, so Fricoulet's objection to Ossipoff's contention is entirely specious. Graffigny seems to have difficulty distinguishing between velocity and acceleration; he continually mistakes the implications of Newton's second law (force equals mass times acceleration), and this confusion is the principal factor making his various suggested means of space flight blatantly nonsensical.

"Why? Why?" grumbled Ossipoff. "You don't seem to have any other words in your mouth. Well, to get to this, of course: to make you recognize that, to make aerial navigation possible with apparatus heavier than air, it's necessary to create power-units weighing no more than 10 kilograms per horsepower of output."

"Why?" said Fricoulet, again.

The old man shrugged his shoulders. "In order that they can lift themselves along with their propellers." Ossipoff looked at Gontran triumphantly. "Isn't that rigorously scientific?" he concluded.

"Which is to say…" The young man said.

"…That it's absolutely false," Fricoulet finished for him, calmly.

The old man stated and turned his interrogative gaze toward the Comte, who nodded his head in agreement. "Absolutely false."

"But Rinfaggy,[35] in his book on *Aerial Navigation*…"

"…Is entirely mistaken," the young engineer continued, gravely, "As you will recognize…."

"Indeed! Let's see, my dear Gontran, please explain…"

The Comte de Flammermont was, however, too fearful of compromising himself to respond to the old man's invitation. He remained silent, thinking it much more prudent to let his friend answer in his stead.

"Firstly, isn't it true that the velocity of 4.9 meters per second that bodies in free fall attain is progressively accelerated? How many centimeters does a heavy object fall in the first tenth of a second?"

Mikhail Ossipoff slapped his forehead. "Only a few centimeters!" he exclaimed. "That's true…but then…"

"Then it's only a matter of combating, each tenth of a second, against a considerably lesser force of gravity…which permit the employment of machines weighing more than ten kilograms per horsepower of output, as you just said, Besides, it's not the helicopter principle that we've applied in the construction of this aeroplane, for it wasn't sufficient for us to have an ascensional force; we also needed a means of moving through the ambient air."

"That's true," Ossipoff replied, dryly. Leaning towards Selena, he murmured: "It's strange how this fellow irritates me; he talks all the time, doubtless repeating parrot-fashion what he's learned from Gontran."

The young woman could scarcely restrain a smile. Designating the Comte de Flammermont with a sideways glance, the old man added: "See what a difference there is between the man who truly understands and the only who has

---

[35] This name is either invented or so badly mangled as to make the intended reference irretrievable. The argument Ossipoff employs is similar in structure, if not in numerical detail, to the one put forward in the first of George Cayley's classic series of articles "On Aerial Navigation" published in *Nicholson's Magazine* in 1809.

only a smattering of science…the modest silence of the former speaks more eloquently in his favor than all the loquacity of the latter."

"By the way, Monsieur Fricoulet," Selena said, to change the subject, "when my father was hit by a bullet, I saw you throw cannonballs of some kind at your enemies. What was in them? Gunpowder? Dynamite?"

"Or selenite?" murmured Gontran.

"Nothing of that sort," Fricoulet retorted. "They were simple receptacles contained liquefied hydrogen chloride. When they reached the ground, the receptacles burst and the acid, suddenly decompressed, was transformed into a corrosive and asphyxiant gas, so effectively that those of our assailants who were not burned and corroded by the jets of acid were choked and poisoned."

What a beautiful thing science is! Gontran thought.

At that moment the barometer indicated an altitude of 1500 meters above sea-level and Mikhail Ossipoff leaned on the guard-rail gazing pensively at the panorama which fled beneath them with vertiginous rapidity. The Ural Mountains were no more than a mass of shadowy hills and a few sprigs of grass; the human habitations had completely disappeared and the capricious shadows of clouds—vaporous spirals sprinkling the limpid atmosphere beneath the aeroplane's enormous wings—were racing over the immense fields.

"A big town!" cried Selena suddenly.

"It's Perm," Fricoulet replied, having consulted his map.

It was, indeed, the capital of the Perm district, a rather large town situated on the Kama at the confluence of three smaller rivers: the Chusovaya, the Iren and the Barola, about 250 *versts* from the Ural Mountans. The aeroplane, whose speed was then 32 meters a second—115 kilometers per hour, almost twice the speed of an express train—passed over Perm at a low altitude. At the sight of it, the inhabitants disappeared into their little houses, releasing cries that reached the aviators' ears as a confused racket. In an instant, the streets were deserted.

At 10 p.m., the *Albatros* passed directly over the town of Vyatka, about 700 kilometers from the Urals. With the aid of a favorable wind the aeroplane had crossed that enormous distance in a little more than five hours. It was making very good progress, but the provision of mineral oil that served the machine as fuel was running out.

Gontran, who was leaning on the guard-rail chatting to Selena, suddenly felt a hand on his shoulder; it was Fricolet, who drew him aside and said: "We're out of oil."

"Well, that seems to be troubling you," said the young Comte. "Do we need it, then?"

The engineer looked at his friend in amazement. "What! Don't you understand how my aeroplane works?"

"Vaguely," Gontran replied, with a smile.

"Mademoiselle Selena's lovely eyes are much more interesting, aren't they?" grumbled Fricoulet. "Know, then, that for lack of oil we'll fall from an altitude of 1500 meters."

Flammermont could not repress a cry, which brought Selena and her father running.

"What is it?" asked the young woman.

"It's…" the young Comte hastened to reply.

"…That Gontran and I have to get to the nearest place where we can obtain mineral oil. The country's resources are something of a mystery to us." Fricoulet, fearing that his friend was about to say something imprudent, had cut him off hurriedly.

Mikhail Ossipoff immediately said: "Petroleum, of which considerable wells exist in the Caucasus, forms the basis of a very important commerce in Russia, which is very widespread. You'll find it even in the smallest town in the region we're crossing."

So much the better, thought the engineer—and he decided that the *Albatros* would make a stop at Popovska, a small town 150 kilometers from Vyatka. Darkness was falling at that very moment, and a landing could be effected without frightening the local inhabitants. They would camp there, and the aeroplane would resume its flight at dawn on the following day.

That was what they did. The descent took place without hindrance and, while Fricoulet, aided by Selena, put up the tent and prepared a meal, Gontran and Ossipoff went to a neighboring village to fill the on-board reservoir with petroleum. The following morning, at dawn, the *Albatros* took off again.

In round numbers the distance between Viatka and St. Petersburg, as the crow flies, is 1000 *versts*, or 1100 kilometers. It was midday when our travelers passed over the capital of all the Russias; as a precaution, Fricoulet went up to a high altitude in order not to attract the attention of its citizens. Selena and her father, leaning over the guard-rail, strove to pierce the low clouds that veiled the city they might never see again.

During the long journey that our travelers had made, however, the wind had turned and had been blowing from the north for several hours; it had become distinctly sharp, and made the cordage of the *Albatros* vibrate as it flew before it like a bird before a storm. Selena, hiding her head in her hands, shivered as she huddled close to her father, frightened by the whistling of the wind and the trembling of the apparatus.

"How fast are we going?" asked Ossipoff, with imperturbable composure.

"About 45 meters a second," Fricoulet replied.

Gontran opened his eyes wide in alarm. "But that's 162 kilometers an hour," he stammered. "Aren't you afraid…?"

"I'm only afraid of one thing," the engineer replied, "and that's falling. Now, we need that speed to combat the breeze and conserve our stability. There's only one thing that worries me…"

As he spoke, he consulted the compass.

"What?" asked Ossipoff.

"That I can no longer steer as I'd like to. I have to veer with the wind and tack as much as I can...it's almost impossible to go against the current."

"Go with it, then."

"That's what I'm obliged to do...but it's drawing us southwards."

For several hours the aeroplane followed the line of the Berlin railway in this fashion. It passed successively over Gatchina, Dunaburg and Vilna. Then, at Orzestkitovsky, it left Russian territory and began flying over the former Poland.[36]

"We're getting lower," the young Comte observed from time to time, dividing his attention between the barometer and Selena.

"I'm very well aware of that," Fricoulet retorted, angrily. He had opened the taps as wide as possible, thus imparting to the machine all the speed of which it was capable and, clinging to the rudder-wheel, persisted in trying to steer northwards.

"Wasn't the wind on your agenda, then, old chap?" asked Gontran, ironically.

"The engineer shrugged his shoulders. "Not a wind like this," he grumbled. "It's blowing at least 40 meters a second...how can you fight it?" And he stamped his foot on the platform.

"Oh well! Don't fight it," said Gontran.

"Oh," murmured Fricolet, his eyes fiery and his lips taut, "to think that man, with all his science, is at the mercy of this impalpable and nameless thing, this blind and brutal force. The wind!"

A tear of rage glittered on the brim of his eyelid, and for another half-hour, he continued the struggle—but there was no point in bursting the boiler and shattering the propeller; the wind was his master.

Finally, having consulted the map, he murmured: "I need a reference-point. I need to know where we are, damn it!"

The *Albatros* descended to some 50 meters above the ground. Leaning over the guard-rail, the engineer tried to question a peasant who was working the land, but the man fled in terror.

"Ah" said Ossipoff, suddenly, examining the map. "Isn't that body of water Lake Balaton?"

"You're right," Fricoulet replied.

The aeroplane was, indeed, over the shore of Lake Balaton—which is to say, in the middle of Austria-Hungary.

---

[36] Poland ceased to exist as a political entity in 1795, when its territory was carved up between the Russian Empire, the Austro-Hungarian Empire and East Prussia, but survived as an idea and a cause until it was reconstituted in 1918.

Almost 13 hours had passed since they had left St. Petersburg, and in that 13 hours they had traveled more than 2000 kilometers, crossing the Niemen, the Vistula, the Danube and doubtless passing over the Carpathian Mountains. In terms of speed, that was good, but not in terms of direction. Alcide Fricoulet had hoped to be further west, but, still dominated by the same current, he was being drawn irresistibly southwards.

At the first town they encountered, Zalaegerszeg, the engineer renewed his supplies of oil and water. Then, as the north wind appeared to be weakening, he set a course due west, and by morning the *Albatros* was flying over the town of Gorizia. The vast sheet of the waters of the Adriatic appeared before the travelers' eyes, gilded by the rays of the rising Sun.

Selena clapped her hands at the superb spectacle. "How beautiful it is!" she cried, enthusiastically. "And how far south the wind had carried us!"

A groan replied to her; it was Fricoulet, protesting in his own fashion against the young woman's joy. "Fortunately," he went on, "we'll be able to steer north-west to reach Switzerland."

"Is that how we'll get to France?" asked the young woman, pulling a face.

The young engineer nodded his head affirmatively.

"Well, I don't compliment you on your itinerary," Selena said. "With its extravagant peaks, Switzerland will oblige us to go up to such a height…"

"Oh, 4000 or 5000 meters, at the most," said Gontran, mockingly.

"You think that's nothing?" Selena continued. "If you'd asked my advice, I'd have suggested Italy, and I'm sure that my father wouldn't have been sorry to see its cheerful and fertile plains instead of that horrible all-white landscape, which will remind us of Siberia."

"Since that's your desire, my dear Selena," Gontran said, "We'll take the road of scholars…all roads lead to Rome, in any case, and what does it matter from which direction we enter France?"

"It's easy for you to talk," muttered Fricoulet.

"Oh, you poor chap," the Comte replied, in the same tone. "What I say is to save your self-respect as an inventor. The wind's stronger than you—better to give way to it and feign deference to Selena's caprice. It's more gallant for the man and less humiliating for the constructor."

Fricolet shrugged his shoulders and, making no reply, gave the rudder-wheel an abrupt turn, which cause the aeroplane to veer south-west. Then, once the appropriate heading had been selected with the aid of the compass, the *Albatros* lost altitude, causing the inhabitants of the Italian heights to cry out in fear and amazement, and slew on with vertiginous rapidity.

The panoramas of Venice, Padua, Verona, Brescia and Bergamo unrolled successively before the dazzled eyes of the celestial voyagers. In the vicinity of Bergamo the young engineer modified the *Albatros*'s course again. In mid-afternoon it passed directly over Turin, heading for the Alps, which they had to cross. For several hours, however, Fricoulet had seemed anxious. His ordinarily cheerful manner was now serious, his lips pursed by the stress of a violent cerebral tension, and his eyes narrowed by concern. His gaze went continually to the meteorological instruments and returned with an indefinable expression to his companions, who were leaning on the guard-rail, absorbed by the magnificent landscape unfolding beneath them.

Suddenly, as he turned round mechanically, Gontran caught sight of one of these glances. He came straight over to the engineer. "Something's worrying you, isn't it?"

Silently, Fricoulet pointed to the madly swinging compass and the rapidly-falling barometer.

"Well, are we in danger?" asked the young Comte.

The engineer shrugged his shoulders. "In this situation we're always in danger," he replied. "Look at those clouds heaped up threateningly over the mountains. Observe the mist spreading through the air, and the warm vapor that seems to bed rising from the ground and enveloping us. All that presages a storm, if I'm not mistaken."

Gontran's gaze immediately went to Selena. "What shall we do?" he murmured, in an anguished tone.

Making no reply, Fricoulet opened the tap wide and the steam rushed into the conduits, whistling. The entire apparatus shook; the propeller hubs groaned and their vanes turned vertiginously—but it was in vain. There were such variations in the strength and direction of the wind that the *Albatros*, like a bird strayed into a whirlwind, fluttered without making any substantial headway.

It was much the same until 5 p.m. The sky had become dark and menacing, and distant rumbles of thunders could be heard on the horizon. Abruptly, without any warning that it was so imminent, the squall arrived like a thunderbolt, bending the trees to the ground and whipping up thick clouds of dust, beneath which the ground disappeared. At that moment that aeroplane was at an altitude of no more than 200 meters, flying over the foothills of the Alps.

"Higher! Higher!" cried Fricoulet, stoking the fire of his machine in an attempt to confront the storm.

The apparatus climbed vertically and went into the clouds—but there, the tempest reigned, perhaps more terribly than in the inferior regions. It took possession of the *Albatros*, which had to resign itself to flee like a vulgar aerostat in spite of its pilot's efforts.

To allow Fricoulet complete freedom of action in maneuvering, the travelers huddled together against the guard-rail and maintained silence. Lightning-flashes streaked the sky, inflaming the atmosphere and splitting the clouds that were coming apart all around the *Albatros*.

Suddenly, the whistling of the steam through the escape-valve fell silent, and the grinding of the propellers stopped. Fricoulet could not restrain a cry of rage, and stood stock still, as if petrified, looking at the extinct lamp with a terrible expression. The petroleum had suddenly run out.

"We're going down!" cried Ossipoff.

"No," murmured Fricoulet, dully. "We're falling."

The aeroplane, deprived of fuel and surrendered to its own weight, was now only retained in the air by the force of its parachute.

Selena suddenly released a terrible scream. "The sea! The sea!"

Indeed, on the horizon, the agitated waves of the Mediterranean rose up, and the apparatus, carried like a feather by the storm, was heading for it with vertiginous speed.

"Are we lost?" Gontran asked his friend.

"Not yet, if I have anything to do with it," the latter replied. Exerting all his strength upon the rudder, in order at least to direct the *Albatros*'s fall, he constrained the aeroplane to obey him again. Suddenly, however, and intense whistle sounded overhead and the planks of the deck seemed to collapse beneath their feet. A lightning strike of unexpected violence had just torn away the two propellers and simultaneously set fire to the fabric of the inclined planes.

Deprived of all its engines of locomotion, the *Albatros* slipped through the layers of air with a violence that the fire could only increase. It seemed inevitable that it would crash into the side of a mountain when, by a desperate effort, the young engineer succeeded in bringing the vast surface of canvas that formed the anterior rudder into a horizontal plane. The fall moderated slightly and, still advancing under the terrible pressure of the gusts of wind, the *Albatros* came to within ten meters of the ground.

"Look out!" shouted Fricoulet, stridently. "Get ready for the impact! Hold tight!"

At the same time, there was a fearful shock; the aeroplane had just touched down. Like a bird falling from the sky, mortally struck by a hunter's bullet, it lay inert, wings extended. The force of the reaction threw the travelers off the platform, rolling on the ground.

Although stunned, Ossipoff was the first to get to his feet; immediately, his eyes went to Selena. The young woman, trembling with fear, ran to her father, who opened his arms. After an emotional embrace, the old scientist said: "What about Monsieur de Flammermont?"

"Present!" the young Comte cried, joyfully, emerging from a crevasse into whose depths he had rolled.

"Well," said Fricoulet, who was busy putting out the fire that was devouring the aeroplane's fabric, "is anything broken?"

"No," the three travelers replied, in unison.

Then Ossipoff, who was looking around curiously, suddenly exclaimed: "But we're in a civilized country, gentlemen! There's an observatory!" He pointed at a singular construction, which emerged from the ground some 200 meters away, somewhat reminiscent of a jockey's cap set on the ground.

"Hurrah!" said Alcide Fricoulet, waving his cap triumphantly. "Hurrah for the *Albatros* and its engineer. That's the Nice Observatory—we're in France!"

Chapter VI
In which Gontran has a bright idea.

While our friends, gathered around the lamentable wreckage of the *Albatros*, consulted one another as to what to do next, a lively agitation reigned in the Nice Observatory. A dozen young people, gathered in a long covered gallery that led from the administration buildings to the library, were discussing the surprising phenomenon they had just witnessed in a heated fashion.

"It was an aerolith," said one. "I recognized all the distinctive characteristics. If you care to recall…"

"And I'm quite ready to prove to you that it was a comet, whose tail has just brushed Mount Boron.[37] You must, in fact, have observed…"

"Neither an aerolith nor a comet, but simply a perfectly natural result of the storm that has just passed over the region…it was a lightning-bolt."

Ironic laughter greeted this declaration, and they all repeated:

"It was an aerolith."

"It was a comet."

"It was lightning."

At the same time, they looked at one another furiously, brandishing the binoculars and telescopes with which they were equipped, ready to transform these peaceful scientific instruments into weapons of war.

"Well, Messieurs," said one of them, who seemed to have preserved a little more self-control than the others, "there's one means of finding out which of us is right."

"What means?"

"Let's go and see. Nothing will be easier, on reaching the place where the strange fall that we're arguing about took place, than to establish whether we're dealing with an aerolith, a bolide or simply a lightning-strike."

This proposal was greeted with enthusiastic cheers. Five minutes later, the whole band emerged from the Observatory and took the road leading down to Nice. Suddenly, as they rounded a corner, they perceived a group of individuals who were engaged in a heated discussion, pointing excitedly at an object extended on the ground.

Immediately, our young people, carried away by curiosity and having no doubt that they were confronted by witnesses to the phenomenon that had divided their opinions, ran to our friends and arrived beside them out of breath.

"What was it that fell?"

"Where has it gone?"

---

[37] I have retained the name used in the text, although the hill on which the Nice Observatory is sited is more commonly known as Mont-Gras.

"Did it cause this damage?"

Ossipoff and his companions, surprised by these questions emerging simultaneously from various mouths, looked at the newcomers with a certain anxiety.

"What are you talking about, Messieurs?" asked the old man.

"The aerolith!"

"The comet!"

"The lightning-bolt."

These responses had no other effect than to persuade Ossipoff that he was dealing with madmen. Even so, he said: "What aerolith? What comet? What lightning-bolt?"

"Didn't you see anything, then?" said the others, utterly disappointed.

The old Russian shook his head. "Nothing at all," he replied. "But who are you, and what do you want."

"We're the student astronomers of the Nice Observatory," one of them replied.

Scarcely had he pronounced these words when Ossipoff precipitated himself on him, seized him by the arm and kissed him frantically on both cheeks, crying: "Astronomers! Astronomers!"

This time it was the turn of the young men to think that they were in the presence of a madman. They took a step back, and the one who had just been subjected to Ossipoff's accolade replied: "Just now, as the storm was ending, we observed a very curious phenomenon, as to the nature of which we're divided. Some claim that it was a fiery aerolith, others the tail of a comet, others a flash of lightning."

A burst of laughter greeted these words. That was Fricoulet—who, taking a step forward, cried: "Well, Messieurs, you're all right and you're all mistaken. What you saw was like an aerolith, for it fell from the sky; it was like a comet, for it possesses a tail, and it was like a lightning-bolt, because it was in flames— and yet it is neither an aerolith, nor a comet, nor a lightning-bolt."

"What is it, then?"

"It is—or, rather, was—an aeroplane," replied the young engineer, pointing to the broken limbs of the *Albatros*, which were lying at his feet, "and it was our fall that you witnessed."

"Who are you, then Messieurs?" they asked, drawing closer to the travelers again.

"Oh, we're no one in particular," Fricoulet replied, modestly. "We're not famous." He pointed at Mikhail Ossipoff. "On the other hand, you should have heard of this gentleman. He's Mikhail Ossipoff."

At this name, known throughout the scientific world, the young men took off their hats respectfully. The one who had spoken before approached the old man. "Monsieur Ossipoff," he said, in an emotional voice, "permit me, in the name of French youth—which knows your work and admires you—to shake you by the hand." Then, after a cordial handshake, he said: "Now, I hope you will do us the great honor of accepting the hospitality of the Observatory. We have guest rooms there, Monsieur Ossipoff, and you have every right to that title."

The old scientists darted a rapid glance at his companions and replied: "In spite of the cordiality of your invitation, Messieurs, I'd decline it for fear of being indiscreet—but the long journey has exhausted my daughter, who might not be able to go as far as Nice, so I therefore accept it wholeheartedly...."

Ossipoff offered his arm to Selena and, accompanied by Fricoulet and Gontran, he headed for the Observatory, followed by the company of young astronomers as if by a guard of honor.

Constructed on the summit of Mount Boron, abut 50 meters above sealevel, the Observatory looked out on one side over the Mediterranean, whose blue shores extended as far as Cape Frejus, and on the other over the valley of the Paillon, with the eternally-white peaks of the Alps on the horizon.

In addition to the climatological conditions indispensable to an observatory, one could not have chosen a more admirable site to rest the eyes of scientists dazzled by the contemplation of celestial beauty. In it, Monsieur Bischoffsheim,[38] to whose generosity the construction of Nice Observatory is due, had combined the work of an artist, a nature-lover and a philanthropic friend of the progress of science. But what has given this scientific establishment a near-universal reputation is its equatorial telescope, presently the most powerful in the entire world. It has a focal length of 18 meters; its objective lens is 76 centimeters in diameter. With its equatorially movable carriage, it weighs no less than 25,000 kilograms, and that enormous mass is controlled by a simple clockwork mechanism. As for the cupola beneath which that gigantic telescope is installed—on of the marvels of metallic construction of the century—it is 21 meters in diameter and more than 30 meters high; its weight is no less than 95,000 kilograms—95 tonnes!

One might believe that such a considerable weight would not be easily maneuverable, but not so. The constructor of this cupola, Monsieur Eiffel,[39] has, in fact, devised a mechanism that renders this enormous construction docile even to the hand of a child. Instead of rolling on metallic castors, like other observatory cupolas, the Nice cupola is balanced on watertight containers floating in a basin of water contained within the sustaining walls, so that the feeblest effort is

---

[38] The philanthropist Raphael Bischoffsheim (1822-1906) founded Nice Observatory in 1881, but it did not become fully operational until 1887, thus creating an anachronism in the narrative.

[39] When this passage was written, Gustave Eiffel (1832-1923) had only just started constructing the tower that was to immortalize his name, for the 1889 Paris Exposition.

sufficient to direct the slot of the enormous hemisphere towards any part of the sky.

While it requires nearly an hour's work at the Paris Observatory to accomplish a complete rotation of the great cupola—which measures no more than 13 meters—a few minutes is sufficient to rotate the enormous cupola of Nice Observatory on its axis.

Needless to say, as early as possible the following morning, Mikhail Ossipoff set about examining every detail of all these marvels. On finding himself once again in the midst of instruments in the company of which he had spent his life, the memory of his suffering immediately vanished, and he surrendered himself to the joy of scanning visually those celestial worlds to which he felt so powerfully attracted.

In the evening, though, when he went to rejoin his friends in the little room in which, to give them more privacy, their supper had been served to them, the old man's face was veiled by a sadness that did not escape Selena's observation.

"What's the matter, Father?" she said, affectionately putting her arm around Ossipoff's neck. "What secret trouble is darkening your features?"

He shook his head and replied in a low voice: "It's nothing, my child. Nothing's wrong, I swear."

Selena looked at him for a moment, then turned to Gontran, her beautiful eyes misted over. The young man understood that the young woman was asking for his help. He drew nearer to the armchair into which the old scientist had sunk, and put a friendly hand on his shoulder. "I'll wager, my dear Monsieur Ossipoff," he said, "that I know what's troubling you."

The old man shivered, but did not reply.

"I'll wager," Gontran went on, "that this famous telescope, which has permitted you, so to speak, to put your finger on the marvels of the Heavens, has something to do with your chagrin."

Ossipoff shook his head. "It has been such a long time," he murmured, "since I perused my dear lunar solitudes. It took me back to the time when I was so happy in St. Petersburg, you see…when I was not what I am today…a miserable exile…"

"It took you back to the time when you formulated your great project…"

Ossipoff seized his hand abruptly and darted a sideways glance at Fricoulet, whose was sitting in a corner immersed in reading a book he had found in the Observatory library. "Don't mention that in front of him," he said, in a low voice. "There's no need to take him into our confidence."

Selena smiled, and said: "My dear Father, there's no mystery about our projects as regards Monsieur Fricoulet. He knows everything."

Ossipoff pulled a face. "Why have you told him?" he stammered.

"Wasn't it necessary, to interest him in your fate? Not only does he know about your projects, but I've promised him in your name to make him a participant in your celestial voyage."

Ossipoff started. "What an idea!" he exclaimed.

"It was only on that condition that he consented to save you," Gontran said.

The old man shrugged his shoulders. "To save me! To save me!" he grumbled. "Because he was able to construct that aeroplane according to your plans! It's his profession, after all. In truth, I think you're very good, my dear Gontran, to be so generous to a fellow who tries to put you in the shade at every opportunity."

"But, if you'll permit…"

"No, I won't permit you to say anything whatsoever in his defense, for I saw quite clearly during the journey…every time I spoke to you, he answered in your stead, purely to make himself seem important…but he's wasting his time."

Gontran looked at Selena, with a glint in his eyes, while making every effort to suppress a smile. "Still, Monsieur Ossipoff," he said, "all that doesn't explain why you're so sad."

The old man seized his hands. "What!" he said. "You haven't guessed the reason? Yes, I'm thinking about that marvelous project, to the preparation of which I've dedicated my entire life…and I'm heart-broken at the thought of being robbed and cheated by a villain, at the very moment when I was about to attain the goal of my efforts."

"But what's preventing you from taking advantage of your renewed liberty to go back to work? A man like you has no need of notes to reconstitute his work. In a few days, you can put your plans and your formula on paper again."

"What about money?" murmured Ossipoff.

"Money?" said Gontran. "Without prying into your private affairs, were you counting on your personal resources to bring your project to fruition?"

"Certainly not—but in St. Petersburg I had a situation that permitted me to hope that I might raise the formidable capital necessary to the great enterprise. People are very interested in celestial matters in Russia, and a public subscription would soon have furnished me with the means to do what I wanted to do."

Fricoulet, who had been listening to the conversation for some minutes, took his nose out of his book and said: "Why not attempt here what you wanted to attempt there? People in France are fond of scientists—not to mention the fact that our quixotic temperament urges us to take up the causes of all victims and unfortunates. Besides, your nationality is sympathetic to us."

As the old man shook his head, the young engineer added: "If I were you, I'd go from city to city, giving lectures on my projects, until I'd accumulated he necessary support."

"Since you assure me of it, Monsieur Fricoulet," Ossipoff replied, "I don't doubt that the plan you suggest has every chance of success—unfortunately, I don't have the time."

"The time!" Flammermont replied, jokingly. "But you're not yet on the point of death, thank God! I've rarely seen a man of your age as robust and resilient."

Selena, saddened by her father's thoughtfulness, smiled softly at Gontran.

"That's not what I mean," said Ossipoff. "You don't understand."

"What do you mean, then?"

"This: that Sharp has certainly not stolen all my plans in order to let them lie dormant in boxes, and that he must have profited from the long months of my detention."

"What of it?"

"So," replied the old man, "there's nothing left for me to do but die. Even supposing that I could assemble the funds necessary to the great enterprise, to put it into operation would require an indispensable period of time...and I won't finish second, outdistanced by that wretch."

"Before abandoning yourself to despair, though," Fricoulet objected, "you need to be certain that Sharp intends to make use of your plans. Even if we assume that he does want to make use of them, it's necessary to acquire the certainty that he's sufficiently far advance to neutralize the efforts that you can make..."

Selena kissed the old man on the forehead. "What Monsieur Fricoulet says is very reasonable, Father," she said. "Come on—you mustn't get discouraged. You have to react. Write to your friends in St. Petersburg to ask for information. If the man intends to utilize your plans, your friends will already have heard talk of it, and they'll be able to tell you whether the situation is as desperate as you fear."

"For my part," added Gontran, "I'll write to my former ambassador asking him to make inquiries—his information will serve as a check on those we obtain from other sources."

Ossipoff and Flammermont immediately sat down at the table and made a start on their correspondence. They had written half a dozen letters apiece when Fricoulet, who had gone out to roam around the Observatory came back in precipitately. "Monsieur Ossipoff," he said, "one of your colleagues from the United States has just arrived at the Observatory."

The scientist put down his pen and raised his head. "What's his name?" he asked.

"Jonathan Farenheit."

Ossipoff seemed to interrogate his memory. "That's odd," he said. "I don't know him."

"Perhaps he's involved himself in astronomy since your departure from St. Petersburg," Gontran suggested.

The young man had made this observation with all the sincerity in the world but, fortunately for him, Ossipoff thought he was joking and replied in the same spirit: "You're probably right…but what is he doing here?"

"One of the students I met told me that he's come to carry out some observations of the Moon with the aid of the big 18-meter telescope."

The old scientist's brows furrowed slightly "With what purpose? Did he tell you?"

"No—but it seems that he's going to give a lecture on that subject in the Observatory library, to which we're invited."

An hour later, Ossipoff offered his arm to his daughter and, accompanied by Gontran and Fricoulet, made his entrance into the room where the entire Observatory staff was already assembled.

A man was sitting in an armchair at one of the ends of the table that occupied the middle of the room, with a stack of files in front of him, through which his fingers were nervously riffling. This was Jonathan Farenheit. His highly-colored face was framed by a full red beard, whose hairs seemed as coarse as wild boar's bristles. His hair, of the same shade, was cut very short, with a meager fringe. His red and bushy eyebrows overhung a set of prominent eyelashes, sheltering small grey eyes that shone in the depths of their orbits, full of malice. The shaven upper lip created, by its lack of a moustache, an impression of cunning and spitefulness that gave the lie to the lower lip, which was markedly curved and replete with bonhomie. The fleshy chin fell in two stages to a wide-open collar, doubtless designed to allow more room to an enormous and apoplectic neck. To judge by his powerful torso, the man had to be almost gigantic in stature, and to judge by the diamonds glittering in his cravat, in his cuffs and on his fingers, he had to be very rich.

"Damn!" Fricoulet murmured in Gontran's ear. "The profession of scientist in free America seems to be very lucrative."

The young man was about to reply when Jonathan Farenheit stood up. "Messieurs," he said, bowing to his audience. "I shall begin by thanking you for the more than congenial welcome that you've given me, although I must confess, in all frankness, that I expected no less from illustrious scientists who belong to the most civilized and most amiable nation in the entire world." At this point the American paused, which permitted his audience to thank him with a slight murmur of approval for the flattering words he had just uttered. "Messieurs," he continued, with a slight smile, "I have a confession to make. I do not belong, properly speaking, to the scientific community. I am simply the president of an American company, which proposes to resolve one of the greatest problems that has confronted the genius of human curiosity for centuries. I'm talking about establishing communication between our terrestrial globe and the celestial worlds that we see gravitating around us."

At that moment, Flammermont, gripped by a painful presentiment, glanced sideways at Mikhail Ossipoff. The old man was leaning slightly forwards, his fingers clenched on the arms of his chair. His face was pale, his forehead covered in sweat, his eyes feverishly bright and his lips partly open as if to cry out.

"Going to the Moon!" exclaimed Jonathan Farenheit. "How many geniuses have devoted themselves to researching that problem? How many human lives have been spent cherishing that dream, reckoned until now to be impossible...mad? Well, Messieurs, that dream is no longer a dream...it is on the point of becoming a reality."

There was another pause here, which permitted the orator to establish that the interest of his audience was increasing.

Jonathan Farenheit went on: "The analysis of the lunar spectrum has permitted the discovery, on our satellite's surface, of considerable deposits of crystallized carbon—which is to say, diamonds. An American company, formed for the exploitation of these deposits, has acquired—for a considerable sum—the plans of a scientist that render practicable a journey from the Earth to the Moon. Before appealing for funds from shareholders, however, it has been decided to carry out an initial voyage to make certain, by sight, of the existence of these deposits. Now, although I have every confidence in the project, I nevertheless desire to have the advice of the scientific world. That's why, while the work is in progress, I'm going from one country to another, exposing the plan in question and asking everyone what they think of it. That, Messieurs, is why I'm here..."

Ossipoff stood up. "Would it be indiscreet, Monsieur," he asked, in a tremulous voice, "to ask you the name of the scientist from whom you obtained these plans?"

"On the contrary, Monsieur," the American replied. "I have every reason to spread throughout the entire world the name of the bold genius thanks to whom humankind will, in a few months, have taken a giant step along the path of progress. That audacious man is the permanent secretary of the St. Petersburg Academy of Sciences; his name is Fedor Sharp."

Ossipoff uttered a terrible cry, while his friends got to their feet alongside him, prey to indignant wrath. "This Sharp is a thief!" cried the old man. "The plans that he has sold did not belong to him."

Jonathan Farenheit seemed surprised; nevertheless, he retained his composure. "That's a serious accusation," he said. "On what do you base it?"

"On this: that the plans to which Sharp claims paternity are mine!"

A murmur of astonishment ran through the audience.

"It's necessary to prove that," objected the American.

Briefly, Ossipoff told the story of the trap that Sharp had laid for him in order to be free to steal the produce of his research and labor. "You doubtless have in those files," he added, "the plans that you have been sold. Well, if you wish, I shall put on a demonstration for these gentlemen."

Jonathan Farenheit nodded his head approvingly, and Ossipoff began: "You know, Messieurs, that a moving object can only conclusively escape terrestrial ground by traveling at great speed. In fact, launched horizontally with an initial velocity of 8000 meters a second, where would such a projectile end up?"

"The projectile would never fall back to Earth," a voice replied. The voice belonged to Gontran; seeing the scientist's eyes fixed upon him, he had assumed that the question—to which Fricoulet had whispered the answer—was addressed to him.

"Yes," Ossipoff continued. "The object would orbit the Earth as a new satellite without ever falling back, maintained in equilibrium by its own tangential momentum, which would then become equal to the intensity of the Earth's gravitational attraction. But the case that concerns us is another one; it is, in fact, a matter of reaching the Moon—of launching a vessel toward the zenith in order to escape the Earth's gravity as rapidly as possible. Now that gravitational attraction, Messieurs, diminishing as the square of the distance, will never become equal to zero, and one can therefore only be freed from it by penetrating the zone of attraction of another celestial body. That is what will probably happen if one were to succeed in launching the vessel with a velocity superior to 11,300 meters a second. I therefore investigated whether human agency could produce a velocity as great as that, and I arrived at a satisfactory solution."

While the scientist was speaking, the American consulted his files and shook his head.

"Two things were necessary to attain the goal I had set myself: a powerful explosive and a cannon capable of launching an engine weighing 3000 kilos over a distance of 80,000 leagues. The explosive, which I named selenite, was a mixture of potassium carbazotate[40] and gelatine; as for the cannon, permit me to sketch it for you with a few strokes of pencil."

He turned to a large blackboard that occupied an entire panel of the wall behind him and rapidly drew a bizarre sketch that made the eyes of the audience grow wide.

"It has been established," he said, while sketching, "that in all artillery pieces, the greater the trajectory traversed in the barrel of the device, the greater will be the muzzle velocity. The best result is obtained when the entire charge burns during the time it takes the shell to leave the piece. If, during the time that the shell is traveling along the barrel, animated by increasing force, one can recharge and ignite a second charge, the muzzle velocity will be further increased. In consequence, to impel a projectile to a considerable velocity, it is necessary to increase the length of the cannon and ignite several charges successively, combining to give the shell an increasingly considerable velocity."

He paused briefly and looked at Jonathan Farenheit, but the latter had his eyes fixed on his papers and his face was impassive.

---

[40] The term "carboazotate" is enigmatic, and presumably invented (this account does not correspond to the formula previously given).

"This," Ossipoff continued, "is the provision I had made for causing several charges to detonate, within a second and at perfectly calculated intervals. I should begin by telling you that my shell would have been 3.50 meters in height and 2 meters in diameter. Now, the cannon in which I would have lodged it would itself have been 40 times as long as that diameter, or 80 meters. That enormous tube would have been founded in steel in a single block, by means of a technique that I have invented as which is much more economical than Bessemer's. Its total weight would have been 600 tonnes—600,000 kilograms— and, as it would have been embedded in the ground its resistance would have been infinite. The most important aspect of my invention, however, was the adjunction to this tube of several powder-chambers situated along the barrel.

Ossipoff paused again at this point. "That's correct, isn't it?" he asked Jonathan Farenheit.

The latter, who was following the scientist's explanation in one of the files spread out before him, replied impassively: "That's correct."

A triumphant smile lit up the scientist's face. He went on: "These powder chambers are made of steel, 15 centimeters thick, in order to be able to resist the most formidable pressures. They number 12, and each of them contains 500 kilograms of selenite. The bottom of the cannon itself contains 1000 kilograms, and I leave an empty space of 50 centimeters between that charge and the bottom of the shell. The powder chambers and the initial charge are all connected to an extremely delicate electrical mechanism. At the exact moment when the projectile has to leave terrestrial ground, a current is released into the basal charge; the charges are ignited; a million cubic meters of gas are instantaneously produced, and the shell is driven forward, in such a way that, as it travels through the tube, it unmasks the orifices of the powder-chambers. The deflagration of the selenite they contain adds further impulsion to that of the initial charge, with the effect that, on leaving the cannon, the projectile is endowed with a velocity of 12 kilometers a second."

Osipoff, electrified by his subject, had pronounced the last sentences of his demonstration in a vibrant tone, and when he finished the audience burst into applause.

The old scientist raised his had to restore silence. "I will add," he said, "that in my plan, the founding of the cannon, the fabrication of the powder and the departure itself were to be effected in the southern hemisphere, not far from the Gambier archipelago, on Pitcairn Island, situated on the 26th degree of latitude. It is, in fact, necessary to find a point on the globe possessing the geographical position indispensable for the cannon to be aimed appropriately at the Moon, and also far enough away from any inhabited place. It is easily understandable, of course, that the instantaneous production of several million cubic meters of explosive gas would inevitable give rise to a terrible atmospheric perturbation, which would destroy everything in the immediate vicinity of the cannon." He fell silent; then, after a moment's pause, he said: "Well, Monsieur Farenheit, have I reproduced almost exactly the information contained in your dossiers?"

The American stood up. "To render homage to the truth," he said, "I have to declare that Mr. Sharp's plans are similar in every respect to the explanations that you have just furnished."

Ossipoff could not retain a cry of joy and, racing towards Farenheit, he shook his hands with a vigorous grip. "Thank you," he stammered. "Thank you, Monsieur!"

"What are you going to do, then?" said Fricoulet.

The American started at that question. "What am I going to go?" he asked. "What do you expect me to do?"

"Well," said the young engineer, "it seems to me that in the presence of the proofs that Monsieur Ossipoff has given you..."

Jonathan Farenheit cut him off with a gesture. "Monsieur," he said, "as I had the honor of telling you at the outset, a company has been formed for the exploitation of the lunar mines with a capital of half-a-billion dollars, of which five millions have already been spent, to pay Mr. Sharp for the plans and to met the expenses of the first exploratory expedition...we are, after all, practical people for whom questions of sentiment count for very little."

"Which is to say?" asked Ossipoff, in a tremulous voice.

"Which is to say that, while finding the profound knowledge that you have of Mr. Sharp's plans bizarre, I don't see that you can prevent us from continuing our project. We have paid for them; we own them; and we intend to exploit our property!"

On hearing these words, the unfortunate Ossipoff felt as if a formidable weight had descended upon his skull. He fell back in his armchair. His eyes closed, his head fell back and he became motionless, devoid of consciousness.

When he came round, the old man was in his bed, his head covered with a bag containing ice and his legs burning under the effect of mustard plasters intended to draw the blood to his lower extremities. Selena was beside him, holding his hand and looking at him anxiously. Slumped in an armchair at the foot of the bed, Gontran de Flammermont was immersed in reading a book that must have been very interesting, to judge by the fever that heated his cheeks and the glitter in his eyes.

"Father!" cried the young woman, seeing the old man open his eyes. "Do you recognize me, Father?"

Ossipoff looked at Selena affectionately, but made no reply for a moment. Then, finally, a sad smile creased his mournful features.

"My child," he stammered. "My beloved Selena." Then, noticing Gontran, who had got to his feet in order to come closer, he put out his hand, saying: "My son."

An emotional silence gripped the three individuals for a few seconds. Eventually, Ossipoff said: "I've been very ill, haven't I?"

"There was a danger of brain fever," Gontran replied.

"And I was in that condition for a long time?"

"It will be ten days tomorrow."

Suddenly, two large tears appeared in the corners of the old man's eye, and he said: "Why aren't I dead? I wouldn't have the pain of seeing of seeing that accursed fellow, that diabolical Sharp, enjoying the fruits of his theft with impunity!"

"Come on, Father," said Selena. "Be reasonable. Don't think about that any more, or you'll fall ill again."

"Especially as all hope is not lost," said Gontran. "At this very moment, my friend Fricoulet is in Nice organizing a great conference, as great as any that has ever been convened."

"What god will it do now?" groans Ossipoff. "You heard what Jonathan Farenheit said the other day. Sharp is too far ahead of us now for me to think of beating him to it."

"Can't you devise a more rapid method?" the young Comte persisted.

Ossipoff shook his head. "My dear friend," he said, "I expended my whole life before arriving at the marvelous result that that wretch has stolen from me—and now death is looming over me—may it come quickly, to relieve me of a burdensome existence."

Gontran looked silently at Selena, whose eyes were swelling with tears, and the young woman's dolor put his heart to the torture.

Suddenly, he uttered a cry of triumph and, seizing the book that he had been reading when Ossipoff had regained consciousness he said in a vibrant voice: "Monsieur Ossipoff, the answer is here!"

Selena and her father thought the young man had gone mad; nevertheless, the scientist asked: "What book is that?"

"A work by Father Martinez da Campadores,[41] the prior of the Society of Jesus at the convent of Salamanca: *The Subterranean World*."

"Well?" prompted Selena—whose heart, involuntarily, had reopened to hope.

"Well, Mademoiselle," cried Flammermont, "the Devil with all the cannons, aeroplanes, balloons, steam-engines and selenite itself, thus far imagined in order to visit other planets. All those means are obsolete, antiquated, out of date…" He paused for breath and went on, in an ironic voice: "And to think that men put their minds to the torture to invent terrible engines and powerful explosives, when nature has taken the trouble to construct apparatus for us that leaves all that human genius has invented far behind!"

---

[41] This individual seems to be fictitious.

Ossipoff too allowed himself to be infected by Gontran's confidence, and asked anxiously: "Explain yourself, my dear friend, I implore you. What natural apparatus are you talking about?"

"Volcanoes, Monsieur Ossipoff!" cried Flammermont, triumphantly.

"Volcanoes!" repeated Ossipoff, utterly bewildered.

"Yes!" said Gontran. "Volcanoes are natural cannons. Surprising results might be obtained from volcanoes, if one succeeded in controlling their power!"

Ossipoff and his daughter looked at Gontran, unable to believe their ears, doubting that the young man was speaking seriously.

The latter riffled through the Spanish scientist's work with his finger. "Hold on," he said. On page 130, Martinez da Campadores gives a table of the speeds of projection observed in different volcanoes. Etna launches stones with a speed of 800 meters per second; Vesuvius 1250 meters; Hecla 1500 meters; Stromboli, 1600 meters…but there are volcanoes in South America that are more powerful. Thus, Pichincha, Cotopaxi and Antisana communicate to the stones that escape their gaping craters an initial velocity of between 3000 and 4000 meters a second." He paused to catch his breath and added: "Well, Monsieur Ossipoff, do you think it's impossible to master the power of these subterranean vapors and regulate their expansion?"

The old scientist uttered a cry of joy. "Ah!" he stammered, in a trembling voice. "Ah, Gontran…my son! You'll save my life!" He drew the young man to him and hugged him in a fit of sincere affection.

At that moment the door opened and Fricoulet appeared on the threshold. "Good!" he said, joyously. "So you've recovered your health, my dear Monsieur Ossipoff—and I'll tell you some news that will hasten your recovery."

"Speak, speak!" Ossipoff hastened to say.

"I've seen the prefect; I've seen the presidents of the various scientific societies of the département. I've told them your story, which interested them greatly, and they've all agreed to play a part in the committee that will sponsor your first lecture. The auditorium of the theater has been graciously put at your disposal, and I have here a list of people rich enough to furnish you with capital, to whom shall send out invitations."

He had said all of this in a single breath, his eyes shining and his face radiant. Then he let himself fall into a chair, sponging his sweat-covered forehead with his handkerchief. To his great surprise, though, his communication did not receive the enthusiastic greeting that he expected.

"My God, my dear Monsieur Fricoulet," replied Ossipoff, with a marked coolness, "I'm very grateful to you for all the trouble you've taken…but I'm obliged to tell you that I'm unable to utilize your services."

The young engineer opened his eyes wide.

"Yes," the old man went on. "While you were running around a great deal, and talking no less, your friend Flammermont, a true scientist, who runs around less and talks less, was quietly studying the means of putting our projects of celestial circumnavigation into operation in spite of everything."

Fricoulet looked at the young Comte in complete bewilderment. Gontran replied, with some embarrassment: "Oh, you're exaggerating, Monsieur Ossipoff. *Doctus cum libro*."[42]

"No, no," insisted the old man. "You're modest in your erudition, my young friend, and that's what sets you apart from false scientists who conceal the semblance of science they parade with their fluency of their chatter." So saying, he glanced disdainfully at Fricoulet.

"So you've found a means of going to the Moon," said the latter, examining Gontran curiously.

"My God!" replied the young Comte. "I was riffling through this volume by Campadores you left on the side-table, when the idea occurred to me that one might be able to use the propulsive force of volcanoes."

Fricoulet thought that his friend had gone mad. He leapt out of his armchair, ran to him and seized his hands. Gontran took the young engineer's attitude as poof of his enthusiasm and added: "Well, what do you think of my proposal?"

Fricoulet was on the point of answering that it was a madness that surpassed all of the cases of mental alienation so far discovered by physicians, but it occurred to him that Ossipoff would be sure to attribute that reply to his jealousy, and he cried: "Magnificent! Sublime! Sheer genius!"

Ossipoff, however, suddenly uttered a desolate exclamation. "Alas," he said, "the proposal, magnificent in theory, is impossible in practice. To utilize the power of a volcano scientifically, it would be necessary to know when an eruption was to take place."

Gontran's expression lengthened considerably. "That's true," he stammered.

"Is that all that's stopping you?" asked Fricoulet. "In that case, Martinez da Campadores can get you over the difficulty." Addressing Gontran, he added: "If you've read the book all the way through, you'll have seen that, at the end, the author includes a table of predictions of volcanic eruptions up to the year 1900. It's based on the principle, universally recognized since, that eruptions are elated to terrestrial magnetism, and that when a volcanic eruption is imminent the compass needle is confused. He therefore studied, for several years, in the very crater of Vesuvius, the relationship that exists between geological phenomena and magnetism, which permitted him to formulate laws regarding the prediction, several years in advance, of great subterranean cataclysms."

"But how did he establish the table?" asked Ossipoff, his voice trembling with emotion.

---

[42] "Learned from a book."

"In a perfectly simple fashion. These laws being established, it follows that the movements of the Earth's crust can be compared to tides, and that they obey an incontestable periodicity determined by the positions of celestial bodies and centrifugal force. Thus, after having carefully calculated the circumstances in which a number of ancient eruptions and earthquakes took place, Martinez set up the very curious table that concludes his book."

While speaking, he had taken the volume from Gontran's hands and he riffled through it rapidly.

"Yes," murmured Ossipoff, "but, admitting that one can know the date of the eruption with certainty, it's still necessary for the volcano to be situated between the 28th north and south parallels in order for the Moon to pass directly overhead, and it's also necessary that the mountain itself should be high enough to avoid a notable diminution of the velocity of departure in consequence of the layers of the atmosphere."

As he concluded this speech with a despairing shake of the head, Fricoulet ran to him, his index-finger posed triumphantly on one of the volume's pages. "Victory!" he cried. "Victory! Here's what Campadores says: *March 28, 1882, formidable eruption of Cotopaxi, terrible earthquakes in the Pastos region.*[43] Now, it seems to me that Cotopaxi, one of the highest mountains in equatorial America, is between the 28th north and south parallels.

A strange gleam ignited in Ossipoff's pupils. He folded his arms across his chest and murmured: "My God! My God! Then the dream isn't insane?"

"But what if the Spanish scientist is mistaken?" said Gontran.

Fricoulet looked at him ironically. "Bah!" he replied. "You only have to invent an apparatus capable of revealing in advance the state of fermentation of the Earth's crust and indicate the proximity of a seismological phenomenon…that's nothing at all. You can do that."

"You're right," Flammermont replied, with imperturbable self-possession. "I thought as much—now, another point: the eruption's predicted for March, and it's already October."

---

[43] In writing this, the authors had the advantage of knowing that Cotopaxi had, indeed, erupted explosively early in 1882, but had they researched the matter more carefully, they would have discovered that the actual eruption began in January, and might have made more provision for that in their subsequent timetabling than they actually do. Cotopaxi was the most active volcano in the world during the 1880s, and was the natural choice for this role. The statement a few lines hence that March 1882 is five months away places this scene in October 1881, which is inconsistent with the earlier statement that August 8 was a Sunday, but later dates in the text are adjusted—albeit crudely and inconsistently—to fit in with the pivotal date of March 1882.

"We'll work twice as hard," Ossipoff retorted. "In five months, we'll succeed in constructing the celestial vehicle to be projected by the volcano and preparing the crater of Cotopaxi for the role of cannon that we want it to play."

"But, Papa," murmured Selena, who saw, fearfully, that the scientist was getting carried away by the idea, "where would we get the money to put such large projects into operation."

Ossipoff smiled in a mysterious manner. Pointing to the telescope that he had brought from Ekaterinburg, which was suspended on the wall by a cord, he said: "Give me that, my dear child."

Then, unscrewing the telescope's objective lens, he up-ended the instrument, causing the precious stones given to him by the criminal Yegor to cascade on to his bed.

The young woman and the two young men put their hands together, dazzled by the milticolored gleams that the emeralds and topazes emitted.

"Wow!" murmured Fricoulet. "Do you know, Monsieur Ossipoff, that there's a fortune here."

"Pooh—800,000 or 900,000 francs at the most. But that's all we'll need, now that Cotopaxi's going to serve as our cannon."

Selena put her arms round her father's neck, joyfully.

Fricoulet took Gontran to one side then and whispered: "How long are you going to keep this joke up?"

"Until my marriage to Selena."

"Even if that only takes place on the Moon?"

Flammermont looked at his friend in bewilderment. "Oh," he said, "I certainly hope things won't go as far as that."

"Me neither—but it's necessary to be ready for anything."

Gontran shrugged his shoulders gently and he replied: "Well, when one's in love, it's not the same as when one's not in love—so may Cupid, god of love, watch over us!"

Chapter VII
The Shell [44]

It was two months later. Gontran de Flammermont, whom Ossipoff had charged with the responsibility of supervising the construction the shell that would carry them into space, according to his plans, had arranged a meeting with the old scientist and his daughter that evening. It was, he had briefly said in his letter, a matter of reporting on the progress the project had made.

As one might imagine, Ossipoff and his daughter presented themselves at the appointed time at the Cail factory in Grenelle, where the colossal engine and its accessory machinery was under construction. There, they met the young Comte, escorted by his inseparable friend Fricoulet, who guided them through the deserted workshops and dark yards to a glazed hangar, into which he admitted them. In the middle of an immense space, the proportions of which seemed almost doubled by the obscurity, stood an enormous mass whose vague contours seemed to gleam in the darkness.

"What's that?" murmured Selena, impressed in spite of herself by the silent darkness surrounding them.

"Stay where you are," Fricoulet replied. As he spoke he drew away from the group comprised by Ossipoff, his daughter and Gontran de Flammermont.

Suddenly, the latter party uttered a triple exclamation of surprise and admiration. By pushing a button, Fricoulet had just lit up an electric lamp suspended from the ceiling of the workshop and the immense block in front of which the visitors had paused emerged from the darkness that enveloped it as if by magic, bathed in light. It resembled one of the ancient pepper-pot-shaped towers of the Middle Ages, made entirely in polished metal, shining like silver.

"The shell!" cried Ossipoff.

"Yes, my dear Monsieur," said Fricoulet, "it's the shell whose plan you gave to Monsieur de Flammermont, and which I have constructed on his instructions.

The old scientist walked around the projectile with an evident air of satisfaction.

"I permitted myself," the former diplomat said, "to make a slight modification to your plan with respect to the metal of the shell. Fearing that it might be too heavy, in fact, I thought of nickel-plated magnesium. You know that the

---

[44] The authors refer to the projectile at this point as a "wagon-obus" [wagon-shell] but subsequently use the two terms singly and interchangeably, also using "véhicule" [vehicle] for this and others spacefaring projectiles; I have also substituted "vehicle" for "wagon," as the latter seems to me to ring false in its English meaning, and it would give a false impression to use "spaceship."

production of magnesium has been fully industrialized, and that it costs little more than 80 francs a kilogram. It is the lightest of metals, for it weighs only a sixth as much as silver and less than half as much as aluminum. Nickel, on the other hand, is as resistant as steel, so I chose it in preference to any other alloy."

The old scientist nodded his head approvingly.

"But a mass like that must have a considerable weight," Selena observed.

"Pooh! About five or six kilos. As you can see, it's been founded and nickeled in separate sections, assembled with the aid of nuts and bolts—which makes it relatively easy to transport."

"We wanted to assemble it," Fricoulet added, "in order to make certain that the whole was in accordance with your views, and also so that it would be easier to reassemble it in the crater of Cotopaxi."

Ossipoff had drawn closer in order to pass his trembling fingers over the polished metal, like a father caressing a child whose advent he has been awaiting impatiently.

Selena too examined the enormous projectile with a grave expression and wide eyes. "We'll have to go inside that?" she murmured.

As the young woman pronounced these words, Gontran pressed a switch, and a hidden door opened in the flank of the shell, turning soundlessly on its hinges and giving access to the interior. "Go in, Mademoiselle, go in," he said, standing aside to let Selena pass. Mikhail Ossipoff almost elbowed her out of the way to get in more rapidly.

Like a jewel-box, the interior of the shell was covered with thick padding. The floor, covered with a thick carpet, was mounted on powerful springs of great elasticity, suspended in such a fashion that, although their solidity was proof against anything, they could yield without breaking to the rudest shocks. Four portholes opened in the walls at the four cardinal points, fitted with glass in order to permit the passengers to see what was happening outside. A circular divan ran along the entire length of the padded wall, and a chandelier hung from the ceiling, bearing four incandescent lamps.

"The fitting-out isn't complete," said Gontran, reading evident signs of satisfaction on the old scientist's face. "The cabinet-maker hasn't yet delivered the only item of furniture with which the room will be equipped—a sort of cupboard-cum-sideboard whose upper section forms a bookcase, with a desk and drawers in the middle, a dressing-table a little lower down and whose lowest section will serve to store our clothes.

"Bravo!" cried Ossipoff. "Those are details of the greatest importance, which I had omitted."

"The cupboard is the invention of our friend Fricoulet," said Gontran.

The young engineer inclined his head modestly, while murmuring in Selena's ear: "This Gontran has an aplomb that I've not seen before; in fact, the cupboard is his and the rest is mine. I admire his clever reversal of roles."

"Oh, Monsieur Fricoulet," implored the young woman, "since your friend's happiness is at stake, sacrifice a little of your self-respect."

"Eh! That's all I do, Mademoiselle, sacrifice my self-respect. More than that, I stamp on it…veritably trample it underfoot…it's unnecessary to ask for more." And he muttered something between his gritted teeth that Selena did not catch—and which, if she had, would undoubtedly not have flattered her. As usual, Fricoulet was cursing women.

Hearing voices behind him, however, Ossipoff abruptly turned round. "What's that?" he demanded, suspiciously.

Fricoulet replied, cheerfully: "Mademoiselle was asking me about the upper part of the shell, and I was explaining that there was another level, to which a ladder formed of crampons fixed into the hull gives access. It's divided into three sections connected by a circular landing, each lighted by a porthole. One will serve as a kitchen, the second as a laboratory, the third as a store-room for oxygen, wine and the various utensils and instruments that we'll need to take with us."

"I see that you've left that part of my plan intact," Ossipoff said to Gontran.

"It seemed absolutely perfect to me," Flammermont relied, gravely, "and I followed your instructions to the letter."

Selena had to summon up all her will-power to repress a strong desire to laugh. "You were just talking about cooking, Monsieur Fricoulet," she said. "Will we have the means to make beef stew?"

"A very simple means, Mademoiselle. We'll carry a Trouvé battery."[45]

"You see," murmured Gontran, "he's also an inventor of new cooking-implements."

Fricoulet was seized by a violent fit of coughing, during which he trod on his friend's toes to impose silence upon him. "We shall carry," he repeated, "a 12-element Trouvé electrical battery, with the materials necessary to keep its working for 240 hours—ten days without a pause. The current produced will feed the incandescent chandelier that you can see suspended there, and also a lamp placed in each room. As for the furnaces, they'll be fueled by alcohol, which, while furnishing an intense heat, will not produce any smoke to pollute the air."

Selena clapped her hands. "Bravo!" she exclaimed. "I've passed the ship-board *cordon bleu* and I promise you succulent menus."

Gontran shook his head.

"Do you doubt my competence, Monsieur?" cried the young woman, as if her self-respect as a housekeeper had been offended.

---

[45] Gustave Trouvé (1839-1902) was an electrical engineer, famous for designing the first electric automobile.

"Me?" cried Flammermont. "God forbid, my dear Selena; what I doubt is being able to appreciate your full value."

"What do you mean?"

"Well, before thinking about putting anything in our stomachs, it's necessary to think about putting something in our lungs. In a word, how shall we breathe? I won't hide from you, Monsieur Ossipoff, that that's a matter that has caused me incessant anxiety, since your plan has no trace of that detail."

"Undoubtedly," said Fricoulet, "Monsieur Ossipoff intends to manufacture respirable air artificially from potassium chloride and manganese dioxide?"

The old scientist made a violent gesture of negation. "Not at all," he replied, "for, to decompose that mixture and produce oxygen requires energetic heating…" He paused to look at Gontran, seemingly interrogating him.

"I have it!" cried the ex-diplomat, to whom Fricoulet had just whispered the response. "You're going to employ Tessié de Motay's method."[46] Privately, he added: *As long as Ossipoff doesn't take it into his head to ask me for an explanation of that…*

But the old man shook his head, his face cheered up by a smile. "I shall make no use of chemistry," he said,

"You've found a new method, then?"

"Not me, but compatriots of yours whose renown in universal: Messieurs Cailletet and Raoul Pictet, who have each succeeded, by different methods, in liquefying gases previously reputed to be incompressible: hydrogen and oxygen. Inspired by them, I've done the same but on a larger scale. With the aid of powerful pressure and a considerable decrease in temperature, I shall liquefy oxygen; if need be, I can solidify it and carry a provision of air in tablet form, but I'd prefer to carry it in steel containers."

"But do you know how much of it you'll need?" said Fricoulet, a trifle anxiously.

"Have no fear, my dear friend. I've calculated that one liter of liquefied oxygen represents 15 cubic meters—15,000 liters, that is—of vital gas. With 100 liters of the liquid, we'll have sufficient provision; in 24 hours we'll only expend a liter of liquid, each of us requiring 150 liters of vital gas per hour."

"But have you considered," Fricoulet objected, "that the air will deteriorate during the voyage."

"To combat that deterioration I'll employ caustic potash, which will absorb the carbon dioxide, and every 48 hours, I'll expel the miasmas produced by pulmonary and cutaneous respiration. What do you think of that, Monsieur de Flammermont?"

---

[46] C. Tessié de Motay (1817-1890) was best known as a pioneer of photography. He also worked on air compression, but did not succeed in liquefying oxygen, as the two next-quoted scientists, Louis-Paul Cailletet (1832-1913) and Raoul Pictet (1846-1929), both did—albeit on a very small scale—in 1877.

"I think, Monsieur," the young man replied, gravely, "that you've thought of everything." So saying, he shook the old man's hands vehemently.

Meanwhile, Selena had headed for the door. Showing Fricoulet the footstep that served to reach the floor of the circular space surrounding them, she asked: "How far above the ground are we?"

"One meter, Mademoiselle."

"And what's in there?" she asked, tapping the inferior part of the shell with the tip of her umbrella.

"Compressed air, Mademoiselle, whose escape will diminish the countershock of the departure."

Gontran suddenly slapped his forehead. "There's one thing you haven't thought of, Monsieur Ossipoff."

"What?"

"That it's quite possible that your shell won't be the right caliber."

The scientist's eyes widened. "Not the right caliber?" he repeated. "What do you mean by that?"

"As a hunter, I know that one of the fundamental principles of ballistics is that, in order to utilize all the energy of an expanding gas, it's absolutely necessary to oppose a resistant surface to it, completely blocking the barrel of the revolver, rifle or cannon in order to avoid leakage causing a diminution of speed."

"Well?"

"Well, your shell is six meters in diameter. Do you know how wide the chimney we'll be using will be?"

Ossipoff grabbed his head in both hands. "God in Heaven!" he exclaimed. "You're right! Why didn't I think of that sooner?" Veritably stunned, he looked at Gontran despairingly, seemingly asking him for a means of countering this inconvenience, which he had not foreseen.

For his part, Gontran looked at Fricoulet, begging him mutely to come to his rescue. A leaden silence weighed upon their shoulders, until the young engineer put the index finger of his right hand to his forehead in a gesture of inspiration. "What's stopping us," he said, speaking slowly, "from setting the caisson of compressed air comprising the base of our shell on a second caisson of greater capacity than the first, all the elements of whose construction we'll take from here, and whose diameter we'll fit exactly to that of the chimney of the volcano."

Everyone listened to him speaking without saying a word.

Fricoulet went on: "In addition to this adjunct countering the objection judiciously raised by my friend Gontran, it will offer a further advantage: under the enormous pressure of subterranean gases, the inferior walls of these caissons will be driven back with such force that the air will escape through tightly-fitted valves set in the superior bulkhead; in that manner, the escape will be gradual and not instantaneous, and our chances of impact will be proportionately diminished."

A smile came to Ossipoff's lips. He looked at the young engineer silently for a moment, then leaned towards Gontran and said: "This young man seems to know his business; if he knew how to talk less and listen more, he might get somewhere." Then, addressing Fricoulet, he said, a trifle disdainfully: "Will you be able to make a design for this caisson and the system of valves?"

Humiliated, Fricoulet replied, dryly: "Monsieur de Flammermont will give you the design tomorrow." And, turning on his heel, he went down the three steps that led down from the projectile.

"Make sure," Ossipoff said to Gontran, "to give me that fellow's design exactly as he gives it to you, without adding anything whatsoever; I want to see what he can do."

The ex-diplomat made a hand gesture indicating that he would conform to his interlocutor's request. Then, after a pause, he said: "But Monsieur Ossipoff, have you considered that once it's in the zone of lunar gravitational attraction, it will fall from a height of almost 30,000 kilometers? Have you thought about deadening the impact?"

The old scientist smiled, and shrugged his shoulders slightly. "Bah!" he said. We'll only be falling at a velocity of 2500 meters per second on impact. Now, in view of the rarefaction of the air, it's not necessary to think about any physical means; I thought that we'd simply furnish the bottom of our wagon with tampons equipped with powerful springs, in order that the shock will be deprived of all its violence for us, enclosed in the interior."

While speaking, Ossipoff darted one last approving glance around the interior of the projectile; then he went down the steps, followed by his daughter and Gontran. "My dear boy," he said, shaking the young Comte's hand warmly, "permit me to congratulate you in all sincerity on having succeeded, in such a short time, in bringing this important part of our plan to fruition. This vehicle is perfectly conceived in every particular, and its interior reflects its exterior. Nothing has been forgotten, and, I repeat, you have progressed with a rapidity that does the greatest honor to your activity and your intelligence."

Alcide Fricoulet had moved closer; he smiled complacently, with his hands behind his back, taking for himself the compliments that were not addressed to him, but to which he was entitled.

"And you haven't seen everything," Gontran said, drawing the scientist toward another part of the workshop. "Here are the machines designed to render the chimney of the volcano cylindrical and calibrate it exactly. Here are the pumps and our workmen's tools—they're all specialists in the tasks for which they'll be employed—and here are the projectile's guide-rails."

Ossipoff could not restrain himself from looking at all the items Gontran pointed out to him, examining them in detail one after another. "But on what plans were all these machines constructed?" he said, finally. "I can't see any here that don't seem to have been specially designed with a view to the role that they're to play within our work."

Flammermont was about to reply—doubtless to tell the truth—when an energetic gesture from Fricoulet commanded him to be silent.

"Well? You're not answering," said the astonished Ossipoff.

"Come on, Gontran," said the young engineer. "Why are you ashamed to say that you are the author of the plans according to which all this has been constructed?"

The old man raised his arms to the heavens. "What genius!" he exclaimed. "And what modesty!" Addressing Fricoulet, he added: "There you are, Monsieur Fricoulet. True scientists are all like that: modest and taciturn—while the others…"

The young engineer frowned slightly. "You're repeating yourself, Monsieur Ossipoff," he grumbled. "You've already told me that."

Ossipoff looked him straight in the eyes and wagged his finger at him. "You're jealous of Monsieur de Flammermont's merit," he murmured. "Which doesn't surprise me at all."

Fricoulet remained silent momentarily, amazed and doubtful that he had heard correctly. Then he suddenly burst out laughing. "Me!" he cried. "Me, jealous of Gontran's scientific merit! Ah, Monsieur Ossipoff, scorn my humble worth and my petty scientific knowledge if you will, but don't suspect my sincere friendship for Monsieur de Flammermont!"

Mademoiselle Ossipoff, who, while roaming around the workshop, had nevertheless kept an ear on the conversation, understood that things were at risk of being spoiled if she did not create a diversion. "Oh, what a strange machine!" she cried, pointing into a corner of the hangar, at a sort of gigantic iron horseshoe enclosing a dial equipped with a stout mobile needle. What's that?"

The old scientist turned round in response to the young woman's exclamation. "It is indeed," he said, joining her, "a bizarre construction."

Fricoulet darted a singular glance at Gontran de Flammermont and whispered in his ear: "Be careful. Do you know what you're doing?"

The ex-diplomat shrugged his shoulders and smiled. "You'll see," he said. Then, not without a certain self-importance, he said aloud: "That, Mademoiselle, is the apparatus that your father asked me to invent."

"A seismograph!" exclaimed Ossipoff.

Gontran inclined his head gravely. "Yes, Monsieur Ossipoff, a seismograph. "The two limbs of the iron horseshoe are nothing less than electromagnets; the telluric currents pass through the coils of these spools and magnetize them. According to the intensity of that magnetization, the needle on the dial deviates to a greater or lesser degree, indicating variations in the intensity of terrestrial magnetism, which an unknown law links to volcanic manifestations and eruptive phenomena."

"Bravo!" cried Fricoulet, who had followed his friend's explanation with some trepidation.

Selena looked at the young engineer and thanked him with a smile for providential role that he consented to play with so much self-abnegation.

Ossipoff, for his part, was overcome with joy. "Ah, my boy!" he exclaimed, in a voice tremulous with emotion, what a scientist you are! I tell you, in truth—me, who has grown old in harness, worn down by scientific research—that I admire you! What ingenuity! What depths of insight! What diversity of knowledge!" In his enthusiasm, he seized Gontran's hands and shook them vigorously.

"So you think this instrument will be able to do what you expect of it?" Fricoulet enquired, to render the comedy even more plausible.

"What!" cried Flammermont. "By this means, I will undertake to inform you, a month in advance, of the fermentation of the deep layers of the globe, and predict the next eruption of Cotopaxi for you."

"All my compliments, my dear chap," the engineer replied.

Doubtless Ossipoff thought he perceived an element of irony in these words, for he looked at Fricoulet furiously and asked him, rather sharply: "Are you, perchance, insulting Monsieur de Flammermont by doubting his success, Monsieur Fricoulet?"

The later raised his arms to the heavens. "Absolutely not," he hastened to retort, "but my friend Gontran's science always plunges me into profound amazement."

The ex-diplomat, who feared that Fricoulet's continual mockery would attract the old scientist's attention, hastened to intervene. "Now, Monsieur Ossipoff," he said, "it only remains for me to take my leave of you."

The old man and the young woman uttered simultaneous exclamations of surprise. "You're leaving!"

"Of course! Isn't it necessary for me to go on ahead of you in order to test my seismograph in the very bosom of Cotopaxi. Besides, if I can rely on the information I've received, means of locomotion are by no means abundant over there, and it will take a full month to organize and gather all the material and personnel necessary to transport my luggage to the summit of Cotopaxi."

"Ah," said Ossipoff, enveloping the young man with his affectionate gaze, "what a precious collaborator! You think of everything. You're right, 100 times over. I never thought about these details." And he added, in a mischievous tone: "You'd never have thought of that, Monsieur Fricoulet."

The engineer bowed his head. "That, no," he said. "I admit it humbly."

Suddenly, Ossipoff leaned towards Gontran's ear. "Why, then, is it you that's going?" he asked. "Wouldn't it be better to send your friend Fricoulet over there? That wouldn't cause us any inconvenience."

Selena, whose face had acquired a veil of sadness on hearing Gontran mention his departure, started to smile. "Indeed," she said, "that's an excellent idea." Without waiting for her fiancé's response, she spoke to the engineer, gazing at him pleadingly. "Monsieur Fricoulet," she said, "surely you won't let your friend leave—you know how much pleasure he'll derive from remaining with me."

Gontran frowned slightly, while a moue of discontent creased his lips. He made an imperceptible signal to Fricoulet, who replied: "My God, Mademoiselle, I'm entirely ready to do whatever Gontran tells me to do. If he tells me to leave, I'll leave; if he wants me to stay, I'll stay. It's for him to judge where I'll be most useful to Monsieur Ossipoff's project." He had pronounced these words with an affected humility that won him the privilege of a slightly softer gaze from the scientist.

Selena clapped her hands. "In that case…" she said, joyfully, turning to Flammermont.

"In that case," the latter replied, "my friend Fricoulet will stay here and I shall leave for South America, the day after tomorrow."

Ossipoff and his daughter started.

"Fricoulet will be a great help to you here," Gontran went on. "He's a mechanic, and you'll need someone like him to supervise the dismantling and packing of all the pieces of machinery that we'll need over there."

The old scientist nodded his head approvingly.

"Then again," said Gontran, "I know the apparatus I've constructed better than anyone, and no one can test it better than I can." With a gesture, he drew Selena to one side. "Dear Selena," he murmured, "you have no idea of the grief that this separation will cause me…but it's for the sake of prudence and in the interests of our love that I'm acting thus."

"Prudence!" repeated the young woman.

"I'm afraid of finding myself alone in Monsieur Ossipoff's presence. Without Fricoulet, my good genius, your father wouldn't take long to strip me of the borrowed vestment in which I've dressed up, and he wouldn't need to scratch very deeply for his finger to scrape away the layer of scientific varnish with which I've coated myself. In going away, on the other hand, my heart will suffer, to be sure—but my prestige will remain intact." He paused momentarily; then, narrowing his eyes in an expression of finality, he went on: "Isn't that wisely calculated?"

A slight smile brightened Selena's sad expression. "Perhaps you're right," she murmured. "But it's very annoying that you're only a fake scientist." She emphasized her regret with a deep sigh.

Ossipoff turned to the young man at that moment. "When are you planning to leave?" he asked.

"I've booked a cabin aboard an American ship that's leaving Le Havre in the morning, the day after tomorrow."

"So soon!" exclaimed Selena.

"In a fortnight I'll be at Colon. I'll cross the isthmus of Panama by rail and re-embark for Guayaquil on the far side. From there I'll go on horseback to Quito, where I'll organize the convoy that you'll need to transport your material. By

129

the first of February next I'll be on the summit of Cotopaxi. I'll test the seismograph and let you know the result of my experiment, whatever it is."

"In code, of course!" cried Ossipoff.

"Naturally. If Martinez da Campadores isn't mistake in his calculations, and if I recognize the precursory signs of an imminent eruption, you'll immediately set out to sea with the ship you've chartered. By doubling Cape Horn at full steam, you can be at Guayaquil by March 1, and on March 10, we'll be reunited in the crater of Cotopaxi…"

Darting a singular glance at the ex-diplomat, which would doubtless have given the old scientist much to think about, Fricoulet added: "Provided, at least, that nothing unforeseen happens…"

Ossipoff shrugged his shoulders. Following on from Flammermont's remarks without paying any heed to the engineer's observation, he said: "Allowing 12 days for the appropriation of the chimney, the reassembly of the shell and all the metallic pieces, we'll be ready, three days before the predicted explosion, to launch ourselves into sidereal space!"

As he pronounced these words, he raised his arms vertically toward the sky in a truly magnificent gesture: the action of a warrior designating the countries he is ready to conquer.

Chapter VIII

In which it is demonstrated once again that Fedor Sharp is a scoundrel.

It was 2 p.m. on January 29. In the dining-room of the Hotel Royal in Brest, Monsieur Ossipoff was smoking his cigar, accompanied by Fricoulet. Selena, sitting by the window, let her gaze wander over the forest of masts bristling on the horizon, but her thoughts were far away beyond the sea, with her absent beloved.

"Do you know, Father," she said, suddenly turning round, "that it's nearly a month since Monsieur de Flammermont left."

"A month, indeed, my girl," the aged scientist replied. "It surely won't be more than a week before we have news."

The young woman pulled a slight face. "It seems to me," she said, "that he might have sent us some already!"

Fricoulet, who was leaning over a map of the Atlantic, raised his head. "Assuming that the voyage was effected without hindrance and that no unexpected difficulty has delayed him, Gontran will only have arrived the day before yesterday. Well, he needs time to carry out the seismographic experiment and send a message—and then, there's the telegraphic transmission. In brief, we can't possibly receive any news for another 48 hours, at least."

"48 hours!" murmured Selena. "That's a long time."

"Unless," said Fricoulet, cheerfully, "little Cupid has lent him his wings to enable him to go faster...but such things died with mythological times and our prosaic epoch is not worthy of the descent of gods from Olympus."

The young woman tapped the ground with the toe of her buttoned-up boot impatiently. "Oh, Monsieur Fricoulet," she said, "it's obvious that, unlike your friend Gontran, you don't have a head filled with scientific ideas. You're always making jokes." She smiled maliciously ass she said it, in response to the reproachful gaze the young engineer directed at her.

"Would you say, Monsieur Fricoulet," said Ossipoff, "that we're entirely ready to depart?"

"Everything was concluded yesterday evening, Monsieur Ossipoff. The last cases were stowed away before my very eyes. I've given orders to keep the engine under pressure, in order that the *Maria Selena* can put to sea two hours after receiving Gontran's message—assuming that everything is favorable." Privately, he added: *Which cost a lot of money, and all of it wasted. It would be better for Gontran if the old man converted his stones into 3% bonds rather than dissipate them in unrealizable follies. Fortunately, this comedy will soon come to an end. When we parted company, Gontran appeared to have understood my reasoning. He'll telegraph from over there that the seismograph has not given any result and that Cotopaxi is extinct. Ossipoff will put the blame on Martinez*

131

da Campadores, calling him a cretin and an idiot—which the chap won't take badly, since he's been dead and buried for some years. Then Gontran will come back and marry Selena, and that will be his punishment for all the time he's lost me.

While he was indulging in this monologue, the young engineer studied Ossipoff with an ironic eye. The latter was carefully checking the list of all the objects that the little company had brought with it.

Suddenly, Selena uttered an exclamation. "Father!" she said. "Father, there's a boy from the telegraph office coming this way." The old man abandoned his task and raced to join his daughter. "He's coming into the hotel," she murmured, in a tremulous voice.

"But we're not the Hotel Royal's only guests," objected Fricoulet, sarcastically. Even so, agitated by a presentiment, without knowing why, he was preparing to go in search of news when the door opened and a waiter came in. "A telegram for Monsieur Ossipoff," he said.

The old scientist ran forward, grabbed the blue envelope, opened it with feverish fingers, and avidly scanned its contents.

"Hurrah!" he cried, waving his arms in the air in a wild gesture. "Hurrah for Cotopaxi! Hurrah for Gontran de Flammermont!" Then, broken by emotion, he fell into a chair. His face was very pale, his lips blue and his eyelids almost closed.

"Father!" said Selena, hurrying over to the old man, full of anxiety.

Fricoulet, for his part, remained motionless, his feet nailed to the floor, with a distraught expression. *Poor man,* he thought. *The dashing of all his hopes has rendered him instantaneously mad. Perhaps, if Gontran had attempted it, the experiment would have yielded good results.* Gripped by remorse, he added: *Sapristi! If we could start again, I'd advise Gontran to go all the way to Cotopaxi and try the seismograph. The hazards are so great...perhaps the instrument would have given the results we expected of it.*

In great distress, furious with himself, he too went to Mikhail Ossipoff, who was beginning to recover. "Poor Monsieur Ossipoff," he murmured, taking him by the hand.

The old man uttered a profound sigh, opened his eyes, then abruptly sat up straight, leapt to his feet and cried: "Hurrah! Hurrah for Gontran de Flammermont!"

Here we go, thought Fricoulet. *It's starting again!*

"My dear Monsieur Fricoulet," said Ossipoff, "would you care to run to the harbor and tell the captain of the *Maria Selena* that we'll be setting sail in two hours. I'll take charge of buckling our suitcases and settling our hotel bill."

The engineer started in confusion. The old man had definitely suffered a mental aberration. He drew Selena to him with a wink of the eye. "Your father doesn't seem to me to be in his normal state," he murmured.

It was Selena's turn to start. "What do you mean?" she asked, not taking her eyes off Ossipoff, who was feverishly putting the pieces of paper scattered on the table in order.

"That the telegram must have struck your father terribly hard, and we need to make a decision."

"To do what?"

"I don't know...at any rate, we can't leave him in his state."

The young woman stared at Fricoulet; a sudden doubt had just entered her mind as to the young engineer's mental equilibrium. As they stood next to one another, Ossipoff turned round and, observing their embarrassment, said: "Well, why are you both standing there like book-ends? Monsieur Fricoulet, you should already have left; as for you, Selena, you'd do better to give me a little help. Come on, what's the matter with you? What are you talking about?"

"It's the telegram, Father," the young woman replied. You didn't show us Monsieur de Flammermont's telegram, so I said to Monsieur Fricoulet that you were doubtless hiding something from us...that perhaps Monsieur de Flammermont is ill...injured..."

Ossipoff snatched the telegram from the portfolio into which he had stuffed it and held it out to Selena.

"Here!" he said. "Read it, and be reassured."

The young woman scanned the form rapidly and passed it to Fricoulet, asking in a low voice: "I don't understand what you were trying to say. This telegram could not have caused my father anything but great joy."

Fricoulet rubbed his eyes forcefully. *I'm seeing things*, he thought. *I'm reading it wrong, or else Gontran has gone mad out there.*

And he re-read these words for a third time:

"Martinez Campadores prediction perfectly accurate. Seismograph indicates imminent eruption. Leave immediately. Regards. Flammermont."

He stood there motionless, dumbstruck, rolling the telegram between his fingers, racking his brains, wondering why Gontran had done this. *I can only put his conduct down to sunstroke*, he thought. *In any case, it's necessary to go all the way; now that he's given the word to depart, we have to depart. I only hope that we'll arrive in time to avert a catastrophe.*

"Well, Monsieur Fricoulet?" cried Ossipoff.

"Just so, Monsieur," replied the young engineer, heading for the door. "I'll run to the harbor and, when you arrive, the *Maria Selena* will be ready to raise anchor."

A fortnight later, thanks to winds blowing from the north-east, the schooner arrived in Aspinwall. The material, carefully packed in enormous boxes, was embarked in a great hurry on the Panama railway. On the other side of the isthmus, it was reloaded on the *Salvador Urquiza*, a 500-tonne coaster that was to transport it to Tacames, on the Las Emeraldas River. There, a steamboat would take it to Quito in the center of the massive Andes Mountains, less distant from Cotopaxi than Guayaquil.

On February 24, at 8 p.m., as Fricoulet was leading on the rear guard-rail, smoking an excellent cigar while his eyes absent-mindedly followed the white foam formed by the propeller in the clear Pacific waves, a sudden intense light irradiated the horizon, reflected from the surface of the ocean like firelight. For a second, everything was red: the horizon, the sky, the sea and the ship itself seemed to be stained with blood. Then the light disappeared; everything became dark again—even darker than before.

Fricoulet had shot bolt upright as if moved by a spring and hurtled towards the hatchway to the lower decks. "Ossipoff!" he shouted. "Ossipoff!"

The old scientist had undoubtedly witnessed the strange phenomenon too, through the porthole in his cabin, for he was running up the steps of the stairway, accompanied by Selena. Behind them came the captain, followed by some of the crew.

"What's happening?" asked Mikhail Ossipoff, dragging Fricoulet toward the side of the ship.

"Over there!" replied the young engineer, extending his arm toward the point on the horizon that had caught fire so suddenly. As he spoke, a frightful and monstrous noise burst forth, like the explosion of 100 artillery batteries firing in unison. Then a sudden tempest descended on the ship, tearing away its sails and bending its masts, while the waves, lifted up by an unknown force, reared up like mountains, lifting the unfortunate ship to a vertiginous height and then letting it fall back into unsoundable gulfs. The sky, however, remained clear, myriad of stars shining as on a night in spring.

Suddenly, the wind dropped, the waves relaxed, the atmosphere became calm and on the sea, congealed like an oil-slick, the ship continued on its way. Ossipoff, who never lost his self-composure, especially when it came to making scientific observations, consulted his watch. The strange cyclone had lasted just two minutes. Everyone on board, passengers and crewmen alike, still under the impression of that incomprehensible cataclysm, looked at one another silently, tremulously and fearfully.

Fricoulet was the first to recover his wits. "My word," he said. "If someone were to tell me that we've been subject to the counter-shock of an eruption, I wouldn't be at all surprised."

A dolorous exclamation replied to him: "Cotopaxi!"

And Ossipoff, his eyes haggard and his hair disordered, clung hard to the rail, his eye fixed on the horizon.

Selena ran to him: "Father! My dear Father!" she stammered, tremulously, her heart wrung by an inexpressible anguish. "What do you mean?"

"I mean that Monsieur Fricoulet's presentiments are accurate—that the light we have seen and the noise we have heard must have been produced by an eruption of Cotopaxi, which is only a few 100 kilometers away."

Moved by the old man's distress, the young engineer hastened to intervene. "Do you really think that was the cause of the tempest that descended upon us? In saying that, I was being a trifle speculative…"

Ossipoff shook his head. "Alas," he replied, "it's only too probable. In consequence of a subterranean cataclysm that no on could foresee, the eruption predicted by Martinez da Campadores for next month has just occurred. And he added, in a broken voice: "Fate is undoubtedly against me, insistent on reducing my projects to nothing."

Suddenly, Selena uttered a terrible scream and collapsed into her father's arms, shaken by convulsive sobs.

"Selena! My beloved daughter!" said the old scientist, fearfully. "What is it? Why these tears?"

The young woman sobbed even harder. Mikhail Ossipoff and Fricoulet, both observing the explosion of this anguish mutely, were unable to deduce its cause and felt powerless to calm her down. Ossipoff limited himself to repeating, as tenderly as possible, the epithets that his paternal affection transmitted from his heart to his lips. "But after all, what's the matter, my darling girl?" he asked, taking advantage of a momentary pause in Selena's sobbing.

Then, in the midst of the young woman's tears and moaning, Fricoulet heard these words: "Cotopaxi! Oh, Gontran…my dear Gontran!"

"What's she saying?" Ossipoff asked, having not caught the meaning of these unintelligible words.

The young engineer frowned, and his features suddenly contracted in the grip of a violent emotion. "Gontran!" he cried. "Oh, the poor fellow!" And his arms fell limp by his sides, in a gesture of defeat and despair. Seeing Ossipoff interrogating him with his gaze, he groaned. "Oh, don't you see that if Cotopaxi has erupted, Gontran has certainly perished, buried by its lava? While you, in your scientific egotism, see nothing in this catastrophe but the ruination of your hopes, your daughter sees the death of her fiancé, and I that of my best friend." He added: "You've sent him to his death—he's a victim of your madness, and you haven't even a single regret for him!" And Fricoulet turned round, hiding his face in his hands to conceal the sincere tears that were streaming down his cheeks.

Ossipoff was devastated. In the first moment, indeed, his mind had been struck by only one thing: the annihilation of his hopes. The idea that Gontran might have died—and what a death!—in the burning lava of the volcano had not even occurred to him. Now, however, he felt a sharp pain in his heart at the thought that the fine boy whose qualities he had appreciated so much, and whom he already loved like a son, had perished. Yes, Fricoulet was right; he was the man who had caused the young Comte's death and broken his daughter's heart forever—the heart of his adored Selena, for whose happiness he would have given the last drop of his blood.

Overwhelmed, he fell to his knees on the deck and took Selena's hands in his own. "Forgive me, my daughter," he murmured. "Yes, I'm a madman. Yes, I'm a wretch, since I've allowed my soul to be invaded by the love of science, when it should only have been full of affection for you."

The flow of Selena's tears redoubled. As for Fricoulet, moved by the despairing attitude of the old man and already regretting the hard words he had addressed to him, he went to him, grabbed him by the shoulders and lifted him up. "No, Monsieur Ossipoff," he said. "No, you're not a wretch. No, you're not a madman…and your daughter forgives you for the death of her fiancé, as I forgive you the death of my friend."

The old man looked at him and stammered: "Do you really mean it?"

"Here's my hand," Fricoulet replied, simply.

Ossipoff shook the hand that the engineer offered to him vigorously. Then, turning to his daughter, he said, in a low voice: "And you, Selena? Will you forgive me too?"

The young woman's only response was to throw herself into her father's arms. He hugged her for a long time. Suddenly, Fricoulet burst out laughing. Putting his hand on the old man's shoulder, he cried: "Shall I tell you something? Well, we're both imbeciles!"

Ossipoff looked at him, his eyes increasingly bewildered. "What do you mean?" he murmured.

"It means that the phenomenon we've just witnessed can't be attributed to an eruption of Cotopaxi."

Selena stood up straight and threw herself into the young engineer's arms. "Oh, tell us, Monsieur Fricoulet, tell us that what you're saying is possible!"

"It's very probable, Mademoiselle, and this is why: we are at this moment, if I'm not mistaken, about 83 degrees and 30 minutes west of the Paris meridian, at a latitude of four degrees north. Well, relative to us, Cotopaxi lies to the south-west. Now, it's on the port side that the phenomenon appeared—which is to say, to the west. The Cordilleras aren't in that direction, so far as I know."

He did not finish. The old scientist had thrown himself upon him impetuously and hugged him. "Oh, my friend, my son!" he cried. "You've brought me back to life."

Selena, for her part, had seized his hands again. "And me!" she said. "You've given Gontran back to me."

"But in that case," said Ossipoff, "What was the cataclysm?"

"Perhaps a submarine volcano?"

"Or even a lightning-strike!"

"Unless it was a ship blowing up in the open sea!"

Each of them offered an opinion, but the old man shook his head.

"I can see only one means of satisfying ourselves as to the cause of that surprising phenomenon," said Fricoulet.

"And what's that, my friend?" asked Ossipoff, who was beginning to mellow toward the young engineer.

"To go and see. Let's set a course westwards and go full steam ahead until we've found something."

The captain was consulted, and immediately changed the ship's direction—but the night passed without the lookout sighting anything on the horizon but the waves of the sea extending to infinity.

At dawn, Fricoulet—who had not quit the deck, continually scanning the darkness with the aid of a telescope—suggested that they set a new course towards the south-west. Suddenly, however, the voice of a seaman on the topsail cried: "Land to port!"

Fricoulet raised his telescope and aimed it in the direction indicated. "Indeed," he said, "I think I can see something out there, far away on the horizon: a little black dot. As for telling whether the dot's a ship, land or only a cloud, I can't."

The captain, leaning over his poop-deck, was also studying the signaled object. "The seaman's right," he said. "It's definitely land that we can see—so what shall we do?"

"Head straight for it at top speed. We need to have clear consciences—we've lost several hours, but perhaps we'll find important information there, from a scientific viewpoint." Ossipoff having spoken thus, the captain increased the steam-pressure and the ship headed straight for the land.

"I didn't know that there was any land at all in this part of the Pacific," Ossipoff said.

The captain consulted his chart and replied: "There's the island of Malpelo, which belongs to Colombia. It's an arid uninhabited rock, doubtless the summit of a submarine mountain."

For two hours they went at full steam and gradually perceived a low tongue of land emerge more distinctly from the waves, on which the telescope did not reveal any hint of vegetation.

The captain called a halt; he did not know the region very well, and had to be careful not to break the hull of his vessel on rocks that might be lurking at water-level. "Are the gentlemen proposing to take the adventure any further?" he asked.

"Of course," said Fricoulet. "We want to go ashore."

A command rang out, and a few minutes later, one of the ship's boats was dancing on the waves, manned by four oarsmen.

"Are you coming with me, Monsieur Ossipoff?" asked the young engineer, as he took his place in the stern of the boat.

Without answering, the old scientist clambered down the rope-ladder and sat down beside his companion. Then they cast off; the oars ploughed the waves with marvelous unanimity, and the boat flew like an arrow in the direction of the island. As they drew closer to the shore, though, they encountered a large quantity of wreckage: plants, bushes, tree-trunks and the corpses of animals, Fricoulet even thought he recognized the horribly mutilated body of a man. *The captain claimed that this island was uninhabited*, he thought. *It doesn't appear so.*

Ossipoff was somber and silent; one might have thought that his mind had been prey to a great preoccupation for some little time.

Finally, they ran aground on a shingle beach, split in many places by deep ravines. Fricoulet bent down and ascertained that these ravines were of very recent origin. *Ah!* he thought. *As the captain said, we're certainly on the summit of a submarine volcano, and it was an eruption that we saw yesterday...just as long as there isn't another one now...that's all I ask.*

Then, leaving the oarsmen in charge of the boat, they advanced into the island's interior, observing traces of the recent disturbance of the soil at every step. The further they went, the more Fricoulet wondered how anything could survive on that Sun-burned land, deprived of all vegetation and situated off the shipping-routes. *And yet*, he thought, *the island was inhabited, since we found corpses.*

Ossipoff, for his part, had remained absolutely silent. Suddenly, he stopped, raised his head and looked the engineer full in the face. "Today is February 25, isn't it?" he asked.

"Indeed—why?"

"You know that in three days the Moon will pass directly overhead, and is also at its perigee—the nearest point of approach to the Earth."

"Yes, I know—but I don't understand."

The old man was on the point of answering, but his lips closed again and he walked on, even more somber and taciturn. At that moment, they were climbing a little hillock elevated a few meters above sea level; they hoped to be able to see the entire islet from the top of this natural observatory. Fricoulet, who reached the summit first, cried: "A man! A man!"

"Dead?" asked Ossipoff.

"No, alive...so alive that he's running towards us at top speed."

Indeed, a bare-headed man with his clothes in tatters arrived as fast as his legs could carry him, seemingly fleeing from some terrible danger. "Save me! Save me!" he cried, in English.

They studied him curiously, moved to pity by the miserable state in which they found him, soiled with mud and blood. His face was distorted by an indescribable terror, his fearful eyes almost popping out of his head.

"Farenheit!" Ossipoff suddenly cried, in a terrible voice. "Jonathan Farenheit!"

These words seemed to have a singular effect on the unfortunate. He slowly straightened up and passed his trembling hands over his forehead as if to wipe away the terror that obsessed him. Then, all of a sudden, his panic-stricken features became serene again; his gaze lost its brutal fixity, and a gleam of intelligence shone in his eyes. He raised his eyes to the two companions and murmured: "Jonathan Farenheit! That's me. Yes, that's my name. But how do you know my name—and who are you?"

Ossipoff had become very pale. "Do you remember your lecture at the Nice Observatory?" he asked. "Do you remember Mikhail Ossipoff?"

The American uttered a terrible scream, and seized the old man's hand. "Ah! It's Providence that has sent you," he said. "If you knew! The monster! The bandit! The scoundrel!"

"Who?" demanded Ossipoff and Fricoulet, in unison. "Who are you talking about?"

"Come! Come…you'll see!" He took the old scientist by the arm, thus obliging him to follow him, and set about running to a spot 200 meters away, where the ground appeared more disturbed and torn up than any other part of the island.

The engineer and his companion could not suppress a cry of horror at the sight of the hideous spectacle that appeared to their eyes. The ground was strewn with unidentifiable debris: twisted pieces of metal and burned pieces of wood, in the midst of which lay about 40 horribly mutilated corpses. One might have thought it a lake of blood, in which floated hacked-off arms, broken legs, unraveled intestines and split heads. The two men felt a cold sweat inundate their limbs, and instinctively turned away from that terrible charnel-house.

Fricoulet was the first to recover a measure of self-possession. "But what's happened?" he demanded of Farenheit. "What formidable scourge struck these men down?"

"Let's step away first," replied the American, drawing his companions with him. "Then I'll tell you the story of this horrible catastrophe." After a few steps, however, his strength abandoned him, his legs bent and the unfortunate would have fallen down if Fricoulet had not grabbed him by the shoulders.

"It's the reaction," murmured Ossipoff, seeing Farenheit suddenly become very pale and close his eyes.

"The best thing, I think, is to carry him to the boat," said the young engineer. "The quicker we get him aboard, the quicker we can give him the care that will bring him round…not to mention that we've lost nearly 24 hours, and we need to make them up, no matter what the cost."

Mikhail Ossipoff grabbed Farenheit's legs while Fricoulet held on to his shoulders, and they headed straight for the place on the shore where they had left the boat and the oarsmen, their progress rendered difficult by the disruption of the ground.

An hour later, the *Salvador Urquiza* resumed its course at full steam, and Jonathan Farenheit was deeply asleep, lying in Ossipoff's own bed. The old scientist had volunteered to watch over the sick man; anxious to hear the story he had been promised, he wanted to be there to lay claim to it as soon as the

American's brain had recovered its intelligence and his lips could pronounce comprehensible words.

Suddenly, in the middle of the night, just as Ossipoff was beginning to doze off, sprawled in a wicker armchair and rocked by the ship, a single word escaped the invalid's lips. It was vague and confused, but it made the old man start.

Farenheit had said: "Sharp!" And he repeated several times. "Sharp! Oh! The bandit! Oh! The wretch!"

Ossipoff leaned over the bed. Farenheit was asleep but he was pronouncing words incoherently and inconsequentially in the grip of a nightmare. The aged scientist shook the sick man brutally; the latter did not budge and continued sleeping. Then Ossipoff ran to Fricoulet's cabin and knocked on the door, with such vigor that the young engineer, waking up with a start, got up in alarm. "What is it? What's up?" he demanded, appearing on the threshold still half-asleep. "Is the ship on fire? Are we sinking?"

"Nothing like that," Ossipoff replied, in a trembling voice. "It's Farenheit."

"Is he dead?" cried the young man, suddenly coming fully awake.

"No, but he's just pronounced a name in his sleep…"

"So what?"

"So what! Get dressed and come to meet me. I'd rather not be alone."

Intrigued and somewhat troubled by the old man's strange manner, Fricoulet got dressed hastily and ran to Farenheit's cabin, where he found Ossipoff bending over the invalid, anxiously watching the movement of his lips.

The young engineer, it will be remembered, was something of a physician. Gently, he pushed Ossipoff aside; then, taking the American's wrist between his thumb and index finger, he started counting his pulse-beats. "The fever's almost died down," he murmured, after a few moments. Taking a little traveling pharmacy out of his pocket, he extracted a small phial, a part of whose contents he poured between the invalid's lips.

The latter remained motionless for a few seconds; then his mouth suddenly opened very wide to give passage to a yawn. His eyelids then began to flutter nervously and lifted up, uncovering abnormally-dilated eyes, while his cheeks reddened slightly. The American gazed around the cabin, vaguely at first, then suddenly fixed his eyes on Ossipoff and his companion. He studied them momentarily as if he did not recognize them, then reached out towards them. "My saviors," he stammered. With Fricoulet's help, he propped himself up on his elbow, and passed his hand over his forehead several times, as if to bring back memories that had taken flight. His features suddenly contracted, and he murmured in a strangled voice: "Oh, it's horrible! It's horrible!"

"What?" demanded Osipoff, anxiously. "Speak—tell us what happened to you."

"Yes, yes—I remember now. Yesterday, after you saved me, I was going to tell you the whole frightful story…and then…I can't remember."

"Yes," said Fricoulet, "you've been rather ill—but you're better now."

"Listen," said Farenheit. "You remember, don't you, that lecture I gave in Nice, which you attended. You know, therefore, that a company had been formed for the exploitation of precious mineral deposits situated in the lunar plains, and that I was president of that company's board of directors."

"Yes," said Ossipoff and Fricoulet in unison. "We know that—but what does it have to do with this horrible catastrophe?"

"What! Everything, Messieurs, everything…for the company had bought the plans of a Russian scientist, by the name of Fedor Sharp, and several members of the board, including me, were to accompany Sharp on his voyage of exploration, which was intended to convince us, by means of our own eyes, that the spectral analyses had not misled us. Well…"

"Well?" asked Ossipoff, anxiously.

"The wretch…the bandit has robbed us. He was supposed to take us as passengers in the shell that the American society's dollars paid for…he abused our generosity. He left on his own, and you've seen the result of the deflagration of that terrible powder. The cannon exploded. All our constructions blew up; almost all of our staff perished. Thanks to a providential stroke of luck, I was on another part of the island and survived."[47]

Ossipoff uttered a terrible exclamation: "Sharp has gone!"

"Yes," replied Jonathan Farenheit. "Gone to the Moon!!!"

"Ah! I'm defeated," murmured the old scientist, collapsing into an armchair.

The American, by contrast, seemed to have recovered all his strength and vigor. "But I shan't give up!" he howled, waving his formidable fists at the void. "I'll follow him, that accursed Sharp, all the way to the Moon! We shall see whether a scoundrel of that sort can cheat free America with impunity! He probably doesn't know how tenacious a son of the United States can be!"

Ossipoff, his head in his hands, was prey to a profound discouragement. "Gone," he repeated, in a broken voice. "He's gone…oh, the villain…the thief…"

"But that's the not only means of getting to the Moon," Farenheit continued. "Is it impossible for a man of genius to find a more rapid means of transit from the Earth to its satellite? Come on, Monsieur Ossipoff….let's see, Monsieur…just give me a means to avenge myself and I'll put all the dollars that the bandit Sharp has left in my bank account at your disposal."

"The means is found, Monsieur Farenheit," replied Fricoulet, "and, as you can see, we're on our way to make use of it."

---

[47] Malpelo Island is actually situated at 30 degrees 59 minutes north latitude, and is thus outside the range earlier specified for the location of the cannon (between 28 degrees north and 28 degrees south), so it is unclear why Sharp and Farenheit would have chosen it as a site.

"And this means is…?"

"A volcanic eruption of Cotopaxi!"

The American started mightily, almost falling out of bed. "Hurrah!" he cried. "Hurrah for Cotopaxi!"

The young engineer shook his head. "Unfortunately," he said, "the eruption won't take place until March 28, and the Moon will pass directly overhead at its perigee—which is to say, at its shortest distance from us, 84,000 leagues—tomorrow. It will draw away from us thereafter and I think it will be materially impossible to reach it on March 28."

"Well then," said Jonathan Farenheit, "let's leave right away!"

"It will take us a month to get the chimney of the volcano ready for its new destination!"

The American uttered a formidable curse.

Ossipoff, however, suddenly sat up, his face radiant and his eyes flashing. "Since March 28 is too far distant," he said, "we'll bring the eruption forward!"

"What do you mean?" asked Fricoulet, bewildered.

"One of your compatriots once shouted in parliament: '*De l'audace, encore de l'audace, et toujours l'audace!*'[48] Well, since Nature isn't ready to further our plans, we'll force her hand. We'll compel the crater of Cotopaxi to hurl us into space when it suits us, and we'll leave for the March's full Moon."

Farenheit released another loud hurrah, which burst like a thunderclap in the silence of the sleeping ship, while Fricoulet, looking at Ossipoff with a mixture of surprise and admiration, muttered: "The diabolical man! He'll do as he says…I'm beginning to think that we'll go no matter what."

---

[48] The cry in question was originally credited to the Revolutionary firebrand Georges Danton, but was subsequently echoed by many other sympathetic souls.

Chapter IX
Preparations for Departure

At the very moment when old Ossipoff, aboard the *Salvador Urquiza*, was in despair at the ruination of his plans, while Selena was mourning her fiancé and Fricoulet his friend, Gontran de Flammermont himself was working with feverish activity to prepare everything that was necessary to transport his companions an their luggage.

On quitting the summit of Cotopaxi after making the observations telegraphed to Ossipoff with the aid of the seismograph, the young man had decided not to make the expedition follow the same route he had followed in arriving—from Guayaquil, that is. He had, in fact, observed how long and perilous the road was from that city to the Andes mountains, not to mention that he strongly doubted that the necessary objects inevitably forgotten on departure from Europe, but which the expedition he had summoned would require, could not be found in Guayaquil. He therefore resolved to go to Quito, a city situated 48 kilometers away, in the very midst of the massive volcanic mountains, and to make that his operational base.

Quito is one of the most important cities in Colombia, even though it is situated 2950 meters above sea level, in the bosom of a desolate and arid region with a harsh and cold climate. It has a population of no less than 80,000, is the capital of the equatorial region, and is an important commercial center.

Gontran was very surprised to find so much movement and animation in a city lost in the midst of the world's highest mountains; he did not know that Quito's inhabitants are renowned as being the most avid pleasure-seekers among all the natives of Colombia—and yet their city hardly shines in the beauty of its monuments and streets. The government is held in scant respect, and highway administration is unknown in Quito, which, apart from the four main roads putting it in communication with the rest of America, only possesses tortuous side-streets, uneven and without any surfacing whatsoever. There are, however, very rich churches in Quito, a library containing more than 100,000 volumes, a university famed through South America and numerous factories. As he passed through it, the young Comte admired the façade of the Jesuit church, richly ornamented according to the most rigorous rules of the Corinthian style, and formed out of a single block of stone nearly 30 feet high.

After establishing his general headquarters in one of the city's most luxurious hotels, he made an agreement with the owner of one of the large barges that plough the waters of the Las Emeraldas River—which maintain constant communication between the coast, the high plateaus and Quito—to transport Mikhail Ossipoff, his companions and luggage to that city. Then he took the road to Cotopaxi again, establishing staging-posts every 15 kilometers, with relays of mules and apartments for the travelers. When that was done, he had only to wait. Finally, on February 26, he perceived the huge barge he had hired coming up river by the force of its oars. Not being able to wait for it to be moored to the quay, he leapt into a boat and had himself taken aboard.

From Ossipoff's arms he passed to Fricoulet's; arriving in front of Selena, however, who was flushed with emotion and in whose eyes tears of joy were shining, he stopped dead.

"Come on," said Ossipoff, gaily, "kiss your fiancée—you deserve it."

"If you knew what I've gone through," the young woman murmured. "We thought you were dead!"

"Dead—me!" Gontrain exclaimed in surprise. "What made you think such a terrible thing?"

The young woman told him, briefly, about the surprising phenomenon that the passengers of the *Salvador Urquiza* had witnessed. "Oh, how I wept!" she murmured.

"Poor Selena!" he said, squeezing her hand tenderly. Then, he suddenly added: "So that brigand Sharp has gone!"

"Ah, but we'll catch him up!" cried Farenheit, coming closer.

At the sight of this unknown man, whose features he could not place, the Comte de Flammermont stepped back. Looking him up and down haughtily, he asked, suspiciously: "Who is this man?"

"Jonathan Farenheit, of the United States," the American replied. "A man that this bandit Sharp has cheated and robbed, and who is counting on you to help him get his hands on the thief!"

"On me?" cried Gontran.

"No need to dissimulate, Monsieur de Flammermont—Mr. Ossipoff has told me everything."

"Everything!"

"Yes, everything: the volcano, the seismograph, and the rest. I see that you're as modest as you're knowledgeable." He held out his huge hand. "Put it there, Monsieur de Flammermont. If you weren't French, you'd make a worthy American!"

After matching the American's grip, the young Comte went to rejoin Fricoulet murmuring to himself: "Here's another one for whom I'm a torch-bearer for science. It's flirting with disaster—Fricoulet will never be able to help me sustain my role."

He was ready to reveal these apprehensions to the engineer, when the latter said to him, mischievously: "Well, you're a fine joker, you know. Didn't we agree before your departure from France on the text of the message you'd send the old madman once you'd arrived? And then you telegraph telling him to come! What does it mean?"

"It means, my dear friend, that I was overcome by remorse during the journey, and instead of staying tranquilly in Aspinwall, as had been agreed, then

144

telegraphing to Monsieur Ossipoff that Cotopaxi was an extinct crater and that there was nothing to be done, I pressed on to the volcano. I experimented with my seismograph...."

"Mine, if it's all the same to you," Fricoulet put in.

"I beg your pardon, my dear chap; I've got so far into character that I sometimes think your ideas an inventions are mine."

"You're quite forgiven. So the seismograph..."

"Worked marvelously."

"Of course! I expected as much. But are you at least sure that you're not mistaken?"

"You'll see for yourself..."

"But the voyage—you've decided to attempt it, then?" Fricoulet asked, seriously.

"Or, at least, to get everything ready. At the last moment, though, something might well crop up that will render it impossible..."

The young engineer shook his head. "At the last moment!" he grumbled. "At the last moment...that's extremely imprudent, for if nothing does crop up..."

"In that case," Gontran retorted, "we'll go. Selena and I shall see whether the honeymoon is more complete at close range than at long distance!"

Fricoulet raised his arms to the Heavens in a despairing gesture. "Oh, love...love!" he said, in a tragic tone.

The following morning, at dawn, an impressive caravan passed out of the gates of Quito. First, marching at the head beside the guide, came Fricoulet who forgot the sidereal goal of the journey in gazing with astonished eyes at the splendid equatorial vegetation, so different from that of our own climes. Then came Gontran, on horseback, escorting Selena, for whom a mule specially chosen by the young man served as a mount. Behind them, similarly astride mules, came Ossipoff and Jonathan Farenheit, their boots almost touching. Afterwards, in two files, also mounted on mules, marched the 25 technicians, fitters, laborers, masons and so on, hired in Quito by the Comte de Flammermont. Bringing up the rear, under the guidance of local men, came 30 pack-animals transporting carefully-packaged materials and metallic sections. In all, there were 45 men and 80 quadrupeds.

After marching all day, they halted at the foot of the superior cone. The mules were unloaded and they camped for the night. After dawn, it was a matter of traveling for at least a kilometer through the eternal snows, and the entirety of the following day was devoted to that.

On leaving the summit of Cotopaxi for the first time, Gontran had taken care to prepare for the climbing of the peak by leaving long, strong rope-ladders behind him, attached to the rocks by iron crampons. In ten hours, they climbed 500 or 600 meters, hoisting their baggage after them by means of an ingenious system of pulleys. They were preparing to continue the climb when Fricoulet, whose sharp eyes were exploring every crack in the rock, noticed an opening through the monstrous rocks heaped up in that titanic chaos. The entire troop slipped through that tortuous tunnel hollowed out by incandescent lava and molten eruptive matter. After an hour's march, Fricoulet, who was at the head, shouted *hurrah* in a resonant voice, multiplied by the echoes. He had just emerged into the very crater of the volcano.

Mikhail Ossipoff precipitated himself towards the "chimneys"—the frightful gaping mouths of giants with entrails of fire—and his gaze tried to sound their dark depths, but he could see nothing except terrible gulfs, whose eternal shadows had never been troubled by any ray of sunlight.

The next day, thanks to Fricoulet's vigilance, everyone was up and about at 4 a.m. The first thing to do was to determine which of the volcano's chimneys would be transformed into a cannon. Several were successively eliminated by the young engineer as too large or too tortuous. He ended up choosing the middle chimney; it measured no more than 100 feet in diameter. Instead of sending back the plumb-line—which measured its depth at 4000 feet, or 1333 meters—Fricoulet decided to explore the barrel of this prodigious cannon himself.

On this subject, a slight dispute flared up between himself and Flammermont, who claimed the honor of descending to the bottom of the crater himself, as if it were his entitlement. He was, in fact, burning with a desire to advertise himself, in Selena's presence, by some act of folly or heroism.

"Come on," Fricoulet suddenly said, "I'll let Monsieur Ossipoff settle the matter. Let him decide whether it's up to you—who is, after all, the soul of the expedition—to endanger its outcome by exposing yourself to some accident." He had pronounced these words in a sincere tone, while addressing an ironic smile to his friend.

Gontran wanted to argue, but the old scientist cut him off. "Monsieur Fricoulet's right," he said. "I formally forbid you to make this descent."

The young engineer turned on his heel without further delay and made his preparations for the perilous expedition. A sort of flying bridge was installed across the abyss; a few paces away, a windlass was fixed, carrying 500 meters of rope that was passed through the throat of a pulley suspended under the bridge. A plank fitted with iron crampons was attached to the end of this rope; Fricoulet took his place upon it, holding a Trouvé electric lamp in one hand and a pick-axe in the other, intended not only to make his decent less perilous by keeping him away from the walls but also to serve as a defensive weapon in the event of his being attacked by some vicious animal.

"Listen," said the young engineer. "I have my revolver in my pocket; when you hear a shot, stop the descent. Two successive shots will tell you that you need to bring me up again, but in a normal fashion. If, by chance, you hear three shots one after another, bring me up as rapidly as possible."

Gontran, more anxious than he wanted to appear, shook his hand effusively. "Don't worry," he said. "I'll be here, and I'll be listening!"

"All right," said the engineer, calmly.

Two men, who were manning the windlass, released the starting-handles, while keeping on the friction-brake, and Fricoulet descended in free fall into the void.

Leaning over the edge of the hole, the young Comte followed his friend's descent with anxious eyes, but the light of the lamp, which faded rapidly, soon vanished entirely...and the rope was still unwinding.

Five minutes went by; then, all of a sudden, like an indistinct echo, the sound of a gunshot reached the lip of the gulf.

"Halt!" commanded Gontran. Lying on his belly on the edge of the crater, he cocked his ear, in the hope of perceiving some indication of what was happening at the bottom—but a deathly silence filled the gigantic funnel, disturbed by a human being for the fist time since its formation.

Ten more minutes went by, full of anguish and terror. Finally, two shots rang out. Four men manned the handles of the windlass and, half an hour later, Fricoulet's head appeared.

Gontran threw himself toward his friend; before he even had time to free himself from the apparatus he had pressed him in his arms several times.

Ossipoff stamped his feet, impatient because these testaments of friendship were delaying the young engineer's story. "Come on," he said. "Let's have it— what are the results of your exploration?"

"In the first place, terrible, absurd fears," replied Fricoulet. "For one thing, I almost broke my legs on arriving to the bottom. Then..."

"But what about the chimney?" the old scientist put in.

"Secondly, I roasted myself by planting my feet on rocks so hot that the soles of my boots were charred all over."

"But what about the volcano?" Ossipoff exclaimed. "You haven't mentioned the volcano. What's your opinion?"

"My opinion is that it's very near to sneezing," Fricoulet retorted. "Thirdly, I dropped my revolver and I feared that I wouldn't be able to put my hands on it, any more than...fourthly, my lamp went out, and it was so dark down there...brrr..."

The old man seized the engineer by the arm. "Well?" he cried, beside himself. "Are you going tell me? Did you go down into the crater simply for the pleasure of gathering impressions of the voyage?"

"Calm down, Monsieur Ossipoff," replied Fricoulet, laughing, "and rest content...we couldn't have wished or hoped for anything better, although, to tell the truth, the well is a trifle deep. The chimney is rigorously vertical—as to that, there's no doubt, since I played the role of plumb-line myself. It narrows at a depth of 15 feet, the inferior part measuring no more than ten meters in diameter; that's exactly the dimension we require. The ground at the bottom is stony, and rests, I think, on an unbreakable mass of obsidian."

"Then the crater isn't even in communication with the fires of the volcano?" cried Ossipoff.

"Certainly not. We're dealing with a stoppered chimney, though which the subterranean gases no longer run."

"In that case, we can't use it!"

"On the contrary—it's exactly what we need."

"I confess that I don't understand you," said the old man.

"It's quite simple, though. We'll be able to work in total security, without fear that some partial trepidation will destroy our preparations, as might happen in any other active crater. Then, when we want to, we'll be able to reduce that rock to dust by means of a few pinches of selenite, and thus open a new path for the subterranean vapors."

"With the result," Gontran added, "that instead of bursting forth when Cotopaxi wishes, it's us who will determine the moment of departure."

"Exactly," said Fricoulet. "This is what we'll do: while the technicians and fitters get busy unpacking all the equipment, we'll install a flying platform that can carry ten men. We'll send that platform down to be bottom of the well. During the descent, the men will scrape away from the 300 meters of the cylindrical section that will serve as a cannon all the rocky asperities that might provide obstacles to the ascension of the projectile."

Ossipoff turned to Gontran. "Is that your opinion?" he asked.

"Absolutely," the ex-diplomat replied in a grave tone. "Isn't it necessary to make the interior of the crater as smooth as the barrel of a cannon?"

The work got under way immediately, in order not to waste a second until it was complete, under the active impulsion of the Russian scientist and the intelligent direction of the young engineer. The crater of Cotopaxi was turned into a human ant-hill, and its ancient echoes repeated the sounds of hammers, saws and pick-axes, while its darkness was dissipated by the vivid glare of 100 Trouvé electric lamps.

In six days, the shell was entirely reassembled, while the chimney was "re-bored" as completely as if it had been the barrel of a steel mortar. When that important work was complete, Fricoulet tested the thickness of the layer of stone that had to be reduced to crumbs; it was not more than 30 feet. What was that to a few kilograms of selenite? Holes were drilled out in the rock and cartridges crammed in to a depth of 15 feet, so as to blast those dozen meters of stone into smithereens. Two copper wires covered in gutta-percha projected from each cartridge, connected to a Bréguet detonator,[49] the system being designed to transmit the igniting spark into the center of the mixture.

---

[49] The Bréguets were a famous family of watchmakers and physicists; this particular reference is to Louis-François-Clément of that ilk (1804-1883), a pioneer of electric induction and telephony.

148

For their part, the technicians did not remain inactive; all the equipment was unpacked and a veritable camp was organized in the depths of Cotopaxi's crater, under the direction of the aged scientist.

One evening, while the principal characters in the story were having a meal in the tent adapted as a dining-room, an argument began between Jonathan Farenheit and Gontran de Flammermont. For the first time since his arrival, the American had consented to accompany the young Comte to the bottom of the crater, but the suffocating heat of the gigantic chamber had obliged him to come up again almost immediately. He was in an execrable humor and hastened to seize every opportunity that presented itself to relax his nerves.

"What's up, Mr. Farenheit?" asked Fricoulet, between two mouthfuls of soup, one perceiving the Yankee's furious appearance.

"What's up? What's up is that I'm beginning to see that grand plan is a simple *fumisterie*, as you say in France—humbug and tomfoolery."

Ossipoff became red with choler, and extended a hand armed with a menacing fork toward the American. "Explain yourself!" he growled. "What do you mean?"

"I mean that, in all probability, only insane minds could come up with the idea of blowing up 50 feet of granite. Do you think that's trivial?"

"It is trivial…for selenite," the old scientist affirmed.

"All right, then—let's assume that your 50 feet of rock can be reduced to dust. To what will they give passage? To nothing. You heard me right: to nothing. Your Spanish Jesuit is a joker, and his predictions of volcanic eruptions are nothing but a farce. Your Cotopaxi is no more a volcano than its monstrous colleague Chimborazo."

Ossipoff had rise to his feet; Fricoulet and Flammermont had done likewise.

"It ill befits you, as an American, Mr. Farenheit," said the young Comte, with marvelous self-composure, "to insult an American volcano."

"Monsieur," Farenheit replied, gravely, "for me, America is the United States. The rest does not concern me."

"Cotopaxi, not a volcano!" exclaimed Ossipoff. "But it's the most frightful ignivomous mouth in the entire world. You're claiming that it's an extinct volcano! Don't you recall the frightful eruption of February 15, 1843, which claimed so many victims?"

Farenheit shook his head. "Besides," Ossipoff went on, "that recent eruption was not the most terrible. In 1698, a rock 1000 feet high was split by the action of subterranean forces. In 1738…"

149

"Eh? Let's get to the Deluge, my dear Monsieur Ossipoff!"[50] cried the American, seeing his companion getting carried away and anticipating a long speech, from which he wanted to be spared.

"In 1738," the aged scientist continued, imperturbably, "Air volcanoes like those of Turbaco,[51] which we would be able to examine by climbing the superior cone of the mountain that bears us, redoubled their activity and produced horrible tempests…"

"Thank…"

"In 1744, the cataclysm was complete; never in human memory had such a grandiose and superhuman spectacle been seen; in the space of a single night, the eternal snows crowning the summit of the mountain melted entirely, giving rise to torrents of water that precipitated down into the valleys, inundating and entirely destroying the town of Tacunga. But that's not all…"

Farhenheit had become resigned; he had rolled a cigarette philosophically and was now impassive, enveloped in clouds of smoke.

"In 1758," the old man went on, "there was a new eruption and an earthquake that shook the bowels of the entire American continent. The equatorial region was particularly tested. At Guayaquil, more than 200 kilometers away, the noise of the volcano was audible day and night, crackling like continual artillery fire. In 1768, it was even better; the roaring of Cotopaxi was heard in Honda, more than 900 kilometers away…but that's still nothing compared with the eruptions of the present century. In 1803, flames rose up more than a kilometer above the crater, illuminating the entire country with an incendiary glow, and stones—entire blocks of stone—were projected into the rarefied atmosphere with initial velocities of 2800 and even 3000 meters per second. And it's this equatorial giant that you believe to extinct and dead because it hasn't spoken for 30 years? Hasn't the ground we've been working told you anything? Haven't you seen the snow melting rapidly? Can't you feel the heat increasing? Can't you hear the entrails of the globe stirring?"

"And what about my seismograph?" cried Gontran. "Do you take it for a fake? Be assured, Mr. Jonathan Farenheit, the predicted eruption will take place; if necessary, we shall hasten and provoke it—and you may be certain that this mountain on which we're standing enclosed in its bosom enough vapor and compressed gas to project our vehicle 300,000 kilometers into space!" He had pronounced these words in a voice vibrant with emotion. In a slightly mocking

---

[50] It is surprising to find Farenheit quoting from Act 3 Scene 3 of Racine's *Les Plaideurs* (1668), in which a loquacious lawyer begins his speech for the defence by referring to the Creation, to which the judge responds: "Avocat, passons au déluge."

[51] Turbaco is a volcanic region of Colombia; air volcanoes are gas vents, which emit gas and mud more-or-less continuously but rarely suffer explosive eruptions.

tone, he added: "Anyway, if you don't trust us, there's still time to back out, you know."

Jonathan Farenheit stood up. "An American never backs down, Monsieur," he said, in a dry tone. "I've said that I'll go with you, and I'd go even if I were sure that I'd fall back and shatter into a 1000 pieces."

Thus ended the argument; it had no other consequence than to tighten the bonds that already united these men, who were bold to the point of temerity. The next day, they began to send the steel vessels of compressed air down the well. They had been assembled in advance; all that remained as to set them in place. Between the granite seat and the first vessel Fricoulet left a space of 50 feet. Then, once the caisson of air was in place, supported by four cast-iron brackets embedded in the wall, the four "guides" designed to steer the shell during its ascent through the narrow section of the well were installed.

In the early days, the rudimentary windlass had been replaced by an enormous crane whose counterweight was a large basket filled with pebbles and lava debris, by means of which the fully-assembled shell was lowered down to the caissons. It was deposited on the twentieth of March. While eight men manning compression-pumps filed the caissons with air, they fitted out the interior of the vehicle and loaded all the provisions necessary to feed the travelers—and God knows that it was not easy work!

Finally, on the evening of March 21, everything was done. 24 days of work had been sufficient for those 45 men to transform the chimney of the volcano into a gigantic cannon capable of projecting the formidable machine containing our voyagers at the sidereal target at which it was aimed.

Ossipoff presided over the last meal that the personnel ate before quitting the crater. During the dessert he got to his feet and pronounced these few words in an emotional voice: "My friends, you remember our agreement; I promised to pay you all a bonus I addition to the wages for your labor on the day when our task was completed. That day has arrived, and I thank all of you—technicians, fitters, experienced laborers who have been with us since we left Europe—for your zeal and devotion. I fix the promised bonus at 50% of your wages. The ship that brought you here is waiting at Aspinwall to take you back to France. Go, then, and go as quickly as possible, without delay and without looking back— for in two days, the volcano in which we are located will explode, and there will never have been a more terrible eruption."

At these words, a dull rumor ran through the crowd of workmen. It seemed that mumblings were agitating the subterranean strata and that old Cotopaxi was waking up after its long sleep to protest against the audacity of these strangers, who were troubling the serenity of its crater, inviolate for so many centuries.

After his little speech, Ossipoff lifted his glass and everyone drank a toast to the success of the expedition. Two hours later, the payments having been made, the workmen and guides withdrew, marveling at the generous fashion in which their services had been remunerated. That same evening, Osipoff, his daughter and their three companions prepared to spend the night alone in the crater.

"When are we leaving, Father?" asked Selena, before going to sleep.

"On March 25, at 6:10 p.m."

"Are you sure that the eruption will take place at that moment? There's no proof that it won't be sooner or later."

Ossipoff shrugged his shoulders gently and replied: "The eruption will take place at the moment that suits me, and that moment is the one I've just indicated to you."

"But how?"

"Quite simply, by means of the Bréguet detonator that the foreman brought with him."

"Ah!" murmured Selena, simply. She said no more, but it was easy to read on her face that her father's reply had not satisfied her.

"You don't seem to have understood," said Ossipoff.

"To tell you the truth…"

"It's quite simple, though," the old scientist went on, complacently. "At a height of 2000 meters, in the mountain-side, there's a naturally-formed grotto. It's in that shelter that the foreman will set up an induction apparatus that can generate a electric current, simply by moving a lever, which will reach the charges embedded in the obsidian rock at the appropriate moment, by means of a conductive wire uncoiled during the descent."

After a few minutes, she asked: "How long will the voyage take?"

"100 hours. I calculated that we'll reach the Moon on March 29, at the moment of its conjunction with the Sun. We could not have chosen a more propitious time."

Satisfied with this response, the young woman let her head fall on to the pillow of her bunk. Five minutes later, she had flown off in a dream to the celestial plain to which her father's genius would transport her, in 48 hours time.

Chapter X
The Final Day on Earth

When the moment came to make the colossal wager whose stake was the knowledge of the mysterious worlds in whose contemplation he had spent the greater part of his life, the aged scientist fell prey to an inexpressible anxiety. To have set himself, for so many years, a problem as gigantic as that of the celestial immensity, and to be on the point of resolving it! You would have to be made of marble, and never, on lifting your eyes to the blue vault of heaven, to have hoped for a miracle that would suddenly transport you into those unknown regions, to be unable to comprehend the emotion that was agitating the old man.

At intervals, however, his ardent desire to know gave way to his paternal love; then, he raised his head and his gaze, leaving his sheets of paper blackened by algebraic calculations, would revert to Selena. The young woman, lying on her camp bed, was sleeping peacefully, with a smile on her face. Doubtless she could see herself, in a dream, united with the man she loved, and that vision was giving her face a radiant expression of contentment.

Mikhail Ossipoff's eyebrows furrowed then, and his lips became anxiously pursed. "Poor child," he murmured. "Have I the right to risk her life in such a perilous enterprise?"

Pensively, his head slumped over his breast, he remained absorbed in his reflections for long moments—for if, on the one hand, the dread of exposing his daughter to all the dangers that he was running tended to instruct him not to take her within him, he was also, on the other hand, worried that she might be left alone in life, responsible for herself, without guidance and support, if he left her on Earth. There was, of course, Gontran, who loved her and would protect her— but in that case, he would deprive himself of the company of the young diplomat, and that was a sacrifice to which he could not reconcile himself. From his viewpoint, Flammermont, with his vast knowledge, was as indispensable to the expedition as he might be himself, and he was conscious of the fact that it might compromise the result to exclude him from participation in the voyage. True, he would still have Alcide Fricoulet—but, even though the old man's initial hostility to the young engineer had almost entirely disappeared, to be gradually succeeded by something akin to friendship, the scientist was nevertheless far from having absolute confidence in Fricoulet. As he had told him many times over, in his eyes, true science was never without a dose of natural modesty, and Ossipoff took the habit that the young engineer had of substituting himself for Flammermont for prideful boasting.

After having debated this important point privately for a long time, Mikhail Ossipoff reached the conclusion that, being unable to trust Fricoulet completely, he had to take Gontran de Flammermont with him—and in consequence, in order not to deprive Selena of her natural protector, he had to take her too.

Having established that, he plunged back into his studies, and the hours of darkness passed rapidly and silently, without him noticing the passage of time. The first rays of the rising Sun were gilding the summit of Cotopaxi when Mikhail Ossipoff put out his lamp—and he too was about to lie down, to seek in a few hours of sleep the strength that he would need in the course of the day, when he heard a gently scratching on the outside of the tent.

He got up, tiptoed toward the canvas flap that served to seal the tent, and lifted it up. Fricoulet appeared in the frame.

"You!" said the old man. "Why are you up so early?"

"Please lower your voice, Monsieur Ossipoff," said the young engineer. "It's necessary that no one suspects that I've come to talk to you." So saying, he pointed at Jonathan Farenheit's tent.

"What's this about?" asked the old man, intrigued by Fricoulet's manner.

"Let's go inside," the latter replied. "I'll explain why I came."

Ossipoff sat down on the foot of his bed; the engineer took possession of a trunk that served as a chair, and leaned toward his companion. "Seriously, Monsieur Ossipoff," he said, "do you really intend to take the worthy Mr. Farenheit with you?"

The old man could not conceal the surprise that this question occasioned. "What do you want me to do, then?" he asked. "You don't, I suppose, intend to abandon the unfortunate on the summit of Cotopaxi?"

"He has only to rejoin the others."

"It's too late now. Remember that the eruption must take place at 6:10 p.m., and that anyone within a radius of several miles from Cotopaxi at that moment is doomed to certain destruction."

"Ah!" said the young engineer, with a gesture of impatience. "Would it be so terrible if that Yankee were to be torn to shreds? Do you suppose that the United States would put on mourning-dress for the loss of that citizen? You have a short memory if you've already forgotten the brutal declaration that he made to you at the Nice Observatory. Without our friend Gontran, who had a bright idea, thanks to divine inspiration, all your projects would have been reduced to nothing. And that's the man—who is nothing to you but an enemy, since he furnished that thief Sharp with the means of making use of his theft—to whom you're going to offer a place in your projectile?"

Ossipoff smiled, and put his hand on Fricoulet's arm. "Don't you understand," he said, in a low hiss, "that it's my vengeance I'm taking with me? Personally, I despise and disdain this Sharp, but if he fell into my hands, I believe that I'd let him go. For Farenheit, on the contrary, it's not the same. His fury is such that he'll pursue his robber as far as the remotest lunar solitudes—and woe betide him if he allows himself to be caught! That will be God's justice. Shouldn't the wretch be punished for his double crime?"

154

"Doubtless, from that particular viewpoint, you're right," the young engineer retorted. "It's no less true that the inclusion of the American will upset your exceedingly well-laid plans. Think about it—an extra traveler!"

"If that's all that's worrying you," the old scientist relied, "you can rest easy. You haven't forgotten that our stores have received provisions of liquid air, water and food somewhat grater than those initially planned. We shall therefore be as well-supplied as we were before, even though Farenheit is an extra passenger."

"Hmm!" grumbled Alcide. "These Yankees have terrible appetites, and this one, in particular, seems to have a stomach that could count for two—not to mention that lungs like his must swallow up at least a cubic meter of gas per hour."

"Bah!" Ossipoff replied. "Our provisions permit us to extend this charity."

Fricoulet shrugged his shoulders impatiently. "With regard to the consumption of air and food," he said, "but there's still the question of weight. Like me, you've observed that the man has a massive build, which will add at least 90 kilograms—have you included that surplus weight in your calculations? I don't think so—for in an enterprise like ours, weight must be rigorously calculated and established."

Ossipoff smiled again, with an air of profound commiseration. "If you knew how small a matter 100 kilos is," he said. "If that were the only anxiety motivating your opposition to Farenheit's departure…"

"It's not the departure I'm worried about," Fricoulet said, "but the arrival. The addition of the Yankee might prevent us from reaching the lunar regions."

At that moment, a new outburst of laughter resounded behind the young man, who turned around immediately, quite astonished.

Selena, leaning on her elbow, had been listening to the conversation for a few moments, and was very amused by the resistance that the young engineer was putting up to the inclusion of the American among his traveling companions. "Oh, Monsieur Fricoulet," she said, "are you really so afraid of not reaching the beautiful Moon?"

"Well, Mademoiselle, you'll admit that it would be a great misfortune to take so much trouble and make such a long journey only to fall short…not to mention that if we don't land up there, the Devil may devour me if I know where we'd end up."

The young woman looked at him with a comically mournful expression. "Oh, Monsieur Fricoulet," he said. "How often have I lamented that you don't have as much science as your friend Gontran! He, at least, doesn't have these uncertainties. He has his itinerary at his fingertips." Then, turning to the old man, she said: "Father, I'd like to know why we're leaving today, although the Moon won't be full for five days. I woke up just now, tormented by that idea and asking myself why we don't wait for that date."

"Quite simply because, in order to land, it's necessary that the Moon be full at the moment of our arrival—which is to say that having the face fully illuminated by the Sun will permit us to see clearly on our arrival—and because our journey will last four days."

Selena, satisfied with this explanation, fell silent for a few seconds, then continued: "Are you certain, though, that the eruption will take place at the precise moment fixed for the departure, and, above all, that it will be violent enough to send us across such a considerable distance."

Ossipoff looked at his daughter anxiously. "Are you afraid?" he asked. "If you are, there's still time to think again."

Selena made a dismissive gesture. "Afraid, me!" she said. "Why would you think I'm afraid, Father? Between you and Monsieur de Flammermont, what have I to fear? Whether it be life or death that awaits me, what does it matter, provided that the two of you are at my sides?"

The old man took the young woman's hands. "Dear child," he murmured.

"I'm a woman, though," Selena said, "and, in consequence, inclined to curiosity. It's therefore quite natural that I want to know I advance what phenomena will surround our departure, simply for fear of mistaking entirely natural effects for dangers."

"In that case," said Ossipoff, replying to his daughter's question, "calm yourself; when the moment comes, the volcano, obedient to my will, will reawaken to release the vapors that have been so long compressed. At a signal from my hand, a path will be opened up to incandescent lava and subterranean gases, whose release will hurl us into space with a velocity of more than 12 kilometers per second."

Selena's forehead creased slightly. "A frightful heat will then surround our vehicle," she murmured. "Won't we be asphyxiated and roasted?"

Ossipoff smiled. "Child," he replied," there's no fear of that; the release of gas will be so abrupt that we'll be expelled from the deep well and Cotopaxi's crater in less than a second. Besides, the heat won't be able to reach us, given that the vehicle is resting on two caissons of compressed air, which block the chimney completely."

"Will these caissons accompany us into space?" asked Selena.

"No, no. Once their role as brakes is over, the compressed air having escaped under the pressure of the subterranean gas, the vessels will probably fall into the crater, or perhaps on the cone—not far, in either case, from the point of departure."

"What a horrible noise we'll hear—what a frightful detonation!" murmured the young woman.

"Don't deceive yourself, Mademoiselle," Fricoulet put in. "We won't hear anything at all."

"Why's that?" she said, marveling already. "Have you found some means of preventing it?"

"No," retorted Ossipoff. "We have no need to worry about that—and to understand why, you have only to remember how many meters sound travels in a second."

"About 300 meters, if I'm not mistaken."

"Well, at the time the noise is produced, our vehicle will be animated by a velocity of 11,000 meters a second at the minimum. You'll easily understand that the sound won't have time to reach us."

"Yes, indeed—I understand…but it's strange, all the same." There was a pause; then the young woman suddenly cried: "But now I think about it, Father, I've cast an eye over the furniture of our vehicle, and I didn't see any trace of bedding. Where shall we sleep at night, when we're in our rooms?"

Ossipoff smiled and shook his head. "You'll understand, my child, that we didn't have the room to install a sitting-room, a dining-room, a kitchen and five bedrooms. The big circular room will therefore be the common room. Messieurs de Flammermont, Fricoulet and Farenheit will sleep there; they'll either lie down on the divans fixed to the wall or in hammocks suspended from the ceiling. The upper floor is divided into three rooms: a kitchen, a laboratory and a store-room. I'll make the kitchen my bedroom; which is to say that I'll hang up my hammock there when fatigue obliges me to rest—during the voyage, of course, we'll be continuously bathed in solar radiation, so night won't exist for us. As for you, the laboratory will be abandoned to you for 12 hours in every 24."

They had reached this point in their conversation when footsteps sounded outside, and the soon heard Flammermont asking whether it would be possible for him to present his respects to Mademoiselle Ossipoff.

"Come in, come in, my dear Gontran," shouted the old man. "Mademoiselle Ossipoff has been awake for some time."

"And has already been waiting for you for some time," the young woman added, laughing.

The canvas flap was lifted up, and the distressed face of the ex-diplomat appeared there at almost the same moment as the grave physiognomy of the American. "Mademoiselle," said the latter, bowing ceremoniously, "I hope that you had a good night."

"An excellent night, Monsieur Farenheit," Selena replied. "Thank you for your alacrity in enquiring after my health, but—as you can see—you and Monsieur de Flammermont have been preceded by Monsieur Fricoulet."

"Bah!" said the engineer, moved to pity by his friend's expression in spite of himself. "One can't expect too much of Gontran. Besides, it's the first time he's had to spend the night in a volcano and his tardiness can be forgiven."

The day passed slowly. In the morning they had finished packing the last things they had to take with them, and without his book and instruments, Mikhail Ossipoff was like a body without a soul. He had, however, conserved a pencil and paper; seated in a crevice in the rock, he killed time by making infinitesimal calculations, to assure himself that he had not forgotten any part of the great problem that he was about to resolve, and that he had taken account of all the variables and probabilities.

Flammermont was so bored that he yawned widely enough to dislocate his jaw—as one says in vulgar terms. Occasionally, his breast also rose under the pressure of a profound sigh. The ex-diplomat was thinking about Paris, his lively and exciting Paris, and—as if to render the departure even sharper—hazard put before his eyes, as a gilded vision, his dear Boulevard des Italiens, with its entire crowd of Parisian silhouettes, the Allée des Poteaux, animated by bold cavaliers and graceful Amazones, and the racecourse at Auteuil on the day of the Grand International, with its queue of mail-coaches. It was like a magic lantern show.

Even the placid Fricoulet was nervous; armed with a small hammer, he soothed his nerves by playing the mineralogist, but even the manner in which the steel fell upon the rock testified to the fact that the engineer was there in body only, and that his mind was elsewhere. Having initially sought to struggle against the various circumstances that had drawn him into this extraordinary adventure involuntarily, and having privately complained to Gontran of the pure folly of Mikhail Ossipoff's project, the engineer had been forced for weeks to hear the journey discussed as a practical and feasible possibility, and had eventually come to consider it as such. As obstacles initially considered to be insurmountable had disappeared, and as the days and hours separating them from the moment of departure had gone by, he had become, if not as convinced a the old scientist himself of the possibility of reaching the Moon, at least as enthusiastic as he was that the attempt should be made to reach it. He frequently abandoned his hammer to consult his watch, in order to calculate the time he had to expend in breaking pebbles before the departure.

As for Jonathan Farenheit, he strode up and down the narrow corridor that circulated within the rock around the central chimney, like a polar bear in its enclosure. While he walked, he frequently clenched his fists, lifted up his arms like sledgehammers, looking furiously to the right and left, muttering muffled curses. As Mikhail Ossipoff had said to Fricoulet, the American had a vindictive soul, and now had only one objective in life: to avenge himself on Fedor Sharp. It should be noted that it was not so much that he wanted to kill Sharp because the latter had killed 40 of his companions, or that he had stolen some $2,000,000 from the society of which he was president, as because he had put one over on him, Jonathan Farenheit, a citizen of free America. The Yankee considered Sharp's conduct to be prejudicial to the honor of the Stars and Stripes, and to punish that insult, he would as readily have descended into the depths of the ocean and taken flight into the immensity of space.

Finally, Fricoulet's repeating watch chimed 12 noon, the hour of the daily meal. They rushed through one last token dinner; then the little troop got read to descend to the bottom of the well to take their place in the cannonball-vehicle.

The more time went by, the more evident the symptoms of an imminent eruption became.

The solfataras and fumaroles were, it is true, dormant, but in the volcanic depths, dull rumblings resounded like distant rolls of thunder; the lava took on a brownish tint again, and, under the influence of the gradually rising temperature, the snows of the upper cone were breaking up and running away in muddy streams. It was still calm, but it was a fearful calm, the precursor of a storm.

Selena, pressing close to her father, looked down into the terrible abyss hollowed out at her feet. The windlass, with its 500 meters of rope, had been left close to the well; Ossipoff and his friends went to it.

"Well," said Flamermont gravely. "Who's going down first?"

To say that the young man was emotionless would have been a lie, but he had noticed Selena's pallor and he wanted to boost her morale by adopting a playful attitude.

Jonathan Farenheit stepped forward. "If you would like me to go down," he said, "I'm ready."

The former diplomat put a hand on his arm. "No, Monsieur," he said. "It ought, if I might express myself thus, to be one of the family." In order to reply to the American's interrogative gaze, he added: "You don't know how to open the manhole that grants entry to the vehicle."

Farenheit made a gesture to indicate that he recognized the soundness of the argument.

"Well," said Fricoulet, in his turn, "you're family—you go."

Without paying any heed to Selena's anxious movement, the young man stepped into the skip suspended from the end of the rope, crouched down in the bottom and said, in a firm voice: "Let it go!"

The ratchet of the windlass was released; the rope began to unwind, and the Comte soon disappeared into the depths of the hole. Leaning over the abyss, Ossipoff and his companions sought to pierce the darkness, cocking their ears to capture any sound that might inform them as to the progress of the descent. All they heard, though, was the monotonous whirr of the rope on the windlass, and the light of the lamp that Gontran had taken with him was almost immediately absorbed by the thick darkness that filled the crater.

A quarter of an hour went by. Then an electric bell rang, indicating that the voyager had arrived at the bottom. The rope was brought back up. Ossipoff took his place in the skip and went down in his turn. Selena went next.

Only Fricoulet and Jonathan Farenheit remained.

"How are we going to do it?" asked the American.

"I don't understand the question."

"How will the last of us get down? It's necessary to unlock the opening of the chimney, which the windlass is obstructing."

The engineer shrugged his shoulders. "Don't worry about that," he said, as he caught the skip that had come up empty. "Embark," he said. "I'll take care of all that."

Once the agreed signal had been sent from the bottom of the abyss by the American, Fricoulet set about removing everything that might be an obstacle to the shell's passage. After half an hour of hard work, he succeeded in withdrawing the flying bridge and the pulley. Then he bucked a large belt around his body, similar to the ones that firemen employ. To the ring of the belt he fixed a small apparatus consisting of two pulleys, over the first of which he coiled the cable, while the second simply played the role of a friction brake. Then, seizing his lamp in one hand and the cable in the other, he let himself slide into the abyss. Two minutes later, to the amazement of his companions, he arrived without undue effort and went into the vehicle in which they were already gathered.

"Monsieur Fricoulet!" exclaimed Selena. "How did you come down 500 meters so easily?"

"By means of the simplest apparatus, Mademoiselle: a *spiral descensor*." He pressed a button then, and the four incandescent lamps came on abruptly, vividly illuminating the interior of the large circular room.

At the sight of the not-very-sumptuous but comfortable and practical layout of the room, Jonathan Farenheit beamed. "Nice!" he said. "Here's something well-planned!" One of the divans was folded down; the Yankee sank his fist into it to judge the quality of its springs. Then he passed his hand over the thick-piled carpet that covered the floor. He leaned back on the padded wall, then unhooked one of the hammocks and suspended it. When this careful inspection was concluded, he smiled again and murmured, in a tone of authentic satisfaction: "We'll do okay here." He turned to Ossipoff, who had watched this little maneuver with a docile impassivity, and said; "All my compliments, my dear sir; here's a vehicle that's nicely kitted out, and if its solidity matches its furniture, I think we'll have a very agreeable journey."

"You're too kind, Mr. Farenheit," the old man replied. "Really too kind…but you haven't yet seen and admired everything." So saying, he opened the storage compartments that contained the casks of water and other liquids, the vegetable conserves and a host of other foodstuffs whose necessity he had foreseen. He folded out the steps of the collapsible ladder, so that his companions might admire the reserves of liquid air, the sparkling kitchen equipment and the flasks in the laboratory situated in the upper part of the nose-cone.

The American's enthusiasm was unbounded. "You'd swear you were in a sleeping-car!" he cried. He shook Gontran's hand, saying: "If you lived in New York, you'd be a millionaire in six months."

Flammermont kept his face straight, but he was secretly entertaining great apprehensions. *Just as long*, he thought, *as we aren't roasted on take-off or blasted into pieces during the journey*. In addition to the fact that he had no desire to alienate the genuine amity that Ossipoff had for him, however, he saw

Fricoulet so resolute, Selena so resigned and Farenheit so impatient that he would have blushed with shame if he thought that anyone suspected his emotion.

That last afternoon seemed interminable. When every last nook and cranny of the projectile had been inspected, the young engineer consulted his chronometer; it was 3 p.m. "In my opinion, Monsieur Ossipoff," he said, "We should now begin our final preparations for departure."

"Already!" that was the word that emerged from all their mouths. At the same time, Selena and Gontran blanched slightly. Although emotional, Jonathan Farenheit kept a straight face.

Only Mikhail Ossipoff remained calm; he turned to Flammermont. "What do you think?" he asked.

"I think that perhaps it would, indeed, be more prudent." And apart from that, he thought that if, by chance, the eruption was early and they were taken unawares, they would be reduced to little pieces.

Fricoulet immediately turned the handle of the automatic air distribution apparatus, and sealed the door of the shell hermetically by means of bolts. Save for the engineer and Ossipoff, the other travelers looked at one another with a certain anxiety, carefully studying the manner in which their lungs were functioning in the new artificially-fabricated air. And each of them thought, privately: *As long as we don't suffocate.*

Gontran had taken out his watch, but the seconds and minutes went by and no indication of asphyxia was manifest. They were definitely breathing, and breathing marvelously.

"Hurrah for Mikhail Ossipoff!" cried Farenheit, throwing his cap in the air to render his enthusiasm more tangible.

Selena, recovered from her initial emotion, busied herself about the vehicle, exactly as if she were in her little house in St. Petersburg. Briskly, she set up the table in the middle of the common room and covered it with a white cloth, on which she set out cutlery.

"What!" cried Flammermont. "We're eating already—but it's only 5 p.m."

"It seems to me that it's preferable to eat before departure," the young woman relied. "What do you think, Father?"

"That's my opinion too," said the old man.

Jonathan Farenheit already had his napkin around his neck. "Let's go," he said, rapping the table with the hilt of his knife. "Let's do honor to this terrestrial meal—perhaps the last one we shall ever eat."

Fricoulet added: "Who knows? Perhaps we'll be supping with Hades this evening?"

This reminiscence of Greek mythology made a slight frisson run over Gontran's epidermis. "You're not very cheerful, you know!" he murmured. Nevertheless, after five minutes, thanks to an excellent Burgundy, the young diplomat had left his apprehensions at the bottom of his glass and, along with his companions, did great honor to Mademoiselle Ossipoff's culinary talents. The captivation was so complete that no one even thought of consulting the clock suspended from one of the vehicle's walls.

They were eating dessert, and Alcide Fricoulet had just filled a round of champagne glasses in preparation for making a toast to Mikhail Ossipoff, when the vehicle suddenly trembled on its base. One might have thought that the one of the powerful supports of the globe had just given way under the weight of the heaped-up Cordilleras; the ground was shaken by a prolonged trepidation, while muffled cracking sounds were heard throughout the granite mass.

They all put down the glasses they were lifting to their lips simultaneously and looked at their neighbors anxiously. The old scientist suddenly sat up straight. "The eruption!" he cried.

"The eruption," repeated Fricoulet, mockingly. "Here's to it!" Emptying his glass in a single draught, he added, in a ringing voice: "Messieurs, I drink to Ossipoff and to Cotopaxi, the two forces—one intellectual, the other brutal—thanks to which we're departing in conquest of unknown worlds."

Everyone followed his example; then all gazes turned to the clock; it marked 5:45 p.m.

"But we're ahead of time," stammered Gontran.

"It's probably only the preliminaries to the eruption," Fricoulet replied, coolly.

"What if we're leaving before the time you indicated?" Jonathan Farenheit said, in his turn.

"That's quite possible."

"What do we do, if so?"

"Wait," said Ossipoff. "One can't fight against the blind forces of nature, especially against eruptions—hold them back and contain them by utilizing their enormous power, perhaps, but command them, never. I've taken measures to bring the explosion forward, in case it doesn't happen until after the time I've appointed for the departure, but I can do nothing to delay it."

No one replied to him, all of them being absorbed in their own thoughts, waiting for the fateful moment that would either activate the aged scientist's audacious project or annihilate it. Outside, the volcanic crepitations and subterranean detonations were increasing; their violence was further magnified with every passing second. Now the vehicle was vibrating, shuddering on its two caissons of compressed air, and with each increasing trepidation, the travelers expected the vapors and the laval matter, finally clearing a passage, to send them into space or break their limbs. In spite of the increasing intensity of the quaking of the ground, however, the meal was concluded without difficulty.

For a moment, Ossipoff, who was listening attentively to the many noises confused in the space, went white; the dreadful thought crossed his mind that if the lava rising through the channels neighboring the chimney in which the vehicle was enclosed were to spread out over the chimney's orifice, the projectile

162

and its voyagers would then be buried beneath a mass of incandescent matter. In the silence that filled the vehicle, the clock struck six times.

"We have ten minutes more to remain on Earth," murmured the old scientist.

"Under the Earth, you mean," observed Gontran.

"Monsieur Ossipoff," said Alcide Fricoulet, "don't you think we should make our final preparations for departure?"

"What preparations?" asked the American.

"Firstly, to make sure that all the items of furniture are firmly attached, that the bolts on the portholes and lashings are screwed all the way down, in order that everything inside the vehicle resists the shock that that it will play the role of a full vessel..." So saying, the engineer carefully inspected the stowage and equipment of the celestial vehicle. He carefully closed all the doors of the glass-fronted cabinets, put a lid on the bichromate piles and bolted the storage lockers.

Eventually, he came down again. "However brutal the shock is," the young man said, "everything should resist the formidable recoil of departure, and the vehicle will behave as if it were a solid block. It's equally necessary that we should be firmly moored. For that, we need to introduce ourselves side by side in the 'padded drawers' I've prepared. In that fashion, the shock of departure won't crush us against the walls of the vehicle with which we comprise a body."

"Brr," murmured Gontran, considering the "drawers" whose lids Fricoulet had just lifted. "They look like coffins!" To set an example for his companions, however, Flammermont slid into the box next to Selena, and the lid was lowered and secured.

Five minutes had gone by during these preparations, and in that short interval the elements had been unleashed in a frightful fashion. Horrible cracking sounds were shaking the buttresses of the mountain, which shook like the metal-plate of an overheated boiler. As the Spanish Jesuit Martinez da Campadores had predicted, the monstrous Cotopaxi had woken up after its long sleep, and subterranean vapors accumulated under enormous pressure were hissing and howling in its gigantic entrails.

"It's as if the 500,000 devils of Hell had fallen to the bottom of this hole," Alcide Fricoulet said, jokingly. He had remained standing while his companions wedged themselves against the walls of their boxes.

"Why aren't you lying down?" asked Gontran.

"Because I still have something to do before the departure," the engineer replied.

"6:08 p.m.!" announced Ossipoff, vibrantly. "Pay attention!"

"We're finally on our way," said the American joyously, rubbing his hands together energetically at the thought that he was finally about to go in pursuit of that scoundrel Sharp.

At the same moment, Fricoulet turned the switch of the commutator-interrupter placed across the wires conducting the current to the incandescent lamps, and the interior of the vehicle was abruptly plunged into darkness. Everyone immediately fell silent, and nothing was to be heard but the sounds of the five explorers' labored breathing and the beating of their hearts. A few seconds went by in mortal anxiety.

Suddenly, a frightful shock shook the entire projectile, threatening to break the steel springs on which the boxes were suspended. The voyagers perceived a dull and prolonged sound, accompanied by shrill whistling; it seemed to pass right through them in an incendiary fashion, and they lost consciousness.

Meanwhile, under the indescribable pressure of several million cubic meters of subterranean gases, the projectile quit the crater of Cotopaxi in a fiery cloud, and sped through the entire terrestrial atmosphere in less than five seconds.

They had not heard the terrible detonation produced by the abrupt release of gases so long accumulated and compressed within the flanks of the volcano. Their vehicle, as Ossipoff had explained to Selena, flew more rapidly than sound, and they were already floating in the absolute void to which a myriad of silver stars lent an incomparable dazzle.

Although the bold voyagers had been able to launch themselves into space, thanks to their speed, without even being conscious of the cataclysm that accompanied their departure, the same was not true for the whole of America. An immense plume of flames, more than 500 meters high, sprang forth above the crater of Cotopaxi and a frightful noise reverberated in the remotest layers of the atmosphere. The fiery plume was seen more than 100 leagues away by two ships at sea, crossing that part of the Pacific Ocean, while the air, violently agitated and driven back by the sudden exhalation of several million cubic meters of hot gas, was transformed into a furious storm-wind, whose ravages were incalculable.

That tempest—animated, according to the observations of the scientists of the New World by a wind-speed of 155 kilometers per hour—raced northeastwards across the Gulf of Mexico, engulfing 15 ships that were sailing peacefully and were unexpectedly seized by whirlwinds and waterspouts. It crossed the United States, lifting roofs, blowing down houses and uprooting centenarian trees; in less than six hours, it vanished into the polar regions of Baffin Bay.

In the regions of equatorial America the terror was immense; an earthquake sent its breaking waves along the entire range of the Andes, from Quito to Valparaiso. But it was, above all, the region of the Codilleras known as the Knot of Pastos, that was most severely tested. The magnificent façade of the Jesuit College in Quito, so admired a few weeks earlier by Gontran de Flammermont, was split from top to bottom to a width of 20 centimeters. Several factory chimneys collapsed and 15 houses were cracked and dismembered, ripe for demolition. 80 leagues away in Guayaquil, the ground abruptly caved in and, 200 meters from the harbor, a crevasse several meters wide suddenly opened up, from which toxic gases emerged.

In brief, there was a general desolation in the two Americas, and the Republic of Ecuador had one more catastrophe to attribute to the activity of the most immense volcano on its soil.

Chapter XI
Mikhail Ossipoff encounters his former colleague
from the Academy of Sciences in space

While the New World was the theater of the terrible catastrophes described in summary at the end of the preceding chapter, the authors of those catastrophes seemed already to have received the just punishment of Heaven due to their frightful sin. In the interior of the shell a deep darkness reigned, which did not permit anything whatsoever to be distinguished; in addition, there was not the slightest noise, nor the least breath, nor even the most imperceptible groan. It was the darkness and silence of the tomb.

Suddenly, a sneeze burst forth, as sharp as a pistol-shot—then a second, and a third, then a whole succession, lasting a least three minutes. It was a certain indication that at least one of the five passengers was alive.

"Saperlipopette!" said a slightly gruff voice. "I must have caught a cold."

Scarcely had these words been mumbled when another sneeze burst forth a short distance away. "Bless you!" said the first voice, joyfully.

"So you're alive, then, Monsieur Fricoulet!" exclaimed the second sneezer.

"What's surprising about that, honorable Monsieur Farenheit?"

"But it doesn't surprise me," retorted the American. "It pleases me."

"You're too kind, Monsieur Farenheit."

"Well, not being fond of solitude, I was already trembling at the thought of finding myself shut up in here in intimate company with four cadavers."

"The conversation might, indeed, have lacked animation," said the young engineer, slightly irritated by the Yankee's egotism. Then, suddenly, in a tremulous voice, he exclaimed: "Why are you talking about cadavers? Do you think that our companions are...?" He did not finish, because anguish gripped his throat.

"Well," said Jonathan Farenheit, impassively, "apart from the two of us, no one's moving or saying a word...it is, therefore, supposable..."

A chill ran through Fricoulet's limbs; overcoming the numbness that immobilized him in his box, he slid down to the floor. Once on the carpet, he dragged himself on his knees along the padded wall, patting it feverishly with his hand. Suddenly, he uttered a cry of joy; his fingers had just encountered the commutator switch. He turned it on its axis, and the incandescent lamps in the chandelier immediately lit up, inundating the interior of the vehicle with light.

"By Heaven!" cried Jonathan. "A little light does a lot of good." So saying, he stood up, stretching his limbs sensuously, making all his joints crack one after another.

Fricoulet, meanwhile, had run to the first "drawer" that was within reach; on the soft quilt, Flammermont lay motionless and stuff, as if death had struck him down in his sleep.

"Gontran!" cried the young engineer, shaking his friend as vigorously as his own weakness permitted—but he might as well have been trying to bring a mannequin to life. In response to Fricoulet's efforts, the young Comte's head rolled to the right and the left, the eyelids closed and the lips taut.

"Dead!" murmured Fricoulet, in alarm.

The American had come closer and, without saying anything, stuck his ear to the Comte's breast. "No more dead than you," he sniggered. "His heart's beating normally."

"In that case," said the engineer, "sit him up for a few seconds—that always helps the lungs to work. I'll be with you directly." He ran to the cupboard, opened it, searched among several small bottles arranged on the shelf for a flask filled with a whitish liquid. He shook it, and then, having uncorked it, passed back and forth under Gontan's nostrils several times.

Almost immediately, the Comte's face contracted, his eyelids fluttered and his lips parted, revealing nervously-clenched teeth. Suddenly, the mouth opened very wide, giving passage to a formidable sneeze.

"Saved!" cried Fricoulet, throwing his arms around his friend's neck.

To his exclamation, though, another exclamation replied, coming from another drawer. "We're off! We're on our way!" It was Mikhail Ossipoff who had pronounced these words, in a vibrant voice. He had sat up, and was shaking his arms feverishly.

"What's the matter?" asked Fricoulet, bewildered.

"Didn't you hear that frightful explosion?" said the old scientist.

"What?"

"It's Cotopaxi that has erupted!"

The engineer and the American looked at one another in surprise; then Farenheit cried: "What you mistook for Cotopaxi was simply Monsieur de Flammermont greeting his return to life with a sneeze."

Gontran, meanwhile, sat on the edge of his drawer alternately rubbing his head and his hips. "Ouch!" he groaned. "I could have fallen from the top of Notre-Dame's towers without my skull hurting any more. As for my hips, they're experiencing exactly the same sensation as a serious thrashing."

Suddenly, the ache in his head and the ache in his hips disappeared, as if by magic. He leapt to the floor and ran to Selena's coffin. The young woman seemed to be asleep.

"Fricoulet!" cried Gontran. "Come quickly—this sleep frightens me!"

With one bound, Ossipoff was beside his daughter, whom he took in his arms as if he were holding a little child, covering her with caresses and kisses.

Fricoulet moved him gently aside and, as he had done for his friend, slowly passed the little bottle with the white liquid under her nostrils. It brought about the same miracle, this time without the accompaniment of any noisy manifestations.

"Dear Father," murmured Selena, coming to and holding out her arms to the old man. Then, perceiving Gontran looking at her anxiously, she added: "Dear Monsieur Gontran..." And she let him have one of her hands, which the young man brushed with his lips.

"Yes! Bravo!" said the engineer, joyfully. "No one's kicked the bucket. A voyage to the Moon is definitely less perilous than I thought."

Scarcely had Ossipoff established that his daughter was out of danger than, abruptly tearing himself away from her caresses, he knelt down on the floor and headed for the center of the vehicle, moving on all fours. Having arrived there, he stopped and undid the cords that retained a section of the carpet, which lifted up to reveal a porthole set in the floor itself. This porthole, measuring no less than 40 centimeters in diameter, was made of glass thick enough for someone to walk on it without fear. In anticipation of the shocks that would accompany the vehicle on its departure, the porthole was protected externally by an iron plate fixed by means of bolts whose securing locknuts were inside.

"The wrench! The wrench!" Ossipoff demanded, feverishly.

Fricoulet ran to the cupboard and took out a wrench, by means of which he attacked the bolts ardently. When the last one was unfastened, the iron plate came away, uncovering the porthole and permitting a view to the rear of the vehicle. Then, with Fricoulet's help, Ossipoff performed a similar operation on four openings pierced in the projectile's side walls, which were protected in the same manner as the first.

"Put out the lights, please," the old scientist ordered, curtly.

The young engineer obeyed immediately. He pushed the stem of the commutator and darkness reigned again within the shell.

Ossipoff hurled himself toward one of the portholes. "Victory!" he cried. "Victory! We've left the Earth—we're heading for the Moon."

Farenheit, his face plastered against the glass, opened his eyes wide without perceiving anything but intense darkness. "By Heaven!" he exclaimed. "I'd like to know, Monsieur Ossipoff, on what you base your affirmation that we've left the Earth."

"Quite simply on the fact that a thick shadow is amassed between the Earth and us! If we'd fallen back on our planet, we'd see the ground all around us, lit by moonlight. If, on the other hand, we'd fallen into the Pacific Ocean, we'd feel the motion of the waves. I therefore repeat: we're on out way."

"If your only evidence for saying that, though," murmured Gontran, "is the darkness that surrounds us, I might observe that the darkness was just as intense in the depths of the crater."

"So what?" asked Ossipoff, ironically.

"So we might very well still be in Cotopaxi's chimney."

Making no reply, the old man took him by the hand and drew him to one of the portholes. "Look," he said. "When you were in the crater, did you see that?" And he pointed through the thick glass at the constellations sparkling with an incomparable gleam, like diamonds in a velvet-lined casket.

"It remains to be seen," muttered Fricoulet, "whether the propulsive force will be sufficient to carry us as far as the lunar sphere of attraction."

"We shall see," replied the aged scientist, dryly.

"Tell me," said Gontran, suddenly, addressing his friend, "Can't we open one of these little windows?"

"What for?"

"To get a little air, of course! It's stifling in here."

Fortunately, the young man had spoken in a low voice, so that Ossipoff did not hear the question clearly. It was Fricoulet who leaned close to his ear and murmured: "But we're floating in the void, imbecile."

The ex-diplomat's face reflected the most profound amazement. "In the void," he repeated. "Have we already passed through the whole of Earth's atmosphere?"

The engineer consulted his watch. "Yes," he said. "21 minutes and 30 seconds ago."

"Where are we now, then?" Gontran asked.

Fricoulet glanced at Ossipoff. "Softly, you fool, softly," he whispered. "If your future father-in-law hears you, it'll be the end of your marriage." Then, muffling his voice, he went on: "The space that we're traveling through at present is filled with a fluid called ether, which is so rarefied that its density represents the absolute vacuum that one obtains by means of pneumatic machines. It is, therefore, absolutely impossible to open the portholes for the entire duration of the voyage…rather than letting in breathable air, the little that we have would escape."

Jonathan Farenheit, who had eavesdropped on this explanation, asked: "But if, Monsieur, as I remember from explanations formerly given to us by the accursed Sharp, the surface of the Moon is almost devoid of air, how are we going to breathe there? Have you got rubber diving-suits and tanks of air, like him?"

"Of course," Fricoulet replied. "You may be quite sure that we haven't embarked on such a long voyage without having anticipated even the most improbable circumstances. Even though the lunar surface, according to the eminent Monsieur Ossipoff's theories, possesses an atmosphere sufficient for human lungs, my friend Flammermont, who is a careful man, has had six complete sets of apparatus constructed, thanks to which we shall be able to move about with impunity in an unbreathable or extremely rarefied atmosphere."

Completely reassured, the American muttered: "Oh, I don't want to be able to breathe for long on the Moon—all I ask is enough breath to get my hands on that villain Sharp and strangle him with these ten fingers. Once that task's over,

I'll only want to go back home." With these words, he turned on his heel and stuck his face to the nearest porthole, while Gontran went to install himself beside Selena at another window.

"But the Moon's nowhere to be seen!" Gontran said, suddenly. "Will she be impolite enough to miss the rendezvous?"

"If you'd like to take the trouble to go up to the first floor," Fricoulet replied, "You can see Mademoiselle Selena's godmother, following her invariable route through the stellar immensity in order to reach, four days hence, the exact spot indicated by us."

"She must already have increased in size since our departure."

"If you want to take account of that, you only have to go up the ladder."

The young Comte briskly climbed the steps and found himself in front of a little open door. He groped his way across the threshold—but in the darkness, his foot bumped into a crouching body, and that clumsiness was greeted by an irritated exclamation.

"What—is that you, my dear Monsieur Ossipoff?" said the young Comte. "What are you doing here, in that posture?"

"Oh, it's you, Flammermont," the old man retorted. "You've arrived just in time. I've been trying for ten minutes to undo the nuts retain the plate of the porthole—I do believe the Devil must have tightened them. Give me a hand."

As he finished this speech, and without waiting for the requested hand, he gave one last wrench, so violent that the last nut gave way and the old man, losing his balance, fell backwards into Gontran—who, falling backwards in his turn, rolled on the floor. The ex-diplomat cried out—not in pain, although the fall had rudely shaken him up, but in surprise, for at the same time as his buttocks hit the ground, a bright light had suddenly inundated the laboratory, striking him full in the face.

"The Moon?" he cried, in an interrogative tone.

But Ossipoff did not reply; with one bound, the old man had got to his feet, and while his companion was getting up, he had had the time to seize a telescope, aim the objective lens at the shining satellite and glue his eye to the ocular lens.

As Gontran, visibly interested, drew nearer to the old scientist, he heard him murmur: "Finally, we'll be able to do a little selenography." The young man heard no more; terrified at the thought of being alone, exposed to the old man's redoubtable questions, he drew away on tiptoe and silently descended the steps of the little stairway.

"Well," said Fricoulet, on seeing him reappear, "did you find the Moon?"

The ex-diplomat put a finger to his lips. "Shh!" he said. "I'm running away from Monsieur Ossipoff, on whose lips I foresee embarrassing questions."

Fricoulet burst out laughing. "Coward," he said.

"You're very generous," Gontran replied. "I'd like to see you do it…if you were risking compromising your happiness by an idiotic response, I don't know whether you'd hold up under interrogation."

The young engineer shrugged his shoulders. "His happiness!" he groaned. "Oh, if I were quite sure that some gross heresy in selenography would snatch me away from that precipice called marriage…" As he murmured these words, a mischievous smile strayed over his lips.

At that moment, Selena, who had climbed up the ladder quietly, came back down and approached the engineer. "Monsieur Fricoulet," she's said, "a good idea has just occurred to me."

"What's that, Mademoiselle?"

"If you were to give Gontran a few astronomical tips while my father is lost in contemplation of his cherished star, that might allow him not to be caught out by the questions that my father might address to him in your absence."

"Bravo!" said the young Comte. "Fricoulet, I appoint you as my personal tutor. As for the price of the lessons, we'll settle that later."

The young engineer pulled a face. Nevertheless, Gontran drew him to one of the portholes and extended his arm toward the stars scintillating in space. "Come on," he said. "Tell me about these constellations."

"First of all," Fricoulet began, "there aren't any constellations. It's the position of the Earth in space that makes stars belonging to different systems and immeasurably distant from one another appear to us to be linked. If we were transported to another star, the entire appearance of the sky would be changed by virtue of the displacement of our observation-point. All the suns that we see shining on dark nights are strewn hapahazardly in the immensity and, I repeat, it's simply perspective that creates constellations. Furthermore, each of these stars is animated by its own motion, sometimes very rapid, quite distinct from its neighbors, which are often moving in the opposite direction."

"So that if we came back in 50,000 years…"

"The appearance of the sky would be completely changed for the Earth's inhabitants and as different from the one we're admiring now than it is from the sky existing several 1000 years ago. Would you like some examples? The Great Bear would be dismembered, David's Chariot would be dismantled, and the Three Kings, who appear to have been traveling together until now, would have turned their backs on one another to move in different directions." The young engineer paused, then continued: Everything changes; everything in the universe is transformed, and it's thanks to that perpetual movement that life develops universally on those spheres, and death will never reign over all the stars of infinity!"

He had pronounced the last words in a ringing tone that demonstrated how dear the subject he was dealing with was to him. He was ready to continue when Gontran put a hand on his arm and said to him, in a tone that was half-serious and half-jesting: "My dear friend, you're a bad professor, for, instead of teaching me to read by making me say C-A-T, cat, you're making a speech. So talk to me very simply—about the Moon, to begin with."

At that moment there was the sound of a formidable yawn. It was Jonathan Farenheit, manifesting in his fashion an invincible desire to sleep—and almost immediately, nothing being as contagious as drowsiness, Gontran and Fricoulet felt themselves gripped by a strong desire to lie down in their hammocks.

"Messieurs," said Selena, darting a glance at the clock hanging on the wall, "It's 11 p.m. The moment has come I think, to go to bed. I'm going to my room, and I wish you a good night." So saying, she politely extended her hand to her companions and disappeared into the upper section of the vehicle.

Five minutes later, the lights were out and our three friends, rolled up in their blankets, were snoring in competition.

An intense radiance entering through the portholes struck Gontran full in the face, waking him up with a start. "Sapristi!" he murmured. "It's broad daylight." And, sitting on the edge of his hammock, he rubbed his sleep-swollen eyelids.

"Are we far from Earth?" asked Farenheit, waking up in his turn.

Fricoulet consulted his watch. "6 a.m.," he said. "It's probable that in ten hours we've covered a far number of kilometers."

"But how many?" Gontran persisted.

"To answer you exactly, I'd have to measure the arc subtended by the Earth and make a fairly simple calculation...but there's no point...you wouldn't understand."

"That might well be true, for my part," replied the young Comte, "for my head's as heavy as lead." With a hint of anxiety, he murmured: "Am I falling ill?" Then, jokingly, he added: "It must be the change of air."

Fricoulet clapped his hands. "Me too," he said. "I've got buzzing in my ears—but you've just opened my eyes to the cause of the disturbance. Of course! It's not the change of air that's making you ill, but the exact opposite; it's necessary to purify the air polluted by our respiration and get rid of the surplus carbon dioxide it contains."

"But how?"

"In a very simple manner."

From a cupboard, Alcide Fricoulet took a bottle containing translucent white crystals, which he poured into several saucers deposited on the floor; then he closed the tap that emitted pure oxygen.

Five minutes later, the crystals—which were noting but caustic potash—had entirely absorbed the carbon dioxide from the room and had transformed it into potassium carbonate. Then the engineer lifted up the saucers, which he put back in place, and opened the oxygen tap again.

"Well," he asked, "is that better?"

"It's like breathing sea air," Gontran replied.

172

"One might think one were in the plains of the Far West," said Jonathan Farenheit, in his turn.

With a single movement, they leapt down from their hammocks and were finishing off by rolling them up in order to put them in the place that they occupied by day when the door to the upper floor opened and Ossipoff appeared at the top of the little stairway, his face all smiles. "Messieurs," he said, cheerfully. "Breakfast is ready—a simple cup of arrowroot. There's nothing better in the morning."

Indeed, Selena came down the stairs behind him, carrying five fuming cups on a tray. With Gontran's, help the table was soon set.

"Hurray for Miss Selena!" cried Jonathan Farenheit. "Here's an arrowroot so good that no housekeeper in the United States could make a better one."

After swallowing the contents of his cup in a few rapid draughts and hastily chewing the slice of toast posed on his plate, Ossipoff got up and went back up to his observatory. Scarcely had he departed when Gontran, concealing a formidable yawn, murmured: "That's that! What are we going to do to occupy our time? It seems to me that we'll get bored stiff."

"You'll not lack for occupation if you care to give me a hand."

"Gladly—to do what?"

"Simply help me make notes on the incidents of our journey: the speed of our vehicle, the indications of the instruments, the sidereal phenomena—in a word, to keep a ship's log."

The young Comte nodded his head energetically. "If you've nothing better to offer, I'm your man." Then, turning to Selena, he said: "And you, Mademoiselle? Can't I be some use to you?"

"I don't think so," she replied, "for my own task is completely foreign to you." So saying, she took a book out of a cupboard, and went to sit down on the divan with it.

"What's that?" asked Gontran. "If it's not indiscreet to ask…"

"Oh, not at all," she replied, smiling. "It's the *Cuisinière bourgeoise*;[52] I'm going to study it seriously, in order to provide sufficiently varied menus with the limited resources on board…you can't help me, at all, you see."

Mortified, Flammermont bowed, with a slight mocking smile, and turned to the American. "Dare I," he asked, "for want of dominoes, propose a game of Wet Finger or Flying Pigeon?"[53]

---

[52] The French equivalent of Mrs. Beeton's *Book of Household Management*.

[53] I have translated the names of these French children's games directly into English; the latter is an elimination game bearing some slight resemblance to the English game "Simon Says." They are, of course, ludicrously ill-fitted for gambling purposes.

Jonathan Farenheit burst out laughing. "Ah, by Heaven!" he said. "That's a good idea…and we'll settle up later—which is to say, that if you care to lend me a small sum…"

The young man's lips creased in a significant grimace. "Thanks for he offer," he said. And he went to lie on the divan, to await impatiently the moment when the mid-day meal would reunite the passengers around the table.

Once they had taken coffee and everyone had returned to their occupations, the unfortunate Comte went to a porthole and stayed there all day, his eyes fixed on the sidereal immensity, interested in spite of himself by the diversity of the spectacles that were offered to him. Sometimes, there were bolides streaking through space on their way from one planet to another, sometimes a comet, reminiscent of a flaming salamander, ran across the sky, whipping the stars with its sparkling tail.

Meanwhile, the journey continued in excellent conditions of security and speed; after 48 hours they had covered some 168,700 kilometers and Ossipoff expected to reach the zone of equal attraction, situated 78,500 leagues from the Earth, in a further 40 hours.

Gontran had finally found a distraction that absorbed all his attention; it was the progressive disappearance of the terrestrial crescent, drowned in the fires of the Sun and the continuous increase in size of the Moon, which appeared at the zenith, similar—as he had said in his first rush of amazement—to an immense silver-plated reflector suspended in the sky. With the aid of a telescope that Ossipoff had lent him, he examined every detail of the planet, veiled by a weak ash-colored light, scattered across which he could distinguish the dark patches of seas and a few brilliant points that he did not hesitate to identify as erupting volcanoes.

They were in the fourth day of the voyage, having already traveled more than 60,000,000 leagues, when a more serious event occurred. It was morning. After having drunk his cup of arrowroot, Gontran, moved by curiosity, had gone up to Monsieur Ossipoff's observatory in order to examine the Moon with the scientist's large telescope. Suddenly, he uttered an exclamation so loud that Fricoulet, thinking there had been an accident, ran to the ladder and climbed anxiously up to his side.

"What happened?" the young engineer asked, breathlessly.

"I've just discovered a satellite of the Moon, my dear chap."

Fricoulet burst into spontaneous laughter.

"What's got into you?" grumbled Gontran, offended by this inappropriate hilarity. "Are you going mad?"

"I think it's more probably you that's mad."

"Why?"

"Because the Moon has no satellite."

"Oh, you think so…"

"I suggest you speak in a lower voice—Monsieur Ossipoff might hear you!"

Flammermont stood up and abandoned the telescope, inviting Fricoulet to take it and saying in an irritated tone: "Here, take my place. If you're not blind, or I'm not seeing things…"

The engineer shrugged his shoulders and took his friend's place. Scarcely had he applied his eye to the objective lens than an exclamation of surprise escaped his lips. "It's really true," he murmured. Then, quitting the instrument, he leaned over the stairway and shouted: "Monsieur Ossipoff! Come up here a minute!"

The old man raced up the steps. "What do you want?" he asked.

"Gontran's just discovered a body—for I hesitate to call it a world—which appears to be motionless in the vicinity of the Moon."

Ossipoff did not need to hear any more. In his turn, he crouched over the telescope and looked through it. He looked for a long time, mute and tremulous. Then, finally, he turned round and seized the young Comte by the arm.

"My dear Gontran—my boy—you're a great man!" Tears were running down the old man's cheeks. Kissing Gontran on both cheeks he said: "You have the honor of having discovered a new minor planet. I now baptize this world Planet Flammermont!"

Fricoulet performed an entrechat and, hurtling down the stairway, ran to Selena. "Mademoiselle," he stammered. "Gontran has just discovered a planet!"

Mademoiselle Ossipoff opened her eyes wide. "How did he do that?" she asked.

"I was looking through the telescope," Gontran replied. "It was no more difficult than that." He shrugged his shoulders, and muttered, aside: "That's how astronomical glory is born, though!"

"I propose a toast to Monsieur de Flammermont," cried Jonathan Farenheit, enthusiastically.

Fricoulet took the glasses out of the cupboard and filled them with Bordeaux. Everyone drank to the young Comte's glory, except Mikhail Ossipoff, who refused to come down, not wanting to take his eyes off the new planet. He remained there alone, absorbed in contemplation, until the evening, not leaving his post even to eat. Suddenly, Fricoulet and Gontran heard him call out.

"Come up here, quickly!" cried the old man.

When they got up there, Ossipoff stood aside, indicating that Gontran should take the telescope. "Go on, my dear friend," he said. "Look!"

The young Comte glued his eye to the ocular lens, and could not help crying out.

"What do you see?" asked the old man.

Instead of answering, Gontran shook his head and yielded his place to Fricoulet. Just as his friend had done the young engineer also uttered an exclamation of surprise.

"Well," said Ossipoff, "this planet..."

"Is not a planet at all," Fricoulet continued. "It's a bolide, a cometary fragment, or a rock projected by a volcano with insufficient velocity for it to attain the point of equal attraction situated between the Earth and the Moon."

Gontran clicked his tongue impatiently. "It's not that," he murmured. "Your cometary fragment has a bizarre form, which is also quite regular and elongated. One might think..." He stopped, afraid of saying something stupid.

"One might think that it's a shell?" Ossipoff prompted, nervously.

"That's it exactly," the young Comte replied, excitedly. "The resemblance struck me immediately, but I didn't dare mention it because it's so implausible..." Suddenly, he slapped his forehead, and added: "Unless it's Sharp!"

Scarcely had he pronounced these words than he regretted them. Mikhail Ossipoff's face took on a mortal pallor, and his legs quivered so much that he was obliged to sit down. "Yes, yes," he stammered. "You're right—it must be Sharp!"

"Eh?" cried Fricoulet. "That's even more implausible! Sharp, at this moment, is on the Moon...unless he fell back to Earth in pieces."

The old man did not reply, but he installed himself at the telescope again and looked through it. Around him, Gontran, Selena, Farenheit and Fricoulet stood motionless and silent, inspecting the aged scientist's face for evidence of what he could see in space.

Dinner time arrived without anyone paying any heed to it; everyone's thoughts were concentrated on the object that Gontran had discovered.

The vehicle was only advancing relatively slowly now; the velocity acquired thanks to the volcanic gases of Cotopaxi was beginning to diminish, increasing the passengers' impatience.

Finally, at about midnight, the object became distinct even to the naked eye, and Ossipoff murmured between his teeth: "Yes, that's definitely what it is. I recognize the shell I designed. It really that devil Sharp who's inside it!"

"Ah!" cried Gontran. "Here's a fine opportunity to avenge yourself; you have your thief, scarcely 400 leagues away."

"So what?" asked the old man.

"Well," Fricoulet replied, "according to Mr. Farenheit, Sharp left Earth on February 24. Today, after more than a month of traveling, he's still in space, without having reached the Moon."

"We understand that as well as you do," Ossipoff said, "but what do you deduce from it?"

"That the projective force of the cannon, or the selenite, was insufficient to take the shell past the danger-point—the zone of equal attraction—and that it is suspended between the two worlds, maintained at the neutral point without the power to pass through it and fall, whether upon the Earth or the Moon."[54]

"And will he remain there forever?" asked Gontran

"Yes—unless something happens to modify that state of affairs."

"What sort of thing?"

"For example, the attraction of a body traveling through space, which would draw the motionless shell after it—until the moment when, obedient to a greater force, it was able to reach some other world."

While Fricoulet was giving this explanation, Jonathan Farenheit, his face close to the porthole, was directing a piercing stare at the shell containing Fedor Sharp. "Ah, the bandit!" he muttered. "There he is, almost within range, without any possibility of getting him into a boxing match." The American's cheeks quivered in anger while he clenched his formidable fists.

Meanwhile, Ossipoff was still crouched over his telescope. "We're heading straight towards him," he murmured.

"So much the better!" cried Jonathan. "Let's knock him down, crush him, smash him into smithereens!"

The scientist shrugged his shoulders.

"Knocking him down is all very well," Gontran said, "and personally, there's nothing I'd like better; while thinking about our vengeance, though, it's also necessary to think about our own skins. What will happen?"

"That depends on our speed," Ossipoff replied. "Assuming that we don't collide with the shell—in which case we and Sharp would fall back to Earth—if we're moving fast enough, we'll uproot him..."

"And he'll rotate around us like a satellite!" cried Gontran de Flammermont. "Shall we see our vehicle become a planet, with a satellite of its own?"

Ossipoff tore himself away from he ocular lens to look at the ex-diplomat in surprise. "You're joking, aren't you?" he said. "You know that the laws of celestial mechanics won't permit that?"

"It would have been charming, though," Gontran murmured, aside. "Sharp's cannonball would have been turning around us, us around the Moon,

---

[54] When Jules Verne refers to a neutral point between the terrestrial and lunar "zones of attraction" in *Autour de la lune*, he is careful to observe that he is simplifying a situation that is actually more complicated, not only because the Earth and Moon are in constant relative motion, but because the Sun's gravitational attraction is by no means trivial in Earth's orbit; Graffigny and Le Faure are not as scrupulous, and thus permit themselves to design and develop an impossible situation. They also imitate Verne in assuming that the weight of the space travelers would remain constant until vanishing at the neutral point, even though Ossipoff has already observed that gravitational attraction varies with the square of the distance from the attracting body—an error perpetuated throughout the text.

the Moon around the Earth, the Earth around the Sun, and the Sun..." The young man could not think of anything around which the Sun might be turning, and shut up.

"Obviously," Fricoulet said, "Sharp won't rotate around us—but he will follow us."

"And thanks to us," Ossipoff said, in a tone of inexpressible rage, "he'll reach the Moon."

"What!" howled Farenheit. "Isn't there any means of sending a torpedo loaded with dynamite to blow him up! Oh, if we were in America..."

"The sad thing is that we're rather a long way from America," said Fricoulet, ironically.

As one might imagine, there was no question of going to sleep. The shell had increased considerably in apparent size, and Ossipoff now estimated its distance at scarcely 100 kilometers. They could see it through the lateral wall of the large room. The night passed in anguish-filled anticipation. For the voyagers, it was a matter of life or death.

At 5 a.m, the two vehicles were no more than ten leagues apart and Ossipoff's telescope reduced that distance to a little less than 100 meters. He was therefore able to make out two thin and emaciated faces glue to the shell's portholes, whose ardent eyes were fixed on the vehicle containing our friends.

The old scientist recognized Fedor Sharp; as for his companion, Jonathan Farenheit declared that it was Voriguin Sanburoff, the assistant and stooge of the former permanent secretary of the St. Petersburg Academy of Sciences—the man with whose complicity Sharp had played him false.

Suddenly, a strange incident occurred; Sharp's shell seemed to quit the point in the sky where it appeared to be mounted, in order to hurtle towards Mikhail Ossipoff's vehicle.

"We're doomed!" cried Flammermont. "It'll hit us!"

The old scientist, who was aiming a sextant at the shell, wiped away the sweat that was inundating his forehead. Fricoulet, for his part, seemed no less anxious, even though he was making every effort to hide his emotion. Only Jonathan Farenheit, oblivious to the danger, uttered cries of joy on seeing the distance that separated him from his enemy diminishing with his own eyes, so to speak.

"Scoundrel!" he groaned. "Blackguard!" And his Herculean fingers opened and closed, as if about the throat of Fedor Sharp.

"Well?" Gontran asked Fricoulet.

"Well, as you see, that animal's shell is following us, and will fall on to the Moon at the same time as ours."

"May he break his bones in the fall!" growled the American, a cruel smile distorting his lips.

Suddenly, the young engineer uttered a cry of rage.

"What is it?" everyone asked.

"That accursed projectile, by its attraction, is pulling us off course!"

"Which means?" cried Selena, anxiously.

"Which means," replied Fricoulet, with great self-possession, "that we won't fall on to the Moon—we'll simply curve around its disk, and be lost in space."

Chapter XII
A Drama in a Cannonball

It is now time to elaborate on the brief explanation furnished by Jonathan Farenheit regarding Sharp's departure.

Strangely enough, since the citizens of the New World are endowed with a practical sense that generally makes them wary of crooks, Jonathan Farenheit had not taken any inference from the very clear declarations made by Mikhail Ossipoff at the Nice Observatory regarding his former colleague from the St. Petersburg Institute of Sciences. He ought to have been on the alert, keeping a close watch on the man to whom he had too lightly entrusted the expenditure of several million dollars. He who has drunk will drink again, says the wisdom of nations, and there is a 93% chance that the man who has stolen on Monday will do the same on Tuesday.

As well as having made the grave error of not taking the revelations of the Russian scientist—whom he initially considered to be mentally unbalanced—more seriously, Jonathan Farenheit had also been so obsessed by the idea that he would go to the Moon himself that, even if someone had shown him Fedor Sharp with his hand in a till, he would still have doubted. Imagine that—to go to the Moon! What an extraordinary thing! And how far such a prodigious voyage would elevated him—a former pig-farmer who had grown rich trading in animal fat—above the level of his fellow citizens!

That was an example of the first point at issue: Farenheit's vainglorious character, which helped to blind him, not merely with respect to Sharp's intellectual merits—the man was a scientist, after all, and audacious—but also his probity and good faith.

Secondly, as a practical man, Farenheit envisaged the voyage as being bound to bring him an ample harvest of dollars; dazzled by Sharp's wonderful promises, he had not hesitated to put the greater part of his fortune into the business, assuming that the Moon's gold and diamond mines would multiply the capital pledged by him and his shareholders 100 times over.

Finally, for some years, he had been a member of a New York circle whose mere title—the Eccentric Club—is self-explanatory. To be accepted as a member of that club, it was necessary to be credited with one of those eccentricities that make a man stand out from the banality of life, of one those traits thanks to which people point to you in the New York streets and say: "He's an original!" In France, people say: "He's a madman!" But that is not all that is required for admission to the circle; the principal preoccupation of members of the Eccentric Club, once admitted, was to be nominated as members of the committee, secretary, vice-president or president. Needless to say, each of these honorific functions could only be acquired by one's own efforts—which is to say, by heaping eccentricity upon eccentricity, madness upon madness.

Now, Jonathan Farenheit had a dream, which was to advertise himself by some action so dramatic that all the members of the Eccentric Club would be constrained to vote him in, by unanimous acclamation, as their president. Unfortunately, he was not alone in being gripped by that ambition and, in spite of all his efforts, whenever the annual elections were held, he saw a fellow member elevated above him to the chair that he coveted so ardently. And then, all of a sudden, when he was beginning to despair, he came across Fedor Sharp, with his vertiginous project of a lunar voyage. He surely had his presidency now! What member of the Eccentric Club would be able to rival him on his return from an excursion of 96,000 leagues through space?

We have now said enough for the reader to understand how the worthy American had deceived himself, until the last moment, with regard to the true sentiments of the former permanent secretary of the St. Petersburg Academy of Sciences. If he had been a different man—if he had kept his eyes open and his ears pricked—he would have glimpsed certain enigmatic smiles and ambiguous phrases that would have awakened his suspicions.

Throughout the time spent on Malpelo Island putting the plans stolen from Mikhail Ossipoff into effect, Fedor Sharp had had frequent conferences with his two assistants, Votiguin and Ladislas Rotterdack. What were they saying? It would have been rather difficult to find out, Sharp having taken the precaution of setting up his tent in an isolated and very exposed spot, so that no indiscreet person would be able to prowl around in the vicinity. But if Farenheit had had ears keen enough to hear what these three men were whispering in low voices, he would have been obliged greatly to revise his opinion of the ex-permanent secretary of the Academy of Sciences.

Sharp, in fact, was not at all concerned with the American, now that, thanks to him and the dollars of the society of which Farenheit was president, he had been able to put Mikhail Ossipoff's great project into execution—a project from which he expected to obtain honor and profit. Yes, profit—for if Fedor Sharp loved science, he loved wealth no less, and his lunar excursion, while permitting him to cover himself with glory, would also permit him to fill his pockets. Moreover, what he plotted so secretly with his two acolytes was also directed to the purpose of ridding himself of the inconvenient encumbrance of Jonathan Farenheit.

Finally, the day of departure arrived. Sharp gathered all the personnel around him and, in a voice that he strove to render emotional, made the following speech: "My dear friends—ah, yes, permit me to give that title to all of you, engineers, overseers, workmen, who have assisted me with so much courage and effort to bring my audacious projects to fruition—my dear friends, thanks to you, we have now arrived at the decisive moment, ready to profit from the most favorable instant to launch ourselves toward the Moon. Permit me, before the emotional moment of the departure, to thank you…"

At this point, Jonathan Farenheit cut in. "And me," he said, in a vibrant tone, "I thank you too, in the name of the Lunar Mining Company, and in the name of the American government, which takes pride in the audacious attempt by one of its members…" He interrupted himself and turned round; voices whispering behind him had attracted his attention. It was Sharp and his friends, exchanging a few words.

"That's understood?" asked the Russian, in conclusion.

"Agreed," replied the others.

The ex-secretary of the Academy of Sciences came forward then, and called for silence with a gesture of his hand.

"At 8:35 p.m.," he said, "the charges of selenite will be ignited, and the projectile in which in which the honorable gentleman Jonathan Farenheit, my friend Voriguin and I will take our places, will take flight for the planetary regions. I therefore request that you re-embark without delay and set out to sea to avoid the terrible shock that the abrupt deflagration of the selenite will cause." He stopped talking.

A formidable cheer escaped the throats of all the workmen; then they filed in front of the voyagers and shook them by the hand. Afterwards, the embarkation process began. The process threatened to last a long time, for the ship had been obliged to anchor some way out to sea for fear of the subsurface rocks that surrounded the island; they had to transport the men to the vessel by means of two rowing-boats.

"But how will the selenite be ignited?" Farenheit suddenly asked.

"My excellent friend Ladislas Rotterdack," Fedor Sharp replied, tranquilly, "will be responsible for starting, at the appropriate moment, the clockwork mechanism that regulates the electric current thanks to which, at a precise second, the cannon's charges will ignite." He turned to Rotterdack and, taking out his chronometer, said: "What time do you have, my friend?"

The other consulted his watch. "7:15 p.m.," he said.

"You're 37 seconds fast, my dear friend," said Sharp, in a perfectly natural tone. "Synchronize your watch with mine, for it's important not to advance the moment of departure by a second." As he spoke, an imperceptible smile played upon his lips. "There," he said. "We have to remain here for a further one hour, 20 minutes and 47 seconds. If you wish, my dear Voriguin, we can take advantage of that respite to carry out one last inspection of the shell's equipment."

Unsuspectingly, Jonathan Farenheit helped the two men to descend, with the aid of a skip, into the depths of the enormous engine; then he busied himself hurrying along the embarkation of the personnel.

Half an hour went by; about 50 workmen still remained on the shore, waiting to climb into the row-boats, when an immense column of fire suddenly sprang from the ground, shaking the island to its foundations, splitting the ground and upsetting the waves. Advancing the fixed departure-time by half an hour, Ladislas Rotterdack had just triggered the mine, launching Fedor Sharp and Voriguin into space by themselves.

The latter pair had successfully resisted the formidable recoil of the departure and the first days of the journey had been effected in the best possible conditions. It was only on the fourth day, on measuring the angular distance between the Earth and its satellite, that Sharp frowned and strangled an oath in his throat.

The shell's velocity was slowing in an alarming fashion.

Very pale, Voriguin murmured: "As long as we get past the neutral point."

The other nodded his head. "We'll certainly get as far as that," he muttered. "At least, I hope so..."

"Perhaps it's because we left early," Voriguin stammered, reproachfully.

"Imbecile!" replied Fedor Sharp. "Do you think I'd so anything so stupid? No, we left at the precise second—but to fool that idiot Farenheit, Ladilas and I had deliberately set our watches back half by an hour."

"After all..." murmured Voriguin, in a resigned tone.

All night, the two men were up and about, checking the deceleration of the shell at hourly intervals. Then, Sharp suddenly uttered a cry of terror. The projectile was motionless at the boundary where the Earth's zone of attraction was counterbalanced by the Moon's.

"Destiny's thunder!" he groaned. "We've stopped." And he let himself fall on to the seat that ran around the vehicle, his features distraught, his eyes haggard, his teeth clenched and his fingernails tearing the upholstery petulantly.

"We're doomed! Doomed!" Voriguin repeated, like some mournful echo. After a few seconds, he fixed his companion with a mad stare and added, in a hoarse voice: "We have no chance of being rescued from here, have we?"

Fedor Sharp replied, in a dejected tone: "We're condemned to remain here eternally, fixed at this point...unless..."

"Unless...?" Voriguin repeated, with a glimmer of hope.

"Unless," Sharp continued, "some foreign influence draws us backwards or forwards from this accursed line of attraction."

"In that case," the other stammered, "we're irredeemably doomed."

A week went by, then another week, and then an entire month without anything happening to modify the situation. From the first day, they had been obliged to lash all the furniture firmly to the floor because it was displaced by the slightest impulsion, the shell no longer having any up or down, by virtue of the complete suppression of gravity. They had to abstain from all excessively violent movements themselves, to avoid unpleasant shocks.

Voriguin, with nothing to do and completely demoralized, spent his time drinking, seeking in drunkenness to forget the terrible death that awaited him. As for Fedor Sharp, with his eye riveted to his telescope, he never ceased searching space in the absurd hope of perceiving some providential cause capable of drawing him out of his eternal immobility. Every day he went to the reservoir of air to calculate how much longer he and his companion still had to live—and more than once, having observed that the provision was rapidly running out, he had darted sharp glances in the direction of the hammock on which Voriguin was snoring peacefully, sleeping off his intoxication. A rictus twisted his thin lips, while his hand clenched in a gesture of strangulation. Voriguin's death would have doubled the lifespan remaining to Fedor Sharp.

"Ah, that wretch Ossipoff!" the ex-permanent secretary of the Academy of Sciences cried one ay, after having scanned the sidereal desert for hours. "Who would have thought that his calculations were false, the propulsive force of his selenite insufficient and his steel fragile?" Striking his fist hard on the table on which lay the calculations he had gone over for the 100th time the day before, he added: "Ah, if not for his powder and his cannon..." The villain gave no thought to the fact that he had only taken possession of that powder and cannon by means of theft.

The following morning he was lying in his hammock, with his eyes closed but not asleep—since he had been imprisoned in the vehicle he had been unable to sleep—when he heard his companion get up.

As was his habit, Voriguin had gone to bed the previous evening half-drunk and Sharp had been obliged to tie him down, following the habit he had acquired when he saw him in that state and for fear of some violence. Astonished that he had been able to fee himself from his bonds, when he usually asked to be untied, the scientist had a presentiment that something abnormal was happening. He turned his head slightly and saw through his lowered eyelashes that Voriguin was, indeed, leaning over the edge of his hammock, examining him intently.

The other remained motionless for a moment; then a hideous smile spread his lips, while a wild gleam came into his eyes. "He's asleep," he murmured. "So much the better...it'll be over quicker." One after the other, he put his legs out of the hammock, placing his feet on the floor. A slight creak made him shiver and he resumed his immobility, his eyes still fixed on Sharp.

The latter continued to simulate sleep.

Reassured, Voriguin took a few steps across the room, but in a direction opposite to that in which the Russian was located, heading for the only item of furniture, which served simultaneously as a bookcase and a storage-unit for instruments and tools. He bent over, searched silently in a cabinet, straightened up and turned round, then marched straight toward Sharp's hammock.

By the light of the lamp that he left on all night to serve as a night-light, Sharp saw a glint of steel in his companion's hand, and a convulsive shudder shook his limbs. The idea that he had had several times, of killing his companion, Voriguin was about to put into execution; he was armed with an enormous ice-pick and intended to stab him in the chest with one well-directed blow.

Sharp sat up abruptly and said, in a terrible voice: "What do you want?"

Surprised to find the man that he had intended to kill in his sleep, without a struggle, was awake, the other took a step back. Then, with a savage snigger, he replied: "What do I want? That's a joke! I want to kill you, of course!"

"What have I done?" asked Sharp.

"You brought me here."

"Is it my fault if that accursed Ossipoff's plans weren't accurate?"

Voriguin shrugged his shoulders. "When one steals," he growled, "one steals intelligently."

"But I'm just as badly off as you are."

"What do I care? It's not to avenge myself, but to live that I'm getting rid of you...the air that you breathe you steal from me." And he came forward, recklessly.

Fedor Sharp had quit his bed and, seizing a stool, had assumed a defensive pose, determined to fight to the last. Immobile, the two adversaries silently looked one another up and down. "To live!" Fedor Sharp finally exclaimed, in a pitying voice. "By how many days, then, do you hope that my death might prolong your life?"

"By as many days as you would live yourself."

"It would advance, rather than delay, your death by several weeks!"

Voriguin laughed. "It would advance your own so much that you're ready to defend your skin. When one has principles, one applies them...since you claim that it doesn't matter whether one dies a few days sooner or later, let yourself be killed without resistance."

This reasoning was logical, and Sharp remained silent for a few moments, with his head bowed, not knowing what to say in response.

"Come on," said the other, in a dull voice. "Let's get on with it. I've already told you that we're one too many. You're the oldest—give way to me voluntarily. If not..." He came forward, his arm raised.

The Russian went very pale. "Listen," he said, finally. "Give me till the end of the day."

Voriguin shrugged his shoulders. "What good would that do?" he said. "You'll use up a few more cubic meters of air needlessly...better to finish it now."

Suddenly, an idea occurred to Sharp. "Perhaps," he murmured, "we really might be able to save ourselves."

An expression of incredulity appeared on Voriguin's face. "Go on, then," he said. "What makes you think that?"

"My calculations and my observations."

"Your observations?" Voriguin sniggered. "What observations?"

"The ones I made last night. I seemed to perceive a celestial body, with the aid of my telescope, a few 1000 leagues away, that might well be capable of modifying our situation."

"You're lying. You'd have woken me up to tell me news like that."

"You were so drunk that it wasn't worth the trouble to try."

Voriguin's lips pursed with profound thought; he was wondering how much credence to lend his companion's words. It seemed very improbable to him—but if it were true...

He watched Fedor Sharp from the corner of his eye, trying to read his thoughts in his face.

Sharp remained impassive, however, looking at his companion from beneath his spectacles, gladly noticing traces of the indecision in which the other was languishing. If Voriguin believed his lie—for he had just lied brazenly, since he had spent the night in his hammock—he would want to see it for himself and he would go up to the makeshift observatory built into the top of the shell. However little time he stayed there, it would be enough to permit Sharp to take an excellent pair of revolvers from the cupboard drawer, which would put him in the position of having all the advantages on his side, if violent conflict became inevitable.

Unfortunately, Voriguin seemed to read the wretch's thought. After remaining motionless and silent for a few moments, he shook his head in a fashion that clearly meant: "Furthermore, what am I risking?" Then he went straight to the drawer, took the revolvers, calmly put them in his pockets, and headed for the ladder that led to the upper floor.

Fedor Sharp's chagrin was so violent that he could not hide it; a livid pallor overwhelmed his features. Seeing that, his assistant burst out laughing. "Hey!" he said, in a jeering tone. "So you wanted to blow someone's brains out, did you, old man? Fortunately, someone still has his head screwed on." Then, laughing in Sharp's face again, he slowly went up the steps.

The Russian sensed that he was doomed. In a few moments, Voriguin would come back down, furious at having been tricked, and would lodge a bullet in his chest. The strength ebbed out of him then, and he remained inert, waiting for the mortal blow.

Suddenly, there was a loud exclamation overhead: a cry of joy and triumph. Almost immediately, the door of the little observatory opened noisily, giving passage to Voriguin, who hurtled down the steps and came to throw himself into Fedor Sharp's arms.

"What's the matter?" cried the latter, straightening up again. "Are you mad?"

"Saved!" stammered Voriguin, so emotional that he was hardly able to speak. "We're saved!"

Sharp was very pale. Mechanically, as if he did not understand the word's meaning, he repeated: "Saved? Saved?"

His accomplice was laughing, singing and gesticulating like a madman. Sharp seized him by the arm and held him still for a moment. "Answer me!" he cried. "What's happened, and why are you claiming that we're saved?"

But Voriguin's joy was too powerful; he sank into a seat, babbling: "Up there…the telescope…an object coming towards us…" And he fainted.

Scarcely believing his ears, Sharp raced up into the nose-cone, but he was trembling so much that it took him a few minutes to adjust the ocular lens. Finally, he succeeded, and he too released a piercing exclamation. Out there in space, an object was advancing at considerable speed. His lie had, therefore, turned out to be true, and chance had sent him a savior.

Suddenly, though, his brows furrowed, his mouth twisted into a grimace of fury and an oath escaped his lips. "Him!" he groaned. "Him again! Always him!" Drunk with rage, he waved his clenched fist in the direction of Mikhail Ossipoff's vehicle.

The joy of being saved, however, swelled his heart, along with the hope that he would now be able to continue on his route and land on the lunar shore. He would, it is true, find himself face to face with his enemy—but that enemy would get him out of the critical situation in which he was languishing and drag him in his wake. "Voriguin!" he cried. "Voriguin!"

The assistant was just coming to; hearing the call, he emerged entirely from his torpor and rejoined Fedor Sharp. "Do you know what that is?" the latter asked.

The other opened his eyes wide at this question. "Good God!" he said. "How should I know? It's doubtless some aerolith…"

Sharp shook his head.

"A comet, perhaps?"

"No," said the Russian, in a hoarse voice strangled by choler. "No, it's Mikhail Ossipoff."

At that name, which he had always heard pronounced as that of a mortal enemy, Voriguin took a step backwards. "Mikhail Ossipoff!" he exclaimed. "I don't understand."

"The swine has found a means to escape, and there he is—he too is attempting to reach the Moon."

Voriguin shuddered and murmured: "Will he get there?"

The Russian shrugged his shoulders furiously. "No doubt," he said. "Or at least, there's every indication of it." He put his eye to the ocular lens of the telescope again. "His velocity is sufficient to carry him across the line of equal attraction," he continued. "He'll run aground…"

"What about us?" asked Voriguin, in a tremulous voice.

"He'll drag us along with him."

Voriguin threw his cap in the air. "Hurrah!" he cried. "Hurrah for Mikhail Ossipoff!"

Fedor Sharp's face darkened. "Yes," he growled. "But what will happen afterwards?"

"Bah!" Voriguin retorted. "Aren't there two of us?" He underlined the sentence with a menacing gesture.

"Hmm," thought the Russian. "Ossipoff won't have set off alone."

For an hour, the two projectiles sailed in convoy, scarcely a few kilometers apart. The ex-permanent secretary of the Academy of Sciences never ceased using the telescope to study the vehicle in which his former colleague and his friends were enclosed. He saw the astonished and curious faces of Gontran de Flammermont, Fricoulet and Selena appear in succession at the portholes. "So they've got an entire crew over there, have they?" he muttered—and he racked his brains to try to figure out what explosive had been powerful enough to launch into space, to such a distance from the Earth, a weight similar to that of the vehicle and its passengers.

Suddenly, though, he pushed his telescope away, crying out in a strangled voice: "Farenheit!"

Voriguin suddenly went pale and his trembling lips repeated the name. "Farenheit?"

"Yes," growled Fedor Sharp. "The accursed American is with them."

"But that's impossible," Voriguin stammered. "You must be mistaken. How do you imagine that the unfortunate Yankee could have escaped? He must have perished with the others."

Sharp stamped his foot impatiently and shoved his companion toward the telescope. "See for yourself," he growled.

Voriguin looked, and he too perceived the menacing face of Jonathan Farenheit glued to the glass of the porthole; he could even make out the American's muscular fist, aimed in their direction. He stepped back and gazed at Fedor Sharp with an expression in which genuine fear could be read. "That man is the Devil," he murmured. "If he gets his hands on us, we're doomed…inasmuch as there's a whole band over there ready to lend him a hand to satisfy his vengeance."

Fedor Sharp made no reply, shaking his head.

"Ah!" groaned the other. "I'd have preferred to choose my own way of dying, if I could…while that American's capable of lynching us."

"You've got the revolvers on you," the Russian replied, dully. "If you want to kill yourself, feel free."

"On the other hand," Voriguin continued, "perhaps their shell won't have enough force to draw us out from here and drag us to the Moon."

"That's already done," Sharp retorted.

Voriguin looked at him fearfully. "Already done!" he stammered.

"Yes," the Russian replied. We're no longer motionless. We're now within the zone on lunar attraction. We're falling." And he remained angrily crouched over his telescope, while Voriguin, so fearful was he of the American, hoped that he might break his back in the fall.

Chapter XIII
A bird's-eye view of the Moon

While Fedor Sharp and his companion, prey to an anguish justly deserved by their infamy, await events tremulously, Mikhail Ossipoff and his friends were no more reassured. Their vehicle's encounter with Sharp's cannonball could have fatal consequences for them. If they deviated from their route even slightly, they might miss their intended target—and then, launched into space, what would become of them?

Overwhelmed. Ossipoff was slumped on the divan, supporting Selena's limp head on his shoulder. Gontran de Flammermont could not tear himself away from the porthole, thinking of the tremendous fall in which the shell might, at any moment, be crushed. Jonathan Farenheit was cursing the freak of chance that had brought him face to face with the traitor and thief without his being able to avenge himself as he deserved before dying.

Only Fricoulet had conserved his self-composure. He had not budged from the observatory, where his eye was glued to the telescope, looking into space. Suddenly, he fell like a bomb into his companions' midst. "Our vehicle is swinging around!" he cried.

Gontran started. "Are we going to stand on our heads?" he murmured.

His friend was the only one who heard this aside, which he treated as a joke.

"Which is to say," he replied, "That we shall have our feet where out heads were—in a word, the nose-cone our shell, which was pointing at the Moon, will be pointing at the Earth in a few minutes' time."

Farenheit moaned with joy. "In that case," he said, "I'll be able to catch up with him."

"How?"

"If we fall on to the surface of the Moon, of course."

Fricoulet raised his eyebrows "Did I say that?" he asked.

"It seems logical to me."

"It may seem logical to you, but it's still doubtful."

Gontran shuddered. "Then...?" he prompted.

"Then...how do I know? We're going to sail around the Moon, veering around its disk. In that case, God alone knows what awaits us."

"Let's entrust ourselves to God, then," murmured Selena. At the same time she looked at Gontran with an expression full of tenderness.

"In any case," Fricoulet added, cheerfully, "whatever happens, we'll be the first to enjoy the spectacle...there's always a silver lining."

Now that the engineer had told them about it, the voyagers were not long delayed in perceiving the rotational movement accomplished by the vehicle. It

189

pivoted gently on its axis, gradually turning its inferior part—the heavier part—toward the Moon. The fall was beginning, but obliquely, as Fricoulet had foreseen and with almost imperceptible force.

That force did not take long to increase, however.

"We're falling 10,000 leagues," murmured the young engineer.

Ossipoff had risen to his feet to measure the distance from the lunar surface again; he estimated it at 45,000 kilometers. Now, with the aid of the telescope's strongest ocular lens—which reduced that distance to 150 kilometers, about 40 leagues—they could easily make out the configuration of that contorted surface. The entire disk appeared, full lit by the Sun's rays and the entranced Ossipoff perceived a host of details that it was impossible to detect from Earth, even with the most powerful optical instruments.

There was, however, still nothing to confirm the presence of living beings on the surface of that stony world; there was nothing but arid rocks, gaping craters, sharp crags, muddled up in an exceedingly complicated orographic network, brightened by a raw and uniform light. If the shell had fallen vertically upon the surface of the Moon, it would have landed not far from the North Pole, but what velocity it retained, partly neutralizing the lunar attraction, was curving it around the entire visible hemisphere and steering it to the south-west of the satellite—whose immense disk was filling the sky, reflecting an intense light.

"We might close the portholes to permit Mademoiselle Selena to sleep for a while," Fricoulet proposed.

"Me, sleep!" cried the young woman. "Not before we get there!"

"Remember, Mademoiselle," the engineer persisted, "that it will take 48 hours, at least."

"Yes, darling," Ossipoff said, in his turn. "The gentleman is right. We ought to get a little rest, in order to be ready to weather the new fatigues that await us. Anyway, there's no shame in sleeping. Look!" And he pointed at Farenheit, who, overwhelmed by fatigue, was snoring peacefully, lying on the divan. Fury taxes strength as heavily as the most violent exercise, and in the 24 hours since he had first spotted his enemy Fedor Sharp, the American had not calmed down. Besides, the panorama of lunar craters did not interest him enough for him to admire it for 48 hours on the trot.

At that moment, the vehicle was passing over the Sea of Humboldt, the Lake of Dreams and the Lake of Death,[55] which, seen from that height, formed greenish patches similar to forests seen from a great distance. Soon, they were directly over the Sea of Serenity.

---

[55] Graffigny gives these names in French; I have chosen to render them straightforwardly into English because a few of the more familiar Latin names are deliberately introduced into the text very shortly, in a calculatedly quirky fashion whose effect would be destroyed if I used the Latin terms here.

Ossipoff, enraptured, could not tear himself away from the contemplation of this world, all of whose mysteries were gradually unveiling themselves to him. "See," he said to his companions, "what an uneven face the Selenian world presents...you recognize, don't you, my dear Gontran, those chains of immense mountains that you can see on your right, which seem to be several kilometers high—they're the Apennines, the Carpathians and the Caucasus." After a pause, the astronomer murmured, as if to himself: "Ah! There's the Sea of Tears, the Marsh of Mists, the Marsh of Putrefaction..."

Gontran jogged Fricoulet's elbow. "Seas?" he whispered in his hear. "Where does he see these seas?"

The young engineer replied in a whisper. "In selenographic terms, 'seas' are what those dark patches are called, whose nature has not yet been determined, and which resemble dry plains."

"There you are," grumbled the Comte, shaking his head. "A bizarre appellation, which seems to me to be totally lacking in logic."

"Thus," Fricoulet went on, "the oval patch that you perceive over there, on the left-hand edge of the disk, is the Sea of Crises."

"*Mare Crisium*, in Molière's Latin," joked Gontran.[56]

"Just so—and beside it, the Marsh of Sleep."

"*Palus Somniorum*."

"Again, just so."

"So called," Gontran added, "because its inhabitants sleep perpetually."

"Its inhabitants!" said the engineer. "If there are any..."

For several hours, the vehicle continued its oblique trajectory towards the Moon in this fashion, permitting the voyagers to study the slightest features of the uneven ground quite easily.

"How far away are we now?" Fricoulet asked.

"About 8000 leagues," Ossipoff replied.

"That's odd," said Gontran. "We seem to be slowing down."

"On the contrary—at present we're traveling, or rather falling, with a velocity of no less than 500 meters a second—which is 30 kilometers a minute."

"Hold on," Gontran suddenly said. "I'm curious to see what the Earth looks like at this distance." He climbed the steps of the little stairway and uncovered the porthole pierced in the nose-cone of the shell.

He uttered a cry of surprise. Lost in the solar glare, the Earth seemed no more than an increasingly slender crescent of exceedingly small dimension. "And that's my native planet!" murmured the young Comte, disdainfully shrug-

---

[56] "Molière's Latin" is Latin—or nonsense imitative of Latin—used for the purposes of pretension. It derives from a famous speech in *Le Médecin malgré lui*, in which the fake doctor blinds his client with a nonsensical speech seasoned with every Latin phrase he knows.

ging his shoulders. As he came back down he asked: "How far from the Earth are we now?"

Fricoulet looked at him in amazement. "Didn't you hear just now that we're 8000 leagues from the Moon?"

"Perfectly."

"Well, 90,000 minus 8000 is 82,000—it's as simple as that."

"Indeed," retorted Gontran, slightly vexed, "but it's necessary to think of it." Then his thoughts abruptly veered in another direction. "But why is it," he said, "that the Earth, seen from here, appears more voluminous to me than the Moon seen from the Earth's surface?"

Fricoulet looked at Gontran in terror, but the old man, absorbed in his contemplation, had not heard. "Don't you love Selena, then, my unfortunate friend?" the engineer murmured, rapidly drawing Gontran to the far end of the room."

The young man was so astounded by this question that he did not reply immediately. Finally, he stammered: "Are you mad?"

"It's you who ought to be asked that question," retorted Fricoulet. "You still love your fiancée and you're doing everything possible not to marry her!"

"I don't understand," Gontran stammered.

"Weren't you just astonished that, at this equal distance, the Earth seems larger than the Moon?"

"So what?"

"Don't you know, then—or, rather, shouldn't you know—that the Moon is 49 times smaller by volume than the planet around which it gravitates…?"

"…In 28 and a half days," Gontran added. "That's true—I recall that now."

Fricoulet put his hand on his friend's shoulder to attract his attention. "Do you also recall," he went on, "that the density of the materials comprising the lunar world is considerably less than that of terrestrial rock; it's only six tenths. That means that the Selenian globe weighs no more than a sphere of water of the same diameter; surface gravity there is extremely feeble—the weakest observed on all the planetary surfaces in the Solar System. It's six times less than the Earth's…"

The young engineer smiled at the seriousness with which Flammermont was listening to him. "Well," he asked, "what do you say to that?"

"I'm doing my best."

"You understand, don't you," Fricoulet added, amicably, "that if I tell you all these details, it's not to show off my scientific knowledge, but quite simply to enable you to reply in a fairly satisfactory fashion when your future father-in-law subjects to you an oral examination?"

The Comte thanked his friend by squeezing his hand firmly.

Then, after a pause, Fricoulet sighed and added: "You know, I'm doing this against my will. I even think I'm committing a crime, betraying our friendship, for I'm contributing to your unhappiness by smoothing the route that will lead you to marriage."

Gontran shrugged his shoulders and laughed. "You great fool!" he said. "Still the same."

"Always," Fricoulet muttered. He turned on his heel, bad-temperedly, and put his face to the porthole to his left, through which he could see the whole lunar panorama.

At that moment, the vehicle was passing directly over the Sea of Vapors, scarcely 20,000 kilometers from the lunar surface, which it was rapidly approaching. It passed over the Circus of Triesnecker and thus arrived over the crater Pallas, whose wrinkled and confused surface stood out with rigorous clarity.

Gontran had come to stand beside his friend, and was absorbed by the spectacle of that fantastic magic lantern. "But it seems to me," he murmured, "that all these mountains are prodigiously high for the world that supports them. I don't believe that there are peaks as monstrous on Earth, even though it's 49 times as voluminous."

"This time," Fricoulet relied, "you're right. They all measure several kilometers in height, and if we were arriving here during one of the phases if the Moon, you'd be able to judge their dimensions even better—for then, lit from the side by the Sun, they'd be projecting dark shadows far over the ground, magnified by their crags and their jagged crests.

Momentarily, the Comte was no longer listening; he was curiously examining a sparkling dot that had appeared in the center of an immense white plain more than 300 leagues wide in the east of the Moon.

"The Circus of Aristarchus," said Fricoulet. "One of the most beautiful specimens of Selenian orography. A few 100 kilometers to the north you can make out its elder brother, Mount Kepler, similarly situated at the center of a whitish plain that advances like a promontory into the Ocean of Tempests.

Gontran stared, mute with astonishment.

"But these mountains," the engineer went on, "are nothing compared with certain others, one of which is nearer to us, and which you see to the north of the Carpathian mountain chain; it's the Circus of Copernicus, which measures no less than 160 kilometers in diameter—almost as large as the surface of Bohemia enclosed in he Carpathian Mountains of Europe."

"I can see it," Flammermont said, finally. "The volcanic circle you're talking about.[57] But I can see two other craters at the foot of Copernicus, which also seem to be enormous."

---

[57] Graffigny and his characters are, of course, assuming that the Moon's craters are volcanic rather than impact craters—an assumption that colors much of their subsequent discussions of the surface features of the satellite.

"Merely an effect of perspective," Fricoulet retorted. "Mounts Stadius and Eratosthenes are much more limited in dimension."

"Are all these mountains, then," said Gontran, "named after philosophers and astronomers?"

Fricoulet laughed. "If you'd read the work of your namesake, the celebrated Flammermont of *Les Continents célestes*, more attentively, you'd know that he likens the Moon to an astronomers' cemetery. 'It's there,' he says, 'that they are buried; when they have quit the Earth, their names are inscribed on the lunar terrain like so many epitaphs.' I've remembered the sentence, which seemed amusing."

At that moment, Ossipoff's head appeared at the top of the ladder leading to the upper part of the shell. "Victory!" cried the aged scientist. "Our speed in increasing...in three hours we'll be flying over Tycho."

"Tycho," cried Fricoulet, in astonishment.

"Yes, Tycho," the old man repeated. "What's extraordinary about that?"

"It's just that the route we're following," the young engineer replied, "takes us over the Seas of Clouds and Humors, not in the direction of Tycho."

Ossipoff relied, a trifle sharply: "You must be mistaken, Monsieur, for I've just this instant realized that our route is veering along the arc of a circle and that we're presently heading due south. An hour ago, we passed directly over the center of the lunar disk, in the middle of the Central Gulf and within sight of the crater Herschel; now we're passing between Guericke and Ptolemy and along two circuses joined by their circular ramparts, Alphonse and Arzachel."

While speaking, the old man had slowly come down the steps and handed Fricoulet a pair of binoculars. "Anyway, see for yourself."

While the engineer studied he configuration of the surface, Ossipoff murmured in Gontran's ear: "Always the same...that boy gets on my nerves, with his scientific pretensions."

At that moment, Fricoulet declared, in a humbled tone: "You're right, Monsieur Ossipoff, "We're following an unknown trajectory, and we're about to describe the entire arc of a circle around the Moon, which will lead us God knows where."

"Surely it will lead us to the Moon," said Gontran.

Fricoulet shrugged his shoulders.

"Monsieur de Flammermont is right," the old scientist replied, dryly. And he added, in a slightly disdainful tone: "Have you calculated the angle of our fall?"

"No, I confess."

"Well, you were wrong to talk without having done so—for you would have established, like me, that we are getting closer and closer to the lunar surface." He had pronounced these words in a scathing fashion that brought a slight blush to Fricoulet's cheeks.

"What does that prove?" the latter asked, impatiently.

Ossipoff looked at him for a moment in bewilderment, then said: "What? You ask what that proves? Simply that we can't turn eternally around the satellite, and that a moment will inevitably arrive when we'll impact with the ground. For example, at the North Pole there are two very high mountain peaks, Doerfel and Leibnitz, which measure no less than 7610 meters in elevation—who knows whether we'll run into them? For my part, I can affirm that we'll land not far from the pole."

"I expect so," replied the engineer, frostily, "but I'm fearful, all the same."

Ossipoff folded his arms. "For what reason, if you please?" he asked, ironically.

"First, because instead of impacting the ground vertically with the bottom of our vehicle, which is furnished with tampons and powerful springs to absorb the force of the shock, we'll hit the mountains side-on, so that the shock will be formidable...then, because we'll be more than seven kilometers high on an icy crater, plunging into the void..."

"It's true," said Gontran in his turn, "that if a native of the Moon were to disembark on the summit of Mont Blanc or Cotopaxi, he wouldn't actually have reached the ground. It'll be the same for us."

"Assuredly," Fricoulet went on. "And it's for that reason, my dear Monsieur Ossipoff, that I hope that your calculations are false, and that we won't end up perched on the summit of Mount Doerfel."

The astronomer clicked his tongue—which, in him, was always a sign of irritation. Then, without saying a word, he climbed the steps and shut himself up in his laboratory.

"He's not happy," murmured Gontran.

"After all," the engineer retorted, "am I obliged always to say the same as him? If he doesn't like contradiction, let him live alone. He annoys me, sometimes..." While grumbling, he resumed his place at the porthole.

The vehicle passed over the craters Walter and Bulialdus; the ground became bumpier and more uneven than ever; long pale streaks extended for hundreds of kilometers, sometimes at the level of the plains, sometimes at the height of the most elevated peaks.

"What are those?" Flammermont asked.

"They're *striae*."

"And what are *striae*?"

"You can judge for yourself far better than terrestrial astronomers can from their observatories 90,000 leagues away."

Gontran nodded his head. "But what's your opinion?" he persisted. "You know very well that I don't know anything. Are they resolidified lava-flows? Are they walls built by the Selenites? You must have an opinion."

"My word," retorted the engineer. "The more I look the more convinced I am of my initial supposition that they're traces of an earthquake."

Gontran smiled and replied: "A moonquake, you mean."

Fricoulet shrugged his shoulders. "A moonquake, if you wish. It must have occurred when the world was still in a viscous state…as it cooled, the crust reformed, conserving traces of the frightful cataclysm on its surface."

"A world that demolishes itself and sticks itself back together!" said Gontran, in jest. "In truth, that's something out of the ordinary. The Selenites must have been terrified by seeing their globe shattered, of course."

Fricoulet looked at his friend to see whether he was talking seriously, but was reassured by the sight of his smile. "The Selenites!" he said, shaking his head. "There probably weren't any at that time…otherwise they'd all have perished in the catastrophe."

At that moment the little door to the observatory opened, and Ossipoff shouted to his companions: "Tycho!" Then his head disappeared.

"Ten minute stop—buffet available!" the engineer murmured, comically. And he took up a position at the window, where Gontran had already preceded him, his eyes growing wide at the sight of the panorama, sublime in its strangeness, that unfolded scarcely 1000 kilometers beneath the projectile.

In the middle of the lumpy ground, dazzling with an intense brightness that the eternal ice with which its sides were covered reflected into space, Tycho, the most monstrous of lunar mountains, loomed up hugely and majestically. At its center, in a vast cavity measuring no less than eight-seven kilometers in diameter, rose a group of mountains, the highest of which rose to 1500 kilometers above the bottom. The mountain that formed the annular ramparts appeared to have an elevation of nearly 5000 kilometers, in the east as in the west. Forming an immense aureole around the crater, luminous streaks extended to all points of the horizon, some of them more than 1000 kilometers long.

"One might think that it was a silver octopus whose tentacles are embracing the lunar world," murmured Gontran, emotion tightening his throat.

Even the skeptical Fricoulet, overwhelmed by admiration, remained mute, unable to remove his eyes from the sublime spectacle.

"Well," cried Ossipoff, in a triumphant voice, appearing at the top of the staircase, "What did I tell you? Do you see that we're veering westwards, while gradually getting lower? Before long, we'll see the craters Clavius, Logomontanus, Maginus, Fabricius, Maurolycus…"

Et ceterus, thought Flammermont.

The scientist continued: "Finally, we'll pass over the summit of Mount Doerfel, at an altitude of a few kilometers."

"But if we pass over everything you mention," Gontran pout in, "we'll end up falling…"

"On the invisible part of the Moon!" said Ossipoff, completing the young Comte's sentence—fortunately for him, since he would certainly have said something stupid. "Yes, exactly, my young friend."

Flammermont bit his lips and remained silent.

At that moment, Jonathan Farenheit woke up. "Where are we?" he murmured, in the initial drowsiness of awakening.

"At Tycho station, my dear sir," Gontran replied. "Perhaps you'd like to get off the train to stretch your legs."

The American stood up and stretched his limbs lazily, making his joints crack. "Ah, by God!" he mumbled, "I wouldn't say no, for in the five days I've been shut up in here I'd begun to fear that my joints would lose their lubrication." Simulating the landing of a mighty punch on an invisible opponent, he added: "I'll need all my strength, though, to flatten that bandit Sharp."

"That's right!" cried Gontran. "What's become of him? While admiring the countryside, we've forgotten about him and his cannonball." He ran to put his face to the porthole on the right and searched the space where Fedor Sharp's projectile had been. "It's no longer there!" he exclaimed.

A forceful oath answered him, and Jonathan Farenheit ran to his side. "Oh, the bandit!" he cried. "He's scared of me and he's run away!" He had pronounced these words in the heat of anger, without considering the impossibility of flight in Sharp's situation. The truth was, however, that the cannonball had disappeared.

Ossipoff searched space carefully with his most powerful telescope. There was nothing—nothing but the sidereal desert pricked by the brilliant points of the stars in spite of the solar light illuminating the sky. The vehicle, at that moment, was crossing the Austral Sea; it was about 6 a.m.

As Gontran was about to ask the old scientist for an explanation of this strange disappearance, an intense, absolute darkness enveloped them. As if a curtain had been drawn, night succeeded day and the densest shadow instantaneously replaced, without any transition, the powerful and dazzling solar radiation.

At the cries of astonishment, amazement—and even terror—that Gontran and Farenheit emitted, Selena awoke. Thinking that something terrible had happened, she ran to her father and tremulously wrapped her arms around him.

"What's happened?" Fricoulet finally asked, having been merely taken by surprise by the phenomenon, without any fear being inspired in him.

Ossipoff kissed his daughter in order to reassure her, and replied: "It's quite simply as I predicted, Monsieur Fricoulet. We've passed over the pole and, in changing hemisphere, we've simply entered the one that isn't sunlit. I'm astonished that you didn't think of that." He turned to Flammermont. "You weren't surprised, were you, my dear Gontran?"

The young man had had time to recover from his emotion. Suppressing a smile, he replied, with an assurance that drew a forceful oath from the American, who had witnessed his alarm: "Given that the visible hemisphere was in daylight, shouldn't we have expected to find the other in darkness?"

"I think it would be prudent to make preparations for the landing now," said Ossipoff.

197

"How far from here do you think we'll touch down?" asked Jonathan Farenheit.

"If my calculations aren't mistaken, about 200 leagues from the pole."

"Ah! We still have time," murmured Selena.

"Not as much as you might think, darling," the aged scientist replied. "At this moment, we're grazing the Moon at a height of 50 leagues, and the further we go the steeper our descent will become. Thus, if you can believe me..."

The electric chandelier was lit; then they checked the cords securing the furniture, tightened the knots, and carefully closed all the hatches. That took an hour.

"Hurry up," said Ossipoff. "We can't be far from touching down now."

As an additional precaution, the metallic plates protecting the portholes had been screwed down again, with the consequence that it was impossible to measure the vehicle's progress.

The hammocks were rolled up and the travelers placed themselves in the padded drawers that had already protected them from the shock of the departure.

A profound silence reigned, troubled only by the ticking of the clock. Everyone fell silent, their throats tightened by anxiety.

Suddenly, a formidable shock shook the entire vehicle. The chandelier came away and the incandescent lamps and shattered into numerous pieces, which cascaded down with a frightful din, while items of furniture, breaking their moorings, smashed into one another in the darkness. Not a single cry was emitted by the travelers—and yet, if ever there was an occasion to shout a triumphant "hurrah," this was it, for Ossipoff and his intrepid companions had just arrived at the goal of their voyage.

They were on the Moon!

Chapter XIV
Ninety Thousand Leagues from Earth

"It is very curious to think that, although the Moon is much smaller than the Earth, the inhabitants of that world, if they exist, must be taller than we are and their buildings, if they have erected any, must have dimensions greater than ours.

"Beings of our size and strength, transported to the Moon, would weigh six times less, while being six times as strong as us; they would be prodigiously light and agile, carrying ten times their own weight and moving masses weighing 1000 kilograms on Earth.

"It is natural to suppose that, not being nailed to the ground like us by the shackles of gravity, they would grow to dimensions that would give them both more weight and solidity. If the Moon were surrounded by a dense enough atmosphere, the Selenites would undoubtedly fly like birds, but it is certain that their atmosphere is insufficient for that organic feat.

"Moreover, not only would it be *possible* for a race of Selenites equal to terrestrial races in muscular strength to construct monuments much higher than ours, but it would also be *necessary* for them to give those constructions gigantic proportions and to set them on considerable and massive bases, to ensure their solidity and duration,

"Now, although skillful observers such as William Herschel, Schröter, Gruithuisen[58] and Littrow[59] have believed that they were able to make out traces of constructions 'made by human hands' with their keen eyes, more attentive examination with the aid of more powerful instruments has proved that these constructions—ramparts, trenches, channels and roads—are not artificial but purely natural formations. The telescope shows us, in reality, no trace of habitation—and yet, a great city there would undoubtedly be easily recognizable.

"Let us remark, however, that it would be easily recognizable if it resembled ours. But nothing proves that lunar beings or objects bear any resemblance whatsoever to terrestrial beings or objects; on the contrary, everything encourages us to think that there is the most extreme dissimilarity between the two regions. Now, it could very well be that we have lunar villages and habitations before our eyes, and constructions made by their hands—if they have hands—

---

[58] Franz von Gruithuisen (1774-1852) published his "discovery" of a city north of Schröter crater in 1824, naming it Wallwerk. Subsequent observers armed with better telescopes could find no trace of it. The next reference on this list remains stubbornly obscure.
[59] Joseph Johann von Littrow (1781-1840).

strewn across the landscape, without it ever being possible for us to suppose that these objects and works were the result of lunar intelligence."

Thus, in one of his books, speaks the French scientist who has done so much for the popularization of astronomy and the diffusion of education throughout the entire world, and with whom Ossipoff, in the first chapter of this story, got Gontran de Flammermont mixed up. How astonished and joyful the illustrious scientist would have been if, like his obscure namesake, he had been able to be transported to the world that he had studied by telescope for so many years and about which he had written so many charming pages.

He would have been able to observe with his own eyes that he was not mistaken in his suppositions, and that his hypotheses, based on well-established scientific data, were justified—in brief, that lunar life was just as he had foreseen and described in the preceding lines.

The Sun had just risen on the hemisphere of the Moon on which Ossipoff's vehicle had fallen. The peaks and the craters of the mountainous regions situated on the side of the disk forever invisible to terrestrial eyes cast vast shadows over the plains extending to their foothills. In the middle of a vast encircled desert—a sort of deep well filled with shadows into which a pale ray of sunlight slid, as if shamefully—stood a bizarre construction, affecting the form of a gigantic cage whose bars were formed of those tall frameworks of scaffolding that constructors use to support their cranes. This cage, which was about four or five meters tall, was conical in form—which is to say that its bars, deeply embedded in the ground, converged towards their summit. Inside the cage, on ground covered by a thick layer of volcanic dust, five bodies were extended side by side, motionless, as if in *rigor mortis*.

These bodies were those of Mikhail Ossipoff and his companions. In a corner, piled up at random, were all the utensils and instruments that their vehicle had contained.

Suddenly, the ray of sunlight that darted a soft and timid light into the crater reached Gontran's face. It required no more than that to extract the sleeper from the profound slumber in which he was plunged. Slowly, his body moved; his stiff limbs extended in a sort of convulsion and his heavy eyelids were raised, uncovering dull and vitreous eyes. He stayed like that for a long moment, lying on his back, his eyes wandering vacantly. Then intelligence reasserted itself, and memory with it, and he was surprised by the spectacle his eyes beheld, so different from the interior of the vehicle in which he had just spent five days and five nights. Perceiving the bodies extended beside him, he uttered a cry of terror.

"Dead!" he said. "They're dead!" Suddenly coming to his feet, he ran to the nearest one. It was Fricoulet. "Alcide!" he said, in a tremulous voice. "Alcide!" At the same time, he tugged him. Bizarrely enough, he lifted him entirely off the ground, holding him suspended above the ground with one hand, when he had only wanted to shake him in order to wake him up.

The young engineer rubbed his eyes, raised his eyelids, yawned lazily and stammered, in a thick voice: "Well, what is it?"

"You're alive!" cried Gontran, joyfully. "You're alive!"

This exclamation woke Fricoulet up completely. "Yes, I'm alive," he replied. "Why shouldn't I be alive? You're very much alive yourself."

Flammermont shook his head. "If you'd seen yourself as I saw you," he said, "lying there, pale and motionless...just like the others..." He pointed to Ossipoff, Selena and Farenheit, who were as still as the stones. "But where are we, then?" he asked, oppressed by the great silence that reigned over that solitude.

He had pronounced these words in a soft voice, but not so quietly that Fricoulet could not hear them. Even so, the engineer exclaimed: "Speak more loudly if you want me to hear you. What was it you just said?"

"You didn't hear?" Gontran repeated, very surprised. Raising his voice, he said: "I was talking reasonably loudly, though. What can have caused that?"

Someone behind them replied: "Probably the composition of the atmosphere."

They turned round and saw Monsieur Ossipoff sitting up, looking around curiously.

"Yes," the old scientist added, speaking loudly, "the rarefaction of the air might be another reason why voices don't carry."

The two young men went to Ossipoff and shook him cordially by the hand. "Nothing broken, Monsieur Ossipoff?" Fricoulet asked.

"No, nothing...at least, it doesn't appear so...but I don't see Selena."

"Your daughter's still asleep," Gontran replied. "She's there, behind you."

"Help me to wake her up, dear boy," said the old man. "I feel quite numb."

The young man seized the old man by the wrists and, bracing himself solidly, pulled him up. He had undoubtedly miscalculated the required force, though—or, rather, was not conscious of his own strength—for Ossipoff came to his feet with a prodigious vigor, slipped out of Gontran's hands, passed over his head like a feather and fell on top of Jonathan Farenheit, who had been sleeping as peacefully as if he were on the mattress of his hammock.

Three cries rang out simultaneously: one of surprise, emitted by Gontran; one of pain, emitted by Ossipoff; and, finally, one of anger, accompanied by a forceful "By God!" The last, as will easily be guessed, was from the powerful lungs of the American, who was dreaming just then that he had finally got his hands on that villain Fedor Sharp. Instinctively, his fingers clenched around the throat of the unfortunate scientist, and squeezed with such violence that they would have caused him to pass from life to death if the others had not run to his rescue.

On seeing the adversary that he had attacked, Jonathan Farenheit became very contrite. As for Flammermont, he showered the old man with apologies.

The latter, still overwhelmed by emotion, contented himself with smiling while undoing his cravat, which was strangling him.

"What's happening?" asked Selena, who had been woken up by the tumult, and hurried over anxiously, to see her father pale and distraught in the midst of his disconcerted companions.

It was the old man, having pulled himself together somewhat, who replied to the young woman's question by saying to Gontran: "You've forgotten, dear boy, that we're on the Moon, and than on the lunar surface, weight is six times less than on Earth—which is to say, equal to 0.164…that's why you lifted me up so easily and why, thanks to he impulse you communicated to me, I slipped out of your grasp to disturb the slumber of the worthy Mr. Farenheit…you won't hold it against me, will you, Jonathan?"

The American offered his huge hand to the scientist and replied: "No—although you interrupted an adorable dream…" As he said these words, blood rushed to Farenheit's face, while his eyes lit up with a dark gleam.

"What were you dreaming, then?" asked Selena.

"That I was strangling that bandit Sharp."

"That's right!" cried Fricoulet, astonished. "That animal has parted company with us." And he added, in jest: "We couldn't have asked for anything better!"

"What's become of him?" asked Gontran. "By what miracle did he disappear?"

Ossipoff smiled. "By a very simple miracle," he replied. "His projectile was an inert object—which is to say that, not being animated, as ours was, by its own velocity, which would have permitted him to combat the lunar attraction, his projectile, once in the zone of attraction into which we dragged him, abandoned us to obey a superior force, and so…."

"Do you think he's fallen far away from here?"

The old man shook his head. "Unless my assumptions are false, Sharp must have fallen on the other hemisphere of the Moon."

Jonathan Farenheit brandished his fists in a menacing fashion. "Oh," he growled, "I'll catch up with him if I have to go all around the world."

"The lunar world," added Fricoulet, jokingly.

"Yes, Monsieur Fricoulet," retorted the furious American. "If I have to, I'll offer a reward of $1,000,000 and I'll contrive a means of locomotion that will permit me to follow the bandit if he leaves the Moon to take refuge on another planet in order to escape me."

"My friends," said Mikhail Ossipoff at that moment, "I think it would be as well to leave the subject of that uninteresting person and think about ourselves."

Gontran lent support to the old man's opinion with a forceful gesture. "Yes," he said. "Let's hold a council. What are we going to do?"

"The most urgent matter, I think, is to devise a way of getting out of this prison—or rather this cage," said Fricoulet, pointing at the tree-trunks surrounding them.

"A cage!" cried Jonathan Farenheit, going pale. "They've dared to put a citizen of free America in a cage!"

"A cage," repeated Ossipoff, joining his hands in an ecstatic gesture. "A cage!" And, running to the barrier that enclosed them, he carefully examined the manner in which the bars were embedded in the ground and joined together above their heads. "Ah, merciful Heaven!" he exclaimed, tremulous with emotion. "These are certainly evidence of the work of an intelligent being!"

Gontran, who had heard him, drew closer. "Then, Monsieur Ossipoff," he said, "you genuinely believe in the existence of a lunar humankind?"

The aged scientist raised his arms to the heavens, staring at the young Comte with eyes wide with amazement. "What!" he said. "You can ask me such a question—you, who, before undertaking this perilous voyage with me, were familiar with the illustrious Flammermont's opinion on that subject? You, who have just found further proof, at this very moment, of the existence of the humankind you seem to be putting in question?"

Utterly nonplussed, Gontran silently hung his head. "Monsieur Ossipoff," he said, after a pause, "would you permit me to ask you a question?"

"Speak, my friend, speak."

"You said just now that you suspect that Sharp has fallen in the other hemisphere."

"Indeed."

"Which one did you mean?"

"The visible hemisphere."

Gontran made a gesture of surprise. "I recall, however," he said, "that a few hours before our fall, when we were surprised to pass with out transition from the most dazzling light to the most profound darkness, you gave us the explanation that we had just passed over the pole and penetrated into the invisible hemisphere."

"Yes—so what?"

"Well, it was dark...while now..."

"While it's now the visible hemisphere that's plunged into darkness."

Gontran shook his head. "Right!" he said. "I hadn't thought of that...but it's quite simple." And he added: "I thought that we were in the visible hemisphere."

"If we were, we probably wouldn't be breathing as easily as we are."

"But there's an atmosphere...."

"Yes, but it must be very thin; if we were to make an excursion into that region, we'd probably, have to make use of our breathing apparatus.

At that moment a strange noise, reminiscent of the crack of a whip, was audible behind them. Selena burst out laughing. "Father," she said, "look at Jonathan—that's the way to destroy our cage."

They turned round and saw the American breaking the young tree-trunks as easily as if they were reeds. While strewing the stripped and broken trees on the ground, he growled: "A citizen of the United States! A resident of New York, shut up like a chicken. By God! They did well to hide—I'd have broken them just like these trees."

Gontran watched this devastation with profound astonishment.

"Try your strength, ladies and gentlemen," said Fricoulet, in joking imitation of the tone of a fairground barker—and he grabbed a young sapling of respectable girth himself, which he snapped without any apparent effort.

Seeing that, the young Comte cried: "If that's how things are, the Selenites can come; the four of us are strong enough to hold them off."

"And me," said Selena, slightly offended. "Don't I count? I assume that my strength has been increased just as much as yours."

Ossipoff could not help smiling at the sight of his daughter's bellicose expression—but his face became suddenly anxious.

"What's the matter, Father?" she asked.

Without answering, the old man went to Gontran. "Have you seen our vehicle?" he asked.

"What did you say?" asked the young man, improvising and ear-trumpet with his hand.

"I asked you if you knew where our vehicle is?"

"How should I know, my dear Monsieur?" Gontran replied. "I fell at the same time as you, and it wasn't five minutes after I ceased sleeping that you woke up yourself." After a pause, he added: "You're quite sure, aren't you, that we're on the Moon?"

The old man shrugged his shoulders gently, then knelt down in the corner where all the instruments were gathered. "Well," he said, "the compass is agitated, with no fixed direction, the barometer indicates 320 millimeters of atmospheric pressure and the hygrometer indicates absolute dryness."

Fricoulet added: "And we're in a crater—look at the truncated form of the walls encircling us. Observe that the opening through which the light reaches us is regular, and situated far above our heads." And he murmured, as if talking to himself: "There's no doubt about it—we're inside the cone of a lunar volcano."

"An extinct volcano, though?" Gontran hastened to ask.

The engineer was opening his mouth to reply and to reassure his friend, when immense forms suddenly surged out of a dark tunnel. "The Selenites!" he cried. "Look out!"

One by one, emerging from a cavern that the voyagers had not noticed, a dozen strange beings of gigantic size were advancing prudently.

Petrified by astonishment, Ossipoff and his companions studied these giants, not without a certain terror.

They were about 12 feet tall, but their structure differed very little from that of Earthly humans—except that the head was surprisingly large and seemed disproportionate to the rest of the body; it was balanced on the end of a long, thin neck, which reposed on narrow and fleshless shoulders. To these shoulders were connected thin arms terminating in hands as large as laundry-beaters. The torso was prodigiously flat, as if it enclosed neither lungs nor intestines; it extended to spindly legs somewhat reminiscent of those of wading birds, as were the voluminous feet on which they stood, thus serving as solid bases for the elevated edifice they supported. The round and beardless face was equipped with two bulging eyes in which no light shone, which gave the face a dull and icy stare; there were no eyelashes, nor eyebrows; by contrast, a mass of hair, which they all wore uniformly, fell in shoulder-length tresses. The mouth, widely cleft, was not rimmed by lips like those of the Earth's inhabitants but resembled a saber-slash across the face. The most distinctive feature of these strange beings was the vast splayed ears, like acoustic funnels, one each side of the head.

Instinctively, Gontran had grabbed a rifle, and had placed himself in front of Selena, determined to kill rather than permit one of these monsters to get near the young woman.

"Peace, Gontran, my friend," said Fricoulet, noticing the young Comte's hostile attitude. "Stay calm, and don't aggravate our situation by attacking these islanders first. There'll still be time to resort to coercive means when we can't do anything else. Let's try to communicate with them first."

"How do you intend to make yourself heard?" asked Flammermont. "You've noticed that our voices scarcely carry when we speak loudly and put our ears close to our mouths—you'll have to try hard, given the size of these fellows!"

The young engineer shrugged his shoulders. "You'll see," he said. He took a few paces forward and, leaping into the air with a slight thrust of his feet, reached a rocky ledge situated about five meters above the ground. "Hey!" he called to his companions. "Am I tall enough now?"

Seeing him perched thus, one of the Selenites—which was marching at the head of the company and seemed to be their leader—appeared to understand the intention with which he had made that rapid ascent and headed in his direction. Once close to him, he made a long speech in a sonorous language whose syllables echoed from the immense walls. From time to time he stopped, looked carefully around at all the Terrans as if to determine whether they had understood, and then resumed talking.[60]

---

[60] The French pronoun used to refer to the Selenite is ambiguous, potentially translatable as "he" or "it." As the physical description contains no reference to sexual organs, the neutral term might be preferable on logical grounds, but sub-

"Sing, my lad, sing," muttered Jonathan Farenheit. "If you think that we understand a single word of your harangue..."

Fricoulet made a signal to the American with his hand, bidding him to be silent. The Selenite perceived the gesture and, presumably taking it for a commanding gesture, deduced that Fricoulet was the strangers' leader. From that moment on he addressed itself directly to him; then he stopped, looking at the engineer and seemingly awaiting a response.

Fricoulet reflected briefly. Then, suddenly, he had a bright idea. That idea was that the whole of the long speech that he had just heard was probably nothing but an enquiry as to where he and his companions came from. He plunged his hand into his pockets, which were always full of the most disparate assortment of objects, and pulled a piece of chalk out of one of them. Rapidly, on the crater's blackened lava wall, he drew two spheres of unequal size, which he connected by means of a straight line to represent the course followed through space by the shell. Then, putting the index-finger of his right hand on the larger sphere, he applied his left hand to his breast.

The Selenite seemed to be following this mime with keen interest. Then Fricoulet pointed to the smaller sphere and extended his arm toward the inhabitant of the Moon. The latter seemed surprised, came closer, and considered the drawing attentively. Then he summoned its companions, which came to look at it, one after the other—after which they drew away, seemed to confer with one another, and then went back into the dark tunnel from which they had emerged.

Ossipoff and his companions looked at one another silently for a moment.

"Well, what do you think of the Lunarians?" asked Gontran.

"They're much as I imagined they would be," the old man replied.

"At any rate, they're not very handsome," murmured Selena.

"For myself," said Fricoulet, "I expected to see beings much stranger and more dissimilar to us than they are."

"Why is that?" asked the old scientist. "Although the conditions of habitability of their world are very different from ours, they originated, as we did, from the solar nebula..."

"Their physiological conformation, however," Fricoulet observed, "does not appear to be absolutely identical to ours. Did you notice those enormous heads, the large pupils of their eyes, and the narrow torso?"

"Of course."

"To what do you attribute that?"

"At present, we can only draw inferences."

"Well, what inferences do you draw?"

"That if the Selenites have very voluminous skulls, it's because their brains are more highly developed than ours..."

---

sequent developments leave no doubt that the authors are assuming that the Selenites have two sexes, as human do, and that those showing initiative are male.

"And it is therefore necessary to conclude," Fricoulet prompted, "that they're more intelligent than us?"

"Perhaps not—but in any case, they ought to possess more acquired knowledge. Now, if their chests are narrow, it's because their lungs are conformed differently from ours, in order to function without hindrance under an atmospheric pressure as low as the one that pertains here. As for the stomach and the abdomen, if they're not as pronounced as those of Terrans, it's because the latter belong to a planet on which it's necessary to eat to live, where the law of life is the law of death, and where the weak are absorbed by the strong."

Selena opened her eyes wide as she listened to her father speaking. "Are there worlds in the universe, Father," she asked, "in which creatures do not eat?"

"It's probable," he old man replied. "It would be sad to think that such a ridiculous function and its consequences are compulsory on every world. It is good for a wretched planet still in a state of infancy, as the Earth is, but that reflects the powerlessness of Nature in proportion to our size...."[61]

"I can't imagine the external form of beings that don't eat," Fricoulet put in.

"It's certain," Ossipoff replied, "that such beings must be clothed in fantastic appearances and strange conformation: men without heads, torsos or limbs—for our brain is nothing but the blossoming of the spinal cord; it's that which makes the skull, and the skull the head. Our legs and arms are only the quadruped's limbs transformed and improved...it's the gradual development of a vertical stance that makes the feet and repeated exercise that makes the hands. The abdomen is merely the envelope of the intestine; the form and length of the intestine depends on the kind of alimentation. In the final analysis, there is not a single cubic centimeter on or within our bodies that isn't due to our vital functioning in the environment that we inhabit."

As Ossipoff concluded this speech, the company of Selenites reappeared. Two of them were pushing a sort of cart in which the scientists and his companions were obliged to embark. Then they went into a long underground tunnel, and after several minutes of vertiginously rapid progress they returned to the light of the Sun. The Terrans now found themselves in the middle of a crater that Fricoulet estimated to be several kilometers wide and which had to be the principal crater of a volcano. This immense arena was bordered by high mountains, whose capriciously jagged summits and sharp peaks extended as far as the eye could see into space. From the bottom of this chimney the sky seemed deep

---

[61] The notion that there might be worlds in which eating is unnecessary (because alimentation could be achieved by breathing) is one of Camille Flammarion's frequent preoccupations, reflected in *Lumen* and elsewhere. It is always coupled in his works with the conviction that the inhabitants of other worlds might not bear the slightest physical resemblance to Earthly life, having been adapted by evolution to very different physical environments.

blue, almost black; in spite of the blinding light of the Sun, a few first-magnitude stars sparkled therein, like enormous diamonds in a jewel-box.

"I'm astonished," murmured Fricoulet, "not to feel any difficulty breathing, even though the pressure is very weak."

"Pooh!" replied Ossipoff. "It corresponds to that indicated by the barometer on the highest peak in the Andes—which is to say, at an altitude of 7500 meters."

"It's claimed, however," Gontran put in, "that at such an altitude one feels the most painful symptoms of 'mountain sickness'—and yet I don't feel anything similar. On the contrary, it seems to me that my lungs are working with marvelous ease. Strangely enough, my stomach remains silent."

"It must be the case," Ossipoff replied, "that the atmosphere in which we are plunged has a composition completely different from that of the Earth, of which I shall take account by analyzing it. What seems certain is that oxygen is found here in a more considerable proportion than the breathable air of our native planet, and that the atmosphere also includes other gases."

Meanwhile, the cart continued to roll across the plain that extended across the bottom of the crater.

Suddenly, Farenheit pointed out a shining mass emerging from the ground in the distance. "Our vehicle!" he cried.

It was indeed the vehicle that had brought the bold travelers far from the Earth. It was embedded a foot deep in the rocky soil and its impact had sprayed dross and lava debris over a fairly wide radius. The glass of one porthole was broken, the base was crumpled and the metal was completely burned through in places.

As he observed this damage, Fricoulet shook his head "God knows how we'll be able to go back," he murmured.

The Selenites had come closer and, pointing to the shell, seemed to be asking for explanations in that respect.

Ossipoff picked up a metal bar that had been dislodged from the vehicle, and by that means, as easily as if he were using a pencil, he drew two spheres of unequal size in the dust, as Fricoulet had on the wall of the volcano. He connected them by means of a straight line and completed the drawing by sketching the shape of the vehicle at a point on the line.

Immediately, one of the Selenites knelt down in order to be within closer range of his interlocutor. Then, by means of an expressive mime, he appeared to ask whether the larger sphere drawn on the ground was a heavenly body.

Ossipoff nodded his head several times. Then, to make himself better understood, the scientist drew the Copernican system in the sand, ranking the planets in the order of their distance from the Sun, which he depicted as an immense sphere. When he reached the Earth he drew the orbit of the Moon and called the giant's particular attention to these two worlds.

The Selenite pointed to the shell in an interrogative manner.

"He's asking if that's the means by which we arrived?" said Fricoulet.[62]

Ossipoff made a gesture signifying "yes."

"Tell them that we're ambassadors sent by the Earth to its satellite," murmured Flammermont, jokingly.

"Rather ask them if they've seen another projectile in these parts like that one," muttered Farenheit, who had not abandoned his quest for vengeance. And he added: "Oh, to be able to get my hands on that scoundrel Sharp..."

Meanwhile, the mute dialogue between the Lunarian and Mikhail Ossipoff continued. The giant put his finger on his tongue; the astronomer shook his head negatively.

"They'll never be able to understand one another," murmured Selena.

She was undoubtedly mistaken, for, at that moment, the Selenite got up and, turning toward his companions, began talking to them animatedly, sometimes pointing to the Terrans and sometimes the diagrams drawn in the sand by Ossipoff. Finally, he took another by the hand and, drawing him closer to the old scientist, pointed to him and said, in a loud voice: "Telinga." He touched Telinga's tongue and then Ossipoff's ear. Afterwards, striking his breast to indicate himself, he said: "Roum Sertchoum."

The one that had just been named Telinga took off a garment consisting of long bands covered with a sort of indecipherable script. At the same time, he mimed drawing characters thereon.

"This one," said Fricoulet to Flammermont, "is evidently one of your illustrious namesake's fellow astronomers. It's probably this one that will be charged with our instruction—for, if I understand the other one's mute language, we're to be taught to talk."

As he finished this speech, the Selenites pointed at the cart. Before getting into it, Ossipoff, by means of an eloquent mime, confided the vehicle to the care of the indigenes. Then the cart got under way again, plunging into a dark underground tunnel. After many turns and detours, it ended up in an immense room lit from one side by daylight. Once in this room they were left alone.

"Prisoners!" exclaimed Jonathan Farenheit, angrily.

Ossipoff put a hand on his arm. "Calm down, Mr. Farenheit," he said, with great self-composure. "There's been a misunderstanding. Life is merely a matter of explaining oneself."

---

[62] The reader might think it odd that Fricoulet does not seem curious as to how the shell's passengers were removed from the crashed shell to the cage, if it was not by the Selenites—who would, in that case, know already that it was the means by which the strangers had arrived—and why they were removed to that location. The question is never addressed, let alone answered, when communication with the Selenites is eventually opened.

The American shrugged his shoulders furiously. "Explaining oneself?" he growled. "And how are you going to explain yourself to these savages, who don't speak a word of English?"

"It's merely a matter of learning their language."

"I'm not going to do that, myself," Farenheit retorted.

"But I am," the old man replied, firmly. "You know that Russians are the foremost linguists in the word."

"Will it take long?" asked the American.

"I can assure you that I'll be able to converse with these people in two days."

The scientist's response amazed the citizen of the United States. "Two days!" he repeated. "That's marvelous."

Fricoulet winked slyly and whispered in Gontran's ear: "Poor man! He doesn't know that the lunar year is only 12 days long, each one of which is equivalent to 29 of ours, plus 12 hours 44 minutes."

The day after their arrival on the lunar surface—only their chronometers could now give the voyagers an exact notion of time, which day and night no longer divided up in the same quantity as on Earth—they saw Telinga come in to the large room that had been assigned to them as a residence.

After forceful gestures—which Fricoulet assured them were cordial greetings—the Selenite stuck out his tongue and placed its finger on it; then he touched their ears and waited.

"He's probably asking whether it's convenient to begin your lessons immediately," said the young engineer, who had formally appointed himself as the little troop's interpreter.

On receiving his friends' affirmative response, Fricoulet turned back to Telinga and gave him to understand that he and his companions were at his disposal. The Selenite bowed and went out.

"What?" exclaimed Gontran, astonished, "He's leaving it at that?"

"Perhaps he's gone to fetch its grammars and dictionaries," Fricoulet replied.

"Do you think that there's a Lhomond and a Littré here?"[63] asked the young Comte.

It was Ossipoff who replied: "Personally, I think that these people's level of education must be much more advanced than ours."

"These savages!" Jonanthan Farenheit protested.

"These savages," the old man replied, coldly, "have the advantage of inhabiting a world much older than ours."

The American stamped his heel furiously—which gesture, to his profound surprise, made a profound dent, in which his leg sank up to the calf. He stifled an oath. "Always that accursed sextuple strength!" he muttered.

"May we know the reason for this excessive anger, Mr. Farenheit?" asked Gontran.

"Well," Farenheit retorted, "didn't Monsieur Ossipoff just say that the Moon is a much older world than Earth?"

"Yes I said that and I repeat it."

"But wasn't the Moon formed from the Earth?"

"That's scientifically exact."

---

[63] The reference is to two of the standard texts used in the French educational system, Abbé Charles-François Lhomond's Latin manual *De viris illustribus* (1775) and Emile Littré's *Dictionnaire de la langue française* (1877).

"Isn't the Moon just a parcel of the gaseous globe rotating on its axis, which cooled gradually, and which we baptized with the name of Earth?"

"A parcel detached from the terrestrial equator by the effect of centrifugal force," added Fricoulet.

"My dear Mr. Farenheit," Ossipoff declared, "you're absolutely right; the Moon is exactly what you say it is—but what of it?"

"Simply this, by God! Since it's true that the Moon is a subsidiary part of the Earth, how can you claim that the world is older than the one from which it was born?"

While the American was speaking, Gontran looked at Fricoulet and nodded his head approvingly. "He's right," he murmured. "I was just thinking the same thing..."

"Shut up!" the engineer whispered in his ear. "What you're saying is stupid."

The young Comte was about to protest when Ossipoff, replying to Farenheit's observation, declared: "You haven't taken into account, my dear Farenheit, that the Moon has only a quarter of the Earth's diameter."

"Well, what does that matter?"

"What! What does it matter?" repeated the aged scientist. "The small matter of the fact that the Moon is 49 times smaller than the Earth."

With slightly pursed lips, the American retorted: "There's no need to tell me that the size of a world depends on its diameter—but, with respect to the matter in hand, I don't see what its size has to do with its age."

Ossipoff manifested his impatience in a slight shrug of the shoulders. *Oh, these ignoramuses*! he thought. Aloud, he said: "But it's precisely because of its small size that the little sun that the Moon once was cooled and crusted over so rapidly, while the Earth's temperature was still too high to permit life to become manifest and to develop. It follows that vital evolution was much more rapid here than on Earth, and that, while the latter was still the abode of gigantic animals, humankind was blossoming on the Moon and making rapid progress toward its apogee."

Doubly humiliated, the American fell silent and lowered his head.

At that moment, the Selenite came back in, carrying a kind of box on his shoulder, which he set down on the ground. He beckoned to the Terrans to come closer. He pointed to their ears while pointing to the box, then to their eyes while pointing at the wall of the room in front of them.

"Do you understand what he's saying?" Gontran asked Fricoulet.

The latter could not suppress a gesture of impatience. "If you were less intent on contemplating Mademoiselle Selena's face," he grumbled, "and were paying more attention to what this man is saying..."

"This Selenite, you mean," the young Comte rectified. Then, with a smile, he added: "But you haven't answered my question."

"Well, he's undoubtedly asking us to listen to the box and watch the wall."

212

While the young engineer was speaking, the Selenite had placed metal cylinders engraved with indecipherable characters in the box; then he had stood a sort of wooden screen against the wall. The screen was covered with white fabric pinned to the wood. Once this equipment was disposed, he made a clicking noise with his tongue to attract the attention of his audience and, seeing that their eyes were fixed on the panel, as he had instructed, he released a small switch.

Immediately, the box emitted a clear and perfectly comprehensible voice, similar in every respect to a human voice, save that it was monotonous—which is to say, invariant in pitch. At the same time, symbols similar to the shadow-figures of a Chinese lantern appeared on the screen.

"What's that?" asked Selena, pointing at the wall in amazement.

On hearing the young woman's voice, the Selenite touched the box, which stopped speaking, and the panel became white again, as before.

"That's bizarre," murmured Fricoulet, then added, abruptly: "If I'm not mistaken, the symbols that appeared must be representations of the syllables or words pronounced by that sort of music box. The system is intended to increase the rapidity of education by teaching a pupil how to pronounce and write words at the same time."

Flammermont shook his head. "That's very nice," he said, "but when I've spent entire hours in front of this Barbary-organ-cum-magic-lantern, how much further forward will I be? I understand how to pronounce a word and I know how to write it, but do I know what it signifies? And when I can repeat, like a parrot, the thousands of words of which these people's language consists…well, what then?"

The young engineer compressed his lips into a dubious moue, and silence reigned again in the room while everyone remained plunged in these reflections.

The Selenite, who had listened to this dialogue patiently, thought that his pupils were ready to resume their lesson and pressed the switch again. Then the box began to speak, and the characters reappeared on the board—but at the same time, the Selenite brought an object out of a case, which he showed to the Terrans.

"A cup!" exclaimed Jonathan Farenheit.

The Selenite pronounced a guttural word, pointing successively at the object it held, the box and the board.

Selena clapped her hands. "I understand!" she said, joyfully. "I understand!"

"And what have you understood?" asked Ossipoff.

"The box pronounces a word, the board writes it and the Selenite displays the object to which it applies." And, with a marvelous linguistic surety, she repeated the word that the Selenite had pronounced. The latter smiled gently, and also repeated the word, nodding his head several times.

With this procedure, the lessons made rapid progress—all the more rapidly because, once the Sun had disappeared over the horizon, the voyagers had nothing else to do but listen to their professor's lessons through the long night.

First, the Selenite taught his pupils the names of the most familiar objects—each of which Mikhail Ossipoff carefully recorded in his notebook, with its Russian, French and English translation, so that it constituted, as Gontran jokingly observed "a little pocket dictionary."

After four lessons, the professor passed on to the mechanics of the language and Selenian grammar. When that was done, the *Terragenes* were soon able to converse with the inhabitants of the satellite.

As he had promised the American, Mikhail Ossipoff rapidly assimilated the warm and sonorous language, which was reminiscent of Hindustani and the dialects of India. He put so much ardor into his studies that it he soon longed to quit the interior of the crater to launch himself upon the exploration of the unknown face of the world, to which he has aspired for so many long years.

One day, while riffling through the volumes of the library put at their disposal—which is to say, making use of the music box, or rather the phonograph, which took the trouble not merely to speak aloud but to reproduce the appearance of the page he was reading, he succeeded in finding a map of the Moon. He hastened to make a sketch of the very clear silhouette projected on the panel—in order, he said, to be able to trace the itinerary of his excursion at a later date.

As on the visible hemisphere of the Moon, the invisible side was sprinkled with large grey patches—"seas" or "oceans"—but were they really expanses of liquid or merely dry plains? That was what Ossipoff yearned to know.

There were also numerous craters, high mountain chains and streaks, as on the visible face. In places, too, there were points marked on the map in a special fashion. On being questioned, Telinga replied that these were cities.

"Cities!" cried Gontran, in amazement. "There are cities in the Moon—doubtless we'll find branches of Bon Marché and Belle Jardinière in these cities. I really need to renew my stock of gloves."

Ossipoff, however, who had not neglected to include a calendar among the most precious objects with which he had equipped the vehicle, consulted it with an impatience equal to that of his companions. If he was anxious to commencing his voyage of exploration, he was no less anxious than Farenheit and Gontran were to see the sunlight reappear.

Finally, the old man announced that the night was ending. "In two hours," he said, "the Sun will rise." Addressing Telinga, he said: "I request an audience with your leader."

"Whenever you like," replied the Selenite.

"Immediately, then, for there's no time to lose."

A few minutes later, Ossipoff and his companions were led into a room, at the back of which half a dozen Lunarians were sitting on bizarrely formed chairs, which Fricoulet declared to be carved out of lava.

214

"Friends," said one of them, "Speak, ambassadors that the *Revolver* [64] has sent to its little worldlet, and your desires will be satisfied."

"We'd like to leave this place," replied the old man.

"Leave? Why?"

"Do you think," Ossipoff asked, "that we have left the Earth and traveled 90,000 leagues, braving the most extreme perils, to reside indefinitely in a crater on your world? The Moon is only the first stage of the celestial voyage we have undertaken, nothing but a station in the exploration of the entire Solar System that we dreamed of carrying out. But before we launch ourselves toward the planets that shine radiantly in your pure sky, we want to visit your world. That's why we're in a hurry to leave here."

"Have you a destination in mind?"

"Our destination is the north of the hemisphere that faces the *Revolver*, in order to witness the spectacle of the full Earth, seen from your globe.

"And in addition," cried Jonathan Farenheit, mingling Selenite idioms with his native tongue and French phrases in his haste, "we want to recover the track of an inhabitant of Earth whom we assume to have fallen in the other hemisphere."

The Selenite made a gesture of alarm. "If he has fallen in the other hemisphere," he said, "he must be dead."

"Dead!" groaned the American, shaking his fists furiously. "The bandit will escape me, then? In any case, I need to be certain of it, and until I've seen his corpse..."

After a few seconds of silence, the Selenite added: "The excursion that you wish to attempt, into the hemisphere from which the *Revolver* can be seen, like a vast and tremulous celestial clock, is impossible."

"Impossible!" exclaimed Ossipoff. "And why is that?"

"Because a formidable belt of mountainous rocks separates the two hemispheres of the Moon, and many obstacles will prevent you from reaching that part of the world: an absolutely arid, sterile and abandoned continent, where you will only find vestiges of what were once flourishing cities, where nothing grows and it impossible to live—even for us, whose constitution is adapted to the rarefaction of the air."

"There's no air!" cried Gontran. He turned to Ossipoff and added: "Then we're all mistaken—my celebrated namesake, you and me..." He had pronounced the last few words with an aplomb that made Fricoulet smile.

---

[64] The text refers to the Earth, presumably employing a deliberately crude translation of a Selenite term, as *Tournante* [rotating], adapting the adjective as a noun. "Revolver" has acquired unfortunate connotations in English, but still seems more appropriate in context than "Turning" or "Spinning," whose noun versions also have awkwardly inapposite meanings.

The old scientist reflected momentarily. "There's certainly a great exaggeration in what the Selenite has just said," he remarked. "Perhaps there isn't a sufficient quantity of air to support life...but however little there is, we'll make do with it."

Jonathan Farenheit's eyes widened immeasurably. "We can't live without breathing," he muttered.

"Eh? Who told you that?" replied Ossipoff, with a gesture of impatience. "Don't we have provisions on liquid air and apparatus?"

Gontran looked anxiously at Selena. "Even so," he objected, "if there are grave dangers to be run, perhaps it would be preferable to abandon the excursion."

The old scientist folded his arms across his chest. "And how shall we continue our voyage then?" he asked.

"What does the exploration of the Moon have to do with our interplanetary excursion?"

"The spectroscope has revealed on the surface of the Moon, not far from the pole, a deposit of a precious mineral, which is the sole means by which we can launch ourselves into space again...but if you're afraid of something, stay here—I'll go alone."

"You shall not go alone, Monsieur Ossipoff!" cried Farenheit. "I shall go with you, and while you search for your mineral, I shall search for that bandit Sharp." He underlined his statement with a forceful gesture.

Gontran protested: "It's not for myself that I fear the dangers or the fatigues of the journey," he replied, "but for Mademoiselle Ossipoff."

The young woman thanked him with a smile. "Thank you, my dear Gontran," she said, "but I'm not afraid; wherever my father goes, I'll go with him."

There was a pause, of which the Selenite took advantage to ask: "Are you quite familiar with the selenographic conformation of the lunar disk on which you are presently standing?"

"*Quite familiar* is perhaps not the exact expression...at any rate, I'm less familiar with it than the other hemisphere.

"The other hemisphere!" repeated the Selenite, in amazement.

"Yes, the visible hemisphere."

"That's not credible."

Ossipoff then set before the indigene's eyes a recent lunar photograph obtained by the skill of the celebrated American astronomer Rutherfurd.[65] The Selenite's astonishment was prodigious. "But how were you able to compile this map," he murmured, "since you have never set foot on our planet?"

---

[65] Lewis Morris Rutherfurd (1816-1892) was an early expert in celestial photography; he donated his collection to Columbia University, where its cream is still displayed.

Ossipoff attempted to explain to the Selenite, briefly, what the photograph was; then he added: "If you were able to give us a guide, however…?"

"Telinga will accompany you."

"And when shall we depart?"

"Tomorrow, at sunrise."

Ossipoff was about to leave the room when Fricoulet turned back and asked: "What means of locomotion shall we employ?"

"They will differ according to the itinerary that you adopt, and according to the rapidity with which you want to travel."

After going to the vehicle to obtain a generous provision of comestibles to provide for their nourishment, the voyagers were ready to launch themselves into new adventures and to brave new dangers. As the first rays of sunlight gilded the summits of the crater that served as their refuge, Telinga came into their room. Seeing their luggage attached to their shoulders, he made a sign bidding them to follow him and set off along the underground route by which they had arrived.

Fortunately, Fricoulet, who thought of everything, had brought a Trouvé electric lamp with him, so he only had to press a button to illuminate the dark and tortuous tunnel through which the little company was moving.

Ossipoff, who was holding the map that he had drawn of this hemisphere of the Moon, asked: "Where are we going?"

"Directly to Chuir, a big city situated at the confluence of the river To," replied the Selenite.

"But by what route?" asked the old man.

"You'll know that in a few moments," Telinga replied, laconically.

At this location the crater abruptly widened out in an immense truncated cone whose jagged summit rose at least 1000 feet into the air. The tunnel ended in a sort of hall measuring almost a kilometer square, lit by sunlight falling from the orifice of the crater. The Selenite, to whom the place was perfectly familiar, uttered a shout that awoke sonorous and prolonged echoes in the interior of the volcano. In response to this summons a vague form emerged from the shadows, which Ossipoff soon recognized as the silhouette of a Selenite. Telinga advanced to meet the other, spent a few moments in conversation, then retraced his steps. "In an hour," he said, "we'll be in Chuir."

The scientists consulted his map and released an exclamation of surprise. "But that's more than 400 *versts* from here," he said. "Have you a means of rapid locomotion at your disposal, then?"

"Perhaps they have railways on the Moon," murmured Gontran.

Jonathan Farenheit shrugged his shoulders and muttered: "Even if they have, it wouldn't be possible to travel such a distance in an hour. The train from New York to San Francisco would only get a quarter as far." And he added, proudly: "And that's the fastest train in the entire world."

On hearing Ossipoff's question, the Selenite had shaken his head. "We are going to Chuir," it said, "by the underground way, but without any force transporting us. The distance is too short for us to have recourse to any but natural means."

The Terrans' astonishment was transformed into bewilderment.

"But then…?" murmured Fricoulet.

He did not finish his sentence. In the middle of the vast hall, emerging from an underground passage, an apparatus had just emerged, as if by magic, sliding noiselessly through the cracks in the lava. It was a sort of boat mounted on skis.

Silently, Telinga ushered his companions to this strange vehicle and they sat down one by one on a bench running along its flank. Then he assumed a standing position at the front, setting his hand on a metal lever.

The Selenite that had brought the vehicle pushed it, without any apparent effort, to the entrance of an underground tunnel, where he abandoned it. Then, as if drawn forward by an invisible force of extraordinary power, the vehicle silently moved into the darkness, with ever-increasing speed.

"I get it," said Fricoulet to his friends. "We're presently sliding down an inclined plane…"

"But we can't go downhill all the time," Gontran objected, "or we'd end up at the center of the Moon instead of staying on the surface."

The young engineer reflected momentarily. "This tunnel," he said, finally, "probably consists of a series of undulations, similar to the fairground ride known as a roller-coaster.[66] When the vehicle has acquired sufficient momentum on a downslope, the curvature probably reverses, then goes down again, and so on, until we arrive."

"Do you think, Monsieur Fricoulet," asked Selena, "that this roller-coaster system could prevail over long distances?"

"I don't see anything against it, provided that the point of departure has sufficient elevation—which would be minimal, by reason of the insignificance of friction."

"In that case," murmured Flammermont, "what will become of steam and electricity?"

The engineer added, in the Selenite language: "If this tunnel is 100 leagues long, its construction is certainly a marvel."

---

[66] The term the authors actually use is "*montagnes russes*," which is now used in France as a generic term for roller-coasters, although the original "Russian mountain" ride—which caused a sensation in Paris in the early years of the 19th century—was more like a helter-skelter, with a continuous but somewhat tortuous descent. Fricoulet's subsequent description is, indeed, more reminiscent of a roller-coaster, although it is exceedingly hard to believe that frictional losses in speed would be as minimal as he seems to think.

"The tunnel," Telinga replied, "was not constructed by our hands; it is simply a natural tube pierced through the underground strata by lava, in the epoch when the lunar world vomited forth its burning entrails through the multitudinous mouths of its volcanoes. These fissures are numerous in our world; that's why we thought of utilizing them to establish communications between our various centers."

"That's marvelous," murmured Ossipoff, ecstatically.

"The unfortunate thing," Gontran said, "is that the route isn't illuminated. A pair of lanterns wouldn't spoil the look of our carriage."

The Selenite, who had the faculty of seeing in the dark, did not understand the Terrans' horror of darkness; fortunately, Fricoulet had his Trouvé lamp, which 'split the blackness' and permitted the voyagers to examine the path they were following as best they could. Soon, though, the speed of the vehicle became excessive, for the slope of the path, far from becoming gentler, became even steeper. They were also obliged to turn their backs on the impetuous current of air that was blowing in their faces, through which the vessel flew like an arrow.

"We're going at nearly 100 meters a second," murmured Ossipoff.

Selena, gripped by vertigo, had hidden her face against her father's breast. Gontran leaned over the side, rolling his eyes anxiously, and Farenheit affected an impassivity belied by the pallor of his cheeks and the quivering of his lips.

Only Fricoulet was perfectly calm; while taking precautions against the possibility of choking, he carefully examined the route the vehicle was following. Suddenly, he cried: "That's definitely it—it's definitely a roller-coaster system. We're climbing again now. Can you feel our speed decreasing? We're only making further progress by virtue of the momentum acquired during the descent, which will decrease until the moment when the vehicle comes to a stop for lack of force."

"Will we arrive soon?" asked Farenheit.

The engineer consulted his watch. "Telinga mentioned an hour," he replied, "and it's now 50 minutes since we set off. We're probably nearly there." And he extended his hand towards a luminous point that appeared in the distance, which rapidly grew in size.

Then the Selenite pressed down on the lever that he held in his hand, and their speed relented further until the moment when they emerged into a crater identical to the one they had left. "Chuir," he said, laconically, indicating the crater.

The travelers got down and followed their guide into a short corridor that led them, in a matter of minutes, to a circus of greater size, broadly illuminated by sunlight.

"A city—this!" exclaimed Farenehiet, pivoting on his heels and widening his eyes. "Damned if I can see a single habitation or inhabitant."

The Selenite smiled. "All the habitations," he said, "are hollowed out in the sides of the mountain. You can make out a great many fissures in the rock, which permit the free penetration of air and sunlight—when the star is shining—but which are closed during the 354-hour night."

"But the map indicates that a river passes through Chuir," Ossipoff observed.

"Certainly; we shall walk to it, for we need to embark there to reach Rouarthwer."

"On the shore of the Central Sea?" asked the scientist, after consulting the map.

"Indeed—and from there we shall go to Maoulideck, the most important city on the Moon, inhabited by several million Selenites, and from which the *Revolver* is sometimes visible."

"Is it on the other hemisphere, then?" Gontran asked.

"No," said Ossipoff, "but it's located in the libration zone."

Ah," said the young man, as if that reply were satisfactory to him. He let Ossipoff take the lead with Telinga, who was giving him details of the region. Slowing his own steps, he joined Fricoulet. "Libration," he murmured. "What's that?"

"For an astronomer, my poor friend," said the engineer, "you don't know anything about anything. Well, what's meant by the term *libration* is an inherent wobbling of the Moon that sometimes allows us to see a little more of its left side, sometimes a little of its right side and sometimes a little beyond its superior or inferior pole."

Meanwhile, they had arrived at a river, which bore a few bizarre constructions that had nothing in common with European boats, but which navigated against the current with a marvelous rapidity. They were reminiscent of buoys about ten meters wide, seemingly devoid of any kind of motor or propeller.

At first, Fricoulet was amazed. *Are we going to board one of those?* he thought. He was not mistaken. Telinga having shouted a summons, one of these singular machines approached the shore, without any pilot becoming visible. The Selenite got down first, sat down on the ring and invited his companions to join him. Then a there was a whistling sound; the water bubbled momentarily and the vessel drew away rapidly. Inevitably, they had scarcely got under way when Fricoulet asked Telinga to explain the surprising phenomenon by which the curious construction could advance at such a prodigious speed.

"By the simplest means," replied the Selenite, "and if you wish to take account yourself of what you call *the works...*"

He took the young man down into the hold, where a pump activated by a motor was taking in water through a tube at the front to expel it at the rear.

"Indeed," murmured the engineer, with a pitying smile, "nothing is simpler." And he added, seeing the banks flee into the distance behind the rapidly-moving boat: "And it works!"

It worked so well that after a day's navigation, the travelers arrived in Rouarthwer.

"Here," said Telinga, "we shall halt for a while to allow you to rest, then we shall resume our journey."

"That's an excellent idea," said Flammermont, "for it's been too long since I had a substantial meal, prepared by Mademoiselle Selena's white hands. Besides, I'm not disposed to imitate the Sun, which doesn't go to bed for 354 hours. Since early infancy I've developed the habit of sleeping every 12 hours, and it's now nearly 16 that we've been on foot, so I propose we postpone the continuation of our journey until tomorrow."

Everyone shared this opinion; they dined copiously on the provisions they had brought from the Terran vehicle and slept in a compartment of the boat, which went on to Maoulideck without stopping again.

The following day—or, at least, 12 hours after going to sleep—when the travelers woke up, the boat was within sight of the capital of the Moon, the only place with habitations that were not hollowed out like moles' burrows but authentic houses, of a bizarre and veritably lunar architecture.

"Here are folk," murmured Flammermont, "who've certainly passed through the Polytechnique or the Centrale—what do you think, Alcide?" And the young Comte directed his friend's attention to an agglomeration of gigantic curvilinear figures, ranging from the cylindrical to the spherical.

"All the masons that have worked in this city," the engineer replied, "have been Xs,[67] that's for sure."

"At any rate," Gontran said, "they aren't from the architecture department of the Ecole des Beaux-Arts, for all this is decidedly ugly."

Selena, who had overheard, smiled and said: "Oh, my dear Monsieur de Flammermont, it's sufficient for something to be associated with science for you to declare it ugly."

The Comte took the young woman's hand and looked at her amorously. "Oh, my dear Selena," he murmured, "what you say isn't strictly true, for you're very closely associated with Monsieur Ossipoff, who is the most scientific person in the world, and yet I've never hesitated to declare you the prettiest and most charming."

The young woman smiled and lowered her eyes.

"If Monsieur Ossipoff were to hear you!" muttered Fricoulet, the sweet talk getting on his nerves.

The worthy scientist had other things on his mind than listening to his daughter's conversation with her fiancé, however. Telinga had just introduced

---

[67] In Parisian slang, "X" is the Ecole Polytechnique—one of the two colleges specializing in practical arts that Gontran has just sneeringly cited—while "un X" is one of its students, "Monsieur X" one of its graduates and "les X" mathematics.

him to the director of the Observatory and, happy to meet a colleague, the old man had plunged into a lengthy discussion of things that were dear to him.

For his part, the Selenite scientist, delighted to make the acquaintance of a Terran, wanted him to stay longer, in order to ask him for information about parts of the sky that were unknown to him—but Telinga declared that if they wanted to be ready to go into the Subvolvan[68] regions before the day's end, they must not lose any time. It was therefore agreed that once Ossipoff's exploration was concluded, the Terrans would come back to Maoulideck, where a great scientific congress would be held, bringing together all the notable scientists of the lunar world in order to listen to their "heavenly brothers". Solely on that condition, the director of the Selenite Observatory consented to let his visitors leave.

Meanwhile, Telinga—who had gone away momentarily—came back, giving evidence of the greatest satisfaction, and approached Fricoulet. "Monsieur," he said, "I shall prove to you that, in respect of the atmospheric domain, our means of locomotion are equal to our land and water vehicles. If you would care to follow me…" And he steered towards a rather high hill, the summit of which the Terrans reached in a few long strides.

Lying on the ground there, they found a sort of vehicle, somewhat reminiscent of the cart that had brought them to Chuir, with the difference that it was longer and almost cigar-shaped.

"If that's his dirigible balloon…" murmured Gontran, completing the sentence by stretching his lips disdainfully.

"My dear chap," Fricoulet replied, "the experiences we've already had should have served to give you better expectations of the Selenite imagination."

"You have confidence in this machine, then?" asked the young Comte.

"Absolute confidence," retorted the engineer, climbing over the edge of the "machine". He then perceived a sort of receptacle in the center, somewhat reminiscent of a cooking-pot.

"Oh, good God!" exclaimed Gontran, who had followed his friend. "Are the Selenites going to make beef stew?"

Ossipoff, his daughter and the American were already seated; the young Comte followed their example.

---

[68] This term (*Subvolves* in French), introduced into the text abruptly and without explanation, is derived from John Kepler's classic *Somnium*, published posthumously in 1634, which describes a visionary lunar voyage in which the side of the Moon facing the Earth is named *Subvolva* and the far side *Privolva*. Kepler's hypothetical account of lunar biology, although very sketchy, is more sophisticated intellectually than Graffigny's; no 19th century writer contrived to surpass its logical acumen, although Verne and Flammarion were capable of similar imaginative ingenuity.

Telinga bent down and dropped some sort of explosive mixture into the "cooking-pot" through an aperture, which he immediately re-sealed. After a few seconds, crackling sounds commenced. "Hold tight," he said. "We're off." At the same time, he opened a tap. Immediately, a prolonged fizzing sound was heard at the rear and the vessel left the ground, impelled by an invisible force, climbing into the air along a diagonal path.

Gontran leaned over the edge, considered this phenomenon open-mouthed, wondering whether he were witnessing a miracle. Fricoulet—who, in his capacity as an engineer, was in a position to understand many things—broke into a smile. "It's quite simple," he said. "The propulsion is obtained by the slow combustion of the mixture. The gases produced escape through a tube situated at the rear, and it's by virtue of the force of the recoil—the reaction of the gas upon the air—that the apparatus moves forwards, sliding on the layers of air like a rocket...or rather a kite."[69]

"It's the same principle as your steam-aeroplane," said Ossipoff to the young Comte.

"Oh," Gontran replied, seriously, with a disdainful shake of the head. "Less complicated..."

Simple as it was, however, the vehicle advanced with marvelous rapidity; the lunar territories passed beneath the travelers before they had time to examine them in detail. For a while, the apparatus followed a long artificially-excavated canal that established communication between two oceans, which Selena jokingly baptized with the name of "the Panama Canal."[70]

"Oh!" said Gontran. "They too have their Ferdinand de Lesseps."

The Central Ocean was succeeded by an immense verdant forest, divided into two equal parts by a broad river, and then by large plains. Then, little by

---

[69] As in his account of his own flying-machine, Fricoulet seems not to understand the actual principle of jet propulsion, confusing his correct attribution of the impulse to the reaction against the expulsion of gas with an incorrect suggestion that a rocket is "pushing against the air" in a manner somehow analogous to a kite. Flammarion knew better, although his accurate calculation of the escape velocity necessary to escape the grip of terrestrial gravity inhibited him from suggesting that jet propulsion might be adequate to its achievement. André Mas, writing in Paris in 1913, was similarly dubious; like the English popularizer of science John Munro—whose theoretical account of the possibilities of space travel in *A Trip to Venus* (1897) includes consideration of a "compound cannon" not unlike Ossipoff's—Mas thought that rockets would only become practicable as a means of propulsion once a vessel was actually in space.

[70] As the earlier chapters of the narrative make clear, the Panama Canal was not operational when the novel was written, but Ferdinand de Lesseps had already begun work on it in 1881, so it was a celebrated work in progress; it was eventually completed in 1914.

little, the region became more uneven, and the horizon was soon seemingly barred by a chain of high mountains, among which was one particular peak of vertiginous altitude. This was Phovethn, the most formidable active volcano on the entire Moon. The crater of this Selenite Cotopaxi measured no less than a league in breadth and it projected rocks, monstrous lava debris and solid blocks of stone as far as the limits of the atmosphere.

"Here's a volcano," said Flammermont, "which would like nothing better than to give us a return ticket to our fatherland."

"Its force would, indeed, undoubtedly be more than sufficient for us to attain the Earth's zone of attraction," Ossipoff replied, "if this face of the Moon did not have the misfortune of never seeing our planet." So saying, he studied the young man carefully, wondering whether he had been speaking seriously or whether he considered what he had said to be a joke.

Meanwhile, Telinga had set a course northwards and the vessel was now flying over an immense sea.

"Where are we going?" Ossipoff asked.

"To Tough," the Selenite replied. "The fuel whose combustion produces the boat's propulsion is almost exhausted, and it's necessary to replaced it before we launch into Subvolvan regions.

It was only after 36 hours of uninterrupted travel that the travelers reached Tough-Todivaslou—the Queen of the North—an important city of the lunar world's northern hemisphere, built near a river in an immense drained marsh.

"It reminds me of Pinsk, in Russia," murmured Ossipoff.

They only stayed in the city just long enough to renew the boat's provisions.

The journey had already lasted two terrestrial days; the Sun was descending gradually toward the horizon, and in three times 24 hours it would cease to illuminate this hemisphere of the Moon, transporting its light and heat to the visible hemisphere. It was, therefore, important to make haste if they wanted to avoid the 15-day night and cross the pole at the same time as the Sun. The second part of the voyage was bound to be much more difficult and more perilous, and the 354 hours of daylight would not be too many to permit Ossipoff to find his precious mineral and allow Jonathan Farenheit to get his hands on Fedor Sharp.

Chapter XVI
The Mountains of Eternal Light

Seated in the bow of the vessel with a strong telescope in his hands, Ossipoff scanned the horizon; his expression, already grave, visibly darkened as the mountains looming up in the distance displayed their elevated peaks and monstrous ramparts more clearly. A hand fell on his shoulder, and he turned to see Selena standing behind him, looking at him anxiously. "Father," she said, "is there some frightful danger that's worrying you?"

"It's those mountains that frighten me," the old man answered, anxiously.

"Why is that? Wasn't that volcano we passed recently just as high?"

"Perhaps—but it didn't have the same location."

"What do you mean by that?"

"That those mountains are situated on the boundary between the two hemispheres and that, in consequence, the air must be very rarefied there."

Selena smiled. "Haven't we got Monsieur Fricoulet's *respirols*?"

The old man pursed his lips disdainfully.

"You don't trust them?" Selena murmured. "Monsieur de Flammermont has examined them, and has told me that he couldn't have done better himself."

"Hmm!" said Ossipoff. "Dear Gontran is indulgent to his friend. I can't understand how a man as replete with talent and education as him can associate himself with such a mediocre individual." He turned to Telinga and asked: "Will we be obliged to fly over those peaks?"

"It is necessary," the Selenite replied. "What other route would you like to take?"

"There must be some less elevated pass, however narrow, between two chains."

"Yes," said the other. "We could find a pass without making a considerable detour, but we can only reach Romounhinch by going straight ahead."

Ossipoff consulted the map that he had drawn up during the long night spent in the volcano. By comparing it with his atlas of lunar geography he established that Romounhinch was the name by which the Selenites designated the Circus of Plato. "But is it necessary to go that far?" he murmured.

"It is the shortest route to get to Notoliders, in the vicinity of which—according to the information you've given me—you will find what you are looking for."

A further comparison of his Terran atlas with his Selenite map told Ossipoff that this new volcano was none other than Archimedes. "But that volcano is a long way into the other hemisphere!" he exclaimed.

"Almost in the center of the Subvolvan region. It, is, moreover, the largest crater on our world after the Circus of Clavius.

225

Ossipoff consulted his instruments. The barometer indicated just 28 centimeters of pressure; the compass was confused, indicating no fixed direction. The old man's eyebrows furrowed violently and he looked at his companions anxiously. Meanwhile, to increase the gravity of the situation, the further the vessel advanced, the more the daylight faded and the darkness deepened. "My friends," he said, trying to keep his voice firm, "I think it's time to put on these items of apparatus."

The *respirols*, as Fricoulet had baptized them, were quite simple. They had been designed to permit their wearers to venture with impunity into the bosom of the most unbreathable and most rarefied atmospheres. Each one consisted of a sort of rubber cagoule falling to the underside of the thorax, hermetically sealed beneath the arms. Two panes of glass set in front of the eyes permitted the wearer to see as clearly as if he were wearing spectacles, and there was an opening in front of the mouth equipped with a valve opening inside and out, in order to permit the evacuation of the gases of pulmonary combustion. This valve also permitted the adjunction of a copper tube designed to be applied to the ear of anyone to whom he wished to speak, when the rarefaction of the air prevented the transmission of sound. In a side-pocket there was a steel cylinder, with a capacity of a quarter of a liter, containing liquid oxygen; when the tap was opened, gas was released and it arrived via a tube in the rubber envelope, which it inflated without being able to escape. This steel cylinder contained a provision of 3000 liters of gaseous oxygen—which is to say, the equivalent of three days' consumption.

With the assistance of the inventor, the travelers were rapidly clad in their respirols. Fricoulet checked all the parts of the apparatus one after another, assuring himself that the tubes were firmly attached and that the fastenings were hermetically sealed. Then he opened the taps and the oxygen distended the folds of the cagoule. So far as the upper parts of their bodies were concerned, each traveler soon resembled a lollipop.

While this was accomplished, Telinga had recharged the apparatus of his vehicle with combustible material, and the voyagers rose up into the air, alternately moving very steeply up and down.

Always roller-coasters, thought Gontran, privately, the respirol making it extremely inconvenient for him to communicate his impressions.

Ossipoff's eyes had not left the needle of his barometer, and he was very glad that his faced was hidden by the rubber cagoule, for his companions would have been veritably alarmed by the alteration of his features. "Damn!" he murmured. "The pressure's diminishing."

Fricoulet, who was also keeping watch on the barometer, applied the end of his "speaker"—as he had nicknamed the acoustic tube—to the scientist's ear. "Before long," he said, "the pressure will be less than that subsisting at an Earthly altitude of 15,000 meters."

Ossipoff nodded his head and murmured: "As long as these rubber hoods don't burst!"

At that moment his gaze fell on Gontran, who was sitting beside Selena, holding the young woman's hands in his, using the expressive language of his eyes to replace the affectionate words that he found it repugnant to address to her "by tube." *What a man!* thought the old scientist, attributing Flammermont's indifference to the threat of death to courage rather than ignorance. Then, solicited by his anguish, he turned to Telinga, who was attentively supervising the maneuvers. He was anxious that the Selenite should not risk even lower pressure in order to get over the mountains.

Suddenly, however, as the vessel flew over a mass of granite barring the horizon, at a prodigious velocity, Telinga brought about an abrupt 50-meter descent in order to enter a breach curving between two masses of brown rocks. Although it was almost completely dark now, the Selenite pressed on boldly into this corridor, avoiding all the obstacles that loomed up incessantly from the shadows with marvelous assurance.

Finally, after ten minutes—which seemed as long as decades to the voyagers—the rocks suddenly opened up, and an enormous and resplendent star appeared over a jagged mountainous horizon.

The Earth! Selena thought.

"The Moon!" cried Gontran, applying his speaker to Ossipoff's ear.

Flamermont understood from the old man's abrupt movement that he had just said something stupid. He hastened to correct himself. "The Moon's moon, that is—isn't the Earth lit up like a satellite of the world we're presently visiting?"

Leaning pensively on the guard-rail, Selena studied the sparkling sphere, 13 times brighter than the full Moon of the most beautiful terrestrial nights. She found it difficult to imagine that she had been born on that distant world, and that a mere five days had sufficed to hollow out an immense and terrifying abyss of 90,000 leagues between her and it.

Even Ossipoff, forgetting the dangers of the situation, glued his eye to his telescope, recognizing the large patches of the oceans, cut across by the brighter tints of the continents. At that moment, it was 2 p.m. in Paris and 4 p.m. in St. Petersburg; the two Americas were emerging from shadow and Asia had disappeared.

While the scientist plunged into contemplation, the boat wound around the buttresses of the monstrous mountains forming a titanic barrier between the two hemispheres. Beyond that barrier, there was a very different region. The panorama offered to the travelers' view was grandiose, presenting no point of comparison with the most savage location that might be encountered on Earth. The almost total rarefaction of the air at the high altitudes they had reached gave the landscape a monotonous aspect.

What immediately struck Gontran—who, as an amateur artist, was amusing himself by sketching in a drawing-pad—was the absolute lack of perspective, by virtue of the absence of half-tones. A harsh light descended from the sky, and everything that was not directly illuminated by the light of the full Earth remained intensely black, so that the remotest plane surfaces seemed as sharp as the nearest—to the extent that the Comte, wanting to depict these rocks and jagged-rimmed craters, could put nothing but ink-stains on his sheet of white paper. "In truth," he murmured, "if I sent a painting in this genre to the Salon, the Impressionists themselves would jeer at me—and yet it's photographically exact!" Sadly, he added: "Sometimes the truth isn't very plausible."

O Boileau, you certainly could not have expected to awaken echoes in lunar landscapes![71]

The further the travelers advanced into the Subvolvan regions, the more the desolate aridity of the rocky regions increased. Jonathan Farenheit never stopped swearing, Selena felt a desire to weep, and even Fricoulet was afflicted by a mortal sadness. As for Gontran, he became profoundly nostalgic in thinking that, at this very moment, that palace of industry the Champs-Elysées, would be spilling forth a crowd racing to witness the great military tournament mounted for the benefit of the poor.

Closing his eyes to rid himself of the monotonous and dreary spectacle of the lunar wilderness, he crossed the 90,000 leagues separating him from Paris with a single imaginative leap and, for several seconds, dazzled his eyes with bright costumes, the gleam of diamonds and the sparkle of gold and steel, while his ears hummed softly to orchestral strains, punctuated by the whinnying of horse and bursts of applause. Suddenly, he started, snatched from his pleasant vision by a voice that murmured in his ear: "Plato."

It was Ossipoff, who, forcing himself to lean over the guard-rail, was pointing down from the vessel at the crater of one of the most curious lunar circuses.

Scarcely had the young man directed his eyes at the panorama unfolding beneath him when he cried: "A forest!"

"What did you say?" asked Ossipoff, divining the young man's astonishment without understanding its cause.

By means of his tube, Gontran repeated the exclamation that he had just uttered.

"Well, what's astonishing about that?" said the old man.

"I thought that all astronomers were agreed in refusing this region of the Moon the slightest vegetation."

"All!" Ossipoff protested. "Not all, for photography proves the contrary. The soil of certain lunar plains and the depths of a few craters, such as Plato, are not photogenic. The majority of the astronomers of the last century had attri-

---

[71] The reference is to the famous critic Nicolas Boileau-Despréaux (1636-1711).

buted the absorption of luminous radiation to vegetation but, as the low density of the atmosphere on the visible surface has now been determined, along with the total absence of rivers or any liquid whatsoever, the present inclination is to deny that vegetation. However, contemporary scientists such as Warren de la Rue, Rutherfurd and Secchi,[72] who are specialists in lunar photography, have held to the contrary opinion that these photogenic differences must originate from vegetal reflection. The green tint in question has been observed in the Sea of Crises and in Plato." Passing Gontran a pieced of paper, he continued: "Here's a drawing by Stanley Williams[73] representing the interior of the circus over which we're flying. Isn't it an exact representation of the actuality?"

The flying boat was, at that moment, almost immobile directly above the crater and the voyagers were able to distinguish clearly that the soil of the circus was covered in vast forests cut through by wide roads. There were objects like molehills at certain crossroads, which Telinga declared to have once been dwellings, and a thick, opaque fog rose in spirals from a few subsurface chimneys, spreading like a misty veil from one edge to the other.

"Stanley Williams' drawing corresponds closely to the actuality," said Fricoulet.

"But I've already seen this map," Gontran said, seriously, "in one of my illustrious namesake's books."

"In *Les Continents célestes*?" said Ossipoff.

"Undoubtedly."

The Selenite, thinking that enough time had been lost in the study of the crater, pressed the lever that he used to steer his vessel, and the aerial voyage continued.

It was then that Fricoulet asked Ossipoff: "If I've understood the objective of this exploration correctly, we're going in search of a means of continuing our interplanetary voyage?"

The scientist replied affirmatively by nodding his head.

"You seriously intend to leave the Moon?"

Ossipoff gestured impatiently. "A worldlet scarcely 800 leagues in diameter!" he exclaimed. "On which the five of us weigh no more than I alone weigh on Earth: a decadent—not to say nearly dead—world, only parts of which are habitable and inhabited!"

"But to launch yourself into space again," Fricoulet objected, "you'll need an agent of projection even more rapid than Cotopaxi, for in the sidereal desert, the leagues are not counted in thousands, but in millions."

---

[72] Warren de la Rue (1815-1889) was the first significant pioneer of celestial photography, although his endeavors were soon outshone by Rutherfurd's. Angelo Secchi (1818-78) was far more significant as an observer of stars than he was as a lunar photographer.

[73] The amateur astronomer Arthur Stanley Williams (1861-1938).

"My dear Monsieur," the old man replied, a trifle haughtily, "I know all that as well as you do. In any case, you may be tranquil. If my calculations are not mistaken, we shall have that high-velocity propulsive agent of which you speak very soon." And to prove to the engineer that he wanted to cut the conversation short, the old scientist turned his back on him and set about examining the panorama with the aid of his telescope.

"Notoliders!" the Selenite said, all of a sudden, extending his hand toward a mountain whose jagged crest rose high into the sky in the distance.

"Mount Archimedes," murmured Ossipoff.

If Plato is the lunar circus that presents the most singular appearance, as seen from Earth, Archimedes is certainly the most remarkable mountain after Tycho. During the full Moon, it appears to Terrans as a brilliant point on their satellite's disk. For Mikhail Ossipoff and his companions, however, who were flying only a few 100 meters over the circus, all the orographical details stood out with a surprising clarity. They were easily able to distinguish the high peaks that rose up from the depths of the crater to an altitude of 1500 meters and the two slopes forming the ring of the circular mountain. Ridges and buttresses extended from the mountain to link up with the distant Apennine Mountains.

The flying boat took nearly an hour to cross the crater of Archimedes, which measures no less than 83 kilometers in diameter.

"What luck," Fricoulet suddenly said to Gontran, "that the Selenites have invented aerial navigation; otherwise, the exploration of this world would be impossible for us."

Making no reply, the young Comte looked at his friend questioningly.

The engineer pointed to the deep ravines that opened across the plain in the midst of which the enormous crater stood. "Look at those clefts," he said. They're certainly more than a kilometer wide; as for their length, they extend to the horizon. Their sides are sheer and, in places, their depths are obstructed by landslides. Well, suppose that instead of arriving by way of the air, we were simply going on foot, *pedibus cum jambis*[74]—what would we do when confronted by crevasses 1,300 meters deep? We'd be stopped."

"We'd make a detour," Gontran objected.

"Of how many kilometers? And who knows whether, north of the declivity, we wouldn't encounter another crevasse that would force us to retrace or steps?"

Flammermont nodded his head affirmatively. "Viewed from the telescope in Pulkova Observatory, these fissures seemed to me to be the dry beds of ancient rivers."

Fricoulet signaled to him to lower his voice. "Be careful of Mikhail Ossipoff, fool," he said. "Remember that there can't be any rivers, lakes or oceans in

---

[74] This mock-Latin phrase used to be employed in France as a comically pretentious way of saying "on foot."

this part of the Moon; the atmospheric pressure is too low to maintain water in its liquid state. As I told you, when we were chatting during the journey, these crevasses are purely geo…no, selenological…in nature."

During this conversation, the flying boat had continued its route and was now no more than 50 kilometers from the Apennine chain, whose elevated crests rose 6000 meters into the sky, extending immoderate shadows over the neighboring plains.

"This time," murmured Fricoulet, "we won't get over."

Mikhail Ossipoff was hunched over the bow of the vessel, studying the terrain with his telescope. Suddenly, he put his instrument down and took a crumpled and discolored piece of paper from his pocket, which he unfolded carefully and examined attentively. Then he resumed his original position, after murmuring a few words in Telinga's ear.

The vessel immediately veered sideways and began to follow the crests of the Apennines, which were succeeded by the less elevated peaks of the Carpathians. Ossipoff set his telescope aside again, and Farenheit immediately took possession of it. Ossipoff took out another, and subjected it to a mysterious operation.

"What are you doing, Father?" asked Selena.

"I'm adding a prism to this telescope."

"A prism?" she repeated. "My God, what for?"

"To convert this telescope into a simplified spectroscope. Thanks to the prism, the light of the terrain on which I focus will be decomposed, and will then be reflected by a polished mirror set in the middle of the tube." Then, addressing Gontran—who also appeared to be listening to the aged scientist's explanation—he added: "You know, my dear friend, that a number of narrow black and colored lines have been distinguished in the solar spectrum, always situated in the same place and of the same hue. Thanks to these fundamental reference-points, it was possible to develop spectroscopy, a science that permits the determination of the composition of any body—of whatever sort—whose luminous spectrum can be observed, by comparing the colors and lines of its spectrum to those of known substances. It's thanks to this method that we know, without any doubt, that there are iron, magnesium and zinc in combination in our Sun, hydrogen in Vega, and gold, platinum, and copper in fusion in other stars."

He paused momentarily and aimed his telescope at the slopes of the Carpathians. Then, shaking his head, he continued: "What I've just told you was in order to explain how, from the St. Petersburg Observatory and thanks to careful spectroscopic research, I recognized in the flames of active lunar volcanoes a substance that has the property of being attracted toward light. I've made careful note of the lines and colors of that substance, and I've inscribed them on the polished glass disposed in the middle of my telescope—with the consequence that by aiming this spectroscopic telescope at the various objects within range, the spectra of those objects will be superimposed on the one already etched and engraved on the glass. I compare them, and when the two spectra are identical, it's because the material I'm aiming at is the one that I'm seeking."

"Is it this substance that will enable you to continue your voyage?" asked Gontran, whose faced reflected a profound bewilderment.

Fricoulet had drawn closer, and there mocking gleam in his eyes. Ossipoff noticed it and replied: "Yes, I thought of utilizing this substance, which has the curious property of moving towards the light."

"But how will you employ it?"

"I'll enclose it in glass spheres attached to each side of our vehicle, and it will carry us toward the Sun. We shall thus be able to visit the worlds that are between the Earth and the central star."

In a skeptical tone, Fricoulet asked: "But how do you propose to land when we want to, rather than hurling ourselves into the solar furnace like a moth burning its wings in a candle-flame?"

Ossipoff shrugged his shoulders. "In order to be master of the direction and velocity of the vehicle, "he replied, "it will be sufficient to shield the receptacles that contain the substance in question from light, and increase or decrease speed in the direction of the attracted surface."

Gontran could not help saying, admiringly: "You have an answer for everything, Monsieur Ossipoff!"

The old scientist shrugged his shoulders slightly and resumed his observation-post beside Jonathan Farenheit, who was standing in the bow as motionless as a statue, with his telescope glued to the ground.

Suddenly, the old man uttered an exclamation and extended his arm, pointing at a column of smoke a few kilometers further on, which seemed to be emerging from the ground and rising swiftly into the air to lose itself in space. "There!" he said, while the telescope trembled in his hand. "There it is!"

Within a few moments, steered diagonally by Telinga's sure hand, the flying boat was swooping down towards the point indicated by Ossipoff. It was a sort of squat cone, the crater of which was projecting swirls of fine, almost impalpable dust in the direction of the Sun shining in the sky. As the voyagers got down, they would certainly have been blinded if the glass lenses encased in their rubber cagoules had not protected their eyes. Immediately, the old scientist took an immense sheet of canvas from the bottom of the boat. With his companions' help, he extended it over the top of the crater, in such a fashion as to intercept the light of the Sun.

As if by a miracle, the eruption ceased. Sacks brought for that purpose were promptly filled with the precious dust and loaded on the boat—which, at a signal from Ossipoff, took off again.

The old scientist was exultant.

"Where are we going now?" asked Telinga.

232

"We're returning, at our convenience, to the Privolvan regions. Don't we have to attend the congress what is to be held in our honor in the capital city?"

The Selenite pressed his lever and the boat, rapidly turning round, headed back towards the invisible hemisphere.

Suddenly, however, Jonathan Farenheit started and turned to Ossipoff. "What are you doing?" he demanded.

"As you can see, we're going back."

"What about Fedor Sharp?" he complained.

The old man raised his arms to the heavens.

"You've taken care of your business," grumbled the American. "I want to take care of mine."

"Trust me," replied Ossipoff. "Do as I've done—renounce your vengeance...all the more so as it can only be exercised now on a cadaver."

Farenheit stifled an oath.

"In addition," added the aged scientist, "time's pressing. The Sun's just above the horizon and I don't want to be surprised by darkness in this wilderness...it would be death for us all."

The American lowered his head; then he went back to his position and, telescope in hand, resumed scanning the landscape that was fleeing rapidly beneath the boat. In the meantime, the other voyagers, for whom the return journey held no surprises, lay down on the cushions to seek reparative rest in a long sleep.

When they woke up, the aerial boat had already left the circus of Plato far behind and was heading at high speed towards a chain of mountains whose elevated summits were vaguely silhouetted on the horizon.

Ossipoff consulted his map. "The north pole!" he exclaimed.

Running to Farenheit, who was still absorbed in his search, he said: "Lend me my telescope, Mr. Farenheit."

The American surrendered the instrument, with an ill grace. "Eh?" he said. "What's there to see at the north pole that's out of the ordinary? More mountains, craters, frightful bare rocks and gulfs."

Ossipoff stared at Farenheit briefly, as if he were looking at a criminal. Then he replied: "At the north pole, Monsieur, we shall see the Mountains of Eternal Light."

The American's eyes widened. Gontran and Selena drew nearer.

The old scientist continued: "Those mountains—some of which Scoresby, Euctemon and Gioja[75] estimate as being up to 28,000 meters in height, and on which the Sun never sets—are one of the wonders of the world that we're visiting."

---

[75] The three named objects are all craters and the height attributed to them is entirely illusory; as with many other craters mentioned in the text, Graffigny's mistaken conviction that they are volcanic turns them into mountains.

"Impossible," murmured Flammermont. Fortunately for him, the rubber hood stifled the sound of his voice.

"But how can such a phenomenon occur, Father?" Selena asked.

"In the simplest fashion in the world, my dear—by virtue of the inclination of the lunar globe on its axis, the Sun never descends more than a degree and a half below the horizon of either pole. Now, by reason of the smallness of the lunar globe, an elevation of 595 meters is sufficient to see a degree and a half beyond the true horizon. In consequence, mountains like those I've cited, attaining 2800 meters of altitude, are eternally lit by the Sun."

"Are the surrounding valleys, then," murmured Gontran, "always in darkness?"

"*In darkness* is a trifle exaggerated," replied Ossipoff, "for while they remain eternally in the shadow of the mountains, they're illuminated by the reflection of the bright light that strikes the high peaks, rotating around them." Then, turning to the American, he said: "Well, Mr. Farenheit, is such a spectacle worthy of your abandoning your search for a few moments?"

"Nothing's worth more than a satisfactory vengeance," the American replied. Picking up his telescope, he became motionless again, leaving his companions to anticipate the sublime panorama that they were about to admire.

Telinga had just modified the heading of the aerial boat slightly, in order to follow the sinuosities of the extending slopes of Mount Scoresby. He passed below the peak of Euctemon, whose height is only 400 meters less than the highest mountains in the Pyrenees, and headed through the rocky ramifications directly for the chains surrounding the boreal pole. To pass over the cyclopean mass of monstrous craters, the Selenite had to ascend to 3000 meters.

Once the chain was behind them, the lunar aeroplane was launched at top speed on a diagonal path that took it down to 1000 meters above the ground, above an isolated mountain with a bowl-shaped crater.

"The north pole!" cried Ossipoff.

Motionless and mute, the Terrans admired the magical spectacle that was suddenly offered to their rapt eyes. Into a black sky, strewn with vividly-shining stars, elevated peaks projected their sharp crests, the enormous shadows of which extended into the distance, darkening entire valleys. On the sunward side, these peaks were as resplendent as glaciers, and their glare was dazzling.

"Look, Mr. Farenheit!" Flammermont said, all of a sudden, tapping the American on the shoulder.

The latter made no response. Leaning over the guard-rail to the point of losing his balance, he remained fixed in complete immobility, his eye glued to his telescope.

"My God!" sniggered the young Comte. "Wouldn't one think that the American is about to swoop down on that bandit Sharp?"

He had not even completed this speech when Farenheit straightened up as if jerked by a spring, and ran to Ossipoff. "It's him!" he cried, gesticulating like a madman. "It's him!"

"Who's *him*?" demanded the old man, furious at being wrenched so rudely from his contemplation.

"Who do you think it is," retorted the American, "if not that thief, that scoundrel, that traitor...?" The emotion tightening his throat stemmed the flood of insults that were rising to his lips.

More emotional than he wished to appear, the old scientist seized the telescope and aimed it in the direction indicated by Farenheit. After a few moments, he cried out in his turn: "I can indeed see a brilliant point down there, only a few kilometers away, which might well be the cannonball...take a look, Gontran..."

He passed the instrument to the young Comte, who passed it on in his turn to Fricoulet, saying: "I'd bet my head that it is indeed Sharp's cannonball."

"Me too," added the engineer. "Except that I don't see any trace of the man himself."

Ossipoff had not waited to instruct Telinga to set down, and no more than a few moments went by before the aerial boat deposited the voyagers on the slope of a crater next to a dented and scorched metallic mass, which the old scientist declared with certainty to be Fedor Sharp's cannonball.

"But what about him?" growled Farenehit. "Where is he?" He darted furious glances all around as he spoke.

"Well," said Fricoulet, tapping the cannonball with his foot, "it's in there that we'll have to look for him."

"In there?" retorted the American. "Do you suppose he's stayed there, then?"

"For the good reason that it was impossible for him to get out." The engineer pointed out to his companions that at least a third of the shell was embedded in the ground, and that the little door fabricated in its side-wall was so solidly buried that all the efforts that the passengers might have made to get out of their prison would have been in vain. He added: "In any case, the prison is surely no more that a tomb now, and I propose to let those who are asleep with in it rest their eternally."

The American did not intend that to happen, though. Before leaving, he wanted to make certain with his own eyes that his enemy really had escaped his vengeance. With the aid of the tools that Ossipoff had chanced to bring with him, he set about attacking the friable soil. Seeing that, Gontran, seized by curiosity, grabbed a pick-axe—and was not long delayed in being imitated by Fricoulet too.

After half an hour, thanks to their colossal strength, sextupled by the Moon, they had excavated a trench around the cannonball wide enough for the door to be opened.

"Look out," muttered the American, putting himself on the defensive. "Let's be on our guard…they might attack us."

The engineer shrugged his shoulders. Introducing the point of a pick-axe into the crack in the door, he exercised such violent leverage that the bolt and the screws securing the lock eventually gave way. He opened it, took a step forward and slid the upper half of his body into the interior of the cannonball—but he came back out immediately, uttering a cry of horror.

"Dead!" he exclaimed. "They're dead!"

Jonathan Farenheit went forward in his turn and, in spite of the hatred he nursed for the ex-permanent secretary of the Academy of Sciences, felt a chill run through his limbs at the sight of the sinister spectacle that was offered to him.

On the floor of the vehicle, a semi-naked corpse lay in the middle of a pool of blood. A horrible injury had almost separated the head from the trunk and—a frightful detail—slices of flesh had been stripped from the thighs. The cadaver had served as a food-supply. Not far away, another corpse was lying, this one fully-dressed. The American hurled himself toward it. He had recognized Fedor Sharp. He picked it up and took it outside the vehicle.

"Dead!" he said, in a somber tone, bowing his head.

"Dead of starvation!" cried Selena, putting her hands together. "Oh, the poor man."

"No," replied Farenheit. "I suspect him of having murdered his companion in order to nourish himself on his flesh."

A cry of horror escaped all their throats.

Chapter XVII
What happened in the cannonball

What had happened?

We left Fedor Sharp and his companion in their cannonball, the former furious on seeing his former colleague on the point of arriving, like him, on the coveted lunar soil, the latter trembling in contemplation of the fate that awaited them if chance should put them in proximity with Jonathan Farenheit's formidable fists.

They remained thus for a long time. Voriguin mentally calculated his remaining chances of avoiding the American's vengeance; Sharp, his eyes fixed on his objective, followed the progress of Mikhail Ossipoff's projectile through space. Suddenly, the latter uttered an exclamation that brought his already-anxious laboratory assistant running to his side.

"What's gone wrong now?" stammered Voriguin.

Without answering, Sharp grabbed him by the shoulders and stuck his face to the telescope. "Look!" he said, briefly.

It was the laboratory assistant's turn to be astonished.

"Damn it!" he said. "That's bizarre!"

"You can see it too?" Sharp said.

"Of course!" the other retorted. "One would have to be blind not to see that the demonic American's cannonball is smaller that it was this morning." He stood up and fixed an anxious gaze on the Russian. "What does it mean?"

Sharp did not reply; he was thinking.

"Are we stopping again?" Voriguin persisted.

Still silent, Sharp climbed the few steps that led to the cannonball's nose-cone. There he uncovered a porthole and looked through it. Out there in space, very distant, a luminous crescent shone in the midst of a host of stars. He picked up a telescope, aimed it for a few seconds, then covered the porthole again, went down the ladder and said to Voriguin: "The shell has turned over."

The other made a fearful gesture. "Turned over?" he exclaimed. "So what?"

Sharp grimaced a smile. "So nothing. It's now the base of the shell that's facing the Moon and the tip that's pointed towards the Earth."

Incredulous, Voriguin dropped to his hands and knees on the floor and looked out. Beneath him, the Moon was extended like a huge world-map. "What about them?" he asked.

Sharp shrugged his shoulders. "What about them?" he sniggered. "They're flying through space."

A joyful gleam came into the laboratory assistant's eye. "Won't they reach the Moon?"

"It's improbable."

On hearing this reassuring reply, Voriguin got to his feet swiftly and attempted to express his joy by means of an entrechat—but he had forgotten that, being so distant from the Earth—the laws of gravity were constantly modifying their effect on the cannonball and its contents, so that he bumped his head against the ceiling of the compartment and fell rather rudely on the floor.

Sharp's austere face cleared as he saw the laboratory assistant grab his head in both hands. "Ha ha! That's what comes of having so few brains," he said.

Voriguin emitted a dull groan; then, without any retort, he went to the telescope and aimed it once again at Mikhail Ossipoff's vehicle. Borne away by an unknown force, it continued to draw away in the direction of the Moon's polar regions.

"To what do you attribute that, Master?" Voriguin asked.

"Doubtless to the influence exerted on their cannonball by ours—an influence sufficient to pull them off course."

The laboratory assistant clapped his hands. "Oh!" he cried. "If what you say were true, it would give me sweet satisfaction to know that the accursed American would fly through space for ever, and that it was our fault! For you're quite certain, aren't you, that they won't reach the lunar surface?"

"One can never be certain of these things, my dear chap," Sharp replied, in a slightly disdainful tone. "One can only deal in probabilities."

"And the probability is…?"

"That Ossipoff will curve around the entire lunar disk and then be lost in infinity."

With a ferocious smile, Voriguin added: "Ha ha! I'd like to be a fly on the wall to see what will happen. It would be interesting, to be sure, when there are no more food-supplies on board. They're capable of drawing straws to see who'll be eaten, as in the song of *Le Petit Navire*."[76] The wretch had already forgotten the bloody scene what had almost taken place between his companion and himself when the savior shell had been spotted in space. Abruptly, his thoughts took another track and, abandoning Ossipoff's projectile, returned to the one containing him. "Well fall, though?" he asked.

---

[76] *Le Petit Navire* [The Little Ship], also known as *La Courte Paille* [The Short Straw] is a seamen's ballad whose French version dates back at least as far as the 16th century. Versions of it exist in most other European languages; the British one, *The Ship in Distress*, was recorded by several 20th century folk singers, including Ewan MacColl. Its central motif, in which shipwreck victims draw straws to determine which of them will be killed and eaten to keep the others alive, is an enduring item of maritime mythology, often exploited or satirized in popular fiction. Like some modern urban legends, it gave rise to actual cases of imitative behavior.

Sharp nodded his head affirmatively.

"And how will we fall?" Voriguin went on.

The scientist consulted his instruments. "It's bizarre," he murmured. "We're following a rigorously perpendicular course."

"And can you tell in advance exactly where we're going to land?"

Sharp knelt down beside the window in the middle of the shell's circular floor, with a plumb line in his right hand and a pair of binoculars in the left. After a brief investigation, he replied: "We're falling into the dead center of the Sea of Serenity."

"Isn't that one of the most curious regions of the satellite?" asked the laboratory assistant.

The scientist got up and nodded his head. "It's one of the most enigmatic, at least," he replied, "for it's subject to changes with regard to which terrestrial astronomers are not in agreement."

"They observe them, though."

"It's the causes of the changes about which they disagree."

"I don't understand."

Sharp bent down again and beckoned to his companion to come closer. "Look," he instructed.

Voriguin strained his eyes. "Well?" he said. "What's extraordinary? It's all the same: mountains, craters, peaks…"

"Don't you see a small rockslide to the right of the Sea of Serenity?"

"Right…beside those shiny outcrops of rock."

"That's the Tumulus of Linné."

"Well?"

"Well, that little circus, hardly perceptible today, was once very obvious, since one finds it marked on maps of the Moon originating in the year 1651. In 1788 the astronomer Schröter observed and described it. In the time of Lohrmann and Mädler that circus presented an internal diameter of 30,000 feet. It was darkly shadowed when lit obliquely; on the other hand, when the Sun was high above the horizon, the whole thing appeared as a white stain. Then, abruptly, in 1866, Schmidt—the director of the Observatory of Athens, one of the astronomers most interested in the Moon—observed that the crater had been replaced by a low-lying white cone with gently-sloping sides.[77] Finally, very re-

---

[77] Johann Schmidt (1824-1878) made the cited claim while compiling a detailed lunar map, first completed in 1868 and improved in 1874. It was based on comparisons of his own observations with earlier lunar maps made by Johann Mädler (1794-1874) and Wilhelm Lohrmann (1796-1840) in the 1830s— although Lorhmann's map was only published posthumously, in a version edited by Schmidt. Mädler and his sponsor William Beer had been adamant that the moon's face was unchanging, and Schimdt was enthusiastic to prove them

cently, the French scientist Flammarion, observing this mysterious point, concluded that the crater had more-or-less crumbled or disintegrated since 1830. And now, as you can see for yourself, it's no more than a whitish dome without any cavity at the center, when it had a circus more than ten kilometers wide 200 years ago."

"And what caused that collapse?" asked Voriguin.

Sharp straightened up and shrugged his shoulders. "We'll know that," he said, "once we've arrived down there."

"But you must have an opinion on the subject," the laboratory assistant persisted. "Is it the action of nature or must we see it as the result of the labor of intelligent beings?"

"I repeat, I don't have any firm idea with respect to the phenomenon. I've only concluded one thing, which is that the astronomers of the terrestrial world are mistaken in propagating the opinion that the lunar world is completely dead and frozen." He paused momentarily, then added: "What strange people they are! Being unable, with the feeble instruments at their disposal, to discover the causes of important changes observed in the lunar surface, they prefer to conclude that the satellite is dead. It's absurd, in truth." He folded his arms and looked at his companion angrily, as if he held him personally responsible for the stupidity of astronomers. "The Moon, a dead world!" he cried. "But that requires a willful denial of the evidence, or putting in doubt the observations made by the most illustrious of our predecessors! The German astronomer Gruithuisen was, no doubt, blind in 1824, when he perceived in the dark region of the Moon in its first quarter, in the same Sea of Fecundity over which we're now flying, an enigmatic glow that measured no less than 100 kilometers in length and 30 in breadth. That glow extended as far as the crater of Copernicus, lasted ten minutes and then disappeared, to reappear shortly afterwards, like a pale flame that shines for a few moments and goes out, to be replaced by flickering electrical palpitations."

"It was doubtless an aurora borealis," stammered Voriguin.

"That's exactly what Gruithuisen thought," said Sharp. After a few moments employed in drawing breath, he continued: "Monsieur Trouvelot[78] has similarly observed evidence of changes in the form of the large crater Eudoxus, which we can see from here. On the twentieth of February 1877, while observing this crater, he was surprised to see a sort of narrow rectilinear wall crossing the circus at its greatest width—and it was not marked on the map. It was orientated east/west and was very high, to judge by the shadow it projected northwards. Well, a year later, on February 17, 1878, the same observer, examining

---

wrong, but later observers have mostly attributed the discrepancy between the maps to observer error.

[78] Etienne Leopold Trouvelot (1827-1895) was an artist who made many drawings of celestial objects.

the crater again, was very surprised to be unable to discover the slightest trace of that wall…"

"And since?" asked Voriguin.

"He has search in vain during the same phases and the same conditions of illumination…"

"Of course!" cried the laboratory assistant. "It has fallen down!"

"It raised itself up by itself, then," retorted Sharp, "since it didn't exist before!"

"A convulsion of the ground, perhaps," the other hazarded.

"In that case," Sharp exclaimed, "why affirm that the Moon is dead? Only animate entities can experience convulsions." Then, furious at Voriguin's silence, he went on: "Well, have you nothing to say? You're just going to stand there, mute as a carp? Answer me—what do you think?"

"But I think the same as you," the laboratory assistant hastened to say. "The people who dare to put it about that the Moon is a dead world are the worst of cretins."

These words appeared to appease the scientist. "Well," he said, in a softer voice, "if you'd like further proof of the vitality of our satellite, look at the green tint that the Sea of Serenity presents. What's that, in your opinion?"

"Hmm!" murmured Voriguin. "I daren't affirm anything…but it seems to me that it's very like vegetation."

Sharp raised his arms into the air triumphantly. "Well done!" he cried. "You're right!"

"Are you certain of that?" asked the other, ingenuously.

"As certain as the astronomer Klein,[79] who attributes that general tint of the Sea of Serenity to a thick and dense vegetal carpet formed of plants of unknown height, while the white streak that cuts the 'sea' in two represents, in his eyes, a sterile desert zone."

Voriguin was pensive; while he appeared to be listening attentively to his companion's explanations, his mind was elsewhere. While Sharp became engrossed in the consideration of theories that divided terrestrial astronomers, the laboratory assistant, whose ideas were more practical, thought about the actual goal of the voyage. In his opinion, it was not to enlighten the scientists of Earth as to the vitality or otherwise of the Moon that the shell had been commissioned and Jonathan Farenheit had put together a company with a capital of several million dollars. The walls of the crater Eudoxus and the vegetation of the Sea of Serenity were certainly interesting, and not lacking in a certain charm, but if, as Sharp had affirmed, life on the Moon, was, so to speak, cost-free, the same was unfortunately not true of life on Earth; it was necessary to think about their return. Now, Vorigin had only consented to accompany Sharp on this perilous

---

[79] The German astronomer Hermann Klein (1844-1914), a prominent member of the Selenographic Society.

voyage on the condition of having a proportional share in the produce of the diamond mines discovered by the scientist's spectroscope—and it seemed to Voriguin that the aforesaid diamond mines were being neglected.

"What are you thinking about?" Sharp asked him, after a brief pause, surprised by his silence and his serious expression.

"I'm thinking about the diamond-fields," the laboratory assistant replied.

An imperceptible scornful smile creased the scientist's thin lips. "What about them?" he said.

"How far away are they from the point where we're gong to set down?"

Sharp consulted a map that was hanging on the wall. "About 500 kilometers," he said.

"Eh? But that's quite a journey!" Voriguin exclaimed.

"Pooh! A week's journey, no more."

"Will we be staying on the Moon for long?"

Sharp shrugged his shoulders. "That depends on circumstances."

The laboratory assistant's face darkened. "It's just that the food-store is almost empty," he said.

"Bah! What are you worried about?" the scientist replied. "In ten hours we'll have arrived—and if there's vegetation on the lunar surface, as I have every reason to suppose, it will be devilishly odd if there aren't foodstuffs there too."

Voriguin shook his head. "Brr!" he muttered. "Better not to think about that." Then, all of a sudden, an idea occurred to him. "But how are we going to get back?" he cried. "We've been entirely preoccupied with getting here, without thinking about getting back."

"In truth, Voriguin," Sharp said, disdainfully, "you're the most pusillanimous man I've ever met!"

"You have a knowledge of science that I don't possess, Master," the laboratory assistant replied, humbly. "That's what gives you such great assurance."

Appeased by these words, the scientist replied: "If you'd only take the trouble to think about it a little, you'd avid a great deal of anxiety. When we left the Earth, it was necessary for us to have an initial velocity sufficient for us to reach the point at which the spheres of attraction of the Earth and the Moon met. Now, that point was 86,856 leagues from our point of departure. To go back, on the other hand, we only have 9,244 leagues to travel to arrive at that point, and to do that, we only need an initial velocity of 2,500 meters a second."

As Sharp spoke, the laboratory assistant's face cleared.

"And then," added the scientist, "We have to take the difference in weight into account. How much did our shell weigh when we left?"

"About 3000 kilos," Voriguin replied.

"Well, down there it will only weigh 500 kilos, which is six times less."

A smile expanded the laboratory assistant's anxiously pursed lips. "All this is better than I thought," he murmured. Then, after a pause, he asked: "How long do you think it will be before we arrive?"

"About eight hours."

"In that case, I ask your permission to get a little rest; all this emotion's worn me out."

Sharp took out his watch. "It's 2 a.m. in St. Petersburg at present," he said, earnestly. "At 10 a.m. precisely, we'll set foot on the Moon."

Voriguin lay down on the divan that ran around the projectile and turned his face to the padded wall. "You can wake me up," he stammered, through a yawn.

Sharp studied him momentarily with a furious expression, then shrugged his shoulders and went to install himself at a little table covered with papers and books. Five minutes later, the sound of snoring filled the vehicle; Voriguin was asleep.

For several hours, Sharp continued his calculations to the sound of that strange music, only putting down his pen to take up his instruments and measure the projectile's the ever-increasing speed.

8 a.m. was chiming when Voriguin stirred on his divan. "Well, anything new?" he asked.

"Nothing…we're still falling, in accordance with the law of gravity."

"Are we far away?"

"Still 2000 leagues to cross."

The laboratory assistant started on hearing these words. "2000 kilometers more!" he exclaimed. "But will there be time to make our preparations for landing?" So saying, he ran to one of the portholes, and an involuntary cry escaped him at the sight of the immense world over which the shell was flying.

The spectacle was, in fact, marvelous. The last buttresses of a mountain chain appeared on the horizon, the summits looming up into space like giants. Then, in the immense greenish plain that extended to infinity, small volcanoes were now clearly distinguishable, with their gaping craters and their sharp peaks, measuring scarcely half a kilometer in diameter. The shell was traveling with a velocity of nearly 10,000 kilometers an hour, and the panorama was becoming more distinct by the second. The mountains that barred the horizon formed a continuous line rising to the altitude of the projectile and the ground seemed to be hollowing out to receive the explorers.

Sharp looked at his watch. "Another half-hour," he said. "Let's get ready for the shock of impact—which, I warn you, will be rude."

Voriguin paled slightly.

The bolts of the portholes were carefully tightened. Then they checked the solidity of the powerful toroidal springs with which the base of the projectile was furnished. Finally, they tested the resistant strength of the hammocks' suspensions.

"Everything's in order," murmured Voriguin.

"Let's go," said Sharp. "We have no more than five minutes. Lie down, Voriguin. I'll put out the incandescent lamps myself."

When the laboratory assistant was installed in his hammock, the scientist turned a switch and plunged the vehicle abruptly into darkness. Then he lay down next to his companion. A deathly silence reigned; side by side, the two men silently waited for the impact—and perhaps, in consequence of it, death.

Suddenly the temperature rose abnormally, the half-light filtering through the portholes from outside disappeared, and a frightful noise resounded. Then a terrific shock shook the shell from the base to the nose-cone. At the same time, the springs of the hammocks broke, with a dry snap that was scarcely audible amid the racket of breaking glass and apparatus, tumbling furniture, collapsing walls and the friction of steel digging into the ground....

Stunned and senseless, the two voyagers rolled unconscious on the floor, which was already strewn with all sorts of debris.

They lay there side by side, motionless and corpse-like, for a long time. The interior of the projectile was dark and silent.

Suddenly, a faint and plaintive groan was heard.

"Sharp!" murmured Voriguin. "Sharp!"

No answer.

He repeated his appeal, with no more success than the first time. Then, summoning up all of his will-power, he dragged himself to the divan in the dark, and pulled himself to his feet. He rummaged in his pocket and took out a match, which he struck on the wall.

He saw Sharp by the flickering light, his limbs stiff and his face bloody. "Thunder!" he groaned. "He's dead!" This thought restored his strength. He ran to the commutator and turned it sharply—but the battery that supplied current to the lamps must have been broken, for no light shone forth.

Voriguin hesitated for a moment, uncertain what to do. The match had gone out, burning his fingers, and the darkness seemed even more intense and frightening following that temporary illumination.

Suddenly, he remembered that he had a candle-stub in his pocket. He struck a match and lit the candle. Sure now of not being plunged back into darkness, he went back to Sharp, knelt down beside him and put a hand on his heart. The heart was beating—feebly, to be sure, but it was beating.

The anguish that had gripped Voriguin at the thought that he was alone, with a cadaver for his only companion, abruptly disappeared, and he set about trying to bring Fedor Sharp round. He observed that the scientist's forehead had struck the corner of the bookcase and that the wound, though slight, was bleeding copiously. Among the debris scattered on the floor, the laboratory assistant perceived a medial kit, which had survived the shock. He opened it and improvised a dressing. Once the hemorrhage was stemmed he resumed trying to bring the wounded man round. He uncorked a phial and passed it back and forth under the nostrils several times.

Finally, Sharp sniffed vigorously. Blood colored his cheeks and he opened his eyes. At first, he looked around in astonishment, seemingly wondering what he was doing there, lying on the floor in the midst of broken furniture and fragments of instruments. Then, memory suddenly flooded back. He put his hand to his head and cried: "We're on the Moon!"

"So it seems," said the laboratory assistant.

"What?" exclaimed the scientist. "It seems so—aren't you sure, then?"

"I confess that I was in much more of a hurry to assure myself that you weren't dead."

Sharp raised his arms to the Heavens. "God be praised!" he exclaimed. "Well, I can tell you that my first action would have been to run to the porthole."

"That doesn't surprise me," muttered Voriguin, ill-temperedly. "You're nothing but an egotist."

"No," said Sharp, "I'm a scientist! Science before all!" As he concluded this reply in his usual dry and jerky voice, his expression suddenly darkened. He had only just noticed the pitiful state of the shell's interior. "Why that light?" he asked, pointing to the candle that Voriguin had placed on a broken door-panel from the bookcase.

"Because the batteries aren't working."

Sharp frowned. "Is it night, then?" he asked.

The laboratory assistant shrugged his shoulders. "All I know," he said, "is that when I came to, the vehicle was in complete darkness."

At this reply, Sharp mumbled a few words that his companion did not hear. "Of course," he said. "That's because we re-sealed the portholes, for fear that the glass might be broken in the fall." And he added: "Give me your arm to help me up, Voriguin, for I feel extremely weak."

When he was upright, he took a few steps, with the support of his assistant. "Ah," he said, "that's better. I think it's this blood-loss that weakened me." He leaned back against the wall of the shell and said to Voriguin: "Before anything else, we need to know where we are. Climb up on the divan, unscrew the plate of the porthole and look out."

The laboratory assistant obeyed, but did not succeed in immediately in exposing the porthole; the bolts had undoubtedly been damaged in the fall; one of them had even snapped. Finally, the plate fell away and a bright ray of light penetrated the interior of the shell. Sharp immediately blew out the candle.

"Well?" he asked, in a tremulous voice.

"We've arrived," Voriguin replied. "At least, I think so—I can see mountains in the distance strongly resembling those we saw when we were still in space."

Sharp uttered a cry of joy. "But where are we, exactly?" he said.

The laboratory assistant pressed his face against the window, standing on tiptoe in order to get a better view of the surroundings. "Without being precise," he said, "I think we must have fallen on the slope of a crater."

"The interior or exterior slope?"

"Exterior—otherwise, I wouldn't see mountains on the horizon, my view being limited..."

"It's doubtless one of the small volcanoes I showed you in the Sea of Serenity," murmured Sharp. After a pause, he exclaimed: "Get down! Get down quickly. We need to get out of here."

Voriguin jumped down to the floor. "Get out of here?" he repeated. "We'll have to take some precautions, I imagine?"

The scientist shrugged his shoulders. "What have we to fear?" he asked. "Too great a difference between the density of the lunar atmosphere and the air in our vehicle."

"Unless the composition of the lunar atmosphere is totally different," Vorigin retorted.

"That's a possibility," Sharp muttered.

"And perhaps fatal," the other added.

Sharp looked at him scornfully. "You didn't come here I suppose, to stay shut up in the vehicle?" he growled.

"You assured me that the atmosphere on the Moon's surface was breathable."

"I still affirm that."

"It's possible—but personally, I doubt it."

The scientist seemed surprised. "Why?" he asked.

To this perfectly natural question, Voriguin made no reply.

"In a word, you're scared," jeered Sharp.

"At least admit that you're scared too," said the laboratory assistant.

"You've braved dangers more serious that this, though."

"I don't deny it," Voriguin protested, "but I'm strongly averse to leaving my bones here and I'd like to take certain precautions."

"What precautions?" Sharp asked.

"That's up to you, not me," the other complained. "You're a man of science, while I..."

A singular smile played on Sharp's lips. "As far as you're concerned," he said. "I know of only one precaution to take."

"Go on."

"Let me go out first. Admit that no experiment on the lunar atmosphere could be as conclusive."

Voriguin stuck out his lips in a significant moue. "Agreed—but if you die..."

"If I die," Sharp replied, "you'll have to decide what to do." And he advanced upon the 'manhole' that served as a door, armed with a wrench with which to unscrew the nuts.

Voriguin put a hand on his arm. Sharp stopped and looked at him in surprise. "What is it now?" he growled.

"Do you think you have the right to risk your life like this?" the laboratory assistant asked.

Sharp could not suppress a start of surprise. "You're joking!" he said.

"No, I'm being serious."

The scientist folded his arms. "You're claiming the right," he said, "to prevent me from disposing of my life as I see fit?"

"Certainly—don't forget that you brought me here and that, consequently, you're responsible for my skin. If you died, what would become of me?"

Sharp burst out laughing. "Ah!" he said. "That's the real reason for the interest you're taking in my health. I find this solicitude quite extraordinary, though, inasmuch as it contrasts markedly with the less-than-benevolent intentions you manifested in my regard two days ago, before the presence of Mikhail Ossipoff's shell was observed in space."

Voriguin lowered his head, frowning and scowling.

"Well?" Sharp went on. "You're not answering…."

The laboratory assistant raised his head again. "When I wanted to kill you," he muttered, "your death assured my life, in the sense that the air you would have ceased to breathe I would have breathed myself. Now, on the contrary, your death would lead to mine. What would become of me, in fact, in these regions of which I know nothing? How would I ever see the Earth again, ignorant as I am of all the things you know?" He had pronounced these final words in a vibrant and angry voice, which gave evidence of the jealousy he felt towards the scientist.

Sharp nodded his head. "Good," he said. "Very well, I understand. Fundamentally, you're right. We're two associates; the existence of each of us represents a social asset that we don't have the right to depreciate." He reflected briefly. "Well, don't worry," he continued. "I promise you to act prudently, so as not to compromise an existence that is so precious to you."

"You promise me?" said Voriguin, incredulously.

"I swear it," said Sharp, more sincere than he had ever been about being minded to risk his life. The he went to the manhole and set about unfastening the bolts. In spite of all his efforts, however, he could not do it. "What's the matter with it?" he grumbled.

"You're doubtless still too weak," retorted the laboratory assistant. "Pass me the implement." He grabbed the wrench and strove vigorously against the steel plate that served as a door. It was in vain, though, the bolts resisted, and the plate did not budge an inch. "Damn it!" he muttered. He threw the wrench across the room and sat down, using the back of his sleeve to wipe the sweat from his brow.

Sharp had gone pale. "Climb back on the divan," he said, "and try to see in what position the shell has fallen."

Voriguin hoisted himself up again. Scarcely had he glanced outside, however, when he released a frightful oath. "It's impossible to get out," he said, in a strangled voice.

"Impossible!" exclaimed Sharp.

"The shell is embedded in the ground to a depth 15 centimeters below the portholes. The door's blocked."

The scientist let himself collapse on to the divan, his limbs shaken by a convulsive tremor. "We'll need all our strength," he said, hoarsely, "to free the bolts on the plate...once the plate is off, we'll attack the ground with the tools we have."

Voriguin shook his head. "You're forgetting that the door opens outwards," he said.

"That's true," murmured Sharp, dejectedly.

There was a long silence between the two men, who were racking their brains trying to think of a means of escaping the inevitable and frightful death that awaited them.

"What if we break a porthole?" Voriguin said, suddenly.

"What good would it do?" said Sharp. "The opening isn't large enough to let us out."

"I know that," the laboratory assistant replied, "but through the opening, by means of a pick-axe, we could clear the doorway."

"But the windows are made of reinforced glass—and, in consequence, unbreakable."

"Ler's try anyway," Voriguin retorted. He bent down, retrieved a strong steel pick-axe from among the objects strewn on the floor, hoisted himself up on the bench and was raising his arms to attack the window when a cry from Sharp stopped him.

"Fool!" howled the scientist. "What are you doing?"

Voruin looked at him in amazement. "I'm going to break this porthole."

"And what if the lunar atmosphere isn't breathable?" stammered Sharp.[80]

"Well?" said the other, uncomprehendingly.

"All the air in the vehicle will rush outside and we'll perish here, asphyxiated. Can you grasp that?"

---

[80] The reader might think it odd that Sharp did not think of this before, when he was enthusiastic to open the door and step outside. The authors appear to have forgotten that they inserted a reference to the breathing apparatus carried by both space vessels into the earlier scene featuring Sharp and Voriguin

Yes, Voriguin had grasped it. He let his pick-axe fall, collapsed on the divan, put his head in his hands and began to sob.

Sharp, seated in a corner, looked at him pityingly.

Suddenly, the other got up, ran to the scientist, grabbed him by his coat collar and shook him furiously, shouting: "You're a swine! You dragged me here, assuring me that it would be possible to live on the Moon—but it's not true, since you'd rather await death here than take the risk of finding air outside."

Sharp struggled in vain; his companion's wrists held him firmly and he could not escape from their grip. Eventually, Voriguin, having got over his anger, let him go, and the scientist rolled on the floor amid the debris of instruments and furniture. Sharp was not the stronger of the two; he hid his anger, silently got to his feet and went up into the vehicle's nose-cone. He stayed there for a long time, considering the situation, seeking a means of getting out of the tomb—but his thoughts went round and round in the same circle and no bright idea came to mind.

When he went back down, Voriguin, moved by hunger, said to him in an ominous voice: "I've checked the contents of the food-store. There are 30 pounds of biscuits left, 15 pounds of tinned meat and 50 liters of cognac. How long do you think we can live on that?"

Sharp thought about it and replied: "We can keep going for a month."

"Provided that we have sufficient air for that."

"Have you checked?"

"No—you know that I'm not very familiar with it. I'm not sure of the calculation to convert liters of liquid into cubic meters of gas, so if you want to see for yourself..."

Making no reply, Sharp headed for the reservoir and examined its contents minutely. He remained silent for a moment, as if he were making a calculation, then said in a dull voice: "We still have six weeks' supply."

Voriguin sighed. "A lot might happen in six weeks," he said.

"You're forgetting that breathing isn't eating, and we only have a month's food."

"Well, that gives us a month," said the laboratory assistant.

Surprised by this philosophical attitude, Sharp looked at his companion. "What are you hoping for, then?" he asked.

The other shook his head. "Perhaps Ossipoff will save us once again."

"You're mad!" exclaimed the scientist, a flush of blood reddening his face. "Ossipoff's traveling through space."

"Is he?" replied the laboratory assistant. "What proof is there that you're not mistaken?"

"Oh!" Sharp bellowed. "Rather death than deliverance by that man!"

"I don't share your opinion."

"We'll see what you think when Jonathan Farenheit gets his hands on you," Sharp retorted.

Voriguin shuddered. He had not thought about the American.

That was the commencement of a frightful existence. The antipathy between the two men that had existed in a latent state could only increase, and was soon transformed into hatred. Each of them, accusing the other of stealing his share of the air and nourishment, was haunted by an obsession: the murder of his companion. They did not speak to one another, and cut meal-times—the only occasions they came together—as short as they could. The rest of the time, Sharp remained shut up in his laboratory, sometimes plunged into rage-filled reveries, sometimes with his eye glued to his telescope, feverishly scanning the horizon.

What did he hope to see out there, on the summits of those high mountains?

Downstairs, Voriguin spent his time lying on the divan, smoking and drinking, as he had done during the month when the shell had remained immobile at the point of equal attraction—except that he drank more moderately, fearful of drunkenness, which might put him at Sharp's mercy.

One day, the latter came down, more depressed and anxious than usual. He had observed that the Sun was descending towards the horizon. Knowing the particular meteorology of the lunar world as he did, he knew that this presaged the long, cold and mortal night. At the same time, a glance at the reservoir informed him of the rapid diminution of the precious breathable gas. When he went back up again after the meal, he took a liter of cognac with him. Voriguin smiled, thinking that the scientist too was seeking forgetfulness in alcohol of the frightful fate that awaited them.

Having arrived in the laboratory, Sharp uncorked the bottle, drank two or three gulps of the liquid, then rummaged in a dark corner and took out a small bottle full of a greenish liquid, which he emptied into the cognac bottle. That done, he seemed calmer, and he waited resignedly for the Sun to disappear beneath the horizon. The most intense darkness then succeeded the vivid sunlight; at the same time, a frightful cold, penetrating the shell, chilled the two companions.

For long hours, each of them prowled around the narrow cage in which they were enclosed, seeking to struggle by means of constant movement against the cold numbing their limbs.

"Oh!" cried Voriguin, in a moment of anger. "To think that I haven't the courage to kill myself!"

A cruel smile distorted Sharp's lips as he continued walking. That extraordinary man did not sleep; understanding that to immobilize himself in sleep would be to immobilize himself in death, he had condemned himself to march without respite. Exhausted, harassed by fatigue, he marched, leaning on the walls of the cannonball, supporting himself on the furniture, his head swimming,

250

his eyelids closed, his legs unsteady, he marched on and on. Such was the force of his will that he slept as he marched. Only once did he stop and prick up his ears. Beneath him, Voroguin's circular promenade had ceased. The scientist nodded his head and murmured: "Who knows? Perhaps I'll have no need to do as I planned?" And he resumed his march.

12 hours passed...then 24...then 48. The room that served as Voriguin's residence was still silent. Then Sharp opened his door slightly, went down the stairway on tiptoe and groped his way around the room. Suddenly, his hands encountered an inert, frozen body and he stood up, releasing a cry of horror. It was Voriguin's body, gripped by the cold in his sleep, and killed by it.

Sharp bent down again, felt for a pulse, sounded the cadaver with a stethoscope, and turned it over. The face and hands were frozen, in the true sense of the word. Then he released a sigh of satisfaction and murmured: "So much the better." He went back to the cannonball's nose-cone then, and resumed his circular march, until the moment when, his stomach racked by hunger, he went back down and headed for the food-store. Scarcely had he plunged his hand into it however, than he uttered a cry of fury and despair.

The store was empty. Voriguin had devoured the few biscuits and little meat that remained before going to sleep; it was that very excess of nourishment that had caused his death, for, gripped by the cold in the midst of a difficult digestion, he had suffered a stroke in his sleep.

Devastated, Sharp let himself fall on to the divan. What good would it do to struggle further against the cold, since hunger had arrived, with tortures 100 times more frightful?

For long hours, fixed in complete immobility, he waited, feeling a mortal numbness gradually invading his limbs, freezing them and stiffening them. Then, all of a sudden, the desire to lived took possession of him, and again he began to walk abut, slowly at first, then more rapidly, to make his blood circulate and regenerate a little warmth. The suffering of his stomach increased by the hour, though; soon it became intolerable, and then, to deceive his hunger, he seized a bottle of cognac and drank several gulps on after another.

As if by magic, the pain eased; a sort of intoxication took possession of him and went to his head—and for a while, he felt quite well. Warmed by the alcohol, he was even able to sit down and get a little rest. Soon, however, the hunger pangs began again, more violent and atrocious, causing him to howl like a wild beast. Then, as he had the first time, he took refuge in alcohol and drank the rest of the bottle of cognac. Doubtless the dose was too strong, or else the alcohol, falling into the empty stomach, acted more rapidly and with greater violence. Either way, a sort of furious madness took possession of him. With his head on fire, his eyes bloody, his mouth drooling hideously and his limbs agitated by a ferocious tremor, he hurled himself, in the darkness, upon the cadaver of the unfortunate Voriguin. And he did the same every time his stomach demanded its daily nourishment.

For hours, he struggled desperately, nauseated by these frightful feasts, horrified by himself; then, when his strength gave out, vanquished by nature, he drank—and, when drunkenness had driven him mad, he ate.

That lasted until the moment when the Sun, climbing above the horizon again, illuminated these scenes of horror. The unfortunate's torture then became more frightful still; while the darkness enveloped him, he could at least escape the hideous spectacle that he offered, as he crouched over the cadaver and hacking slices off it with a knife—but now...

Then again, with the light, warmth returned—and the body, which the cold had conserved, began to decompose rapidly, infecting the air with poisonous miasmas. Sensing that there was death in the polluted atmosphere he was breathing, Sharp tried to break one of the portholes with the pick-axe, but in vain. The implement's iron head was blunted, and the haft broke without it being able to crack the glass.

In desperation, with his courage and strength exhausted, sensing the futility of further struggle, Sharp then lay down beside Voriguin's corpse and waited. When Jonathan Farenheit's piercing eyes spotted the cannonball in which his enemy was imprisoned, he had only fallen unconscious a few hours before.

Chapter XVIII
A solar eclipse and a lunar tide

Fricoulet, as we know, had a smattering of medical knowledge. In spite of the horror and disgust that the ex-permanent secretary of the Academy of Sciences inspired in him, he knelt down next to Sharp, unbuttoned his clothing and carefully applied a stethoscope to his chest.

"This man isn't dead," he declared, eventually. "He's merely in a coma."

Scarcely had he pronounced these words than the American hurried towards him. "Save him," he implored. "Save him, Monsieur Fricoulet, and half of what I possess is yours."

The young engineer looked at him in total surprise. "What!" he said. "Is that you talking, Mr. Farenheit? Whence comes this sudden interest in a scoundrel whom you wanted to strangle with your own hands a little while ago? If your hatred always transforms itself in that manner, I envy the fate of your enemies." He had pronounced these words in a slightly mocking tone which made the American blush.

"It's not Fedor Sharp's carcass that I care about," Farenheit replied. "It's my vengeance." And he added, with a glint in his eye: "That man belongs to me."

Ossipoff came forward. "I beg your pardon, Monsieur," he said, "but that man was my enemy before he was yours. I hope you will not dispute that priority." The old scientist had put such authority into these words that Farenheit stared at him in surprise. "You'll see," he murmured, mockingly, "that I shall be obliged to put this blackguard Sharp in chains."

Farenheit, presumably recognizing that Ossipoff's claim was just, turned on his heel, cursing.

"What are you going to do?" the old man asked Fricoulet.

"Whatever you decide."

"Can you save him?"

The engineer shrugged his shoulders. "One can try, at least. When I was an intern in a Paris hospital, I saw a man who remained in a cataleptic state for several weeks. The same might happen with Sharp. I'll put him into the spare respirol, which we brought in case of an accident."

"And afterwards?"

"Afterwards, we'll have to wait for Nature to take its course."

Having said that, Fricoulet and Gontran carried Fedor Sharp's body to the aerial boat, where they laid him out on the cushions. As they were about to embark, Fricoulet noticed that their guide looked worried, and that his gaze was interrogating the horizon with an expression of evident anxiety.

"What's the matter?" asked the engineer.

"I anticipate bad weather," the Selenite replied, laconically.

Ossipoff and his companions turned round. "Bad weather!" they repeated, in astonishment.

"I've already said, and you must already have seen for yourselves," Telinga replied, "that this is the most inhospitable part of the Moon. The cause of that is these immense forests, which condense and retain in their yellowed foliage the little humidity present in the atmosphere. It is not rare to see true clouds form here, which dissolve into rain or opaque fogs and, in the process of their condensation, produce violent displacements of air. These winds, eddying as they blow through the mountain gorges, carry off branches, small pieces of pumice-stone and even lava debris torn away from the flanks of craters."

"But these tempestuous rains of stone must be dangerous," observed Gontran.

"Very dangerous."

"And you anticipate something similar?"

Telinga made an expansive gesture indicating the sky. "Everything makes me dread an imminent perturbation of the atmosphere," he replied.

"What can we do?" asked Ossipoff.

"Flee, as quickly as possible." Scarcely had he pronounced these words than Flammermont was assisting Selena to take her seat in the aerial skiff. Farenheit sat down between the two young men.

"What direction should we take?" asked the old scientist.

"We'll doubtless head north-west," replied Fricoulet, consulting his map. "When we arrive at the level of the lunar equator, we'll cross the circle of mountains and we'll end up, still in daylight, in the other hemisphere not far from Chuir."

"Still in daylight," Ossipoff repeated. "We'll have to hurry."

"Oh, have no fear of that," said Telinga. "We have 2000 kilometers to travel…it will take less than 30 hours."

"Unless there's an accident," murmured Gontran.

Everything was ready. Telinga was the last to embark; he turned his steering-mechanism and pressed down the control-levers. Immediately, a loud bang was heard at the stern of the boat; a jet of gas gushed into the air and the apparatus, finding its purchase on the rarefied fluid, rose up through the atmospheric layers.

Suddenly, though, as if they had only awaiting a signal, all the humid particles held in suspension in the air condensed. Heavy ink-black spirals emerged from the vegetal masses, twisting in the air like titanic serpents and gathering into thick clouds, which soon covered the Sea of Serenity.

Gontran leaned toward Fricoulet. "I'm sure," he said, "that in spite of their improved telescopes, terrestrial astronomers have not witnessed such a phenomenon; this, at least, would have convinced them of the existence of a lunar atmosphere."

254

"You're mistaken, my dear friend," the engineer replied. "All astronomers have observed, as you are doing at this moment, occasional clouds covering an entire region of the planet."

"Have these people an interest in denying the evidence, then?" cried Flammermont.

"If you doubt what I say," the engineer retorted, slightly piqued by his friend's incredulity, "you can ask old Ossipoff."

Gontran turned to the scientists and told him about the discussion. "My God!" he replied. "Monsieur Fricoulet is not mistaken, but he's not entirely right either. These clouds have not, strictly speaking, been seen—but that is the only rational explanation that can be given for the singular occultation of known craters that seem to disappear for irregular periods, and also for certain details of lunar orthography that have been apparent at certain times to certain astronomers while not existing at others. For instance, in the middle of the Sea of Vapors, in a passage well-known to selenographers, there's a little crater named Hyginus, cut in two by some sort of river traced in a straight line and clearly recognizable. Now, north-west of this crater, no one has ever observed a circus measuring half a league in diameter."

"But the circus exists?"

"I've seen it, studied and photographed it. Similarly, in the Sea of Nectar there's a little crater six kilometers in diameter, which Mädler and Lohrmann— two conscientious observers—did not see. Schmidt perceived it for the first time in 1851 and it's clearly distinguishable on a photograph taken by Rutherfurd in 1865. Now, in 1875 the English selenographer Neison[81] examined, described and drew that same region with the most minute care and the most exact measurements, without finding any trace of that volcano. Last year, however, it was clearly discernible by means of the Pulkova equatorial."

"What conclusion to you draw from that?" the Comte de Flammermont asked, gravely, seemingly following the old man's explanations with great interest.

"The theory that I've always advocated and which turns out to be true—the phenomenon that we're witnessing at present proves it—is that the lunar volcanoes emit fumes or that atmospheric vapor condenses in fogs above these regions and mask them from terrestrial observers, as is the case for an aeronaut flying a few leagues above Vesuvius during an eruption."

While the old scientist was furnishing these detailed explanations to Gontran, the aerial boat had quit the luxuriant regions of the Sea of Serenity. The Tumulus of Linné had disappeared over the horizon and, after going around the little crater of Bessel at a considerable altitude, our voyagers were now flying over a gigantic granite rampart that seemed to serve as an enclosure for the dark and velvety plain of the Sea of Serenity.

---

[81] Edmund Neison (1849-1940).

"What are these mountains that we're crossing, Father?" asked Selena.

"To the left," the old man replied, "We have the circus of Pliny, to the right is Menelaus."

That name awoke ideas in Gontran's mind of an entirely different order than those belonging to lunar orthography. If he had been listening intently, Ossipoff would have heard the young man humming a chorus from an operetta unmistakably reminiscent of *La Belle Hélène*.[82]

Fricoulet nudged his companion with his elbow. "Are you mad?" he muttered.

"It's the association of ideas," Gontran retorted. "The crater Menelaus reminded me of Mademoiselle Schneider and her *roulades*." He released a deep sigh—and, to divert himself from his dark thoughts, turned abruptly to Ossipoff and asked: "What's that sharp peak outlined on the horizon, beyond Menelaus on the right?"

"Sulpicius Gallus. From here you can make out the bizarre broken buttresses that connect it to the orographic system of Manilius."

"Manilius!" repeated Farenheit.

"A large crater that we can't see from here, because we're more than 100 leagues away from it."

Fricoulet, who was consulting his map frequently, extended his arm towards a dark and immense stain just beginning to reveal appear in the distance. "Isn't that the Sea of Tranquility?" he asked.

"Indeed it is," said Ossipoff.

The Sun, mid-way through its course, was at its zenith at that moment, pouring torrents of hot light upon the lunar soil. Suddenly, the star appeared to darken.

"By God!" cried Jonathan Farenheit. "We aren't going fast enough—here's the night."

Gontran and Selena, who were chatting to one another, interrupted their conversation. "Night!" repeated the young man. "It's true, though—the horizon's getting noticeably darker." He tapped Ossipoff on the shoulder; the latter was utterly absorbed, along with Fricoulet, in the study of their map.

"What is it?" the old man asked. As he spoke he raised his head, and uttered a cry of surprise. Darkness was overtaking the sky. "Am I mistaken in my

---

[82] Jacques Offenbach's light opera about the incident that sparked to Trojan War, *La Belle Hélène*, which had a libretto by Henri Meilhac and Ludovic Halévy, opened at the Théâtre des Variétés in Paris in December 1864, with the slightly long-in-the-tooth Hortense Schneider playing the eponymous heroine. The fact that Gontran appears to have seen Mlle. Schneider playing the role adds some slight confusion to the story's chronology; we have been told that he was "25 or 26" when the story began, in March 1881, so he can only have been a child in 1864.

calculations then?" he murmured. "The day is definitely 354 hours long, though…and only half of that has elapsed." He turned round on hearing a loud burst of laughter behind him. He saw Fricoulet holding his sides.

"What's up with you?" the old man demanded, curtly. "Whence comes this hilarity?"

"From Gontran and Farenheit's fearful expressions." The engineer pointed at his two companions, who were looking up, waving their arms in the air, seemingly alarmed by their consideration of the day star, whose disk was disappearing rapidly.

Ossipoff stamped his foot angrily. "To laugh like that," he said, "you must have an explanation of this phenomenon."

"An eclipse," replied Fricoulet.

"An eclipse?" repeated the old man, bewildered.

"Yes, an eclipse of the Sun."

"Of the Moon, you mean?" retorted Gontran, mockingly.

Fricoulet shrugged his shoulders. "No," he said, "but by the Earth." And he added, by way of response to the gesture of incredulity that greeted these words: "Our native planet is now in conjunction with the Sun, passing in front of the central star and masking it—because, seen from the Moon, it is four times as large. As you can see, it's quite simple and not at all dangerous."

"But will it last a long time?" Farenheit asked.

"Well, the eclipse is total, and will certainly not last less than two hours."

"We'll be obliged to stop, then," said Selena.

"Why?" countered Fricoulet.

"Do you think that it will be possible to navigate in such darkness?"

The engineer turned to Telinga.

"Dangerous," the Selenite said, laconically. "Fog…"

Fricoulet rummaged in a compartment built into the stern of the boat and took out a lamp, to which he attached a silvered reflector. By means of a cord he attached the lamp firmly to the skiff's prow; then, bringing the two poles together, he produced a dazzling light, whose rays the reflector projected ten meters ahead. "Like that," he said, "we won't break our nose."

After a brief pause, Selena asked the old scientist: "Is it like this in every conjunction of the Earth, Father?"

"No, my dear," Ossipoff replied. "The Sun, in its daily course, usually passes to the north or south of the planet Earth, motionless in space—but it sometimes happens, by virtue of the combined movements of the two heavenly bodies, that the radiant star passes directly behind its vassal, as at the present moment. Then it becomes invisible from the Moon, which falls back into darkness. These eclipses are not frequent, though, and there'is little need to worry about them, since they take place in deserted regions."

Jonathan Farenheit thumped the guard-rail with his fist. "What about us?" he growled. "Do you take us for rocks, then?"

"Not at all—but we're in a very exceptional situation. For myself, I'm delighted by the circumstance, which will permit me to study the edges of the Sun, the luminous crown and the zodiacal light." The old scientist rubbed his hands together with evident satisfaction.

Selena was thoughtful, though. After a pause, she said: "But if the Earth is hiding the Sun from us because it's in conjunction with it, and the two bodies are in the same alignment, the Moon must be full for the Earth's inhabitants, mustn't it?"

"Yes, my love."

"So they're witnessing an eclipse of the Moon?"

"How's that?" said Gontran.

"Since the Earth is intercepting the solar rays, they can't be reflected from the lunar ground; consequently, the satellite becomes dark."

"That's true," observed the young man.

"But what are you getting at?" asked the old man.

"I thought that terrestrial astronomers had drawn up tables predicting lunar eclipses. You ought, therefore, to have anticipated the present phenomenon." And so saying, she smiled slyly.

Fricoulet clapped his hands joyfully. "Bravo, Mademoiselle!" he exclaimed. "That's logic, or I don't know it—all my compliments, especially as logic isn't generally the dominant quality of your sex."

"Oh, one can't think of everything," grumbled the old scientist. "While I was thinking of the danger that this initially-inexplicable phenomenon might pose to my daughter, I didn't have that table of predictions present in my memory." He shrugged his shoulders ill-humoredly and, picking up his binoculars, plunged himself into an attentive examination of the Sun, which presented a most peculiar appearance at that moment.

Telinga seemed anxious, however. In spite of the rapidity with which the boat was flying through the air, it was being overtaken by the fog whose formation our friends had observed above the vegetal masses of the Selenian forests, and was now traveling in the midst of swirling dust, which would have blinded the travelers had it not been for the lenses that protected the openings in their respirols.

"We are going off course," murmured Telinga.

"Wouldn't it preferable to stop?" Fricoulet asked it. "With so little control over the vessel, you risk crashing into some unknown peak."

"Stop?" repeated Telinga. "To do that it would be necessary to land and that would be very dangerous." As he concluded this speech, a crackling sound became audible in the distance. A violent pitching motion shook the aerial apparatus, breaking the lamp's conductive wires, while monstrous masses seemed to be shuddering in the darkness under the pressure of unknown forces. The mountains seemed to be collapsing, the craters filling up with avalanches of stones and fantastic landslips.

It was a frightful chaos, a general upheaval; one might have thought that the poor lunar planet was coming apart at the seams.

"It's an earthquake!" cried Jonathan Farenheit, crouching down at the guard-rail.

"A moonquake, rather!" Fricoulet retorted, mockingly, his voice drowned out by the roaring of the tempest.

Telinga made every effort to maintain the apparatus in the eye of the wind; it was shaking violently, threatening to capsize, like a boat in a furious sea.

Immediately the storm had started, on Fricoulet's advice, the voyagers had attached themselves together by means of a strong rope, as fishermen do, in order to avoid being thrown out of the vessel. The intense darkness that reigned further increased the horror of the cataclysm. Telinga had stopped trying to steer the boat—which, enveloped by the aerial eddies, was driven in an unknown direction.

Ossipoff, careless of the torment, remained in contemplation on the Sun—which, entirely masked by the Earth, still revealed its presence by luminous projections forming a fiery aureole around the planet.

"Our native world is doing us a bad turn!" grumbled Fricoulet.

Eventually, after two hours of that frightful scene—two hours that seemed as long as two centuries—a bright ray of light suddenly lanced from behind the terrestrial sphere and the entire region was suddenly illuminated. Then, insensibly, the light increased as the planet unmasked the radiant star, which inundated the Selenian mountains and seas with its warmth once again.

Immediately, Telinga made preparations to land. He feared that the apparatus had sustained some damage, and wanted to make a detailed examination.

"Where are we, then?" asked Flammermont. "Isn't there a possibility that the tempest has carried us far away from our route?"

"It's more than probable," murmured Fricoulet, "but maps aren't made for dogs, and Monsieur Ossipoff will be able to enlighten us."

The old scientist had, indeed, unfolded his map on the ground, and was examining it attentively.

"Well?" prompted the engineer, surprised by his long silence. "Where are we, Monsieur Ossipoff?"

The old man raised his head and said, in an anxious voice: "I don't recognize the place!"

Fricoulet could not help starting in surprise. "What are you saying?" he stammered.

"The truth," growled Ossipoff. "Everything's changed. I don't see anything on the map that resembles that cyclopean aggregation of rocks near which we've come down. See for yourself." And he handed the map to the engineer.

"Oh, I trust you implicitly," replied the latter, who had no reason—quite the contrary—to doubt the old man's affirmation. But he added: "Perhaps Telinga can enlighten us."

When consulted, the Selenite declared that he could not be sure but believed that they were some way west of the Sea of Fecundity, at a very high latitude.

"What makes you think that?" asked Ossipoff.

"The position of the Sun," Telinga replied, pointing to the day-star shining at the zenith. "In any case," he added, "we shall orientate ourselves more easily when we are flying at a certain height and can see a vast range of territory."

They embarked. The apparatus left the ground and, in a few minutes, rose up to an altitude of 300 feet. Leaning over the map, Ossipoff and Fricoulet tried in vain to recognize the terrain, but none of the details on the map corresponded with the panorama extended beneath their feet.

"Hold on," said the old scientist, extending his hand. "If it were not for the irregular form of the little circus on the right, I'd swear that what we see down there are the twin craters to which Beer and Mädler gave the name Messier.

The engineer examined the point indicated by Ossipoff for some time, with the aid of the binoculars. "Indeed," he replied, "I can clearly see the two white bands that extend eastwards and make the craters resemble a double-headed comet...but that's impossible."

"Yes," said Ossipoff, "that's impossible. I've studied those two craters several times from the Observatory at Pulkova, and found them in absolute conformity with the descriptions of Schröter and Beer/Mädler." And with the confidence of a prodigious memory, he quoted the actual text of the observations made by these astronomers: "They are identically similar to one another: their diameters, shapes, heights, depths, the colors of their arenas and rings and the positions of a few hills founded on the buttresses all resemble one another so closely that the fact can only be explained as a strange freak of chance or by an unknown law of nature." He paused momentarily, then added: "Instead of that, what do we have before our eyes? Two circuses that do not resemble one another in any respect: the nearer one is elliptical and its long axis runs from east to west, while the other is oval, to be sure, but in the other direction." He bowed his head and murmured: "I'm reduced to conjectures."

The old man put his head in his hands and plunged into a profound meditation.

"Are we lost, then?" asked Gontran, coming closer.

Fricoulet shrugged his shoulders.

"What a pity," the young Comte exclaimed, "that we didn't think of dropping pebbles along our route like Petit Poucet."[83]

---

[83] The reference is to the central character of one of Charles Perrault's famous fairy tales; the story is usually known in English as "Hop o'my Thumb," although the English version of the folktale that Perrault adapted is more familiar as "Tom Thumb."

The engineer could not help smiling. "If Petit Poucet had had an earth-quake to deal with," he replied, "he wouldn't have found his way back, for the pebbles would have been scattered and buried."

"Well," replied Gontran, "the craters are for us what the pebbles were for Petit Poucet. Why shouldn't they, too, have been scattered, buried or deformed?"

Fricoulet uttered an exclamation and ran to Ossipoff. "Gontran," he said, "has just discovered the solution of the puzzle that confronts us."

"And what is that solution?"

"That the change of form which put us off the track must be attributed to the frightful upheaval whose phases were hidden from us by the eclipse."

A gleam appeared in Ossipoff's eye. "Right," he said. "I admit that the two craters really are those of Messier and that they've been deformed by the cataclysm that we witnessed. But to what can we attribute the upheaval?"

Gontran made a gesture that might have signified: "This time, you're asking too much of me." After a brief silence, however, he replied. "To a moon-quake, produced by a volcanic eruption."

Fricoulet grabbed his friend's arm. "Fool," he whispered in the ex-diplomat's ear. "You're forgetting that there are no active volcanoes on the Moon."

Although he was speaking in a low voice, the engineer was overheard by Ossipoff, who cried out in a tone of supreme satisfaction; "No volcanoes on the Moon, Monsieur Fricoulet! In truth, I thought you rather weak in astronomical matters but I didn't expect such heresy!" Addressing himself to Flammermont, he went on: "Well, Gontran, what do you think?"

"The fact is," stammered the young Comte, "that my friend Fricoulet's observation astonishes me."

"Really?" exclaimed the engineer, sarcastically.

Ossipoff folded his arms. "Is it necessary to remind you," he said, "of the number of astronomers who have been unable to explain the changes observed on the lunar surface except by volcanoes?"

Fricoulet made a gesture with his hand to indicate the needlessness of that enumeration, but the old scientist took no notice of it and continued: "Your compatriot Laplace, Monsieur Fricoulet, believed in lunar volcanoes, as did Herschel, Lalande, Maskelyne and many others.[84] I've already mentioned the

---

[84] The four individuals cited here are Pierre-Simon, Marquis de Laplace (1749-1827), William Herschel (1738-1822), Jérome Lalande (1732-1807) and Nevil Maskelyne (1732-1811). Their dates provide a striking illustration of the obsolescence of Ossipoff's opinion. The only relatively recent observation he cites in this speech, credited to Grower in 1865, is stubbornly obscure. As the argument progresses, it retreats even further in time, to the opinions of the pioneering lunar map-maker Johannes Helvelius (1629-1696).

new volcano near Ukert, in the valley of Hyginus, the Tumulus of Linné and the crater Eudoxus. You've just seen the revolution produced in the twin craters of Messier. Hold on, better still—I've just remembered a fact that will convince you. In 1788, Schröter perceived a tiny light in the lunar Alps analogous to a star of the fifth magnitude, which remained visible for a quarter of an hour. In 1865, an English astronomer, Grower, saw a luminous point in the same place, which shone for 30 minutes and then disappeared..." Ossipoff paused briefly, then added, defiantly: "Would you like to tell me what that could have been, if not a volcano?"

"But Monsieur..." Fricoulet began.

The old scientist did not allow him to continue. "Do you know what a French astronomer who has studied the Moon more than anyone else—your friend Gontran's namesake—says on the subject? Listen: 'In the month of May 1867, to the left of the bright mountain Aristarchus, a very bright luminous point appeared, presenting the appearance of a volcano. Although little disposed to admit the existence of active volcanoes on the Moon, I have always retained from that observation the impression of having witnessed a lunar volcanic eruption, perhaps not of flames but at least of phosphorescent matter. The point is, at any rate, so remarkable that, since the 17th century, several astronomers—notably Helvelius and Herschel—have considered it to be an active volcano, and such was Herschel's conviction of its reality that the astronomer wrote, in 1787: *The volcano is burning with great violence; the objects situated close to the crater are feebly lit; the eruption resembles the one that I witnessed on May 4, 1783.* The actual diameter of the volcanic light was about 5000 meters and its intensity appeared to be greater than that of a comet which was then on the horizon.'"

Breathless after this long quotation, the old man stopped to get his breath back. Then, victoriously, he asked: "Well, Monsieur Fricoulet, what do you say to that? Are you convinced?"

The engineer smiled and said: "Would you think me a cretin, Monsieur Ossipoff, if I were to confess to you that I'm not convinced?"

The old man looked at him with a pitying expression. "What do you think, then?" he said.

"That the changes we are observing at this moment are due neither to an agitation of the selenological strata nor to a volcanic eruption."

Ossipoff raised his arms to the heavens in despair. "How absurd!" he exclaimed. Ironically, he added: "Then to what, in your opinion, should we attribute these phenomena?"

"Quite simply, to a tide."

This response, offered in a tranquil tone, caused the aged scientist to choke. "A tide!" he stammered. "You think that it was a tide that..." He was unable to say more, but, turning to Flammermont, he made a sign indicating that, in his view, the engineer had suddenly gone out of his mind.

The smiling Fricoulet shrugged his shoulders. "Before making a premature judgment of the state of my faculties, hear me out. Personally, I attribute that general upheaval, that titanic disruption of the terrain and that collapse of rocks to the combined attraction of the Earth and the Sun, during their alignment. That attraction was strong enough—perhaps assisted by other unknown forces—to move the ground considerably, changing the form of craters, upsetting the disposition of mountains, thus producing a tide of lunar fragments, since water does not exist on this face of the Moon."

Ossipoff was no longer laughing; he was thoughtful.

Suddenly, Telinga got up. "I recognize the region," he said, curtly.

"And where are we?" asked Gontran.

"We are in the equatorial region of the lunar disk, skirting the Sea of Crises."

"*Mare Crisium,*" murmured Flammermont, self-importantly.

"You've already said that," Fricoulet whispered in his ear.

"Within 24 hours, we shall cross the equator," the Selenite continued.

Jonathan Farenheit rubbed his hands together. "Bravo!" he muttered. "I've had enough of white mountains and black sky—not to mentioned that we have mummified air in this rubber sack...although we've seen some funny things here...." He interrupted himself to say: "Only one thing interested me—that was seeing the Earth serve as the Moon." And he burst out laughing.

Mikhail Ossipoff looked at the American pityingly and then turned to Gontran, letting the words "*Vulgum pecus!*"[85] fall from disdainful lips.

The young Comte replied: "For myself, I'm delighted by this exploration, which has convinced me once again that the cycle of physical manifestations has not reached a conclusion on the surface of our satellite. The forces of nature are incommensurable, and to measure them by our stature would be to tax them with impotence. They operate everywhere, and their mysterious impulsion moves the rocks in the craters of volcanoes as they move the stars in the immensity of the skies."

The old man looked at Gontran tenderly.

Fricoulet tugged his friend's sleeve. "Nice turn of phrase!" he murmured, mockingly. "Where did you get it?"

"From *Les Continents célestes* by my namesake Flammermont!"

---

[85] A contemptuous Latin insult, somewhat akin to "Riff-raff!"

Chapter XIX
In which Fedor Sharp gets up to his old tricks

It was in the dead of night that the aerial boat reached Maoulideck, the capital city of the Moon, where the Selenite congress was meeting. A room was put at the disposal of the voyagers to permit them to wait not only for the light of day, which would only shine again in three times 24 hours, but also for the hour fixed for the Lunarians' assembly—which is to say, the 240th hour after sunrise.

Fedor Sharp, still in a coma, was laid down in one corner and the sacks of mineral piled up in another. Then, after arranging themselves comfortably to wait for daylight, they began planning the next voyage. Ossipoff had declared that he wanted to leave as soon as possible, to take advantage of the favorable position of Venus relative to the Moon. The old scientist was impatient with the darkness, by virtue of which he was forced to remain inactive and waste precious time.

"What, my dear Monsieur Ossipoff!" said Fricoulet, in jest. "You want to explore other worlds, and you've no more patience than that! How do you now that you won't find spheres in which night is eternal, whose inhabitants might take centuries to decide to make the slightest movement?"

"That's quite possible," Flammermont added, seriously. "There are so many worlds in space that one might as easily encounter one on which everyone sleeps eternally as one on which no one ever sleeps."

When he was in a bad mood, the old scientist did not care for jokes, so he turned his back on the two young people to sit down and study the progress of Venus through space by the light of a Trouvé lamp.

Finally, the Sun appeared and everyone was ready to carry out the old man's instructions.

"My dear Monsieur Ossipoff," Fricoulet suddenly said. "I've just had a good idea."

The old scientist had adopted the principle of mistrusting the engineer's ideas to begin with, ready to declare them excellent only when they had been put into execution. He frowned slightly; then, in a voice that was not at all welcoming, he said: "Go on."

"Well," said Fricoulet, lowering his voice mysteriously, "we ought to try to leave the Selenites with a marvelous opinion of the ambassadors from the *Revolver*."

"And how should we do that, in your opinion?" asked the scientist.

"Leave the Moon on the very day of the congress."

Ossipoff nodded his head approvingly.

"Better than that," said Gontran. "Let's set off from the very bosom of the congress."

The engineer and the old man arched their eyebrows interrogatively.

"Since we know the place where the Selenites will meet to admire us and listen to us, let's transport our vehicle there, and prepare it as rapidly as possible. When the last word is pronounced, while the applause is still greeting your resounding oration, we'll take off before their astonished eyes."

"Like Mohammed under the beards and noses of the Muslims," said Selena.

"Or better still," Fricoulet said in his turn, smiling slyly, "like Godard in some traveling fair in the vicinity of Paris."[86] And he added: "We only need the local Orpheus to salute us with the sound of trumpets."

Ossipoff, however, remained serious.

"Well?" asked Gontran.

The old man did not reply right away. It is certain that if a similar suggestion had been made by Fricoulet alone, the old scientist would have been suspicious of it, thinking it a joke, but in his mind, Flammermont was much too serious a man for him to think of not paying attention to anything coming from him. He therefore reflected for a few moments, and finally said: "I don't see any problem that would prevent that being done—without having examined our vehicle in detail, though, I think it might have sustained a good deal of damage."

"It's easy to find out," said Fricoulet, laughing covertly to see the old man accepting, without any discussion, this original manner of departure. It was decided forthwith that the little company would go to Chuir without losing a moment—from where, with the aid of what Gontran called the roller-coaster, they would go in search of the projectile and the equipment, in order to bring them to the crater chosen for the departure.

When they were about to embark, however, Jonathan Farenheit firmly refused to follow his companions. "Go without me," he said. "I'll stay here. You can easily find some Selenite to replace me."

"But what's the matter?" the others asked, in surprise.

The American's lips creased into a ferocious rictus. "It's just that I've appointed myself as Fedor Sharp's guard and nurse, and I can't leave him…"

"Why, that's true!" cried Fricoulet. "We're forgetting our friend Fedor. Bandit though he is, we can't abandon him in his present state."

"Messieurs," said Selena, in her turn, "There's one very simple thing we can do. All four of you can leave for Chuir; as for me, who can't be of any use to you out there, I'll stay here and look after the patient."

On hearing his fiancée make this offer, Flammermont went slight pale, and his face expressed the most determined opposition. "Monsieur Ossipoff," he said, turning to the old man, "I beg you not to leave Mademoiselle Selena alone with that man."

---

[86] The reference is presumably to the prolific composer of popular music Benjamin Godard (1849-1895).

"What are you afraid of?" asked the young woman. "The unfortunate, as you see, is incapable of moving a muscle; if he weren't breathing, he'd be assumed to be dead."

"I know that, my dear Selena," replied the young Comte "but what do you expect? It worries me to think of you staying here alone with him."

All gazes were turned to the old man. "It's true," he said, "that it would certainly be preferable not to deprive ourselves of Mr. Farenheit's services...but it's better for him to stay here with Sharp instead of my daughter. I know that there's nothing to fear, but we shouldn't tempt the Devil."

It was with these words that the old scientist, his daughter and their two companions embarked once again in the flying boat to go to Chuir, leaving the American installed at the dying man's bedside—for it was impossible to consider Fedor Sharp as anything else but moribund. More than a week had passed since the day when Sharp's enemies had found him in the Mountains of Eternal Light, and, still extended motionless on his bed, he would have seemed dead had not Fricoulet assured himself from time to time that his heart was still beating—feebly, it is true—and if the engineer had not succeeded, every 12 hours, in introducing a half-cube's worth of Liebig[87] dissolved in a little water between his teeth.

This did not prevent Jonathan Farenheit from watching him as closely as if he dreaded some escape attempt on the part of the living corpse. The American's hatred, apparently soothed over time, had awakened more strongly than ever as soon as hazard had brought him face to face with his enemy. He would not, however, lay a finger on him when he was in this state; he could be rude, brutal and resentful—manifest all the faults in the world, in brief—but in reality, his was an honest and loyal nature. He prayed to God, however, for a miracle that would restore Fedor Sharp to health. If such a thing should happen, oh how different things would be! And as he thought about that, a ferocious rictus pulled back his lips, uncovering his long yellow teeth, while his formidable hairy fists closed in a feverish clench.

Unfortunately for the American's plans for vengeance, God did not seem at all disposed to work a miracle; when Ossipoff came back after three days with the vehicle, Sharp was in exactly the same state as when he had left. Taking note of that, Farenheit lost patience—not to mention that he did not like to see his companions working while he spent his days wandering around the room where the invalid lay, like a wild beast in its cage—and therefore decided to abandon

---

[87] The chemist Justus von Liebig (1803-1887) invented a manufacturing process for beef extract and set up the Liebig Extract of Meat Company (Lemco) to exploit it. Initially marketed as a viscous liquid, the extract was also produced in a soluble solid form frequently carried by 19th century explorers. It is still familiar in England as the basic ingredient of Bovril and the Lemco-trademarked Oxo cube.

his sentry-duty and join the others in the crater where they were busy repairing the vehicle.

The shell had suffered somewhat during the terrible fall that had deposited it on the lunar soil. The base, or inferior part, was buckled and deformed in several places and the Terrans required a great deal of effort and many hours of work to restore its former impermeability. Mikhail Ossipoff was so knowledgeable, though, Fricoulet so ingenious, Gontran so adroit and Farenheit so strong, that they achieved this goal quite rapidly.

When the projectile's exterior had been repaired, they went on to the interior, but that work was trivial compared to what they had already completed; it was simply a matter of reassembling the bookcases, re-securing the floorboards, replacing the broken incandescent lamps, screwing in the chandelier, laying down new conductive wires and putting new zinc plates in the batteries. When all that was done, and the vehicle was restored to its original state, they busied themselves refilling the reservoirs of air by liquefying—by means of apparatus Ossipoff had brought with him—the oxygen contained in the lunar atmosphere.

Now, there was no more to do but furnish the vehicle with its new means of locomotion.

Ossipoff had some carefully nailed-up boxes, whose contents he had kept absolutely secret throughout the voyage, brought from the laboratory. These boxes had been transported to the room put at the Terrans' disposal. The sacks of mineral gathered in the Subvolvan regions were piled in the corner opposite Fedor Sharp's bunk and protected from the light by a tarpaulin.

Half a dozen crystal spheres about 50 centimeters in diameter, carefully wrapped in straw and protected from the least shock by rubber tampons, were taken out of the opened boxes.

"Well, Monsieur Ossipoff," said Fricoulet, "you're a careful man. These receptacles that you mentioned the other day for the purpose containing your mineral—here they are."

"Precisely, Monsieur Fricoulet," replied the old man. Then, observing visible traces of anxiety on the young man's face, he added: "Have you, by chance, some observation to make to me? What are you thinking?"

"I'm wondering what means we'll use to land."

Ossipoff shrugged his shoulders. "Nothing more simple," he said. "These transparent spheres will be enclosed in other metallic spheres, which you see here. By uncovering these metallic spheres to a greater or lesser extent, by a mechanism operated from inside, the mineral will be exposed to the luminous rays to varying degrees, and we'll regulate our speed in that fashion."

Fricoulet shook his head, and was certainly about to raise another objection, but Gontran got in ahead of him. "That's the question of speed settled, my dear Monsieur," he said, "but the question of direction remains. If light becomes the motor of our projectile, we'll never be able to steer in any other direction than sunwards."

A sly smile lit up the engineer's face, and he added in his turn: "With the result that we can only visit the planets orbiting between the Earth and the Sun—Venus and Mercury, that is. As for the planets external to the Earth's orbit, like Mars, Saturn and many others...we won't be able to think of going there."

The old scientist reflected, his head on his breast.

"Then again," Flammermont went on, desirous of showing off his astronomical knowledge, "How long will this new voyage last? Have you considered that it's more than 20,000,000 leagues from the Earth to Mercury...it will take whole months to cross such enormous distances." He fell silent.

It seemed that the old man was crushed by the weight of these objections; with his arms folded, his eyes fixed on the ground and his brows violently furrowed, he remained plunged in profound meditation.

"By God!" Jonathan Farenheit suddenly cried, having not so far said anything. "Why don't you coat the exterior wall of your vehicle with the mineral. The greater the impressionable surface you have, the greater your speed will be."

Ossipoff raised his head and stared fixedly at the American. Then he hurled himself towards him and grabbed his hands, which he shook warmly. "You're a genius, Mr. Farenheit!" he cried. He turned to Gontran and Fricoulet.

"No, we won't be traveling for years, Monsieur de Flammermont," he said, victoriously. "No, Monsieur Fricoulet, we won't always be traveling towards the Sun. As dear Mr. Farenheit has just said, we have a sufficiently respectable number of square meters on our vehicle to maximize our speed. As for the direction, we shall obtain that by disposing a large platform around the vehicle, one side of which will be coated by the mineral while the other is painted black. This platform will be composed of plates pivoting in such a manner that by exposing one face or another to the light one can change direction."[88]

He took a pencil from his pocket, made a few rapid calculations on the wall of the room, and added: "The maximum speed that we shall be able to attain

---

[88] It is not obvious these improvisations would work, or that Ossipoff's calculation makes sense. If the attraction imparted by the photophilic mineral is a force analogous to gravity or electromagnetism, then it would impart a constant acceleration rather than a constant velocity, which would increase markedly as the vehicle got closer to the Sun; even if there were some reason to suppose that increasing the exposed surface area would bring about a proportional increase in the force acting on the craft, switching that surface for a plain black one would surely only result in the substitution of a constant velocity maintained by momentum for the former acceleration, certainly not a change in direction. This facilitating invention was not without influence, however; a similar photophilic substance plays a key role in Octave Jonquel and Théo Varlet's L'Epopée martien (1921-22; tr. in a Black Coat Press edition as The Martian Epic).

might be as high as 20,000 meters per second, which is 18,000 leagues an hour. To reach Mercury, therefore, will require a little more than 40 days of traveling." He looked around in search of approval, but those audacious men found the old man's project so extravagant that no one responded. "Bah!" he muttered, through gritted teeth. "They don't understand—but experience will convince them."

However little confidence Gontran and the American had in the theory, and however mistrustful Fricoulet might be, everyone nevertheless set to work doggedly. They prepared a viscous paint to which the precious mineral was added, having first been purified, carefully sifted and purged of the foreign elements it contained. Farenheit, transformed into a plasterer, was charged with extending this preparation over the exterior walls of the vehicle. In the meantime, Fricoulet, aided by Gontran, fabricated a platform composed of 24 sections, each mounted on an axis that cut through the wall and allowed them to pivot on themselves at the travelers' command, in order to present one face or the other to the luminous rays.

Finally, on the very morning of the day fixed for the congress to meet, the Terrans completed their task and left the shell in the middle of the crater, ready to depart, in order to get a few hours' rest.

"What are we going to do with Sharp?" Fricoulet asked Ossipoff, when they got back to their temporary lodgings.

A frown informed the engineer that this question was something of an embarrassment to the old man. "I don't know," the latter replied, after a few seconds.

"We can't abandon the poor man in that state, though," Selena murmured, in a voice full of pity.

"For the moment, he's certainly not much more than a corpse," added Fricoulet.

Farenheit extended his hand. "Would you like to entrust the job of looking after him to me?" he asked.

"You!" cried Ossipoff.

"Yes, me. I'll give you my word of honor to do everything possible to save him—but once he's up and about, I resume my former liberty, and then...." The glint in his eye finished his sentence more significantly than the most forceful words could have done.

"Are you abandoning us, then?" cried Flammermont.

"My dear sir," replied the American, "In encumbering you with my presence when the shell left Earth, I had but one objective—to get to the Moon and, once there, to go in search of that scoundrel Sharp. Now I have him, I shan't leave him. I have no reason to extend my peregrinations any further."

Ossipoff shrugged his shoulders in a surprised manner. "What?" he exclaimed. "Don't you care about going to admire at close range all the celestial marvels that solicit your attention even when you perceive them at a distance of millions of leagues?"

The American shook his head. "To be frank, Monsieur Ossipoff," he replied, "I must confess that I've always been much more interested in the raising of pigs and the pork-fat trade than the stars and planets. For the moment, I'd much prefer to contemplate the face of Fedor Sharp, villain that he is, than to admire Mars or Saturn, however magical the spectacles they promise me." And with these words, pronounced in a tone that admitted no rely, the American crossed the threshold of the room that served as the Terrans' dwelling. Scarcely had he taken a few paces, though, than he raised his arms to the heavens in a gesture of fury, and a strangle exclamation escaped his lips: "Sharp...Sharp!"

He could say no more, and is mouth remained wide open in the midst of his apoplectic face, in which his round eyes were like two stains shining like furnaces. His companions had come running and were staring, mute with amazement, at the bunk on which Sharp had been lying for a fortnight.

It was empty.

"The clown's tricked us!" cried Gontran, furiously.

Ospoff turned to Fricoulet and asked him, in a mocking tone: "Well, Monsieur, how ill did you say he was?"

"I'll run after him, Monsieur Ossipoff," the engineer replied, "and if I find him, I swear that I'll bring him back, dead or alive." So saying, he leapt upon a carbine suspended from the wall and raced outside. Gontran and Farenheit set off at his heels, leaving the old man and his distressed daughter behind.

The three men came back four hours later, exhausted and with heads bowed. They had been unable to find any trace of the fugitive anywhere.

"We must be on our guard," growled Farenheit. "The bandit is capable of doing us a bad turn."

As he finished this speech, Telinga came in search of them to take them to the crater in which a vast crowd, under the presidency of the eminent Selenite scientists, was waiting for them.

In the midst of an imposing silence, the director of the Selenite Observatory stood up and made the following speech in a vibrant tone:

"My dear compatriots, all of you who have responded to our call and have traveled enormous distances to gather in this enclosure, know that the space that separates the Revolver from our world has been crossed by audacious inhabitants of that planet, curious to study our humble sphere in the course of their journey.

"Thus, the great veil is torn away, the mysteries of nature are brought into the light, and, before the complete extinction of life on its surface, our world will have received the assurance that another life is developing alongside it, and that, while it continues to roll, inert and frozen, though the infinite space of the heavens, another humankind, younger and superior to ours, will pursue its ascendant march towards progress and perfection.

"What more prodigious fact is there than that to which we are witness? What more moving event has there been in the annals of our planet? From this moment on, we are entering into direct communication with our other brothers in Infinity. Before disappearing, our humankind will have seen them, and obtained the assurance from them that the Worlds of the Heavens are the abode of intelligent and happy beings."

Here the orator paused briefly, which permitted Gontran to murmur in Fricoulet's ear: "Strike up the band!"

Turning toward Ossipoff, the Selenite resumed: "And now illustrious scientist, tell us about the Earth and give us a detailed account of your voyage, that our scribes might record it on a special page in our history."

The old man got up, and began the story of his adventures.

When he got to the point of saying that the most powerful motive for his voyage had been the ardent desire to know whether or not the Moon was inhabited, Telinga asked him: "Do people on the Revolver not believe in the habitability of other worlds, then—and that of the Moon, in particular?"

"To tell the truth," Ossipoff replied, "nine-tenth of humankind take very little interest in the planets and stars, hardly knowing their names." So saying, he glanced scornfully at Jonathan Farenheit. "As for the rest—by which I mean the scientific world—in spite of the efforts of our philosophers, they dispute the question of the plurality of worlds bitterly. The most celebrated among us consider the Earth to be the only place where creatures can exist; for them, the other planets are absolutely deserted, for the simple reason that they do not resemble the terraqueous ball that gave birth to them. As to the specific matter of the Moon, this, or very nearly, is the language they use: 'Long deprived of all liquid and any aerial envelope, the Moon is not subject to any terrestrial meteorological phenomena; it has neither rain, nor clouds, nor wind, nor hail, nor storms. It is a solid and arid mass, desolate and silent, without the slightest vestige of vegetation, where it is evident that no animal could find the means of subsistence. If, however, the Moon has inhabitants, they can only be creatures devoid of all impressionability, sentiment and movement, reduced to the condition of brute bodies, inert substances, etc. etc...' "

These words were greeted by a loud clicking of tongues sounded by 12,000 giants. That explosion of gaiety might almost have been heard on Earth.

"This reasoning by terrestrial astronomers," Telinga retorted, immediately, "proves that they have very poor optical instruments with which to study our planet, and that their understanding is blind to the manifestations of nature. Rather than you, would we not he entitled to claim that your world is uninhabitable, by virtue of the differences it presents from ours: its tumultuous meteorological regime, its heavy atmosphere and its continually agitated oceans? Could we not say, with reason, that your planet has no other reason for existence than to serve the regions of Subvolva as a lighthouse and clock?"

After satisfying his indignation with these few words, the Selenite sat down, and Ossipoff added: "So, it was only after many difficulties that I was able to quit my native planet and launch myself into space…"

Telinga interrupted again. "But what about the two Terrans that you encountered in the Mountains of Eternal Light?"

Ossipoff became red with anger. "One of those two—the one that is dead—is unknown to me," he said. "The other is a wretch who succeeded in stealing my method of interlunary locomotion…and while a volcano furnished me with the propulsion I needed, he constructed the cannon that I had invented and launched himself toward your world."

"To exploit its diamond-fields!" cried the thunderous voice of Jonathan Farenheit. "Those precious diggings that only existed in the thief's imagination!"

As he finished, a long thin silhouette surged from behind a crack in the rock, and a strident voice cried: "Jonathan Farenheit, you're a liar!"

The man who had spoken was Fedor Sharp, who was standing still in the middle of the circus, not far from the tarpaulin covering the vehicle, looking his enemies up and down with a mocking gaze, seemingly challenging them.

Ossipoff and the American stood up as one. The former was dumbstruck with amazement, but the latter would have hurled himself forward if Fricoulet and Gontran had not thrown their arms around him. "Let me go!" he cried. "Let me go—I want to avenge myself!" But his companions, who wanted to serve justice by taking Sharp alive, felt bound by that obligation to prevent Farenheit from reaching the wretch.

In the assembly, the tumult reached its peak; all the Selenites were standing up, seeing to divine from the Terrans' gestures what was being said in a language incomprehensible to them.

Suddenly, Ossipoff said to Sharp: "Fedor Sharp, you are a traitor and a thief. I blush for Russia, my fatherland, which gave birth to you, and for the St. Petersburg Institute of Sciences, which admitted you into its ranks. Your infamous conduct calls for vengeance; the very circumstances permit us to punish you. We are departing, never to return, and we shall leave you here, on this unknown world, without a friend, without sustenance, in the midst of a population hostile to deceit, which will hold you in the most profound scorn. May God take pity on you soon and summon you to Him…"

Sharp replied to these words, which the old man had spoken in a sorrowful tone with a mocking laugh. "Ah!" he retorted, looking at his former colleague with an expression full of hatred. "You're departing, are you, Mikhail Ossipoff? For you, the glory and the joy of having satisfied your thirst for the infinite—and for me, nothing but death! Well, that won't happen."

As this speech ended, Farenheit finally succeeded in freeing himself from the grip of the two young men, and hurled himself toward Fedor Sharp—but the latter never took his eyes of him. On seeing him come running, followed by Ossipoff and the other Terrans, he took out a metallic tube with the approximate form and dimensions of a rifle cartridge and threw it at the group united against him.

There was a frightful bang. Ossipoff and his friends were surrounded by flames and smoke. The ground gave way beneath their feet and they fell, amid rocks pulverized by the explosion. Farenheit, struck full in the chest by the murderous blast of the selenite-stuffed projectile, writhed in the most horrible agony.

Profiting from the stupor and the general panic, Fedor Sharp ran toward Selena, who lay unconscious beside her father, and seized her in his arms; then he fled as fast as his legs could carry him to the middle of the circus. He disappeared under the canvas that was shielding the shell from the light.

Already, those Terrrans who were only stunned were coming round.

"My daughter!" cried Ossipoff, observing Selena's disappearance.

Gontran uttered a cry of fury. "That bandit's capable of holding her as a hostage," he said.

A Selenite who had followed Sharp's movements pointed to the center of the circus. "There," he said. "The man has taken refuge there with your companion." As he completed this speech, the tarpaulin fell away, uncovering the shell, which sparkled like a diamond in the sunlight.

Ossipoff and his companions ran forward, a poignant anguish in their hearts—but before they had covered half the distance, the shell, obedient to the light that was attracting it, rose up and shot into space like a lightning-bolt, carrying Fedor Sharp and his enemy's daughter away.

On seeing this, Mikhail Ossipoff collapsed into Fricoulet's arms, while Flammermont, maddened by impotent range, waved his fist threateningly at the Infinite.

Chapter XX
Our heroes experience hunger pangs

Alcide Fricoulet was what is called a "fine fellow"—and if, for reasons that he kept secret, he did not like women, at least he had a generous heart. So, while privately applauding the incident that saved his friend Gontran from the hell of marriage, he could not help simultaneously deploring that same incident, which had struck the Comte de Flammermont such a cruel blow.

Like a madman, the latter shouted and gesticulated, insulting Sharp, appealing to Selena, vainly scanning the immensity in which no trace of the vehicle could any longer be seen amid the solar radiation.

"Gontran!" cried the engineer. "Gontran!" But the young man, entirely in the grip of grief, did not hear him and continued to absorb himself in his search.

Fricoulet then shifted his attention to Ossipoff, who had fainted in his arms in response to the violence of emotion. With his legs limp, his body inert and his head dangling, the old man remained motionless; without the labored breath that escaped his constricted throat, he could have passed for a dead man. Fricoulet, the only one had conserved his composure—and with reason, since he was neither Selena's father nor her fiancé—felt the necessity of taking a decision. "I can't stay here forever," he murmured. "The old man needs help. As for Gontran, he'll be distraught for a while."

Only then did he perceive that the audience that had gathered for the congress was gradually leaving the crater. In the distance, long files of Selenites were disappearing into tunnels, like a family of rabbits disturbed in their play by a stranger. *Egotists!* thought Fricoulet. *Not one among them has come to find out what happened.*

At that moment a hand fell on his shoulder. He turned round and recognized Telinga. "Hey!" exclaimed the engineer. "Would you ever have imagined that such scoundrels might exist on the luminous world that illuminates the region of Subvolva by night?"

The Selenite shook its head without making any reply. Then, after a pause, he said: "You must hurry."

"Me, hurry?" Fricoulet replied. "Hurry to do what?"

"Leave here."

The engineer looked at his interlocutor in bewilderment. "But where do you want us to go?" he asked.

Telinga placed his index finger on the young man's forehead.

"No, no!" he exclaimed. "Don't worry, I'm in my right mind—but I don't understand why you're telling me to hurry away from here."

"Night," replied the Selenite, laconically—and extended his arm toward the horizon. The summits of the neighboring mountains and craters were gradually blurring, and the growing shadow of their volcanic battlements was extending toward the Terrans. At he same time, in the deep azure of the sky, whose impassive and bleak serenity was untroubled by any cloud, the stars were beginning to shine.

"Brrr!" said Fricoulet, suddenly. "One might think that a cloak of ice were falling on one's shoulders."

"It's necessary not to delay," observed Telinga. "The Selenites, whose constitution is better adapted these abrupt changes in temperature, are already returning to their warm underground dwellings. Believe me, it would be dangerous for you and your friends to stay here any longer."

"You're right," Fricoulet replied. "I'm already chilled to the bone." With as much ease as if he had weighed no more than a feather, the engineer lifted Ossipoff up and threw him over his shoulder. Then he ran to Gontran, took him by the arm and dragged him towards the large room put at their disposal by the director of the Maoulideck Observatory. He had only taken a few steps when he suddenly stopped. "What about Farenheit?" he exclaimed. Wholly preoccupied with Ossipoff's condition and Gontran's distress, Fricoulet had forgotten all about the American, the memory of whom had returned to him abruptly at that moment.

"I can't abandon the unfortunate like this," he said—and, in spite of Telinga's observations, he strode back purposefully to the place where Farenheit had fallen.

Struck full in the chest by the murderous blast of Sharp's cartridge, the American lay on the ground; his limbs were stiff, his rage-convulsed face was rigid, his eyes were glazed and his fist was still clamped on the butt of his revolver, in the attitude in which death had seized him.

"But he's alive!" cried Fricoulet, deceived by that appearance of movement.

Telinga shook its head. "The cold has already taken possession of him," it murmured. "The soul has fled into the higher spheres, and we have nothing but the mortal husk before our eyes."

"I must at least give him a grave," the engineer insisted.

"The ground is already frozen," the Selenite replied. "You would exhaust yourself in vain trying to dig into it. Futhermore, it is a needless precaution. The cold will desiccate the body and mummify it. When the Sun shines again, you can do what seems to you to be necessary."

Fricoulet looked at his companion's corpse sadly. Followed by Telinga, he fled the profound shadow cast by the summits that was invading the circus behind him, enveloping with deathly silence the titanic rocks at the foot of which, seized by the frightful cold of space, Farenheit's grimacing corpse was freezing.

Having arrived in the room that had already served as their habitation for 15 times 24 hours, in which they would be forced to await the Sun's return, Fricoulet laid the old man down on Fedor Sharp's bunk. Then he rummaged in one of the many pockets with which his garments were equipped and took out a candle-stub, which he lit. In its flickering light the room soon took on a sinister and funereal aspect. Monstrous shadows where cast by the room's projections, making the three Terrans gathered in a corner seem even smaller.

"Damn!" said Fricoulet. "It's not cheerful here!" He shook his shoulders abruptly to shake off the veil of sadness that threatened to envelop him like a shroud. Then he went to Flammermont—who had let himself fall on to a bunk and was sitting there with his head slumped on to his breast and his eyes fixed on the ground, engulfed by a desperate torpor—and put a hand on his shoulder.

The young Comte shuddered, raised his head and looked at his friend with the initial stupor of a man abruptly woken from sleep imprinted on his features.

"Come on, Gontran," said the engineer. "Come on—be a man! What the Devil…? In truth, I'm ashamed to see you downcast like this."

Flammermont shrugged his shoulders helplessly and murmured a single word in a heartbroken voice: "Selena!"

Fricoulet became suddenly impatient and stamped his foot. "What?" he cried. "You sit there, unmoving, as inert as a crater, despairing and calling to Selena! Do you think that's the way you'll get her back?"

"Get her back!" Gontran murmured. "She's lost, alas—lost forever!" After a brief pause, he went on, bitterly: "Oh, why didn't that swine kill me along with Farenheit? At least it would be an end to suffering."

Fricoulet raised his arms to the heavens. "That's perfect selfishness, and no mistake!" he exclaimed. "What about us? Don't we count for anything in your affection? Have I, in particular, no right to that for which you'd end your existence so cheaply?" He paused, then resumed: "Would you ever have been able to lay a finger on that happiness whose loss has driven you to despair if I hadn't made you a stepladder to bring you within reach of it?"

"What are you getting at?" Flammermont asked.

"Quite simply, this: that something even worse than Mademoiselle Selena's abduction could have come between you and your matrimonial intentions."

The young Comte looked at his friend, wide-eyed with bewilderment. "I understand less and less," he stammered.

"Grief must be clouding your mind. Does what I'm saying not seem clear to you, genius? Imagine that, instead of kidnapping your fiancée, that rascal Sharp might have left on his own."

At this suggestion, Gontran released a profound sigh. "Alas!" he said.

"And imagine, too," the engineer went on, "that instead of killing poor Mr. Farenheit before his departure, it might have been me that Sharp had struck down." He paused, then folded his arms. "Don't you think that Selena would then have been even more lost to you than she is at present? Oh, my poor friend! Monsieur Ossipoff would have perceived the scientific ignorance of his future son-in-law for sure."

"Well, what does Monsieur Ossipoff's opinion matter to me now?" Flammermon riposted. I only consented to play that comedy for love of his daughter. My happiness is lost forever...."

The engineer cut him off with a curt gesture. "Lost?" he said. "Why's that?"

Gontran sat up straight, as if impelled by a spring. "What do you mean?" he stammered, in a tremulous voice.

"That I consider your happiness to be compromised, but not lost."

The Comte grabbed his hands. "Go on!" he said, in anguish. "Do you have some hope? Some plan?"

"Plan, no—but in any case, I'm not in despair. I'm furious, enraged; I could strangle Sharp with infinite joy—but with respect to Mademoiselle Ossipoff, if I were in your place, I wouldn't despair until I found her dead."

"Find her?" murmured Gontran. "Do you think that's possible?"

"Is anything impossible for men like us?" replied the engineer, with a casual shrug of his shoulders. And then, glad to see Gontran emerge from the initial torpor into which the disappearance of his fiancée had plunged him, he exclaimed: "Let's go! *Sursum corda!*[89] Let this misfortune, far from beating us down, put the Devil in our bodies instead, to bring us forth triumphant from the gigantic struggle that we're waging against the Infinite!"

A groan resounded behind the engineer and Ossipoff's dolorous voice was heard: "Alas, it's not a matter of us struggling against the Infinite, but against our own nature. Why are you talking about going in pursuit of Sharp, Monsieur Fricoulet, when we'll be nothing but corpses in a few hours?"

The young engineer could not restrain a start of surprise. "What?" he said "You too! You're confessing yourself beaten?" Then, suddenly standing up straight, enthused by the very difficulty of the obstacles that had to be vanquished, he cried in a vibrant voice: "Well, since you, her father, and you, her fiancé, are abandoning her, I'll be the one to go to Mademoiselle Selena's rescue!"

Gontran seized his friend's hand and shook it energetically. "I'm at your disposal, Fricoulet," he said, in a firm voice. "What you tell me to do, I'll do; wherever you go, I'll go—for, in truth, I'm ashamed of my dejection and despair!"

"Fool that you are," exclaimed the old man, "haven't you considered the fact that, by taking possession of our shell, that wretch has not merely robbed us of the means of leaving the lunar surface, but also of our means of subsistence?"

Gontran went very pale. "What do you mean?" he stammered.

"That we have no more to do but die of hunger. We no longer have any food, nor water, nor air..."

---

[89] This injunction, borrowed from the Latin mass, translates as "lift up your hearts!"

"Come on!" Flammermont retorted. "The Selenites find means of subsistence."

"Because the aliments of which they make use contain the nutritive elements necessary to their organic make-up."

"But why are you so sure that our stomachs can't accommodate them too?"

The old man cut him off with a despairing gesture. "Do you think that I waited until today to find that out? Chemical analysis has demonstrated that we are not compatible with Lunarian alimentation."

These words were greeted by a groan and a cry of rage, the first uttered by Gontran and the second released by Fricoulet's lips. The three men looked at one another for a few seconds, silent and depressed. The situation was, indeed, terrible; to struggle against the impossible was still at the level of their audacity, but to struggle against starvation...

It was the engineer who spoke first. "To die of hunger!" he exclaimed. "After traveling more than 90,000 leagues, to die of hunger on the Moon! In truth, that would be stupid, and if the good Terran astronomers ever found out about it, they'd burst out laughing at their telescopes!" And he began striding back and forth across the room.

"You can call it stupid if you wish," retorted Flammermont, "but it's no less true that we're confronted with an empty larder!"

"To be sure, we still have the resource of dancing," the engineer went on, "but although hygienic, I don't know that dancing has ever been considered as a fortifying exercise." After a pause, he went on. "Let's see, we are three men to whom, as is undeniable, none of the secrets of modern science is unknown—and we can't find the means of sustaining ourselves in the world that we've reached? That's absolutely unthinkable!"

Gontran shook his head. "It's easy for you to talk," he said. "To invent a system of locomotion that allows you to travel millions of leagues astride a ray of light or an electric current...to travel the planetary immensity...to visit the Sun and the stars—that's nothing! But to invent a leg of mutton or a beefsteak without having the primary ingredient—which is to say, a sheep or an ox—to hand...that, I declare, is beyond my scope."

Fricoulet snapped his fingers impatiently. "My word!" he said. "You'll persuade me that you're as bourgeois as all the bourgeoisie who crowd the tables in Duval's soup-shops or the 32-*sou* restaurants of the Palais-Royal. Do you still believe that legs of mutton and lamb cutlets are indispensable to human existence?" He waved his arms in the air and cried: "What will the people of the 20th century say, when they read that people still believed such things in the enlightened era that we claim to inhabit?"

So saying, Fricoulet had turned to Ossipoff as if to demand his approval— but the old man had not heard a single word of what the two friends had been saying. Crouched on his bunk, he seemed to be fully occupied in blackening a blank page in his notebook with figures and diagrams. Finally, he raised his head and exclaimed: "Sharp won't reach Venus for 25 days. It's still a month until the planet arrives in conjunction with the Sun and at its greatest proximity to Earth, from which it's only separated by some 12,000,000 leagues."

"Futility," murmured the young Comte bitterly. "It's really not worth the trouble of talking about it."

"Have you taken account in your calculations of the reduced weight that the shell is carrying?" Fricoulet asked.

"Of course—and I've found that the duration of the journey will be reduced by 4 days 18 hours 14 minutes and 13 seconds, by virtue of the elimination of the 285 kilos that the four of us represent."

"But Sharp's weight must be set against that diminution."

Ossipoff nodded. "I've thought of that. Sharp weighs 80 kilos; those 80 kilos subtracted from 285 leave 205 kilos as the lightening of the shell, which represent, in effect, an augmentation of speed that translates as four days..."

"...18 hours, 14 minutes and 13 seconds less in the duration of he voyage," Gontran put in.

"That's right."

"And what do these calculations imply?" the young Comte asked, mockingly.

"Simply this," replied Fricoulet, cutting off the old man unceremoniously. "That we need to find a means of locomotion rapid enough to us to arrive on Venus in 25 days as well, in order to catch that scoundrel Sharp and rescue Mademoiselle Selena."

Ossipoff silently extended his hand to the young engineer and shook hands with him firmly.

"In truth, my poor friend," Gontran said, "aren't you deluding yourself with false hope?"

"What?" exclaimed Fricoulet. "I repeat that the three of us will be able to overcome the most insurmountable difficulties. In any case, I have adopted as a motto an adage as old as the world, but which has always been successful for those who have faith in it: 'Heaven helps those who help themselves.'" He clapped his friend on the shoulder and added: "As for you, your lack of self-confidence comes from an excess of modesty...love of science has already accomplished miracles for you. You can't tell me that Mademoiselle Selena isn't capable of making you do things more surprising still..."

In spite of his sadness, the young Comte could not help smiling.

After a brief pause, the young engineer went on: "So, in consequence of that rogue Sharp's theft, we're almost in the same situation as Robinson Crusoe on his island, but with the difference that Robinson could gather fruit from the trees—which, without making him fat, at least prevented him from dying of hunger...while we..." Suddenly, he interrupted himself, slapped his forehead in a gesture of inspiration. Kneeling on the ground, he took a box from under Monsieur Ossipoff's bed, which he opened. It contained a few dozen biscuits and four tins of preserves. "There you are—a good deed never goes unrewarded," he said.

"What's that?" asked the old man.

"A kindness of Mademoiselle Selena's with regard to Sharp. Not wishing to abandon him here without resources, she demanded that I leave him this little reserve, without mentioning it to anyone."

"That child has always had a heart of gold," murmured the old scientist, tenderly.

"And that good deed will work to her advantage too," replied Fricoulet.

"What do you mean?" asked Gontran.

"In order that we can get her back from her kidnapper, it will be necessary for us to construct a means of locomotion—and for that, we'll need time, and during that time, our stomachs will claim their due."

Flammermont pointed to the contents of the box. "Is that what you're counting on to sustain all three of us?"

"No, just to give us the time to construct other aliments."

"Construct!" exclaimed Gontran. "It's a nice word." Seriously, he added: "Then you're going back to your original idea of fabricating legs of mutton and lamb cutlets?"

On hearing these words, Ossipoff looked at Fricoulet with a surprised expression. "Monsieur de Flammermont's joking, isn't he?" he said.

"Certainly, as that's not what I'm thinking."

"Explain yourself, then," said Gontran, a trifle piqued.

"I simply want to find a means of procuring us assimilable elements and permitting our organic system to repair the everyday losses caused by the expenditure of strength to which we'll be subject."

Flammermont shrugged his shoulders. "There, you see," he said. "You're back to my sheep, whose legs are, I believe, the only assimilable substances capable of rendering us the reparative services of which you speak."

"My poor friend," retorted Fricoulet, "the loss of your fiancée has completely turned your head—otherwise, you'd recall that in that foodstuffs, the basis of human nutrition, useless water accounts for four-fifths of the weight. The remaining fifth consists of solid materials such as albumin, fibrin, creatin, gelatin, chondrine, etc."

"I'm in agreement with you on that point," replied Flammermont, ironically. "So let's fabricate food, for water we have in quantity…come on! Where are we going to find your albumin, fibrin, etc., etc…?"

Ossipoff answered him. "No need for all that, my dear boy—for, among the substances that make up food, there's a certain number absolutely irrelevant to nutrition, being completely useless—chondrin and gelatin, for example. Others, like fibrin and albumin, aren't simple substances but compounds, following known proportions, of oxygen, hydrogen, carbon and nitrogen. We therefore have no need of bread and meat for our nourishment; all our efforts must be devoted to the extraction of the truly nutritive substances from Selenian materials and adapting them to us."

"In other words," said Fricoulet, "synthesizing them."

Gontran, on whose lips a mocking smile had been playing for a few seconds, folded his arms and exclaimed: "In truth, I admire you. If I've understood your explanations correctly, it's simply a matter of devoting ourselves to the work of chemical analysis. Now, the first thing we need—an indispensable thing, when it comes to mounting this fine project—is instruments. Now..."

Fricoulet, whose eyes were wandering around the room, started. "No need to say more," he interrupted, triumphantly. "I anticipated your objection, and this is what will answer it magnificently."

He ran to the other side of the room, rummaged in a shadowy corner for a few seconds, and emerged dragging a box carefully along the ground. He deposited it at Flammermont's feet.

"What's that?" asked the latter.

"Well?" said Ossipoff, in his turn.

"It's your box of instruments."

"How's that?"

"You know very well—it's the box that we put aside in order to analyze, when the opportunity arose, the lunar atmosphere. Now, the various events that overtook us during our sojourn caused us, by a stroke of good luck, to postpone that study indefinitely. The box was forgotten and left here—it will do the job for us, I promise you." Rapping on the lid, he said to Flammermont, jokingly: "With this, as you'll see, we're going to fabricate legs of mutton and four-pound loaves, since those aliments are absolutely necessary to your well-being."

Once the box was opened, the old scientist could not contain an exclamation of pleasure at the sight of the instruments buried in the straw. "A eudiometer, an aneroid, thermometers, a compass, test-tubes, a box of reagents!" he murmured, while his face became clearer at every discovery he made. "There's more here than we'll need." After a moment he added: "Let's take things in order. The first thing to do is to make sure of the composition of the air we're breathing and he importance of the atmosphere—don't you agree, my dear Gontran?"

"Absolutely, absolutely," the young man repeated twice over. Privately, he added, while scratching his ear: *Provided that he doesn't take it into his head to consult me about the cookery he's going to do.* With this thought, he darted an imploring glance at Fricoulet.

The latter understood his mute prayer and, suppressing a smile, asked the old man: "What method are we..." Immediately, he corrected himself: "...are you going to use?"

The aged scientist reflected briefly. "My God! At first I thought of the eudiometric method devised by Gay-Lussac[90]...but as you know, it can only be used on very small quantities of gas, by which reason there's a wide margin of error. Now, in the situation we're in, I can't afford to make mistakes, and I need to obtain scrupulously exact results..."

"In that case," Fricoulet exclaimed, "employ phosphorus...it's the simplest method and the quickest!"

"That's what I thought," Ossipoff replied, dryly. He took a wine-glass from the box of reagents, which he filled to a depth of two-thirds with distilled water. Then, he plunged graduated test-tube into the water which contained exactly five cubic centimeters of air—after which, he inserted a long stick of damp phosphorus into the tube. Having done that, he put the apparatus in a corner and set about unpacking the other instruments.

The young Comte, who had watched this operation curiously, drew Fricoulet aside and whispered in his ear: "Explain it to me."

"The stick of phosphorus that you can see glowing in the dark," the engineer replied in a low voice, "absorbs oxygen from the ambient air and combines with it. Soon, when the phosphorus is no longer surrounded by white fumes and has lost all its radiance, Ossipoff will withdraw the test-tube and, as it's graduated, he'll only have to return the new volume of gas to the initial pressure to establish what fraction of it has disappeared, absorbed by the phosphorus."

"That's the oxygen, isn't it?" said Gontran.

"Indeed—and the gas remaining in the test-tube will be the nitrogen..."

"Unless the composition of the lunar atmosphere differs from that of the terrestrial atmosphere—as I've heard Monsieur Ossipoff suggest several times."

At that moment, the old man uttered an exclamation and pointed to Fricoulet's candle. "We're soon going to find ourselves in darkness," he said. The wick was, indeed, charring and only emitting a flickering light.

"Oh, if only we could make gas!" sighed Gontran.

Ossipoff clapped his hands. "Why not?" he said. "I mean liquid gas. It's quite simple, since we have alcohol and turpentine." And while he made up the mixture in an ordinary glass flask, Fricoulet fabricated a wick with the aid of a cotton ribbon—which, plunged into the liquid and ignited, immediately flared up, distributing a bright light.

Gontran was amazed. *Oh, these men of science!* he thought.

Ossipoff was already thinking about something else; while arranging his instruments, he said: "We shouldn't restrict ourselves to the air, for water must also contribute to our nutrition. Like me, you must have noticed that the lunar water has a taste quite different from that of terrestrial rivers and seas. I think

---

[90] Joseph-Louis Gay-Lussac (1778-1850) introduced many instruments of chemical analysis still in use, especially those related to the isolation and measurement of gases.

that its analysis will reveal to us some element of which we might be able to make use. I propose to make that analysis by means of the electric battery, which will give us the relationship of the volumes of gas, and then by evaporation, which will leave residues the nature of which it will be easy for us to determine. Do you approve of that manner of procedure?"

Gontran, to whom this question was specifically addressed, nodded his head as if he understood. "Certainly," he replied. "That's the procedure I think we should follow, if..."

"If...?"

"If we were in possession of the indispensable instrument—which is to say, the electric battery."

"That's no obstacle," said Fricoulet. "We can construct one easily." In response to the young Comte's interrogative gaze, he went on: "The zinc that lines this box, the copper coins that we have in our pockets, and finally, a piece of cloth borrowed from our clothing—aren't those all the constitutive elements of a battery? We'll steep them in water to which a little sulfuric acid has been added, and the current we obtain will be sufficient to electrolyze the liquid..." As Gontran became enraptured, the young engineer added: "There's nothing new in the procedure—it dates from 1800, and was employed by Nicholson and Carlisle to make the first analysis of terrestrial water."[91] While speaking, he had cut a piece from one of the tails of his frock-coat into roundels, while Ossipoff was doing the same to zinc removed from the lid of the box.

Flammermont watched them assemble the battery, shaking his head dubiously. In spite of the explanations he had been given, he could not imagine that all these manipulations would result in anything nutritive and stomachable. *If they can do what they claim,* he thought, *the terrestrial expression 'living on air' will be found to be true—and that would be too bizarre!* Suddenly, he uttered a slight exclamation that attracted the attention of Ossipoff and his companion.

"What's the matter?" Fricoulet asked.

"The stick of phosphorus has gone out," Flammermont replied.

The old man left the battery in the hands of the engineer and went to the apparatus. After withdrawing the phosophrus from the test-tube and rapidly making his calculations he triumphantly exclaimed "Hurrah! I wasn't mistaken in my suppositions."

"Have you, by chance, found a sheep in that test-tube?" asked the young Comte, jokingly.

---

[91] William Nicholson (1753-1815), assisted by Anthony Carlisle (1768-1842), electrolyzed water into its component gases within a matter of months of building his own version of a Voltaic pile, thus pioneering a vital technique in chemical analysis.

Ossipoff smiled and replied: "No, but something that might certainly replace the flesh of that quadruped." Gontran opened his eyes wide as Selena's father continued: "Instead of being composed, as on Earth, of 79 parts of nitrogen for 21 parts of oxygen, the air that we are breathing is composed of equal volumes of those two gases!"

"That's why we're not experiencing any difficulty because of the low air pressure," said Fricoulet.

A few moments later, Ossipoff and the engineer were bent over the voltameter silently examining the bubbles of gas forming in the battery and filling the test-tubes.

"That's bizarre," murmured the old man.

Fricoulet took a drop of water submitted to the analysis and spread it over his hand. "Of course!" he said. "I was sure of it!"

"Of what were you sure?" asked the old scientist.

The engineer examined the drop of water meticulously and replied: "Like the air, this water does not have the same composition as on Earth."

"What do you mean?"

"That it contains twice as much oxygen as terrestrial water and that it is composed of three volumes of that gas for one of hydrogen."

"But in that case," said Gontran, "It's oxygenated water!"

"Definitely."

"It's undrinkable!"

"Not at all, but it's necessary to distil it in order to get ride of its surplus oxygen."

Ossipoff said nothing, however; with his lips pursed, his eyes half-obscured by lowered lids and his chin in his hand, he appeared to be plunged in profound meditation.

"What are you thinking, Monsieur Ossipoff?" asked Gontran.

"I'm thinking that we have oxygen, hydrogen and nitrogen…but that what we still have to do is to find carbon."

"Carbon!" exclaimed he young Comte. "What would you do with it if you had it?"

"I would put it in the presence, in certain proportions, of the substances we already possess—and that combination would give birth to the substance destined to serve us as nourishment."

On hearing these words, Gontran shrugged his shoulders prodigiously. "Oh, of course!" he murmured. "I should have expected that!"

Fricoulet jogged his elbow and leaned towards him "A true scientist," he whispered, "should expect everything."

Flammermont accepted this advice and promised himself to dissimulate, in future, any astonishment capable of making Ossipoff suspicious of the scientific capabilities of his future son-in-law.

Meanwhile, the old man remained silent, his gaze fixed on his bottles of reagents and his apparatus. Suddenly, his companions heard him repeat several times, as if speaking to himself: "That's it—yes, that's it." Then he beckoned them to come closer and said to them: "This is how we'll proceed. We'll begin by extracting oxygen and hydrogen from the water by means of the battery. We'll use phosphorus to absorb oxygen from the air to collect pure nitrogen. As for carbon, we'll produce it in the form of graphite. Then, by familiar methods, we'll produce, on the one hand, pure oxygen in the solid state and, on the other, a nutritive compound, a small volume of which will possess extraordinary qualities of assimilation. By that means, we'll be sure of our lungs and our stomachs."[92] He turned to Flammermont. "When we arrive at that result, I'll appeal to all your intelligence, my dear boy, to procure us a new means of locomotion to launch us in pursuit of Sharp."

The sweet vision of his fiancée doubtless passed before the young man's eyes at that moment, for he cried out in a vibrant voice: "Count on me, Monsieur Ossipoff. If it only depends on my determination, we'll catch up with the rogue, even if it's on the Sun!"

Overcome by a surge of emotion, the old man hugged the young man to his breast and held him tightly for some time.

Meanwhile, Fricoulet carefully examined the state of the larder—which is to say, the contents of the box that Selena's foresight had left for the benefit of Sharp. "My friends," he said, "I think it's important to set about the task without delay, for we have only four days' nourishment in hand, at the most: 33 biscuits and five half-pound tins of preserves—that's all."

"Plus a bar of chocolate that I put in my pocket to nibble during the congress," Gontran added. "I'll add it to the pot." So saying, he brought out the precious comestible and gave it to Fricoulet, who took charge of the little colony's rations.

---

[92] The authors' casual reference to *procédés connus* [familiar methods] is disingenuous. The advent of organic chemistry had informed 19th century scientists that foodstuffs were mostly composed of carbon, hydrogen, oxygen and nitrogen, and the notion of synthesizing food from those elements by chemical methods was commonplace in French scientific romance, having been advertised as a likely future triumph of science by the chemist Marcellin Berthelot. Le Faure and Graffigny were not to know that the entire 20th century would elapse without any technological substitute for the ingenuity of plant photosynthesis being discovered, but they are still overreaching vastly in regarding the problem as easily soluble, just as they are in casually describing lunar "water" as "oxygenated" (although the proportional formula sketched out is not that of hydrogen peroxide, which is poisonous). The reader might be tempted to wonder what resources Selenite organic chemistry might have provided for the castaways, had Ossipoff bothered to investigate it.

Chapter XXI
In which Gontran has another good idea

"Alcide!"

"Gontran!"

"I can't do any more."

"Come on—a little more courage."

"Oh, I have courage—it's my stomach that hasn't. I haven't provided its daily ration for 30 hours; it's resisting and demanding its entitlement."

The young Comte had pronounced these words in a feeble voice that made a deep impression on Fricoulet. The engineer, who was using a compression pump to liquefy and solidify nitrogen and oxygen,[93] immediately abandoned his task and ran to Flammermont. "What?" he said, trying to make a joke of it. "You aren't capable of going more than two days without eating. You make a deplorable explorer, you know."

Gontran shook his head. "Oh," he aid, "I'd give one of my limbs to be sat down in front of a cutlet *au cresson* or a beefsteak *aux pommes*..."

"Everyone has his whims," replied the engineer, smiling.

"Yes, and if this goes on, that whim will be transformed into madness. I can feel it—my head is becoming empty, my ideas are getting confused and, at the same time..." He put his hands to his breast in a dolorous gesture. "Oh, I'm suffering," he sighed.

"And nothing to get your teeth into, poor chap," said Fricoulet, affectionately. "Oh, if things had gone as Ossipoff hoped—but you've seen with your own eyes the difficulties he's encountered. Twice already, he's started over...hence the delay—but now he claims to be certain of success."

Gontran shook his head. "If his success is delayed any longer, it'll come too late," he grumbled.

As he said this, the old man—whose silhouette was visible at the far end of the room, bent over his retorts—uttered an exclamation of triumph. "Gontran! Fricoulet!" he called.

The two young man ran over, arriving just in time to catch Mikhail Ossipoff in their arms. He too was exhausted by hunger but had struggled nevertheless, with indomitable energy, until the moment of victory. With an unaccus-

---

[93] The liquefaction of oxygen and nitrogen, let alone their solidification, requires far more technical sophistication than a "compression pump," as Graffigny must surely have known. On the other hand, the reader might wonder, here and elsewhere in the narrative, why the characters become desperate with hunger after such brief periods of starvation.

tomed effort, he extended his hand towards a receptacle at the bottom of which a blackish gelatinous substance was visible. "There," he succeeded in stammering. "Eat...quickly...quickly..." His head slumped backwards and he became motionless, as if unconscious.

Gontran and Fricoulet looked at one another, terrified.

"Dead!" exclaimed the young Comte. "He's dead."

"No," replied the engineer, "but he's not far off. Help me to carry him to his bunk—then we'll figure out what to do."

When the old man was lying down, the upper part of his body slightly raised up to facilitate the functioning of his lungs, the young Comte and his companion went back to the retorts that Ossipoff had used to compose the alimentary preparation that was to ensure the existence of our voyagers.

"So that's what we have to absorb," murmured Gontran, pulling a face.

"So he claims, at least..."

"But suppose we poison ourselves."

"Impossible, given that all the elementary substances that went into it are absolutely inoffensive."[94]

"In any case, simply looking at that, I can feel my appetite going away. Pooh! It looks like licorice paste."

Without paying any heed to Gontran's repugnance, however, Fricoulet had uncorked the receptacle and brought out a walnut-sized lump of the composition the tip of his knife, which he swallowed after chewing it for some time. Flammermont stared at him with such a strange expression that he could not help bursting into laughter.

"Well?" asked Gontran.

The engineer clicked his tongue against his palate. "Hmm...it's a trifle insipid—that's the sole reproach one can address to it. Here, taste it yourself..."

"And you think," Gontran complained, "that this will suffice to prevent our dying of starvation?"

"In theory, it ought to be sufficient. In any case, it won't be long before we know what to expect from it." For the third time, he took a little of the precious substance on the end of his knife and, going back to Ossipoff, introduced it into his mouth, not without a good deal of trouble unclenching his teeth.

Meanwhile, Flammermont, staying where he was, seemed to be silently studying the effects produced on his organism by the absorption of this bizarre aliment. "It's strange," he murmured, finally. "My empty head seems to be filling up, my ideas seem clearer and my hunger pangs are disappearing. It's very strange." Then, addressing Fricoulet, he said: "Do you feel the same?"

---

[94] Given that the deadliest organic poisons and the most nutritious aliments are made up of exactly the same elements, this cry of "impossible!" seems a trifle overstated.

"Me? At this moment, I'm in the same condition as if I'd just left the table after a hearty meal."

"Indeed—but it'll be very monotonous to nourish ourselves on licorice," said Gontran, piteously.

"Go on!" exclaimed the engineer. "Are you, then, one of those people who live to eat? Me, I eat to live…"

Gradually, Ossipoff opened his eyes. His pale cheeks took on a little color. At first, he appeared very surprised to find himself lying down. "Was I asleep?" he stammered.

"No, my dear Monsieur Ossipoff," Fricoulet replied, in jest, "you died of starvation."

The old man passed his hand over his forehead. "Oh, yes," he said. "I remember." Abruptly leaping off his bunk, he grabbed the young men's arms, one after the other, and cried: "Saved! We're saved!"

"Hmm!" murmured Gontran. "Provided that we aren't victims of an illusion. I'd be more reassured if I'd absorbed a couple of cutlets…if only from the visual point of view…"

Ossipoff shrugged his shoulders. "Now that our existence is assured," he said, "we need to find a means we can employ to set off in pursuit of Sharp."

"I propose," said Flammermont, immediately, "that we go to the Mountains of Eternal Light."

"Good God—to do what?" exclaimed the engineer.

"To seek out the scoundrel's shell and coat it, as we did with ours, with the radiothermic mineral, in order to launch ourselves in pursuit of the wretch without losing any time."

Fricoulet shook his head. "My poor friend," he said, "before preoccupying ourselves with the means that we'll employ to get our hands on that gentleman, it would be more logical to find out first exactly where he's gone—for, following the direction he's taken, we'll be able…"

Ossipoff did not let him finish his sentence. "What!" he cried. "Sharp can only have taken one route—the one we must take ourselves. He's flying directly towards the Sun, and in a fortnight or thereabouts, he'll reach Venus."

The engineer stuck out his lips in an expressive moue. "What you just said, Monsieur," he replied, "would seem plausible in any other circumstances—but it's necessary to take account of the scant desire that Sharp must have to be caught by us. Now, he will certainly suppose that you, being Selena's father, Gontran, being her fiancé, and I, being your friend, will employ all means imaginable to rescue his victim." A profound groan issuing from Flammermont's breast underlined Fricoulet's words. The latter raised his hand. "Let me continue," he said.

Before he could resume his reasoning, however, the young Comte exclaimed: "Of course! You're right—all that we've already done will give him an idea of what we can do. Personally, if I were in his place, I'd fly on through space, without stopping. I'd overshoot Venus..."

"To go and burn yourself in the Sun, no?" said Ossipoff, in his turn.[95] The old man studied Flammermont pityingly. Leaning toward the engineer, he murmured in his ear: "His affection for my poor Selena must be profound to make him forget the most elementary notions of astronomy like this, for it's obvious that by not landing on Venus..."

"It's necessary to make a decision, though!" Flammermont exclaimed, violently. He stamped his foot in rage and added: "Oh, science is nothing but a vain word!" Prey to a genuine despair, he took his head in his hands and fell silent, anguished.

At that moment, the echo of footsteps approaching their room became audible, muffled at first and then more clearly. "Someone's coming," murmured Ossipoff. "Telinga, no doubt." As he finished speaking, a gigantic shadow extended along the floor of the tunnel; the shadow was, indeed, that of their guide.

"Greetings, friends," the Selenite said, in a curt and metallic voice.

"Greetings," replied Ossipoff. "How is it that we see you standing up, when all your compatriots are deeply asleep?"

"I've come back from Wandoung to bring you news."

"News?" all three of them repeated. "News of whom?"

"Of the Terran who took possession of your apparatus and the young woman."

In the grip of the emotion occasioned by these words, Ossipoff sat down on his bunk, almost fainting, incapable of saying a word. As for Gontran, he ran to Telinga and seized its hands. "Praise God!" he exclaimed. "Has the wretch fallen back on lunar soil? Oh, if only that were the case!" His eyes shone with a hateful gleam and his eyebrows, deeply furrowed, offered evidence enough of the ideas of vengeance that were haunting his mind.

"Fallen back? But that's impossible. Mathematically, the projectile must reach Venus." The person who had spoken was none other than Ossipoff. His affection for his daughter and his hatred for Sharp were not as strong as his love of science. He preferred to see his enemy escape him, thanks to a system of locomotion he had invented, to being mistaken in his calculations and projections...

Gontran had paid no attention to the old man's words, because another thought—a frightful thought—had just occurred to him. "But Selena would have been killed in the fall!" he exclaimed.

He had pronounced these words in the Selenite language, addressing himself to Telinga. Very surprised, the latter asked: "What fall?"

"Didn't you just say that you were bringing us news of the villain?"

---

[95] There is an untranslatable play on words here; the verb *brûler* [to burn] is also used metaphorically to mean "to overshoot."

289

"Yes, indeed."

"How can you have any if he hasn't fallen back on the Moon?"

Telinga shook its head. "At this moment," it replied, "the Terran is flying through space at high speed, heading for Tihy, which he seems to want to reach—but he is still far away and will not arrive until the time when daylight has come to gild the high summits of the circus of Wandoung."

"It's from the Observatory that you've been able to determine the progress of the vehicle?" asked Gontran.

"What are you thinking, my dear friend?" exclaimed Ossipoff. "Remember that it's now five days—that is to say, five times 24 hours—since Sharp left...now, according to our calculations, he's traveling at 75,000 kilometers an hour. He must, therefore, be 2,300,000 leagues from the Moon. You'll agree with me that no optical instrument, however powerful, could permit the perception at such a distance of a body whose surface area is as small as that of our vehicle."

Gontran bowed his head, convinced that he had said something stupid and once again regretting that he had such a hasty tongue.

"Sharp must, however, have been seen from somewhere" Fricoulet put in, "since Telinga says so." So saying, he looked at the Selenite.

The latter replied, gravely: "The progress of the Terran through space has indeed, been observed—but not by us, the Lunarians."

"By whom, then?" asked the young engineer.

"By the inhabitants of Tihy—the planet you call Venus."

The three voyagers stood there open-mouthed and wide-eyed, unable to believe their ears.

"It appears," murmured Gontran, "that there's an optical telegraphic service between the Moon and Venus."

Fricoulet shrugged his shoulders. "Your love for Selena is making you lose your mind," he stammered.

Ossipoff looked at the young engineer severely. "Monsieur de Flammermont may be closer to the truth than you think," he said. Then, he said to the Lunarian: "You must have observed the amazement into which the words you've just pronounced have thrown us. Please explain."

"Centuries ago," Telinga replied, "our astronomers noticed intermittent shining points on the surface of Tihy, which appeared to change in form and intensity. They judged that they were signals designed to establish communication between the planet and other worlds, and all their efforts, for many years, were devoted to securing a relationship with our brilliant neighbor. They succeeded, thanks to agreed signals, which the luminous centers of Tihy understand and repeat."

Ossipoff listened to this speech, utterly dumbfounded. Unable to restrain his curiosity, he interrupted the Lunarian. "But what method do you employ?" he asked.

"There is a metal in our surface that has the curious property of conducting electricity, following which it emits light to an equivalent degree of brightness."

"That's selenium," said Fricoulet.

"Don't interrupt!" exclaimed Ossipoff. "Especially to say things that everyone knows as well as you do."

The impassive Telinga continued: "With this metal we have constructed an immense, very bright, reflector, the focal point of which is connected by wires to an electrical generator and an apparatus for transmitting speech."

"But that's a telephone!" exclaimed Gontran.

"Or rather a photophone," Fricoulet added.

"Thanks to the light accumulated at the focal point of the reflector by a host of small mirrors, all of whose rays converge at the same point, the sound is transmitted to the receptive apparatus installed by the Venusians on the highest mountain of their globe. The ray of light carries the sound vibrations through space and our own voices reach our celestial brothers, while theirs arrive here."

"It's prodigious…prodigious," murmured Ossipoff. Then, after a pause, he asked: "But what sort of receiver do you have?"

"Our transmitter itself serves that purpose, transforming the luminous waves that arrive at the reflector into sound waves. Do you understand now how I can bring you news of the Terran? Immediately after the catastrophe, I left for Wandoung. Taking advantage of the final hours of solar light, I put myself in communication with Tihy, whose inhabitants gave me the reply that I've given you."

"Prodigious, prodigious," the old savant continued to repeat, in a whisper. The memory of Sharp, and even his daughter, was far away; his mind was entirely taken up with the thought that two worlds orbiting millions of leagues from one another could communicate with one another—and he thought, in humiliation, of his natal globe, alone and isolated in the midst of sidereal space.

He was snatched out of these reflections by an exclamation uttered by Flammermont. "I have an idea!" the young Comte said. "Might this light that carries voices on its wings be powerful enough to carry us as well?" He had expressed himself in his own language, with the result that Telinga was unable to understand the cause of the amazement into which Ossipoff and Fricoulet had suddenly fallen.

The old man was the first to recover his composure. "What do you mean by that?" he asked.

"Well," Gontran replied, without embarrassment, "they can send messages as far as Venus—why can't we follow the same route?"

"Explain what your mean," said Ossipoff.

Fricoulet tugged at his friend's coat-tail to recommend silence, but in vain. Flammermont replied: "Since electricity is a force, I imagine that if we could accumulate all that contained in light and utilize it to activate a motor, we'd have an infallible means of reaching Sharp swiftly and getting Selena away from him."

As he heard Gontran speak, the engineer seemed to be standing on hot coals; he coughed in a significant fashion, but in vain; he rolled his eyes at him in a terrifying fashion, but it was futile. *The fool!* he thought. *He's done for now. My word—he must have gone mad!*

"Not as mad as all that," Gontran replied, a trifle bitterly, having caught the last few words as they were murmured, "for if I were mad, it would be necessary to admit hat Monsieur Ossipoff has also gone mad! Haven't you heard him repeat several times that light, heat and sound are nothing but movement and force? Well, if we could utilize all these vibrations and oscillations that travel through the ether and intersect..." He paused, and asked, ingenuously: "And why shouldn't we utilize them?"

Ossipoff drew closer to him, his eyes wide open, shining with a strange gleam. Then, all of a sudden, he grabbed his arms and cried: "Oh, my dear boy! You haven't said that lightly! I can already sense and divine that a plan is germinating in your mind."

The young Comte tried to deny it.

"You must try something, at least," the old man persisted. "Remember that Selena's fate is in your hands. To get her back will require a miracle—and you alone are capable of accomplishing that miracle."

Fricoulet bit his lip to prevent himself bursting into laughter. It became even worse when he heard his friend—speaking slowly, as if he were tracking the phases of an idea slowly hatching in his brain—say to the old man: "We can admit, can't we, that the atoms moving in the ray of light that the reflector reflects set off in a straight line at an immense speed. What prevents the utilization of those atoms for the continuation of our voyage?"

The engineer was unable to listen further; he leaned close to Gontran's ear. "You're rambling, my dear friend," he whispered—but he was obliged to lower his head beneath the triumphant gaze that Gontran was directed at him on hearing Telinga declare that the Lunarians had already undertaken trials by means of the Wandoung apparatus, transmitting light objects on rays of light.

"Indeed!" the young Comte cried, folding his arms. "I'd be very glad to hear your explanations on that subject. "What machine did you employ?"

"A simple hollow sphere, which was placed at the center of the great reflector I mentioned," Telinga replied. "A deep and continuous sound acts on the transmission apparatus, whose poles are connected to a powerful electric battery. Under the influence of the vibrations stored therein, the sphere, suspended in the network of electrical and luminous oscillations, escapes with unusual rapidity and moves in a straight line until the vibrations became so weak that the sphere is no longer animated by any movement and is forced to stop. In the same way, if the sound and the luminous ray are interrupted while it is traveling, the sphere stops and falls back."

"Well?" demanded Flammermont, addressing Fricoulet. "What do you have to say to that?"

"Nothing," replied the engineer, "absolutely nothing, except that I'll put myself entirely at your disposal to construct, according to your plans, a sphere similar to that mentioned by Telinga, but of sufficient size to contain all three of us."

He had pronounced these words with such magnificent seriousness that Ossipoff was captivated and murmured in an audible whisper: "Well done! There's the modesty I like to see. It's a great pity that the boy isn't always like that."

The old man frowned, though, on hearing the engineer murmur, in a low voice: "The lunar soil must certainly have special properties utterly different from those we find in our terrestrial soil, for the Devil may take me if such a plan could succeed on our native planet."

"How is it, Monsieur Fricoulet," Mikhail Ossipoff exclaimed, "that you are so prejudiced against the future? The few scientific notions that you possess ought to allow you, more than common mortals, to estimate the true value of the marvelous discoveries to which the 19th century alone has given birth—and those discoveries should have given you some inkling of the miracles that future centuries hold in reserve for us." After this small admonition, the old scientist turned to Telinga. "It's urgent," he said, "that you give us the plans of the system that you've just mentioned."

"If you and your companions had let me finish what I was saying," the Selenite replied, "you would know that all the pieces of an apparatus once constructed by audacious Selenites who proposed to visit Venus are in Maoulideck, in the tunnels leading to the Observatory."

Ossipoff uttered a cry of joy. "What does this apparatus do?" he asked.

"The apparatus was never tried, the government of that time having decided that it would not be wise to compromise the perfect happiness enjoyed by our planet by establishing relations with a world whose mores and state of civilization were unknown to us."

"But you think," the old man asked, anxiously, "that this apparatus might be put at our disposal?"

Before Telinga could reply, Gontran had moved closer to Fricoulet. "Well," he said, "you mocked me a little while ago, but what do you think now?"

"The innocents shall have full hands," growled the engineer. He turned to the Selenite and said: "But if your apparatus is similar in every respect to the one you've described to us, the reflector must be at least a kilometer in diameter."

"Why is that?"

"Remember that it's a matter of transporting a projectile over a distance of 12,000,000 leagues."

"Pardon me," said Ossipoff, "but it's only 6,000,000, since that's the distance at which the zones of attraction of the Moon and Venus meet."

"Now," said the Selenite in its turn, "the constructors of the apparatus judged that transporting a projectile over such a derisory distance would only require a reflector measuring 50 meters in height and 250 meters wide."

The engineer made a face. "That's not much," he murmured. Addressing Ossipoff, he said "Don't you think so?"

The old man did not answer. For several seconds he had been engaged in a series of calculations that had covered no less than three pages of his notebook with figures. Finally, he uttered a sigh of relief, held out his calculations to Flammermont and said: "See whether that's correct, my dear Gontran." Then he addressed Telinga. "If it's not inconvenient," he said, "I'll use Maoulideck as a point of departure. That city's situation, at the center of your hemisphere, will permit me to rise up vertically, in order to escape the influence of weight more rapidly and simultaneously take advantage of the entire influence of the electric vibrations...."

The Selenite approved this with a mute nod of his head.

"You're quite certain," asked Flammermont, who was examining the calculations submitted to him by Ossipoff with imperturbable seriousness, "that no error has been made?"

The old man shivered and drew closer to the young man. "Might I be mistaken, by chance?" he asked. "After all, it's quite possible."

"No, no," Gontran replied, hastily. "It's just the rapidity with which we'll complete the journey, in your estimation, that astonishes me."

"You need have no fear from that point of view. I've calculated that Venus' zone of attraction is only two and a half days away; allowing as much for the fall, that makes five terrestrial days..."

"But in that case," Gontran exclaimed, "we can reach Venus before Sharp can land there himself."

Fricoulet's expression was dubious. "Damn!" he said. "You're getting ahead of yourself! Remember that while we're here, immobilized in darkness, the scoundrel's still traveling; nine more days still separate us from the sunrise, and by the time we can see clearly—and only then will we be able to make useful preparations for our departure—he'll have no more than 3,000,000 leagues to cover."

As Gontran's and Monsieur Ossipoff's expressions darkened, Ossipoff said to him: "Anyway, what does it matter whether we arrive before or after him. The main thing is to catch up with him—which is inevitable if, as Telinga affirms, all the pieces of the apparatus are intact.

"For my part," declared the Selenite. "I promise to have everything prepared by the 200th hour of the day."

Scarcely had the first rays of sunlight gilding the crenellated summits of the craters brought heat and light back to the surface of the invisible hemisphere than the Selenites set to work under the direction of Telinga. While some were busy on the summit of a peak overlooking Maoulideck, setting up immense mirrors designed to concentrate all the Sun's light at the focal point of the parabolic reflector, others were putting together the 500 plates of selenium that formed the reflector itself.

Ossipoff and his companions were no less active. Having made a lengthy examination of the strange vehicle in which they would be required to continue their voyage, they had agreed to subject it to an important transformation on which the success of their bold enterprise would depend.

The vehicle was a hollow sphere made entirely of selenium, measuring no less than ten meters in diameter. In its lower part, a one-meter opening has been made, cut transversally by four stalks, the intersection of which supported a selenium axis. The extremity of that axis served to support, by courtesy of bronze rollers on an iron track, a sort of observatory dome, in such a manner that the room—in which the voyagers would be accommodated—could remain immobile in spite of the rotation of the sphere.

Gontran, to whom Fricoulet was giving a minute description of all the pieces of this strange vehicle, murmured in his ear: "That sphere rotates?"

"Certainly. Doesn't a bullet rotate as it exits the device that fired it?" He took the young Comte aside. "There's no point in asking you, is there, whether you know what William Crookes the great English scientist, meant by atomic bombardment?"

"No point, indeed, in asking me," Flammermont replied, smiling, "for you're convinced that I don't know anything about it."

"Well," Fricoulet continued, "matter is in a state of eternal and powerful motion; the further matter is dissociated, the more that movement is freed from the shackles of cohesion. Now, as the millions of vibrations produced by that telephonic roundel are stored in the sphere, the molecules of air that act against the walls of the sphere are set in motion, as if by thousands of little fingers, and impress an incalculable velocity upon it. Do you understand?"

"I understand hardly anything—but the main thing is that you're quite certain that this machine is functional."

"And how could it be otherwise?" replied the engineer. "Look at this telephone transmitter, the roundel of which is less than three meters in diameter, and these formidable electromagnets, which will made it vibrate, and this Voltaic battery."

While listening silently to his friend's explanations, however, Flammermont seemed worried. "What are you thinking about?" Fricoulet asked him, abruptly.

"My God!" replied the young Comte. "Doubtless you'll laugh at me, but I just had a dreadful thought."

"What?"

"At a certain distance from the lunar surface, the vibrant waves will no longer have enough force to carry us forward."

The engineer frowned. "Of course," he said. "That might well happen." Then, addressing Ossipoff, he said: "Monsieur de Flammermont thinks that our motive force won't be sufficient to last is till the end of the journey."

"On what do you base that supposition, dear boy?" asked the old man.

Gontran found himself completely at a loss and glanced at Fricoulet desperately. Fortunately, the young engineer replied in his stead and handed Ossipoff a page from his notebook. On that page, the following formula was inscribed in pencil:

$$A = \frac{\sqrt{L189+v}}{V+P} = 980,400$$

"What's that?" asked the old man, opening his eyes wide.

"That," replied Fricoulet, "is the mathematical proof that our friend Gontran is right." As the old man was already turning to Flammermont, the engineer hastened to reply to the question that his friend had been asked. "The three of us," he said, "weigh 250 kilograms. Now, taking account of the continuous loss of motive force the further we travel, it's easy to calculate that, by necessity, there will come a moment when that continually-diminishing force becomes absolutely ineffective. That's why, representing the speed of the apparatus as v and multiplying it by L189, the intensity of gravity at the lunar surface, I divide them by V, Venus, plus P, our weight. I take the square root and I arrive at this result: we shall come to a halt 980,400 kilometers from the Moon."[96]

Monsieur Ossipoff had listened to the young engineer's calculations without interrupting. When the latter had finished, the old man remained plunged into thought for a few seconds more. Eventually, he murmured: "That's correct...quite correct. But then..." He looked at his two companions in turn and added: "It will be necessary for one of us to stay here to lighten the apparatus."

Fricoulet smiled. "In that case," he said, "I see no one but me who can play the role of the abandoned, for neither you nor Gontran, one a father and the other a fiancé, can avoid the duty incumbent upon you to run after Selena's kidnapper.

---

[96] It is impossible to make any sense of this formula or the associated "explanation;" either it has been drastically misrendered or it is calculated gibberish—Molière's science, as it were. The notion that light waves lose energy as they plough through the luminiferous ether seems plausible, on the basis of an analogy with sound waves in air or actual waves on the surface of water, but is somewhat out of keeping with the calculations of stellar distances cited later in the text, which assume the constancy of the velocity of light.

"I dared not ask that of you," added the old man, "but since you recognize yourself that there's no way to do otherwise…"

This plan was not at all to Flamermont's taste, though. Separate himself from Fricoulet! Fricoulet, his inspiration, then man who held out the pole to him to get him out of dangerous waters in which Ossipoff's embarrassing questions might plunge him at any moment. He might as well renounce Selena right away. No, this could not be, and it would not be! Fricoulet was part of Gontran; the engineer was the diplomat's scientific face. To separate them from one another would be to destroy entirely the Flammermont that Monsieur Ossipoff knew, who had seduced Selena's father.

"Well, what's the matter?" asked the old man, suddenly, noticing the absorbed demeanor of his future son-in-law. "Anyone would think that the arrangement didn't suit you."

"Alcide is a childhood friend," replied the young man, with admirably well-feigned emotion, "and you'll understand that I can't abandon him gladly."

"Would you prefer to renounce Selena?" countered the scientist, not without a certain bitterness.

"God forbid!" cried the young Comte, heatedly, "but since it's a matter of weight that's troubling us, could we not dispense with part of the apparatus rather than dispensing with Fricoulet?"

The old scientist shrugged expansively. "Dispense with the apparatus!" he exclaimed. "You don't, I suppose, intend to fly on the luminous ray yourself, like an atom."

"Would that really be impossible?" the young man riposted. Then, without leaving Ossipoff—whose haggard eyes ere looking at him in astonishment— time to recover from that enormity, he went on gravely: "Although I don't have any such audacity in mind, it seems to me that by looking hard, we might find a means of making our vehicle lighter." He spoke slowly, emphasizing his words and punctuating his phrases, watching Fricoulet from the corner of his eye. The latter, while appearing to by deep in thought, was performing an expressive mime.

"As Telinga has told me that we can be ready to depart in four times 24 hours," Ossipoff replied, "think about what you've just said—and if you find the means of which you speak, I'll be the first to adopt it. You can't think that I can easily resign myself to leaving Monsieur Fricoulet behind." With a grimace that contradicted the words he had just spoken, he shook the engineer's hand, then added: "But if, in spite of all your efforts, the apparatus must remain as it presently is and it's necessary to lighten the load…"

"Then," Fricoulet continued, smiling, "you'll throw me overboard like a sack of ballast."

Ossipoff nodded his head affirmatively and, turning on his heel, went to rejoin Telinga, in whose company he had to go to Fedor Sharp's vehicle in order to search it with the utmost care for objects he might need, such as blankets, spare clothing, scientific apparatus, weapons, etc.

As soon as the two young men were alone, Flammermont exclaimed: "Well, you're a nice one! You know that I don't understand a damned word of all these combinations of speed, weight and so on, but you amuse yourself by making me juggle with figures and then hang me out to dry!"

The engineer shrugged his shoulders. "You have such amazing aplomb," he said, "that I'm always on the lookout for occasions for you to deploy it."

"That's all well and good," Gontran retorted, in a piqued tone, "but it's no less true that you've given me a hare to chase, and it's necessary that I kill that hare."

"Bah! You'll kill it. Don't worry—you know full well that I understand this sort of thing. Just give me a few hours and you'll be satisfied."

"I don't matter—it's Ossipoff that has to be satisfied.

"Very well—he will be."

With these words, leaving Flammermont to supervise the work, the engineer went back underground in order to be able conduct his meditation and research in peace.

In less than an hour, he returned to the Comte in triumph.

"Well?" said the latter.

"Here it is—look." And before his friend's eyes he made a rapid sketch, saying: "Given that our total weight is too great for the apparatus to be able to transport us all the way to Venus, it was necessary to reduce that weight. Two means of doing that presented themselves: to get rid of me, or to get rid of the apparatus. You opted for the second means—I expected no less of your friendship."

"I beg your pardon!" Gontran exclaimed. "I never mentioned getting rid of the apparatus."

"That's where we're not in agreement, for that's what my plan is based on."

"Do you intend us to make the voyage sitting astride an electric current?"

"You're joking—but I'm being serious, and I'll convince you of it. The new calculations that I've just made establish that the apparatus, as it's presently set up, will be sufficient to take us as far as the confines of the lunar zone of attraction; once there, of course, the vibratory waves will have no further influence on it, so we'll abandon it."

"That's easy to say!" Gontran exclaimed. "We'll abandon it! But what will become of us?"

Fricoulet smiled at his friend's anxiety. "We'll stay where we are," he continued, "which is to say, in the three-meters-high and three-meters-broad cabin enclosed in the upper part of the sphere."

Flammermont's bewilderment was increasing. "But the cabin's part of the apparatus," he objected.

"At this moment, yes. But this is my innovation. Instead of linking it indissolubly with the sphere by means of rivets, as it is now, I'll attach it by means of nuts and bolts, in such a way that it can be rendered independent of it at the desired moment."

Gontran clapped his hands. "I get it!" he cried. "It's perfectly simple."

"You get it," said the engineer, sarcastically.

"Of course! When we reach the limit of the zone of lunar attraction, we'll abandon the sphere, which has become useless, and continue the voyage in our cabin."

Fricoulet could not help laughing. "Fortunately," he said, Monsieur Osipoff can't hear you. If he could, he'd have a sorry opinion of you. Fool! You'd let yourself fall 6,000,000 leagues in that selenium cube!"

"Do you see any reason why not?"

"Many—first of all...but I don't have time to explain all that. I'd rather continue explaining my plan. Around my sphere, in an equatorial position, I extend a circular surface made entirely of selenium, 30 meters in diameter. To that surface, our cabin is attached by metallic cables, with the effect that, once we're rid of the encumbering sphere, we'll continue our voyage with our cabin forming a gondola, suspended from a vast rigid parachute, the surface area of which will measure no less than 300 square meters. In that fashion, not only will the apparatus be lightened sufficiently to permit me to take part in our voyage, but will also allow us to take Selenite companions, if they're minded to do it."

As he finished this speech, Fricoulet rolled on the ground, dragging his friend Gontran down with him. The latter, to show the engineer how enthusiastic he was about his invention, had bounded forward to hug him, without thinking about the special conditions of density and weight on the world where they were. With his sextupled strength, he had cannoned into the unfortunate Fricoulet's torso with the force of a catapult.

"Ficthre!" groaned the engineer, feeling himself anxiously. "Can you think before you act?" Having convinced himself that nothing was broken, he added: "In future, spare me your gestures of friendship—they're too dangerous." On seeing Gontran's crestfallen expression, though, he started laughing and took him by the hand. "No hard feelings, eh? Now let's get busy putting the plan you've just submitted to me into execution."

"What!" Gontran exclaimed. "You want..."

"Certainly I want you to pass for its discoverer in Ossipoff's eyes. Anyway, as you said yourself, it's childishly simple—Christopher Columbus's egg."

Five days after this conversation, the immense selenium parachute surrounded the sphere, attached by cables to the cabin in which the voyagers were to take their places. The sphere itself, suspended from two metal masts, was placed at the focal point of the parabolic reflector. All that remained was to "center" the mirrors, and the departure had been fixed for the following day.

After loading all the objects that they intended to take with them, Ossipoff and his companions had decided to get a few hours' rest. In order not to waste their time in unnecessary comings and goings, though, they had lain down on the bunks accommodated in the new vehicle, so that when they woke up they would only have to give the signal to take off. Worn out by the accumulated fatigue of the previous days, they were sleeping, as the saying goes, with closed fists, filling the cabin with sonorous snoring, when a sudden dreadfully loud noise brought them to their feet.

For a second, they looked at one another helplessly, searching one another's eyes for an explanation of their abrupt awakening.

Fricoulet was the first to exclaim: "Our friend Telinga surely wouldn't do us the bad turn of sending us into space without warning?"

Gontran shook his head. "No," he said, "it seemed to me to be more like the sound of an avalanche falling on top of us. Perhaps some rocks have been dislodged from the rim of the crater."

Ossipoff shrugged his shoulders and muttered laconically: "One's as likely as the other."

"In any case," said Fricoulet, "there's a very simple means of finding out what's happened, and that's to go and see." So saying, he climbed the ladder giving access to one of the portholes that served as doors.

He was about to leave the cabin when Gontran exclaimed: "God forgive me, but there's someone walking around underneath us."

"In the sphere!" exclaimed the engineer. "Go on! You're dreaming..." Nevertheless, he came back down, knelt down at put his ear to the cabin floor.

When he got up again, his features were imprinted with profound amazement. "I don't know if it's walking," he said, in a low voice, "but something unusual is happening down there, at any rate, for I can hear a noise I can't quite define."

He had scarcely finished speaking when a roll of thunder burst forth beneath the voyagers' feet. In the initial moment of fright they leapt into the air.

"What's this devilment!" cried Fricoulet.

A second roll was heard, then a third and a fourth, as dull and continuous as the first.

"My word, Messieurs," said Gontran, "you can follow me or not, as you wish, but for myself, I want to know what I'm dealing with." He took a revolver from the wall, which had been hung there along with several other weapons, checked that it was loaded and advanced toward the exit-hole.

"We'll go with you," said the engineer, "but you amuse me with your precautions. Are you expecting to find Comanche Indians down there?"

The young Comte did not react to the joke, for the good reason that he had not heard it. Without worrying about whether or not his companions were following him he had grabbed hold of the rigid ladder that ran from the cabin along the entire depth of the sphere to the lower section. Without hesitation, with the

300

revolver in his fist, he went into the dark hole formed by the metal sphere and marched straight ahead. Suddenly, however, there was a loud bang, whose echoes, striking the selenium walls and rebounding like a volley from a tennis racket, multiplied deafeningly and terrifyingly.

Gontran was no scientist, but he was a courageous man; this assault, far from stopping him, only excited him further and set him running in the direction from which it seemed to have come. There was a second bang and he heard a bullet whistle past his ear. Then he fired his revolver six times, at hazard, threw away the useless weapon, and hurled himself forward. Suddenly, from the shadows, arms gripped him. His fingers found a throat and squeezed it vigorously. His unknown adversary tottered, dragging him down as he fell.

"Help me! Help me!" Flammermont shouted.

At that moment, Ossipoff arrived, followed by Fricoulet—who, being a careful man, had armed himself with magnesium rods. He set fire to one and the darkness immediately dissipated. The newcomers saw a confused mass comprising Gontran and his adversary, on whose stomach he was crouched.

"Great God!" cried the young man, keeping backwards. "It's Farenheit!"

"Farenheit!" repeated Ossipoff and Fricoulet simultaneously, as they leaned over the body immobile at heir feet, dumbfounded.

It was, indeed, the American, thin and fleshless—freeze-dried, so to speak—whose livid and leathery face the magnesium illuminated. When the initial moment of stupefaction had passed, Ossipoff declared that it was vital to transport the unfortunate to the cabin as soon as possible, in order to give him the care that his condition required.

"I haven't killed him, have I?" Gontran asked. "I fear that I might have squeezed too hard."

Making no reply, Fricoulet threw the American on his back as if he were as light as a feather, and carried him back up to the cockpit. "The poor devil's dying of hunger," he said, after examining him. "First of all, let's try to get him to absorb a little of our nutritive paste."

With great difficulty, they succeeded in unclenching the American's teeth and introducing a little of the aliment into his mouth, then waited anxiously to see what effect it would produce.

"How do you explain this resurrection?" asked Flammermont, who could not, even now, believe his eyes.

"Quite simply. First, it's necessary to assume that the cartridge that scoundrel Sharp threw, rather than killing Farenheit, only wounded him. When we abandoned him, fleeing the night, the cold gripped him. Now, you know that cold preserves, and that certain animals—eels, for example—are able to stay alive even after being frozen. It's probably a similar phenomenon that affected Farenheit."

"It's the sunlight that's unfrozen him, then?" said Gontran, smiling.

"As you quite rightly say."

"But how can his conduct be explained?"

"That's not in the scientific domain. I can't enlighten you as to that—but you can ask him yourself."

At that moment, the American began to stir on his bed. His lips became pink and a little blood appeared in his cheeks, where the prominent cheekbones seemed ready to cave in. For several seconds his teeth rattled like castanets in a formidable chewing motion; then, without opening his eyes, he murmured in a cavernous voice: "Eat, eat, eat..." As Fricoulet had foreseen this demand, he had a large ball of paste ready at his fingertips. Taking advantage of a moment when the American's mouth opened wide, he introduced it therein.

The effect was virtually instantaneous. Farenheit sat up; his eyelids lifted; his eyes fixed themselves successively on the people surrounding him—and then he extended his arms toward them. "By God!" he said. "So it wasn't that scoundrel Sharp who built this metal balloon I was trying to destroy."

Ossipoff could not suppress a groan. "Destroy!" he cried.

"What do you expect? On coming round, in that frightful desert, I dragged myself a few kilometers as best I could—then, all of a sudden, I saw all these preparations for departure. I thought it was Sharp, trying to escape me again. Rage took hold of me and I decided to die, if necessary, provided that I died avenging myself."

"Then he's the one you thought you were shooting at just now?" asked Gontran.

"Of course—fortunately, my hand was shaking. He interrupted himself, with a covetous gleam in his eye. "Oh," he said, "I could gladly eat a beef roast washed down with a glass of port."

Fricoulet and Gontran looked at one another, sorrowfully. "The only means of satisfying that desire," the young engineer said, finally, "is for you to go to sleep and hope that Morpheus sends you a gastronomic dream. As for us, our larder consists of this." And he pointed to the paste fabricated by Ossipoff.

The American pulled a face, and then, following Fricoulet's advice, lay down on his side and went to sleep.

"Well, Monsieur Fricoulet, are you beginning to be convinced?" asked Ossipoff in a mocking tone.

"I've more than begun, my dear Monsieur, I'm convinced—absolutely convinced. That doesn't prevent me from being amazed by the success..." The engineer turned to Flammermont. "What about you, Gontran?" he asked.

The young Comte shrugged his shoulders slightly and replied, in a rather casual tone: "Oh, as for me, you know full well that I never had the shadow of a doubt, even for an instant."

"Besides," said the old man, in his turn, "isn't he the one who came up with this ingenious idea, thanks to which we can continue our voyage. It would be astonishing if he had conceived any anxieties on the subject."

Fricoulet hid the joyful gleam that these words ignited in his eyes behind half-lowered lids, but he had difficulty not bursting into laughter when Gontran said, gravely: "What gives me great confidence in myself is the persuasion I have that the word *impossible* isn't French..."

A groan was heard behind them; they turned and saw Farenheit sitting on the edge of the cushion that served him as a bunk. "The word *impossible* isn't American either," he said, churlishly.

Fricoulet smiled slightly and replied: "You're striking proof of that—for the Devil may take me if I ever expected to see you living after the strange adventure that overtook you..."

"You have to go to the Moon to see such things," said Gontran, in his turn.

"Why is that?" retorted Ossipoff. "Have we not methods of conservation of foodstuffs by cold on Earth?"

"With the difference that the sheep and oxen thus conserved don't come back to life, while Mr. Farenheit has."

"We've forgotten to ask how you are," said Gontran.

The American stretched his arms forcefully, making his joints crack like pistol shots, and replied: "Not bad, thanks. I just feel rather stiff—that's doubtless the effect of the hibernation...but a little exercise will restore all my elasticity." So saying, he made as if to get up.

A gesture from Fricoulet stopped him. "A little exercise," the engineer repeated. "But where the Devil do you expect to take it? You have only the cage in which we're located in which to take a stroll, and you'll confess that space is severely lacking."

A profound disappointment was painted on the Yankee's face. "By God!" he groaned. "Indeed, it's not much." Then, in a one of amazement, he immediately added: "Right! Where are we?"

"In our new vehicle—the one that you were trying to destroy when Monsieur Flammermont intervened, fortunately for you and for us."

Farenheit looked around, in frank dissatisfaction. "Pooh!" he murmured, pulling a face. "It's less comfortable than the other one."

"What do you expect?" replied Gontran. "Needs must when the Devil drives—we should think ourselves fortunate that a providential combination of circumstances has permitted us to continue our voyage—otherwise, I would have had to renounce all hope forever of recovering my dear Selena, and you all hope of getting your hands on your friend Sharp again."

At that name, which always had the effect of making him furious, the American sat up straight on his bed, with his teeth clenched, his fists clenched and his eyes ablaze. But then a singular phenomenon occurred; projected by the force of his impulse, he bumped his head on the upper wall of the projectile and fell back on top of Ossipoff, who was quietly occupied in writing his notes of the voyage. Taken by surprise, the old man lost his balance and tried to hold on to Gontran, whom he dragged down in his fall. All three of them rolled on the floor, while Fricoulet laughed himself to tears.

Ossipoff was the first to get up. "What's happening?" he mumbled. "What's all the commotion?"

The engineer held his sides, incapable of saying a word. It was Gontran who replied, while rubbing his knees. "The commotion was caused by a falling body, of course!"

"A bolide!" exclaimed Ossipoff.

Farenheit, who had also got up, went to the old man. "I was ready to make my apologies to you," he said, "but as you're making use of such unpleasant expressions with regard to me…"

Fricoulet's hilarity was immediately redoubled, and it was impossible for Gontran to remain serious any longer. Farenheit and Ossipoff looked one another in the whites of the eyes, like two bulldogs ready to fight.

"But, my dear Mr. Farenheit," the young Comte succeeded in saying, "the worthy Monsieur Ossipoff had no intention of insulting you."

"Even so," complained the American. "Bolide!"

"Is the name given, in astronomy, to certain errant bodies in space. Now, you'll agree that, being in space, you played a somewhat similar role."

The Yankee's face cleared. He took another step forward and held out his open hand to the old man. "Shake, Monsieur Ossipoff," he said, with dignity, "to prove that you don't hold it against me that I fell astride your shoulders as if you were a vaulting-horse."

"I gladly accept your apology," replied the old scientist, shaking Farenheit's hand, "but I'd be very grateful to you if you'd explain what caused you to make that ardent manifestation."

"I don't know what to tell you, and I'm as surprised by you are by what happened."

Fricoulet, whose had finally mastered his hilarity, then explained that the American had made an abrupt movement, without reflecting that the further away they got from the Moon, the more they escaped the effects of gravity, already so feeble on the satellite's surface.

On hearing these words, the American nearly signaled his amazement with a start no less formidable than the first; having learned from experience, though, and mistrusting his nervous nature, he clung to the cushions of the divan with both hands and exclaimed: "By God! Did I just hear you say *the further away we get from the Moon*?"

"You heard me perfectly well, Mr. Farenheit."

"We're no longer on the Moon?"

"It's now more than an hour since we left."

The worthy American's alarm was comical to behold. He raced to one of the portholes and remained there for a few moments, with his nose glued to the thick glass, looking out into the immensity. Convinced of the reality, he came back. "Right!" he said. "How come you were able to leave the lunar surface, on which we seemed to be stranded forever?"

Ossipoff pointed to Gontran. "It's Monsieur de Flammermont, again, to whom we owe this marvelous application of electrical forces."

The American shook the young Comte's hand vigorously. "In the name of my hatred, thanks," he said, in a deep voice. "And I promise, if we succeed in getting our hands on that blackguard Sharp for a second time, not to let him escape. He'll pay for all his misdeeds at a stroke."

"Pardon me," replied Gontran, whose face had paled slightly, "but you'll agree that Sharp belongs partly to me now. Have I not to avenge my fiancée, my beloved Selena?"

Farenheit paused briefly, then said: "Let's not argue about it now. There'll be time enough to discuss the matter when the scoundrel's at our disposal."

"There's a very simple means of settling it, after having discussed it," joked Fricoulet. "You can throw dice for Sharp's skin, or draw straws…"

While the three men were chatting in this fashion, Osssipoff attentively consulted the instruments suspended from the cabin walls. "There we go," he said, rubbing his hands in satisfaction. "The voyage is progressing well. The barometer only marks 350 milimeters, but the weather's good anyway. The hygrometer indicates very moderate humidity and the ozometric papers are intact."

"Are you certain that we're heading in the right direction?" Fricoulet asked.

"I've submitted all my calculations to Monsieur de Flammermont," the old man replied, "and he's confirmed their accuracy."

The American studied the young man—who maintained an imperturbable seriousness—with a strange expression.

"In any case," said the Comte, "If you doubt it, you have only to consult the compass."

Ossipoff straightened up and looked at Flammermont in surprise. *Oh good*, thought the latter. *I've just said something stupid.* He was convinced of it even before Ossipoff said, in a slightly bitter tone: "You're joking, of course...you know perfectly well that the indications of the compass don't relate to anything in the medium we're in, and that it's no use to us so far from any attraction."

Gontran bit his lip, utterly confused. Suddenly, though, he had an inspiration of genius and pointed at the portholes through which the constellations shining in the sidereal immensity were visible. "I meant those stars," he said, in a vibrant voice, "which are as many celestial compasses by which we can track our progress."

A smile played on the old man's lips. Immediately, he replied: "I beg your pardon, dear boy. I must admit that such a heresy, on your part, would astonish me." Having said that, in an affectionate tone, Ossipoff resumed his occupations, while Gontran went to sit next to Fricoulet.

"I admire you sincerely, my friend," the engineer murmured. "I'm profoundly hostile to your marriage, God knows, but I must confess that if you finally succeed in espousing the woman you love...well, you certainly won't have stolen her."

"Love seems to increase my imagination tenfold," the young Comte replied.

Farenheit came over to them at that moment. "How far away are we now, in your estimation, from the Moon?" he asked.

"Pooh!" replied Fricoulet, consulting his watch. "Without being able to tell you exactly, I can testify that we must be about 100,000 kilometers away."

The American opened his eyes wide. "100,000 kilometers!" he repeated. "But you just said that we only left an hour ago."

"Well, at a rate of 28,000 meters a second...what's that?"

"100,800 kilometers an hour," replied the Yankee—who, as a tradesman, had a talent for mental arithmetic.

"So, when I told you 100,000 kilometers, I wasn't far off."

"But that will take us 500,000 leagues a day...or in 24 hours, at least."

"Rigorously precise," said the engineer, enjoying Farenheit's amazement. He added: "In ten hours, we'll reach the neutral point—that is to say, the one at which the attractions of the Moon and Venus are contiguous."

The American was thoughtful; he was performing prodigies of mental arithmetic. "But on Earth, at that rate," he murmured, "it would only take us a minute and a half to cross the Atlantic."

"I haven't made the calculation," Fricoulet riposted, "but it must be about right, given the proportions."

Gontran sighed.

"What's the matter?" asked the engineer.

"If we'd had a similar means of locomotion at our disposal when we left Earth, we'd have reached the Moon in three hours."

"You're right…but since it's done now, what have you to regret?"

"The lost time…which will never be recovered," Flammermont replied, gravely, raising his voice so that Ossipoff could hear him.

"Time is money," added Farenheit, no less gravely. Suddenly, the American uttered a slight exclamation of surprise. "What's that?" he asked, pointing at a corner of the cabin. "They look like diving suits…."

"You're not mistaken," the young Comte replied, with a smile. "They are diving suits."

"Are we going to travel underwater, then?" asked the American.

"No—in the void." From his interlocutor's surprised expression, Fricoulet deduced that his reply was meaningless to him. "Briefly," he said, "you'll understand that the electrical force that is propelling us forward will, according to our calculations, be sufficient to get us into the Venusian zone of attraction—but there it will stop, and the apparatus will be no further use to us. On the contrary, its weight will only render our fall more rapid—which is to say, more dangerous. Do you understand?"

The American replied affirmatively.

"Then, we'll abandon the sphere that supports us and continue our voyage in this cabin, transformed into a gondola. That's why we've brought these devices with us, designed in the past by adventurous Selenites. Whereas diving-suits serve to protect the body against the pressure of water, however, these guarantee it against the mortal effect of the abrupt disappearance of atmospheric pressure…there!"

"Very ingenious," murmured the American. Stifling an enormous yawn with his hand, he added: "By God! I seem to be falling asleep."

"There's nothing astonishing in that," Fricoulet replied, very seriously. "For a fortnight, you've done nothing but that. You don't get over such bad habits in a matter of hours."

"What do you advise, then?" asked Farenheit, interrogating him with his gaze.

"Take a nap, to begin with. Then we'll see…"

This advice doubtless coincided exactly with the American's secret desire for, after muttering an incomprehensible goodnight, he stretched himself out on the cushions and was not long delayed in filling the cabin with sonorous snoring.

Five minutes later, Fricoulet said in his turn: "Mr. Farenheit's full of common sense. It's past midnight in Paris now; it's the hour when honest men go to sleep." He rolled himself up in his travel-blanket and stammered, somnolently: "I wish you good night, Messieurs…"

Only a few minutes had gone by when a shrill sound was heard, dominating he American's *basso profundo*; it was the engineer, adding his part to the concert of snores. Gontran tried to fight, but in vain. Drowsiness claimed him. "It's definitely contagious," he murmured. Addressing Ossipoff, who was still busy writing, he said: "Is there anything to see between the Moon and the orbit of Venus?"

The scientist looked up, slightly surprised. "Absolutely nothing," he said, "as you know."

"In that case," retorted the young Comte, "As nothing else offers itself to me by way of recreation, I ask your permission to get a few hours' sleep."

The old man shook his hand and Gontran took his place on the cushions beside his companions. He soon fell into a strange dream. After recovering Selena, he married her, and they spent their honeymoon touring the celestial worlds. Soon, transformed into stars themselves and united for eternity in the celestial immensity, they became the favorite stars of terrestrial lovers.

Left alone, Mikhail Ossipoff had let his head fall into his hands and was also dreaming about his beloved daughter, who had disappeared in space. Would he ever see the girl he had sacrificed to his passion for science again? Would the desperate attempt he was making at this moment have any other result than to carry him one step further into the intersidereal desert? Oh, if only, at least, Sharp might fall into his hands! And it was no longer the rancor of the scientist but the hatred of the father that swelled the old man's heart and made the blood boil in his veins…

Little by little, however, his thoughts became clearer; the silhouettes of Sharp and Selena faded away into a sort of mist. Soon, they disappeared completely and all sensation of life disappeared. Mikhail Ossipoff was also fast asleep.

It was 11 a.m. on the Yankee's chronometer when a vigorous hand shook the old man, who woke up with a start.

"What's the matter?" he stammered, surprised to have dozed off in that position. "What's happening?"

"Nothing, Monsieur," the American replied, "but it's getting late…"

The old man looked around. Gontran was trimming his beard with the aid of a small pocket mirror and Fricoulet was using a micrometer to measure the arc subtended by the plant Venus, which was framed in a porthole in the ceiling.

Ossipoff went toward him, excitedly. "Well?" he demanded, with a slight anxiety in his voice.

The engineer calmly replied: "Telinga's predictions were correct. It's 20 hours since we left the lunar surface, and we've already crossed 1,800,000 kilometers. "We've already completed a sixth of our journey. We're exactly where we need to be…" Surrendering his place to the old man, he added: "See for yourself, anyway. You can already make out the phases of Venus."

"Venus has phases!" exclaimed Gontran. Fricoulet looked at him in a terrible fashion, and the young Comte immediately continued, in a loud voice: "Yes, Mr. Farenheit, Venus has phases like the Moon."

"But I never doubted it," the American replied, in a plaintive voice.

The engineer came to stand in front of him and declared, in a professorial voice. "Venus has been baptized with various names by Terrans: sometimes it's the Shepherd's Star or the Morning Star, sometimes Vesper and sometimes Lucifer. It's the second planet of the Solar System and it orbits the central star—the Sun—at a mean distance of 26,750,000 leagues."

"And the Earth?" queried the American.

It was Gontran who spoke, in a self-important tone. "The Earth is further away from the Sun than Venus. Its orbit has a radius of 148,000,000 kilometers, or 37,000,000 leagues."

Fricoulet looked at him in surprise. "You're more of a scientist than I thought," he whispered in his ear.

"*Doctus cum libro!*" replied Flammermont, smiling.

"What do you mean?"

Gontran winked, and pointed to his traveling-blanket. "Guess what I've got hidden under there," he said.

"How should I know?"

"A book I found in Sharp's cannonball."

"A book?"

"Yes, *Les Continents célestes*. I brought it with me, and while you were all asleep just now, I spent two hours boning up on Venus…"

"Bah!"

"And I promise you that I know my subject. Ossipoff can give me an oral…with my *vade mecum*,[97] I no longer have anything to fear…"

"Except that you forgot the phases…"

"That's true—I forgot them."

While the two friends chatted in this fashion, Farenheit talked astronomy with Mikhail Ossipoff to pass the time. "There's nothing else beyond the Earth, is there?" he asked.

"What about Mars, at 56,000,000 leagues—doesn't that count for anything?" said Ossipoff, catching his breath at such ignorance.

The American, who had no reason to pose as a fount of astronomical knowledge with respect to the old man, replied to Ossipoff's suffocation with a slight shrug of indifference. Then, clicking his tongue in irritation, he muttered: "Mars! The patron planet of soldiers—that's one I'd eliminate from the celestial map, if it could be done."

"Bah!" said Fricoulet and Gontran, in unison. "Why's that?"

---

[97] *Vade mecum* ["go with me"] was once used as a flippant general term for all pocket reference books. Les *Terres du ciel*, of which *Les Continents célestes* is an obvious analogue, would have made a very inconvenient *vade mecum*, as it is a very weighty quarto volume.

"Because I'm a tradesman...and war puts an end to commerce. If you knew the harm the Civil War did to the pork-fat trade...my losses were numbered in millions of dollars that year..."

"You don't like soldiers, then?" asked Flammermont, laughing.

"I consider them to be a useless element of society. Look, have we in the United States an army? And our affairs are no worse for it...on the contrary."

"You're in favor of the suppression of permanent armies?" said the engineer.

"Absolutely. I only like uniforms in the theater...and the uniforms of the last century at that, with huge hats and white feathers, sparkling breastplates, silk scarves, velvet doublets...from the decorative point of view, that's quite pretty. In life, though...an honorable tradesman at his counter makes more of an impression on me than a colonel at the head of his regiment."

"Ugh!" replied Flammermont. "Your situation as a citizen of free America permits you to utter such paradoxes, but you'd change your tune if, like us, you were obliged to play your part in the European concert."

Fricoulet began to laugh and Ossipoff nodded his head in approval of the young Comte's reply.

By way of response, Farenheit released a dull groan and, turning slowly on his heel, described a circular promenade with his gaze, taking visual inventory of the equipment that the travelers had brought with them. "Say!" he exclaimed. "It seems to me that you haven't given much thought to the rigors of temperature. If we find that Venus has nights of 15 times 24 hours, like the Moon..."

"On that score, you can rest easy," Gontran replied. "On Venus we'll find days and nights alternating regularly, exactly as on our native planet, except that the quantity differs..."

"Really?" said he American. "Why?"

"Simply because, the orbit followed by Venus being interior, and therefore shorter, instead of being composed of 365 and a third days, as on Earth, the Venusian year only has 280 and a third days."[98]

Farenheit scratched his head energetically, which was, in him, an indication of intense cerebral tension. "While having a smaller orbit, though," he said, "Venus might spend as much time completing it as Earth takes to complete its own."

"It might," Fricoulet replied, "but it doesn't. There's even a law establishing that the planets rotate more rapidly around the Sun the closer they are. Thus, Mercury travels at 47 kilometers a second, or more than a million leagues a day,

---

[98] In fact, Venus's days are very long, equivalent to 243 of ours, and its "year" is only equivalent to 224.7 Earthly days; the former figure was unknown to contemporary astronomers, but there is no reason for Fricoulet to misquote the latter, especially as he is correct in citing the planet's orbital velocity as 35 kps. Either Graffigny or the authors' amanuensis must have slipped up.

Venus 35 kilometers a second, or 750,000 leagues a day, the Earth 29 kilometers and 643,000 leagues, Mars 24 kilometers and 214,000 leagues, Saturn 10 kilometers and 205,000 leagues, Uranus 7 kilometers and 144,000 leagues."

The engineer had reeled off this long tirade without hesitation, which made the American open his marveling eyes wide. "What a memory!" he murmured. "But if you think I'll remember a single one of those figures..." And he added: "What does it matter, anyway—the main thing is that we'll find conditions out there very similar to those on Earth..."

"Oh, similar in every respect," Flammermont hastened to say. "Its axial rotation takes exactly 23 hours, 21 minutes, 22 seconds; the duration of the day is very nearly the same."

"Except that the year's shorter," observed the American.

"Indeed—but what does that matter to us, who have no intention of spending a year there?" said Gontran. Getting carried away by his subject, he continued: "Add to that the same density, the same atmosphere, the same gravity, the same volume...you might say that Venus is the Earth's younger sister." He jogged Fricoulet's elbow and whispered: "Hey! Haven't I studied them hard, my *Continents célestes*?"

A few words from Ossipoff, however, diminished the young man's self-satisfaction almost immediately. "You're very hasty to offer your opinions, it seems to me," the old scientist said. "When we arrive, you'll see that Venus is far from being the enchanting abode you imagine..."

"Why is that?" asked the young Comte, almost involuntarily.

"One single figure—the one that every astronomer has written beside the planet Venus—will give you your answer. That figure is 55 degrees."

Flammermont was none the wiser; quite the contrary, the figure embarrassed him considerably. At first he said nothing, and, as the possibility of a further question from Ossipoff hung over his head, the unfortunate turned his pleading gaze to Fricoulet.

The engineer, understanding this mute supplication, said to Farenheit: "Yes, my dear Mr. Farenheit, these figures have their eloquence, and this 55 degrees, which represents the angle formed to the ecliptic plane by the rotational axis of Venus contains, in itself alone, everything that is special about the planet: seasons, climates, the length of days, celestial aspects, vegetation, animal life, etc., etc."[99]

---

[99] The figure for the axial inclination of Venus given in modern textbooks is 178 degrees, which is only two degrees from the vertical (it is rendered in that fashion because Venus' south magnetic pole is "above" the ecliptic rather than below it). The datum was very difficult to ascertain by means of optical telescopes because of the obscuring cloud cover, and the highly imaginative "measurements" made by Giovanni Cassini in the 17th century cast a long shadow over subsequent attempts.

The Yankee listened open-mouthed, wondering why he had been dragged into it. He was even more surprised when the engineer continued, after a brief mocking laugh: "Ah, my lad, you've got a taste for celestial matters! What I've just told you intrigues you, and you want to know what that figure of 55 degrees really means…"

The American made an energetic gesture of negation. Fricoulet took no notice of it and cried: "Why deny it, Mr. Farenheit? I appeal to Monsieur Ossipoff—in what circumstances could curiosity be more legitimate than when it's a matter of lifting the veil that will reveal the mysteries of celestial infinity to us? So there's no point in your denying it. It's written on your face: your eyes are sparkling with curiosity and your lips brimming with questions."

Quite astounded by this flood of words, the American nevertheless found the strength to utter a burst of disdainful laughter. "In truth," he tried to say, "if my eyes are sparkling and my lips brimming, I don't understand…"

"But of course!" exclaimed Fricoulet, with perfectly feigned impatience. "How can you understand? You keep interrupting me. Know, then, that Venus has a mass almost equal to that of our native planet and a density 90% that of the Earth, but even though the surface gravity is almost the same as our globe's, Venus is not Paradise. Far from it—mass, density and weight don't make for happiness…"

The American's bewilderment was increasing, to the extent that his lips, quite mechanically, stammered: "Why?"

"Why? Well, it's that 55 degrees that's the cause, of course." He had seized one of the buttons on the unfortunate Farenheit's jacket, and there was nothing the latter could do about it. Not understanding the engineer's intention, Farenheit took it for an act of aggression and took a step backwards.

The young man reassured him with a gesture and continued, smiling: "By virtue of that axial inclination, the seasons, which succeed one another on Venus every 56 days, are very abrupt. The polar zone extends as far as 35 degrees from the equator, and by the same token, the tropical regions extend to 35 degrees from the poles, with the result that two zones, much larger than the temperate zones of our globe, encroach upon one another continually, belonging simultaneously to polar and tropical climates. These regions are therefore subjected to enormous changes in temperature."

"You complained about the heat on the Moon!" said Ossipoff, intervening in the conversation. "Know that on Venus, in summer, the Sun turns around the pole, rising spirally and dispatching a quantity of light almost twice as great as that which it transmits to Earth."

"As for winter," said Fricoulet in his turn, "the cold must be comparable to that which reigns on the Moon during the 350 hour night, for the Sun never gets near the horizon and stays considerably below it."

"The equatorial regions are no more favored than the polar regions; every year, they have two summers during which the Sun climbs to the zenith and pours forth rays that are certainly more ardent than those which roast our equatorial regions…"

"Well?" Fricoulet asked. "Do you understand now?"

"I don't know whether I understand or not," replied the unfortunate Yankee, who was utterly overwhelmed, in a dejected tone. "All I know is that it's stiflingly hot in here." He had taken off his cap and was sponging his sweat-covered forehead.

"It is very warm in here, in fact," Fricoulet admitted. To Gontran, he said: "What's the matter? You're as red as a lobster."

"I'm dying," murmured the young Comte, taking off his coat.

"It's doubtless the Sun," said Ossipoff. "The further we go, the closer we get to it. The exterior walls of the vehicle must be red hot."

"Indeed," murmured Flammermont, "it must be the Sun; our distance therefrom is palpably diminishing."

"Oh, palpably," replied the old man. "2,000,000 leagues out of 37,000,000…that's not very much…"

Farenheit was panting like an ox. "By God!" he groaned. "It must be unbearable on your diabolical planet!"

"Don't worry, my dear Mr. Farenheit," Ossipoff replied, smiling. "That diabolical planet, as you call it, doubtless because you think it's as hot as Hell, has a very thick envelope of clouds to protect it from the solar heat, so the temperature there isn't much higher than on Earth. That's very fortunate for its inhabitants, but very inconvenient for astronomers, who have only been able to perceive Venusian geography through gaps in that cloudy veil…"

"So we only have imperfect data, believed to be unreliable," Gontran said, earnestly.

Fricoulet, however, could no longer keep still. He wandered about the cabin, taking off items of clothing one by one, until he was only dressed in his shirt and underpants. "This heat is intolerable!" he shouted, suddenly, in veritable agony.

"What do you want us to do about it?" asked the old man, dryly. "You knew what you were exposing yourself to in coming with us. You could have stayed with Telinga."

"Isn't there any means of shielding ourselves from the solar rays?" asked Gontran, grieved by his friend's apparent distress.

"I have an idea!" said the American. "If we were to moisten all our blankets and hang them on the walls, the evaporation…"

"Yes," gasped Fricoulet, completely breathless. "We can try that…"

He bent down to pick up one of the blankets that had slipped on to the floor, but immediately uttered a cry of pain and got up very pale, his eyes distraught.

"What's wrong?" asked the voyagers, hurrying toward him.

"The floor is red hot," Fricoulet replied.

"Red hot! That's not possible!" they exclaimed, all at the same time.

"See for yourselves!" retorted the engineer, a trifle bitterly.

The America bent down and put out his hand. "By God!" he said. "Monsieur Fricoulet is right." As he finished this sentence, there was a rather violent shock beneath their feet, and they all fell into a sitting position on the circular divan.

"Damn it!" groaned Fricoulet. "What's happening down there?"

"It appears," Ossipoff replied, "that the castors sustaining the floor have just jammed."

Fricoulet's pallor increased. "Oh!" he said, in a low voice. "That's serious…"

"Serious?" exclaimed Gontran. "Why's that?"

"Because…" He stopped, and murmured: "What good will it do to frighten them?" He turned to Ossipoff. "How distant are we from the neutral point?"

The old man reflected for a few seconds and replied, confidently: "1000 kilometers."

"How long will it take to travel that distance?"

"About two hours."[100]

The engineer's face darkened. "We'll never make it that far," he muttered.

Everyone looked at him anxiously.

"But what are you thinking?" asked Gontran. "Come on—say it. We're men, after all, and if we must die…well, we'll die. Personally, I'd prefer to know what's happening to me…and I presume these gentlemen are of the same opinion."

"Certainly," they said.

"Before answering," Fricoulet said, "let me make certain…" He took a pair of pincers from his instrument-case, went to a corner of the cabin, gripped a ring and pulled it with all his might. It lifted up a square panel in the floor mounted on hinges like a door. At the same moment, a jet of flame shot up to the top of the metallic dome. The engineer let the panel fall back. "That's what I feared," he said, hoarsely.

"What's that?" they asked, prey to the most profound amazement.

"Obviously," Fricoulet retorted, "it's a fire…"

"A fire!"

"Yes. We're on fire, caused by the pivots of the floor seizing up. That's the explanation of the intolerable heat in here. You wanted to know…now you know."

---

[100] This calculation seems a trifle odd, since we were told a little while ago that the vehicle was traveling at a little over 100,000 kilometers an hour—but we have also been told that it is decelerating continually as its propulsive force declines.

The cause the engineer had cited was the only plausible explanation for the sudden fire. The pivot must be red hot, for the floor made of selenium—well known as a good conductor of heat—had become burning hot, even for feet clad in strong boots. Their soles were scorching and threatening to burst into flames at any moment.

Obedient to the same impulse, they all climbed up on to the circular divan.

"What can we do?" asked Ossipoff.

"By God!" cried the American, "Is there anything else to do but extinguish the fire?"

"If you have a means of cooling that metal," said Fricoulet, angrily, "I'm ready to employ it."

"Let's douse it," suggested Gontran.

They all raced to the water-bottles hanging on the walls and emptied their contents on to the floor. On contact with the hot metal, though, the water was transformed into hot vapor. The vehicle's atmosphere became completely opaque, so that the voyagers could no longer see one another, and the noise of the vaporization made it difficult for them to hear one another.

"Let's separate ourselves from the sphere!" Farenheit shouted, madly, throwing himself toward the levers that controlled the attachments.

Ossipoff and Fricoulet hurled themselves upon him. "Wretch!" howled the old man, "You're insane!"

"Immediate death rather than this infernal torture!" groaned the Yankee, making unimaginable efforts to extract himself from the grip of his two companions.

Fricoulet had drawn his revolver. "If you won't be still, Mr. Farenheit," he said, with deadly calmness, "I'll blow your brains out."

"What does it matter?" roared the American, who was out of his mind. "I'm in too much pain."

Suddenly, Gontran had an inspiration. "What about Sharp?" he asked. "Are you renouncing your vengeance, then?"

These words produced a complete transformation in the American's attitude. He let go of the levers voluntarily and retreated into a corner, where he remained immobile, moaning in pain.

"Two hours," said Ossipoff. "I ask for two hours. Then, we can abandon the sphere without any risk, for we'll have penetrated the Venusian zone of attraction."

They were two terrible, frightful hours, during which the voyagers gave proof of admirable courage and superhuman strength. They never ceased soaking the floor, which the continual friction of the pivot had rendered red hot in its entirety, and which emitted a torrid heat.

Ossipoff only took his eyes off his chronometer to measure the arc subtended by Venus with a micrometer.

Finally, he cried in a hoarse voice: "In ten minutes we'll arrive at the neutral point—get ready!"

It was high time; the thermometer marked 42 degrees Centigrade, and the travelers were breathless. Nevertheless, the approach of deliverance gave them new strength; already they had attached everything that they wanted to keep aboard solidly to the walls, and they put on their diving suits skillfully.

The suits were made of an elastic fabric like rubber, in which the limbs and the torso were hermetically enclosed. The fabric itself was supported by a network of extremely fine metallic springs of remarkable elasticity, so as to resist the expansion of the gas contained in the travelers' living tissues. The head was protected by an oval selenium helmet reminiscent of the respirols that Ossipoff and his companions had already used to explore the visible hemisphere of the Moon. They hastily packed a few tablets of solidified oxygen in receptacles built into the interior of the helmets; the air would deteriorate, even though the products of pulmonary combustion would be evacuated through a valve located on top of the head.

"Are you ready?" Ossipoff asked. Everyone replied affirmatively, each of them holding in his hand the helmet in which his head would be imprisoned. "Release the bolts," he instructed. "Each of them pressed down on a lever connected to one of the four bolts, and the cabin was no longer attached to the apparatus, except by the central pivot.

"Follow my instructions to the letter," the old man said then. "In a few seconds, as soon as we've penetrated the Venusian zone of attraction, we'll turn over, as we did when we arrived on the Moon, so that our feet will be where our heads are at present. Imitate my movements exactly and hold on hard to the attachments disposed around the cupola, on the bottom of which we'll find ourselves standing."

He fell silent and quickly screwed his helmet on to the collar of his suit, while his companions did the same. Then, when he saw that they were firmly and resolutely attached to the hand-grips, he ran to the control-mechanism operating the central bolt and grabbed it firmly in one hand, while he lifted the other in a gesture that signified: "Pay attention!"

Chapter XXIII
Three million leagues by parachute

Mikhail Ossipoff operated the control-mechanism while Fricoulet pressed down with all his strength on the cables that reached the exterior by passing through wadded holes. They barely had time to grab hold of the hand-grips; with a terrible shock, the sphere separated from its alveolus and the voyagers found themselves caught in a kind of whirlwind, which prevented them having any consciousness of the rotation that the apparatus performed. They closed their eyes instinctively, and clung to the cords with all the strength of desperation, their hearts wrung by the prospect of the frightful death that awaited them.

When they recovered their self-composure they found themselves crouched in the rounded dome of the cabin, which now formed the floor under their feet. Above their heads, retained by a dozen selenium cables, the immense parachute extended its metallic surface.

Mikhail Ossipoff turned to Gontran and applied his "speaker" to the escape-valve of his helmet. These speakers had been slightly modified to alleviate inconveniences discovered during the excursion to the Moon's visible hemisphere. Instead of being straight, they were strongly curved; one end connected to a little valve pierced in the helmet in front of the mouth and the other was adapted to the escape valve situated, as we have said, at the top of the helmet. In this way, the voyagers could talk to one another without interruption, taking turns as they would in the open air. It was only necessary to apply the end of a speaker to the escape valve of the person with whom one wished to converse.

"Well," said Mikhail Ossipoff, "we're now definitely on our way to Venus."

"How long before we arrive?"

"About 40 hours."

"40 hours! We'll never be able to go so long without eating—at least, I won't."

"But there's no need to fast until our arrival; we only need to introduce into our helmets a provision of the nutritive product we fabricated in Maoulideck, and the artificial air that we breathe will become nutritive in its turn."

"Perfect. I won't try to hide the fact that I had some anxiety on that score, for—I don't know if you're like me—I find that emotion makes me enormously hungry." And he added privately, with a profound sigh: *A beefsteak* aux pommes *or a simple cutlet* au cresson…*O sheep and oxen of my childhood, shall I ever see you again!* Then, pursuant to the idea of a kind of alimentation more in tune with his stomach's tastes and habits, he said: "40 hours is a long time. Isn't there any means of speeding up the fall?"

"If you can find a means, I'd like nothing better than to employ it."

It seemed to Gontran that in pronouncing these words, Ossipoff's voice had taken on a hint of mockery. It was, therefore, with some hesitation that he replied; "What if we were to reduce the surface area of the parachute?" He understood that he had been right to hesitate when he saw the old man shrug his shoulders.

"We're falling through the void," the latter growled, "so that parachute has no effect." With these words, pronounced in an irritated tone, Ossipoff removed his speaker and turned on his heel.

Poor Gontran was still quite nonplussed by this abrupt interruption of the conversation when Fricoulet came over and put himself in communication.

"Another gaffe?" he asked.

"Lower your voice," retorted the young Comte.

"You're forgetting that he can't hear what we're saying. What happened?"

Briefly, Flammermont told his friend about the suggestion he had made to the old scientist for reducing the journey-time.

"Bah!" replied the engineer. "There's no need to worry about such a small thing. After the gymnastics we've just performed, it's permissible to have had your head turned upside-down." Laughing, he added: "All the more so as it's the exact truth, since our heads are now where our feet were a little while ago. Then, seriously, he asked: "How do you feel?"

"Why, quite well. What about you?"

"The absence of atmosphere isn't troubling you?"

"Not at all."

"There we go! So much the better."

The engineer was about to cut off communication when his friend caught him by the arm and asked: "What's that little shining dot we can see out there?"

The engineer turned to look in the direction indicated.

"Do you think it might be our vibratory sphere?" Gontran went on.

"Perhaps," Fricoulet replied, distractedly. After a brief pause, he added: "No, it isn't...like us, the sphere must be falling towards Venus."

"Then what is that thing?"

"Of course!" said Fricoulet. "That thing is simply the Moon—the excellent Selene, whose company we quite three days ago. Now, do you see that large star shining with a bluish light a little further away?"

"One would have to be myopic not to see it. So what?"

"That's the Earth."

"That's not possible!"

Fricoulet slapped him on the shoulder. "There's an exclamation that would certainly compromise your marriage," he said, "if Monsieur Ossipoff heard it. My poor Gontran, you haven't the slightest idea where you were born, and I now understand how mistaken those people are who say that travel broadens the mind."

"That's not very polite," retorted Flammermont.

"For you," the engineer went on, imperturbably, "the sublimities of creation remain a closed book. The globe that gave birth to you is a veritable world…"

"…Measuring 12,000 kilometers in breadth, rotating on its axis in 24 hours and around the Sun with a velocity of 29 and a half kilometers per second, completing an orbit 74,000,000 leagues in diameter in 365 days." Flammermont had pronounced this without pausing, in one breath, in the same monotonous voice that a schoolboy employs in reciting his lesson. Having drawn breath, he added: "You see what a good memory I have, my dear chap; I was 12 when I learned that at the Lycée Henri IV."

"Didn't you, in fact, read it very recently in *Les Continents célestes*?"

Flammermont shrugged his shoulders. Without answering the question, he asked: "Is there any risk in going to sleep trussed up like this?"

"Look!" said the engineer, pointing at Farenheit, lying at the bottom of the gondola, rolled up in his blanket and sleeping peacefully.

"Wake me up when we're within sight of Venus," said Gontran, lying down beside the American.

The engineer went over to Mikhail Ossipoff, who was leaning over the guard-rail, with his eye glued to the ocular lens of a telescope discovered in Sharp's vehicle, sounding the celestial immensity. Fricoulet put himself in communication with him. "Well, Monsieur Ossipoff," he said, "can you see anything?"

"Nothing yet—but I'm on the lookout for a propitious moment to make a few preliminary studies of the world we're heading towards."

"I thought the thickness of the Venusian atmosphere made all geographical observation very difficult, not to say impossible.

"For terrestrial astronomers perhaps—but for us, floating in the void…anyway, look."

The engineer had leaned a long way over the guard-rail but he could not make anything out; the disk of Venus, melted into a kind of mist, allowed none of the details of its surface to be seen, especially by the naked eye. "We're quite certain of the existence of an atmosphere, aren't we?" he said.

"Of course!" retorted the old scientist. "It's as clear as day, not only that we have irrefutable proof of its existence, but that we also know its height, density and composition. Already, you can see how rounded and truncated the extremities of the Venus crescent's horns appear to be…" He sniggered briefly and added: "Although you don't know much about astronomy, you must know that that bluntness is entirely due to the presence of an atmosphere. On the other hand, on studying Venus spectroscopically, astronomers have recognized the absorption lines due to an atmosphere containing water vapor, analogous to the terrestrial atmosphere, but denser."

"Weren't those astronomers Tacchini and Vogel?" said the engineer.[101]

The old scientist could not retain an exclamation of surprise. "How do you know that?" he murmured.

"By listening to Monsieur de Flammermont, who was talking to me about Venus just now," Fricoulet replied, imperturbably.

Ossipoff nodded his head, which clearly signified: "Gontran! There's a man who knows a great many things!" Then he continued: "He must also have told you that all the terrestrial observers noticed the atmosphere of the world, like a luminous aureole surrounding it, during the transit of the planet across the Sun."

"He also told me," Fricoulet hastened to add, "that, based on very precise measurements, it has been calculated that the atmosphere in question measures no less that 194 kilometers in height—which is to say that it's twice as high as the Earth's atmosphere, and denser."

"So you see, Monsieur," the scientist replied, "that you were wrong to be anxious. You'll be able to breathe as well on Venus as on Earth...the air might perhaps be richer in oxygen, but that's not an inconvenience."

"On the contrary." With these words, Fricoulet turned away, leaving Ossipoff to strain his eyes for a few hours more, seeking to solve the mysteries of the Venusian world, and went to take his place in the bottom of the gondola, next to Gontran.

How long was he asleep? A long time, no doubt, for when he awoke, shaken by an energetic hand, he perceived—to his great amazement—Mikhail Ossipoff standing over him, disencumbered of his diving-suit. Immediately, he realized how far the apparatus had traveled while he had been asleep. Dexterously, he took off his selenium helmet and exclaimed: "We're already in the Venusian atmosphere!"

"Whether you like it or not, yes, Monsieur," the old man replied, mockingly. "In 15 hours, we've covered several 100,000 leagues."[102]

"15 hours!" exclaimed Fricoulet. "I've slept for 15 hours?" Slightly confused, he added: "It's the Sun, no doubt." Then, leaning towards Flammermont, he applied his speaker to the valve of his helmet. "Let's go!" he cried, in a thunderous voice. "On your feet—we're here!"

The young man, waking up with a start, made such a violent movement that Farenheit also sat up, abruptly snatched from his slumber. No words could describe the bewilderment of the two sleepers on seeing their traveling companions liberated from the diving-suits that had imprisoned them.

---

[101] Pietro Tacchini (1838-1905) and Hermann Carl Vogel (1841-1907).

[102] A little while ago, it was going to take 40 hours and the point was forcibly made that there was no way to reduce that journey time.

Without needing to be told, they released themselves rapidly, avid to breathe veritable air. Their nostrils dilated and their mouths opened wide to inhale the greatest possible quantity of the cool and vivifying atmosphere, which penetrated their lungs and send new life flowing through their entire being.

"One could believe that one were on Earth," murmured Gontran, in the grip of unalloyed bliss.

Farenheit breathed the air in avidly, continually repeating: "Air! Real air! Like American air!"

The old scientist had unpacked his instruments and suspended them from the strings of the parachute.

"What does the thermometer say?" asked Fricoulet.

"It indicates 30 degrees Centigrade, and the barometer 780 millimeters."

The engineer rubbed his hands. "We can't be more than 20 kilometers away, can we?" he said.

"Only a few hours of traveling," Ossipoff replied.

Meanwhile, Farenheit had picked up his traveling-blanket and thrown it over his shoulders like a shawl. "Brrr," he complained. "It isn't warm, you know. We were grilled a little while ago, now we're freezing, and it wouldn't take much more to catch a chill."[103]

"It's an advance notification of the temperature that awaits us on Venus," said Gontran, following the American's example.

"It's proof of the density of the atmosphere, which forms a screen between the planet and the Sun whose thickness protects it from the solar rays." Ossipoff had taken his place at the guard-rail again, telescope in hand, and was impatiently examining the new world that was silhouetted in space.

"You'll ruin your eyes doing that, my dear Monsieur," said Fricoulet, shrugging his shoulders. As he spoke, and with no warning of the abrupt change in temperature, the mists cleared, the grey clouds fleeing in all directions, and Venus appeared to the Terran's marveling eyes, radiantly illuminated by the Sun.

"Finally!" murmured Ossipoff.

By a curious phenomenon of perspective—which the aeronauts of our world cannot describe, never having been launched to such prodigious heights—the planet extended an immense panorama beneath the voyagers' feet, whose horizon appeared to be at eye-level, thus forming a gigantic funnel ready to receive those who were arriving there from the depths of space.

"One thing that astonishes me," Fricoulet said, suddenly, "is that we're not closer to the ground—we're at least 15 kilometers away, which I find unusual, given that the attraction of this globe is almost as great as that of the Earth."

---

[103] This reaction is surprising, given that we have just been told that the temperature is 30 degrees Centigrade; the figure might have been misprinted.

Ossipoff, who had heard the engineer's observation, turned to him and said: "You're doubtless leaving out of account the action of the parachute, which is playing the role of a powerful brake. Then again, when you mention the Earth, I'm obliged to remind you that the Venusian atmosphere is twice as dense as the terrestrial atmosphere. Moreover you can see that we're breathing perfectly well at an altitude of 15 kilometers, a league and a half higher than the point at which Sivel and Crocé-Spinelli,[104] the courageous terrestrial aeronauts, died; you can imagine, in consequence, the density of this air at ground level."

"But we'll be drowned and crushed by the pressure!" cried Flammermont.

Fricoulet shook his head. "You're mistaken," he replied. "We'll adapt to the pressure gradually, and the action of our lungs will become progressively accustomed to the density of the air. One can live perfectly well at a pressure of four and a half atmospheres—on Earth, divers and hydraulic engineers working in caissons, subject to pressures even more considerable, don't die. Don't worry, my dear chap—we'll find our sojourn on this new world quite comfortable."

"Oh, I'm not afraid for myself," protested Flammermont.

"For whom, then?"

"For Selena—her fragile constitution…"

"Can only draw elements of force and vigor from the excess of oxygen that the Venusian atmosphere contains."

Gontran seemed to be relieved of a keen anxiety, and his care-worn face cleared somewhat.

"Ah, my dear boy," Ossipoff said to him, "it's very unfortunate that you went to sleep 24 hours ago. You'd certainly have experienced great pleasure in studying the planet's phases with me."

"It's very kind of you to think of me," the young man replied, with the utmost seriousness, "but fatigue knocked me out. Before going to sleep, though, I was able to observe that Venus resembled the Moon in its first quarter yesterday."

"That's quite easy to understand," added the old man, hastily giving an explanation that no one had asked for. "The orbit of Venus being interior to that of Earth, that planet sometimes turns its illuminated face towards us, sometimes its dark hemisphere, and sometimes parts of each."

"When is Venus closest to the Earth?" asked Farenheit.

The old man sighed profoundly. "Unfortunately," he said, "that's when it's new and completely dark. When it's full, it's on the far side of the Sun—which is to say, more than 60,000,000 leagues away instead of ten. That's one of the causes of the difficulty that we experience in studying the world's geography; when it's closest to us, one can only see a tiny part of it."

---

[104] Théodore Sivel (1834-1875) and Joseph Croce-Spinelli (1845-1875) were asphyxiated while trying to break their own height record for a balloon ascent; they were buried in a common grave at Pére-Lachaise.

"Personally," declared Gontran, earnestly, "I know that my illustrious namesake has not been able, thus far, to distinguish clearly the markings observed by certain other astronomers on Venus's disk."

"Bravo!" Fricoulet whispered in his ear, truly amazed by his friend's aplomb.

"*Continents célestes* page 163," Flammermont retorted, in the same fashion.

"What did you say?" asked the old man, abruptly turning round, having already taken up his telescope again.

It was the engineer who replied. "Gontran was in the process of giving me some very interesting details of the work already done by Bianchini, Cassini, Denning…"[105]

"It's Bianchini who has had the most success, for he managed to draw up a rudimentary map showing three seas in the equatorial region and one in the polar region. The map also features continents, promontories, straits…"

"But it was in 1726 that Bianchini drew that map," Fricoulet said, "and since that time, it must have been considerable augmented and modified."

"Absolutely false, my dear Monsieur," replied the aged scientist. "Not only has that map not been modified, but its indications have not even been verified, in spite of the progress in optics."

"But to make studies that no one coming after him has been able to check," said Farenheit, "Bianchini must have had marvelous instruments."

"It's to the purity of the fine Italian sky, above all, that Bianchini must owe the discoveries he has made."

"Or thought he made…" Gontran put in.

The old man shuddered. "What are you saying?" he said, in an anxious tone.

"I'm saying, *or thought he made*—for my illustrious namesake has been unable to make out these features clearly…"

"*Errare humanum est*," declared Ossipoff sententiously. "Still, if Bianchini was the victim of an optical illusion, Cassini, Webb, Denning and others were equally mistaken, for they too have seen these features—oceans, continents and promontories."[106]

He had pronounced these words in a vibrant and slightly aggressive tone, causing Flammermont to reply dryly: "You'll permit me to hold to the opinion of my illustrious namesake, for, with respect to these continents, who knows?"

---

[105] The amateur William Frederick Denning (1848-1931) is the odd man out in this set, the others being the Italian pioneers Francesco Bianchini (1662-1729) and Giovani Domenico Cassini (1625-1712).
[106] The astronomer cited for the first time is Thomas William Webb (1807-1885).

"I've already told you, and I repeat, that by virtue of its location in space, Venus presents considerable difficulties to those who venture to study it, which militate against our having as exact a notion of it as we have, for example, of the Moon or Mars. However in 1833 and 1836 the selenographers Beer and Mädler drew a likeness of Venus. Their drawings were revised in 1847 by Gruithuisen, and in 1881 by Niesten,[107] at the Brussels Observatory."

"That's all well and good," said Farenheit, curtly, "but what was the result?"

"The result is that we're certain of the existence of very high mountains on Venus; the geographical relief is considerable and, the forces in action of the Earth being similarly active on this world, it follows that there are volcanoes, mountain chains—but as for precise measurements of their location, we have none."

"So, *Les Continents célestes* is right!" cried Flammermont, triumphantly.

"Did I say that it was wrong?" replied the aged scientist, in a piqued tone.

To provide a diversion, Fricoulet asked: "I've sometimes heard the thesis advanced that Venus has a satellite."[108]

Gontran considered his friend in amazement, thinking that he had gone mad, but his surprise was greater still when he heard Ossipoff reply, while nodding his head: "Indeed, many astronomers have believed that they saw the satellite you mention. For myself, despite the numerous papers published on the subject, I persist in thinking of its existence as problematic. On the other hand, you might reply to me that it's difficult to admit that scientists like Cassini, Horrebow, Short and Montaigne were bad observers, or could have been victims of an optical illusion."

"How can it be explained, then?"

"For me, there are two possible explanations: either they mistook a small planet passing through the same optical field for a satellite of Venus, or that satellite, being very small, is only visible from Earth in very exceptional conditions."

"It might also be the case," Gontran put in, "that, since these observations were made, the satellite might have fallen on to the planet."

"That hypothesis is not entirely implausible; no natural law forbids such a phenomenon from occurring."

---

[107] Louis Niesten (1844-1920).

[108] The controversy relating to the alleged satellite of Venus first observed by Cassini in 1672 and 1686 endured for more than two centuries; it even acquired a name (Neith). Others who reported sighting it included James Short in 1740, Andreas Mayer in 1759, Joseph Louis Lagrange in 1761 and Christian Horrebow in 1768. J. H. Lambert wrote a treatise on the subject in 1777, but glimpses of the supposed satellite became scarcer in the 19th century, when optical instruments improved markedly.

They had reached this point in their conversation when Fricoulet, who had taken out his chronometer, suddenly exclaimed: "What the Devil! How is it that we aren't descending more rapidly? We should have arrived some time ago."

"It seems that we aren't moving at all," added Farenheit.

"I beg your pardon," Gontran countered, "we are, in fact, moving—but in a horizontal sense rather than a vertical one." He put out his arm in front of him and declared: "We're making rapid progress in that direction."

The cloudy screen, which had opened momentarily, had closed again, and the voyagers were plunged once again into the thick mass of the atmosphere. After checking the young Comte's affirmation and establishing that the apparatus was, indeed, being borne along with prodigious speed by a powerful air current, the old scientist cried: "But we mustn't let ourselves go off course! We have to go down, as quickly as possible, wherever we are…if not…"

He made a tragic gesture.

"The parachute's too light," said Jonathan Farenheit.

"Or the atmosphere's too dense," riposted the engineer.

"But what can we do?" complained the American.

"It's impossible to make ourselves any heavier," Ossipoff murmured.

They all looked at one another anxiously, not knowing what decision to make.

"Cut the strings connecting us to the parachute," the American said, suddenly. "Let ourselves fall, at God's mercy."

Fricoulet shrugged his shoulders. "That's madness!" he murmured.

"There are times in life," growled Farenheit, "when mad things are the only things one can reasonable do."

"But that mad thing has just given me an idea," said Flammermont, in his turn.

Ossipoff seized his hands. "Tell us, my dear friend—quickly!"

"I think that if we were to reduce the resistant force of the parachute, we'd fall more rapidly."

"Easy to say," grumbled the American, humiliated by the scant success of his suggestion, "but not to do."

"If we could reduce the surface area of the parachute," suggested the old scientist.

"Genius!" cried the engineer. He rummage in his tool-box, took out some steel pincers, which he tucked into his belt, and cried: "Let me do it—it's my job." With one bond, he leapt on to the guard-rail and grabbed one of the selenium cables that connected the gondola to the parachute in both hands, then pulled himself up—but weight, almost negligible on the Moon, had resumed its empire, and it seemed to the young man that he had become as heavy as lead.

"Fricoulet!" called Flammermont. "Fricoulet!"

But the engineer made no reply and kept climbing, albeit slowly. In spite of his strength, he thought several times that he was about to faint. Finally, his hands reached the edge of the metal plateau, and he clung on to it desperately. Exhausted by the ascent along ten meters of cable no thicker than his little finger, however, his attempts to haul himself up by an operation of his muscles known in gymnastic terminology as a re-establishment were in vain; he could not do it. He was about to give way to discouragement when his foot encountered a goose-foot—as a suture of two threads is called—and, by bracing himself against it, he was finally able to haul himself up on to the parachute. The most difficult part was over, and the courageous engineer, after catching his breath briefly, crawled over the polished surface of the parachute on his hands and knees, using his pincers at intervals to draw out the screws connecting the selenium plates together.

"Come down! Come down!" cried Ossipoff, suddenly. "We're falling!"

Fricoulet removed a few more plates, which he hurled into space; then he calmly put the pincers back in his belt, let himself slide down a cable, and rejoined his companions, who were waiting for him anxiously. They were, indeed, falling with vertiginous rapidity, passing through the layers of cloud like an arrow.

Suddenly, there was a loud bang, like the sound of ten simultaneous thunderclaps; an intense, blinding light seemed to set the sky aflame, falling on to the parachute like firelight. At the same time the wind, suddenly unleashed, took possession of the apparatus and dragged it toward the ground in a frightful whirlwind.

"A storm!" shouted Mikhail Ossipoff, at the top of his voice, to reassure his companions.

"The sea! The sea!" cried Gontran, in his turn. He was leaning out of the gondola, trying to see through the fiery clouds. Under the force of the wind, the veil that hid the ground had just been torn apart, and a sheet of water appeared a kilometer below the apparatus, extending as far as the eye could see, raising monstrous waves crowned with electric sparks, with a horrible noise.

The spinning parachute fell like a stone.

"Boats! I can see boats!" howled Farenheit, making himself heard in spite of the whistling of the tempest.

"We're bound to take a serious bath," retorted Fricoulet. "Those boats will save us."

They were the last words spoken. The gondola had just slid into the crest of a wave; a mountain of water collapsed upon them, capsizing them, rolling them over like a piece of wreckage. Then, drawn by the weight of the parachute—which had also crashed into the sea—it went straight down, dragging Ossipoff and his bold companions into the mysterious depths of the Venusian ocean.

Chapter XXIV
A dip in the Venusian ocean

Scarcely two minutes had gone by since the moment when the gondola had been engulfed by the waves when a head appeared on the surface of the ocean. That head was Jonathan Farenheit's. While going down vertically, the American had kept his composure; it was not, in any case, his first shipwreck. In the course of numerous crossings that the pork-fat trade had forced him to make from America to Europe and *vice versa*, Farenheit had, as the saying has it, "drunk from the big cup" more than once. In addition, far from clinging to the rail of the gondola, as his companions had, he had abandoned the apparatus almost immediately and had come back to the surface with a vigorous thrust. In the midst of supreme peril, he had suddenly remembered the boats sighted by Fricoulet and, confident of his strength and his skill, he had resolved to try anything to escape death.

An enormous wave, carrying him along, hoisted him up to its crest, and from that liquid observatory he was able to dart a rapid glance around the immensity that surrounded him. *Come on!* he thought. *As I descend with the wave, which is collapsing into a bottomless pit, it's a matter of staying on the surface…it will be the very devil if one of those ships doesn't pass close by…*

For anyone but a strong swimmer like him, a similar project would have been folly; the stormy sea was hurling monstrous waves at the sky, whipped and ripped by the tempest howling through the air—but the water and Farenheit were old acquaintances; without trying to fight, he devoted all his efforts to not being submerged, and he succeeded.

Suddenly, as he was lifted up again to the summit of a wave, he uttered a scream of rage and disappointment. The boats on which he had pinned his hopes had disappeared. Had they foundered as they fled before the tempest?

As far as the eye could see, the sea was deserted. Enormous masses of water were rushing to assault one another, with a formidable racket. The clouds in the sky were racing like a herd of galloping horses, driven by a terrible wind, momentarily bloodied by bolts of lightning, and large luminous sparks were dancing on the summits of the waves, casting livid light into the abysms hollowed out by the wind.

Farenheit felt his heart gripped by an inexpressible anguish. On the horizon, there was nothing but the tempest, around him, nothing but the infuriated liquid immensity. What good would it do to struggle? His desire for life had had no other end than the satisfaction of his thirst for vengeance against Sharp; now that he had no hope of imminent salvation, persistence would have no other effect than to prolong his agony. Then, with no other regret in his heart than that of dying before having satisfied his hatred, he folded his arms, immobilized his legs, and allowed himself to be swallowed up by an enormous wave that loomed over him.

"The humankind that reigns on the world of Venus," writes Camille Flammarion, "must offer the greatest resemblance to ours, and also, probably, the greatest moral resemblance. One may suppose, even so—Venus having being born later than the Earth—that its humankind is more recent than ours. Are its populations still in the Stone Age? All conjectures in this regard are, however, evidently superfluous, the paleontological successions possibly having taken a course on that planet different from our own. On the other hand, it is in the mildest climates that humankind is at its most active, and Venus is a world more various and certainly more turbulent than the Earth. In the final analysis, the best conclusion to draw from these general considerations of the state of the planet is that *life must be little different there than it is on our world*."

The first of our voyagers who was able to establish the truth of the above-mentioned philosophical suppositions with his own eyes was Flammermont, when he opened his eyes in response to the impression of a bizarre odor sensed by his nostrils and transmitted to his brain.

A first, prey to an entirely natural and easily comprehensible phenomenon, he thought that he was no longer alive, having already been transported to another astral existence. "Of course!" he said. "How stupid I am! I'm dead!"

As he pronounced these words, he let his head fall back heavily. Immediately, though, he uttered an exclamation and sat up. The echo of his words had struck his ears distinctly, at the same time as a rather abrupt impact had bruised his skull. "Morbleu!" he groaned. "It seems, however, that I'm alive"—and to convince himself that he was not mistaken, he opened and closed his eyes several times, sniffed the air, worked his jaws, slowly passed his hands over the various parts of is body and finally put one of his hands on his breast. His heart was beating strongly, and the blood was circulating freely in his arteries. The young man released a profound sigh of satisfaction then; he liked this state of affairs better, all things considered; it conserved the hope of seeing Selena again.

He became doubtful again, however, when his gaze, as it played around him, fell on two bodies lying not far away, rigid and seemingly lifeless. These two bodies were those of Mikhail Ossipoff and Alcide Fricoulet. On seeing that, the sensation of reality returned to him fully, and the veil obscuring his memory was completely torn away. "Saved!" he exclaimed. "We've been saved?"

He ran to the engineer and put his ear to his breast. The heart was beating feebly. Passing on to Ossipoff then, he established that he old scientist was also counted among the number of the living. Only then did his mind, freed from all preoccupations, pose two questions. Where were they, he and his companions? And who had snatched them from the jaws of death?

In trying to resolve the first of these questions, he also resolve the second, for the gaze that he paraded around him in a circle showed him a square room with wooden walls, furnished with wooden bunks on which he and his friends had been set down. At the same time, he saw a group of individuals in a dark corner, who were watching him with a suspicion filled with curiosity.

"Human beings!" he cried, joyfully—and he advanced toward them. They recoiled, however, and Gontran saw then that they were armed, and appeared to be quite ready to use the pikes and javelins they held in their hands. "My word!" he murmured. "Am I dreaming or am I really awake? But these are Egyptians that I have before me! Or, at least, they resemble them strikingly."

He could not take his eyes off these individuals, clad in short white tunics, bare-legged below the knee, and also baring their arms and their necks. Their feet were enclosed in shoes that were also made of cloth, but red in color, their ankles imprisoned by interlaced cords. Their heads were remarkable for the total absence of hair but their rather elongated faces, with deep-set almond-shaped eyes, were framed by long black curly beards. "They're doubtless Venusians," murmured the young Comte, whose amazement caused him to forget his friends.

Seeing the Terran unmoving, the indigenes were reassured and took a few paces toward him, with their weapons in their left hands and their right hands extended. Gontran did the same—which is to say that, while remaining in the same place so as not to alarm them, he too reached out his hand in a sign of peaceful intent. Immediately, the Venusian began talking to one another in a sonorous language accompanied by a great many lively and rapid gestures.

"Well," murmured Gontran, in disappointment, after listening for several seconds, "it's going to be devilishly difficult to talk to these fellows." And he added, while curling his moustache: "The planetary worlds ought to follow our example—the French language should be the only one adopted for international usage."

Nevertheless, he listened with unimaginable concentration, seizing shreds of phases, words and syllables, and his mind worked overtime. *If I weren't afraid of making a fool of myself*, he thought, *I'd wager that there echoes of Burnouf in this language. Might we, by chance, be in the presence of compatriots of Epaminondas and Themistocles?*[109]

He was distracted from these reflections by one of the Venusians, who came forward, touched his hand and then prostrated himself at his feet and kissed them. Initially taken by surprise, Gontran bent down, lifted the Venusian up. Remembering certain accounts of voyages through primitive lands, and in spite of his intense repugnance, he kissed the individual on the mouth. The other's face immediately lit up. He made a gesture to his companions, who went to

---

[109] Jean-Louis Burnouf (1775-1844) was the professor of Latin eloquence at the Collège de France, and produced many of the translation used in the French education system. Epaminondas was a notable Theban of the 5th century BC, Themistocles a notable Athenian of the previous century.

Fricoulet and Ossipoff, undressed them rapidly and set about rubbing them with a prodigious vigor.

In the meantime, the Venusian addressed a long discourse to Flammermont—who, in spite of his sustained attention and the considerable efforts he made to remember his classical education, understood absolutely none of it. Despairing of ever achieving a better result, he ended up shaking his head and pointing to his ears to indicate to the Venusian that his eloquence was entirely wasted.

The indigene seemed quite mortified, and expressed his disappointment by means of an exclamation whose consonance struck Gontran's ear strangely. "Damn," he muttered. "That's definitely Greek—let's have a go."

Slowly and gravely, emphasizing the words, he intoned the first two verses of Homer's *Iliad*—the only ones his memory had conserved during the ten years since he had left the Lycée Henri IV. The Venusian seemed surprised. He grabbed Gontran's hand and called to one of his companions. Pointing to the young man's tongue and his own ears, seemed to be demanding a second opinion on what he had just heard.

Obligingly, Flammermont complied with this desire, and began again, more slowly still. There was a sudden outburst of laughter behind him. He immediately interrupted himself and turned around to see Fricoulet sitting on the edge of his bed, clutching his sides.

"Gontran talking Greek!" the engineer exclaimed. "There's a prodigy!" Raising his arms to Heaven in a tragicomic gesture, he added: "O shade of Burnouf, how amazed you must be!" Then, to the young Comte, he said: "Continue, my dear chap, I beg you. You appear to be captivating these gentlemen with the charm of your reminiscences. I don't want to break the charm…"

Ossipoff, whom the energetic friction of the Venusians had also brought round, put an end to the engineer's mockery. "In truth, Monsieur Fricoulet," he declared, dryly, "I don't understand you. To listen to you, one would think that you didn't know your friend. Since when has Monsieur Flammermont ever said or done anything that has not worked to our advantage?"

While the Terrans were talking among themselves, the Venusians fell silent, listening curiously to this incomprehensible language and communicating their impressions with expressive and rapid mimes.

"Let's see," said Ossipoff, addressing Gontran. "Explain to me why you're reciting verses from Homer to these people."

"Quite simply, my dear Monsieur," the young man replied, "because I thought I noticed some analogies between the long speech that was made to me a little while ago and the vague memories I've retained of my classical Greek."

The old man nodded his head. "Nothing's impossible," he murmured, pensively.

The Venusians' attention, abandoning Flammermont, was entirely diverted to Mikhail Ossipoff, whose long white beard and venerable appearance seemed to impress them considerably. He perceived the effect that he had on the indigenes and, addressing the one who appeared to be the leader—the same one to whom Gontran had recited Homer—began to speak the language of the great poet of antiquity.

The Venusian listened attentively, appearing, if not to understand, at least to divine what the old scientist was saying. Then, when the later had finished, he spoke in his turn. Afterwards, making a sign, he opened a door in the partition-wall and disappeared, followed by his companions.

"Well," said Gontran, "where are we? How were we saved? Do they know anything about the whereabouts of Sharp and Selena?"

"How do you expect me know all that, my poor friend?" countered Ossipoff.

"Didn't you ask them?"

"Of course—but they didn't reply."

"Or, at least, you didn't understand their reply," Fricoulet objected.

"Before worrying about that," replied the old man, "it's necessary to know whether they understood my question."

"What did you say, then? You were talking for quite a long time."

"I was talking simply to provoke a response, in order to see for myself whether Gontran's suppositions were well-founded."

"And?"

"And I'm convinced that, without being the same, there are resemblances between these people's language and the Ionian dialect...vague, to be sure, but of which I can nevertheless make use to establish communication with them—rapidly, I think."[110]

"At any rate," muttered Fricoulet, "although I'm not curious by nature, I'd like to know where we are." So saying, he began to wander around the room, rummaging around and scrupulously examining every corner.

He and his friends found that they were in a sort of box that was about ten meters long by five broad and four high. The ceiling above their heads was rounded in the dimension of breath; the floor was flat, resonating like bronze

---

[110] The reader might feel that the homology of languages is taking the authors' theory of parallel evolution to a ludicrous extreme, but the notion that the evolution of Earthly languages had followed a rational and determinate pattern was not uncommon at the time. The narrative device was so very convenient for fictitious interplanetary travelers that it was widely adopted in scientific romance and science fiction, along with an understandable nationalistic bias—in George Griffith's cosmic tour story *A Honeymoon in Space* (1900), which was probably inspired by the *Aventures extraordinaires*, the tourists find decadent Martians speaking degraded English, and unhesitatingly attributed that to the fact that English represents the summit of linguistic evolution, much as human form represents the acme of biological evolution.

beneath their feet. Two stout torches made of red wax, fixed to the wall, illuminated the box with an indecisive and bloody light.

At one end of the room, an enormous metal pillar stretched from floor to ceiling; at the other end was a barred cage, from which a dull and confused noise emerged, similar to the breathing of a congested chest. "Oh—what's that?" murmured Fricoulet, when his ears were suddenly struck by this noise.

"Hey!" exclaimed Gontran, pointing at three holes pieced in the wall at ceiling level. "If we can get up there, perhaps we can see something through those little windows that will enlighten us."

"You're right," said Fricoulet—and he leapt up on to the circular bench that ran along the wall. Once perched on it, though, he uttered an exclamation of disappointment; he was still a meter below the level of the holes.

"Don't move," said Gontran, who had just had an idea. "You'll see..." He climbed on to the bench in his turn; then, gripping Fricoulet's upper body as he might have gripped a tree-trunk, he hoisted himself up on to his shoulders, on which he knelt. Hardly had he moved his face closer to the aperture pierced in the wall and glanced through, though, than he started, so abruptly that Fricoulet tottered.

Gontran, feeling insecure on his mobile observatory, hastened to jump down to the floor. There was such a profound amazement in his expression that Fricoulet and Ossipoff both exclaimed at the same time: "What is it? What did you see?"

"I'll give you three guesses," said Flammermont.

"We're in no mood to guess riddles," the engineer replied. "Speak—where are we?"

"On the sea-bed," retorted the young Comte.

"The sea-bed!" cried Fricoulet. "You're joking! First, what makes you think...?

"That we're underwater? Fish and marine plants, of course!"

As Fricoulet shrugged his shoulders, Ossipoff said in his turn: "It's not impossible that we're in the hold of a Venusian boat."

"You haven't understood me, Monsieur Ossipoff," Gontran replied, confidently. "When I said that we're on the sea-bed, I meant you to understand that we're a considerable distance below the level of the Ocean."

"It's not a boat, then," Fricoulet concluded, immediately.

The scientist folded his arms. "And why shouldn't it be a boat?" he asked, a trifle bitterly.

"Because," the engineer replied, with a brief snigger, "the Venusians haven't yet arrived at such a degree of civilization that submarine navigation could be familiar to them."

Ossipoff shrugged his shoulders.

"In my opinion," Gontran muttered, "that's a secondary matter for the time being, whether we like it or not. What's more important is that I'm dying of hunger."

The engineer opened and closed his jaws several times, murmuring: "It seems to me, too, that I could eat with great pleasure."

"In any case," added Flammermont, "I hope that we really are on a submarine boat." As Fricoulet looked at him interrogatively, he went on, in an amiable tone: "Because people familiar with submarine navigation must also be familiar with the husbandry of sheep and oxen."

That sally made the old scientist smile.

"What do you expect?" asked Gontran. "I'm suffering from cutlet nostalgia."

He had scarcely completed this sentence when the door opened, giving passage to the Venusian who had already engaged the voyagers in conversation. Behind him came other indigenes bearing bowls, which they deposited on the bench, pointing alternately to the bowls and their mouths.

"For all the people in the Universe," Fricoulet said, "that's a gesture whose significance is unmistakable. Let's eat, then…" He sat down beside a broad and deep wooden bowl filled to the brim with a sort of brown stew that emitted a spicy perfume that was not at all disagreeable. Boldly, he plunged his fingers in, Oriental fashion, and put a small piece in his mouth' he chewed it for some time, methodically analyzing the different substances contained in the culinary concoction. Finally, he clicked his tongue against his palate and declared in a serious tone: "A vegetable similar to celery…a sauce containing a fatty material which, if it's not extracted from some sort of plant, indicates the presence in this world of a quadruped similar to a sheep." Without saying any more, he set about eating as well as he could with his fingers—"Father Adam's fork," as he said, jokingly.

Gontran, having searched his pockets in vain for a traveling kit containing all the slender instruments necessary for a meal, was constrained to imitate his friend, his appetite being greater than his repugnance.

As for Ossipoff, he had drawn the Venusian aside and was trying, by means of expressive gestures, to obtain the information he desired. At first, the indigene looked at the scientist without interrupting him, studying his slightest gestures, making every effort to discern his meaning. He seemed to have understood, and was ready to reply by means of the same mute language when one of his companions came over and spoke to him.

Swiftly, the Venusian went to the cage that had intrigued Fricoulet and pronounced a few guttural sounds. The noise immediately ceased and it seemed to Ossipoff that a movement of oscillation he had already noticed also ceased. The Venusian took him by the hand and drew him into a neighboring room, much smaller than the other, in which ten individuals were doggedly operating instruments that Ossipoff immediately recognized as pumps of a primitive sort.

Suddenly, a curt command rang out; the pumps stopped and the men who were manning them applied themselves to chains, which they hauled forcefully. Slowly, almost imperceptibly, the metallic plates forming the ceiling slid apart, and a sparkling light filtering through the gasps gradually began to illuminate the room in which the travelers were. They soon released an exclamation of surprise on seeing a radiant sky above their heads, from which rays of ardent sunlight fell like a rain of fire. All around them, as far as the eye could see, the Ocean extended its sluggish blue waves, gently rocking the boat they supported.

At the same time as this strange vessel emerged on to the surface, the enormous metal pillar that had already attracted the attention of Ossipoff and his companions elongated and extended itself like the tube of a telescope; each cylindrical element emerged from the one that preceded it, and a sail, unrolling around this singular mast, was soon deployed, orientated by a part of the crew.

Gontran's eyes grew wide, as if he were watching some ingenious conjuring trick. "Well, well," he murmured, addressing a sly glance to Fricoulet, "These Venusians aren't so stupid after all."

"Except," growled the engineer, a trifle put out, "that their boats must be slow movers. Have you noticed the rounded shape of the bow? These boats are veritable clogs."

"Very fortunate, though, that this clog picked you up, Monsieur Fricoulet," Ossipoff sniggered.

The engineer did not hear him. Leaning over the side in the stern of the boat, he carefully examined a sort of drum open for three-quarters of its circumference, in which there was a flat-bladed propeller about a meter in diameter. "I get it!" he exclaimed, eventually.

"What's happening?" asked Gontran, coming to join him.

"That cage that we saw inside the boat…"

"What about it?"

"The vague forms that we could see within it, harnessed to a wheel, must certainly be driving this rudimentary propeller. In truth, it's quite ingenious…"

Flammermont remained pensive for a few moments, then eventually said: "In your opinion, why do these people have two modes of navigation?"

"Undoubtedly to avid the disastrous effects of frequent and terrible tempests, of which we encountered a specimen a few hours ago," Fricoulet replied. "How do you expect similar vessels to be able to combat elements unleashed to that extent? I don't know whether even the great transatlantic liners of our world would be capable of withstanding them. When the weather's fine, they navigate in the open air, making use of a sail, as at this moment; when a storm breaks out, they dive in search of calm water some little way beneath the agitated waves, in the midst of which they continue their voyage peacefully, with the aid of their propeller."

"They submerge," muttered Gontran. "That's easy to say—but how?"

"I can't be sure, but the simplest method would surely be to fill reservoirs with water."

Gontran shook his head.

"What's the matter?" asked Fricoulet, surprised.

"*Les Continents célestes* has led me astray, for I'm damned if I expected to find a humankind more advanced than ours on Venus."

The engineer interrogated his friend by raising his eyebrows. "Well, submarine boats aren't commonplace on Earth!" the young Comte replied.

"Certainly—but you're completely mistaken if you conclude that it's a consequence of the relative degree of civilization on Venus! Personally, I suppose that the inhabitants of this world, despite the submarine boats that surprise you so much, have scarcely reached the Bronze Age. All their constructions are metallic, but if they're good founders, they're poor navigators and technologists. Their propeller's less effective than a helical one, and as for their engine—their human engine—it's just barely sufficient."

While Fricoulet and Gontran were chatting, leaning against the side of the boat and breathing in the sea air appreciatively, Mikhail Ossipoff and the Venusian were making every effort to reach a mutual understanding. First of all, the indigene had spread out a map in front of him, drawn in red lines on a square of yellowish cloth, and the old scientist had not been long delayed in identifying the markings perceived telescopically by the astronomer Bianchini among those that this sketchy representation of the Venusian world-map set before his eyes. He could not retain a sudden joyful exclamation, and put his finger on certain bizarre characters traced on the map. "Vellina!" he said, examining the Venusian's face curiously.

The latter appeared surprised at first and stared at his interlocutor. Then, clapping his hands, he repeated: "Vellina!"

Ossipoff called his companions. "Hurrah!" he said. "I've found the key to their language."

The two young men could not believe their ears. "You can understand him, then," said Gontran. "You can talk to him. Have you asked about Selena?"

The old man shook his head. "You're going a little too quickly, my dear boy," he replied. "I've just discovered a very important fact—that the writing of these people is made up of hieroglyphs, exactly like that of the Egyptians. Fortunately, my love of languages has made me a disciple of Champollion—that's why I was immediately able to read what was written on their map."[111]

A profound disappointment was painted on Flammermont's features.

---

[111] Jean-François Champollion was the first Orientalist to decipher Egyptian hieroglyphs, translating part of the Rosetta stone—but that involved understanding the referents of the symbols, not being able to pronounce them, since they are not phonetic symbols, so his achievement cannot explain what Ossipoff seems to have accomplished in discovering a common pronunciation.

"But don't worry," added the old man. "I already have two precious elements: I can read their language, and their language has many analogies with ancient Greek. That's more than I need in order to be able, with a little persistence, to reach an understanding with them within a few days."

The Sun had already set five times while our voyagers had been sailing the Venusian Ocean—seeing no other horizon but a completely liquid one, immense and deserted—when, as Gontran and Fricoulet were idling sadly on deck one afternoon, Ossipoff came towards them excitedly. From his radiant expression they deduced that he had important news to tell them and they went to meet him.

"I have news," he called to them from a distance. When he had joined them he added: "I've succeeded in making myself understood to Brahmes."

"Who's Brahmes?"

"The captain of this boat."

"What about Selena?" asked Gontran, anxiously.

The old man shook his head sadly. "On that subject, unfortunately," he said, "I haven't been able to learn anything—but we shouldn't despair. From what I understand, Brahmes is coming back from a long voyage, and an event like the one that I attempted to explain to him could easily have occurred without his being aware of it."

"But what are we waiting for?" cried Gontran, seething with impatience. "With all these delays, we're losing time."

"Calm down, my boy, and let me finish. This boat's final destination is Tahorti, an important city in which we'll doubtless obtain news."

"When will we arrive there?"

"In five days, if the weather's good—but we have to stop in Vellina first." He unfolded the map and showed the young men a point marked in the middle of the ocean.

"Vellina! Is that a city?" demanded Fricoulet.

"A city on an island, if so," said Gontran. "But I don't see any sign of dry land."

"Perhaps it's a submarine city," said Fricoulet, in jest.

Ossipoff looked at him furiously.

"Come on," said the engineer. "In a world where submarine navigation is so highly developed…" He broke off on seeing a Venusian coming rapidly towards them; he addressed a few words to Ossipoff, who seemed astonished.

"Brahmes want us to go down to the cabin, because the boat is going to dive."

"What! Dive?" cried Flammermont, looking around in surprise. "But there's no hint of bad weather. The sea's like oil and the sky's superb."

The Venusian evidently guessed what the young man had said, for he laconically pronounced: "Vellina!"

"Of course!" Fricoulet exclaimed, in his turn. "You'll see that I was right just now—Vellina is a submarine city!"

Ossipoff shrugged his shoulders, and all three of them went down the few steps leading to the room in which they had initially found themselves, after their shipwreck. Then, in response to a command from Brahmes, the sail was folded away, the mast was retracted into its tube, the panels were sealed and the Terrans heard the water rushing into the reservoirs.

"We're going down," said Gontran.

The boat was, indeed, immersed, and fell like a dead weight to the bottom of the sea.

"But we're not going forward," the engineer said, in his turn.

"How do you know that?" asked Ossipoff, sharply.

"Simply by virtue of the fact that the human engine isn't functioning," replied the engineer, pointing to the cage located at the rear, from which mo sound was escaping. As he finished the sentence, though, the wheel that set the flat-bladed propeller in motion began to grate. "I spoke too soon," Fricoulet said. "We're on the move."

Intrigued, the three voyagers awaited the outcome of this adventure in silence. Fricoulet had his watch in is hand, keeping track of the minutes.

A quarter of an hour passed; then they felt a shock, and the propeller stopped.

"We've just touched bottom," Gotran declared.

Brahmes came in at that moment and beckoned Ossipoff to follow him. All four of them went up on to the deck, already relieved of its metal cover, and the Terrans could not retain an exclamation of surprise at the sight of he spectacle offered to their eyes. The boast on which they were traveling had run aground on a beach of fine sand covered by a few scant centimeters of water, on which a quantity of other boats similar to theirs in all respects were moored. On raising their heads, they saw, 20 meters above them, the vault of a natural crypt formed amid the rocks, and flaming red wax torches everywhere, similar to those that illuminated Brahmes' boat but thicker, flooding the surroundings with fiery light.

A numerous and busy crowd was moving around the boats, unloading those that had just arrived and stowing numerous packages aboard those that were ready to depart. Ossipoff and his friends were, however, amazed and almost horrified to see strange and hideous beings mingling with the Venusians, from whom they were entirely different. Their structure was very nearly human, but smaller; they went completely nude, their bodies being covered by thick glossy fur like that of seals. Their short legs terminated in large, flat webbed feet, like ducks' feet. Long, thin arms emanated from the top of the torso, terminating in hands that were also webbed. The rounded head, as hairy as the rest of the body, rested directly on the shoulders. Two glaucous eyes devoid of the light of intelligence opened in a bestial face divided horizontally by a large mouth garnished with sharp teeth. On each side of the head, in the place where the ears should have been, a mobile membrane similar to the gill of a fish opened partially at frequent intervals.

"Axolotls," said Fricoulet, after scrupulously studying several of the monsters that were talking to Brahmes.

The latter listened to them with increasing surprise; finally, he turned to Ossipoff and said a few rapid words to him. The old man immediately became anxious. Addressing his companions. He said: "They've just told Brahmes that an individual similar in all respects to us has been picked up by a boat and brought here."

"Sharp!" cried Gontran, all a-tremble. "It's Sharp!"

"Unless it's Farenheit," Fricoulet put in.

"Oh, don't delay Monsieur Ossipoff, I beg you," Flammermont continued, seizing the old man by the arm. "Let's run…"

Brahmes obligingly offered to accompany the old scientist in his search. Taking as a guide one of the strange beings who had brought him the news, he left his companions to supervise the unloading of the boat by themselves.

While they walked, he gave Ossipoff an explanation of the inhabitants of this strange submarine land, which the latter transmitted to his friends. Although they were inferior in nature and intelligence to the other peoples of Venus, no one was reluctant to trade with them, for their soil contained mineral riches of every sort. Their strange conformation permitted them to live and breathe in the water by means of gills like those of fish, but they could also live on the planetary surface and Brahmes told the Terrans that some peoples even recruited their slaves from the aquatic tribes. Their houses resembled immense beehives in their form; like the latter, they were pierced in their underside by a hole that allowed their inhabitants to go in and out.

"They doubtless operate like Earthly water-spiders," Fricoulet explained to the astonished Gontran. "They allow themselves to drift up to the surface of the sea but their own lightness; there they take their provision of air and swim back down to their habitations."

"But one thing I don't quite understand," said Gontran, "or, rather, don't understand at all, is the complete absence of water in this part of the ocean."

"It's simply because the fissures in the rock are filled with air that the water can't get in there," the engineer replied.

The axolotl had stopped in front of a dwelling into which it crawled. Soon, the Terrans heard the noise of some sort of struggle in the interior, accompanied by forceful oaths, and a voice cried in English: "By God! Can't one rest in peace is this accursed land?"

"Farenheit!" cried Mikhail Ossipoff. "Jonathan Farenheit!"

He had not finished the last word when the American came out of the narrow opening on all fours, leapt to his feet and hurled himself towards his traveling comparisons with his arms outspread. "You! You!" he cried, in a voice into which sincere emotion put a tremor. "By God! I never expected to see you again! By God!" And the worthy Yankee, in spite of unimaginable efforts to hide his distress, had tears brimming in his eyes. Gontran noticed that but, being aware of the American's principles with regard to self-possession, was afraid offending him; he said nothing and contented himself with shaking his hand energetically.

After they had told one another, briefly, how they had been saved, Ossipoff asked: "Have you heard any mention of Sharp?"

The American shrugged his shoulders furiously. "I might well have heard mention of him," he complained, "without being any the wiser—these animals speak neither English not French, and as my parents completely forgot to teach me the local patois..."

When they returned to the boat, it had taken on its cargo and was only waiting for its passengers to depart. Brhahmes offered to delay his departure for 24 hours in order to permit Ossipoff's party to take stock with their own eyes of the mineral wealth of the submarine land, but they were all too anxious to find out what had become of Sharp to delay the moment of their arrival in Tahorti, even for five minutes.

Unfortunately, that city—the very same, according to Brahmes, in which the optical telephone post that put Venus in communication with the Moon was located—was on the far side of the Equatorial Ocean, nearly 800 leagues from Vellina. Fricoulet, who estimated that the submarine boat could not travel faster than four leagues an hour, calculated that the voyage would take at least eight days.

Ossipoff took advantage of this interval by holding long conversations with Brahmes about the planet and its civilization. He acquired the conviction that, in general, the Venusian race was much less knowledgeable and inferior in all but a few respects to the Earthly human race.

"These people, you see," the scientist said, to summarize his impressions, "can be compared to the earliest civilizations on Earth: the Chaldeans, the Egyptians and the Greeks." In certain matters, they were more advanced, but in general, their sciences were only at their outset. The only motive force they knew was that of humans and animals, although hey also made use of wind and water, the natural forces they had at their disposal. Although electricity and its forces were known to them, they had no knowledge of steam-power, balloons and a great number of other applications of science. In astronomy, though, they had succeeded in making an accurate calculation of their situation in the universe; they knew that the Sun was the center of the Celestial System and they knew of the existence of the Earth, Mercury, Mars and Jupiter.

Finally, after nine days of navigation, the boat carrying our voyagers came within sight of Tahorti. In a few more hours, they would know whether they had crossed the 12,000,000 leagues separating Venus from the Moon in vain.

Chapter XXV
Venusian Excursions

As one can imagine, those few hours seemed as long as centuries to the Terrans. Fricoulet tried in vain to extract them from the muteness into which each of them had enclosed himself; they would reply in monosyllables and then silence would reign between the voyagers again. Sometimes, they did not even reply at all, contenting themselves with simple nods of the head or shrugs of the shoulders.

Ossipoff, installed in the bow of the boat, had balanced his telescope on the rail, and his eye remained glued to its ocular lens, searching the horizon for the first indication of the coast on which they were about to land. Gontran, immobile in a corner, bleakly considered the progress—to slow in his view—of the hands of the watch he held in his hand. As for Farenheit, to cover up his impatience, he marched back and forth along the vessel's deck with long strides, like a bear prowling around its cage.

Finally, Ossipoff spotted a low coastline barring the horizon with a long blue line, which rapidly became more apparent, eventually rounding out into a profound gulf full of boats similar to the one that was carrying them.

Less than an hour afterwards they disembarked and headed, under Brahmes' guidance, towards the city where, before anything else, they were to be introduced to the king.

After a few steps taken in silence, Gontran—who was marching in front of his companions—suddenly stopped, arising his arms in a gesture of amazement. "A mushroom-field!" he cried.

"My word, it's true!" said the engineer, in his turn—and, with a gesture calling Brahmes to him, he pointed with his hand to request an explanation of the singular panorama extending before them.

On the side of a low hill whose foot bathed in the Central Ocean, an agglomeration of bizarre and uniform constructions was laid out, disposed with geometric regularity in long avenues departing from the summit to extend all the way to the sea, like the vanes of an enormous fan. These avenues were bordered to the right and left by dwellings whose umbelliform roofs overlapped one another like the scales of fish, or as Roman soldiers once disposed their shields—*testudo* fashion, as historians put it—to mount an assault and protect themselves from the missiles that beleaguered forces might rain down on them from above.

It was in Fricoulet's mind that the sight of the singular city awoke this memory of antiquity. "Your comparison is very just," Flammermont retorted, "but, given that we're dealing with a human intelligence, you must admit that there has to be some reason for this mode of construction."

"It resembles an army of umbrellas, don't you think?" said Farenheit.

"Mr. Farenheit might perhaps have provided the explanation we're looking for, without realizing it," said the engineer.

The American straightened up and an expression of offended dignity crossed his face. "What!" he said. "Without realizing it? By God, by virtue of your saying that, I understand perfectly well that these people could not have built their city any other way, and I'd wager $100 to a red cent that all the cities of the Venusian world must resemble it."

"Bah!" said Gontran, with a mocking smile. "And what reasons furnish you with support for that thesis?"

"The reasons that the honorable Monsieur Ossipoff himself has furnished."

The old scientist, very surprised to be dragged into the argument, directed an interrogatory gaze at the American.

"By God!" groaned Farenheit. "Was I dreaming a few days ago when, talking about the special climatology of this planet, you gave us details of the deluges of water that must result from the thickness of the clouds floating in its atmosphere? Anyway, we've experienced a rather convincing specimen ourselves, I think…"

"So you think that's the cause to which it's necessary to attribute this." The engineer said.

Ossipoff had turned to Brahmes and was listening intently to what the Venusian was telling him. "Mr. Farenheit is right," he said, after a few seconds. "All these roofs that you see are formed from bronze plates adapted to one another in such a way as to form an enormous carapace over which the torrents of water that fall from the sky at certain times of year flow without any infiltration. Thanks to the disposition of the city, these torrents empty into the Central Ocean without having done any damage.

"But the streets must be washed away," objected Gontran.

"The streets, it appears, are paved with bronze."

While they were talking, the little company had reached the first houses of the city. There they found another cause for astonishment. Their guide took them into one of the dwellings. Fricoulet, notebook in hand, made sketches accompanied by rapid notes. When Farhenheit has mentioned umbrellas he certainly had not known how accurate he was; these houses were, in fact, nothing more than enormous metallic umbrellas backed up against one another. The shaft of the instrument was provided by an enormous bronze pillar rising from the floor to the roof, supporting the three floors comprising the dwelling. The walls were formed of reservoirs filled with water, 20 centimeters in breadth. The roof itself, convex externally but flat internally, was also transformed into a vast basin. By its constant evaporation, this water protected the inhabitants against the heat of the Sun.

"Remember," said Ossipoff to his astonished companions, "that for the Venusians, the Sun is twice as large and hot as for the inhabitants of Earth. It is therefore necessary for them to protect themselves against its powerful effects."

"The inhabitants, the inhabitants," muttered Flammermont. "I'd be curious to see them—for until I see evidence to the contrary, this city seems to me to be abandoned and deserted."

"Perhaps it's market day," said Fricoulet, in jest.

"Unless some festival retains the population outside," Farenheit said, in his turn.

At that moment, Brahmes—who had left them to go in search of news—came back and said to Ossipoff: "The entire city is in turmoil. An enormous, gigantic mass, whose provenance no one can explain, was found a few days ago, floating on the surface of a sea in the other hemisphere."

A joyful exclamation escaped Gontran's lips. "Selena!" he sighed, thinking that he would see his dear fiancée again.

"I'll be able to settle my account with that scoundrel Sharp," growled Farenheit, clenching his huge fists and waving them in the air.

And both of them, without paying any heed to other possible explanations, raced outside, shouting: "Where are they? Where are they?"

"Wait," said Ossipoff, running after them with Fricoulet. "You're running off like madmen, without knowing where you're going. At least let Brahmes guide us."

"Excuse me, my dear Monsieur Ossipoff," replied the young Comte, "but I can't wait much longer to see Mademoiselle Selena."

"Do you think I can wait any longer to see my dear child?"

The Venusian had taken the head of the little company and took them at a rapid pace into the heart of the city. To do that, given the particular disposition of the streets, it was necessary to go uphill, and the Terrans, who had not made much use of their legs for several weeks, had some difficulty keeping up with their guide. Finally, they arrived, sweating and panting, at the very top of the hill, at the center of which all the capital's avenues ended, like the spokes of a wheel. There they were obliged to stop; in front of them, in an immense plaza measuring several kilometers across, a compact and variegated crowd was crammed, crying and gesticulating.

Ossipoff frowned and murmured, bitterly: "That's why the city is deserted. Everyone's here to give an ovation to that wretch Sharp."

Farenheit gave voice to a mocking laugh that strongly resembled a roar. "Patience, patience," he growled. "Things will change, and we'll be laughing soon enough." As he spoke, a glint of hatred shone in the American's eyes.

All the faces were turned in the direction of a monumental dwelling built on the summit of the hill, 20 meters above the other houses forming a semi-circular enclosure around an entire half of the plaza.

"That's the royal palace!" said Brahmes to Ossipoff. "That's where the strange thing I mentioned to you has been brought, and all the people have assembled here to see it."

"And that's where we have to go?" asked Fricoulet, alarmed by the prospect of crossing that human sea, whose swelling waves stretched as far as the eye could see.

At that moment, an exclamation of surprise rang out. One of the Venusians in front of them had just turned round and caught sight of them. He attracted the attention of his neighbor with a gesture, who did the same for his. In less than five minutes, the entire crowd had turned around to look at the Terrans, pushing, jostling and crushing one another to get a better view of them and see them at closer range.

To begin with, the indigenes' curiosity was restrained by the initial anxiety and indecision that gripped them at the sight of these beings, who were new to them—but it did not take them long to grow bolder. Little by little, the circle formed around Ossipoff and his companions tightened. Soon, one Venusian bolder than the others put out a hand and touched Farenheit's coat with his fingertips.

The latter took a step back, in a dignified manner. "By God!" he moaned. "Do they take us for curious animals?"

"Which is humiliating for a citizen of free America," replied Fricoulet, mockingly. "They're right, after all, for that's what we are, we foreigners who have the pretension to be civilized. Remember the crowds that flock to the Jardin d'Acclimation in summer to press around cages containing specimens of some savage tribe."

As he finished this speech, a frightful scream rang out and a movement of recoil was immediately produced. It was a Venusian who, very intrigued by the monocle framed in Gontran's optical arch, had wanted to take account of the strange thing by touching it. Without thinking, Flammermont had straightened his arm and his closed fist had struck the indigene in the middle of his chest. The Venusian had uttered a scream of pain and the frightened crowd had immediately drawn back.

"What you've just done is the ultimate imprudence," declared Ossipoff.

"Was I supposed to let that savage paw me?" asked the young man, disgustedly.

"Perhaps you'll be obliged to let yourself be pawed anyway," the old man retorted. "If I'm not mistaken, the whole lot are about to fall on us."

There was, in fact, an extraordinary animation in the crowd; fists wielding batons were appearing overhead; there were even a few hands armed with bronze weapons resembling large daggers, but which were held in the middle, like double-ended staves. With one movement, the four men drew their revolvers and set themselves back-to-back in order to face the assailants on all sides, getting ready to ward off the first attack.

"All the same," Ossipoff murmured, "Brahmes is taking a long time to come back. If he takes much longer, he'll find us torn to pieces."

Suddenly, an immense clamor went up and there was a mighty surge. The first ranks of Venusians found themselves shoved towards the Terrans in spite of themselves. Four shots rang out; Ossipoff and his companions had discharged their pistols into the air simultaneously.

There was an indescribable panic and a frightful tumult: a deafening clamor, mingling cries of fright and the howls of pain of those whom the strongest crushed in their flight. Seeing the unexcited success obtained by this first discharge, the Terrans fired a second, which accentuated the debacle.

In less than five minutes the plaza was completely deserted. The Venusians had gone back to their homes—in which, no doubt, they would barricade themselves strongly. Fricoulet burst into loud laughter. "Oh, these non-civilized people have their advantages. No peace officer in Paris ever obtained a similar result by gentleness and conciliatory words."

"Since Brahmes isn't coming back to us," Ossipoff said, "let's go to him." So saying, he advanced toward the palace, followed by his companions.

As they drew close, a panel 20 meters high was suddenly displaced, rolling back on bronze castors with a thunderous noise, revealing a large bay window about 15 meters square, through which the Terrans saw a spectacle that struck them with astonishment and admiration.

In the middle of an immense hall, on a throne made entirely of polished bronze, sparkling like gold, lay a Venusian. His legs, ringed by shining bands, were resting on purple cushions. The upper part of his body, enveloped by a sort of white toga decorated with stars and suns, was sustained by yellow cushions enriched with a metal unknown to the Terrans but which seemed to glow like hot coals. On his head, a sort of tiara of the same metal seemed to float above the Venusian like a resplendent star. The throne and the individual himself were, moreover, inundated by a dazzling light which genuinely gave an impression of divinity.

All around, the room was dark, fill of mysterious shadows in which a murmur of contained respiration was audible. Ossipoff's eyes, gradually becoming accustomed to the obscurity, soon perceived bodies arranged in a circle, as still as statues, kneeling on the floor in an attitude of prostration, with their foreheads touching the tiles between two supportive elbows, with the forearms raised, holding open hands formed like cups above their necks. On each of these pairs of hands a kind of brazier was placed in which an ardent fire burned with gilded flames, all the light of which was concentrated by mirrors of polished bronze on the throne and the quasi-divine individual it supported. Above the throne, in an immense receptacle, white crackling flames were sparkling; relayed from mirror to mirror, they too converged on the throne, as resplendent as a star in the midst of a dark night.

344

The statue thus irradiated stared at Ossipoff and his companions, who had instinctively bowed their heads. Then, without any gesture or movement, it made a small clicking sound with its tongue. Immediately, all the prostrated bodies emerge from their immobility, slid noiselessly over the bronze tiles, withdrawing backwards, and disappeared, melting into the shadows as genies and fairies disappear. Then the statue raised its hand. At that sign, a Venusian kneeling next to the throne stood up and, also moving backwards and half-bent over, came to find the Terrans.

It was Brahmes. "The king," he said to Ossipoff, "consents to grant you an audience; you may approach. Through me, he is already familiar with your adventures. Explain to him what you want."

"You have told me," the old man replied "that a strange thing has been brought here, found a few days ago in one of the Oceans of your world. I want to know what has become of the beings it contained."

Brahmes translated these words for the king—whose lips, after a few moments of silence—gave voice to a confused murmur of curt and sonorous speech.

The Venusian's face soon reflected a profound astonishment. "The king," he said, "does not understand what you mean. The object in question was empty."

"Empty!" cried Ossipoff, stupefied. His eyelids closed, his legs buckled and he would have fallen if his companions, who had drawn nearer on seeing him go pale, had not supported him in their arms.

"What's happening?" they asked, their hearts gripped—for various reasons—by a horrible anguish.

The old scientist, suddenly letting his head fall into his hands, began sobbing.

Flammermont then released a heart-rending cry. "Dead! Selena's dead! But tell us, Monsieur Ossipoff—you can see full well that you're putting us to the torture."

"Disappeared!" stammered the old man. "No one has seen either her or Sharp."

Gontran was overwhelmed; leaning on Fricoulet, he looked around with vague and haggard eyes.

Farenheit spat out a string of the most expressive Yankee curses between gritted teeth, while his fingers clutched mechanically at an invisible prey.

"What! Disappeared?" exclaimed the engineer, who was the only one of the Terrans to have maintained his self-composure. "That requires explanation—ask Brahmes for further details."

In a trembling voice punctuated by tears, Ossipoff begged Brahmes to ask the king in what circumstances the find he had mentioned to the Terrans had been made.

After having listened religiously while His Venusian Majesty spoke, Brahmes turned to the old man. "About the same time as you landed on our world, it seems, our astronomers detected an object in space that seemed to be heading toward us. At first, it was thought that it was something to do with the mysterious emissary from other celestial worlds who had visited our world a few days earlier…"

Ossipoff shuddered and grabbed the dumbfounded Venusian by the wrist. "What are you saying?" he cried. "Who is this mysterious emissary you're talking about?"

"A being similar in all respects to you, who came from the Moon and said that he was originally from a world visible from here, which he called *the Earth*."

"Sharp! That's Sharp!" groaned Farenheit.

"Yes, that's Sharp," Ossipoff repeated. "On that subject there is no possible doubt." And, in a tremulous voice, he asked Brahmes: "This individual…what has become of him?"

"He stayed here for some while," the Venusian replied. "After that, he continued his voyage."

The old man's knees buckled. "My God!" he stammered. Then, after a momentary pause, he said: "But he wasn't alone, was he? He had a companion with him—a young woman?"

"The voyager was alone…"

"Who knows whether the wretch might not have got rid of the poor child by throwing her into space," sobbed Ossipoff.

A roar greeted these words; it was Farenheit, thrown into a fury by the possibility that his enemy had committed this new crime. "By God!" he howled, gnashing his teeth. "Will God not let me get my hands on that bandit!"

Crushed, and prey to a profound despair, Gontran remained motionless with his head on his breast. This was the end of the dream of love that he had nursed for so long, and which had driven him so many millions of leagues from his native planet. Selena was lost to him forever; he might as well die.

The engineer, who had neither Gontran's love for Selena, nor Farenheit's hatred for Sharp in his heart, was the only one who had remained calm. While lavishing his consolations on both, he asked himself whether it was acceptable that he should be stopped dead in his tracks after coming several million leagues from the Boulevard Montparnasse to make a tour of the celestial world. He answered, squarely, *no*. "Come on," he said, "in all matters, it's necessary not to get carried away. Let's examine the situation calmly. First of all, Monsieur Ossipoff, you're wrong to deduce that Mademoiselle Selena is dead from the fact that no one has seen her. Villain though he is, Sharp is nevertheless and intelligent man, and it would have been an incredible stupidity on his part to set his companion at liberty."

"What would he be risking in a country like this one?" Ossipoff said, sadly. "The poor child would have been incapable of making herself understood."

"In whatever part of the Universe to which you might be transported," the engineer replied, "and in any epoch, tears have their eloquence, and your daughter's supplications would have attracted the sympathy of these people."

"So what do you conclude from that?" asked Gontran, raising his head, with a glimmer of hope in his eye.

"That Sharp must have carefully imprisoned Mademoiselle Selena in the vehicle and arranged things in such a manner as to shield her from all gazes."

Farenheit nodded his head several times. "What Monsieur Fricoulet says makes good sense," he muttered. Perhaps the American had no absolute conviction regarding the continued existence of the young woman, but his role seemed to him to be to appear to believe it. Otherwise, his discouraged companions might renounce their pursuit of Fedor Sharp, and that would put an end to his quest for vengeance.

"Sincerely," Fricoulet went on, "I can see no reason at all why Sharp should have done any violence to your daughter. He's a swindler and a scoundrel, but there's no proof that he has the stuff of a murderer in him." Clapping Flammermont amicably on the shoulder, he added: "So, let's not lose courage and let's seek some means by which we might catch up with this fellow."

"Catch up with him!" murmured Gontran, dejectedly. "Do we even know what direction he's taken?"

"He can only have taken one…the one that we plan to take ourselves."

"We need to be certain."

"Certain!" exclaimed the engineer. "But there's not the shadow of a doubt. Given the means of locomotion that he has stolen, he's obliged to continue towards the Sun—there's no doubt that Mercury will be the next station he visits."

"Now," Ossipoff went on, recovering his courage along with a glimmer of hope, "Mercury having passed its aphelion five days ago, the planet will arrive in five days at its shortest distance from Venus—which is to say, 10,000,000 leagues. Sharp will take about 17 days to cover those 10,000,000 leagues…"

"What does it matter how fast he's getting away from us," grumbled Farenheit, "since we have no means of following him at present?"

That doesn't lack logic, thought Fricoulet. Shrugging his shoulders, however, he turned to Gontran and said: "Remember that you've already got us out of difficulty twice. This time, too, you can do it again."

Flammermont seized him by the wrist. "My dear Alcide," he growled, "I'm not in a mood for joking, and I beg you…"

Ossipoff, however, who had overheard the engineer's observation, leaned closer to the young man and said, in a pleading voice: "My boy…my son…"

"My dear Monsieur," Gontran replied, "I have a broken heart. How can you expect me to have a sufficiently lucid mind…" And yet he murmured, with a sigh: "Oh, if only we still had our sphere…"

"What would we do with it?"

"Isn't it in the vicinity of this city that the mountain is located on whose summit the telegraphic apparatus linking Venus to the Moon is situated?"

"Certainly—what are you getting at?"

"That we would be able to utilize that apparatus."

"To return to the Moon?" grumbled Farenheit.

"What? No—to continue our voyage."

"I don't understand," murmured the American.

"That's because you find comprehension difficult, my dear Mr. Farenheit," replied the young Comte. "Anyway, this discussion is futile, since the sphere isn't in our possession."

Throughout his dialogue, the king had remained on his throne, frozen in his majestic immobility, his gaze fixed on the Terrans, attempting to deduce from their gestures what they were saying. Brahmes, similarly immobile, was waiting, either for them to address him or for the king to give human order.

Suddenly, Fricoulet uttered an exclamation. "I've just thought," he said to Ossipoff, "that in our rage at seeing Sharp escape us for a second time, we haven't thought to ask these people what the strange apparatus is that they have found and brought here. Since it's obvious now that it isn't the blackguard's shell, what can it be?"

Farenheit slapped his forehead. "By God!" he groaned. "It's our sphere!"

Ossipoff laughed sardonically. "That's impossible," he said.

"We can always make sure," replied the engineer. "Ask Brahmes."

The Venusian immediately transmitted the old man's question to the king, who let fall an almost imperceptible murmur from his barely-open lips.

Brahmes bowed, went rapidly to the far side of the hall, and swept aside a large curtain with an abrupt gesture.

The Terrans could not retain a cry of surprise and joy. It was their sphere that had just appeared before them, sparkling in the shadows.

Forgetting the presence of His Venusian Majesty, Fricoulet performed an untidy entrechat. As for the American, he threw his cap in the air, repeating three times in a sonorous voice: "Hurrah! Hurrah! Hurrah!" In the meantime, Ossipoff and Gontran fell into one another's arms and kissed one another on the cheeks. Finally, each of them having manifested his joy in his own fashion, Ossipoff asked the Venusian to explain his companions' intentions to the king.

"On leaving Wourch, the beautiful double planet that you admire from here on clear nights," he said, "we thought we would be able to rejoin the voyager that you have seen on your world a few days ago—who has already departed, you say. We ask, in consequence that you will allow us similarly to continue our voyage, by permitting us to use your reflector..."

By means of the interpreter's voice, the king replied very graciously that he was entirely at the disposal of the bold explorers, but that the emigration would begin on the following day, and, in consequence, the Terrans would have to postpone the execution of their project for two months. On hearing this reply, Ossipoff emitted a dull groan. As for Gontran, he stamped his foot and asked what this joke signified.

Brahmes, for whom the young Comte's observation was translated, replied: "The peoples of our world are in perpetual migration, in quest of the temperate environment indispensable to life. Twice a year we pass from one hemisphere into the other, fleeing either the destructive ardor of the solstice or the cold darkness of the pole. Tomorrow is the day on which, according to the royal statues, we must set off on the march to the southern hemisphere."

"We aren't subjects of His Venusian Majesty!" exclaimed Gontran, "and his statutes are a dead letter so far as we're concerned. Emigrate if you please, but we have business here and we'll stay."

Brahmes did not understand Flammermont's words, but he guessed their meaning. "I doubt," he said, "that your companions and you have a constitution that can withstand the glacial cold that will imprison this region in a coffin of ice for two months. It's certain death that awaits you."

"I don't doubt the truth of what you say," the old man replied, sadly, "but the delay you're demanding of us would destroy any hope of ever catching up with the man we're pursuing. Dying of cold or dying of despair is all one to us."

The king, for whom this heart-rending reply was translated, remained silent for a few moments; then, abandoning his impassivity for the first time, he gesticulated in an extremely excited fashion while talking to Brahmes.

The latter, when His Majesty had stopped talking, turned to the old scientist. "This," he said, "is what is proposed to you. You will follow the emigration, for, as I told you just now, you cannot stay here. The inhabitants of the land of Boos, whom you have seen in their element and whose physical constitution can tolerate the most rigorous cold, will start dismantling the reflector on Mount Itnounh today, and will transport the sections, one by one, to the summit of the highest mountain on our globe, which is in the very center of the country to which we are going. If this is agreeable to you, orders will be given immediately for the people of Boos, who serve us as slaves, to be put at the disposal of the king."

As one might imagine, this proposition, transmitted by Ossipoff to his companions was accepted by them with enthusiasm. They begged Brahmes to thank His Majesty warmly on their behalf. The latter topped off his generosity by declaring his desire to responsibility for meeting all the voyagers' material needs.

The next day, as Brahmes had told them, there was an indescribable brouhaha throughout the city: a general upheaval. In front of every dwelling a cart drew up, on to which the inhabitants loaded their furniture and primitive utensils. When the house was empty, it was sealed by means of a bronze plate, and the cart went to take up its position at the foot of the hill, on the shore of the Central Ocean, where the general rendezvous was arranged.

That evening, the royal carts, each one pulled by 50 inhabitants of Boos, set off on the march. Behind them, quarter by quarter and street by street, the entire procession set off. One might have thought it a gigantic and fantastic caravan, marching tumultuously beneath the starry sky, plowing a formidable course across the desert.

That march lasted eight days, during which the Terrans might easily have believed that they were on an excursion through some Oriental country, so strong was the heat, and also by reason of the marvelous fauna and flora that they were able to admire and study.

On arrival at the destination of their journey, they found a region similar in every respect to the one they had left; on the shore of a blue and waveless sea, on the rump of a high hill, a bronze city was arrayed, deploying its fan-like avenues on the torrid ground. Not far away, cutting the horizon in a dark line, was a chain of mountains, whose summits were lost in the clouds.

"Well," muttered Ossipoff, his eyes fixed in that direction, "that's definitely it."

"One might think that you recognized it," grumbled the American, in a mocking tone.

"Certainly I recognize it," retorted the old man. "It's one of the regions I've explored most frequently—by telescope. Thus, the peak that you see there, on your right, which appears to be the highest of all, has been measured several times—first by Shröter in 1789, then in 1833 and 1836 by Beer and Mädler...and also by myself, a few years ago. Well, we all agreed in giving that peak a height of about 40 kilometers."

"And we'll have to climb it on foot?" Farenheit complained.

"Unless you intend to go up on a funicular railway," retorted Fricoulet, sarcastically.

The American shrugged his shoulders furiously. "It's so many weeks since I've made use of my legs," he said, "that my joints are rusty, and I honestly don't know whether I have the necessary strength...."

"We might be able to hire natives of the land of Boos," Gontran said, laughing. "They could replace the mules that are used in certain ascents in Switzerland."

Ossipoff shook his head pensively. "It'll take us at least a week to get up there," he murmured.

"The fact is," Fricoulet added, "that Mont Blanc is a vulgar molehill beside that monstrous summit."

"Will we still be able to breathe when we get to the top?" the American asked, with some slight anxiety in his voice.

"There's nothing to fear from that point of view," the engineer replied. "If the worst comes to the worst, we have our respirols, but I doubt that we'll need to make use of them. The atmosphere ought to be dense enough to allow our terrestrial lungs to function with ease." While they were talking, the Terrans, guided by Brahmes, had set off walking; they were soon engaged on a zigzag road snaking between enormous rocks.

For nearly an hour they climbed, sweating, panting, whining and cursing; then the signal to halt was abruptly given, and Ossipoff—to whom the Venusian had spoken animatedly—went over to Farenheit. "Don't worry, Mr. Farenheit," he said. "Your legs won't be put to the trouble of effusing you the service that you demand of them. Thanks to the Venusians—who need, it seems, to have access to a hospital at the very top of the mountain—we shall go up without fatigue, in a very simple and comfortable vehicle.

"A vehicle!" cried Farenheit, intrigued. "What sort of vehicle?" As he spoke, a large cart emerged from a cleft in the rocks, mounted on a dozen bronze wheels, low and very large. At the front, attached to a sort of abbreviated helm, was a bronze chain that extended up the side of the mountain as far as the eyes could see.

"But that's the system used by the tugs that operate between Rouen and Paris," said Gontran.

On being interrogated, Brahmes explained that, on the opposite slope of the mountain, an army of natives of Boos, harnessed to the chain, would descend to the plain, thus forming a counterweight.

All the voyagers' luggage and equipment was rapidly loaded on to the cart, as were the various pieces of the reflector that were to be installed on the summit of the mountain. Then the signal to depart was given, and the ascent commenced.

In 24 hours, after several halts effected at various heights—doubtless to permit the human machine to get some rest—they arrived at a height of 30 kilometers. There, they abandoned the vehicle and had to continue the journey on foot, in the midst of a layer of cloud so thick that they could not see ten paces in front of them, along enormous precipices the mere sight of which gave them vertigo.

Finally, after 60 hours of superhuman fatigue, and after having miraculously avoided the death that lay in wait for them at almost every step, Ossipoff and his companions arrived on the plateau that crowned the mountain, looming 42 kilometers above the level of the Venusian oceans. There, they took a short rest before unpacking the apparatus; on the following day, the work commenced—a gigantic, insane task, to the successful completion of which the energy and the determination of the Terrans was entirely adequate. Fortunately, Brahmes, invested for the occasion with all the royal authority, had taken the mission to heart, and did not give the army of slaves working under his orders a moment's rest.

"Alcide," Gontran suddenly said to Fricoulet, "there's one thing bothering me."

"What?"

351

"In a voyage of the sort that we've undertaken, the guiding principle of getting from planet to planet is to take advantage of the moments when they're closest to one another, isn't it?"

"Certainly—that's the ABC of logic."

"So, to go from the Earth to the Moon, we took advantage of its perigee."

"Just as Sharp, in departing in our stead, took advantage of the moment at which the Moon and Venus were at their greatest proximity to one another— which is to say, their periaphrodite..."[112]

"And if I'm not mistaken, he has applied the same principle in departing for Mercury a month ago?"

"Exactly—but where are you going with this?"

"To ask you this question: at what point in its orbit will Mercury be when we quit this world?"

"If, as is probable, we can leave tomorrow. Mercury will be in quadrature with the Sun—which is to say that, relative to a straight line between that star and the planet on which we find ourselves, it will form a right angle."

"Which means," murmured Gontran, fearfully, "that it's no longer 9,000,000 leagues that we have to travel?"

"No, it will be 13,500,000 leagues."[113]

The young Comte started violently. "In that case, there's no point in leaving—we won't reach Mercury."

"Calm down. To fellows like us, a few million leagues more or less are of scant importance. Within a week, the planet of traders and thieves will give us hospitality."

---

[112] The text has "periaplerodite," which must be a typesetter's error occasioned by unclear handwriting in the manuscript; the authors have improvised the word, as others have since, by analogy with perihelion, to mean "closest point to Venus" (Aphrodite being of course, the Greek equaivalent of the Roman goddess Venus).

[113] The mean distance between Mercury and Venus, when they are in conjunction, is nearer to 50 million kilometers than "nine million leagues" (36 million kilometers), although the eccentricity of Mercury's orbit introduces a large variation into the calculation. At quadrature, applying Pythagoras' theorem gives a mean distance between Venus and Mercury of approximately 124 million kilometers, or 31 million leagues, although the actual distance to be traveled would be greater because of the motion of the destination planet.

Chapter XXVI
Through Interplanetary Space

With his face glued to one of the portholes of the cabin, Mikhail Ossipoff was curiously staring into space. Fricoulet, with his inevitable notebook in his hand, was totting up columns of figures. Jonathan Farenheit was fast asleep, snoring. Gontran, sitting beside his friend on the divan, with his elbows on his knees and his head in his hands, was as motionless as a statue.

Suddenly, a profound and heart-rending sigh uttered by his friend made the engineer shiver. He suspended his calculations and placed a hand gently on Flammermont's shoulder. "What's up?" he murmured. "Are you bored?"

The young Comte shook his head. "I've just calculated," he replied, "that it's been exactly 18 months since I asked for Selena's hand."

Fricoulet uttered a small satanic laugh. "And you're doubtless unhappy," he said shrugging his shoulders, "to find yourself no further forward today than you were 18 months ago—but you don't know how lucky you are, my friend." And he added, in a declamatory tone, raising his eyes toward the ceiling of the cabin: "*O fortunatos nimium…*"[114]

Flammeront sat up straight. "You'll exhaust my patience eventually, with your eternal jokes, Alcide," he complained. "I love Selena; I mean to marry her."

"What are you complaining about? Are not the moments in which one pays court to one's fiancée the happiest of the marriage…?"

"Do you call this paying court?" exclaimed Flammermont. "You're not taking this very seriously, are you?"

"That's the only way to avoid perceiving its reciprocal faults…"

"In the meantime, I feel that I'm being ridiculed…I'm turning into the Wandering Jew."

"Voyages are the making of youth," said the engineer, sarcastically. "Personally, in spite of anything you might say, I persist in blessing the various incidents that delay the moment when you will put the collar of slavery about your neck."

That phrase made Ossipoff shiver. For some moments, his attention had been distracted by the young men's conversation; he turned his back on the porthole abruptly, and addressed himself to Fricoulet. "That's an expression, Monsieur, which, in respect of my daughter, seems offensive."

---

[114] The quotation is from Virgil's *Georgics*; the phrase itself refers to excessive happiness, but the full line, implicit in the ellipsis, translates as "O how happy farmers would be if they would only count their blessings."

"Oh! You have your opinions on astronomy, Monsieur; I have mine on marriage—that's all."

The old man frowned and said to Flammermont: "I'm astonished, my dear Gontran, that you permit this gentleman, even though he's your friend, to express himself in this fashion when he speaks about your fiancée."

"His fiancée!" Fricoulet cried, comically. "You'll admit, Monsieur Ossipoff, that she's scarcely that. Gontran said so himself just now."

"Alcide!" said the young Comte, severely.

"Is what Monsieur Fricoulet just said true?" demand Ossipoff, turning to Gontran.

The latter, greatly embarrassed, was scarcely able to reply. "My God!" he stammered. "You'll agree yourself that the situation is strange. I asked you for your daughter's hand 18 months ago, in St. Petersburg. Today, we're..."

"1,500,000 leagues from the planet Venus," said Fricoulet, consulting his notebook.

"1,500,000 leagues from the planet Venus," repeated Gontran, "and I'm beginning to think that I'm not as far from St. Petersburg as I am from the cherished day when I'll be able to lead my dear Selena to the altar."

Mikhail Ossipoff folded his arms across his chest. "In truth," he said, in a slightly acerbic tone, "I didn't expect to hear you speak in that fashion. Is it me who came to find you to ask for your hand? Is it me who forced you to make the declaration that you made to me in the observatory at Pulkova, and which I recall word for word: 'millions, billions and trillions of leagues could not intimidate a love such as mine!' "

The old man fell silent momentarily, crushing Gontran with a stare that made him bow his head. Then, he added, with a little snigger: "Nothing forced you to say that! You spoke of trillions of leagues, and after the few paltry millions that you've covered, here you are, already regretting what you said."

"Monsieur Ossipoff," replied Gontran, with exaggerated dignity, "you're giving one of my friend Fricoulet's bad jokes a meaning that he certainly did not intend to give it. I regret nothing of what I have done; I would do it again....but if you see me so somber and so anxious, do not seek the cause anywhere but in my great affection for Mademoiselle Selena." He had pronounced these words in an earnest and profound voice, full of emotion.

Without saying a word, the old man held out his hand. Behind them, an oath burst forth; it was Farenheit, who had been listening to the conversation silently since waking up a little while before. "By God!" he groaned. "And to think that all this is the fault of that scoundrel, that wretch..." His teeth grated, his cheeks trembled and his hands opened and closed convulsively in a gesture of strangulation. "We'll never get our hands on him," he added, furiously.

"Have patience, Mr. Farenheit," replied Fricoulet. "In four days we'll be on Mercury, and there's at least a hope that you'll be able to savor the sweetness of vengeance there."

"Vengeance," murmured the American, "is a dish best consumed hot, like soup."

The engineer shook his head. "Well," he said, "that's a mater of taste. It's said that gourmets prefer it cold."

"Now then," said Farenheit, addressing Ossipoff, "I hope that as soon as your daughter's recovered and that rogue Sharp is punished, we'll make tracks as fast as possible to return to Earth."

Ossipoff shivered briefly. A dark veil extended over his face, the muscles of which suddenly contracted. He replied in a dull and indistinct voice: "If possible."

The American started. "What do you mean, *if possible*? By God, it had better be! I'm not like Monsieur de Flammermont, me—I haven't signed on for a tour of the sidereal world. Glory's not my thing. I'm not an astronomer, I'm just a simple pig-merchant...I've as much use for astronomy as a fish for an apple..." He paused momentarily to draw breath and then continued: "My business needs me. Then again, the shareholders in my Lunar Diamond Company might think that I've done the dirty on them. Finally, it'll soon be time for the election for the presidency of the Eccentric Club...and I've done enough for my election to be a sure thing. So, I warn you, as soon as I've settled my account with Sharp, I'll demand to go back."

"What about you, Monsieur Fricoulet?" asked Ossipoff, not without anxiety, "are you as impatient as Mr. Farenheit to return to our native planet?"

"To tell the truth, Monsieur Ossipoff," the young engineer replied, "I won't hide from you that this journey through the worlds is beginning to seem monotonous—and although I don't fatten pigs on the Boulevard Montparnasse, have no shareholders to whom I must render my accounts and have not put forward my candidacy for the presidency of any association, eccentric or otherwise, I would gladly follow in Mr. Farenheit's footsteps."

The old man reflected for a few moments, then turned to Flammermont. "You've heard what these gentlemen have said, my dear Gontran. As nothing, fundamentally, obliges them to continue the voyage in our company, it's necessary for you to find a means of facilitating their return to our point of departure—the Earth, that is. In consequence, I shall leave it to you to think about that means." With that, he turned on his heel and resumed his position at the porthole.

Farenheit seemed to be satisfied, but his attitude contrasted strangely with the pained expression on Fricoulet's face. Flammermont, for his part, looked at his friend, smiling ironically.

"There we are, then!" muttered the engineer. "Better to tell us straight out that we're tied to him indissolubly."

"What?" said the American, pricking up his ears.

Gontran trod on Fricoulet's toes; the latter pulled a face, but understood the warning and shut up.

"You were saying?" Farenheit persisted.

"Me? Nothing...although, now I recall...I meant to say that Monsieur de Flammermont's situation is very difficult. There's no doubt, of course, that he'll find a means of repatriating us...except that, whatever means he comes up with, he'll have to put into execution."

"Damn!" said Farenheit. "Mercury's a world like any other, I imagine..."

"Like any other!" muttered the engineer. "That depends what you mean by it. Remember that Mercury is scarcely 57,250,000 kilometers away from the Sun—14,300,000 leagues, that is—that its diameter measures no more than 1,200 leagues and that its volume is only 38% of that of the Earth."[115]

"Well, what does all that matter?"

Fricoulet's face reflected a profound amazement. He turned to Gontran. "Do you hear?" he cried. "He's asking why a world's distance from the Sun, diameter and volume matter. Savage that you are, it matters a great deal that Mercury is the smallest planet in the entire Solar System and that it's also the nearest to the central star."

"So?"

"So Mercury can't be a world like any other—not to mention that its orbit is very eccentric; which is to say that it's formed as an ellipse with the Sun at one of its foci...to the extent that the difference between the aphelion and the perihelion is 6,000,000 leagues. Six million—that's a fair amount for an orbit that only measures 28,000,000 leagues in diameter, which the planet goes round in 88 days..."

"In 88 days?" repeated Gontran, in astonishment. "Its year is only 88 days?"

"And do you know what the consequence is of that rapid progress? It's that a Terran infant transported to Mercury would know how to read and write at scarcely one year of age, that a boy of five would be an adult, and that we'd be centenarians."[116]

"88 day years," murmured Flammermont. "That would make children and concierges happy."

"Why's that?" asked Fricoulet.

"Because of the Christmas presents, of course."

Fricoulet shook his head. "For my part," he said, "I doubt that Mercurian civilization has got that far."

---

[115] The first two figures are not much different from those cited in modern reference books, but the figure for the relative volumes of Mercury and Earth seems to have been miscalculated; Mercury's volume is only 0.056 of Earth's.

[116] This statement, although intended humorously, is nevertheless somewhat confused.

"I read in *Les Continents célestes*, though, that the intensity of solar heat, ten times greater than on Earth, must have caused life to develop on the surface of Mercury with an incredible rapidity."

Ossipoff turned round. "That supposition does not seem to be correct," he said, "for telescopic and spectroscopic observations have established, in an irrefutable manner, that Mercury is surrounded by a considerable atmosphere, very thick, in which a quantity of cloud floats and which protects the planet against the destructive ardor of solar radiation when it is at its perihelion. It similarly prevents the overly rapid evaporation of heat when Mercury is at its aphelion..."

"So?"

"So I conclude, while taking account of the intensity of the heat, that this world, being the last-born of the Universe, must be in the same state as the Earth was in its primary epoch."

Farenheit's face had become anxious. "In those conditions," he said, "I'm afraid that Monsieur de Flammermont will not be able to find a way for me to see the starry flag of the United States again any time soon."

The young man shrugged his shoulders. "What do you expect, Mr. Farenheit?" he said. "Nothing's impossible and I'll just have to rack my brains if I don't find any humankind on Mercury capable of lending me a hand. I hope that you won't be condemned to enjoy our society any longer than you desire." He assumed an earnest expression to address Osipoff. "However," he said, "while recognizing the sound foundation of your reasoning, especially with respect to the age of Mercury, it seems to me that in his *Cosmotheoros*, the illustrious astronomer Huygens established the existence of a humankind similar to ours."

The old man burst out laughing. "According to the theories of Huygens, as to those of Fontenelle, the inhabitants of Mercury will be little beings, lively and agile, always on the move, and as black as the natives of Ethiopia. I don't believe in that humankind any more than the one invented by Baron Holberg in his novelistic account of Nicholas Klim's voyage to the subterranean planets. The plant-men and guitar-men imagined by him have no more reason to exist than Fontenelle's Ethiopians, Huygens' humans and those of the *Voyage au monde de Mercure* published in the 18th century."[117]

His companions, including Farenheit, were listening to him with evident interest; by way of conclusion, the old man added: "For the scientist and the phi-

---

[117] Ludvig Holberg's *Nicolai Klimii Iter Subterraneum* (1741; tr. as *A Journey to the World Underground by Nicholas Klimius*) features a series of "planets" orbiting a central Sun inside a hollow Earth, inhabited by various kinds of fantastic hybrid beings. The anonymous *Relation du monde de Mercure* [An Account of the world of Mercury] (1750), which was reprinted in Charles Garnier's classic collection of imaginary voyages in 1787, was the work of the Chevalier de Béthune; it features winged humanoid Mercurians whose exotic anthropology is described in some detail.

losopher, it's already a considerable effort to imagine the existing humankinds, without being further preoccupied with the forms that future humankinds might affect. Let's let a few centuries go by, and our remote descendants can then attempt to solve such problems..."[118] With these words he returned to his observation-post, leaving the American quite disconcerted by these revelations.

"What are you doing there?" asked Gontran, seeing Fricoulet attentively examining a sort of dial fixed to the extremity of the central pillar of the sphere.

"As you can see, I'm consulting my 'rapidimeter'." When the young Comte raised his eyebrows questioningly, he added: "It's an indicator of my own invention, by means of which I can assure myself, at any moment, that the luminous waves are still reaching the sphere and activating it with the same force."

"Very practical," Gontran approved, "but how does it work?"

"Listen—I'll make it as clear as possible, it's up to you to understand it if you can. What sustains and propel our vehicle in space? The vibrations emitted by the Venusian reflector. I employ an infinitesimal fraction of these vibrations to activate a radiometer turning in a glass ampoule; two gear-wheels guide the needle that rotates in front of the dial. As long as the radiometer moves at great speed the needle is pushed to the extremity of its range; if, for one reason or another, the movement slows down, a spring will bring the needle back towards zero. Do you understand?"

"Well enough," replied Gontran, whose eyes no longer left the rapidimeter, "that I felt a shiver run through my limbs. So, when that needle reaches zero..."

"If it reaches zero before we reach the attractive zone of Mercury, we'll fall back on Venus." Seeing the deplorable effect this declaration had on his friend, the engineer added: "Don't worry, though—there's no reason for any such accident to occur. Then again, should it do so, we're sufficiently accustomed to falls not to fear them any longer."

"It's not the fear of breaking my bones that makes me tremble," Gontran retorted, "it's the time we'd lose in retracing out steps while Sharp continues to move forward." So saying, he studied the instrument anxiously. "At this moment," he said "how are we doing?"

"We're flying at top speed. If my calculations are exact, we'll have passed the neutral point within 48 hours."

---

[118] This casual dismissal of the potential ambitions of serious speculative fiction would be rather remarkable, even if we did not know that, when these words first saw print, Camille Flammarion had recently addressed the question robustly, in the expanded version of *Lumen* published in 1887. Graffigny could not have known, however, that H. G. Wells had recently published "The Chronic Argonauts" in his *Science Schools Journal*, thus beginning the definitive rewriting of the prospectus of futuristic scientific romance that would culminate in the 1895 publication of *The Time Machine*.

Farenheit rubbed his hands together energetically. "Then the accident can go ahead and happen," he growled. "We'd fall, but what would it matter, since we'd fall on Mercury?" He concluded his observation with a formidable yawn. "This Senegalese temperature makes one sleepy, don't you think?" he asked, lying down on the divan.

"It's evidently contagious," joked Fricoulet, on seeing Gontran lie down too, in his usual place.

"That's quite possible," replied the young man, in a loud enough voice to be heard by Ossipoff—and summoned his friend to his side by winking his eye. "Shh!" he said. "I ant to take advantage of Monsieur Ossipoff's absorption in his contemplation to study Mercury a little."

The engineer was amazed. "You've got a singular fashion of studying the planets," he replied, in the same hushed tone...unless you're imploring Morpheus to send you astronomical dreams, I don't see how..."

Flammermont smiled thinly and took a book from beneath his traveling blanket, which he opened. "What about *Les Continents célestes*? Do they count for nothing?"

"Understood," Fricoulet replied. "Oh well, I'll leave you to your lesson—study hard. I also have a little work to do..." And he went to install himself at a porthole next to the one at which the old man was stationed with his telescope.

Less than a quarter of an hour had gone by when the engineer's ears were disagreeably struck by two sonorous noises of different pitch, which filled the cabin. He turned round and saw that Gontran had slumped forward, with his nose in the work of his illustrious namesake, and was mingling his snores with those of the American.

40 hours went by thus, in desperate monotony for Flammermont and Jonathan Farenheit, the former sighing over Selena and the second roaring after Sharp; then, when one had sighed enough and the other roared enough, they sought to forget their sterile love and impotent hatred in sleep. As for Ossipoff and Fricoulet, they scarcely left their observation portholes except to take such rest as was strictly necessary to keep their strength up; the rest of their time was spent with an eye glued to the telescope or a hand blackening a notebook with interminable calculations.

They were approaching the end of the second day when Gontran, impatient at seeing Fricoulet sitting in the same place, still absorbed in his algebraic calculations, went over to him. "We'll be imprisoned in this cage for years, then," he said, "and for years, you'll be gazing and calculating."

"It won't be years," the engineer replied, "it'll be centuries that are necessary, not to understand, but to begin to understand, the Universe."

"But what are you doing at this moment?"

"I'm answering—or, rather, trying to answer—a delicate astronomical question."

Gontran raised his arms to the heavens. "Another one!" he exclaimed. "But isn't astronomy full of delicate questions?"

"There's a star, classified by Groombridge under the number 1830,[119] which plunges scientists into a profound perplexity because of its prodigious speed of translation."

"The 'fixed' stars move, then?" put in the young Comte.

Fricoulet grabbed his arm, indicating Mikhail Ossipoff with an inclination of his head. Fortunately, the old man, absorbed by his contemplation of the sky, had not heard anything. "Do they move?" retorted the engineer. "Absolutely— and with a certain rapidity. Thus, the one I'm talking about, Groombridge 1830, travels at 320 kilometers a second."

Gontran's eyes grew round. "320 kilometers a second!" he stammered.

"That's what creates the supposition that it doesn't belong to our visible Universe, for a body attracted by the suns that we know doesn't attain a velocity superior to 40 kilometers over second."

"And what's the purpose of your research?"

"To elucidate the origin and provenance of this star, which is emerging from the depths of immeasurable infinity."

Gontran shrugged his shoulders, and murmured, with a mocking smile: "And that's how scientists spend their time and use up the genius that their Creator has given them!" He sniggered, and added, in a disdainful tone: "Don't you think that it would be more useful to your peers to seek to resolve the social problems by which our poor humankind is weighed down than to wear yourself out in sterile studies of Groombridge 1830?"

Fricoulet was about to reply when his friend added: "And when one thinks that this star, whose destiny preoccupies you, might have been extinct for 20,000 years—that the world from which its luminous ray sprang probably went to join the old moons centuries ago!"

These words, which betrayed a certain scorn on the young man's part for the science so dear to Ossipoff, nevertheless contained an appearance of logic. At first Fricoulet was somewhat nonplussed.

At that moment, a thunderous "By God!" burst forth behind them.

All three of them turned round simultaneously, and saw Jonathan Farenheit standing as still as a statue, his hair standing on end in horror, his features convulsed and his eyes wide, with an expression of indescribable fear covering his

---

[119] Groombridge 1830 (the figure is the year of its identification) was shown by Friedrich Argelander in 1842 to have the greatest proper motion then known, although it was subsequently overtaken by Kapteyn's Star and Barnard's Star. Its unusual motion is no longer considered to be particularly puzzling, as Groombridge 1830 is now known to be a "halo star" rotating around the galaxy's rim.

face. Both his arms were extended and the index fingers of both his fingers were pointing at the rapidimeter.

Fricoulet was the first to realize the meaning of that tragic immobility. He ran to the instrument and uttered a cry of fright. "Stopped!"

That single word made Ossipoff and Flammermont blanch, and they repeated, with one voice: "Stopped!"

The needle did, indeed, stand at zero.

Farenheit, having emerged from his stupor, tore at his hair. "If only we were in Mercury's zone of attraction!" he groaned.

"Unfortunately," replied Fricoulet, "we're still in that of Venus." And he added, darting an interrogative glance at Ossipoff: "But what the Devil can have happened?"

The old man replied with a shrug of his shoulders.

"Perhaps it's your rapidimeter that's out of order," Gontran suggested, snatching at that last hope.

"It's hardly probable," replied the engineer. "In any case, there's a very simple way of settling the matter, and that's to go and see."

Without swaying anything further, he put on his diving-suit, and carefully screwed down the metallic helmet, after introducing a tablet of solidified oxygen into it. Lifting up the trapdoor fitted into the floor of the cabin, he went down the stairway that led to the interior of the sphere. The first thing he observed, thanks to the magnesium lantern with which he was equipped, was that the central axis around which the sphere rotated was immobile. Apart from that, everything was in as good a condition as at the moment of departure. Very puzzled, he was about to go back to the cabin when, moved by an inexplicable presentiment, he went down to the final steps leading to the inferior aperture of the sphere, and leaned over the abyss.

An exclamation escaped his throat. He had expected to see below him, in space, the luminous point that the focal point of the reflector ought to form on Venus, thanks to whose radiation the sphere was sustained in space—but the space was dark. The luminous point was extinct; the planet itself had disappeared.

Swiftly, the engineer rejoined his companions. He took off the diving-suit and, for the first time since they had left the Earth, the marks of profound despair appeared on his face. "My friends," he said, in a grave voice, "this time we're doomed." In a few words, he told them what he had discovered.

"But what can have happened?" groaned Farenheit.

"Something quite simple," replied Ossipoff. "Something I anticipated, but which I didn't want to mention to you at the time of departure. In the aftermath of one of the meteorological cataclysms so frequent on the surface of Venus, a layer of cloud has interposed itself between the Sun and the reflector."

"We're going to fall back on Venus, then?" complained the American, whose features were contorted by rage.

"It's probable," Ossipoff replied. "We might already be falling—that's something else that's easy to verify."

From one of his pockets he took a little apparatus in the form of an elongated metal frame. Two slender wires, one of which was movable, traversed the frame vertically. By moving the two wires closer to or further away from one another, by means of a screw, one could measure the diameter of any object. The old man attached the instrument to the ocular lens of his telescope and said to Fricoulet: "Here, see for yourself."

The engineer aimed the instrument at the Sun, and turned the adjustment screw slightly to enlarge the distance between the two wires to the appropriate distance.

"Well?" asked Ossipoff, after a brief interval.

"The two threads are tangential to the edges of the Sun."

"What measurement do you obtain?"

"65 minutes," Fricoulet replied, abandoning the instrument.

"We'll check it in a quarter of an hour."

Needless to say, those 15 minutes seemed as long as 15 centuries to the unfortunates, whose chests were constricted by anguish.

Mikhail Ossipoff alone conserved his self-composure. From the moment that they were no longer moving forwards, they were falling—but might they be falling elsewhere than on Venus? With his watch in his hand, he watched the minute-hand impassively as it slowly made its way around the dial.

"Look," he said, finally.

Again, Fricoulet put his eye to the telescope.

"Well?" said the old man. "You ought to observe a perceptible diminution in the solar disk." Then, watching the screw that the engineer was gently turning between his fingers, he suddenly said: "What are you doing? Have you lost your head? Don't you see that you're drawing the wires apart rather than moving them closer?"

Fricoulet did not reply. Pale, with his lips pursed and his breast swollen by labored respiration, he clutched the telescope in his left hand while his right hand maneuvered the micrometer.

Finally, in a choked voice, he stammered: "Monsieur Ossipoff, the solar disk isn't diminishing."

"What do you mean, it isn't diminishing? That's impossible. We aren't at the neutral point, and, in consequence, can't be immobile. Emotion's clouding your vision. The disk must be diminishing."

The engineer straightened up and, passing his hand over his brow, which was soaked with cold sweat, murmured: "You're right. It's doubtless emotion that's spoiling my vision."

"But what do you see?"

"The solar disk is increasing."

Ossipoff started violently at these words. "You're mad!" he exclaimed, shrugging his shoulders.

Unceremoniously, he shoved Fricoulet aside and took his place, but scarcely had he applied his eye to the ocular lens than he uttered a stifled exclamation and stepped back, raising his arms into the air in a gesture of stupefaction. "It's prodigious, incomprehensible, supernatural...you're right. To me, too, it seems that the disk has grown. It now measures 65 minutes, 18 seconds!"

For a moment, all four of them looked at one another in silence, overwhelmed by the incomprehensible phenomenon.

"By God!" cried Farenheit, all of a sudden. "We're changing position, for the solar rays are now coming in through the side portholes."

"It's the apparatus that's turning," declare Fricoulet.

"So we're falling, then?" asked Flammermont, anxiously.

"Of course!"

"But where?" roared the American, prey to a frightful over-excitement. "On Venus? On the Moon? On the Earth? Come on, say something. You're scientists, and it's your job to know these things." He had seized Gontran by the collar of his jacket, putting him on the spot. A frightful scream, uttered by Ossipoff, made him let go.

Everyone looked at the old man. He was horribly pale and, leaning against the wall of the cabin, he seemed to be about to lose consciousness. Suddenly, he covered his face with his hands and murmured: "Oh, it's horrible! It's horrible!"

"Please, Monsieur Ossipoff!" implored Fricoulet. "Tell us what it is. If you know how the phenomenon has been produced, explain it to us—whatever the consequences might be!"

The old man fixed them with a stare in which there as a glimmer of madness, and stammered: "We're falling into the Sun!"

Farenheit uttered a formidable curse, while, in his impotent rage, he waved his fists menacingly at the entire immensity, which was black and bleak, in spite of the dazzling rays of the Sun, where death—a frightful, horrible death—awaited them.

Gontran de Flammermont let himself collapse on to the divan, paralyzed—and there he stayed for long hours, devoid of movement and thought, as if death had struck him already, mechanically babbling a single name over and over: "Selena."

Ossipoff had returned to his telescope, to measure the slow but continuous growth of the solar disk. As for Fricoulet, alone in a corner of the cabin, his notebook in his hand, he surrendered himself to gigantic algebraic operations, blackening the paper with figures and trigonometric diagrams, careless of the ocean of flame by which he and his companions would be engulfed in a few hours time.

Little by little, the temperature was rising, and, inside the cabin, the overheated air was becoming unbreathable. The American, who was prowling like a bear in a cage, went to the thermometer; it marked 42 degrees Centigrade. "By God!" he groaned. "Are we cowardly enough to wait until we're in that frightful furnace, then? In any case, personally, I've made up my mind not to wait any longer." And his hand groped for his revolver.

"My friends," Ossipoff said then, in a pleading voice, turning his anguished face toward them, "will you forgive me for having dragged you to your doom?" His eyes full of tears, his features convulsed and his hair disordered, the old man offered an image of the most profound despair.

Without saying a word, Gontran and the American offered him their hands.

"And you, Monsieur Fricoulet?" said the old scientist. "Will you forgive me?"

As he finished speaking, the engineer leapt to his feet and cried, in a vibrant voice: "I forgive you, all the more willingly because there is nothing for which you need to be forgiven—for the very simple reason that it is not our doom to which you have dragged us, but our goal!"

Ossipoff looked at Gontran, shaking his head. "The poor boy is mad!" he murmured.

"Not as mad as all that, Monsieur Ossipoff, not as mad as all that. While you were despairing, I was working, and I've found that our velocity, presently 20,000 meters per second, is still increasing."

"We'll only arrive more rapidly in the ardent furnace that will devour us," complained the American.

"Not at all," retorted the engineer. "Given our velocity, in conformity with the laws of celestial mechanics, we shall describe a curve around the Sun, open or closed: a parabola, a hyperbola or an ellipse. Well, I've just calculated that curve, and do you know?—it converges with the orbit of Mercury, with which we shan't be long in catching up. Within 24 hours, we'll make contact with Mercury…" So saying, he held out his calculations to Ossipoff, triumphantly.

The latter passed the sheet of paper to Gontran, stammering: "Here, see for yourself…I'm so anxious…"

Fricoulet shrugged his shoulders ironically; then, going to the young Comte, he took him by the hand. "You know," he murmured in his ear, "you were definitely born under an unlucky star." As Flammermont looked at him in astonishment, he added: "I'm beginning to believe that your marriage to Selena will end up being made."

Chapter XXVII
Gontran recovers Selena and Farenheit gets news of Sharp

"The planet Mercury was one of the five planets known throughout antiquity but it was undoubtedly the last to be discovered and identified; the most ancient astronomical measurement that has been handed down to us dates from 265 B.C., the 294th year of the era of Nabonassar, 60 years after the death of Alexander the Great.[120] We also possess Chinese observations of Mercury, of which the most ancient dates from 118 B.C.

"Because of its proximity to the Sun, Mercury is only visible to us in the evening or the morning, never in the middle of the night, and always in the twilight. That is why, at the times of the first observations, it was believed—as with Venus—that there were two different planets, one of the morning and the other of the evening..."

"Gontran! Are you asleep?"

Hearing himself called, the young man swiftly shut the copy of *Les Continents célestes* that he had been busy perusing, hid it under his blanket, and turned to face Ossipoff. "No, my dear Monsieur," he replied. "I was merely drowsy. What can I do for you?"

"If it wouldn't be too inconvenient for you to get up, I beg you to come and join me."

Flammermont concealed a yawn; nevertheless, he got up.

"Here," the old man said to him, standing away from his telescope. "Take a look. I don't know whether I ought to attribute it to the ardor of the Sun's rays, but I've had rather feeble eyesight for some time."

While Ossipoff was speaking, the young man had applied his eye to the ocular lens. "Well, what do you want to know?" he asked.

"In what form do you perceive that planet?"

"As you must have perceived it yourself—in the form of its first quarter."

"Good—but examine carefully, I beg you, the two horns of the crescent. Do you notice anything?"

Gontran paused momentarily before relying. "My word," he said, "no—I don't see anything odd."

---

[120] Nabonassar was king of Chaldea from 747 to 734 B.C. and the "Era of Nabonassar" used in ancient chronology was calculated from the year of his succession, so 265 B.C. was actually the 482nd year of that era. Alexander the Great died in 323 B.C. Flammarion quotes dates from the Era of Nabonassar in *Les Terres du ciel*, but gets them right.

Ossipoff's eyebrows contracted. "Then I must be mistaken," he murmured, "and Schröter, Noble and Burton[121] with me." In a louder voice he added: "Mercury's two horns seem to you to be absolutely identical?"

The young man was silent for several seconds; then he said: "No, the austral horn is nowhere near as sharp as the other…one might think that it is blunted."

Ossipoff uttered a cry of triumph.

"It really is!" he stammered, emotionally. "It really is!" After a pause, he went on: "Some of us, among terrestrial astronomers, have thought that we noticed that inequality between the two Mercurian horns…and that observation has a considerable importance, since it establishes the existence on the planet of uneven ground."

"I'm curious to know," said Farenheit, butting into the conversation, "how you can deduce that logically."

"Nothing simpler. It's sufficient to admit that there exists, near to that meridional horn, a very high mountainous plateau, which interrupts the light of the Sun and prevents it from reaching the point that the horn would extend without such a preeminence."

"But that hypothesis is also Flammermont's!" exclaimed Fricoulet.

"My hypothesis?" said Gontran.

"No—your namesake's."

"That's proof," the young Comte said, gravely, "that great minds often think alike, when it's a matter of resolving the eternal problems of Nature."

"And have you," asked Farenheit, in a skeptical tone, "done the same as for the Moon—which is to say, measured the Mercurian mountains?"

Ossipoff favored the American with a disdainful glance. "You're like St. Thomas, my poor Mr. Farenheit," he replied. "You only believe in things that you can touch with your finger."

Fricoulet nodded his head significantly. "May it please God that he doesn't touch it too rudely," he muttered. "With such a fall, God knows what would happen to our bones."

A slight shiver ran through the American's limbs; nevertheless, he put on a brave face and addressed himself to Ossipoff. "You still haven't answered me," he said.

"Schröter, calculating the degree of truncation of the crescent, estimated the height of certain Mercurian peaks at the 250th part of the planet's diameter—which gives them about 19 kilometers…"

"Pooh!" said Farenheit. "What's that beside the mountains of Venus?"

---

[121] Charles E. Burton (1846-1882) was better known for lending early support to the Martian canal hypothesis.

"Almost nothing, indeed—but it may appear to be a more respectable height if you consider that the highest mountain on our world, Gauri Sankar in the Himalayas, measures no more than 8840 meters.

"And the Mercurian volcanoes?" asked Gontran, assuming an air of expertise. "What do you think of them, Monsieur Ossipoff?"

"I agree with your illustrious compatriot, my dear Monsieur de Flammermont, that perhaps they exist, but they are in any case invisible to our terrestrial observers."

"Are Schröter and Huggins[122] mistaken, then?"

"I won't hide it from you that that's my opinion. At the Observatory of Pulkova I've conducted the most scrupulous searches, but it was impossible for me to find the luminous patch that both of them thought they had observed on the planet, not far from its center."

Farenheit, who was examining the thermometer attentively, suddenly exclaimed: "It's only 39 degrees!"

"Proof that we're drawing away from the Sun," said Fricoulet.

"Of course! To get closer to Mercury, that's necessary," said Gontran, laughing.

"How far away from it are we?" asked the American.

"Only a few 100,000 leagues," the engineer replied. "Furthermore, we must now be within its zone of attraction, and the rapidity of the fall will increase further."

The planet now seemed to occupy one entire side of the sky, and its black mass, like a colossal cannonball stood out clearly against the dark background of space. For some time, the voyagers contemplated the new world in silence with their eyes glued to the portholes. It was, so to speak, visibly increasing in size. They had to land there, but God alone knew how. That question was seriously tormenting Farenheit and Flammermont. The latter approached Fricoulet and murmured in his ear: "You seem to be looking forward to the prospect our fall with a good deal of equanimity. We've avoided the Sun, but I'm afraid that the fate that awaits us on Mercury might not be much more enviable."

The engineer shrugged his shoulders, in a philosophically insouciant fashion. "What do you expect?" he replied. "We've stuck our little finger in the gears—it's necessary that our entire bodies pas through."

"If that's all that you can say to reassure me…"

"Well, what else can I say? We're falling—you know that as well as I do. We're even falling at high speed. What will result from our encounter with the Mercurian surface? It's impossible to foresee that."

Gontran's face darkened visibly. Fricoulet noticed it, and added, with a mocking laugh: "I know how you feel. If I were in your shoes, it would annoy me considerably to risk seeing my fiancée again in the condition of meat

---

[122] Sir William Huggins (1824-1910).

367

paste…but it's necessary to look on the bright side and say that, after all, life is a vale of tears…"

Flammermont stamped his foot impatiently. "Alcide!" he complained. "You're really getting on my nerves!"

"It's the effect of the torrid heat in here…"

"You have no hope, then? It's the end?"

The engineer started. "Are you mad?" he cried. "Why the end? Even if there were 99 chances in 100 that we'll be smashed up, there's still, in an adventure like the one in which we're involved, one fraction unknown in which to invest our hope. That's what I'm doing, and I suggest that you do likewise."

Gontran shook his head. The unknown fraction to which Fricoulet was pinning his hopes did not inspire much confidence in him. "When we fell on the Moon," he said, "the vehicle's springs reduced the shock. When we landed on Venus, we had a parachute—and then again, plunging into the Ocean is always less dangerous than coming down on land…but in the circumstances in which we now find ourselves, we have no trump card in hand to save us."

"You're forgetting the manner in which the aeroplane landed on Mont Boron," Fricoulet retorted. "On that day, as at this moment, we were falling through the air like a stone."

"With the difference that we were falling a few 100 meters, while today we're falling a few 100,000 leagues."

Fricoulet smiled. "Fortunately, to counterbalance that enormous difference, we have in our favor the fact that weight on Mercury's surface is only half of what it is on Earth." [123]

The young Comte opened his eyes wide.

"You're mocking me," he said. "I'm not a scientist, but I'm not an imbecile who can be made to believe that black is white."

"Far be it from me to think that, my dear chap," replied the engineer, "but if, instead of falling asleep over *Les Continents célestes*, as you did yesterday, you had studied your namesake's work a little harder, you'd know that it's by studying the perturbation produced on comets that pass close by it that we have succeeded in determining the exact mass of Mercury…"

Gontran slapped his forehead. "I've got it," he said. "I remember now—it was Le Verrier, wasn't it, who was the first to achieve that result by studying Encke's comet…and the conclusion…" [124]

---

[123] Modern figures give Mercury's surface gravity as 0.38 of Earth's.

[124] Urbain Le Verrier (1811-1877) was able to study Encke's Comet—first discovered in 1786 by Pierre Méchain—because it had an unusually short period of 3.3 years, whose calculation of J. F. Encke gave the comet its name. Encke's Comet is also unusual in cutting across Mercury's orbit.

"Is that the Mercurian globe weighs about five times less than the terrestrial globe, and that weight, on its surface, is about half what it is on our native planet."[125]

"That's true, that's true...I read all that," murmured Gontran, slightly humiliated by his poor memory. "In that case, we have only half as much chance of being reduced to pulp as we would if we were falling on Earth."

"Perfectly logical," said Fricoulet, with an approving nod of the head.

"So that's 50 chances in 100 that we have of breaking our heads, not 99, as you claimed just now," said Farenheit, in his turn.

"Scrupulously exact, Mr. Farenheit."

The American manifested his joy with an entrechat, but a few words from the engineer were sufficient to cool his enthusiasm.

"Don't forget, however, that we're falling from a height of 500,000 leagues, that we weigh, including the apparatus, 1000 kilograms, and that, multiplying the height by the square of the time of the fall, we should hit the Mercurian surface with a velocity of 12 kilometers a second.

Gontran and Farenheit cried out in fright.

"Given that the weight is reduced by half, let's halve that velocity—but you'll agree with me that it's still sufficient to reduce us to our simplest expression."

Flammermont folded his arms across his chest. "To judge by your calm tone," he said, "I swear that one would think that there isn't a word of truth in what you just said. You remind me of a nurse terrifying her children with the story of the bogeyman or Bluebeard."

"I wish to Heaven it were not so," replied the engineer. "Unfortunately, Mercury is there to convince us of the reality."

Beneath the apparatus, indeed, the planet extended its enormous and terrifying mass, whose titanic ruggedness still seemed very vague, bathed in a thick gaseous atmosphere.

The American took Gontran's hands in his. "Come on, Monsieur de Flammermont," he said, in a slightly anguished voice. "You've got us out of trouble too often already for one more time..."

Ossipoff had his back turned, which permitted the young Comte to be able to raise his arms to the heavens in a gesture signifying his impotence, without compromising himself. The American was tenacious, though; he did not release his prey. "By God!" he growled. "Think of your reputation, your glory, your love...and my hatred too...and get us out of this alive." Clenching his fists, he added: "By God! If I were a scientist like you, instead of a simple pig-merchant, I wouldn't want it said that I'd left my fiancée in the hands of a wretch like Fedor Sharp. Come on—think! Think!"

Gontran made a gesture of impatience.

---

[125] Actually, Mercury's mass is only 0.055 that of the Earth.

"Think, eh?" he cried. "That's easy to say. You think it's enough to rack one's brains to find an idea. I'd like to see you do it..."

He remained silent and still for a few moments, his head bowed, in a meditative attitude. "My God!" he said, suddenly, looking at Fricoulet. "I've got an idea..."

Farenheit uttered an exclamation of joy. "I was sure of it!" he cried. "It's impossible that a man like you..."

The young Comte imposed silence on the over-exuberant American with a gesture and turned to Fricoulet. "Why don't we do what mariners do when a ship is about to sink—throw everything we can into the sea to lighten ourselves."

Farenheit was presumably taken in by Flammermont's stroke of genius, for his face visibly lengthened. "Pooh!" he murmured. "When we've got rid of our weapons, our clothes, the few remaining instruments and the provisions we still have to eat, we'll only be 100 kilograms lighter—and then what?"

"The fact is," said Fricoulet, in his turn, "that it's not worth the trouble of throwing ballast overboard when we have so little to throw."

Gontran shook his head. "You haven't understood me," he said. "There's no question, in my view, of getting rid of our weapons, clothes and everything indispensable to our existence."

"In that case," said the American, "unless we throw ourselves overboard..."

"I know what you mean!" Fricoulet suddenly exclaimed, examining his friend attentively as if to read his thoughts in his face.

"You do?"

"At least, I think so."

"Well?"

"It's bold, but it's not impossible." He went over to Ossipoff, who was continuing his studies, careless of the death to which he and his companions were hurtling with vertiginous rapidity. "My dear Monsieur," he said, "the minutes are too precious to be spent counting the stars. Would you please lend us the assistance of your wisdom and knowledge?"

The old scientist abandoned his telescope, grumbling.

"The situation is grave," Fricoulet began. "Very grave. In a few hours we'll land on Mercury, and God only knows what will be left of us after that landing."

Ossipoff shrugged his shoulders, meaning that there was nothing he could do about it.

The engineer continued. "Staring from the principle that the lighter we are, the less chance our fall has of being mortal,[126] Monsieur de Flammermont proposes that we lighten ourselves by 300 kilos."

---

[126] As Galileo is famously reputed to have demonstrated at the Leaning Tower of Pisa, lighter bodies fall just as fast as heavier ones, provided that the effect of air

The old savant started. "But that's a third of the weight of the entire apparatus," he said.

"It is, in fact, the weight of the cabin in which we are presently lodged."

Ossipoff opened his eyes wide. "You want us to separate ourselves from the cabin?" he asked Gontran.

"But you're mad!" cried Farenheit.

Completely nonplussed, the young man kept quiet.

"Why shouldn't we separate ourselves from it?" Fricoulet said. "Isn't the apparatus constructed in such a fashion that the two parts comprising it can be separated from one another? How did we land on Venus, if you please?"

"The situation isn't the same," Ossipoff retorted. "It was the sphere, not the cabin, that we abandoned, and we had a parachute, while at present..."

"At present, it's a matter of doing on Mercury the opposite of what we did on Venus. Besides, have you another means? If so, we're ready to examine it and adopt it, if it's preferable to ours."

"No, I haven't," the old scientist replied, dryly.

"By God!" complained the American. "You might have found one if you'd racked your brains a little, instead of hypnotizing yourself with your eye screwed to your telescope."

Ossipoff shrugged his shoulders meekly, and was doubtless about to return to his beloved instrument, but Fricoulet stopped him. "No, my dear Monsieur" he said. "Leave the continuation of your studies until later. At the moment, it's a matter of all of us getting down to work, for time's pressing."

The old man released a sigh.

"This is what we're going to do," the engineer continued. "You and Mr. Farenheit will package up, as carefully as possible, all the objects contained in the cabin that you think are indispensable. Gontran and I will attach them as we go along to the circular floor that runs along the interior wall of the sphere."

No sooner was this said than the work was begun; in two hours, the cabin was entirely cleared of everything it contained.

"What about the selenium wires that attached us to the parachute?" asked Farenheit. "Shall we abandon them?"

Fricoulet reflected for a few moments, then replied: "No—they might be useful afterwards."

"For what?"

"Attaching ourselves securely. Later perhaps, we'll be able to dispense with them."

His gaze traced a circle around him; having established that nothing had been forgotten, he said: "Let's go. Everyone down below!"

---

resistance is negligible. Given that the sphere is falling through the void, this principle would be strictly applicable; Fricoulet and Ossipoff would surely be aware of that, although Gontran presumably would not.

One after another they went down and, following the engineer's instructions, took their places on the floor, to which Fricoulet attached them solidly, as he had said, with the metal wires.

"What about you?" Gontran asked.

"Don't worry about me," he replied. "I'm going back up to jettison the ballast when the time comes."

An hour went by, and then two, while the voyagers, reduced to almost complete immobility, waited with anguish in their hearts for the engineer to rejoin them.

Suddenly, there was a cracking sound; a powerful shock shook the sphere, and Fricoulet appeared on the first step of the stairway, crying: "It's done! Now, by the grace of God…"

He sat down next to his companions and passed a selenium cable around his body and the central axis, as fishermen tie themselves to the mast of their boat in anticipation of a storm.

They were falling, not in a spin, as Farenheit had dreaded, but vertically, like the lead of a plumb-line. Because all four of them were gathered in the inferior part of the sphere, they accumulated a weight of more than 200 kilograms at a single point, which gave the apparatus an immutable fixity.

They were falling, and through the gaping aperture at their feet they saw the Mercurian panorama approaching them with vertiginous rapidity, filling the entire space. The exact configuration of the ground now appeared to them as clearly as if they were floating in a balloon at a height of a few kilometers. The mountains launched their sharp peaks towards them, while projecting gigantic shadows from their bases, and expanses of water glowed with the fiery reflections of the last rays of the setting Sun. Mute with amazement, clinging to the lines that attached them to the sphere, the voyagers kept their eyes riveted to the world that was attracting them with irresistible force, wondering anxiously whether the moment of impact might be the moment of death.

They were falling…falling…

Suddenly, there was a frightful shock, accompanied by a terrible noise; one would have thought that the vehicle had shattered into tiny pieces.

The four Terrans uttered screams of terror.

"Mercury!" shouted Fricoulet, in jest. "The whole world's coming down!" He had not finished when a new shock, less violent, almost broke their attachments. Then, immediately afterwards, one after another, came a third and a fourth…soon, rolling madly, the sphere began to tumble downwards.

The voyagers, sometimes upside-down and sometimes the right way up, were blinded by thick dust, deafened by the thunderous noise the metal made as it rolled over the ground and bewildered by the sensation of being borne away by that inexplicable whirlwind. What had happened was, however, quite simple. In its fall, the sphere had met one of the high mountains of Mercury half way up; the violence of the impact had caused the sphere to rebound, like a balloon, to a height of some 50 meters; then it had fallen further on, and rebounded again, until the moment when, exhausting its force in successive bounds, it had begun to roll down the side of the mountain, knocking down trees, dislodging rocks and crossing ravines and streams, like an avalanche. In less than ten minutes, it arrived on the plain after a journey of eight kilometers; then it stopped.

"Oof!" sighed Fricoulet. "I thought it would never end." Prudently, he waited for a few seconds. "However," he added, "this time I believe we've arrived. What do you think?" No one replied to this question. "Damn!" he muttered. "My friends don't have solid heads—just as long as we haven't lost one or two of them along the way…"

Rapidly, he rid himself of the wire that bound him to the metal pivot, rummaged in his pocket and bought out his little magnesium torch, which immediately dispersed a dazzling light within the sphere. His three companions were all there; he let out a sigh of relief. On looking at them, though, he burst out laughing almost immediately. In a state of collapse, with their heads slumped on their breasts, their arms hanging down alongside their bodies and their legs limp, they looked for all the world like the marionettes maneuvered in the *Guignols* of the Champs-Elysées for the amusement of children and soldiers. Cut the strings that make one of the aforementioned marionettes move, and you would have an almost exact idea of the appearance of the unfortunate Terrans…

"The fact is," the engineer murmured, "that one would have to have a damned strong heart in one's breast to withstand such a singular means of traveling." While speaking, he untied his companions one by one and laid them out on the circular floor. After that, he went outside to investigate the lie of the land.

Night had fallen and everything around the young man was dark and silent. It seemed to him, however, that he could hear a confused murmur not far away, similar to that produced by the waters of a stream running over pebbles. As he stood still, not knowing which way to go, a star suddenly appeared in the clear sky, where numerous stars were sparkling, burning incomparably brightly amid the nocturnal fires illuminating space, whose gentle and indecisive light fell upon Fricoulet. At the same time the surrounding landscape emerged from the shadows, almost distinctly outlined, although blurred by the evening mist.

"Thank you, Venus," the engineer said, blithely, nodding his head in the direction of the radiant star.

Looking around him, then, he observed that he was at the foot of a very high mountain, on the edge of a forest whose trees had stopped the sphere. Not far away, snaking down the mountain-side, a stream was singing in a crystalline voice, reflecting the discreet light of Venus in its waters.

It only took Fricoulet five minutes to grab the first receptacle that came to hand from the sphere, run to the stream, fill it up and come back to throw the contents in his companions' faces. Hardly had the liquid touched their skin, however, when Mikhail Ossipoff and his two companions in misfortune began to scream horribly.

"Fire! Fire!" howled Farenheit, leaping to his feet. Then, noticing Fricoulet standing at the entrance to the sphere, looking at his friend in bewilderment, he groaned: "By God! What's this dirty trick?" And he advanced upon the engineer with his fists raised threateningly.

"Now then, now then!" retorted the engineer. "Is that how you thank me for the care I've given you?"

"A funny sort of care, in truth," said Ossipoff, in his turn. "A singular fashion of bring people round, dousing them in boiling water!"

"Boiling water?" repeated Fricoulet. "Have you gone mad?"

"Isn't it you that's gone mad?" cried Gontran, dolorously mopping his face with his handkerchief.

"Hot water?" the engineer continued. "But I just fetched it from that stream…over there!"

He had not finished speaking when Farenheit ran out, in order to be the first to check it out. Forgetful of the special laws regulating weight on the surface of a world that was new to him, though, he arrived at the place indicated by Fricoulet in a single bound, even though it was ten meters away. He fell into the stream, in which he sank up to his knees.

There were screams, curses and lamentations then, which were still pouring forth when they pulled the unfortunate Yankee out, with the skin on his legs almost coming away.

"Damn it!" murmured Fricoulet, while applying an improvised dressing. "There's nothing like bathing one's feet in a hot water to clear the head."

Gontran, greatly amused by the American's grimaces, came to shake his hand energetically. "Thank you, Mr. Farenheit," he said. "Thank you!"

"For what?" asked the other, astonished.

"For having given us, by virtue of that little accident, certain proof that the ground on which we're standing at this moment really is the surface of Mercury."

Farenheit looked hard at his interlocutor, to see whether he was mocking him, but Flammermont's serious expression fooled him and he stifled the ill-tempered words he was about to pronounce with a groan.

"Did you think, then, Gontran," Ossipoff said, "that we needed such proof to know where we are?"

The young man sketched a vague gesture. "My God!" he stammered. "Perhaps it wasn't entirely necessary."

"I'd say more—that it was needless." Raising his arms toward the sky, the scientist added: "Do we not have, there above our heads, a marvelous indicator, which, better than any other, can guide us on our way and inform us of our position?"

"It is, indeed, true," said Gontran, "that by the positions of the stars…"

Fricoulet interrupted him. "Permit me, however, to observe, Monsieur Ossipoff, that the sky, seen from Mercury or other planets, is absolutely the same as when seen from Earth. Do we not perceive there, almost at the zenith, the seven stars of the Great Bear? Isn't that Orion on our left, and Rigel, shining not far from the Pleiades? On our right, do we not see Arcturus, Vega, Procyon and Capella? Thus, we can scarcely have recourse to the starry vault to reassure ourselves that we're really on the Mercurian surface."

Ossipoff greeted these words with brief mocking laughter.

"You're forgetting," he said, "that Venus can shine with such an intense light for the planet Mercury alone. If that doesn't seem conclusive to you....there's Mars, over there...there's Jupiter...and finally, there's the Earth. Tell me, from which world in the sidereal system can one perceive the different planets I've just named, in those positions and with those dimensions?" He looked at the engineer triumphantly.

"Take note," replied Fricoulet, "that I had no need of what you have just told me to form an opinion as to the world on which we're standing—but I must insist on the point that, by virtue of the prodigious distance of the stars, the perspectives don't change, and that..."

"Pardon me," said Gontran, looking Fricoulet up and down disdainfully, "But is this little astronomical discourse addressed to me?"

"Not at all, not at all," the engineer hastened to reply. "It was for Mr. Farenheit's benefit."

"By God!" grumbled the latter, considering his calves with a piteous expression. "The boiling water from the stream's turned them scarlet! If you're talking to me you're wasting your time, for I care about all that as much as..." He finished his sentence by flicking his thumbnail against his teeth.

To describe Ossipoff's scornful expression, on hearing the American express himself thus, would be impossible. He pivoted on his heels and shrugged his shoulders—but was utterly amazed to see Flammermont draw away at a run and then, after a few strides, take off into the air with a prodigious leap.

"Gontran!" cried Fricoulet. "Gontran, what are you doing?"

"I've got it!" replied the young Comte. "I've got it!" He was brandishing something at the end of his arm. The darkness did not allow them to distinguish it clearly, but it appeared to be struggling violently. At the same time, piercing and desperate cries became audible, disturbing the majestic silence of the night and awakening mysterious echoes in the depths of the immense forest.

Meanwhile, Gontran had touched down and briskly returned to his companions. "There," he said, laughing. "This will make a succulent meal." And he held up a strange animal, which bore a certain resemblance to a bird, in the sense that it was provided with membranous wings like a bat's. Its head, which had only one eye, placed in the middle of the forehead, was equipped with a long curling tube that widened out, at its extremity, like the mouth of a hunting-horn. It had no paws, but its wings were furnished with hook-like claws, which the animal obviously used to suspend itself from tree-branches when resting.

The Terrans, especially Fricoulet, studied this creature with an interest mingled with amazement.

"And you think that's good to eat?" asked Farenheit, in whose eyes the flying creature had no other interest than the culinary adaptation that might be made of it.

"My word! You're asking me a question I can no more answer than you can—as nothing in Nature is created without a purpose, however, it's perhaps permissible to think that the animal is edible. Thus, if your heart tells you so…"

"No, not the heart but the stomach," replied Gontran, who was already preparing the creature enthusiastically. "I don't know whether that nutriment made of mastic on the Moon or the plants we minced on Venus suited your stomachs, but this bird has awakened carnivorous appetite in mine."

While the young Comte was speaking, Farenheit had collected some twigs, which he heaped up; then, striking a match, he set light to the improvised pyre, which was soon transformed into a veritable brazier. A few minutes later, the Mercurian flyer, threaded on to a branch of green wood by way of a spit, was sizzling over the flames, spreading a pleasant odor of hot fat through the atmosphere—which our voyagers' nostrils savored appreciatively.

As he watched over his roast, Gontran became pensive.

"What are you thinking, dear boy?" asked Mikhail Ossipoff.

"I'm thinking that we're going to encounter many difficulties traveling rapidly through this unknown world, with no map of any sort to guide us—unless that rogue Sharp hasn't robbed us of everything."

"We have nothing to grieve over with respect to a Mercurian map," the old man replied, "since terrestrial astronomers have never been able to study this planet well enough to be able to draw one. Your apprehension is vain, though—what's 15,000 kilometers around to people like us?"

"Especially given that," added Fricoulet, "constituted as we are, it's exactly as if we were equipped with seven league boots."

"To the table! To the table!" cried the American, at that moment.

"But your roast can't be done yet," declared Flamermont.

"I beg your pardon," retorted Farenheit, watch in hand. "It's been on the fire for ten minutes."

"All right—but it'll be bloody."

"Pardon? Those ten minutes are really 40."

"I don't understand."

"Since Mercury completes its voyage round the Sun in a quarter of the time that the Earth takes to complete its own, the minutes on this planet must be worth four times as much as terrestrial minutes."

No one replied, everyone being too hungry to refute this bizarre theory.

While gnawing one of the flyer's wings, Farenheit said: "So, if I've understood what you were saying during the journey, Mercury is an uninhabited world?"

376

Fricoulet shrugged his shoulders. "How can you say such things when you have proof to the contrary in your hand?"

The American rounded his eyes. "This isn't proof," he replied, "it's a bird's wing."

"What is that bird," riposted the engineer, "if not an inhabitant of Mercury?"

At the unexpected sally, the American burst out laughing, and Gontran shared his hilarity.

"In truth," said the young man, "you want to claim that this bird with a trunk is a representative of Mercurian humankind?"[127]

"Why not?"

"Take note, my dear Gontran," said Ossipoff, in his turn, "that Mercury is a very young planet, and its humankind ought to correspond to the terrestrial Quaternary period. On the other hand, it could be that the succession of living species might be different from that on our world, and that Mercurian humankind has a form quite different from the one affected on the other planets."

Gontran had remained nonplussed during this explanation; when the old man had finished, he pulled a disgusted face and threw away the piece of meat he had been about to eat hungrily.

"What's got into you?" asked Fricoulet, whose mouth was full.

"I feel like a cannibal!" declared Flammermont.

"Bah!" growled the American. "An inhabitant of Mercury! That's of no consequence—and anyway, it had only to warn you."

Abruptly, without any transition, night gave way to day.

Scarcely had the Sun appeared on the horizon than it rose rapidly into the sky, deluging the planet with torrents of light and heat. While his companions were sponging their foreheads, Ossipoff, careless of sunstroke, had seized his telescope. Aiming it at the radiant star, he measured its diameter with the aid of a micrometer.

"That's exactly right," he murmured, in a satisfied tone. "75 minutes."

"What about the Earth?" asked the American. "What diameter does that present?"

"Less than half as much—only 32 minutes."

"We can't get under way now," said Fricoulet, "not without being roasted alive, at least. If you ask me, we ought to lie down beneath the thick and impenetrable vault formed by the foliage of the trees, and sleep while we wait for the night."

---

[127] The authors are evidently using *humanité* [humankind] here merely to signify "dominant species" rather than to signify any closer biological kinship between the voyagers and their meal; even so, it is hardly surprising that Gontran reacts as he does, and perhaps a little odd that the narrative voice has no obvious sympathy with his sentiment.

When dusk fell, enveloping the landscape with a soft and warm gilded light, the voyagers prepared to leave. They took nothing with them but their weapons, indispensable in case they encountered Sharp, and a few cubes of the nutritive paste, in case no inhabitant of Mercury came within their range. They left the sphere and all its contents next to the stream, with no fear that any thief would get his hands on it.

"What are we going to do to make sure we don't get lost?" asked Flammermont.

"According to my observations," the old scientist replied, "we must presently be on the edge of the tropical zone. Navigating by the stars, nothing should be easier than for us to circle the planet by set a course eastwards."

"But there must certainly be seas and oceans on this unknown world! How are we going to cross them?"

"We'll think about that."

While chatting, they had set off, and five minutes had sufficed for them to cover a kilometer. They went on at that speed until midnight or thereabouts, crossing arid plains, going over steep hills, clearing a path—with great difficulty—through forests of titanic trees festooned with enormous lianas, and inextricable thickets through which they had to fight their way, like tiny insects in the webs of immense spiders.

Then, all of a sudden, the sky darkened. The atmosphere filled up with thick clouds, behind which the twinkling stars vanished, and opaque shadows descended upon the planet like a shroud. The voyagers were forced to call a halt and wait for daylight.

At dawn, as they prepared to set off again, desirous of taking advantage of the brief interval in which the heat was bearable to cover a few more leagues, Mikhail Ossipoff—who had taken the lead—suddenly stopped. "Water!" he exclaimed. "Water!" Extending his hand, he showed his companions a liquid expanse, which reflected the Sun's golden rays not far away. On the shore, the verdant foliage of gigantic trees hung down, seeming to exude a delightful coolness into the surroundings. "If you ask me, my friends," said the scientist, "We should push on that far, then stop to await the dusk."

"How far away do you think that oasis is?" asked the American, sponging his forehead.

"15 kilometers, at the most," Fricoulet replied.

"That'll take us half an hour. A little courage, and we can enjoy a delightful rest until the evening."

With these words, pronounced in an encouraging tone by Flammermont, they started walking again. Strangely enough, though, the voyagers, although going forward, did not seem to be getting any closer to their goal. The water was still sparkling and the trees continued to extend their tresses toward the sky, but it seemed that the region retreated as Ossipoff and his companions approached.

The American took out his watch. "We've already been marching for 15 minutes," he grumbled. "15 minutes to make 15 kilometers! That's inadmissible—you were mistaken in your estimate of the distance, my dear Monsieur Fricoulet."

"That's quite possible," replied the latter, who was examining the horizon pensively, putting his hand over his eyes to shade them from the Sun.

"Mind you," said Gontran, in his turn, "there's something strange and abnormal about what's happening. Have you noticed that the water and those trees look just the same as they did some while ago? Now, the principles of optics…"

The engineer clapped his hands. "I've got it!" he exclaimed. "I can explain the phenomenon—it's a mirage. We're victims of an optical illusion similar to those that often present themselves in the African desert."

"A mirage," repeated Farenheit, in a disappointed tone. "That water doesn't exist, then?"

"That's not such a great pity," Gontran observed, "for it would be very hot. It's the shade of the trees that I regret."

"Let's not despair," said Fricoulet, swiftly. "Let's walk on a little; it's quite possible that the landscape really exists."

The voyagers' steadfastness was submitted to a rude proof; the country they were passing through was a sort of arid desert. As far as they eye could see, nothing was visible but dry yellow soil—not a single tree or blade of grass, but sand and more sand, and, above their heads, in the clear sky, the enormous disk of the Sun, pouring forth its torrential radiation, which charred their limbs and corroded their entrails.

Finally, their strength exhausted, they stopped. A canvas tent was extended on four poles and the voyagers lay down in the square shadow that the primitive shelter projected on the burning ground until the evening.

When the day star had been replaced in the sidereal immensity by the gentler light of Venus, the voyagers abandoned their encampment, determined to march as far as necessary to get out of that desolate land.

About midnight, after traveling 50 kilometers, they passed into a new region and the vegetation reappeared, even more luxuriant than in the place where they had come down. The desert sands were succeeded by a fertile and grassy plain; in the distance, they heard the murmur of running water rippling over stones.

"Farenheit! Farenheit!" called Ossipoff, seeing the American go on ahead. "Where are you going?"

"To take a bath," he replied, without stopping.

"The fool will scald himself!" said Flammermont, running after him.

Farenheit had a few strides in hand, with the result that he disappeared beneath the tall trees before the young man had caught up with him.

Suddenly the American uttered a cry of joy. Like a silver sheet, a liquid immensity extended in front of him, its surface reflecting the twinkling stars crowding the firmament. "By God!" he muttered, hastening his steps, "Even if that water's hot enough to cook eggs, a bath in it will seem cool by comparison with the Sun's rays."

In two bounds he reached the bank, stripped off his clothes—only retaining his underpants—and went into the water. Although warm, the water did indeed seem to him to be lower in temperature than the hot atmosphere of the day, and he plunged into it with unexpected sensuality, diving, floating and drawing himself along with skilful strokes, good swimmer that he was.

Without noticing it, Farenheit had drawn some distance away from the shore, and had given no thought to drawing his aquatic exercises to a close, when suddenly, a few meters away from him, the water became very turbulent, and a dark mass surfaced, heading for the shore. Immediately, the idea of crocodiles occurred to him—and, in spite of the water temperature, a cold chill ran down his spine. Instinctively, his hand sought his revolver in its usual place—but he was in his underpants. "By God!" he groaned. "As long as my friends arrive in time!"

Meanwhile, the disquieting mass had landed, and was slowly and painfully hoisting itself out of the water, emitting formidable growls. By the light of Venus, the American made out, albeit rather vaguely, an enormous body terminating in a tail, which appeared to measure no less than 50 or 60 meters. The anterior part of the animal seemed to form nothing but a head: a monstrous, frightful head, which terminated in a rigid trunk shaped like a trumpet, similar to the one with which the head of the Mercurian inhabitant the voyagers had eaten had been equipped.

From where he was, Farenheit could hear the monster's powerful breathing. Disturbing the atmospheric layers, it produced violent currents of air whose movement reached the swimmer. The latter was ill at ease, and cursed the ill-conceived idea he had had of taking a bath.

Suddenly, he heard a terrible scream, with nothing human about it. Immediately, though, an anguished voice coming from the shore called for help!

"By God!" muttered Farenheit. "What's happening? Has the monster attacked my friends?" Without considering that his movements might attract the animal's attention, he began swimming vigorously, making a slight detour in order to land as quickly as possible and lend a strong hand to his companions.

"Help! Help!" repeated the same voice.

The American went forward rapidly. "Courage!" he shouted. "Courage! I'm coming!"

As if to reply to him, the monster released a howl that rent the air frightfully; one might have taken it for the screech of a steam-driven siren.

As Farenheit came out of the water, he perceived a white shape clinging to a bush. "Hold on!" he cried. "Hold on, here I am!"

"Help me, Monsieur Farenheit! Help me!"

"Mademoiselle Selena!" exclaimed the American, so stupefied that he stopped dead.

"Quickly, quickly! I can't hold on any longer!"

The white shape seemed to separate from the tree and, struggling all the while, advanced toward the monster, whose trunk, aimed towards her, was like a gulf ready to swallow her up.

At that moment, a loud noise broke out beneath the trees; it was Ossipoff and his companions, running in search of Farenheit. "Shoot! Shoot!" the American shouted to them, powerless to save the young woman from the inevitable death that awaited her.

A volley of shots burst forth, awakening echoes in the distance like the rumbling of thunder. Frightened by the noise, to which its ears were completely unaccustomed, and perhaps struck by one of the bullets, the Mercurian monster uttered a horrible groan and plunged into the lake, disappearing before the Terrans' eyes.

"Selena!" cried Gontran, desperately, bounding toward the white form extended on the ground.

Ossipoff arrived next to his daughter's body almost at the same time as the young man. "My child!" he moaned. "My beloved daughter! It's you! It's really you that I see." He had knelt down and taken her in his arms, cradling her like an infant.

Fricoulet moved Gontran slightly to one side and put his hand on the young woman's chest. "She's only fainted," he declared. "Don't worry, Monsieur Ossipoff—and you too, Gontran. Don't despair, it's absolutely nothing. If you want, we can go back at a forced march to the place where we left the sphere. There, in my pharmaceutical bag, I can find the medicines Mademoiselle Selena needs."

"But how can we transport her?" said Ossipoff.

"In a very simple manner," declared Farenheit, who had finished getting dressed. "You'll see."

He broke two long and flexible branches from the nearest tree, to which he attached the old man's ample frock-coat, like a canvas extended on a camp-bed. They laid the young woman on it; then he and Gontran put the shafts of the improvised litter on their shoulders and set off at the double, followed by Fricoulet and Ossipoff.

Every 20 kilometers the porters were relieved; every 40 kilometers they stopped for ten minutes to rest.

When dawn broke, the voyagers were back in the sphere, gathered around Selena—who, having emerged from her torpor thanks to the intelligent ministrations of Fricoulet, was smiling at them softly.

Of the four voyagers, Farenheit was certainly the one who manifested the greatest joy on seeing the young woman come round. "How good you are, Mr.

Farenheit," she said, holding out her hand to him, "And how much pleasure it seems to give you to see me again."

"Of course!" the American replied. "I assume that you'll be able to give me news of that wretch Sharp!"

"Me!" she replied, in astonishment. "I can't tell you anything, except that he left four days ago."

"Left!" cried Ossipoff and his companions. "For what destination?"

"For the Sun."

"But what about you?"

"He abandoned me here, because I was an excess weight in the vehicle that might compromise his voyage."

Gontran clenched his fists in fury. "Oh, the wretch...the wretch! He'll pay dearly for that!"

Farenheit responded with a roar: "For that, you'll have to get your hands on him. As we're stuck here for the rest of our lives, without any hope of ever seeing our native planet again..."

"What does it matter?" murmured Ossipoff, lost in the joy of holding his beloved daughter in his arms.

"By God!" grumbled the American. "That's easy for you to say—you've recovered your daughter...but Sharp has escaped me yet again."

"And this time for good," sniggered Fricoulet.

Farenheit shrugged his shoulders and went away in search of inhabitants of Mercury on which he could vent his fury. In fact, he came back after half an hour bearing a chaplet of birds attached to his belt, similar in all respects to the one that Gontran had killed.

"Good hunting!" said Fricoulet, rubbing his hands with evident contentment.

"Do you know that something very strange is happening in the sky?" the American replied. "There's a star that seems to be visibly increasing in size."

The engineer shrugged his shoulders, laughing. "Optical illusion," he said.

"I assure you that I saw it clearly, especially as the star's light illuminates a whole region of space."

The American spoke so definitely and in so convincing a manner that Fricoulet followed him outside. Scarcely had he lifted his eyes to the sky than he raced back in and armed himself with Ossipoff's telescope. He aimed it at the point indicated by the American. "A comet!" he cried. "A comet!"

Everyone came to join him, including Selena. The old scientist snatched the instrument from the engineer's hands, directed it towards the star, and stood there for a long time, engrossed in contemplation. Finally, he murmured: "It is, indeed, a comet." Then, looking around the neighborhood, he said: "If you ask me, we should establish ourselves provisionally at the top of that little hill down there; we'll be admirably placed to devote ourselves to our astronomical observations; at the same time, from the hygienic point of view, we'll be less exposed to the solar radiation."

By virtue of the low weight at the planet's surface, the four Terrans soon managed to roll the sphere to the place indicated by the aged scientist. It was a little wooded eminence, raised about 50 meters above ground level and descending a gentle slope to the stream in which Farenheit had taken an ill-advised footbath on the day before last.

When he awoke the next morning, Ossipoff's first concern was to climb the internal stairway that led to the top of the sphere, where he had installed his optical instruments. In response to the exclamations he made, his companions joined him, and perceived the previous evening's meteor advancing toward the Sun with vertiginous rapidity, extending a vast tail across the sky.

After remaining silent for a moment, dazzled by the magical spectacle, Selena asked: "Every comet has a name, doesn't it, Father? What's that one called?"

The astronomer shook his head doubtfully. "I don't know," he replied.

"What? You don't know? But I thought…"

"You thought wrong," he replied, in a slightly dry tone. "These errant bodies, baptized with the name of comets, are as numerous in space as the fish in the bosom of the sea. It might well be that we have a new comet before our eyes, arriving from infinity, which our Sun has deflected from its course."

At that moment, Gontran took a step backwards. "I say," he said. "Isn't there a danger that this comet will crash into us. It seems to be heading directly for us."

Fricoulet, examining the heavenly body attentively, murmured: "You might well be right in your prognostication, for it will certainly intersect Mercury's orbit." A moment later, he added: "That, of course, might well be the end—who can tell, in fact, what might result from such a collision?"

All day, despite the fiery torrent pouring from the sky, the Terrans remained at their observation-post, watching in terror as the star that might be bringing their death increased in magnitude. The three parts of the comet could now be clearly distinguished: the enormous, monstrous head, surrounded by its luminous tresses, next to which the solar light paled, and the tail, sweeping space with its flaming plume.

As night approached, the atmosphere seemed to catch fire all of a sudden; the heat became stifling, the air grew thinner and, under the burden of an inexplicable asphyxia, the voyagers lost consciousness.

Chapter XXVIII
Riding a Comet

"Now then! That's a bit much!" Sitting up on his elbow, Flammermont studied his companions, who were lying around him in various positions and sleeping profoundly. The young man had just woken up, and his eyes, as they opened, had naturally turned in Selena's direction. But was Gontran not yet fully awake, or was he the victim of an optical illusion? The graceful face of the young woman still seemed to him to be as black as ink. He looked at the other voyagers. All of them seemed to have been plunged into soot-bath from top to toe.

"Let's see," he stammered, "Let's see—I must be dreaming...or perhaps, while I was asleep, some inexplicable accident has overtaken my retinas." He tried to rub his eyes, but an abrupt movement stopped his hands half-way. His hands, too, were black, and his white twill suit appeared to have been starched with black dye.

"What! That really is a bit much!" Not without difficulty, still numbed by the strange sleep that had knocked him out along with his companions, he got to his feet, went to Fricoulet and shook him violently by his shoulders.

"Eh? What? What's happening?" groaned the startled engineer. Then, perceiving Gontran, who was leaning over him anxiously, he burst out laughing. "Oh, that's very good!" he said. "You need some soap, my poor friend—unless your skin is so sensitive that 24 hours of Sun have transformed you into an Ethiopian." He writhed with laughter—and his hilarity increased when he saw that everyone around him had been subjected to the same fate as Flammermont. "Oh, what a fine set of heads!" he exclaimed. "Look, Gontran—Ossipoff's, with his hairy and bushy beard, looks exactly like a wolf's head. Ha ha! And Farenheit's...no, Farenheit's worth his weight in gold!" Eventually, he succeeded in recovering his self-control and asked: "What is this joke?"

"It was to get an explanation," Gontran muttered, "that I came to wake you up. You're mocking the others, but if you take the trouble to look at yourself..." He had taken a small grooming-kit from his pocket and held out a tiny mirror to the engineer, just large enough for him to see one eye and the end of his nose therein.

Fricoulet saw the face of the most successful Auvergnian that had ever embellished a coal-merchant's shop. "Oh, that's very good! It's marvelous!" he exclaimed, through tears of laughter.

"You'd be much better employed explaining the cause of this phenomenon to me," Gontran grumbled.

The engineer looked around, hoping to find some clue in the neighborhood that would put him on the track of what he sought. Nothing had changed; as on the previous evening, he and his companions were on the summit of the hill on to which they had rolled the sphere. Down below, in the valley depths, blurred by a sort of mist, was the rounded dome of the forest. The noise of the stream tinkling over its pebbles was audible. He got to his feet then, and looked up; the sky was darkened by a kind of fog that was falling in a fine drizzle, or rather an impalpable dust; it was spreading over the ground, giving the plants and the trees a uniform and desolate grey tint.

"Have you ever visited a coal-mining region?" the engineer asked, suddenly.

"No—why?"

"Because our surroundings have exactly the same appearance; one could swear that what's floating in the air is coal-dust."

"That doesn't tell us…"

"Why we're so utterly ridiculous—you're right…but perhaps Monsieur Ossipoff can enlighten us on that subject." And he went over to the old man, with the intention of waking him up.

Gontran stopped him. Plannting himself in front of his friend, he said, desolately: "Do I look as grotesque as all that?"

"Grotesque, no—but you do look like a native from African." Immediately, he added: "A respectable one, of course."

The young Comte made a desperate gesture. "But I don't want Selena to see me like this."

Fricoulet shrugged. "What inconvenience is there in that, since she's in exactly the same state? On the contrary, you and she form the best-matched couple one can imagine—from the viewpoint of color, that is."

"Oh, that's quite different," murmured Gontran. "A woman is always beautiful."

Fricoulet pulled a face. "If you're so worried about your image," he said, "it might perhaps be as well for us to have a wash. The stream's close at hand—let's hurry to make our ablutions before the others wake up."

In a few strides, the two friends went down the side of the hill, raising clouds of the fine and impalpable dust in which the ground was covered at every step. Gontran who had drawn a few meters ahead of Fricoulet, uttered a cry of desperation, pointing to the stream. "Ink!" he said. "It's ink that's running there, I swear. It's enough to drive one mad!"

The engineer knelt down on the bank, took a few drops of water in the palm of his hand and observed, to his amazement, that the stream too had been subjected to a transformation analogous to their own.

"Well?" said Flammermont.

"I don't understand it at all."

At that moment, exclamations burst forth from the direction of the camp, and the two young men, thinking that there had been an accident, hastened to rejoin their companions.

The latter, having awoken, were standing up, gesticulating like lunatics and speaking with extreme rapidity. "It's a practical joke, I tell you," Farenheit howled. "Now, as it's not carnival time, I don't accept that anyone can abuse my sleep to ridicule me in this manner."

"But you're in error, my dear Mr. Farenheit. How can you think that Monsieur de Flammermont, being such a serious and well-brought-up fellow, could ever...? As for young Fricoulet, though—that one, I could readily believe..."

"No, Papa," Selena said, in her turn. "Gontran would certainly not have allowed Monsieur Fricoulet to daub me in this fashion."

"What, then? What?" roared the American, drawing his revolver. "I cannot tolerate such an insult to the starry flag of the United States!"

Mocking laughter burst out behind him, making Farenheit turn round. He found himself face to face with the engineer. "By God!" he exclaimed. "You too!"

"Yes, me too—like you, like Gontran, like the trees, like the stream itself..." He clapped the American on the shoulder amicably. "Calm down, Mr. Farenheit," he said. "The author of this amiable tomfoolery—for it's a literal fireplace-builder's farce[128]—is not among us. She's above us, and beyond the reach of your fists...for I suppose that this is simply the work of Dame Nature."

Ossipoff straightened up abruptly. "What do you suppose, then?" he murmured.

"Me? Nothing at all—except that we're in the presence of a phenomenon that's presumably unique to the planet on which we presently find ourselves."

The American folded his arms and, addressing the old man, said to him with surprising animation: "And you think I'll be content with that? Me, whom you've dragged into this unexpected and unprecedented adventure! When a phenomenon presents itself, it's your job, as scientists, to explain to the ignorant..."

"Or to imbeciles," said Fricoulet.

"Or to imbeciles," repeated the American, "the cause of the phenomenon...and you can shut up! You have nothing to say! No, my dear sir, that can't be allowed. Since you're an expert on the sky, you're supposed to understand the things that happen there. Error, Monsieur Ossipoff, error! You'll answer..." And he aimed the barrel of his revolver at the old man's breast.

Selena screamed, and Gontran, hurling himself upon the American, disarmed him.

Coldly, Farenheit picked up his carbine and loaded it.

"Now then!" cried Fricoulet. "You're mad! Is it because you're disguised as a blackface that you've become so ferocious?"

---

[128] This wordplay does not translate; the literal meaning of *fumisterie*, whose metaphorical meaning I have translated as "tomfoolery," refers to the work of a fireplace-installer.

Ossipoff, impassive thus far, advanced toward the American with his fists clenched, in a threatening manner. "Leave him alone," he growled. "Leave him—I'll settle this myself."

Fricoulet put his arms round him. "You think so, Monsieur Ossipoff?" he exclaimed. "But you're losing your head too! What the Devil's going on? Come on—a little self-control. Two men like you and Mr. Farenheit can't use your fists to settle a trivial disagreement like this." While speaing, he made every effort to restrain the old man, who was struggling and shouting, howling like a fanatic.

Abruptly, Farenheit freed the arms on to which Gontran was hanging, and shook him off so violently and unexpectedly that the poor young man was thrown backwards, landing with his limbs in the air 50 meters away. Then, putting his carbine over his shoulder, the American turned on his heel and strode away. In a few seconds, he had disappeared.

Gontran came back furiously, proffering death-threats. "Where is he?" he growled. "Where is he?"

No one answered him. Ossipoff, seated on the ground, was already absorbed in a series of gigantic calculations accompanied by bizarre diagrams. Selena, her face hidden in hr hands, was weeping copiously and uttering plaintive whining sounds.

Gontran walked around and around the sphere like a horse in a riding-school, grinding his teeth and shaking his fists at the sky. Suddenly, the hazard of his course having brought him level with the young woman, he stopped short and said, in a bitter—almost insolent—voice: "In truth, Mademoiselle, I'd be very grateful if you'd tell me the cause of your despair. Why these tears? Presumably, it's because Nature has decided to blacken my complexion..." He shook his head and added, with a mocking laugh: "Of course! I understand, poor imbecile that I was...it was my physical appearance that pleased you, nothing else...and the physique having deteriorated, from your viewpoint, your affection has flowed away with your tears...but if the beauty of my soul, Mademoiselle, had counted for anything in the love that you attempted to cultivate for me, you would not be as dejected as you are...for what is the material envelope, I ask you, by comparison...?"

He stopped and noticed Fricoulet, who was listening to him speak and staring at him in bewilderment. "Moreover," he continued, "your attitude offers me superabundant proof that you only possess a very imperfect notion of esthetics. Fricoulet will tell you that there are handsome black men, just as there are handsome white men...esthetics has this in common with morality: that it depends on education...it changes with the latitudes..."

He spoke rapidly, cutting his sentences short and mincing his words, in such a way that Fricoulet was unable to interrupt him. "Morality..." repeated the young Comte, with a burst of strange laughter. "Here, Mademoiselle, are things that you probably do not know…certain tribes of Tierra del Fuego have the custom of eating their old people…"

At these words, Selena released a piercing scream and precipitated herself toward her father, shielding him with her body. "Look out, Father," she said. "Monsieur de Flammermont wants to eat you."

The old man's pencil paused. "What does it mater?" he replied, coldly. "I'll give him my body, on condition that he leaves me my head, to make calculations." And he plunged back into his reckonings.

Gontran shrugged his shoulders and continued: "It's the same for beauty; if I belonged to certain tribes of Oceania, I'd be able to take great exception to the fact that you wear neither feathers in your hair, nor shells in your ears, nor a ring in your nose."

Selena straightened up, and said, in a voice full of dignity: "If it is necessary for me to renounce the customs of my native land in order to please you, Monsieur, it is because you no longer love me. Very well, Monsieur, I release you from your promise." Dissolving in tears, she threw herself into her father's arms, knocking him over.

Fricoulet watched the bizarre scene, mutely and impassively. He put his head in his hands and murmured: "My word, I'm going mad!" Then, going to Selena, he said, in a dispassionate tone: "Don't cry like this, Mademoiselle. One fiancé lost, ten found. If he releases you from your promise, would you care to consider me and ask Monsieur your father to ask for my hand?"

Immediately, Gontran replied: "If that's the way it is, I demand to return to Paris. I sacrificed my career because of that old ingrate; I left my family and my fatherland for that shrew…but now that it's all off…"

He interrupted himself abruptly and seized Fricoulet by the throat as the latter cried out, in a furious voice: "Ingrate! Shrew! Take back those epithets, or…" A menacing gesture completed the sentence.

"Why are you getting mixed up in it?" complained the young Comte.

"I'm defending the honor of my new family," replied the engineer.

During this exchange, Ossipoff impassively continued his calculations and Selena wept even more copiously.

"Anyway," Fricoulet went on, in a ringing voice, accompanying his words with disordered gestures, "what are you doing here? Now that you're no longer Mademoiselle Selena's fiancé, you're becoming a nuisance, an intruder…go back where you came from and leave us to enjoy our honeymoon in peace."

"But that's all I ask!" howled Flammermont. "I only ask to return to my position in St. Petersburg. Diplomacy, that's my job—as for marriage, it was no more than a temporary whim."

"In that case, what's keeping you?"

The young man shrugged his shoulders. "Do you imagine, by chance that I can return on foot?"

"Is it the means of locomotion that you lack?" growled he engineer, taking out his notebook—in which he scribbled a few illegible lines. "Here—look at this, and tell me what you think of it!"

Gontran opened his eyes wide.

"That?" he stammered. "That?"

"Eh? Yes! What? You, a scientist, don't understand that I've just invented a machine that will enable you to reach the stars?"

"But I want to go to France."

"Well, all roads lead to Rome. Distance is a meaningless word. The stars are as near to one another as the molecules in a steel bar. To abandon this world in fusion, we only have to step on to another one. Well, step!"

While listening to his friend speaking, Gontran had selected a blond, very dry Havana from his cigar case. After having squeezed it next to his ear, like a veritable connoisseur, he delicately cut off the end with his pocket-knife and put it to his lips, sniffing it delicately and rolling it appreciatively between his fingers. Then, taking a match, he lit it. By some strange and inexplicable phenomenon, the match flared up and produced a frightful explosion. At the same time, an intense light, unbearably bright, lit up the sky.

All of them, Gontran first of all, uttered a cry of amazement. Mikhail Ossipoff raised his head from his algebraic calculations and looked at the match very attentively. It projected a light similar to that of an electric bulb over a radius of 25 meters. Flammermont stood there, totally nonplussed, his cigar in one hand and the match in the other, utterly perplexed as to which one he ought to use to ignite the other.

The old scientist got up, and examined this inexplicable phenomenon at length. "Singular...singular..." he stammered, his brow furrowed and his eyelids lowered. "Could it be...?" Turning slowly on his heel and putting his hand above his eyes to give his visual range further extent, he examined the landscape in an anxious fashion.

At that moment, they saw Jonathan Farenheit climbing the side of the hill with giant strides. "By God!" he exclaimed, stopping breathlessly a few paces away. "You're all still standing...I was horribly afraid..." And he sponged his sweat-soaked forehead with his handkerchief.

"What's the matter?" asked Gontran. "And why all this emotion?"

The American turned to the young man. "Do you know," he said, "a funny thing just happened to me—very nearly the same that we experienced the day before yesterday with respect to the water and the trees, in the desert."

"A mirage!" cried the Terrans.

"Yes, a mirage...I seemed to see an immense fire suddenly shining at the top of that hill...a sort of beacon, projecting its light at me. Then I thought that some danger was threatening you—that's why I came running."

Flammermont took a match from his pocket and held it out to the American. "The fire—the beacon," he said. "Here it is."

Farenheit stamped his foot angrily. "Come on," he said. "The practical jokes are starting again. I might as well go away…all the more so as I've seen some very strange things down there…" He had not finished this sentence when he found himself surrounded.

"Strange things," repeated Mikhail Ossipoff, in a bizarre tone. "What were they?"

"Firstly, the region has completely changed since yesterday. The forest on the edge of which our sphere came down, which we went through before going into that frightful desert where we nearly perished, no longer exists."

"No longer exists!" exclaimed Gontran. "You're joking, Mr. Farenheit!" And he pointed toward the trees that raised up their leafy crowns at the foot of the hill.

Fricoulet looked at Ossipoff, putting his finger to his forehead in a significant gesture and indicating the American with an imperceptible inclination of his head.

"My poor Farenheit," the old man said, "you've been the victim of a mirage. You can see the trees perfectly well from here, as we can ourselves."

"Yes, I see them, and I still see them down below—but the forest that measured several leagues in extent yesterday is only a few meters deep today."

"Bah! What is there now in place of the trees?"

"A strange, entirely unfamiliar, country with mountains of diamond."

The listeners shrugged their shoulders, looking at him compassionately.

"You think I'm an idiot," he complained. "I'm no more one than you are, and if I hadn't been mistakenly worried about the danger you were running, I'd already have explored that fantastic and marvelous country. Anyway, you have only to come with me…"

"In that case, Mr. Farenheit," replied Flammermont, "leave us, content with your fairy tales…"

"They're no more fairy tales than your story of the match, my dear chap."

"Oh—that's a bit strong!" Gontran retorted—and, by immediately striking the match that he was holding in his fingers, he produced a phenomenon identical to the first.

The American, surprised by the blinding light that suddenly burst forth in his face, leapt backwards with a mighty "By God!"

Suddenly, Mikhail Ossipoff exclaimed, in an anxious tone: "My friends, my good friends…inexplicable and incomprehensible changes must have occurred here, while we were asleep. This nervous overexcitement to which are all prey, and the formidable explosion produced by a mere match are two proofs—one mental and the other material—that a profound perturbation must have taken place in the atmosphere."

"That's right!" murmured Gontran. "Perhaps the air on the surface of Mercury isn't composed of the same elements as on the surfaces of other planets."

390

"Whatever its composition might be, there's no reason why it shouldn't be the same today as it was yesterday," Fricoulet riposted. "And yet, it's certain…"

"What's certain?"

"Certain that the match experiment is conclusive, for I recall that at the Ecole des Arts et Métiers, the professor often had us detonate pure oxygen by means of a simple match."[129]

"Yes!" exclaimed Ossipoff. "It's definitely pure oxygen that we're breathing. Could any other cause be responsible for the kind of madness that has suddenly struck us? Only…"

"Only what?" demanded the other Terrans, in chorus.

"I wonder how this sudden change in the atmosphere could have been produced."

"Perhaps," suggested Flammermont, timidly, "it's a manifestation of the comet's influence."

The old scientist slapped his forehead. "That's right," he said. "The comet! I'd completely forgotten about it."

"But what's become of it?" asked Fricoulet, pirouetting on his heels, looking upwards, searching all four cardinal points of the sky.

"It's disappeared."

"Disappeared!" exclaimed Osipoff. "That's not possible." He ran to his telescope and aimed it successively in every direction. "Nothing!" he stammered, in amazement. "Absolutely nothing! That's quite incomprehensible." He turned to Flammermont. "How do you explain that?" he asked.

"I don't explain it," the young man replied, with marvelous self-composure. "I merely make the observation."

"Well?" said Farenheit. "In the presence of these surprising and incomprehensible facts, will you continue to doubt what I said a little while ago?"

"Your mountains of diamond?"

"Yes, my mountains of diamond. Follow me, and you won't be long delayed in assuring yourselves that they really exist." He turned on his heel and went down the hill, fooled by his companions, whose initial skepticism had given way to a certain anxiety. Into what new adventure had they been plunged?

Bizarrely enough, as the level of the ground decreased, the air that they were breathing seemed no longer to be the same. As they went downhill, the fever burning in their blood abated, their heads cleared and their nerves relaxed;

---

[129] It is not the oxygen that is exploding, but the match that burns more rapidly—and hence more brightly, although not as productively as the authors seem to think—in pure oxygen than in air. Like several other passages in the narrative, this chapter borrows materials from Jules Verne, who dramatized the intoxicant effects of oxygen in "*Le docteur Ox*" and a famous sequence in *Autour de la lune*, and used a tangential comet strike to precipitate highly improbable anomalous phenomena in *Hector Servadac*.

in brief, they gradually became themselves again. They seemed distanced from themselves as they made these observations, scarcely daring to look at one another, ashamed of falling prey to the temporary insanity that had made them say such ridiculous things.

Eventually, they arrived at the steam in which Fricoulet and Gontran had tried in vain to make their ablutions. They crossed it with a single bound and found themselves at the edge of the forest, into which they went. After taking a few steps, they stopped dead, all in unison, on perceiving a landscape through the trees that they did not remember having seen the day before.

"The mirage, always the mirage," Fricoulet complained.

Nevertheless, he started walking again, carefully, and advanced to the point at which the forest suddenly stopped. One might have thought that a giant hand had torn away the piece of ground on which the Terrans were standing, in order to transplant it to another world, totally different from the one in which the Mercurian trees had taken root. As far as the eye could see, the eye embraced black soil covered in fine dust, sparkling in the sunlight like charcoal dust. Here and there, enormous masses emerged from it, also black and shiny, like burnished silver. Cutting across this plain, running from north to south, swept the black waters of a river, above which floated an impalpable grey cloud. Finally, the horizon was barred by a chain of high mountains, sparkling as all the fires of the Sun played over their surfaces—which, polished like mirrors, reflected an iridescent radiance as far as the Terrans, just as the enormous facets of gigantic brilliants might have done.

Mute with astonishment, Ossipoff and his companions remained motionless beneath the trees, considering the strange land that extended before them, a few meters below he level of the forest itself.

"Well?" cried Farenheit, after giving them time to admire it. "Well, was I as mad as you claimed, when I told you I'd seen mountains of diamond?" And he extended his hand triumphantly toward the radiant horizon.

"Of diamond...of diamond..." muttered Fricoulet. "There's nothing to prove that they aren't mere rock crystal."

The American remained silent for a moment, somewhat abashed. Then he replied, abruptly: "There's nothing to prove that they aren't diamond."

"Agreed!" retorted the engineer. "It will suffice, after all, to obtain a specimen..."

He had no sooner pronounced these words than Farenheit jumped down the bank that separated the truncated forest on whose edge the companions had paused from the other ground, and set off in the direction of the mountains, the objects of his desire.

After a few strides, the Terrans saw him stop, look down at his feet, and then bend down, doubtless to pick up an object that had attracted his attention. Suddenly, though, as if struck by a thunderbolt, the American fell down and lay still.

Obedient to the impulse of his generous nature, and thinking that there had been a simple accident, Flammermont ran to help Jonathan Farenheit. Arriving beside him, he leaned over—but, exactly like his companion, the young man had scarcely bent down than he fell like a dead weight.

Selena uttered a terrible cry and tried to run forward—but Ossipoff seized her by the shoulders, saying: "Reckless!" Turning to Fricoulet, he said, rapidly: "There must be a harmful gas at ground level. How can we save those unfortunates?" Then, to his sobbing daughter, he said: "Come on, don't panic. Give us time to think. The two of us ought to be able to come up with an idea, damn it!"

"I've got it!" exclaimed Fricoulet. "Wait for me here, and don't budge."

Running flat out in the direction of the hill, he disappeared into the trees. A few minutes later, he reappeared, having put on a respirol. Signaling to the old man to keep his hopes up, he precipitated himself toward the place where Flammermont and Farenheit were lying side by side. He kicked up clouds of opaque black dust all around him as he went. He loaded the two inert bodies on to his shoulders, one after the other and came back toward Ossipoff, still running. Then, wrenching off his respirol, he called to the old man: "Take charge of Gontran—I'll keep the American—and quickly, back to the sphere!"

Without asking for an explanation, Ossipoff took Flammermont on his back, and followed the engineer, who was running in front of him, as rapidly as possible. They reached the top of the hill in a few strides. There, they laid the two invalids down, side by side, and Fricoulet, putting his mouth to theirs, set about blowing the air from his own lungs into theirs, as one does with drowned men.

"But why bring them here?" murmured Selena, watching the results of the rescue anxiously.

"Because the air we're breathing is composed of pure oxygen, so the medication I'm applying will be more powerful."

As the engineer finished this speech, the American sat up on his elbow, welcoming his return to life with a formidable sneeze. One might have thought that Gontran was only waiting for this signal to emerge from his torpor, and his sneeze replied to the American's like a faithful echo. "Brrr!" said the latter, shaking his limbs. "What an unpleasant sensation!"

"I didn't feel anything, myself," said Flammermont, in his turn. "It was as if a blow from a sledgehammer had landed on the back of my neck."

"There's definitely a layer of unbreathable gas on the surface of the soil," affirmed Ossipoff. "Ammonia, carbon dioxide, or something of the sort. What can that signify?"

In his turn, Fricoulet said: "Carbon dioxide at the bottom, pure oxygen higher up…it's inexplicable."

"Unless," Gontran said, returning to his subject, "you adopt my idea regarding the influence of the comet."

"Eh?" said Fricoulet. "The comet...the comet...that's easy to say—but if it had been able to exercised any such influence on Mercury it would surely have done so while it was nearby...while now, we can no longer even see it."

"Indeed," added Ossipoff. "What Monsieur Fricoulet says seems logical to me. I've searched the sky in every direction, but can't find any trace of the comet anywhere. It must, therefore, be so far away now that its influence can no longer be admitted."

Loud laughter burst forth. The explosion of hilarity was due to Farenheit. "You remind me," he said, "of the story of a distraught peasant who went in search for his donkey while he was perched on top of it. You're searching for the comet in the sky, when that's what's carrying you." He looked triumphantly at the Terrans, who were staring at him in complete bewilderment.

"According to you, then," stammered Ossipoff, "we're no longer on the planet Mercury?"

"Of course!" said Fricoulet, having thought about it. "It must be admitted that we're on another world, since the entire landscape has changed." Suddenly, he slapped his forehead. "And I've just remembered something that we've forgotten—do you remember yesterday evening, when we were studying the rapid progress of the comet, that a strange sleep took possession of us and laid us out?"

"So what?"

"So, it must have been the atmosphere, which became rarefied by virtue of the comet's approach...perhaps, that night, it made contact with Mercury and, in the aftermath of that collision, an infinitesimal part of the planet became stuck to the surface of the star, which is where we are at present..."

"But in that case," stammered Selena "where are we going?"

Fricoulet raised his arms into the air. "How should I know?" he replied.

"By finding out which comet it is that we're riding."

"It's doubtful," sniggered the American, "that we'll find a Town Hall that can inform us on that subject."

The old scientist reflected. "There might be a means..." he said. He looked in a box, took out a barometer, consulted it and declared: "The barometer indicates a height of 400 feet above sea-level, correcting for the depth of the atmosphere. At that height, sight extends in every direction to a distance of 12 kilometers." He turned slowly on his heel and extended his hand. "It's easy to observe that the horizon here is much closer; the world we're on is therefore smaller than Mercury and its diameter can be estimated at about 800 kilometers. As to its nature, I'll answer for the judgment that this comet is in a period of formation that corresponds to the Tertiary epoch; it's a carbon sphere, since we encounter all the allotropic states of that element here: soot, graphite, carbon dioxide and others..."

The American made an impatient gesture. "All that," he cried, "doesn't tell us where the comet is heading."

"Given the fashion in which it cut across the orbit of Mercury, it's probable that it will go around the Sun before taking the route to its aphelion."

"But what's the name of the comet?" the American continued, imperturbably.

"What?" said Ossipoff, exasperated. "I don't know that any more than you do. I'll need more than a month of observations in order to establish all its coordinates. Anyway, if its name interests you as much as that, ask it yourself."

"Doomed! We're doomed!" muttered Farenheit, angrily.

"No!" retorted Gontran, in a vibrant voice. "We're riding through the Heavens in the manner of the genies of olden times, on a diamond hippogriff with a mane and tail of flame."

Chapter XXIX
In which Vulcan does Gontran de Flammermont a bad turn

"Oxygen is necessary, but it's necessary not to have too much of it," Fricoulet had declared, making allusion to the mental perturbations to which he and his companions had been victim. They had, therefore, abandoned the summit of the Mercurian hill to establish their camp—which is to say, the sphere itself—half way down, in a place where a scrupulous analysis of the air had indicated a mixture of nitrogen sufficient for the good functioning of the Terrans' organism.

Once the installation was complete, Ossipoff declared an intention to devote himself exclusively to the studies necessary for him to establish what Gontran referred to jokingly as the "civil estate" of their vehicle. He left it to his companions to provide their everyday material needs, which was no mean task.

In a council held by Gontran, Fricoulet, Farenheit and Selena, it had been decided that they would hold in reserve, only to be used as a last resort, what remained of the provision of alimentary paste fabricated on the Moon, and that they would seek means of existence on the world on which they were living.

First, they had minutely explored the Mercurian fragment stuck to the surface of the cometary nucleus, which represented a surface area of about one square kilometer. For people like the Terrans, who had seven league boots, that was a matter of a few minutes, but the situation was too serious for them to take that exploration lightly. Thus, they had divided the Mercurian territory into three segments, each meeting at the same point—the summit of the hill—and then, dividing the work among themselves, the men had each set out to search a segment, testing the depth of the soil, moving the rocks, examining the plants and climbing the trees. In brief, they did not leave a square inch whose resources they did not know precisely, from the culinary point of view. Then, each of them having made his report on the portion of the terrain allocated to him, the other two had begun the work of the first again, in order that nothing would be forgotten.

After some ten days, that Terrans knew exactly what quantity and quality of victuals might be appropriated to their larder. A flock of Mercurian inhabitants—which is to say, the horn-mouthed birds—had shared the Terrans' fate and had been caught by the cometary attraction; they numbered exactly 61. At first, Farenheit had proposed killing them in order to be sure of having them to hand at the desired moment, but Fricoulet had made the observation that it was unnecessary, in view of the fact that the birds could not escape their native isle, experience having demonstrated that the air above the cometary soil was unbreathable by them. "Let's leave them alive, then," he had declared. "They're trapped here as if in a poultry-yard, and we can sacrifice them according to our needs."

They had then discovered, living in holes a little way beneath the surface, bizarre animals which were lizard-like in form, save that they were equipped with a large number of legs and were as large as rabbits, whose fur they also had. A culinary experiment had been carried out on one of them, which had been perfectly successful—which had given no mediocre delight to Gontran, whose stomach had conserved the memory of Ossipoff's theories regarding the representatives of Mercurian humanity and who therefore only nibbled when an individual belonging to the planet's winged class appeared on the table. When a census was scrupulously taken, these interesting animals had given a respectable figure of 233.

If you add to these furry and feathered comestibles certain plants that Selena had had the idea of cooking and seasoning with the fat of the former, you will know as well as the voyagers themselves what the contents of their larder were.

When this work was done, the results were communicated to Ossipoff, whose face darkened. "Hmm!" he murmured. "That's only enough to support us for six months, and not in luxury."

Farenheit's face lengthened immeasurably on hearing these words. "By God!" he grumbled. "How long do you think we're going to stay here?"

The scientist shook his head pensively. "Eh?" he said. "Perhaps a good six years, if my calculations are correct."

A unanimous exclamation greeted these words. "Six years!" repeated Gontran, in alarm. "You don't think so, my dear Monsieur Ossipoff."

"On the contrary, I certainly do think so," replied the old man, rubbing his hands in a satisfied manner. Then, seeing the doubtful expressions painted on every face, he added: "At present, I have every reason to believe that we are on the comet discovered by Tuttle, an American—your compatriot, Mr. Farenheit." [130]

"A fine discovery," grumbled the latter. "He'd have done better to have discovered something else."

Ossipoff fixed the Yankee with a gaze full of compassion. "If he hadn't discovered it, that wouldn't have prevented us from encountering it or being carried away by it—and at least it was a scientific glory to the credit of the United States."

Farenheit's national pride was undoubtedly pleasantly titillated by that reply, for he immediately fell silent.

---

[130] Horace Parnell Tuttle (1839-1923) was an avid comet-hunter who sighted several of them; the one most often associated with his name, then as now, is the long-period comet nowadays known as Swift-Tuttle, discovered in 1862, but this one is the short-period comet now known as 8P/Tuttle, which he first sighted in January 1858 and whose return he observed in the summer of 1871; the body was subsequently identified as having first been sighted during an earlier passage in 1790.

"But, Papa," said Selena, in her turn, "on what do you base your affirmation?"

"I affirm nothing; I merely suppose. First, the dimension of the comet that is carrying us is identical to Tuttle's. Then, the angle at which it intersected Mercury's orbit and the date at which the conjunction occurred…"

"If it really is that one, then," Gontran said, "where is it taking us?"

"First it will take us round the Sun; then, successively, we'll cross the orbits of Venus, the Earth, Mars and Jupiter…"

As the old man advanced in his enumeration, Flammermont's face gradually darkened. "Where, then, will this insane journey end?" he murmured.

"In the vicinity of Saturn…a trip of about 370,000,000 leagues," Fricoulet riposted, lightly. "Trivial, what?"[131]

"You can laugh," complained the young Comte, "but if you think it amuses me to be transformed into a celestial Wandering Jew, you're mistaken….for all of this doesn't bring the date of my marriage any closer."

The engineer shrugged his shoulders. *All the same*, he thought, *if this excursion has no other result than that, I don't think he has any grounds for complaint.*

A vague hope lingered in Flammermont's heart, though. "What if you're mistaken, my dear Monsieur Ossipoff?" he said, abruptly. "What if the comet that's carrying us isn't the one that you suppose it to be?"

"Oh, that would be quite different," replied the old man.

"Ah!" said Gontran, with an air of satisfaction.

"Yes," the old man continued, "if I'm mistaken, this comet will describe a parabola in space."

"With the result that…?"

"With the result that we'll be transported toward Infinity."

Selena put her hands together in a desperate gesture. "And we'll never see the Earth again?" she murmured.

"Never," Ossipoff replied. "You seem desolate at that idea—as if terrestrial humankind were something to regret."

The young woman made no reply, but Gontran exclaimed: "But this journey must end somewhere."

"I don't see any reason for that."

---

[131] As usual, the authors are following in the footsteps of literary precedent; the comet featured in Verne's *Hector Servadac* heads back toward the Sun soon after passing beyond the orbit of Jupiter. In Albert Robida's farcical alternative account of Servadac's comet, featured in *Voyages très extraordinaires de Saturnin Farandoul* (1879; tr. in a Black Coat Press edition as *The Adventures of Saturnin Farandoul*), it impacts with Saturn in the same (highly improbable) tangential fashion that it had earlier impacted with the Earth and the comet in the present text has impacted with Mercury.

"I can see one, though," retorted Flammermont, folding his arms. "I can't play the role of fiancé forever. It's a supernumerary position that has lasted rather a long time, and needs to be converted into a permanent entitlement before much longer."

The old man's only response was to raise his arms into the air.

"In any case," the young man continued, "when everything comestible that planet contains has been consumed, it will be very advisable to stock our larder."

"Alas," murmured the old man, "that's what distresses me." He added, with a surge of enthusiasm: "It would have been so wonderful, though, to fly beyond the known worlds, into infinity itself!"

"Where would that get us?" muttered Farenheit.

"If you ask me," Flammermont said, "we should stop on Vulcan."[132]

Mikhail Ossipoff started violently. At the same time, Fricoulet gave his friend a forceful dig in the ribs, and murmured in his ear: "Imbecile!"

The young Comte's bewilderment was total. He turned successively to the old man and the engineer, saying: "What? What's happening? Why that tragic expression, Monsieur Ossipoff—and you, Alcide, why are you looking at me like that?"

"Oh, the fool, the fool!" muttered Fricoulet.

Ossipoff planted himself two feet in front of Flammermont. "Vulcan!" she shouted in his face. "Vulcan!"

"Well, what about Vulcan? What do you mean?"

---

[132] As the ensuing passage testifies, the Vulcan controversy was a hot topic in astronomical circles in the late 19th century. One of the century's great triumphs was Urbain Le Verrier's prediction of the position of a new planet, Neptune, which was confirmed by observation in 1846. Le Verrier had calculated the planet's position after a mathematical analysis of anomalies in the orbit of Uranus, following a suggestion by François Arago, the director of the Paris Observatoire. Arago had also suggested that he examine anomalies in the orbit of Mercury, and Le Verrier—not unnaturally—also tried to account for these by hypothesizing the existence of another planet, Vulcan; he published the hypothesis in 1859, and then received a letter from the amateur astronomer Edmond Modeste Lescabault (1814-1894) claiming to have seen Vulcan transiting in Sun earlier that year. The new "discovery" caused a sensation—Lescarbault was awarded the Legion d'honneur in 1860, but the calculation of Vulcan's orbit that Le Verrier, based on Lescarbault's observation, gave rise to unfulfilled predictions, and he spent the rest of his life making successive amendments to it. During the solar eclipse of July 29, 1878, two American believers in Vulcan, Lewis Swift (1820-1913) and James Craig Watson (1838-1880) recorded separate observations of it, but other hunters failed to spot it and the Swift/Watson observations were widely dismissed as errors.

"Did you just advise us to stop on Vulcan?"

"Yes, of course—what's strange about that?"

The old man gave voice to a dry and mocking laugh. Then, folding his arms, with his face indignant and his lips pursed, he said: "So you believe in Vulcan?"

This question struck the young man like a cobble-stone thrown at his breast. *Aargh!* he thought. *I've said something stupid!*

He hesitated before replying, not knowing how he might be able to trick the old man—then, doubtless by some miracle, a certain passage in *Les Continents célestes,* which he had read a few days earlier, came back to his memory with a marvelous lucidity. Immediately, he understood how he could get himself out of trouble.

"So you believe in Vulcan, do you?" repeated Ossipoff, looking him up and down disdainfully.

"And why should I not believe in it?" asked the young man, boldly.

"In truth, I admire you!" the old man exclaimed. "To endow the celestial system with a new planet, you only require the affirmation of an army physician who declared, after examining the Sun for an hour, that he had seen a round black stain pass across the solar disk?" He laughed again, and added: "But that is not sufficient, Monsieur; one fabricates a planet not with one's imagination, but with one's eyes."

"You will grant me, however," replied Gontran, beginning to be intimidated by the old man's attitude, "that Le Verrier is not just anyone, and that if the affirmation made by Dr. Lescarbault had been based on a mere optical illusion, the illustrious astronomer would not have used it as a point of departure for the studies he pursued without interruption from 1858 to 1876."

"You're doubtless forgetting," Ossipoff riposted, "the prediction made by Le Verrier that the famous planet would pass in front of the solar disk on March 22, 1877, which held all the astronomers in the world breathless—who got nothing for their trouble, for nothing appeared on the solar disk on the aforementioned day."

Flammermont was a trifle nonplussed, when Fricoulet came to his aid. "On July 29, 1878, however, during the recent eclipse of the Sun, did not Messieurs Watson and Swift announce that they had seen, in the direction of Venus, very close to the eclipsed Sun, two intramercurial planets? They were, I believe, two American astronomers."

Farenheit who had been listening to the debate with total disinterest, suddenly straightened up and, throwing his cap into the air with an indescribable enthusiasm, cried: "Hurrah! Hurrah for Watson and Swift...for discovering the planet Vulcan, that it really exists!" Precipitating himself toward Gontran, he shook his hand energetically, saying: "You're a scientist—a true scientist!"

Ossipoff shrugged his shoulders and looked at the American disdainfully, then turned to Gontran. "Monsieur Fricoulet is forgetting to tell you that the scientific world, more than reasonably excited by that declaration, devoted itself to observation and established that the two famous intramercurial planets were none other than the two stars Theta and Zeta Cancri." He paused for a moment to give his declaration time to take effect, and added: "Now, Mr. Farenheit, you are free to shout *Hurrah!* for your American astronomers."

The Yankee, however, out of stubbornness as much as national pride, replied: "They discovered the comet that is carrying us. Why should Vulcan, also discovered by them, not exist?"

The old man realized that he had no way to reply to such reasoning. Besides, Gontran, suddenly remembering another argument drawn from *Les Continents célestes*, asked: "What about the orbit calculated by the German astronomer Oppolzer?"[133]

"That orbit has had the same fate as the preceding items—it has also been recognized as false. You see, Monsieur de Flammermont, what the arguments on which your opinion is based are worth. Personally, I won't hide from you that I'm very displeased with you, in consequence of this disagreement between us."

"But, my dear Monsieur Ossipoff..." the young man stammered.

"To live happily as a family," Ossipoff replied, shaking his head, "there must be unity; it is necessary to have a perfect similarity of opinions and ideas. Until now, I have been able to believe that that was the situation with us; I perceive, with distress, that I was mistaken. From today onwards, there is an abyss between us." And with these words, pronounced with a dolorous dignity, the old man turned on his heel and went down the hill, in order to hide his chagrin beneath the tall trees of the forest.

For a moment, Gontran and Selena remained motionless, looking at one another in amazement, asking themselves whether it was necessary to see in Ossipoff's words a decisive rupture in their beautiful project of union.

"Gontran!" murmured the young woman, sadly.

"Selena!" he replied, taking her by the hands. Then, abruptly, he exclaimed: "To the Devil with Vulcan and those who invented it! Don't cry, my beloved. I'll run to find your father to make honorable amends."

"Oh, Gontran," she said, looking at her fiancé admiringly, "you'd sacrifice your opinions?"

"For you, Selena, what wouldn't I do? Wait for me for a minute, and we'll return, Monsieur Ossipoff and I, hand in hand, like a son-in-law and a father-in-law between whom no cloud exists."

He was already setting off when Fricoulet, who was watching him, seized his arm. "One moment," he said.

"Eh?" Gontran exclaimed. "Let me go! Can't you see that she's crying?"

"She'll cry more later, if I let you go."

"Why?"

---

[133] Theodore von Oppolzer (1841-1886).

"Because what you're doing is obviously stupid."

"Stupid?"

"Undoubtedly." Lowering his voice because of Farenheit, who was listening, he went on: "What are you going to say to Monsieur Ossipoff? That you were mistaken, that you didn't understand what you read in *Les Continents célestes*, that Vulcan doesn't exist—in brief, you want to give him the proof that you're no more an astronomer than Mr. Farenheit..."

"But when a great astronomer like Le Verrier is mistaken," replied Flammermont, "it seems to me that..."

"It seems wrong, for that great astronomer isn't soliciting the hand of Mademoiselle Selena, as you are. What does his error matter, in consequence?"

Selena ran to the engineer. "Monsieur Fricoulet," she implored him, smiling through her tears, "you're so good—help us with your advice. Tell us what we must do. Gontran is no astronomer; he doesn't know...guide us...and whether he likes it or not, whatever you decide, I promise that he'll do it..."

The engineer remained silent for a few moments, wearing the gloomy expression he had every time it was a matter of doing something to get the cart carrying the two fiancés' matrimonial hopes back on the road. Finally, in a surly voice, he said: "Since you've asked my advice, I think the best thing for Gontran to do is to continue to play his role as he began it. Every day, one encounters scientists in the Academies and Institutes who don't agree on any scientific matter, but who co-exist happily nevertheless."

"You saw, however," said Gontran, shaking his head, "how Monsieur Ossipoff greeted my theory regarding the existence of Vulcan."

Fricoulet shrugged his shoulders brusquely. "That doesn't prove anything," he replied. "The man was surprised, at first—that's understandable. Give him time to get used to the idea that his future son-in-law might also have his personal opinions, and you'll see that it will all sort itself out."

"You're certain?" asked Selena, anxiously.

"Of course! But it's necessary that Gontran doesn't back down and that he's ready to recommence the battle if need be—and, most of all, that he doesn't allow your father to see through him. All would be lost." Then, clapping the young Comte on the shoulder, amicably, he said: "Let's go, fair-weather scientist. Lend me your *Continents célestes*, and come into the trees to prepare arguments that will defeat the skill of Monsieur Ossipoff!"

When it was time for the evening meal, the old man came to sit down in his usual place. He was somber and silent, enveloped in a cold and offended dignity. Facing him, Gontran—affecting a similar attitude—ate in an anxious fashion, darting covert glances at Fricoulet, who found it very difficult not to burst out laughing.

The engineer waited impatiently for an opportunity to present itself to renew the morning's discussion. It was Farenheit who provided that opportunity, quite naturally, by asking the old man: "Would you care to make a bet with me, Monsieur Ossipoff?"

"What bet?" growled the scientist, still annoyed with the American for what he had said that morning.

"That my illustrious compatriots Watson and Swift were not mistaken in observing the existence of a new planet in the vicinity of the Sun."

Ossipoff uttered a roar. "Now then!" he cried. "Are you determined to make me angry? I said what I had to say on the subject this morning—let's not go back to it." Then, in spite of himself, he asked: "What basis do you have for saying such a thing, you who have not the slightest knowledge of astronomical matters?"

"The fact that Americans are cool and methodical people who don't get carried away, like Russians and Frenchmen..."

The old man laughed loudly. "If you've no other argument than that to offer for the existence of Vulcan..." he said.

At that moment, Flammeront, whose eyes never left Fricoulet, thought he saw in his friend's face that it was time to take the offensive.

"Pardon me, Monsieur Ossipoff," he said, in a glacial tone, "for returning to a subject that is disagreeable to you, but I can't let the words you've just pronounced pass without protest. They cast further doubt on the discoveries of the illustrious Le Verrier, and..."

Ossipoff cut him short with a gesture as trenchant as a saber-thrust. "I told you, and I repeat, that Le Verrier has discovered nothing."

"It is, however, impossible that astronomers belonging to the various nationalities of the world, having made the same observations for 20 years, are all mistaken."

"They *are* mistaken, having mistaken some sunspot for a new world."

Gontran folded his arms and declared, in a challenging tone: "In that case, would you like to tell me how you explain the perturbations in Mercury's motion?"

"Any way you like, except by means of the planet Vulcan, which no more exists in the Heavens than in my eye."

"Was it not, however, the irregularities observed in the motion of Uranus that led Le Verrier to search for and discover the planet Neptune? Therefore..."

"Therefore, it must be the same with regard to Mercury, mustn't it? That's a grave error."

"What!" cried Gontran, simulating great overexcitement. "You haven't answered me—how do you explain it?"

"The increase of 31 seconds that the arc of Mercury presents in the movement of its perihelion over a century?[134] Quite simply by its passage through a

---

[134] Modern measurements of the precession of Mercury's perihelion give a figure of 43 seconds of arc per century; Graffigny could not know it, but the ano-

cloud of particles gravitating around the Sun, too small to be distinguished from the Earth…but as for a planet, no, no…a thousand times no…"

"Monsieur Ossipoff," said Fricoulet in his turn, laughing surreptitiously, "have you seen the particles of which you speak?"

"No—but why ask that question?"

"Because I'd like to know why you admit the existence of these particles, without having observed them, when you deny that of a world that some people claim to have seen."

As the old man did not reply immediately, Farenheit took his silence for defeat. Clapping his enormous hands in the oxygenated air so that they clashed like laundry beaters, he exclaimed: "Bravo, Monsieur Fricoulet! Bravo, Monsieur de Flammermont! I renew my proposition, Monsieur Ossipoff—would you like to bet with me on the existence of Vulcan. I'll wager $100."

"It's ridiculous," muttered the old scientist.

"Ridiculous! If you say so…but if you're as certain as you appear to be of the non-existence of the planet, you won't reject my offer. If you win, you can use the $100 to buy a little souvenir for Mademoiselle Selena, for the occasion of her marriage."

A profound sigh escaped Gontran's breast.

"It's ridiculous," Ossipoff repeated, again.

"Will you bet or won't you?"

"But how will we know who has won?" asked Selena.

"Nothing will be easier," the old man replied, "given the route that the comet is following. If it exists, we'll be bound to encounter Vulcan." To Gontran, he said: "By the way, you haven't told me which orbit you prefer: Le Verrier's, Watson and Swift's or Oppolzer's?"

The young man replied without hesitation: "Le Verrier's, which takes the planet round the Sun in 33 days."

Ossipoff sniggered. "And which is steeply inclined to the ecliptic—which explains the rarity of its appearances. That's very intelligent on Le Verrier's part, and yours too. Well, I repeat, if Vulcan exists, we're bound to encounter it—so let's wait and see."

They did, indeed, wait for several days to pass, during which the sky was searched in every direction by Gontran and Farenheit—but fruitlessly. To play his role as a committed scientist, Flammermont had to spend long hours with is eye glued to the telescope as if he were expecting to greet the appearance of the oft-discussed star, about which he cared, privately, as much as a fish for an apple. As for Farenheit, from the moment that his compatriots, inhabitants of the

---

maly would become a crucial element of the argument regarding Albert Einstein's theory of relativity, which provided an alternative explanation of the precession that was generally regarded as successful and became established as a key item of empirical support for the theory.

United States, had affirmed the existence of Vulcan, he believed in it too, and he wanted to be the first to tell Ossipoff that he had lost his $100.

The old man shrugged his shoulders pityingly on seeing his two companions' efforts, and even Fricoulet could not help sniggering. As for Selena, she privately hoped that Gontran might be right, and silently implored God to work a miracle in his favor by creating the planet on which her happiness was now dependent from scratch.

Such was everyone's preoccupation that they forgot the frightful heat that was increasing further every day; had it not been for the thick atmospheric layer that surrounded the cometary nucleus, the Terrans would already have suffered sunstroke beneath the intense arrows of the Sun. The comet was now no more than 15,000,000 leagues from the all-devouring center of the system and it was drawing closer with every hour that passed. Only the nights brought a hint of freshness, attenuating the overwhelming day-time temperature. Then, Farenheit and Gontran, one armed with a pair of marine binoculars retrieved from the bottom of a box and the other with Ossipoff's telescope, took up their observation-posts and stayed there until dawn, doggedly inspecting space.

One morning, when Fricoulet's chronometer marked half past three and Flammermont was sighing very softly, with his nose crushed against the telescope, an exclamation from the American made him start.

"By God!" said Farenheit. "I've got it! I've got it!" Immediately, to manifest his joy, he started dancing a frenzied jig.

"You've got it!" cried Gontran, running to him. "What have you got?"

"Why, the planet, of course! The planet Vulcan."

"That's not possible," the young man replied, full of incredulity.

"What! Not possible? Didn't you see it, then, as I did just now? You had your eye stuck to your instrument, though."

Not wishing to admit that he had been asleep, the young Comte shook his head. "No," he said, "I didn't see anything…"

"Well," said the American, handing him his binoculars. "Look through those…and tell me what you see."

Scarcely had Gontran aimed the instrument in the direction indicated by Farenheit that he released a cry of surprise in his turn and hurled himself toward the sphere, where Ossipoff, his daughter and Fricoulet were asleep. "Vulcan!" he said. "Vulcan!" And he shook the old scientist and the engineer roughly. Both of them got to their feet, prey to the bewilderment inseparable from an abrupt awakening.

"Vulcan!" repeated Flammermont, in a voice strangled by emotion. "Vulcan!" Seizing Ossipoff by the arm, he dragged him outside. "Look!" he said, pointing into spaced. "Look!"

"But that's the constellation Aquila that you're pointing to," the old man retorted. "What is there to see there?"

Fricoulet, who had already taken possession of Farenheit's binoculars and had aimed it at the constellation indicated by Flammermont, cried: "Yes, Monsieur Ossipoff-it is, indeed, in the direction of Aquila that it's necessary to look...not far from Vega..."

Shaking his head incredulously, the old scientist put his eye to the ocular lens. Immediately, his hands were seized by a convulsive frisson, his lips trembled and he had to lean on his daughter's shoulder, so great was his emotion. "God in Heaven!" he exclaimed, after several seconds. "I've just seen a new star!"

"And a star that's in the exact position in which Vulcan ought to be, according to your own words," replied Gontran, in a biting tone.

"Moreover," added Fricoulet, his eyes still at the binoculars, "We're heading for an encounter with that star; within two days we'll be able to study its configuration, and even its geography."

Prey to an extraordinary emotion, Ossipoff had aimed the telescope into space again.

"Well, Monsieur Ossipoff?" asked Flammermont, with a mocking smile, "what do you think of that sunspot?"

The old man went to him, with his head lowered and a piteous expression. "Oh, my dear boy," he murmured, holding out his hand. "How many apologies do I have to make...?"

"Then you agree that the honorable gentlemen Watson and Swift were not imbeciles?" said Farenheit, in his turn.

Ossipoff raised the cloth cap that covered his skull. "Mr. Farenheit," he replied, "accept all my apologies, in your name and those of your illustrious compatriots."

The American assumed a dignified attitude and replied: "I accept them, Monsieur Ossipoff, while asking you to remember this example, which proves how wrong it is to accuse anyone of thoughtlessness without having the proof in one's hands." He turned to Gontran. "I want to tell you publicly that you are a great man and a true scientist," he said, "whom I am happy to know and to appreciate at his real value." He folded his arms across his chest and added: "Do you know what I shall do with the money lost by the honorable Monsieur Ossipoff? It will be the initial nucleus of a sum that I shall devote to the founding of an Observatory high in the Cordilleras." As they looked at him with curiosity and astonishment, he went on: "Perhaps I don't know anything about it, but I want to be the Bischoffsheim of America...and I hope that Monsieur de Flammermont will do me the honor of accepting the directorship of the new establishment."

At this unexpected proposition, Gontran remained flabbergasted. Fricoulet had to turn away to hide the formidable burst of laughter that rose from his throat to his lips. As for Ossipoff, no human face ever reflected such bewilderment.

"It's agreed, then," added the American, with a cavalier gesture, "that if Monsieur de Flammermont has need of an assistant, I certainly won't prevent him coming an arrangement with you, my dear Ossipoff."

Chapter XXX
In which the hour of vengeance finally chimes

As might be imagined, our voyagers did not sleep that night. Somber, glum and humiliated, Mikhail Ossipoff took possession of the rudimentary observatory established in the upper part of the sphere and, with his eye riveted to his telescope, absorbed himself in the contemplation of Vulcan. From time to time, abandoning his instrument, he seized his notebook, which he covered with figures and algebraic formulas. His companions were gathered a short distance away, chatting about the prodigious event, commenting on it and discussing it with forceful gestures and exclamations.

Gontran was radiant, and received the American's compliments with admirably feigned modesty, wondering what miracle of chance had led him, at exactly the right moment, to adopt a scientific theory contrary to that of Monsieur Ossipoff, but capable of further augmenting his prestige in the old man's eyes.

As far Selena, she was exultant, first because her father's aggressive attitude with regard to Gontran during the last few days had pained her enormously, as well as beginning to give birth in his mind to suspicions of her fiancé's ignorance of astronomical matters. Already, several inspirations of veritable genius had occurred to him, which had got Mikhail Ossipoff himself out of trouble; already, several of his audacious theories, which the old scientist qualified as follies and Fricoulet as absurdities, had been confirmed, and here was another...

My God! she thought, with an upbeat emotion in her heart. *Will Monsieur de Flammermont be a man of science?* Covertly, she darted an admiring glance at her fiancé.

Fricoulet was prey to a double sentiment: doubt and bewilderment. The discovery made by his friend, although he had checked it with his own eyes, seemed to him even now to be abnormal, illogical, anti-scientific and anti-natural. While grumbling, he continually aimed Farenheit's binoculars at the dark immensity in which the planet appeared, scarcely larger than a dot, black and immobile in its vertiginous course. "Absurd...absurd!" he muttered when, his eyes fatigued by his observation, he passed the instrument to the American, who was also desirous of contemplating the new star.

"Why absurd?" replied Flammermont. "Because it pleased a host of scientists of greater or lesser quality to declare that Vulcan did not exist, should we deny the evidence? That's what's absurd." And he added, in a vibrant voice: "I'd like to know how you reconcile your political principles with your scientific ones! You detest autocratic government, but you're a partisan of absolutism in scientific matters. You execrate Louis XIV's 'such is our pleasure,' but you admit into your mouth the Monsieur X or Monsieur Z who gravely decrees the laws of the Universe from the depths of his dusty study or the heights of his incomplete observatory…" The young Comte emphasized this sentence with a brief laugh, then continued: "Me, I'm like St. Thomas—I don't much care for all your calculations, and of all those people who pontificate about what's happening millions of leagues from insular Earth, I ask: 'have you been there to see?' "

Fricoulet was astounded. He remained silent momentarily; then, shrugging his shoulders, he replied, with imperturbable seriousness: "But if you don't believe in calculations or scientific deductions—if, for you to believe in the existence of a planet or a star, it's necessary for you to see it with your own eyes—on what did you base your opinion relative to Vulcan? Do you think that Le Verrier and Dr. Lescarbaut *had been there to see*, as you so aptly put it, when they affirmed the existence of an intramercurial planet?" So saying, he transfixed Gontran with his little grey eyes, full of a malicious gleam.

Addressing himself to Flammermont, Jonathan Farenheit cried: "Don't reply, old chap—it's surely jealousy that dictates these words to Monsieur Fricoulet." Looking the engineer up and down scornfully, he said: "It's not just anyone who can discover planets!"

At that moment, Ossippoff's voice was heard. "Gontran!" shouted the old man. "Would you climb up here for a moment?"

The young man frowned. "Hmm," he murmured, anxiously. "What does he want?"

"Doubtless to ask you to establish Vulcan's coordinates," Fricoulet replied.

Flammermont looked at his friend interrogatively. "Coordinates?" he repeated.

"Which is to say, to give the new world a sort of civil estate: mass, density, surface gravity, orbit…"

The unfortunate Comte made a gesture of alarm.

"Gontran," the old man repeated. "Are you coming?"

"Here goes," moaned Selena's fiancé—and he set foot on the interior stairway that led to the top of the sphere, like a condemned man mounting to the scaffold.

The engineer ran to him and whispered in his ear: "A very small world whose diameter doesn't exceed a few 100 kilometers; orbit steeply inclined to the plane of the ecliptic, which explains the rarity of its passages over the solar disk. As for the rest, your eyes are too tired by long observation to be able to furnish you with accurate information. Do you understand?"

"Thanks," murmured Gontran, squeezing his hand amicably.

A few seconds later, a series of exclamations was heard to resound in the improvised observatory, soon followed by the sound of someone hurrying down the stairway—and old Ossipoff appeared, followed by the stupefied Gontran. "Vulcan!" stammered the old man, in a strangled voice. "It's not a spherical planet…it's a prismatic rock, a polyhedral fragment, an irregular bolide!"

"Hang on!" cried Flammermont. "I protest against the epithet bolide!"

"You can protest all you like," replied Ossipoff, "The evidence is there, against which you're battling in vain."

"The evidence demonstrates that the body in question is not a sphere, that's true—but nothing proves that it belongs to the class of bolides."

Mikhail Ossipoff did not like to be contradicted, and favored Gontran with an irritated stare. Flammermont, for his part, felt that he had gone too far to retreat and played his role as conscientiously as possible; he looked back at the old man with frank displeasure.

A new scene was on the point of breaking out. Fricoulet intervened. "Messieurs," he said, in a conciliatory voice, "I believe that it would be silly to go one arguing about this subject. In a few hours, the world carrying us will have made rapid progress through space, so that we shall be able to undertake a detailed study from the body we occupy—so postpone your appreciations until you can see with your own eyes which of you is correct."

Selena hastened to add: "That's well said, Monsieur Fricoulet. All the more because one planet more or less isn't worth the trouble of two men of your worth sulking for a single instant." Then, understanding the need for a distraction, she went on: "I'm a little like St. Thomas myself, my dear Father, and I think it's good to touch something with one's finger to be convinced…all the more so because even the greatest scientists can't think of everything…or know everything."

"What are you getting at?" asked Ossipoff.

"I'm getting at the world that is carrying us," replied the young woman, "And I'm asking myself how it is that two men filled with knowledge, like you, dear Father, and you, Monsieur de Flammermont, were unable to foresee the singular fashion in which we passed from Mercury to this comet."

"For the sole reason," riposted Ossipoff, a trifle piqued, "that, comets being foreign to our world—the majority of them, at least, arriving from infinity and returning there—it's absolutely impossible to predict their appearance."

"Their appearance, no doubt," said Fricoulet, who never missed an opportunity to enrage the aged scientist, "but not their return. Of the 40 comets that have been recognized, there are, I believe ten whose periodicity has been established and verified—and, if your suppositions are just, the one that is carrying us is one of them. Therefore…"

"Therefore," added Farenheit, "it should have been easy for you, whose job it is, to foresee what has happened to us."

"That's very easy for you to say," retorted Ossipoff. "It's obvious that you don't understand it at all. Then again, I had other things on my mind than comets."

"Very well," declared Fricoulet. "If that's the reason, so be it—but don't tell us that it wasn't possible to know the precise date on which Comet Tuttle would intersect the orbit of Mercury. Its last passage was observed in 1871, and as its period is 13 years and 81 days, it's sufficient to be able to count on one's fingers to know that its reappearance would take place in 1884."[135]

"My God!" stammered Selena, admiringly. "How does it come about that such things are so accurately predictable?"

Gontran smiled. "18 centuries ago," he said, "Seneca declared that 'comets move regularly in paths prescribed by Nature' and he affirmed that posterity would be astonished that his era could be mistaken about such an incontestable truth—but it wasn't until 1758 that comets, having frightened everyone with their sudden appearances, became celestial phenomena of a purely natural order, thanks to Newton and Halley."

"I remember having seen drawings as primitive in artistry as in thought, representing comets whose tresses contained blood-stained daggers," observed Selena.

Farenheit shrugged his shoulders. "What savages!" he muttered.

"Not at all," declared Fricoulet. "The year 1557 is not so far away and Ambroise Paré[136] was no donkey...and yet comets still had a mysterious and terrifying allure in that era, and in the eyes of educated men—as the description of Charles IX's surgeon confirms."

Flammermont, to whose memory a few lines from *L'Astronomie du peuple* had suddenly returned, declared professorially: "It was only in 1758 that, thanks to the studies of Halley, Seneca's prophecy was justified, Halley having understood that, according to the laws of universal attraction, the motion of comets must describe very long curves, calculated the turn of the great comet of 1682. The event proved him right and, on the twelfth of March 1759, the date indicated by the astronomer, the star reappeared in the sky. From that moment on, it was firmly established that comets orbit the Sun..."[137]

"Just like vulgar planets—but following a more elongated orbit."

"Didn't you say just now, though," objected Selena, "that some of them arrive from infinity and return there?"

---

[135] This date is not entirely consistent either with the intervals of time spent by the voyagers on the Moon and Venus (after taking off from Earth in March 1882). More seriously, it is not consistent with the actual periodicity of 8P/Tuttle, which is 13.6 years; the authors should surely have been aware that its actual perihelion when it reappeared after Tuttle's second sighting, was in the early months of 1885, not 1884.

[136] The memoirist Ambroise Paré (1510-1590) was the chief surgeon to four French kings: Henri II, François II, Charles IX and Henri III.

[137] All three of the dates in this paragraph—which I have corrected—are misquoted in the original text, although it should have been easy enough to copy them out of Flammarion's *Astronomie populaire* or any other textbook dealing with comets and their history.

"You're absolutely right, Mademoiselle—but to enable you to understand that, I would have to give you an explanation of the theory of the parabola that would certainly bore you greatly, and with which, to tell the truth, my scientific knowledge would perhaps only permit me to furnish you imperfectly."

"With respect to their composition, though," Selena went on, "do all comets resemble the one on which we're located?"

"No, the greater number of them are simple nebulous masses, aggregations of cosmic matter devoid of consistency. They're vaporous traces, gaseous clouds..."

"Perhaps no more than optical illusions," murmured Flammermont.

Fricoulet trod heavily on his foot and, without giving the old man time to think about it, he replied: "You're forgetting, Monsieur Ossipoff, that the great comet of 1811 had a solid nucleus measuring no less than 1089 leagues in diameter; that of 1858 similarly possessed one of 9000 kilometers."

"And the nucleus of the comet of 1769 was 4000 leagues in diameter!" exclaimed Gontran.

Farenheit, who was yawning as he listened to this conversation, suddenly asked: "I thought that the distinctive sign of a comet was its tail. How is it that the one carrying us is deprived of that appendage?"

"First of all," said Ossipoff, "it's an error to suppose that all comets have tails; there are some that don't, just as there are some which possess several."

"By way of compensation, no doubt," murmured Flammermont, in jest.

"Then again," the old man continued, "there's no proof at all that the world on which we're riding lacks that caudal ornament..."

The American burst out laughing. "You're joking," he said. "Either that or you're trying to make me think I'm short-sighted. According to you, the tails of comets are thousands and thousands of leagues in length. Now, you'll admit that, if that were so, we couldn't be better placed to measure that of our comet...but there's no trace of it." Turning to the east, he put out his hand to indicate infinite space, illuminated only by the light of the stars.

Ossipoff uttered a mocking laugh. "If that's the direction in which you're searching for it," he said, "I understand why you haven't found it..."

The American opened his eyes wide. "By God!" he grumbled. "What's the joke now, and in which direction to you expect me to search for the comet's tail, if not the direction opposite to the one in which we're traveling?" Gradually, anger took hold of him; agitating his arms in chaotic gestures, he exclaimed: "We're going from west to east, so..."[138]

---

[138] So, according to Farenheit's own logic, he ought to be looking for the tail in the other direction. This entire passage is very confused; Fricoulet also reverses his own meaning by referring to the comet's aphelion when he means its perihelion, while Ossipoff appears to have forgotten that they saw the comet's tail while it was approaching them when he suggests that it might not have one, and

Ossipoff smiled pityingly and looked at Flammermnt, pointing to Jonathan Farenheit by means of a wink. "*Vulgum pecus!*" he murmured.

Gontran shrugged his shoulders in a gesture of ironic commiseration.

"Now then!" said the Yankee. "Explain it to me!"

"With the greatest pleasure, Mr. Farenheit. Like a great many of your peers, who have never taken it into heir heads to raise their eyes to he sidereal immensity, you thin that the tails of comets *follow* them in their course…it's a profound error. That caudal appendage is always opposed to the Sun, as it is the luminous shadow of the comet."

"With the result," Fricoulet added, "that if the tail follows the comet, or very nearly, when it is before its aphelion, it precedes it, by contrast, after that point."

"With the result," Gontran added, "that, in the situation presently occupied by the comet. In relation to the Sun, it's to our right that we need to seek the luminous trail."

The American folded his arms furiously. "By God!" he howled. "Am I blind, then, since I've seen none—absolutely none?"

"No, my dear Mr. Farenheit, you're not blind—but it might perfectly well be that the comet serving us as a mount has no tail…that it's one of those."

"And of what is the tail made, Father dear?" asked Selena.

The old man shook his head.

"That's a very embarrassing question, my dear child," he replied, "given that, until now, everyone has been reduced to mere conjectures."

"But at the end of the day, you must have an opinion."

"For me, I think that it's a matter of mere appearance, of a special mode of the vibration of the ether, compressed by the comet—something like a cloud incessantly forming and evaporating in the wake of the comet."

"That's the opinion of the author of *L'Astronomie du peuple*," Gontran put in, with imperturbable self-composure.

"In truth," replied Ossipoff, "it's not the first time I've found myself in accord with that great mind, and that gives me great pleasure." He shrugged his shoulders and added: "Besides, as I was just saying, at present we know very little about these strange worlds, which circulate through the Universes, putting them in touch with one another, like celestial messengers. It's only a century and a half since the study of comets was initiated, and what can one learn in 150 years?"

With these words, he went inside the sphere and laboriously climbed the steps leading to his observatory.

"There goes a man who will fall back into his Vulcanesque contemplation," murmured Fricoulet, lightly.

---

then suggests a hypotheses to explain such tails which, if correct, would place the tail behind the comet, exactly where Farenheit expects to find it.

Gontran shivered, and drew him aside. "Tell me," he said, "do you think a planet can affect any other form than a spherical one?"

The engineer looked at his friend in astonishment. "Why are you asking me that?" he said.

"Because of Vulcan. The word has a bizarre shape, and I can't deny that it makes me anxious."

"Ah!" said Fricoulet. "You're no longer as convinced as you were a little while ago of he existence of the intramercurial planet."

"*Errare humanum est*," said our headmaster at the Lycée Henri IV.

"But he added: *Perseverare autem diabolicum*—do you remember that?"[139]

"Of course, as I have nothing *diabolicum* in my nature."

"So you don't persist in your opinion?"

"I don't say that, only…"

"Only you're strongly tempted to ditch Le Verrier and Dr. Lescarbault, no?"

"I'd like you to give me your opinion—because, you see, if what I saw wasn't Vulcan…"

"It will put paid to your marriage to Mademoiselle Selena—yes, that's true…Ossipoff would send you packing, and he'd be right; you've humiliated him with your discovery."

"Eh? It was that imbecile Farenheit and his observatory, most of all. Anyway, I want to ask you for a favor."

"What?"

"To go up and look through the telescope."

"What good will that do you?"

"To be subsequently informed of my fate. This uncertainty's torturing me…"

"Gladly…give me a moment."

Flammermont accompanied his friend to the foot of the stairway and sat down anxiously on the bottom step.

Inside the sphere, rolled up in his blanket, Farenheit was already sound asleep. Behind the tent-canvas that provided Selena with a kind of separate bedroom, the young woman's calm and gentle breathing could be heard, similar to the fluttering of a butterfly's wings.

"Oh, my happiness," Gontran murmured, "what shall I have had to endure in order to attain you?"

A whispered appeal caused him to raise his head; in the clear square of sky outlined in the shadows of the sphere by the upper aperture of the stairway he saw Fricoulet's silhouette leaning toward him. "Psst! Psst!" said the engineer.

---

[139] The full quotation, generally attributed to Seneca, translates as "To err is human, to persist [in error] is diabolical."

Flammermont stood up. "What is it?" he asked, in a low voice.

"Come up quickly, without making any noise. Monsieur Ossipoff's asleep."

As lightly as a sylph, the young Comte climbed the steps and was soon on the stairhead, at Fricoulet's side. With a nod of the head, the latter indicated Mikhail Ossipoff, crouching by the telescope with his hands on his knees and his chin on his chest. Heavy breathing passed through his slightly open lips, troubling the silence with a sonorous hum.

"Shh!" said the engineer, putting his finger to his mouth. "Keep an eye on him while I examine Vulcan." He went to the telescope, stepping over the old man's body, and aimed the instrument in the direction in which the planet had been seen.

He observed for a long time; then he shivered abruptly and muttered, in a dull voice: "Unbelievable! It's not possible."

"What?" Gontran demanded, gripped by anxiety. "What's not possible?"

The engineer did not reply immediately. Crouched over the telescope, he was staring as intently as he could.

"Tell me, then!" begged the young Comte.

Fricoulet stood aside, took his friend by the arm and dragged him to the stairway, saying only one word, imperatively: "Come on!" A few seconds later, they were down below. "Fool!" said the engineer, then. "Do you know what that pretended planet that you have discovered is? It's the cannonball that Sharp stole from us!"

Gontran started violently. "Are you quite sure?" he murmured, in a strangled voice.

"As sure as I see you standing there…it's our cannonball, falling with vertiginous speed—and, what's more, falling on our comet."

"Great God! What can we do? I'm doomed. Ossipoff will never forgive me."

Fricoulet rubbed his hands together. "So much the better!" he muttered. "In losing the amity of the father, you'll also lose the affection of the daughter, and you'll avoid the chains with which you were preparing to weigh yourself down." And in his enthusiasm he threw his cap in their air, crying: "Long live liberty!"

Gontran grabbed him by the arms and shook him roughly. "Shut up, you fool!" he growled. "Shut up—and if you don't want me to kill myself in front of you, find a way to get me out of this."

"Eh?" grumbled the engineer, impressed in spite of himself by the somber force with which Flammermont had pronounced these words. "You're obviously mistaking me for your Newfoundland dog; since we've undertaken this celestial excursion I've already plunged into the water several times to save you—it's getting rather boring, to tell the truth…especially as it's a matter of facilitating something contrary to my principles: your marriage."

Gontran took his hands. "I'm begging you," he said. "You're my friend, almost my brother."

"It's for exactly that reason…"

"Would you rather I were dead or married?" Flammermont demanded.

"Dead!"

"I swear to you that if you haven't found a way to save me by sunrise, I'll kill myself."

Fricoulet seemed to be prey to a profound indecision. "Listen," he said, finally. "Yet again, I'll do the impossible…for it's truly impossible to persuade old Ossipoff that black is white."

"Oh, you're a good fellow!" stammered the young Comte.

"Rather say I'm stupid," the engineer replied, sullenly.

"Then let's say that you're stupid, for I can't contradict you—and tell me how you're going to get me out of this."

"I'll begin by making it impossible for the old man to observe the transformation of the so-called Vulcan into Sharp's shell."

"How will you do that?"

"To do that, I'll have to go back upstairs. If chance decides that Ossipoff's continuing his little nap, all will be well…"

He came back after five minutes, holding a little object in his hand that he showed to Flammermont, smiling.

"What's that thing?" the latter asked, squinting.

"Merely the objective lens of the telescope."

"What will he say when he finds out?"

"He can say whatever he likes; the important thing is that he won't be able to track the shell in its fall." The lens disappeared into his pocket, and he added: "Now, we must get ready to leave."

"What? Leave!" cried Gontran, with a start.

"Yes—we're going to confront Sharp."

Flammermont clenched is fists in fury. "Oh, the scoundrel!" he growled. "We're finally going to get our hands on him."

"Uh oh!" replied the engineer. "If you want to get a result, you'll have to put a muffler on your rancor. Sharp might be anything you like—a thief, a murderer, a creature unworthy of any pity—but as it's him who holds your happiness in his hands, it's necessary to treat him gently."

Gontran listened to Fricoulet speaking, doubting what his ears were hearing. "I confess," he said, "that I don't understand a word you're saying."

"We'll discuss that as we travel," replied the engineer. "The most urgent thing is to get under way."

A few moments later the two friends silently left the camp; they had each put on a respirol. Gontran was carrying the American's marine binoculars; Fricoulet had his portable electric lamp in his hand, whose reflector projected a luminous beam 50 meters ahead, thanks to which they could navigate as easily as in broad daylight.

When the first solar darts were launched over the horizon, Gontran and his companion had covered about 60 kilometers. In front of them, a vast extent of grayish liquid, sparkling like a burnished silver mirror, barred their way. Gontran uttered an exclamation of disappointment. "What are we to do?" he murmured.

Fricoulet, who was scanning the horizon with the aid of the binoculars, made an abrupt movement, then remained motionless for a few more minutes, leaning forward as if attracted by a spectacle of the greatest interest. Then he passed he instrument to his companion and simply said: "Look."

In the distance, floating on the surface of that bizarre ocean, a mass appeared, its whitish hue standing out against the dark liquid surrounding it. One might have thought it a gigantic marine buoy, reflecting the Sun's rays like a metallic mirror.

"Sharp!" exclaimed Flammermont.

"Yes," replied the engineer, applying his speaking tube to the opening built into the upper part of Gontran's helmet. "It's Sharp's cannonball—which, in accordance with my anticipations, has fallen into that cometary ocean."

The young Comte launched into a chaotic pantomime.

Fricoulet nodded his head to indicate that he had understood. "What are we going to do, you're asking, to take possession of the vehicle and its contents? That'll be the simplest thing in the world. Now, either this sheet of water that we have in front of us, and which I've baptized, perhaps mistakenly, with the name of ocean, is only a shallow marsh—in which case, we can reach the shell on foot, *pedibus cum jambis*—or we'll sink, and then we'll pause to build some sort of raft."

"A raft!" retorted Flammermont. "But for that we'll have to go back to the camp, cut trees from the Mecurian forest and transport them here. Apart from the fact that it'll be a formidable task, Ossipoff will get his hands on us."

"Come on," said the engineer. "Don't lost heart in advance. There'll be time for that if we can't employ the simpler and more natural means, which is to make use of our legs."

This dialogue had taken place at the top of rather high cliffs, which fell sheer from their black and powdery crests to the mirror-like liquid. Using footholds and handholds in the bizarre rocks, the two companions were soon able to arrive at the bottom, where small grey waves beat heavily and silently.

Fricoulet bent down and cupped a few drops of the strange liquid in the palm of his hand, which he studied attentively for a few minutes. "It's not water," he murmured into Gontran's helmet.

The latter shrugged his shoulders, indicating that the chemical composition of the liquid was of no interest to him.

"Imprudent," replied Fricoulet, "Since an opportunity is presenting itself for you to prepare your reply to one of the questions that Ossipoff might ask you—so take advantage of the opportunity and remember if you can that what you have before your eyes is a combination of hydrogen, carbon and oxygen. The light mist that you see floating on the surface is carbon dioxide...in brief, it's a sort of foaming soda-water."

Fricoulet continued talking, but he talked in vain; Gontran, uninterested in these scientific questions, had taken a few strides forward, which had immediately taken him 100 meters from the shore. At that distance, the liquid scarcely came up to his ankles, so he waved his arms in the air triumphantly, inviting the engineer to join him.

Fricoulet lengthened his stride and rapidly caught up with his friend, who resumed his forward march. As they advanced, they sank more deeply into the mobile sheet, which sparkled like a sheet of mercury, but they only sank only gradually as they descended a gentle slope—perhaps a tenth of a millimeter per meter—with the result that after some two hours, the liquid reached the level of their chests.

The further they advanced, the more difficult their march became, but reason of the heavy liquid mass through which they had to move—which lifted them up like corks from time to time, by reason of their lightness, making them lose their footing and their equilibrium, forcing them to resort to uncomfortable gymnastics. It was also the case, however, that the shell was now clearly visible in every detail: an enormous mass sparkling in the ardent rays of the Sun, floating on the surface with surprising lightness.

Fricoulet signaled to his friend to stop. Then, adjusting his speaker to his helmet, he said: "If you ask me, you should stay here while I go on. There's no need for us both to tire ourselves out, when one of us can do the job—all the more so as it might be very easy to lose one's footing out there and have to start swimming. Now, I think I recall that you're not a strong swimmer."

"At school," Flammermont replied, "they only put us in a cold bath once a week, with the result that I was unable to make measurable progress—but I can do it well enough to get myself out of trouble."

"That's not necessary at present. Stay here and rest, for you'll need all your muscular strength soon enough."

"Have you got your revolver?" Gontran asked.

"Yes, I have—why ask?"

"Because that wretch is capable of ambushing you."

"You can rest easy on that subject. According to what old Ossipoff has told me, Fedor Sharp possesses enough scientific acumen to know what would happen to him if he even stuck his nose out of one of the portholes. Whatever his evil intentions toward me might be, therefore, it will be absolutely impossible for him to make them manifest. On that note, I'm going—wait for me, and be ready to join me as soon as I give the signal." He drew away and, as resumed his progress toward the shell as rapidly as possible.

After an hour of troublesome effort, sometimes walking, sometimes swimming, he finally reached it, weary and exhausted, almost ready to drop. With a final effort, he grabbed hold of one of the machine's exterior bolts just as his strength ran out. When he had recovered his breath, he hoisted himself up to one of the portholes in order to look inside the cannonball, and found himself face to face with Sharp, only separated from his enemy by the thick glass against which the other's face was plastered as he examined with extreme curiosity the being whose selenium helmet gave him a fantastic and terrifying appearance. "Ha ha!" muttered Fricoulet. "The worthy Fedor seems to me to be considerably less than reassured. So much the better—we'll bring things to an end more easily."

With these words, he attached the extremity of a metal wire that he had taken the precaution of bring with him to one of the shell's flaps, and retraced his steps, unreeling the cable behind him as he went. After covering 100 meters, he came to a sudden halt. He had just felt solid ground beneath his feet and the extremity of the tether was now in his hands. He tied it around his body and made a signal to Gontran, inviting him to rejoin him.

The young Comte, whose curiosity multiplied his strength and courage tenfold, caught up with him rapidly. Then, following his friend's instructions, he also harnessed himself to the wire. Both of them, demanding from their muscles all the force of which they were capable, set out for the shore, dragging behind them the enormous metal mass, which, by reason of its low weight and the extreme density of the liquid, slid over the surface like a sled on ice.

Finally, after two hours of dogged effort, out of breath, with their bodies soaked in sweat and sunburned, they fell exhausted on to the shore, where they remained inert for some time.

A slight noise made them prick up their ears and drew them out of their torpor. Fricoulet sat up on his elbow and listened; then he leaned toward Flammermont. "If I'm not mistaken," he said, "Sharp's unscrewing the bolts and getting ready to come out."

Gontran started violently.

The engineer seized him by the arm. "If you love Selena," he said, authoritatively, "you'll swear to me not to do anything or say anything that I haven't authorized you to do or say. With respect to this wretch, remain as calm and as indifferent as if you did not know him. If not, I'll leave you to it and you can sort things out with Ossipoff as best you can."

Gontran put out his hand mutely.

"I have your oath," Fricouet went on. "That's enough for me. Now, listen to me. Sharp will come out, but as soon as he sets foot outside, what happened to you and Farenheit will happen to him. He'll fall down, asphyxiated. We'll run to him immediately, and put him back in his shell, into which we'll accompany him. There, we'll bring him round and have a chat at our ease."

As he finished these words, an exclamation rang out, followed by a dull thud. It was Fedor Sharp, who, in accordance with Fricoulet's expectations, had just fallen over, his face already blackened and his eyes bloodshot. The two friends leapt upon him, one seizing him by the shoulders and the other by the legs, and, without losing a moment, transported him to one of the shell's circular cushions.

Ten minutes later, Gontran and Fricoulet, divested of their helmets, were comfortably ensconced on the padding of the divan. Each of them was holding a revolver in his right hand, and a glass full of an excellent port—with which the shell's stores had been abundantly supplied ever since the departure from Cotopaxi—in the other.

"My God!" said Fricoulet, moistening his lips with the odorant liquid. "How good it is to feel at home!" He clinked glasses with Flammermont and added, lightly: "To the health of the excellent Monsieur Sharp."

A profound sigh attracted their attention to the sick man, who thus advertised his return to consciousness, emphasizing the manifestation with tremors in his arms and legs.

"Look out," said Gontran, "the scoundrel's coming round."

"I entreat you," said Fricoulet, "not to use such expressions, or my plan will come unstuck."

"But you haven't told me what your plan is."

"It doesn't matter—its purpose is to save you."

At that moment, Sharp sat up on his cushion and rubbed his eyes with his closed fists for some time, like someone awakening from a long sleep. Then he became suddenly immobile, dumbfounded by the sight of the two men who were looking at him, smiling. He tried to cry out then, but his voice stuck in his throat. He tried to get up, but the two revolver barrels aimed at him commanded him to be still.

"My dear Gontran," Fricoulet said, still smiling, "would you do me the honor of introducing me to the estimable Monsieur Sharp." Seeing that Flammermont was having a great deal of difficulty restraining his indignation, he added: "On seeing you again, after such a long time, my friend Gontran is experiencing an emotion so profound that, as you can see, joy is rendering him mute—but I, who don't have the same reasons as he does for being emotional on seeing you, will tell you who I am myself. My name is Alcide Fricoulet; I'm an engineer—and if Mikhail Ossipoff has been able to carry out the wonderful intersidereal expedition, the idea of which you borrowed from him, in spite of everything, it's to some extent thanks to me."

Sharp's already-livid face became even paler, and his blanched lips contracted nervously.

420

"I tell you that," Fricoulet continued, "not in order to boast—my friend Monsieur Flammermont will confirm that, from the viewpoint of modesty, the violet is nothing by comparison with me—but in order that we can get to know one another better. Is that understood?"

The ex-permanent secretary of the St. Petersburg Institute of Sciences did not reply immediately. Eventually, he decided to ask, in a cavernous voice. "What do you want?"

"To persuade you that you're in our hands and that you'll have do as we wish. You've guessed, of course, that if we didn't have any need of you, the little tricks you've already played would have got your brains blown out." So saying, he passed the barrel of his revolver beneath the trembling wretch's nose. "Yes, Monsieur Sharp," Fricoulet went on, "We have need of you. 'One often has need of one more rascally than oneself,' La Fontaine has said; we'll furnish the proof of it. First of all, is it really necessary to demonstrate to you that certain death awaits you, and that all those you have played false will compete for the bloodthirsty pleasure of sending you to join the old moons? No—you must know as well as we do the sentiments professed in your regard by Mikhail Ossipoff, Gontran de Flammermont and Jonathan Farenheit."

Fedor Sharp took on a greenish tint.

"I alone had some sympathy with you on the day when, by abducting Mademoiselle Selena, you made it impossible for my friend Gontran to marry her—but, thanks to your cowardice and your inhumanity, we've recovered Mademoiselle Selena, with the result that the abyss into which I wanted to prevent Monsieur de Flammermont from falling is once again hollowed out beneath his feet. That's why I hold an implacable and personal grudge against you, which I shall consent not to take out on your villainous flesh...on one condition."

"What's that?" murmured the wretch.

"That in the course of your peregrinations around the Sun, you have indubitably established the existence of the planet Vulcan."

Sharp almost jumped off his cushion. "What!" he cried. "You're mad."

"Mad? Why is that?"

"Because no one is better placed than I am to deny the existence of that planet, brainchild of the optical illusion of some and the over-enthusiastic imagination of others."

"Monsieur de Flammermont, however," said Fricoulet, still smiling, "not only believes in Vulcan but also observed its passage across the solar disk not 24 hours ago."

Sharp remained open-mouthed for a moment, uncertain as to whether the engineer was being serious or mocking him. Finally, he uttered a little snigger and addressed himself directly to Gontran. "I wish you would explain that to me, Monsieur..." he began.

Fricoulet cut him off. "Explanations," he said, harshly, "are unnecessary. The situation is this: have you, or have you not, established the existence of

421

Vulcan? If the answer is yes. Monsieur de Flammermont will forgive you for having abducted his fiancée and abandoned her, at the risk of her dying of starvation. Furthermore, we'll undertake to reconcile you with Ossipoff and Farenheit. If not, the tricks you've played will deprive your vile soul of its vile envelope."

"I believe in the existence of Vulcan," Fedor Sharp made haste to say, "and I'm willing to swear to that before the entire Universe."

"In that case, my dear Monsieur Sharp, Gontran and I are your friends. Keep your promise…and we'll keep ours."

The wretch held out his hands, which the two young men shook as a sign of reconciliation—but not without a grimace of disgust. "Now let's go," said Fricoulet, getting to his feet. "The others must be getting mortally anxious; it's time to rejoin them."

"One moment," said Gontran. "Let me tidy myself up a bit."

So saying, he went to the cupboard and released a sigh of satisfaction on observing that his effects were in the same condition in which he had left them. Swiftly, he donned a pair of nankeen trousers and a light jacket, and completed the transformation by putting on a straw Panama hat.

"You look as if you're about to go fishing with a rod and line," said Fricoulet, laughing.

"Or about to come back," replied the young Comte. "For that's a fine catch that we've made."

Rapidly, the engineer followed his friend's example. Then, having donned their respirols and making Sharp put on his own, all three of them went out of the shell. After carefully closing the door behind them, they set off back to the camp.

The Sun was beginning to disappear over the horizon when they arrived at the foot of the Mercurian hill that served as their refuge. There they took off their helmets and deliberated as to the course to follow with a view to effecting a reconciliation between Sharp and his enemies. Fricoulet proposed that he should go on ahead as an ambassador and negotiate the matter. Gontran, on the other hand, opined that they should tackle the matter squarely, to see what effect that the sudden appearance of the wretch would have on those who had complained about him, and act according to the circumstances. It was the latter opinion that prevailed and the little troop set about slowly climbing the wooded hill on which the selenium sphere stood, illuminated by the dazzling light of Venus.

On perceiving Gontran, who was marching in the lead, Selena uttered a cry of joy and ran to the young man, with her arms extended. "Finally!" she said, with tears in her voice. "There you are, you bad boy. If you knew how anxious we've been…"

"Pardon me, my dear Selena," Flammermont replied. "I was working for our happiness."

Farenheit had come running in response to the young woman's call. "By God!" said the Americam. "It's high time you came back. I was starting to go mad. The old man's taken his telescope apart and reassembled it four times over...one of the lenses seems to be missing. He's in a frightful fury—listen to that!"

High above, in the makeshift observatory organized in the top of the sphere, furious speech was audible, punctuated by curses and exclamations of despair.

"Monsieur Ossipoff!" Fricoulet shouted. "Monsieur Ossipoff! Come down a moment—we have something very interesting to tell you."

When the old man had joined them, the engineer turned round to Sharp, whom he had left lurking in a dark corner, and came back leading the wretch by the hand.

When he appeared in the circle of light formed by the selenium lamp, amazement made Ossipoff and the American take several steps backward. Then, all of a sudden., without saying a word, Farenheit hurled himself forward, his arms widespread and his hands open: formidable pincers that were about to wring the ex-permanent secretary's neck.

Fortunately, Gontran de Flammermont positioned himself between the two men. At the same time, the old man, clinging on to the American's coat-tails, dragged him backwards. "One moment, Mr. Farenheit," he said, in a firm voice. "This man belongs as much to me as to you. He was my enemy before he was yours; you will therefore agree that my vengeance ought to be exacted before yours."

"Your credit is privileged," said Fricoulet, laughing.

The American was fuming. "What!" he groaned. "This man has cheated me, ruined me, attempted to murder me, and I must calmly fold my arms? Oh no! Lynch law is not a vain phrase."

Sharp turned to him. "I beg your pardon, Mr. Farenheit," he said, with marvelous self-composure, "but it's wrong of you to accuse me of having ruined you. What did I promise you? Diamond mines—well, I've delivered more than I promised, since you're in an entire land made of diamond at this moment."

"It's not your fault that I'm here, you wretch!" growled Farenheit.

"It's yours!" retorted Sharp. "Bah! Does one pay attention to such details in your country? In America, you fire off revolver shots as you raise your hats, but you're no better off for it."

The American was about to reply, but Ossipoff cut him off. "This wretch belongs to me and I won't permit anyone to raise a hand against him until I declare my vengeance satisfied."

A mocking smile played on the lips of the ex-permanent secretary. "Your vengeance!" he repeated, in a sardonic tone. "Before going in search of whatever torture of refined cruelty you might be able to inflict on my hide for all my misdeeds, let me ask you whether astronomical questions still impassion you as they did in the past?"

A trifle nonplussed by this question, Ossipoff replied, after a momentary pause: "I don't understand the reason for your question."

"It's because I have a bargain to propose."

"A bargain! What?"

"During the 20 days that the journey I've made through space in the vicinity of the Sun lasted, I devoted myself to a profound study of the central star of the Universe. I've been able to find explanations for many phenomena that have plunged terrestrial astronomers into profound amazement for centuries. These studies and observations I've committed, day by day, to a notebook. Let me live, pardon me, accept me as a collaborator in the excursion you have undertaken, and that notebook is yours."

"Never!" howled Farenheit. "Never! Don't accept, Monsieur Ossipoff! It's a fool's bargain!"

The old man reflected, with his head bowed; eventually, he looked up, his features contracted by a profound emotion, and replied, simply: "Fedor Sharp, in the name of science, I accept."

"But we'd find these notes after your death," the American said.

"You'd find nothing but pieces of paper covered with incomprehensible symbols."

Ossipoff turned to Selena. "My child," he said, "Will you consent to forget what this man has done to you?"

"If you forgive him, Father," the young woman replied, "I shall forgive him."

"What about you, Monsieur de Flammermont?"

"I put one condition on my forgiveness," declared the former diplomat, "and that is that Monsieur Sharp will tell us sincerely what he thinks about the planet Vulcan."

There was a pause, and everyone—except the American, to whom the question as of no importance—looked anxiously at Fedor Sharp. As the latter appeared to hesitate, a small click was heard in the darkness; it was Fricoulet cocking his revolver.

Sharp shivered, and in a slightly tremulous voice, he said: "I have seen the planet Vulcan with my own eyes and I have established that, in accordance with the prognostications of Le Verrier, it describes an orbit around the central star in 33 days. Actually, it's more of a nebulous mass than a world, properly speaking."

Ossipoff suddenly became pale and leaned toward Gontran's ear. "Forgive me," he said, "and let's forget our dispute. In matters of astronomy, I'm a mere child by comparison with you."

Chapter XXXI
The Suburbs of the Sun

Wednesday, March 25. Alone. Here I am, alone now—and it seemed odd, on waking up, not to see the young woman lying in her hammock. At first, with my memory still numbed by sleep, I looked for her, and then I suddenly remembered what had happened the day before: my calculations, clearly establishing the excessive weight of the projectile—an excess corresponding, almost to the gram, of Selena's weight—my hesitations, my scruples and, finally, my abrupt decision.

Could I, for a mere question of humanity, renounce this celestial exploration, which will surround my name with an aureole of unimaginable glory? Could I sacrifice to that young woman the gigantic step that my voyage is making for science?

Then again, I was beginning to get attached to that child, so gentle and so lovable, and beside her pure victim's silhouette I was beginning to look too much like an executioner...that was like a living remorse. Yes, from every point of view, I did well to abandon her. I have no regrets.

Thursday, March 26. This morning, I experienced the same thing as yesterday. When I awoke, my eyes immediately looked for Selena...she made a singular impression on me.

Bah! I'll get used to it.

I'm now 4,000,000 leagues from Mercury. What a journey to make in 48 hours! And my velocity is increasing!

I've measured the diameter of the Sun with the aid of the micrometer, and the dimension is increasing, so to speak, visibly. The projectile is flying through space with vertiginous rapidity. The calculations give me nearly 40 kilometers a second.

Friday, March 27. Last night I was woken up by the intolerable heat. It seemed to me that I was in a red-hot furnace. Although I was virtually naked, my body was inundated by an abundant sweat, which transformed itself without any discontinuity into a thick cloud of vapor.

The interior of the projectile seemed to be on fire. At firs, I thought there really was a fire; I got up precipitately and realized that a dazzling red light was coming through the portholes, which tinted the surrounding objects and my own body the color of blood.

Quickly, to my telescope!

A marvelous spectacle! In velvety black space, extinguishing with its splendid light all the stars in the firmament, a bright and sparkling meteor flew by with unprecedented rapidity, sweeping the immensity with a luminous train in which I was enveloped myself, and which was emitting the suffocating heat that had woken me up.

It's a comet—doubtless Tuttle's; that's the only one that can be crossing the sky in this location, at this time. I've consulted my horary; Tuttle's comet was sighted in 1871; its period is 13 years; this is 1884—it's certainly that one.

I note here, from memory, its aphelion, which is 10.483; its perihelion, which is 1.030; and the eccentricity of its orbit, 0.821.[140] Tuttle's orbit cuts across the orbits of all the planets in the plane of the ecliptic, passes Saturn, reaches its aphelion after 13 years and returns towards our system, after traveling millions and millions of leagues. That's the vehicle I need to travel the interplanetary immensity!—instead of this miserable fragment of metal that's carrying me.

Saturday, March 28. The heat has diminished, I'm breathing more easily. Measured by the micrometer, the Sun's diameter has grown. I'm looking for the comet. In less than a day it's lost itself in space; thanks to my telescope, I find it again out here, far away, on the sidereal horizon. It will cross Mercury's orbit.

I've been making calculations all day, and I've established that Tuttle's comet will almost certainly collide with Mercury. What will the result of the impact be? One comet fewer in the Solar System, no doubt.

Suddenly, the thought of Selena came back to mind; poor child, it's implacable death that awaits her...my God! Just as long as she doesn't suffer too much. I'm a wretch!

Sunday, March 29. I spent a sleepless night. The thought of the horrible cataclysm that's brewing kept my eyes wide open for long hours. Anguish drained me of all strength I didn't even have the courage to go to the porthole to study the two stars marching towards their mutual impact.

Poor Selena! As long as her curses don't bring me bad luck!

The heat is increasing terribly as I get nearer to the Sun. To distract my mind from the thought of Selena, I'm calmly examining the eventualities that await me. Either I continue to head straight toward the Sun, and then, at a distance of 10,000,000 leagues, I'll fall into the central star and—having been burned, turned to ash and volatilized—disappear as impalpable matter into the great All...or I won't reach the attractive zone and, under the impulse of my velocity, I'll take a turn around the Sun and continue my journey.

---

[140] These figures correspond very closely to those given in modern textbooks, and are accidentally revealing; the first, given in astronomical units, confirms that the comet in question gets no closer to the Sun than the orbit of Earth, and cannot possibly be in the location where Sharp has encountered it.

To distract me and soothe my thoughts—which keep on turning, in spite of myself, to Mercury and Selena—I'm trying to verify the calculations to which research on the Sun has given rise. In one day, I've finished that work and I've established the exactitude of all the figures obtained.

Night is approaching, but I'm not sleepy, so I'll try to pass the time. Taking the Earth as a point of comparison, I've established the following: the Sun weighs 5,875 sextillion kilograms; it would require 324,000 Earths as a counterweight;[141] the terrestrial diameter is 180th part of the solar diameter; the central star is, in volume, 1,279,000 times more immense than my native planet. As for the distance, I find that an express train, traveling 60 kilometers an hour, would take 266 years to go from the Earth to the Sun.[142]

These infantilisms have taken me though till morning. I can no longer resist…it's preferable that I know what will become of me…I'll run to the porthole and aim my telescope into infinity, in the direction where Mercury ought to be if the comet has not annihilated it in a formidable impact…

O joy! The planet is there, following its usual orbit as of previous days. I breathe more freely, as if a formidable weight has been lifted from my breast; God, who has just worked a miracle, has consented to protect Selena…it seems to me that the death of that child would have struck me a deadly blow.

Exhausted by anguish and insomnia. I'll lie down in my hammock and go to sleep.

Wednesday, April 1. Nothing to record on Monday and yesterday; the vehicle is continuing in its course toward the Sun, whose enormous disk now fills the horizon. The light is so bright that I've had to cover the portholes with a quadruple layer of black crêpe in order not to be blinded.

What terrible, frightful heat! My skin, desiccated, is flaking off, my lungs, exhausted by the fiery air I'm breathing, function painfully, with a whistling sound that alarms me; it seems that my breast is swelling up, that all my bones are cracking…

What will happen?

I feel that it's certain death I'm heading for…another few 100,000 kilometers and I'll fall down, stifled.

Should I go backwards, instead of going around the central star and launching myself into infinity? Nothing is simpler. I have here, within range of my hand, the cords controlling the movement of the ring with which the shell is surrounded; with a single, scarcely perceptible action, I can turn around!

---

[141] The figure comparing the Sun's mass with Earth's is not far removed from modern estimates, as is the comparing its volume, but modern textbooks quote the mass in metric terms as 2×10^{27} tonnes.

[142] Actually, it would take about 284 years.

No, curiosity draws me on; the marvelous and unknown world attracts me...closer! And closer yet!

Thursday, April 2. It's definite; I'm going forward! That being firmly established, and my mind almost free of the thought of Selena. I'm resuming my study of the Sun. The spots that I've observed on the face of the disk since my departure from Mercury have changed position...

I've established the exactitude of the parallel drawn by a French astronomer between terrestrial gravity, which varies in intensity from the equator to the poles, and the rotation of the solar patches, whose velocity is proportional to their latitude. It was sufficient, to arrive at that certainty, for me to follow the progress of three patches across the disk of the Sun for the whole day, one at the equator, one at 15 degrees of latitude and the other at 38 degrees of latitude. The first gave me, for its complete rotation around the star, a period of 24 days and a half, the second a period of 25 days and two hours, and the third a period of 27 days.

It was impossible for me, from the position in occupy in space, to follow a patch beyond 38 degrees, but it can be presumed that the rapidity of rotation will diminish progressively from latitude to latitude all the way to the pole.

I can scarcely do better than compare that surface rotation to that of an ocean enveloping a globe, which turns more slowly than it does, and less and less rapidly from the equator to the poles.

In 1611, the sublime genius who called himself Galileo measured that rotation, which his predecessors had only observed: Fabricius, Kepler and Giordano Bruno, who was burned in Rome for his astronomical opinions! Would we, who are so proud of our love of science, be ready, like our ancestors, to confess our faith on the pyre? I doubt it....and yet, here I am! O, to suffer 1000 deaths, to return to my native planet for a few minutes, only to die, while bearing the conviction that my name would pass into posterity!

Thanks to my telescope, the ocular lens of which I took care to darken powerfully, I can devote myself to interesting studies of the central star. At this short distance, the photosphere is clearly apparent to me in every detail, a dark network illuminated here and there, irregularly but in considerable quantity, by luminous points. It is these luminous points—whose totality, according to the American Langley,[143] represents barely a fifth of the solar surface—that produce the light and heat. What would happen if their number were to increase or decrease? Death for the planets that its rays vivify—death by calcinations or cold!

I observed at the same time the inequality of heat and light projected by these luminous specks, which, according to their distance from the center of the solar disk, vary in intensity by a factor of five. Is it necessary to conclude from

---

[143] Samuel Pierpoint Langley (1834-1906).

that, like Père Secchi, the existence around the Sun of a slender and absorbent atmospheric layer? I reserve that question for later study.

Friday, April 3. On awakening, my head feels as heavy as lead; I can scarcely open my eyes; my eyelids are inflamed, the pupils are stinging me horribly—the fatal consequences of yesterday's studies.

Am I falling ill at the very moment when I'm ready to lift the veil that envelops the unknown? Should I stay in bed? Perhaps tomorrow...

No, tomorrow I might be dead....or something might set me back. I'm avid to know. To work—let's extract from nature the secrets that attract me.

Great God! What a marvelous spectacle. There, before my eyes, close at hand—thanks to the telescope, at an apparent distance of only a few 1000 kilometers—the solar mass appears to be in upheaval, twisting in titanic convulsions. Here, the photosphere splits, tears and seems to fly into space in sparkling floss. There, it is hollowed out in immeasurable gulfs filled with vertiginous whirlwinds, at the bottom of which appear, as darker stains, the luminous Sun in combustion, through clouds of vapor lit by the glare of a formidable fire.

My amazement scarcely leaves me sufficient lucidity of mind to make a few scientific observations—measured with the micrometer, one of the gulfs is 800,000 kilometers in diameter!

For hours, I've remained here, immobilized in my stupefaction, my eyes riveted to the gaseous lava rising from that formidable pit as from the depths of a volcano, pouring out on to the photospheric surface, forming a sort of incandescent ring all around, running towards its point of origin in luminous threads. No doubt I'm witnessing the formation of those patches that astronomers over the centuries have taken successively for clouds, mountains, volcanic eruptions and immense scoria.

Wilson[144] alone was right; sunspots are cavities whose depths, though sparkling, appear dark by comparison with the photosphere.

I can do no more. I'm exhausted. I scarcely have the strength to grope my way to my hammock—for my eyelids are so swollen that I can't open my eyes...

---

[144] Alaxander Wilson (1714-1786) was both right and wrong; sunspots really are "cavities" (his word was "depressions") in the solar surface, not mountain-tops, but it is not the case that they are dark because they allow glimpses of a dark core within a bright shell, as Wilson thought. The "proof" lent to Wilson's hypothesis by early spectroscropic analyses in 1861—on which de Graffigny, having no inkling of the fact that the Sun's heat is actually produced by nuclear fusion, is presumably relying—was not as far-reaching as some interpreters thought, so Sharp's "observations" give a misleading account of the actual processes ongoing within the Sun.

Monday, April 6. Yesterday and the day before I stayed in bed, in the absolute impossibility of making a movement, and in a state of almost total blindness. For a time, I feared that I might by blind for the rest of my life.

The rest of my life! Bitter derision! Death is stalking me. I'm choking; my lungs function with increasing difficulty. It's fire that I'm breathing, and 15,000,000 leagues still separate me from the Sun. The prospect of imminent death gives me strength and, this morning, even though I can hardly see, I've got out of bed and dragged myself to my telescope.

The solar perturbation observed on previous days has calmed somewhat; curiosity prompts me to count the sunspots. Their number has increased considerably; there again I find confirmation of laws established by terrestrial astronomers, according to which the solar surface is animated by a dependably regular motion of flux and reflux. Every 11 years, the number of sunspots, eruptions and solar storms reaches a maximum and then decreases for seven and a half years; having attained its minimum, it increases again to its maximum, which it reaches in a period of three and a half years. The present phase is certainly that indicated by the maximum of the solar tide; that was the cause of the phenomena observed two days ago.

God, how I'm suffering! The hot ocular lens burns me painfully; it's impossible for me to maneuver the telescope, whose metal absorbs the heat that the superheated air contained in the tube discharges. It's necessary for me to renounce my studies—or, at least, abandon my telescope and devote myself to a few spectroscopic observations of the corona.

I observe the presence of that cloud of solid corpuscles, which forms a belt around the Sun which certainly extends as far as the Earth; incessantly launched into space by solar eruptions, and incessantly falling back on the star that produces them, these corpuscles, illuminated by the luminous rays, produce what people on Earth call the zodiacal light. Is it also to them that the perturbations observed in Mercury's motion must be attributed? One interesting question among many, which I expect to resolve—and simultaneously settle the question of the intramercurial planet discovered by Le Verrier.

I recall now a long dissertation with which Mikhail Ossipoff lulled us to sleep at the Institute of Sciences several years ago, on the subject of projections of solar matter—rising, he said, with a velocity of 267 kilometers per second to heights sometimes surpassing 80,000 kilometers. That poor colleague has made a profound error; these projections have a much lower velocity—but the matter disseminated in space, and temporarily invisible, reappears as a vapor that cools and becomes visible along its entire length within a few seconds.

Tuesday, April 5. Although half-suffocated by the temperature of the vehicle, I'm continuing my spectroscopic studies and my calculations.

The corona is very dense to an extent of 500,000 kilometers around the solar globe. Of the chromosphere, where the immense whirlwinds known as sunspots are produced, I can see nothing but a formidable ocean of fire, forming the second envelope of the Sun. As for the photosphere, it appears to be neither solid, nor liquid, nor gaseous, but seems to be composed, like terrestrial clouds, of mobile particles, and to be dancing on an ocean of gas of enormous weight and cohesion.

Although suffering frightfully, I've succeeded in analyzing the composition of the solar mass itself, and I've identified in the spectroscope the 450 black lines characteristic of iron in combustion in its gaseous state, the 118 of titanium, the 75 of calcium, the 57 of manganese and the 33 of nickel. I recognize, besides, traces of cobalt, chromium, sodium, barium, magnesium, copper, potassium, and finally hydrogen and oxygen, at a very high temperature.

My chronometer marks 4 p.m. I can't continue any longer. The instruments are slipping out of my hands, my head is resonating with an infernal hum...everything is dancing around me...I'm losing my sense of reality. My sight is growing dark...my breast no longer swells...it seems that my heart is stopping. Is this death?

Thursday, April 9. I write that date at random, not knowing exactly how much time I remained in the comatose state from which I've just emerged.

I was awakened a little while ago by a sensation of relative coolness; it seemed to me that it was a resurrection. I was lying on the floor in the midst of my instruments. Although weak, I dragged myself to the thermometer; it marks 65 degrees. On the day on which the accident that I described on the previous page occurred, it stood at nearly 80 degrees.

I feel a sensation of incredible, but purely physical, well-being. My head is still heavy, it's true, but my blood appears to be circulating freely and I'm breathing easily. The furniture-column is within my range; I was able to extend my hand and take a carafe of eau-de-vie from a shelf and drain it by half. Revived, I got to my feet and, supporting myself with my hands on the wall, I made my way to my telescope!

Curses! The micrometer indicates a sensible diminution in the solar disk. Instead of going forward, I'm moving away...or rather, I'm falling! What has happened? In consequence of what phenomenon have I been snatched from the attractive power of light to roll through space?

A relatively uninteresting question, though—the why doesn't matter; it's sufficient that I observe the fact.

All day, I've remained immobile, my eyes riveted to the telescope. The day star is moving away in space; its diameter is decreasing. At the same time the thermometer is falling...falling....

Close enough to touch the goal...and then, nothing more! It's atrocious! I'm afraid of going mad with rage.

The realization of my impotence falls upon my skull like a lead weight.

I'm going to bed and to sleep.

Sunday, April 12. It's been two days since I had the courage to write a line. Idiotically, I remained lying in my hammock, careless of the fate that awaits me, thinking about only one thing: the awakening that drives me to despair.

Oh, to approach the furnace, even to fall into it and be devoured by the oceans of fire! But before then, to see, to contemplate—to have, if only for a few seconds, consciousness of the secrets of that marvel!

But no, the dream is over. Infinity has tempted me and infinity has absorbed me. For all eternity, I will roll like this, an inert and purposeless mass, through the starry spaces.

May God have pity on me and let me die quickly!

Tuesday, April 14. It's the end. The fall is becoming more precipitous…and the vision of Selena is haunting me again.

Will she stand before me like this until my eyelids are closed by the finger of death?

Selena…Selena…forgive me!

Here ended the notes made by Sharp in the course of his voyage—which, in accordance with his promise, he had given to Mikhail Ossipoff. When the latter, very thoughtful and mentally obsessed by the scientific revelations he had just read, had closed the notebook, the young woman got up and marched straight to her father's former enemy, with her hand extended.

"Monsieur Sharp," she said, with an adorable smile, "when you believed you were about to die, your last thought was to regret the harm that you had done me. I therefore have every reason to believe that that regret is sincere. Here is my hand; I forgive you." Enveloping Gontran—who was frowning as he listened to her—with the gaze of an enchantress, she added: "I expect all those who have some sympathy or affection for me to do likewise."

The ex-permanent secretary of the St. Petersburg Academy of Sciences formed a grimace that resembled a smile and, after having stammered a few unintelligible words by way of thanks, fell back into a somber reverie.

Farenheit had listened, motionless and silent, to what Ossipoff had read aloud. It seemed that the account of the frightful dread that his enemy had experienced had not weakened the hatred that the American had sworn against him. His eyes fixed on the ground, tugging his large beard angrily and nervously biting his lip—an indication, in him, of an irritation contained with great difficulty—Farenheit maintained that posture for a long time, as indifferent to the amicable chatter of Gontran and Selena as to Fricoulet's mocking comments. Suddenly, as if coming to a decision, he stood up, went over to Flammermont and touched his shoulder with the tip of his bony finger. "My dear sir," he said, "I want to talk to you."

"I'm listening, Mr. Farenheit."

The American shook his head. "Our conversation must be private."

Gontran got up, linked arms with the American, and went down the hill with him, stopping beneath the first trees of the Mercurian forest. "What's this about?" he said.

"I'd like to ask you a great favor."

"I'm entirely at your disposal, and if it's in my power, consider it done."

These words earned the young man one of those handshakes to which the inhabitants of the New World are accustomed, which almost dislocate the shoulder.

"Here's the thing," said Farenheit. "By virtue of the priority that Monsieur Ossipoff claims to have over me, I'm obliged to renounce my vengeance upon that wretch Sharp. On the other hand, living in company with the scoundrel who ruined me and tried to murder me is impossible..."

"But what do you want you do, my poor Mr. Farenheit?"

"What I want to do," muttered the Yankee, "is to get away."

Gontran opened his eyes wide. *Is he going mad?* he thought.

As if he had divined the young man's thought, Farenheit replied: "You're asking yourself whether I'm in my right mind. Don't worry—I've never had a clearer head in my life. So, I repeat...I want to get away. I want to go back to the Earth, and the favor I have to ask of you is that you help me accomplish that project."

The young man uttered a fervent exclamation, while waving his arms in the air in a chaotic gesture. "Me!" he said, finally, when his initial suffocation had passed. "You were counting on me to..." He stopped, strangled by an irresistible desire to laugh. "But what you're asking of me is impossible!" he continued, after a few moments.

"Impossible? Why?"

Flammermont was about to tell the truth: that he was the last person of whom one might demand such a service. Fortunately, though, he reflected on the imprudence of such a confession and abruptly changed his expression. "Because," he replied, "we're so far from Earth that—for the moment, at least—it's futile to think of repatriating ourselves..."

"Bah!" said a mocking voice behind him.

With one movement, the two men turned and saw Fricoulet.

The latter advanced toward them. "I'll begin," he said, "by offering you my most sincere apologies for having overheard part of your conversation—but you were raising your voices so loudly that they reached my ears...fortunately for you, Mr. Farenheit."

While Flammermont started in surprise on hearing his friend speak in this manner, the American ran to the engineer and gave him a bone-breaking handshake. "Then you think...." he stammered.

"I think that Gontran has not studied the matter sufficiently—in which he is, of course, following the example of Monsieur Ossipoff and Citizen Sharp."

"What do you mean?"

"That none of you three, in calculating the route that the comet will follow, has taken account of planetary perturbations."

"Eh?" retorted the young Comte, with an emphatic shrug of the shoulders. "What do planetary perturbations matter to us?"

"A great deal—and if you care to listen to me for a few moments, you'll come round to my opinion. The comet that is carrying us, being much lighter than the different worlds whose orbits it crosses, is strongly influenced by them—to the extent that the curve it is following is no longer regular, but is formed of a succession of sinuosities inflected toward the planets in proximity to which it passes. Now, if my calculations are accurate, one of the most accentuated sinuosities will be that provoked by the Earth's attraction."

Flammermont nodded his head. "At what distance do you expect us to pass our native world?"

"Pooh! Scarcely 2,000,000 leagues—which is to say that the tail of our comet will envelop the entire Earth."

"But won't that have any harmful result for our compatriots?" asked Farenheit, a trifle anxiously.

"That's something we can't know. If, by chance, it's carbon that is the dominant element in the caudal appendage of the world we're riding, it might result in a partial poisoning or even a general asphyxiation of the human race."

The Yankee uttered an alarmed exclamation.

"What would be even more serious," Fricoulet continued, "is if the nucleus itself were to crash into the Earth: a continent smashed…a kingdom crushed…Paris or New York pulverized…they would certainly be the least consequences of such a collision."

Farenheit had straightened up; he was very pale. "By God!" he groaned, in a strangled voice. "The United States destroyed! But that would be the end of the world!"

The two young men could not help smiling at this formidable national pride.

"The end of the New World, at least," added Gontran.

"Don't worry, Mr. Farenheit," Fricoulet went on. "No such thing will happen…this time, at least. Besides, the great Arago has calculated that the odds against a comet hitting the Earth during its flight through space are 280 million to one. Our native planet has already, on two separate occasions, passed through the tail of Biela's comet without suffering any other damage than a hail of aeroliths and shooting stars. [145]

---

[145] The atypical comet discovered by Wilhelm von Biela in 1826, which had a periodicity of only 6.6 years, split into two before disintegrating completely; the consequent meteor showers were easily attributable to the comet. It is understandable that many contemporary astronomers and writers of scientific romance

The American breathed deeply, his heart freed from a dire anguish.

"You think it's not unreasonable to imagine returning to Earth, then?" said Flammermont.

"My dear friend," the engineer replied, gravely, "When people have been made enough to undertake the vertiginous folly that we have undertaken, the more unreasonable they are, in my opinion, the closer they are to the truth."

"2,000,000 leagues, though?"

"We've already covered a good 30,000,000."

"That's true, but the conditions weren't the same."

"What do conditions matter to men like us?"

"Are you ready to make the attempt, then?"

"Absolutely—I'm beginning to feel nostalgic for the Boulevard Montparnasse. Then again, to tell you the truth, old Ossipoff's conversation isn't much of a distraction. Fedor Sharp is repulsive—and as for Mademoiselle Selena, I'm obliged to admit that she's very charming, but she's your fiancée, alas, and that situation of future execution…"

"Alcide!" Gontran complained, furrowing his brows.

"What do you expect, my dear chap? It's stronger than me. I detest the institution called marriage and I have a supreme horror of women; thus, I repeat, Mademoiselle Selena, whom, in any other circumstances I might perhaps find sympathetic, gets on my nerves terribly, because I know that you're going to marry her some day. My conclusion is that I'm entirely disposed to accompany Mr. Farenheit and attempt to go back home."

"But I'll be ruined!" Flammermont exclaimed, involuntarily. "You know full well that, without you…" Prudently, he did not finish his sentence.

"In that case, come with us," said the engineer.

"Abandon Selena! Do you think I would?"

"Persuade old Ossipoff to come with us."

"You know full well that he'll never consent, before having accomplished the circular voyage that he's planned."

"In that case, leave the father and kidnap the daughter."

Gontran shrugged his shoulders magnificently. "I'm an honest man," he replied, with dignity.

Fricoulet made a gesture of impatience. "Well," he grumbled, "you can't force us into eternal exile. You're welcome to roam the celestial world at your leisure, but don't prevent us from taking advantage of an opportunity, which might never present itself again, to see our motherland again…"

A terrible perplexity was painted on Flammermont's features.

"Remember," the engineer went on, "that there's no reason why this clodhopping journey should ever reach a conclusion. When he's visited the known

---

were ready to believe that such melodramatic events might be more frequent than they now appear to be.

worlds, Ossipoff will want to go on to the unknown ones. All that will take time, and while you have a perfect right, with regard to Selena, to spend your future like this, you'll both be so old and exhausted that you'll only want one thing: eternal sleep." Folding his arms comically, he added: "Just between us, your role as a perpetual fiancé is beginning to seem ridiculous, and it's high time that the mayor settled that situation."

"You're right," Gontran replied, utterly disconcerted. "Absolutely right—but what can I do?"

"Make all your preparations with a view to departure…and when the moment comes, we'll act."

"In what manner?"

"That, we can't know yet. Everything depends on circumstances. For the moment, we're not concerned with that, but with the means to employ in getting away."

"And do you have that means?"

"Very nearly."

Farenheit and the young Comte drew nearer to the engineer, curiously "What is it?" the asked, simultaneously.

"A balloon."

A double exclamation of surprise replied to this word. The American spoke first. "You're not thinking of leaving here in a balloon! Traveling 2,000,000 leagues through space in a balloon is crazy!"

The engineer looked at them both, calmly. "Why is it crazy?" he replied. "As I told you a little while ago, the tail of the comet that's carrying us will, at a given moment, extend as far as the Earth. Once we're in the terrestrial atmosphere, it will be sufficient to open the valve to set foot on our native planet."

Gontran, mouth agape and eyes wide open, listened to his friend's speech, thinking that it was a hoax. After a moment's reflection, though, he said: "Admitting that the route through space of which you speak is open to us…it's the balloon we lack."

"What about our selenium sphere? Doesn't that count?"

This time, Flammermont's bewilderment was complete.

"What?" cried Farenheit. "You're thinking of using that metal machine?"

"Why not? The sphere's weight, compared to its volume, is minimal, and once full of gas, it will be powerful enough to transport all the voyagers who entrust themselves to it to Paris or New York."

"Gas…gas," repeated Farenheit, shaking his head. "I'd like to know how you expect to find that."

"I don't have any such expectation, simply the intention of manufacturing it." While speaking, he took the inevitable notebook out of his pocket and scribbled rapidly on one of the pages. "Here," he said, eventually, "is the calculation I've made, taking account of the intensity of the surface gravity on the world we're on."

They read:

Weight of selenium sphere	*400 kilograms.*
Weight of six voyagers	*300 kilograms.*
Apparatus, rigging, gondola, etc.	*250 kilograms.*
Luggage, food, instruments, etc.	*250 kilograms.*
Total	*1,200 kilograms.*

"Our sphere measures exactly 10.50 meters in diameter, or 630 cubic meters of capacity," Fricoulet continued. "By filling it with pure hydrogen—which, by virtue of the great density of the atmosphere that surrounds us, gas an ascensional force of two and a half kilograms—we'll have sufficient force to lift us all with a breach of equilibrium more than sufficient to allow us to reach our goal."

"What will that difference of equilibrium be?" Gontran asked.

"That of the sphere filled with pure hydrogen, everything included and ready to depart, and the weight of air displaced—no less than 300 kilograms."

"You have an answer for everything, then," said Flammermont. "It only remains to set to work."

"And as soon as possible, for even though we have three months before us, we haven't a moment to lose."

"Three months!" cried Farenheit, in a disappointed tone. "I have to tolerate the sad and repulsive appearance of that devil Sharp for three more months!"

"What do you expect, Mr. Farenheit? You'll have to arm yourself with patience."

"If you only knew how my fingers are itching to get within range of that wretch and fasten themselves around his throat! Seriously, you think there's no other means of getting out of here before the time you've just specified?"

"I said three months, for that's certainly the minimum time that it will take the comet to reach Earth's orbit. Fortunately for us, in fact, for we won't be ready."

"Not ready!" exclaimed Gontran. "But one can do a great many things in three months."

"We don't have three months," Fricoulet continued, "because we have to deduct the time during which we'll be obliged to go underground to flee the solar fire. Within a few days, it will be impossible for us to remain where we are….and we'll have to stay underground until the comet, having passed its perihelion, had resumed its journey toward its aphelion. Only then can we begin work…is that agreed?"

"It's agreed."

As a sign of alliance, the three men shook hands.

"Above all, not a word to anyone—even Mademoiselle Selena."

Gontran blushed slightly. "I'll be as mute as a carp!"

When they went back up to the camp, Ossipoff's daughter had already gone to bed. Up above, on the observation platform, they could hear the old scientist arguing with Fedor Sharp in loud voices.

"So be it, my dear colleague," said the latter, bitterly, "I yield to your reasoning; I admit that the solar protuberances are produced by incandescent gaseous masses—but what force projects them in that manner into the superior regions? On that point, I believe you'll agree with me in attributing the phenomena to low specific gravity."

"Not at all, not at all," replied Ossipoff. "The phenomena are nothing other than veritable eruptions, due to a propulsive force born within the Sun itself. How, otherwise, can we explain the protuberances? If the latter were due solely to the lightness of the gas, they would simply rise up in a straight line. Does what I just said seem logical to you?"

Sharp uttered a sort of grunt, which might, strictly speaking, have qualified as acquiescence.

"As for the origin of the masses of hydrogen thus projected," Ossipoff went on, "I cannot admit that they originate in the Sun itself, as you affirmed just now."

"For what reason, if you please?"

"The reasons, if you please, are twofold. The first is that the volume of the Sun would be diminished by them, since the number of daily eruptions averages 200; the second is that the ambient atmosphere would increase indefinitely by virtue of the adjunction of that gas, which arrives there from every direction."

"Then what's your opinion, my dear colleague?"

"That, by virtue of a phenomenon we can now explore, the gaseous masses projected by the Sun fall back on its surface, to be projected again and to fall again."

"And so on, until the end of time," retorted Fedor Sharp, in a mocking voice.

"Exactly like the jet of water in the Tuileries," whispered Gontran in Fricoulet's ear. The latter shut him up with a jab of his elbow in order to listen to the ex-permanent secretary's reply.

"You do understand, my dear colleague," he said, "that your argument about the diminution of the solar mass can't be sustained for an instant. The hydrogen contained in the interior of the Sun is subject to such a formidable pressure and, on the other hand, it occupies a space so large, that for the eruptions by which it recovers its liberty to deflate the central star would take millions and millions of centuries."

"Then what would happen?"

"What would happen, no doubt, is that the Sun would go out, as other suns have doubtless done before it... Nature is not immutable, my dear colleague; it's eternal transformation that makes eternal life."

Ossipoff remained silent for a moment. Then the two young men heard an impatient click of a tongue, followed by these words pronounced in a dry tone: "It's getting late...we should get some rest."

"As you wish, my dear colleague," Fedor Sharp replied, softly.

The two young men only just had time to jump into their hammocks; the scientists' footsteps were already resonating on the stairway.

"You know," said the engineer, leaning over toward Flammermont, "it seems to me that your future father-in-law has been stumped."

"It'll only make him grumpier tomorrow, mark my words."

"I think you'd better look over your *Continents célestes*," retorted Fricoulet.

"We'll see about that when it's light. For now, I'm going to sleep. Goodnight!"

And Flammermont was not long delayed in going to sleep, to dream that the selenium balloon that had carried them through space had just set down on the racecourse at Longchamp on the day of the Grand Prix.

Chapter XXXII
The Selenium Balloon

Since the day of their reconciliation, Mikhail Ossipoff and Fedor Sharp had established a rota between themselves, which ensured that the celestial phenomena would not remain unobserved for an instant. Two days after the scene that has just been reported, therefore, Sharp, perched on the platform of the observatory, was doing his astronomical shift when he suddenly uttered a loud cry. Immediately, all the members of the little colony abandoned their occupations and ran to the stairway, surrounding the ex-permanent secretary in a matter of minutes.

The latter, his limbs agitated by a nervous tremor, was clutching the telescope in both hands; he kept his eye glued to the ocular lens, without paying any heed to the questions that were addressed to him. Finally, Fricoulet took hold of him and wrenched him away from the instrument, muttering: "Come on, you're playing games. What did that cry that brought us running signify?"

"You don't disturb people for nothing," complained the American.

Sharp, who was struggling, succeeded in escaping the hands that held him. "The Sun!" he stammered. "The Sun!" And he hastened to resume his place at the telescope.

Ossipoff, seized by a presentiment, leapt on the marine binoculars that Farenheit wore constantly around his neck and aimed them at the flaming star. "Great God!" he exclaimed. Then he fell silent, entirely given over to contemplation.

Seeing that, Fricoulet threw himself downstairs and climbed back up armed with one of the spare telescopes found in Fedor Sharp's shell. A few moments later, the entire colony was installed on the platform studying the Sun, some with the aid of telescopes, others with binoculars. All of them stood still, mute and breathless, fixed in a stupefied immobility.

In truth, the spectacle the offered itself to them was fantastic. It seemed that the entirety of the occidental nimbus of the Sun had suddenly exploded, and that a formidable blaze had been projected into space from the flanks of the star. It was as if whirlwinds of flame, in which rockets blazed with marvelous intensity, extended for several 1000 kilometers. Gradually, however, the eruption appeared to calm down; the glare of the flames diminished, and there was soon nothing but a mass of faintly iridescent gas, floating 240,000 kilometers from the solar surface, about 88,000 kilometers deep and 160,000 long. This mass seemed tranquil, even motionless, and it was attached to the solar surface by three or four vertical columns, shining with an exceedingly bright light, and, by contrast, animated by a lively movement.

Suddenly, without any anterior perturbation to presage it, a titanic dust-cloud appeared, coming from the solar mass. The gaseous cloud tore apart and broke up, scattering into space in brilliant threads, which climbed, in less than ten minutes, to a height of 300,000 kilometers. As they rose up, they diminished in size and brightness, melting into space like bursting soap-bubbles. Soon, nothing remained to recall the memory of that marvelous firework display but a few hazy clouds with, close to the chromosphere, a few slightly brighter flames.

Soon, a flaming cloud emerged from the solar surface, small in dimension at first, but which grew rapidly to considerable proportions. Jets of flame sprang forth from the flanks of the cloud, which began by colliding tumultuously with one another as if they were losing their balance, until a sudden surge of solar pressure, doubtless more violent than its predecessors, raised them up to a height of 80,000 kilometers. Once there, they evaporated.

The Terrans waited for some time, hoping that the admirable vision might appear once again to their dazzled eyes—but the solar disk had resumed its ordinary appearance, offering no presumption of a further eruption. They remained mute, though. Immobilized by the spell of the magnificent spectacle.

Fricoulet broke the silence first. "My word!" he exclaimed, in a voice still tremulous with emotion. "That alone was worth the trip."

"It beats the *1001 Nights*," said Gontran, in his turn, rubbing his eyes, which were still dazzled by the magical panorama.

Even Farenheit, who was usually refractory in the face of celestial matters, appeared prey to an unaccustomed agitation.

"Finally, Mr. Farenheit," said Selena, wagging her finger at him, "I've seen you enthralled."

"Enthralled, me!" replied the Yankee, stiffening in response to the word as if it were an insult. "You're mistaken, Miss Selena. I'm not enthralled…I'm merely regretting that one can't organize pleasure-trips from New York to the suburbs of the Sun. One could make money like crazy."

Fricoulet burst out laughing. "It's evident," he said, "that you don't have capital invested in the Niagara Falls—solar eruptions would, I think, provide them with serious competition."

Meanwhile, Mikhail Ossipoff and Fedor Sharp busied themselves making fair copies of the algebraic notes succinctly made in the course of their observations.

"Well?" said Ossipoff, suddenly, after having checked his calculations one last time.

"Well?" replied Fedor Sharp, interrogatively, having stopped writing. "What results do you have my dear colleague?"

"If I'm not mistaken, my dear colleague," Selena's father replied, in his turn, "I find for the first phase of the phenomenon—which is to say, that sort of gaseous cloud extended over the solar nimbus—two seconds of height and three minutes 15 seconds of width. Is that correct?"

"That's correct," replied the other, in a honeyed tone, covertly furious at not having been able to find his colleague's astronomical science at fault.

"Then, for the second phase," Ossipoff continued, "I believe I observed that each of the items of debris measured 16 seconds in length and two to three seconds in width." He stopped, waiting for a gesture of approval from Sharp, but the other remained mute. Then the old man concluded by adding: "Finally, the greatest height to which, in my reckoning, the aforementioned items of debris were projected, is 7 minutes 49 seconds."

Sharp closed his notebook with a loud click, while Ossipoff closed his own silently, with a little ironic smile on his lips.

Farenheit came toward them then. "Gentlemen," he said, "I presume that all the calculations to which you have just devoted yourself are of undeniable interest, but it would be no less interesting, in my opinion, to occupy yourselves with a means of keeping us safe during the perihelion of the world that is carrying us."

Before either of the two scientists said anything, Flammermont added, in a grave tone: "If my calculations are accurate, we shall pass only 230,000 leagues from the central star—which is to say, at a distance 160 times smaller than that which separates it from our native planet, and our situation will be similar to having to support on Earth, one a day in August, not the heat of 160 suns, but the square of that number: 25,600."

Farenheit released a groan of terror. "Brrrr! Your calculations make my blood run cold."

The engineer could not help smiling. "Although it describes your impression precisely, Mr. Farenheit, your expression is slightly inappropriate. An iron sphere equal in size to the Earth and raised to a similar temperature would take 50,000 years to cool down."

"By God!" muttered the American. "In that case, I must renounce all hope of ever seeing New York again."

"Why is that?"

"For three reasons: I'm not made of iron; I'm not as big as the Earth; and I don't have 50,000 years to live." And he looked at the scientists desperately.

"Well, my dear colleague," declared Fedor Sharp, slyly, "what becomes of your theory of universal habitability in the present case? It seems to me to be slightly compromised."

Ossipoff shrugged his shoulders. "If you want my opinion, my dear colleague," he replied, "it's this: given the rapidity with which our comet is moving in its orbit—more than 500 kilometers a second—I'm convinced that, in spite of the furnace that it has to pass through, it won't have time to warm up very profoundly. Perhaps its surface will have to suffer, but by taking certain precautions...."

"Hmm!" said Sharp, shaking his head dubiously.

"Do you remember the comet of 1843, my dear colleague?" retorted the old man. "It was not 230,000 leagues away, as we shall be, but only a mere 31,000 leagues. Now, as the admirable phenomenon that we have just witnessed has proved, the flaming materials that the central star emits from its bosom are sometimes thrown to a height of 80,000 leagues. It was therefore necessary for that comet to pass through that brazier—which, according to the anticipations of science, should have consumed it, volatilized it and annihilated it. Well, it came out of it absolutely intact and undisturbed in its progress."

"Comets doubtless belong to the race of salamanders," murmured Gontran.

Fedor Sharp's face had lengthened immeasurably. Then the ex-permanent secretary raised his arms into the air and declared, in a gruff tone, that he withdrew any responsibility for anything that might happen in future.

"Very good," muttered Farenheit. "It's not only my responsibility that I want to withdrew, but myself."

"Don't worry, Mr. Farenheit," said Fricoulet, who had overheard the American's reflection. "My friend Gontran has, I think, found an excellent means of sheltering us from the solar radiation."

"Me!" the young Comte tried to say—but the engineer shut him up with an elbow discreetly jabbed into his ribs.

"We'll transport everything the sphere contains into the shell; then we'll push the shell out over to the surface of the sea from which we fished it out, until the plumb-line gives us sufficient depth. Then we'll shut ourselves in the projectile, which will sink under our weight; thus submerged, we'll wait until the comet, after going around the Sun, has resumed its route towards its aphelion."

"That's very clever," said Ossipoff, "but what about our astronomical observations?"

"Ah!" said the engineer. "For this, you'll have to put your instruments away for a few days."

Sharp folded his arms. "Then we'd have come so far for nothing!" he complained. "That's impossible."

"Listen," said Gontran, putting a hand on is shoulder. "You're at liberty not to follow us, and to let yourself be volatilized by the Sun."

"A fine death, full of poetry, and out of the ordinary," added Fricoulet, with a snigger.

"It's a kind of suicide that's not available to everyone," Farenheit declared, coldly.

"Unfortunately," the engineer added, "We can't leave you free to act as you wish...your body is useful to us."

"Useful!" stammered Sharp, his voice catching in his throat. He thought that his companions, going back on their word, were proposing to do away with him.

"Yes," Fricoulet repeated, "useful as weight. The six of us, according to Monsieur de Flammermont's calculations, add up to the weight strictly necessary for the immersion of the shell. A few kilograms less, and we wouldn't be able to attain the necessary depth. You see, therefore, that you're indispensable to us."

"And what's more," added Selena smiling, "you don't have the right to get any thinner."

Gontran suddenly uttered a slight exclamation. "But what are we going to do to get out of it—for we're gong to have to float up to the surface at the appropriate time?"

The engineer gestured with his hand, instructing him not to worry. "Given," he said, "that we do indeed have to surface again, it's necessary that the liquid mass that protects us against the solar heat should perform its duty until the end and not evaporate."

"What about the sphere?" asked Farenheit. "Isn't there a danger that it will be damaged, raised to the temperature of red hot iron, and that it might take several months to cool down. How will we make use of it then?"

"Bah!" replied Ossipoff. "We have the shell now."

The American was about to reply that the shell could not replace the sphere in the role for which the latter was destined, but Fricoulet silenced him with an imperative glance. "In the situation in which we find ourselves," he said, in an indifferent tone, "how can we know whether we'll have need of any of the objects we presently possess? We'll take the sphere with us and immerse it at the same time as ourselves."

That same day, the Terrans tried to figure out how to transport everything that it was important for them to retain to the shore of the liquid expanse into which they intended to sink.

Within 48 hours, they had constructed a sort of hurdle out of branches, beneath which, in the guise of wheels they fitted two slightly-polished tree-trunks for and aft. Iron crampons were fixed to the hurdle, curved like hooks in order to penetrate the two extremities of the tree-trunks, thus forming a sort of axle around which the masses of wood could rotate. The sphere and everything it contained was loaded on to this primitive chariot, and the five men hitched themselves to the selenium cables adapted as traces for the occasion.

Selena, offered the opportunity to climb on to the improvised carriage, refused forcefully, not wanting to increase her friends' fatigue and already disappointed by not being able to lend them some assistance.

It took three full days—or, rather, three nights, since they rested while the Sun shot its fiery darts at the comet—to attain their objective, but once they were there, matters made rapid progress. In a few hours, the transfer of movable objects from the sphere to the shell was completed, and the shell itself, drawing the selenium sphere in its wake, was put into the water and pushed out to sea.

It was not until they were about two leagues from the shore that the sounding-line indicated a depth of 20 meters—the depth estimated as necessary to shield the Terrans from the radiation of the solar furnace.

Thanks to Fricoulet's ingenuity, the embarkation was accomplished very comfortably. The engineer had the idea of unscrewing the porthole accommodated in the upper part of the shell, which served to illuminate the makeshift observatory established in the vehicle's nose-cone. Selena—who, being unable to swim, had made the journey seated on the platform of the sphere—had no difficulty in passing from the platform to the porthole by means of a plank that served as a bridge. Afterwards, the Terrans climbed up to the aperture one by one by means of a rope-ladder, then vanished into the device. When only Fricoulet remained, the rim of the porthole was grazing the surface of the liquid expanse so closely that it sufficed for the engineer to dive head-first into the shell, where he fell into Gontran's arms, while Ossipoff and Sharp, standing at the ready, screwed down the hatchway again. All this was done so rapidly that they scarcely shipped 20 liters.

"Oof!" cried Fricoulet, taking off his respirol after having turned on the air tap. "Things are going very smoothly."

"Do you think we're sinking?" Gontran asked.

"If that were not the case, your calculations would be at fault," replied the engineer. "Fortunately, they're correct, as you can easily convince yourself." It was, indeed, easy to observe through the portholes that they were sinking, and that the descent was taking place rapidly. Only a few minutes elapsed before there was a slight shock.

"We've arrived," Ossipoff declared.

"A singular sea-bathing station," Gontran could not help saying. "In heatwaves, our compatriots go to plant their tents on some beach or other, at Trouville, Dieppe or the like. For us, being more refined, the sea breeze is insufficient—we go to the sea-bed in search of coolness."

This whimsy awoke no echo. Ossipoff and Fedor Sharp had plunged into one of the interminable scientific disputes that blew up between them at the slightest provocation. Farenheit, exhausted by the incessant fatigue of the previous days, was drowsing on the divan while awaiting the meal that Selena was busy preparing. Fricoulet, seated in a corner, was totting up his figures. Flammermont stifled a sonorous yawn and, not even having the resource of exchanging ideas with his companions, resigned himself to following the American's example and going to sleep.

He was woken up be the sound of irritated voices.

"I tell you that it is…"

"I tell you that it's not…"

"What you claim is absurd."

"What you contend is not common sense."

"Look at my calculations…"

"Look at mine…"

Gontran opened his eyes and saw Ossipoff and Sharp standing none-to-nose a short distance away, their eyes sparkling and their faces swollen, each brandishing his notebook menacingly.

The young man got up and joined them. "Monsieur Sharp, I entreat you…my dear Monsieur Ossipoff, I beg you…for the sake of self-respect…your scientific dispute…" Gradually, they drew apart; then when they were out of one another's reach and his intervention seemed to have calmed them somewhat, he said: "Let's see—what are you arguing about?"

"The course of the comet that's carrying us."

Fricoulet looked up. "That," he said, "is a discussion whose subject seems to me rather premature—for, if the solar heat is going to volatilize the aforesaid comet…"

Ossipoff shook his head in a sign of forceful negation. "The data that I revealed just now prove superabundantly that it's necessary to set that eventuality aside."

"Very good," muttered the engineer, resuming his calculations.

"Therefore," Ossipoff went on, "my excellent colleague, Monsieur Sharp, claims that the comet's orbit will intersect the Earth's orbit at a distance of about 2,000,000 leagues from our native planet."

Fricoulet shuddered and left his seat, coming to strand beside Gontran. "What about you?" he asked. "What do you presume, Monsieur Ossipoff?"

"That the influence of the Sun on the cometary nucleus will manifest itself by a westward deviation of its orbit—a deviation that I estimate at about 6,000,000 leagues."

The two young men uttered stifled exclamations, at the same time as a furious oath exploded behind them. "By God!" howled Farenheit. "That's too much!"

The old scientist looked at the American in astonishment. "What's the matter?" he asked. Then, as if the embarrassed and discomfited expressions had suddenly clarified his mind, he exclaimed: "Ah! I've got it…your long conversation the other day…the selenium sphere that you were determined to keep in spite of its uselessness…that's it, of course! You made a plan to reach the Earth by balloon while the comet was close by…"

"But we want to take you with us, Monsieur Ossipoff," the young Comte declared.

"I don't doubt it, my friend" the old man retorted, with a smile, "and I'm grateful for your good intentions—which, fortunately, are unnecessary."

"Fortunately…" murmured Flammermont. "From your point of view, perhaps, but from mine and Selna's it's entirely different."

"Bah!" Ossipoff replied, indulgently. "You'll be all the happier later—not to mention that you didn't let me finish. If the perturbation induced in the comet's course by the Sun takes us further away from Earth, it will, on the other hand, take us to within 20,000 kilometers of Mars."

That's precisely what I dispute," cried Fedor Sharp. "It's mathematically impossible for the distance to be so minimal... Otherwise, we'd have to pass between Mars and its satellites."

"I beg your pardon," Ossipoff replied, "it's not the planet Mars itself I was talking about, but its system.

The furious expression of Sharp's face disappeared immediately. "In that case," he said, in a softer voice, "you're right. Given that it's the Martian system you're talking about, my calculations agree with yours." And he put out his hand to shake the one that Ossipoff held out to him.

"A fortunate inspiration you had, my dear Gontran," the latter added, "to conserve the sphere and immerse it with us, for it will still permit us to leave the comet and land, if not on Mars itself, at least on one of its satellites."

"I proposed," the young man said, "to fill it with hydrogen gas."

"An excellent idea. Thanks to the balloon's metallic envelope, it will be possible for us to conserve our gas indefinitely."

"But Father," said Selena, who had been listening for some while, "isn't the selenium too heavy for the role you want it to play?"

It was Fricoulet who got in ahead of the old man and replied. "You need have no fear of that, Mademoiselle," he said. "The density of the metal is no problem, since we're on a world whose gravity is less than half of that at the Earth's surface. Besides, Gontran has told me that a balloon made entirely of copper was made in France a few years ago."

"That's not possible!" the young woman exclaimed.

"I beg your pardon, Mademoiselle, but the aeronaut who carried out that experiment in Paris—in 1845, I think—wasn't just anyone."

"It was Dupuis-Delcourt, wasn't it?" asked Ossipoff.[146]

"Your memory is correct, my dear Monsieur, and that was the precedent that gave Gontran the idea of utilizing our selenium sphere to repatriate ourselves."

"Unfortunately, as I told you just now, the comet isn't taking us in the direction of the Earth at all, but that of Mars—or, rather, its first satellite, Deimos."

"Head for Deimos, then," said Flammermont. Privately, he added: *The Martians, who are supposed to have arrived at the culminating point of their civilization, might perhaps be familiar with the institution of marriage—and then, oh Selena...* And, delighted by the prospect of a prompt denouement to his

---

[146] Jules-François Dupuis-Delcourt (1802-1864) was the most prolific early writer of textbooks and practical manuals of aeronautics, but the balloon he constructed out of copper strips weighed 770 lbs. and never got off the ground.

situation as a perpetual fiancé, the young man ran to the young woman and kissed her hands ecstatically.

After a fortnight of this subaquatic reclusion, Ossipoff and Fedor Sharp having reached agreement—which required no less than 48 hours of heated and bittersweet debate—in declaring that the comet had resumed its progress towards its aphelion, the Terrans decided to come out of their cockleshell. This decision was, however, easier to make than to carry out; in order to get out of the vehicle, it was necessary to get it back to the surface—and to do that, it was necessary for its weight to be reduced.

"If you wish," said Farenheit to his companions, "I'll be the one to lighten the shell's burden. I'm a good swimmer, and 50 fathoms above my head doesn't trouble me at all. I'll get up there quicker than you."

This offer was accepted. As they had done when it was a matter of sinking like a stone, thanks to Fricoulet's introduction into the projectile, Ossipoff and Sharp grasped the hatchway, ready to unscrew it at an agreed signal. As for Farenheit, he placed himself directly below the hatchway with his head encased in his respirol and his legs flexed, ready to straighten up when the hatchway had produced the opening necessary to his passage.

Finally, Gontran gave the signal. The hatchway was scarcely open when the American, launched by a violent contraction of his muscles, shot out like an arrow. Then the opening was hermetically sealed.

"Hey!" said Fricoulet, triumphantly. "Not a drop of water! That was a lovely maneuver."

Ossipoff and Sharp looked at one another in astonishment. "Too good, in my opinion," murmured the former.

"And in mine," said the second in his turn. "There's some mystery here."

"All the more so," exclaimed Selena, "as we're not moving at all. It's as if Mr. Farenheit weight no more than a man of straw."

"That's true!" exclaimed Gontran, leaping to on of the vehicle's lateral portholes. Scarcely was he there than he uttered an exclamation of amazement. "There's no more water!"

"No more water!" repeated the Terrans' voices, like so many echoes, on perceiving around the shell, for as far as the eye could see, a kind of ocean of black dust, reflecting the gentle light of Venus. Then, as one, they all turned around to look at one another with bewildered expressions.

"What can it mean?" asked Fedor Sharp and Gontran de Flammermont, in chorus.

"Quite simply," replied Fricoulet, "that, as we anticipated, the solar heat at perihelion was such that the liquid mass beneath which we were immersed has volatilized, and that we're now resting on the bed of the cometary sea whose evaporation prevented us from being roasted.

"That seems to be the only plausible explanation," said Ossipoff.

"At any rate," added Selena, "it's certain that we can get out of here with dry feet."

Suddenly, Fricoulet exclaimed: "We're forgetting poor Farenheit. What's become of him?"

In the blink of an eye, the Terrans had put on their respirols and opened the manhole. They rushed outside. Gontran, who was in the lead, stumbled over Farenheit's body, extended motionless on the ground. With Fricoulet's help, he lifted him up and carried him into the shell. There, his helmet was opened and they found a deep gash on his head, from which blood was flowing abundantly.

"It's nothing," the engineer declared, applying a cloth strip impregnated with arnica to the wound. "He'll come round in a few minutes."

"But how could that have happened to him?" asked Selena.

"In the simplest imaginable fashion. "He launched himself through the hatchway with the full force of his legs, but instead of encountering the liquid mass that ought to have sustained him until he reached the surface he encountered empty space, and fell head-first on to the bed of the cometary ocean."

"That's it exactly, my dear Fricoulet," stammered the wounded man, in a slightly weak voice, having opened his eyes at that moment. Then, rubbing his eyes, he added in a more forceful tone: "By God, what a shock! I saw, as you say in France, 36,000 candles."

"Here!" said Gontran, handing him a glass of port. "This will put you back on your feet."

The Amerian drained the glass in a single gulp, then leapt to his feet. "Now, to work!" he declared.

They all put their respirols on again and immediately began making preparations for departure. They sought out the makeshift chariot on which they had brought the sphere from the Mercurian hill in the location where they had left it before the immersion, and they rolled it to the place where Sharp's shell had been immersed. Then the shell and the sphere were loaded on to the chariot and the Terrans—slowly and with difficulty—took the route back to their initial encampment.

At every step, however, they experienced further surprises, occasioned by the complete transformation of the landscape. Where, 15 days earlier, they had crossed a plain, it was now necessary for them to climb a hill; to their left, where a chain of mountains with sparkling peaks had formerly loomed up, the ground seemed to have been leveled off as if by a giant's axe; to the right, by contrast, where the down-sloping ground had hollowed out a funnel, there presently stood a monstrous peak. Here, they had been obliged to cross a sort of miry marsh which, completely dried out, was now transformed into a profound depression full of black and blinding dust; there, on the contrary, where they had previously walked with dry feet, a spring had emerged, running brim-full over a newly-hollowed bed.

Just as long as our hill, Fricoulet thought, *hasn't also been transformed, volatilized or evaporated...that would complicate things considerably.*

Fortunately, this dread was vain. When they arrived, after ten days of prodigious effort, in sight of their former encampment, they found everything in the state in which they had left it; the bed of the stream, however, was dry, and the charred and desiccated forest trees extended their blackened and leafless branches into the air.

"There!" said Gontran, finally taking off his respirol. "That's one of His Excellency the Sun's jokes. This is charcoal underfoot."

The following day, they set to work in with a view to preparing the selenium sphere for the new role that it was destined to play. While Gontran and Fedor Sharp transformed the floor of the former cabin into a valve designed to be fitted to the superior part of the metallic balloon, Osipoff constructed a gondola from a sort of plant that grew on the Mercurian hill, large enough to contain all of them and yet surprisingly light.

For his part, Fricoulet did not remain inactive. With Farenheit's help, he constructed a gigantic barrel—a sort of tun with a volume of 2000 liters—which was provided with hoops by courtesy of the plant that served for the fabrication of the gondola. It was filled with iron ore, of which the engineer had found a deposit not far from the hill on which the Terrans had taken refuge. Two other barrels of smaller dimension were similarly fabricated, and joined to the first by strips of canvas steeped in gutta-percha; they would serve as gas-filters.

When that was done, it was necessary to get busy with the manufacture of the sulfuric acid necessary to the decomposition of the iron. While Gontran and Sharp, having completed their, were making a suitable excavation into a water-tight cistern, Fricoulet, with the aid of a Pifre insulator recovered from the shell,[147] distilled the strange liquid extant on the comet's surface. Before long, the cistern was filled with the water in sufficient quantity for them to be able to busy themselves with the manufacture of the gas. Not far away, the ever-questing Fricoulet had discovered a deposit of pyritic shale; he had these nuggets grilled in contact with the air; that gave him a certain quantity of crystalline iron sulfate, which he introduced into earthen vessels places on a hot fire and connected to glass bulbs. Under the influence of the heat, the iron sulfate decomposed; sulfuric acid condensed in the bulbs and all that remained in the vessels was colcothar[148] or "English rouge," the residue of the manufacture. An immense wooden tub, constructed in the same fashion as the barrel, was filled with this acid and mixed with twice its own weight of distilled water. After that,

---

[147] Abel Pifre's work on insulation led directly to his pioneering work in solar energy capture and storage, his most famous invention being a solar-powered printing press—but most of that work was done after 1889.

[148] Colcothar was the name improvised for the mixture of iron oxides resulting from this once-commonplace industrial process.

to obtain hydrogen, it was sufficient to put the mixture in contact with the iron ore in the barrel.

All these preparations had taken nearly two months of relentless labor: two months during which the skill and patience of the Terrans, even more than their strength, was put to a rude proof; two months during which astronomical study was put on one side, to the point at which a spider might have spun a web over the objective lens of the telescope.

Gontran's astonishment was, in consequence, considerable when he aimed the instrument into space one evening and perceived his native planet, with its continents bizarrely marked out upon the dark stains of its oceans, the white patches of its polar snows, and its swirls of cloud extending through the atmosphere. He released a profound sigh.

"What's the matter?" Fricoulet asked him, coming over to him.

Extending his hand toward the Earth in a tragic gesture, Flammermont replied: "Is it not there, alas that the municipal official is to be found, before whom I aspire to appear in company with my dear Selena?"

The engineer burst into laughter. "Eh? Don't you find that the atmosphere that surrounds the Earth is affecting the tricolor tint of the aforementioned municipal official's sash? It's the torture of Tantalus." And he added: "We've already had *Mignon aspirant au ciel*—now we have *Gontran aspirant au maire*."[149]

The engineer would doubtless have continued in that vein for some time had he not been interrupted by Ossipoff's voice.

"Monsieur Fricoulet," the old man said, "we'll need to be ready for departure in 48 hours. How long do you think it will take to load the gas into the sphere?"

"Exactly 48 hours, Monsieur Ossipoff," the young man replied, having thought about it for a few minutes.

"It's necessary, then, for you to get to work immediately…for I repeat, the moment is approaching when we'll need to leave this place."

Two days later, the sphere—having been filled with hydrogen with the aid of a reciprocating pump, which had extracted the atmospheric air and replaced it with the gas—was swaying at the summit of the hill, contained by a sort of wide-meshed net formed by selenium wires crudely attached to the cabin, parachute-fashion. The gondola, full of stones, was fixed at the extremity of this net to prevent the apparatus from flying off into space.

---

[149] "Mignon aspirant au ciel" [Mignon yearning for Heaven] originated in 1839 as a water-color by Ary Scheffer (1795-1856) but achieved international celebrity as a mass-produced inspirational engraving by Aristide Louis. The heroine's attitude was often used in literary comparison and parody; Fricoulet's dig at Gontran's yearning for the Town Hall, where the civil formalities of his marriage would be required to take place, is a trifle cruel.

While his companions were busy loading everything they needed to take into the aerial skiff, Ossipoff, his eye glued to his telescope, was scanning the celestial immensity. Suddenly, he clicked his tongue impatiently, thus attracting Fricoulet's attention.

"What is it?" the engineer asked.

"Deimos isn't there."

"Damn! Was his Papa, Professor Hall, mistaken in thinking that he had discovered him? After all, it's perfectly possible that Mars has no satellites at all."[150]

The old man shook his head and frowned. "Hall was clear-sighted," he replied, "and now I've found the key to the mystery. The satellite we're looking for is, at present, at the other extreme of its orbit, hidden by Mars and more than 40,000 kilometers away from us."

"What are we going to do, then?" asked Gontran.

Ossipoff remained pensive for a while. "There might be one means," he said, finally. "That's to change our plan and, instead of aiming for Deimos, attempt to land on Phobos, from which we'll scarcely be separated, in six hours time, by a few 1000 kilometers. What do you think, Monsieur de Flammermont?" In serious situations the old man renounced the familiar modes of address that he was accustomed to employ with regard to his future son-in-law.

"My dear Monsieur," said the young Comte. "I can only approve of the idea."

"All the more so," Fricoulet said, "as Phobos is only 6000 kilometers away from Mars—it will be easier for us to jump from the satellite to the planet."

The aged scientist was undoubtedly about to launch into some supplementary explanation, but a noisy argument suddenly broke out between Sharp and Farenheit, distracting his attention and that of the two young men. The argument concerned a voluminous package, carefully wrapped in canvas, which the American had just introduced into the gondola, and which Sharp wanted to throw out—because, he said, it was not on the list of objects to be transported.

"By God!" Farenheit complained. "Have I not, like everyone else, worked on the construction of this balloon? Don't I have the right...?"

"No," interjected the ex-permanent secretary. "You don't have the right to compromise the success of the expedition with unnecessary excess weight."

Farenheit's face became apoplectic. "Unnecessary!" he replied, grinding his teeth. "Yes, certainly, this excess would be unnecessary if you hadn't robbed me, stripped me bare and ruined me, as you have done."

Sharp advanced toward him, fists raised. The American struck a defensive pose. At that moment, Ossipoff intervened. "Come on," he said, "What's happening?"

---

[150] Asaph Hall (1829-1907) discovered the oft-anticipated satellites of Mars in circumstances detailed later in the text.

"What's happening," roared Farenheit, "is that this blackguard, whose deadly advice has wiped out my fortune, wants to prevent me from rebuilding it."

"How's that?"

"Oh, I just put a fragment of crystallized carbon in the gondola, which, if I ever have the chance to see New York again, might slightly defray the losses and hardships that I'll have suffered. Isn't that fair?"

"Certainly, my dear Mr. Farenheit," replied the old man, and I don't think a few books more or less…"

Fricoulet, who had just cast a glance over Farenheit's baggage, said: "But this weighs at least 60 kilos."

"In that case," Ossipoff went on, "Fedor Sharp is right. We can't take a supplementary weight as considerable as that."

Bizarrely enough, the American appeared to calm down at once, and he murmured: "Your calculations can't be exact, though. If, by chance, the ascensional force of the sphere were greater than you imagine…"

"Hold on, Mr. Farenheit," said the engineer, "there's a means of reconciliation. Leave your rock in the gondola for now; before taking off we'll test the force of the balloon. If it's insufficient, you'll sacrifice your 60 kilos. Is that agreeable to you?"

A singular smile creased the American's lips. "Suits me," he muttered. And he continued loading baggage as if nothing had happened.

Soon, the loading was finished and it was necessary to proceed with the embarkation.

Selena and Gontran were installed first, then Ossipoff and Fricoulet joined them. After that, Farenheit also took his place in the gondola. Fedor Sharp had wanted to be the last, in order to verify the force of the balloon personally. His animosity against the American was such that he was anticipating great pleasure at the thought of making him throw his block of diamond overboard like a vulgar sack of ballast.

The selenium sphere was now only attached to the cometary soil by a cable woven from the same plant that had provided the barrel-hoops, and it was swaying lightly; little tremors seemingly bore witness to its desire to gain its liberty.

"You see! You see!" cried Farenheit, triumphantly. "I was right! My surcharge won't prevent the balloon from lifting off."

"What about me?" replied Fedor Sharp, mockingly. "Do you think I weight no more than a feather?" So saying, he suspended himself from the rim of the gondola—whose bottom immediately struck the ground hard. "Come on," he sniggered, letting go of the gondola to grab the cable with both hands, "it's necessary to sacrifice your little millions—unless, at least, you prefer to surrender your place to it and stay here."

"There's something else you haven't thought of!" roared the American— and before anyone had time to stop him he opened his knife and cut the cable retaining the selenium balloon with a single stroke.

The balloon rose rapidly into the sky, while Fedor Sharp, losing his balance, rolled like a ball to the bottom of the Mercurian hill. A cry of horror escaped the throats of the voyagers; even Ossipoff threw himself toward Farenheit, with his arms raised in a threatening manner. "Wretch!" he exclaimed.

The American looked him up and down, with his arms folded and a mocking smile on his lips. "There!" he said. "That's what's called killing two birds with one stone. I've repaired the breach made in my fortune, and I've satisfied my vengeance."

"But I gave my word that the past was forgotten, villain!" howled the old man.

"Proof that you have a very easy-going memory. Anyway, you haven't broken your word. I'm willing to testify—in writing, if necessary—that I alone planned and carried out this execrable deed."

Mikhail Ossipoff, leaning over the edge of the gondola, scanned the space below him, searching the sparkling infinity for the cometary nucleus, now scarcely perceptible. Fricoulet looked at Gontran, and a skeptical smile played on his lips. "Poor devil!" he said. "And we promised him to keep him alive."

"Proof that we made our promise wantonly," replied the young Comte, "since Providence did not wish to ratify it."

In less than half an hour, they had covered nearly 100 kilometers. Lost in the solar radiation, the comet was invisible to the naked eye. The increasingly rarefied air had constrained the voyagers to don their respirols, and the intensity of its gravity was diminishing rapidly.

When Ossipoff's timetable marked midnight, they had traveled about 4000 kilometers and were virtually weightless, to the extent that the Terrans had to attach themselves to the gondola to avoid being thrown overboard by their slightest movement. Suddenly, the apparatus appeared to perform a pirouette, and the appearance of the sky suddenly changed.

"We've just penetrated the Martian zone of attraction," Ossipoff told Gontran, by way of his speaker.

"And that's doubtless Phobos that we see beneath us," Flammermont replied, by the same means, pointing to a little ball a few 100 kilometers away in space, which seemed to be enveloped by a reddish radiation.

The old scientist nodded his head affirmatively. Suspending himself from the metallic wire that controlled the valve, he opened it all the way, thus permitting a certain quantity of gas to escape. Immediately, the heavier balloon began to descend and the star they had to reach increased in size with a vertiginous rapidity before the Terrans marveling eyes. It seemed that they were immobile in space and that Phobos was racing to meet them.

"How long do you think the descent will last?" asked Flammermont.

454

Ossipoff darted a rapid glance at his instruments. "About an hour," he replied.

For a while longer he left the valve half-open, then closed it. He dropped a metallic cable overboard, to which a selenium bar curved in the form of a hook had been fixed, by way of an anchor.

Suddenly, the gondola received a shock; it had just touched the ground. Then, after lifting up again, the balloon fell back a few 100 meters further on, to rise up and fall back once again. After that, it began sliding on its side, dragging the gondola—to which the voyagers, roughly shaken, clung with all their might.

Finally, they came to an abrupt and conclusive halt. The anchor had evidently just dug in and immobilized the sphere—which, retained by its cable, swayed back and forth a few meters above the soil. Leaning over the edge, the Terrans examined the strange configuration of the new world on which they had landed, with anxious curiosity.

By virtue of a singular optical illusion, it seemed to them that the ground was covered with a sort of net, with a regular and rather narrow mesh, which extended as far as the eye could see.

"Oh!" Ossipoff said, immediately, to Gontran. "We must lose no time investigating one of the most interesting questions of astronomy." In response to the young man's interrogative expression, he added: "I'm talking about the canals of Mars. Perhaps what we see here, beneath our feet, will serve as a clue to resolve that curious problem right away."

Meanwhile, Fricoulet, aided by Farenheit, had thrown the rope ladder that would enable the voyagers to leave their vehicle out of the gondola. The American went down first; then it was Selena's turn. After that, Ossipoff and Gontran also climbed over the edge to rejoin their companions. Fricoulet was about to follow them when, all of a sudden, the sphere—which the old scientist had not completely drained of hydrogen and which had just been lightened by the departure of the greater part of its load—exerted such a formidable tension on its cable that the anchor broke free and it regained its liberty. Before the Terrans had time to realize what was happening, the metallic balloon was no more than a dot in the sky.

"Fricoulet! Fricoulet!" cried Flammermont, waving his arms desperately in the direction in which his friend had just disappeared—but the young man's voice did not get past the envelope of his respirol.

"Don't be afraid," said Ossipoff, putting a hand on his shoulder. "The young man may not be very knowledgeable but he's very courageous. Besides, he knows more about balloons than astronomy…I have an idea that he'll get himself out of this." Then, drawing Gontran's attention to the ground with a gesture, he asked him: "What do you think of this?"

He showed him a veritable metal net on which he had set his foot, in one of the knots of which the balloon's hook had taken hold. What was the net covering? It was impossible to get an idea, by reason of the relative darkness that reigned on Phobos; it seemed that a perpetual opaque fog hid the appearance of the little world on which they had landed from the Terrans' eyes.

Receiving no answer, Ossipoff repeated the question. Gontran remained mute, plunged as he was in profound reflection. In addition to the fact that the accident that had overtaken Fricoulet was troubling him greatly, he was not without anxiety with regard to the modification that the sudden disappearance of his source of inspiration would bring to his relationship with the old scientist—not to mention that the gondola had carried off, along with all the luggage, the blessed copy of *Les Continents célestes* that had rendered him so much service. Deprived at a stroke of his prompter and his *vade mecum*, Flammermont thought it would be absolutely impossible to continue to play the role that he has sustained so cleverly for several months. Was it necessary for him, after so many proofs, to renounce the hope of ever becoming Selena's husband? No, that could not be, that would not be! And he begged the Martian divinities to send him an inspiration.

Amazed by this mutism, Ossipoff shouted at him with all the force of his lungs: "Are you deaf?"

Gontran shook his head negatively and placed his index finger on the point of his respirol corresponding to his mouth.

"Mute!" exclaimed the old man. "You're mute?" Turning to his daughter, he said: "The poor boy! How exquisitely sensitive he is! The loss of his friend has produced such an upset that he's suddenly lost the power of speech."

The young woman threw herself into her father's arms. Her rubber mask prevented anyone from seeing the tears that were running down her cheeks, but it was easy to divine from her breast, which was rising and falling in abrupt jerks, that she was sobbing.

"There, there, darling," said Ossipoff, softened by that great distress. "It's the initial emotion…with time, it will pass."

Suddenly, Farenheit—who had remained silent until then, positively dumbfounded by the loss of his precious diamond rock—began to gesticulate, waving his arms about wildly.

His companions ran to him, and uttered cries of horror on perceiving that one of the American's feet had been gripped by claws of some sort emerging from inside the net. These claws were fitted at the extremity of long membranous wings, which themselves belonged to a hairy body, along which they extended, attached to the anterior and posterior limbs, which closely resembled the arms and legs of the human species. To a rather long neck was attached a proportionate head: a completely hairless head in which two animated glaucous eyes gleamed between lashless lids. The nose was long and mobile, like a tapir's trunk; the mouth, entirely round, was rimmed with powerful lips, partly opened to reveal formidable jaws. Hanging on to the metallic net by its claws, this strange and horrible being had seized the American by the lower leg.

Finally, with a violent effort, Farenheit freed himself, leapt 20 feet into the air, and came down again 50 meters away.

"A singular world and singular inhabitants," muttered Ossipoff. He drew his daughter away, half-dead with fright

Gontran, who was only partly reassured, followed them. *Perhaps*, he thought, *the net is designed for no other reason than to transform Phobos into a vast aviary...* And he added, with a profound sigh: *O imperfection and inanity of human science! What would the gentlemen of the Observatoire de Paris say if they could see through their telescopes that the Martian satellite is surrounded by a net like a vulgar chignon!*

"If you ask me," said Farenheit to the old man, "We should try to get away from this cage thing; apart from the fact that these vile beings inspire a profound disgust in me, walking on it isn't at all easy, and to maintain one's balance it's necessary to perform acrobatic exercises that have never been my forte."

"Bah!" replied the old scientist. "So far as this world's inhabitants are concerned, what have you to fear? By reason of our weight, which is 100 times less than on the Earth's surface, our strength will be 600 times greater. You could break the skull of one of these individuals with a flick, as if with a sledgehammer blow. As for walking, if you care to try it out, you'll see that a simple pressure of the foot will carry you like a bird for four kilometers. Go ahead and try it, if you're not convinced."

The American shook his head. "I'd be too scared of losing you," he replied.

"On the other hand," Ossipoff went on, "I'd like nothing better than to walk for a while. Firstly, it would get the numbness out of our legs, and secondly, I wouldn't be displeased to get a better idea of this microscopic world...."

"Microscopic!" Farenheit repeated.

"Why, yes! What other label would you put on a worldlet that we could explore in its entirety in ten hours?"

For five hours the Terrans marched, or rather advanced, at a steady speed, by a series of successive bounds of equal height. Suddenly, however, without any transition, night fell and thick darkness overtook Phobos. At the same time, an enormous sparkling star rose above the horizon, similar to a gigantic Moon.

"Mars!" Ossipoff declared.

"Phobos has rotated," said Selena.

"No, darling," the old man relied. "Like all satellites, Phobos always presents the same face to its planet. We're the ones who have turned, having just passed from the solar face to the Martian face."

"It's frightening to see!" cried the young woman, hiding her face in her hands. "One might think that the mass is about to fall on us and smash us to pieces."

The old scientist smiled gently and shook his head. "The sensation you're experiencing doesn't surprise me at all," he said. "It would be the same for the inhabitants of our planet if they suddenly saw the apparent diameter of the Moon become 24 times larger and its volume 6400 times greater."

"6400 times!"

"Yes, that's the exact proportion of Mars by comparison with the Moon...it would be enough to make Mr. Farenheit fear for his beloved United States."

Eventually, after an hour's progress by Marslight, the voyagers came to a place where the metallic mesh seemed to come to an end. It was near the summit of a hill, which Ossipoff immediately declared to have an elevation of 100 meters, and on which they decided unanimously to get a little rest.

"Tomorrow," Ossipoff said to Gontran, who was still struck dumb, "we'll continue on our way, and perhaps we'll obtain news of Monsieur Fricoulet."

A few moments later, in spite of his anxiety, Flammermont was sound asleep—in which he was imitated by his dear Selena and by Farenheit. As for Ossipoff, gently taking possession of the marine binoculars that the American was wearing around his neck, he aimed them at the Martian landscape displayed before his avid eyes.

One of the most singular and remarkable things about the celestial system is the difference that exists between the movement of the two satellites of Mars around their planet. While one of them, Deimos, orbits in 30 hours 17 minutes and 54 seconds, the planet itself rotates in 24 hours, 37 minutes and 23 seconds; in consequence that satellite appears to move slowly from east to west in the Martian sky. If the duration of its revolution were equal to the duration of Mars's rotation, it would be constantly visible to the inhabitants of one hemisphere, and unknown to the inhabitants of the other. The difference between that revolution and that rotation being 5 hours 41 minutes, the result is that Deimos seems to accomplish its circuit of the Martian sky in 131 hours—which is five Martian days. If, therefore, the inhabitants of the planet have, like their terrestrial brothers, a calendar regulated by the revolutionary period of their satellite, the months would be no more than five days long—which, for a year of 608 days, gives a total of 133 months.[151]

Very different conditions apply to the revolution of Phobos, the nearer satellite, which completes its entire orbit in the space of 7 hours 39 minutes. From the difference between this movement and that of Mars, which rotates in the same direction in 24 hours 37 minutes, it results that the satellite rises in the west and sets in the east, after having traversed the Martian sky with a velocity corresponding to the difference between the two movements—which is to say, about 11 hours. This is a unique example in the system of the world.

This special condition of revolution was particularly favorable to the examination of Mars that Mikhail Ossipoff wanted to make; carried by Phobos as if by a celestial racehorse at the gallop, he would race all the way around the new world, whose faces would file past his delighted eyes.

The Sun was rising on the part of the continent Huygens that is bathed by the Huggins Sea, and the satellite, overtaking in its rapid course the more slowly-rotating planet, followed the day star. As if he were in a balloon, the old scientist floated above bizarrely outlined oceans in the midst of yellowish continents, striped haphazardly by numerous streams extending in every direction. In the equatorial region, the continents Herschel and Copernicus appeared to him clearly; then to the north the Lands of Fontana. Laplace and Le Verrier; to the

---

[151] The Martian year is approximately 687 terrestrial days, or 660 Martian days, in duration.

south the isles of Green, Jacob, Cassini, Rosse, Secchi and the isthmus of Niester attaching the Land of Hall to that of Green. [152]

Dark amid the brighter oceans, bathing the equatorial coasts, the Newton Ocean and the Maraldi and Flammarion Seas extended. Then there was the strange Sablier Sea, which, after winding its bizarre contours between the continents Herschel and Copernicus, was linked to the Delambre and Beer Seas. Eventually, shining in the sunlight with an admirable brightness, the white patch of the polar snows extended from the fiftieth degree, almost at the tip of Le Verrier Land, to the South Pole.

For long hours, the scientist remained motionless, his chest strangely constricted, his gaze fixed in a sort of hypnosis on the world he had studied from the Pulkova Observatory at a distance of 19,000,000 leagues, from which he was now separated by only a few 1000 kilometers. Successively, he saw the Kepler Ocean, with the Kaiser Gulf and the curious Mediian Bay, so bizarrely cut out by the waters, and then the continents of Galileoi and Huygens, bathed to the south by the Schiaparelli Sea and to the north by the Oueman Sea, appeared and disappeared in the oriental occident.

At that moment, Phobos, drawn by its rotation, presented the face on which the Terrans had stopped to the Sun, and day dawned abruptly, without transition. Mikhail Ossipoff released a sight of regret at having been thus interrupted in his contemplative studies. Then he straightened up, and only then did the memory of his companions return to him. He turned to look at them, lying on the ground in the same positions in which drownsiness had taken them by surprise a few hours earlier, still asleep.

For a moment, he hesitated over waking them; unlike him, they did not have the passion for science that devoured his entire being to make them forget their fatigue; they were exhausted—but he thought about Fricoulet, who, given his knowledge of aerial navigation, might perhaps have succeeded in landing on the world on which they were located, and in search of whom it was necessary to set out as soon as possible. He went to Farenheit, who happened to be nearest to him, and applied his speaker to the sleeper's helmet. "Ahoy!" he cried. "Get up!"

This summons resonated in the selenium helmet with a terrible loudness— so terrible that the frightened American bounded to his feet. That same bound, though, by virtue of his body's scant weight, launched him 1000 meters into the air. "By God!" grumbled the citizen of the United States, on perceiving his

---

[152] I have transcribed the names employed by the authors, which derive from Flammarion's maps, although modern maps of Mars use a terminology derived, with appropriate modifications, from the competing maps drawn up by Schiaparelli. The authors occasionally acknowledge the competition by citing Schiaparelli's names as alternatives to Flammarion's.

companions below him, who seemed to him to be reduced to half their size, "I'm a dead man, or at least badly damaged!"

Instinctively, he closed his eyes so as not to witness his fall. To his great surprise, though, several seconds passed, then one…two…three…four minutes, and no point of contact had yet been made between Phobos and himself. Then he risked opening his eyes. How great was his amazement and bewilderment on observing that he was still at least a dozen meters from the ground, and that he was descending no more rapidly than a feather released in mid-air. Beneath him, Mikhail Ossipoff, Selena and Gontran were waving their arms desperately.

Finally, with a slowness that did not lack majesty, the American arrived within range, and was immediately grabbed by the feet by the Comte de Flammermont, impatient to regain possession of his traveling companion.

Immediately, Ossipoff signaled that he wanted to enter into communication with the young man. When the two speakers were adjusted, the old man exclaimed, victoriously: "Hey! Mr. Farenheit has just given us proof that Proctor was correct in his prognostications regarding the satellites of Mars."[153]

Gontran felt a slight shiver run down his spine at the thought that Ossipoff might take it into his head to engage in an astronomical discussion; he had already opened his mouth to reply with a non-commital "Ah!" when he suddenly remembered the mutism with which his prudence had suggested to him that he declare himself afflicted the day before. He therefore suppressed the interjection that as ready to escape his lips and contented himself with sketching a vague gesture with his head, which might have passed for an affirmation as easily as a negation.

Ossipoff, however, gripped by the urge of scientific communication, continued. "On the basis that the diameter of Phobos might, at the maximum, be 32 kilometers—which is to say, 100th of the lunar diameter—the English astronomer established that the surface area of Phobos must be 1/10,000th that of the Moon and that it volume, compared to that of the Earth's satellite, must be in the proportion of one in a million."[154] He paused momentarily, then added: "You can see the consequences immediately, can't you? The intensity of a world's surface gravity being proportional to its mass and density, as Proctor takes the Moon as a term of comparison with respect to the volume of Phobos, it is not unreasonable for us to imitate him with respect to its mass and density. It therefore follows that the intensity of gravity here is 100 times weaker than on the

---

[153] Richard Anthony Proctor (1837-1888), a prolific popularizer of astronomy, produced the first good map of Mars in 1869; like Asaph Hall, he took advantage of conjunction of 1877 to make an assiduous search for the planet's satellites, and eventually observed one of them, but not in time to claim credit for its discovery.

[154] The actual diameter of Phobos is 27 kilometers, at its longest (its shape is rather irregular).

surface of the Moon, or 600 times weaker than on the Earth's surface…have you got that?"

Gontran nodded his head several times.

"That's why Mr. Farenheit," Ossipoff said, by way of conclusion, "whose terrestrial weight is 74 kilos, weighs no more than 115 grams here—which permits him to jump, as he has just done, by the simple pressure of his feet…"

The old man, taking his fact as his point of departure, was undoubtedly about to launch into one of those philosophical dissertations to which he was accustomed, when a hand falling on his shoulder made him turn round. He found himself face to face with Farenheit—who immediately put himself in communication with him and said in a surly tone: "What are we going to do now?"

"Continue our exploration. We can't think of leaving Phobos without having done everything in our power to retrieve Monsieur Fricoulet. Don't you think so, Mr. Farenheit?"

"How can you ask me such a question?" replied the American. "Not only does humanity make it our duty to conduct such a search, but our own interests concur."

Misunderstanding the meaning of his words, Ossipoff shrugged his shoulders and replied in a scornful tone: "On that score, you have nothing to fear; from the viewpoint of our personal interests, it's 1000 times preferable that Providence has separated us from Monsieur Fricoulet and left us Gontran, whose science and ingenuity have got us out of trouble several times. Monsieur Fricoulet is, perhaps, a charming fellow, but he's the fifth wheel on a cart…"

Farenheit shook his head. "You haven't understood me. I meant that by finding the engineer, we'd also be getting back our food stores. Now I don't know if your stomach is mute, but mine is claiming its due with unparalleled energy. By God! 16 hours without eating!"

The old man slapped his forehead despairingly. "My poor Selena!" he murmured. Then, to the American, he said: "Let's get going! We need to march until our air-supply is exhausted. Let's hope that Providence, which has not abandoned us heretofore, is still watching over us, and that we'll find Monsieur Fricoulet before it's too late." With these words, he adjusted his respirol and gave the signal to depart.

In a few bounds, they descended the side of the hill on the summit of which they had spent the night, and found themselves on a plain of strange appearance. Immense fields extended as far as the eyes could see, churned up and turned over from top to bottom, occasionally forming hillocks 12 to 15 meters high. They were reminiscent, albeit on a gigantic scale, of the waste ground in the suburbs of large towns into which detritus of every sort is tipped—but it was all deserted, sterile and uncultivated; here were neither vegetables nor animals. A profound, sinister, implacable silence covered these disordered plains with its heavy and terrifying wing.

For several hours the Terrans struggled through the midst of this inextricable chaos. Their strength ran out, however; in the meantime, they were tormented frightfully by hunger, and above all by thirst—and into their breathless lungs, a thin and polluted air no longer transported life, but asphyxia.

Leaning on Gontran's arm, Selena dragged herself painfully along behind her father, who seemed not to be feeling any of the suffering endured by his companions, and marched with a light step. Bringing up the rear, stumbling at every step and complaining incessantly, was Jonathan Farenheit.

Finally, they came out of that desolate and devastated region, and walking became less difficult. Suddenly, Gontran uttered an exclamation and stopped. Selena's hand had jus released the arm that had been supporting her, and the young woman, sliding to the ground, remained lying there, motionless. Alarmed, Flammermont fell to his knees. Hastily unscrewing the selenium apparatus that imprisoned her, he perceived her pale and discolored face, her closed eyelids—whose long lashes cast a shadow over her cheek—her blanched lips and her slender nostrils. The contours of the immobile nostrils were slightly blackened by the commencement of asphyxia.

"Selena!" he moaned. "Selena!"—but this tender appeal was arrested by the walls of his selenium helmet. At the same time, a thick veil descended upon his eyes. With an incredible effort, his lungs dilated to breathe in the last puff of respirable air—but in vain. The supply had run out. The respiratory bellows expanded, closed again, expended anew. His face contracted and his fingers clenched upon the ground in a gesture of agony; then he fell backwards. Even at the approach of death, his last thought was to seize his fiancée's hand once more and to press it to his breast.

"By God!" groaned Farenheit, who had fallen some way behind the little troop but reached the two young people in a few bounds. "They're dead! They're dead!" Forgetting that his respirol would stifle the sound of his voice, he set about shouting at Mikhail Ossipoff with the full force of his lungs. The latter, not knowing what was happening behind him, continued placidly on his way.

Torn between the desire to alert the old man and a perfectly understandable reluctance to leave Gontran and Selena alone, the American stayed where he was, hesitating over the two bodies extended at his feet. All of a sudden, he saw Mikhail Ossipoff stop, totter as he put his hands to his head, then beat the air with his arms and spin around several times before finally falling down.

Farenheit thought that he was going mad, and was abruptly gripped by the sensation of the frightful solitude in which he found himself, on this unknown world, between the corpses of his companions. In a movement of despair, he raised his eyes to the heavens to beg for divine mercy.

As if in response to his prayer, a black dot appeared in the east, visibly increasing in size, seemingly heading toward Phobos. "My God!" murmured the American, his heart wrung by an inexpressible anguish. "May that be help that

Your generosity and benevolence is sending us!" As he finished this speech, he found incredible difficulty breathing, and his lungs produced a sort of hiss as they collapsed, empty.

By God! he thought. *That's how these unfortunates died—and what I'll die of too...lack of air.* He looked back at the black dot and his eyes, already obscured by a light mist, thought they could distinguish, in the midst of the solar radiation, a strange apparatus moving through space with a magical rapidity.

"As long as they see us!" he murmured. "A few minutes' delay could cost all four of us our lives."

An idea came to him then—which was scarcely his habit, but the instinct of self-preservation let a light into his thick suet-merchant's skull. Rapidly, he unbuttoned his vestment and unrolled a long, wide strip of flannel that was wrapped around his body in the manner of our zouaves—except that, by an eccentricity that could only be entertained by a man as excessively full of patriotic pride as Farenheit, this girdle was colored blue and sprinkled with stars, as was the flag of the United States.

He waved this makeshift flag desperately, at arm's length, exhausting the strength that the asphyxia had left him in one last effort. Then his mind was illuminated, as if by lightning; he suddenly remembered the adventure that had overtaken him a few hours earlier, by virtue of his incredible lightness.

He bent his legs and put all his remaining strength and courage into straightening them, launching himself into space like an arrow, dragging his long girdle behind him. With the little lucidity that his frightful agony left him, he had thought of doing that, not so much to reach the savior dot that was advancing towards Phobos as, at least, to be more easily visible to it.

Had he calculated correctly? That was what he could not know, for, suddenly defeated in his struggle against asphyxia, having exhausted the last gasp of air contained in his respirol, he closed his eyes and opened his mouth wide in one last intake of breath. Then his convulsed limbs stiffened in the immobility of death—and the body of Jonathan Farenheit, rolled up in the folds of the starry girdle as if by a shroud, began its slow and almost imperceptible fall upon Phobos.

"By God!" said the American, sitting up on his elbows and rubbing his eyes energetically. "What a terrible dream I've just had!"

"A bad dream! Not at all, my dear Mr. Farenheit—you've very nearly gone west!"

At the sound of this voice, Farenheit shivered and rubbed his eyes harder. "I'm dreaming now, then—for I'm damned if that isn't Monsieur Fricoulet's voice that I thought I heard."

"Don't think, but be certain, my dear Mr. Farenheit—for it's certainly Monsieur Fricoulet in the flesh and bone who's speaking to you." So saying, the engineer—smiling mischievously, as was his habit—shook Farenheit's hand energetically.

The latter leapt down from the seat on which he was lying and looked at the young man with eyes full of bewilderment. "My word, it's true!" he murmured, as if he had needed the testimony of his eyes in order to believe the engineer's words. Then, after a moment of astounded stupor, the American looked around, and his face reflected the most profound astonishment. "Where am I, then?" he said.

"In an apparatus belonging to the Martians."

"Then the black dot that I saw in space…"

"The black dot was me, racing to your rescue. Thanks to your ingenious idea, I had no need to devote myself to a long and dangerous search to find you."

Farenheit's features darkened with an anxious frown, and he asked: "What about the others? What's become of them? Did you manage to bring them back to life, as you did me?" As he posed that question, the American's voice had a slight tremor.

"Would you see me in such good spirits, Mr. Farenheit," Fricoulet replied, a trifle dryly, "if anything had happened to our friends?" Extending his hand toward a dark corner that had escaped the American's investigations, he said: "There's Monsieur de Flammermont, for one. He's resting at the moment, for he suffered more than the others from the crisis, and even I was afraid that I might not be able to bring him back to life. Fortunately, thanks to his strong constitution, I've snatched him back from Pluto's somber realm."

"What about Monsieur Ossipoff and his daughter?"

"They're in the next room, where it's necessary that I pay them a visit now."

"I'll accompany you, if you'll allow it."

"Unfortunately, I can't allow it. For one thing, you're very tired and a little nap will do you the world of good; for another, being forced to absent myself, I don't want to leave Gontran all alone."

The American stifled a formidable yawn. "By God!" he murmured, "I'm as hungry as all the devils in hell!"

Fricoulet went to a shelf, on which stood a little flask. He picked it up and uncorked it. "Here," he said, holding it out to Farenheit. "Drink a mouthful of this—but only one mouthful, or you'll give yourself indigestion."

The American thought that the engineer was about to laugh, but the other spoke very seriously as he added: "It's in this liquid form that the Martians absorb the substance necessary to the support of their muscular strength. It's the quintessential product, raised to the highest power, of one of the aliments in use on the planet."

Farenheit looked suspiciously at the flask he was holding in his hand. "These people aren't gourmets," he said. "By this method, they deprive themselves of one of greatest pleasures there is on the surface of our world—the pleasure of the table."

Fricoulet shook his head. "These people have but one passion, albeit a mad and excessive one, pushed it its ultimate limits: curiosity. To extract from Nature the greatest possible number of secrets—that's the goal to which, from generation to generation, over the centuries, their efforts are devoted." He uttered a little mocking laugh and continued: "Ah, Mr. Farenheit, despite your pragmatic outlook on life, how far distant you are from these people, and how antiquated your famous motto *Time is money* sounds beside theirs! Which is to say that, compared to the Martians, the most agile, hard-working, restless Yankee is nothing but a dormouse…or a snail."

"Hang on! Hang on!"

"For them, time is so precious that they scarcely rest. As for meals, they do without, replacing them by what you hold in your hand—just time enough to uncork the flask, to bend the elbow, and it's done…to go more quickly, in fact, they've refined the liquid to its quintessence. Try a little."

The American said no more; he was convinced—and, deep down, a trifle humiliated. The activity of the citizens of the United States had been surpassed. He put the flask to his lips and swallowed a mouthful of it contents. He pulled a face and gave it back to Fricoulet.

"I'll put it up here," said the engineer, replacing it on the shelf. "If Gontran wakes up before I come back, make him drink the same, for he too must have prodigious hunger pangs." With that, the young man headed for the far end of the room.

He lifted the curtain and found himself face to face with Mikhail Ossipoff. The old man immediately asked, anxiously: "How is Monsieur de Flammermont?"

"Have no fear, he's resting—but I don't see Mademoiselle Selena."

"Here I am," said the young woman, appearing in the doorway. Then, putting her hands to her abdomen with a painful expression, she moaned; "My God, I'm hungry!"

The engineer nodded his head in an understanding manner and, as he had done with Farenheit, made Selena and her father drink a mouthful of the contents of a flask that he took from his pocket. "Now that you're fed…" he began.

Ossipoff did not let him continue. "Before anything else," he said, "tell me where we are."

"On the national balloon that maintains a service between Mars and its satellites."

The old man started in amazement. "Really!" he said. "It's a balloon? But I see nothing that resembles one."

The engineer smiled, took out his notebook, and rapidly scribbled a sketch on a blank page, which he showed to Ossipoff.

The old scientist's faced reflected the most profound bewilderment.

466

"Certainly," declared Farenheit, "this is an apparatus that will have the same effect on you that it had on me at first—this species of large cylinder defies all the ideas of aerial navigation that we have on Earth...and yet, do you recall the numerous models affecting the form of a cigar that you might have seen at various expositions? There's some analogy between them and the apparatus that's carrying us."

"That's quite possible," murmured Ossipoff.

"I'll resume my explanation," said the engineer. "The cylinder that you see there, which appears to me to be made of a sort of metallic fabric, measures no less than 60 meters in length by 12 in diameter. Its various sections are traversed along its entire length by a tube, in which there's an axis around which the apparatus—driven by an electric motor placed in the gondola—turns at a rate of between four and five cycles per second. What you see there, on the external surface of the apparatus, is a propeller 25 meters in diameter, making three complete turns, which gives it a span of 50 meters. The result is that the apparatus advances at about two meters a second, or about seven kilometers and hour."

Mikhail Ossipoff was literally stunned, as if hypnotized by Fricoulet's drawing.

Selena whose ignorance sheltered her from excessive astonishment, and who had, in any case, had a surfeit of the extraordinary, asked the engineer: "Have we left Phobos, then?"

"Yes, Mademoiselle—about three hours ago...with the consequence that we'll arrive on Mars in about five hours.

The young woman clapped her hands. "We've left Phobos! What luck! We're no longer running the risk of seeing those frightful creatures!" Then she interrupted herself abruptly. "That's right," she said to Fricoulet, "you don't understand—you haven't seen them. Can you imagine that we landed, not on the actual ground of the satellite, but on a sort of gigantic cage in which hideous monsters were enclosed?"

The engineer burst out laughing. "Yes, yes," he said. "I know what it is—or, at least, I think so. If I've understood what was explained to me, Phobos is nothing but a penitentiary colony: a sort of celestial convict prison, where the Martians send those among them whose vices render them dangerous to society."

"But what's the purpose of the net?"

"To prevent the prisoners from flying to the planet. Being equipped with wings, that probably wouldn't be impossible for them."

"In that case," cried Selena, her hands meeting in a gesture of fright, "those winged monsters with the sinister appearance are the Martians?"

"Yes, and despite the disgust and terror that they appear to inspire in you, Mademoiselle, these monsters seem to me to have arrived at a degree of perfection much superior to that of our world. It won't be long, in any case, before you have proof of it—but it's probable that the types glimpsed by you through the latticework are the sum of all the moral and physical ugliness of the globe."

"But how can they live in air so rarefied?" the young woman went on. "Without your miraculous appearance, we'd have been done for."

"Your reasoning might be false, Mademoiselle, in the sense that the lungs of these folk are doubtless less demanding than ours. On the other hand, it might perfectly well be that they're sent to Phobos precisely because of the rarefaction of the air, in order to relieve them, gradually and without suffering, of all muscular strength. The asphyxia that renders the convicts apathetic and devoid of energy might be a punishment like any other."

"My dear Monsieur Fricoulet," said Ossipoff at that moment, "Would it be possible to make a tour of this vehicle?"

"Certainly—but for that, you'll have to put on your respirols."

"What?" said Selena. "It's necessary to imprison ourselves in those helmets again?"

"Undoubtedly—but this time there's nothing to fear, for we have our supply of solidified oxygen with us. Then again, your father's curiosity will be satisfied in a few minutes." As they went to put on their respirols, the engineer added: "One last recommendation: be as sober as possible in your movements, for a single slightly-exaggerated gesture might throw you overboard—and this time, you'd be irredeemably lost." With these words he climbed a small ladder, followed by Ossipoff and Selena. A few moments later, all three found themselves standing on a sort of deck serving as the roof of a lodgment, from which and around which ran a metal border.

Above their heads, turning with vertiginous rapidity, the gigantic cylinder extended its enormous moving mass, which surrounded the propeller that appeared to them as a diaphanous outline. In a forward direction, the gondola narrowed like the prow of a ship and the balloon was elongated into a point, cleaving through space almost soundlessly. It was there, by courtesy of a little ladder about 30 meters high, that the Terrans went into the tube in the middle of which the central axis rotated; then, having passed along its entire length, they re-emerged at the rear, near the rudder—a vast circular surface that could be tilted at will in any direction.

Once there, Ossipoff put himself in communication with Fricoulet. "But this apparatus can nether move not steer by itself...it must have a crew?"

The engineer signaled to his friends to follow him and went inside through a narrow opening pierced in the stern of the gondola, hermetically sealed by a sort of lid. Once here, all three took off their respirols and Fricoulet then invited Ossipoff to admire the engine-room, in which incomprehensible machines—bearing no resemblance to any that the old man had seen on Earth—were manufacturing, without heat or sound, the electricity that activated the motors in order to make the gigantic cylindrical balloon rotate on its axis and spin its helical aerofoils.

Half a dozen strange beings were coming and going around the machinery, seemingly indifferent to the Terrans' presence. As the engineer had suggested, there was a considerable difference between the convicts of Phobos—the vile creatures, half-reptile and half-bird, that they had glimpsed through the mesh of the protective net—and the individuals that were in front of them, with their proud bearing, their noble gait and the remarkable intelligence readable in their gaze. They were a little more than two meters in height. The round head was attached to a powerful neck and the remarkably large eyes shone with a vivid gleam which became fatiguing at length. The toothless jaws projected forwards in the form of a beak. The short and profound ears were hairy, as were the cheeks and the skull. The limbs were long and seemed robust, although slender, and a membrane similar to those of bats joined them together.

Fricoulet explained that this membrane served them as both wings and a parachute. At rest, as they were at present, the membrane completely replaced clothing for them, rather like a sort of toga in which they draped themselves, not without nobility. The engineer added that some among them, who moved in the highest intellectual circles, painted the membrane with highly artistic colors.

"And you dared to say, just now, that these creatures are not ugly!" said Selena.

"From your point of view, without doubt, they're frightening," replied the engineer, "but beauty isn't everything, not only in this world but in the Universe entire. Now, what I've seen of their planet has been sufficient to convince me that these people have attained a degree of civilization that we shall not attain for several centuries."

While chatting, the Terrans had gone into the interior of the gondola again and were heading toward the cabin in which Gontran had remained, in Farenheit's care. Fricoulet, who went ahead of the old man and Selena, was about to cross the threshold when the sound of raised voices reached him and immobilized him. He gestured to his companions to remain silent and all three of them pricked up their ears.

"By God!" howled Farenheit, "I tell you that it was an American who discovered these satellites...or Monsieur Ossipoff doesn't know what he's saying."

"Agreed," replied Flammermont. "Who would think of contesting that Hall deserves credit for that discovery? I'm merely saying that although he, being favored by the maximum proximity of the Earth and Mars, actually saw the satellites of the latter planet, others before him had foreseen them."

"Get away!"

"There's no *get away* about it, and these lines I find quoted in my illustrious namesake's *Les Continents célestes* were certainly not written by Hall...they're from the pen of Voltaire, who wrote them in his romance *Micromégas* in 1750: 'On leaving Jupiter, our voyagers crossed a space of about a 100,000,000 leagues and skirted Mars. They saw two moons serving that planet, which have escaped the eyes of our astronomers. I know that Père Castel will write to dispute the existence of these two moons; but I am in agreement with those arguing by analogy. These good philosophers know how difficult it would be for Mars, being so distant from the Sun, to have less than two moons...' "[155]

Gontran shut the book firmly and asked, ironically: "What do you think of that, Mr. Farenheit?"

"I think that Voltaire, not being an astronomer, said that at random, and that an unexpected stroke of luck made his prediction come true."

"It must be admitted, at any rate," Gontran retorted, "that it was a truth that was in the air—no pun intended—for Swift, the celebrated author of *Gulliver's Travels*, not only mentions two 'lesser stars or satellites, which revolve around Mars,' but even gives precise information about one of these satellites; thus, according to him, the one nearer to the planet 'revolves in the space of ten hours, and the more distant in 21 hours.' "[156]

"I'd make the same reply as for Voltaire—Swift said that at random."

"Not so," declared Flammermont. "They both worked by analogy."

"What do you mean by that?" Farenheit complained.

"I mean that from the fact that Earth has one satellite, Jupiter four and Saturn eight, it is presumable that Mars, situated between Earth and Jupiter, would have two. That's mathematics."

As if blinded by the evidence of this reasoning, Farenheit fell silent for a few seconds; then, finally, he muttered: "It doesn't alter the fact that it was a man from America who discovered the satellites of Mars."

The door opened then and Ossipoff replied: "Not a man from America, Mr. Farenheit, but a woman from America. It's an authenticated fact that, after having spent several nights fruitlessly searching for the presumed satellites of Mars,

---

[155] This quote from *Micromégas* (which was actually published in 1752) omits one minor phrase, which offers Père Castel a backhanded compliment in suggesting that he will write "pleasantly enough." The use of the future tense may seem odd; the reference is inserted because the Jesuit mathematician Louis Bertrand Castel (1688-1757) had published a *Traité de physique de la pesanteur universelle des corps* [Treatise on the Physics of the Universal Gravitation of Bodies] (1724) that opposed Isaac Newton's theory, without reference to empirical data, on the grounds that it was irrational and overcomplicated, and Voltaire— one of Newton's chief defenders in France—is suggesting that Castel was the kind of man who would routinely deny facts if he found them unesthetic.

[156] The second of these quotes from Chapter III of Part III of the book generally known as *Gulliver's Travels* is slightly mistaken; the figure Swift gives is actually "21 and a half hours." The great satirist goes on to explain that the squares of these times are in proportion to the satellites' distances from the planet, thus providing an illustration of the universal law of gravitation—that being the principal importance of the discovery, from the viewpoint of the astronomers of Laputa.

Hall was about to renounce the continuation of his search in despair, when his wife arrived and insisted firmly that he devote 'one more evening' to it."

"That's not important," the American replied. "What has to be established is that the honor of the discovery reverts to the United States."

"No one thought of denying it," my dear Mr. Farenheit, said Fricoulet in his turn.

"The moral of the story," said Selena, darting a malicious glance at the engineer, "is that wives can sometimes be useful."

Fricoulet was doubtless about to reply, but Gontran advanced toward him and hugged him. "Ah!" he said, in an emotional voice. "I didn't expect to see you again."

"A miracle!" cried Ossipoff. "You've recovered your voice!"

"In recovering Fricoulet," replied the young Comte, with a smile addressed to Selena, "I've recovered everything that I had lost." Then, after a further accolade, he added: "But by what miracle have you rejoined us?"

The engineer shrugged his shoulders slightly and replied in an affected tone that brought a slight frown to Ossipoff's face: "No need for miracles, my dear chap; a little intelligence and skill were sufficient. Scarcely had the metallic balloon taken to the skies again than I perceived the material impossibility of my being able to come down again to join you, so I abandoned myself to Providence and let myself be carried along for a few hours. Having traveled a few 100 kilometers, the balloon turned a somersault, by virtue of which I recognized that I had just penetrated the attractive zone of Mars. From that moment on, I had a chance of being saved."

"What—of being saved?" Farenheit interjected.

"Assuredly—for, instead of Phobos, I would be able to land on Mars. I immediately maneuvered in that direction. I pulled hard on the cable controlling the valve, opening it wide enough to let three quarters of the gas escape. Then began a frightful, vertiginous, formidable fall; in less than half an hour I fell 5000 kilometers. I was obliged to put on my respirol in order not to be stifled. As I clung to the edge, it was as if I were fascinated by the world whose force of attraction was increasing with every second, on which I would inevitably crash."

"Poor Monsieur Fricoulet," murmured Selena. "What terrible emotions you must have experienced…"

"My God, Mademoiselle, would I seem boastful to you if I were to confess, in all sincerity, that the thought of death never crossed my mind for an instant? On the contrary—I was very calm, and while falling, I calculated the velocity at which I was about to establish contact between my poor body and the surface of Mars. I also tried to extrapolate what the result of that encounter would be."

"Ah, that's the man I know you to be!" cried Gontran, taking pride himself in his friend's courage.

"In brief," the engineer went on, "I was barely 100 meters from the ground when my vertical fall was suddenly halted and I found myself drawn along horizontally by an unknown force with uncommon velocity. I covered 40 kilometers thus, and a vast extent of water soon appeared beneath me, shining in the sunlight. It was the Kepler Ocean. If hazard dictated that my fall would be completed in that liquid element, I had a chance of getting out of it..."

"The element?" asked Gontran.

"No, the situation I was in. Unfortunately, I continued to fly horizontally and, after crossing the ocean, began flying over solid ground again. Gradually, however, my speed relented, and I arrived at a sort of metallic apparatus, where I stopped."

"What was it?" Ossipoff asked, with keen interest.

"I understood, from some summary explanations that were given to me afterwards, that the Martians have established a means of very rapid locomotion on their world, based on the formation of violent air-currents that push vehicles from one relay station to another. I had been caught in one of these air-currents and my balloon, forming a vehicle, had thus miraculously escaped the death that awaited me. As you can imagine, my first concern was to try to rejoin you. That wasn't easy, I can tell you; finally, after much effort, I succeeded in making these people understand the situation you were in. I then persuaded them to charter this balloon in order to permit me to search for you...and here we are..." Then, letting himself fall into a chair, exhausted by his narration, the engineer added: "That, certainly, is a story compared with which that of Théramène[157] is nothing at all; I'm completely out of breath."

Farenheit, who had listened to all these explanations with great attention, went over to Fricoulet. "My dear sir," he said, "I'd like to ask you a question."

"Ask, Mr. Farenheit, ask."

"You mentioned an ocean just now...so they exist on this world?"

"Indubitably, my dear Mr. Farenheit. Their areography has been known to everyone for some time."

"Areography?" Selena repeated, interrogatively.

"The geography of Mars, if you prefer, Mademoiselle—from the Greek Ares, equivalent to the Roman Mars."

Farenheit sniggered audibly. "The geography of the Moon was known for a long time too—selenography, as you call it in that impossible language of scientists. Seas are found there on the maps that were drawn up, but it seems that words change their meaning in astronomy, since the spaces designated on the lunar map by the name of 'seas' are only immense arid and desiccated plains, without the slightest trace of water..."

---

[157] Théramène is a character in Racine's *Phèdre*; the narration that made his name proverbial in this fashion was his account of the death of his pupil, Hippolyte.

"But since I tell you that I have seen the Kepler Ocean with my own eyes..." protested Fricoulet.

"You're like Saint Thomas, Mr. Farenheit," Mikhail Ossipoff put in, mockingly, "you only believe in things you've seen...but if it had ever occurred to you, during your terrestrial existence, to look through a telescope, you would have been convinced of the existence of the Martian seas without actually needing to make the voyage."[158]

"A little voyage," Flammermont sniggered, "of some 19,000,000 leagues."

"14,000,000 only, if you please," observed the old scientist. "To study a world, one does not choose the moment when it is furthest away."

"Let's say 14,000,000," said Farenheit, folding his arms. "And you want me to believe that it is possible at such a distance to establish the presence of water on a planet?"

"You admit yourself that one of your compatriots has discovered Deimos and Phobos—two worldlets a few kilometers in diameter—but you doubt that it has been possible to study Mars, whose diameter is nearly 1700 leagues and its circumference of 5375 leagues? If you take the trouble to reflect a little, you'll avoid many unnecessary words."

The American stamped his foot violently. "Don't put words into my mouth that I haven't said," he muttered. "It's one thing to recognize bodies existing in space—that's what telescopes are made for—and another thing entirely to claim to study infinitely petty details."

"But my dear Mr. Farenheit," aid Gontran, maliciously, "telescopes are made for that too."

"Monsieur de Flammermont is right," Ossipoff added. "Thanks to the marvelous instruments that progress has put at the disposal of modern science, one can affirm the existence of facts occurring millions of leagues away with as much certainty as if one could lay a finger on them. Thus, I will go further still in my affirmation; not only is there water on the surface of Mars but that water has the same chemical composition as ours. Not only are there seas, but we also know their depth. We know, for example, that the deepest are in the vicinity of the equator and the torrid zone, like the Schiaparelli Sea, the Flammarion Sea,

---

[158] This may seem odd to the modern readers, but it was not until the observations made from Percival Lowell's Flagstaff Observatory in the 1890s became the basis for the elaborate mythology of the canals of Mars that the idea took hold that Mars was a world that had become direly arid, whose inhabitants had been forced by necessity to transport water from the poles in order to sustain their decadent civilization. In the 1880s, Camille Flammarion's writings, and those of other popularizers, not only still held to the notion that the Martian "seas" really were vast expanses of water, but took it for granted that the fact was manifest to the eye of the experienced observer, as Ossipoff here maintains.

the Kepler Ocean and the Newton Ocean, while those in the polar regions, such as the Mädler, Faye and Beer Seas, are not as deep."

Farenheit's amazement was indescribably profound.

"On would think, I'd swear, that you've never gone up in a balloon!" Ossipoff exclaimed.

"My word, no," Farenheit replied. "My trade in animal fats does not require ascensions, and my liking for solid ground has always prevented me from indulging in such perilous exercises."

"Well, my dear Mr. Farenheit, if you had gone up in a balloon, you would not be surprised that, in spite of the 14,000,000 leagues that separate us from Mars, one can know the relative depth of its seas. It depends on the relative darkness of the color that the appearance of large masses of liquid present. The darker the hue, the greater the depth."

"Can one not equally deduce," asked Fricoulet, "the degree of salinity of the different seas, for it's proven that the saltier an expanse of water is, the darker it seems? Now, as the salinity depends on evaporation, it's quite natural that the darker seas—which is to say, the saltiest—are found in the equatorial regions."

Ossipoff inclined his head slightly, in a movement full of approving condescension.

The American remained silent for a few moments, then suddenly clicked his fingers. "Anyway," he said, "it doesn't matter to me whether the seas are salty and deep or not. The man thing, for me, is that we can breathe at our ease, freely, without being obliged to shut ourselves up again in those selenium cages." He favored the respirols piled up in a corner with a dirty look.

"In that regard," said Fricoulet, laughing, "you can be tranquil, my dear Mr. Farenheit—the planet Mars is provided with an atmosphere whose composition is identical to ours. Spectral studies leave no doubt on that subject. If you like rain and cloud too, you will have what you need to be content, for the Martian atmosphere is rich in water vapor."

"But in view of the lesser intensity of gravity at the Martian surface," Gontran objected, "the density of its atmosphere must be almost ineffectual, and it probably follows that there is a rarefaction similar to that on the summits of the highest terrestrial mountains."

The American's radiant expression darkened again. "It's respirols again, then?" he groaned.

Fricoulet clicked his tongue impatiently. "If what you say were the case," he replied to Flammermont, "the Martian seas would be dry, all their contents having long been volatilized into space, instead of being transformed, after their evaporation, into vapor—clouds and fogs—to fall again thereafter on to the surface of the planet in the form of rain. Then again, the snows that surround the poles, instead of being simple caps in the polar regions, would bury the entire planet in a shroud, transforming Mars into a block of ice."

Gontran seemed rather annoyed by this explanation, furnished in front of Ossipoff; as for Farenheit, his expression cleared again.

"Now that you've reassured Mr. Farenheit," said Selena, in her turn, with a smile, "I'd like you to reassure me too, Monsieur Fricoulet."

The engineer bowed. "Entirely at your disposal, Mademoiselle," he murmured.

"You know that I'm sensitive to cold," the young woman said.

"Yes, I know—and your cometary sojourn must certainly have developed that natural disposition further—but why mention it to me?"

"Because I suppose that it can't be very warm on your Mars."

The engineer's eyes widened. "I'm curious to know on what you base that supposition?"

"On what I was told by Gontran."

Scarcely had the engineer posed the question than he regretted it, for he had anticipated the response almost immediately, so he muffled the final words of her reply with a loud and obstinate fit of coughing. Then he said: "Yes, yes, I see where you're coming from. You're one of those who believe that the temperature of the planets is determined by their distance from the Sun and that Mars, in consequence of being 19,000,000 leagues further away from the central star than Earth, must enjoy Siberian temperatures."

The young woman indicated with a nod that this was correct.

"Well, that's a mistake," Fricoulet continued. "The temperature depends on the composition of the atmosphere, which acts as a greenhouse. With respect to the solar heat, it allows it to reach the surface of the ground, and then retains it, opposing itself to its dissipation in space. Air, properly speaking—that is to say, oxygen and nitrogen—only plays an insignificant role in the mechanism that I've just explained; only water vapor has an influence on heat, by reason of its absorbent power, 6000 times superior to that of dry air."[159]

Selena clapped her hands. "I get it!" she exclaimed. "You said just now that the spectroscope had discovered a considerably quantity of water vapor in the Martian atmosphere, so the temperature…"

"May be colder or warmer than on Earth, or perhaps even equal to it, depending on circumstance—but in any event, I don't think we'll have to suffer overmuch."

---

[159] The "hothouse effect" by virtue of which atmospheres may act as heat traps was first described by Jean-Baptiste-Joseph, Baron Fourier (1768-1830); unlike Fricoulet, however, Fourier recognized the importance of carbon dioxide as well as that of water vapor. When the authors wrote this passage, however, they were unaware of the calculations made in the 1890s by Svante Arrhenius, who asserted in consequence that doubling the amount of the carbon dioxide in the Earth's atmosphere would result in a mean temperature increase of five degrees Celsius.

"Besides," Farenheit said, "if these Martians are as advanced in their civilization as you claim, they must certainly have infallible means of protecting themselves from cold and heat."

"It's probable." Having said that, Fricoulet put on his respirol, screwed on his selenium helmet and went up on deck, looking for Ossipoff—whom he found leaning over the rampart, devouring the landscape extended beneath them with his eyes.

"How well one can take account of the Martian topography, eh?" said the scientist, immediately putting himself in communication with the engineer.

"It's true," the young man replied, "that from a few 100 kilometers one has things more clearly in view than one has from several million leagues."

"How different it is from our globe! While three-quarters of the terrestrial surface is covered with water and our vastest continents are, properly speaking, only gigantic islands, here it's the other way around. The seas and the continents are in almost the same proportion, but in favor of the continents."

"And in consequence, curiously enough," Fricoulet continued, "all its seas are, in effect, Mediterranean." As he finished these words a hand fell on his shoulder. He turned round and saw Gontran, who signaled that he wanted to talk to him. Immediately, the two speakers were adapted to the two helmets.

"What is it?"

"It's just," replied the young Comte, "that I'm straining my eyes in vain to discover the bloody gleam that has made Mars the warrior planet, of which I can see absolutely nothing."

"Which isn't at all surprising, given that the reddish—or, to be strictly accurate, orange-yellow—tint is more appreciable to the naked eye than through a telescope. It has been remarked in observatories that the tint diminishes in intensity the more the instrumental magnification increases. That's why you can't even make it out."

"A reddish atmosphere ought, however, to give everything it surrounds an appearance of the same hue."

"Heresy, dear chap, heresy—for, if the coloration were due to the atmosphere, it would be more intense at the edges than in the center, by reason of the atmospheric thickness traversed by the luminous rays."

"Is it necessary to attribute it to the soil itself?"

"If Ossipoff heard you, he'd have a fit," said the engineer, "for that hypothesis is in flagrant contradiction with what we know about the world of Mars. How, indeed, can we admit that the age-long effect of the four elements that engender life—water, air, earth and fire—have remained ineffectual, and that no vegetation has dressed the surface of Mars?"

"So it's the vegetation! But you must know something about that, since you arrived there."

"On that subject, I can't give you any information. For one thing, I landed on Mars at night—but even if it had been broad daylight. I'd have been too overcome by anguish to take any notice of it."

Gontran remained silent for a moment. "In that case," he said, "pending further instructions, what I'd better do is to adopt the vegetation theory, if Ossipoff interrogates me?"

"Pooh! It's of little importance. Just remember that Mars is 5375 leagues in circumference, and that, by comparison with the terrestrial globe, its surface area is 27%, its volume 16%, its weight a fifth and its density 69%—which means that the intensity of gravity at its surface is a third of what it is on the Earth's surface. Can you remember all that?"

"I think so—but is that all?"

"No, remember this, too: that Mars rotates on its axis in 24 hours, 37 minutes and 27 seconds, and around the Sun in 660 days—which makes its year twice as long as ours."[160]

"And consequently, its seasons..."

"I'll stop you there, for that's one of the characteristic differences between this world and ours. Not only is the duration of the seasons longer, but it's unequal, by reason of its elongated orbit. Thus, while spring and summer last 191 and 181 days, autumn and winter only last 149 and 147 days."

The engineer was doubtless about to continue his explanations when a Martian approached and signaled to him that it was necessary to descend into the cabin.

THE STORY CONTINUES IN VOLUME II

[160] These figures are all reasonably accurate except the last, although the figure of 660 is closer to the actual number of Martian days in a Martian year (670) than the figure of 608 previously given.

BLACK COAT PRESS

M. Allain & P. Souvestre. *The Daughter of Fantômas*
Anicet-Bourgeois. *Rocambole*
Guy d'Armen. *Doc Ardan: The City of Gold and Lepers*
Aloysius Bertrand. *Gaspard de la Nuit*
A. Bisson & G. Livet. *Nick Carter vs. Fantômas*
Félix Bodin. *The Novel of the Future*
Lucien Dabril. *Rocambole*
V. Darlay & H. de Gorsse. *Lupin vs. Holmes: The Stage Play*
C.I. Defontenay. *Star (Psi Cassiopeia)*
Charles Derennes: *The People of the Pole*
Alexandre Dumas. *The Return of Lord Ruthven*
J.-C. Dunyach. *The Night Orchid: Conan Doyle in Toulouse*
J.-C. Dunyach. *The Thieves of Silence*
Paul Féval: *Anne of the Isles*
Paul Féval. *The Blackcoats: The Companions of the Treasure*
Paul Féval. *The Blackcoats: The Invisible Weapon*
Paul Féval. *The Blackcoats: The Parisian Jungle*
Paul Féval. *The Blackcoats: 'Salem Street*
Paul Féval. *Captain Phantom*
Paul Féval. *Gentlemen of the Night*
Paul Féval. *John Devil*
Paul Féval. *Knightshade*
Paul Féval. *Revenants*
Paul Féval. *Vampire City*
Paul Féval. *The Vampire Countess*
Paul Féval. *The Wandering Jew's Daughter*
Paul Féval, *fils. Felifax, the Tiger-Man*
Emile Gaboriau. *Monsieur Lecoq*
Arnould Galopin. *Doctor Omega*
V. Hugo, Foucher & Meurice. *The Hunchback of Notre-Dame*
O. Joncquel & Theo Varlet. *The Martian Epic*
Jean de La Hire. *The Nyctalope on Mars*
Jean de La Hire. *The Nyctalope vs. Lucifer*
Jean de La Hire. *Enter the Nyctalope*
Steve Leadley. *Sherlock Holmes - The Circle of Blood*
Maurice Leblanc. *Lupin vs. Holmes: The Hollow Needle*
Maurice Leblanc. *Lupin vs. Holmes: The Blonde Phantom*
Gustave Le Rouge. *The Vampires of Mars*
Jules Lermina. *Panic in Paris*
Gaston Leroux. *Chéri-Bibi*
Gaston Leroux. *The Phantom of the Opera*